PENGUIN  BOOKS

THE OLD WIVES' TALE

Arnold Bennett was born in Hanley, Staffordshire, in 1867. After a secondary school education, he worked first for his father, a self-taught solicitor, and then moved to London as a shorthand clerk with a firm of solicitors. He began to write to make extra money and in 1893 became assistant editor and subsequently editor of the weekly magazine, *Woman*, reviewing books and writing articles on general subjects, something he continued to do all his life. His first novel, *A Man from the North*, appeared in 1898 and in 1900 he finished *The Grand Babylon Hotel*, published in 1902, and began *Anna of the Five Towns* (1902), in which he first started to use the Potteries of his boyhood as a setting for his novels. In these contrasting works, he also reveals his lifelong fascination for, on the one hand, the worlds of luxury and opulence, and on the other, puritanism and people who can endure hard work.

In 1903 Arnold Bennett moved to Paris, where he met people such as Turgenev and the composer, Ravel. In 1907 he married a Frenchwoman (from whom he separated in 1921) and in the following year they returned to England. *The Old Wives' Tale* (1908) was written in France and shows Bennett's main influences, the first being that of his own background and the second that of the French realists such as Flaubert, Maupassant and Balzac. In it, Bennett also reveals his own preoccupations with the effects of time and history on the lives of ordinary people.

This was followed by the Clayhanger trilogy: *Clayhanger* (1910), *Hilda Lessways* (1911) and *These Twain* (1916). His works also include several plays, two volumes of short stories and several other novels. He died in 1931.

•

John Wain was born in Stoke-on-Trent in 1925 and educated at the High School, Newcastle-under-Lyme, and St John's College, Oxford. He lectured in English at the University of Reading until 1955, since when he has devoted himself to full-time writing. He has published novels, short stories, poetry and critical essays. His biography, *Samuel Johnson*, was awarded the James Tait Black Memorial Prize and the Heinemann Award. He has also edited James Hogg's *The Private Memoirs and Confessions of a Justified Sinner* for the Penguin Classics. For his services to literature he was awarded the C.B.E. in 1984 and is an honorary D. Litt. of two universities, Keele and Loughborough.

Arnold Bennett

THE OLD WIVES' TALE

Introduction and Notes by
John Wain

PENGUIN BOOKS

PENGUIN BOOKS

Published by the Penguin Group
27 Wrights Lane, London W8 5TZ, England
Viking Penguin Inc., 40 West 23rd Street, New York, New York 10010, USA
Penguin Books Australia Ltd, Ringwood, Victoria, Australia
Penguin Books Canada Ltd, 2801 John Street, Markham, Ontario, Canada L3R 1B4
Penguin Books (NZ) Ltd, 182–190 Wairau Road, Auckland 10, New Zealand

Penguin Books Ltd, Registered Offices: Harmondsworth, Middlesex, England

First published 1908
Published in the Penguin English Library 1983
Reprinted in Penguin Classics 1986, 1987

Preface copyright 1911 by George H. Doran Co.
Introduction and Notes copyright © John Wain, 1983
All rights reserved

Printed and bound in Great Britain by
Cox & Wyman Ltd, Reading
Set in Linotron Sabon by
Rowland Phototypesetting Ltd
Bury St Edmunds, Suffolk

CONTENTS

INTRODUCTION

The Old Wives' Tale has three claims to fame. It is one of the most successful attempts, if not *the* most successful, to rival in English the achievement of the French realistic novel from Balzac down through Flaubert, Zola and Maupassant. It is one of the most complete and satisfying novels of English provincial life. And it is a standing proof that a writer of the male sex can write with real perception about the imaginative and emotional lives of women.

As time hastens by, this rich and bountiful book takes on added benefits. Bennett was an historical novelist, not in the sense that his characters wear period costume and utter strange oaths, but in the sense that the main subject of his important works is the effect of time on human lives. Above and beyond his chosen human subjects, there is always the goddess History herself, benign, sardonic, accusing, according to her mood. 'The Old Wives' Tale,' the young J. B. Priestley noted, 'has two suffering heroines, Constance and Sophia Baines, and three conquering heroes, Time, Mutability and Death.' Knowing that History must be the over-arching presence, Bennett planned his story to begin in the misty distance of the 1860s and to finish at the moment he took up his pen to write it, in 1907. He wanted it, that is, to span the immense gulf from Ancient to Modern. But to us, who see the modern of 1907 as separated from us by seismic upheavals and long, slow marches, its historical patina is enriched. The up-to-date, progressive elevation from which Bennett viewed mid-Victorian England is now further behind us than mid-Victorian England was behind him. Which means that his novel must either be forgotten, hopelessly out-dated and flung aside, or must survive as a classic – that is, an abiding statement, a work of art that speaks for its time so effectively that it will be read as long as that time has any place in the collective memory.

Of these two alternative fates for the book, the reading public has already chosen the second. Hence this edition.

I

'What am I to do with poor Arnold? He'll never be able to earn his own living.' Most fathers fail to assess their sons correctly, but this judgement by Enoch Bennett (1843–1902) must surely stand out even so. But then Arnold, the oldest of a brood of nine children of whom six survived, was a retiring lad with a stammer, who seemed unlikely to push himself forward; such gifts as he displayed were verbal – he won two literary prizes, one for verse and one for prose, during his school days – and literary promise did not enter much into the consciousness of a busy man in the Potteries in the 1870s.

In other respects it was a fortunate environment for a nascent writer. The pottery towns were growing very fast. When Josiah Wedgwood opened up the industry at the end of the eighteenth century, the six villages strung along the valley of the Trent – Longton, Fenton, Stoke, Hanley, Burslem and Tunstall – were villages and nothing more. There was a tradition of skill in clay-working, but it was no more than could have been paralleled, in those decentralized days, in most areas of England. Nor was the local clay anything out of the ordinary; Wedgwood fetched his clay all the way from Cornwall. It was the presence of a small but high-quality coalfield that decided the generation of Wedgwood and Spode that these six villages could become the centre of the pottery industry. And this they brought about; so resoundingly that to this day the Potteries is the only district in England that is known by the name of a trade.

The six villages grew into towns; the population boomed; in the classic manner of unplanned industry, factories and houses mushroomed in a mad jumble on the sides of the steep little hills of which the district is composed; and over it all hung a thick canopy of smoke. Where there's muck there's brass, not that much brass seems to have found its way into the pockets of the miners and potters who made it possible. The place grew from its rural beginnings into the twelfth largest gathering of population in England, until finally, in 1910, the absurdity of calling it by six names instead of one, and of having six mayors, six corporations, six town halls, though the eye could not see any boundaries, was conceded and the City of Stoke-on-Trent came into being.

We must picture the Potteries of Arnold Bennett's boyhood as a place whose dominating ethos was that of work. For lotus-eating or elegant trifling, the district was simply not organized, though the kind of recreations that appeal to ordinary people flourished well enough – choral singing, fit-up travelling theatres, and of course football (Stoke City F.C. is one of the oldest in the country). An energetic, competitive, individualistic place, it bred characters like Bennett *père*, who after starting his working life in a pot-bank, set up a pawnbrokery combined with a drapery and sewing business, studied law in such leisure as he had, and at the age of thirty-four qualified as a solicitor, practising in Hanley for the rest of his life.

As for Arnold, he began tamely enough with a secondary school education and a grounding in law in his father's office. At the age of twenty-one he moved to London, to take a job as a shorthand clerk with a firm of solicitors. One step at a time! He had behind him some small successes in local journalism, and he had a general willingness to use his pen to make extra money, if this proved feasible.

It proved feasible. He won a parody competition in a weekly paper. Leaving the law office, he became assistant editor of *Woman*, reviewing books and writing general articles, many of them under feminine names such as 'Barbara' and 'Sarah Volatile'. More work flowed in: he did it rapidly and competently. He began to write seriously, using a part of his mind that was not called into play by his money-earning work. Not that he ever despised money-earning work. His attitude, throughout life, was that everything he wrote should be as excellent as he could make it, though he distinguished between the kinds of excellence needed by different *genres*.

Mr James G. Hepburn, in the Introduction to the first volume of his invaluable edition of Bennett's letters, has given us a glimpse of his remarkable energy and industry:

By the end of 1900 Bennett was doing more work of more sorts than seems credible. He was editor (until September) of one journal, and a mainstay of two others. He was reviewing books at the rate of more than

one a day, and also writing literary criticism of a high order. He counted
the number of articles he wrote during the year as 196. Also during the
year he wrote six short stories, one one-act play, two full-length plays
(collaborating with Eden Phillpotts and Arthur Hooley), one sensational
novel (*The Grand Babylon Hotel*, soon to have a sensational success),
and most of the first draft of *Anna of the Five Towns* (which was to please
the serious critics almost as much as *The Grand Babylon Hotel* pleased
the public). In addition, he advised the C. Arthur Pearson organization on
fifty manuscripts of books.

Amid this staggering output, the backward-looking eye
catches one detail in particular. Bennett had begun the literary
use of his native background. Already in 1895 he had published
in *The Yellow Book* a grim and intense short story, 'A Letter
Home', in which 'home' is 'Bursley, Staffordshire'. But in *Anna*
he launched out fairly as chronicler of the district, making up
place-names which were easily penetrated by the people back
home, but which, especially when read by the large public who
took care never to go near the Potteries, nudged his settings away
from pure documentary and in the direction of imaginative literature. His biggest change was to make the Six Towns into
five, for the sake of euphony – surely a wise decision, though
one long resented by the inhabitants of Fenton, the town he left
out.

So Bennett wrote and wrote: devising, describing, judging,
reporting, but always writing. Fulfilment was not, however, to
come from industry alone. London had much to offer; but, for a
young man who felt certain that the initiative in European fiction
had passed from English writers to French, Paris had more.
Bennett moved to Paris in 1903, some five years after setting out
as a professional writer.

Three years is the average length, in England, of a university
education. Paris was Arnold Bennett's university and he stayed
there five. He was young, alert, receptive, and he was living amid
an incredible whirl of creative activity. The best way for us
nowadays to get an impression of what Paris was like at that time
is to read Roger Shattuck's brilliant book, *The Banquet Years*,
which surveys Paris during, roughly, the fifteen years on either
side of 1900 and includes in its purview both the social scene and
the arts – painting, music, theatre, poetry. It was a time of

confidence, of daring experimentation, of seemingly inexhaustible energy; to read about it is to feel, even at this distance of time, that the possibilities of life and art are unlimited if we would just let them be so.

Arnold Bennett is not mentioned in Mr Shattuck's book. But he was there, noticing everything, appreciating and assessing everything, compensating gloriously for the narrowness of his youth in Burslem without for a moment jettisoning the gifts that Burslem had given him – the shrewdness, the pertinacity, the meticulous eye for detail and instinct for craftsmanship. He acquired perfect French; he made friends who included such men as the composer Maurice Ravel and the writer Marcel Schwob, who among other things had made the French translation of *Hamlet* in which Sarah Bernhardt swept her audiences along on a tide of emotion, so compellingly that she was to go on doing so even as a very old lady with a wooden leg. He attended concerts, operas, plays. He bought a book every day. He was not 'educating himself'. I doubt whether such a thing as a self-educated person really exists; certainly Arnold Bennett was not one. Paris educated him; and in his work he offered back to France, like a true artist, some of the richness she had given him.

II

For Bennett had not crossed the Channel out of idle curiosity or for diversion. He had gone to France with the intention of writing a masterpiece. And ever since the illumination that came to him on that evening in 1903, when the obese and ungainly middle-aged woman sat at his table in the restaurant, he had been increasingly convinced that this masterpiece would be 'The History of Two Old Women', soon to be re-titled in his mind 'The Old Wives' Tale'. But first, the conditions had to be right. He needed peace, order, comfort. Marriage and a settled background appealed to him strongly. In 1906 he made a try for this domestic happiness, becoming engaged to an American young lady, Eleanor Green. The engagement did not last. But the following summer he proposed again, to a charming and accomplished young Frenchwoman, Marguerite Soulié. He was accepted. The marriage was to last until 1921; and, whatever were the strains that finally tore it apart, its early days were happy and peaceful.

This happiness and peace bore fruit immediately in solid work. The couple rented a house at Les Sablons, on the edge of the Forest of Fontainebleau. By good fortune the landlord and his wife were an elderly couple whose memories went back nearly forty years to the Siege of Paris in 1870, and could supply details of what life had been in those days: though the chief thing they supplied, as Bennett tells the reader in his Preface, was confirmation of something that he had always suspected: the big events, that get into the history books, are, from the point of view of ordinary life, a background. Whatever is happening on the public scene, one's own struggle goes on, and Bennett noted with interest in his *Journal* that when he questioned the old couple, 'they seemed *only to attach importance to the siege because I did. Like inhabitants of picturesque town or curious village.*' The italics are Bennett's. He was really impressed by this circumstance.

Armed with the insight thus gained, and with the printed sources that he names in his Preface, Bennett set to work amid the *ordre et beauté* of his new home. And such work! Only those who know the back-breaking toil of writing a novel are likely to appreciate the astonishing fact that *The Old Wives' Tale*, all two hundred thousand words of it, was finished – not just drafted but finally finished, ready for the printer – in eleven months: months in which he also wrote short stories, plays, a guide to literary taste, innumerable articles, and a brilliant comic novel, *Buried Alive*.

The completing of *The Old Wives' Tale*, with or without this accompanying torrent of subsidiary work, was not only a personal achievement. It was the long-promised fulfilment of a literary programme. Twenty years' study of the French novel had borne fruit in English.

III

To the young Arnold Bennett, casting a critical eye back at his predecessors in the art of fiction, the classic English novel of the eighteenth and nineteenth centuries appeared energetic but woolly, original and inventive but careless, lacking in that cool, scrupulous craftsmanship demanded by the scientific objectivity so necessary in modern times – as 'modern' was understood in the later years of the nineteenth century. With the large-scale confidence of youth, he made this block judgement without pausing much to consider the obvious exceptions; he seems, for instance, to have taken little interest in Jane Austen – surprising, that, for one would have expected him to be fascinated by her exposition of feminine psychology and by the perfection of her self-limited art. His main conclusion, however, was surely right, or at any rate right for him, which is what matters to an artist. The way ahead lay in the study of the French novel. And so we find the young Bennett quoting with approval Stendhal's remark that a novelist, before sitting down to his day's work, ought to read through a few pages of the Civil Code – i.e. something dry and precise, concerned only with definition, which would help to discipline him against the purple patch and the lyric flight that draws attention away from the book's march along its main highway. And we find him at the age of thirty-two writing in his *Journal*:

As regards fiction, it seems to me that only within the last few years have we absorbed from France that passion for the artistic shapely presentation of truth, and that feeling for words as words, which animated Flaubert, the de Goncourts, and de Maupassant . . . None of the (so-called) great masters of English nineteenth-century fiction had (if I am right) a deep artistic interest in form and treatment; they were absorbed in 'subject'.

That reference to 'the last few years' is almost certainly a bow in the direction of George Moore, who, though his language was English, had more the temperament and approach of a Continental than an English writer, and who had pioneered the adaptation into English of the methods of the French realists and even, in *A Mummer's Wife*, opened Bennett's eyes to the notion of using the pottery towns as a setting for fiction by placing his scene in Hanley.

There is plenty of 'subject' in *The Old Wives' Tale*, of course, but nothing to get in the way of that 'artistic shapely presentation of truth'. The book is beautifully crafted, built as it is on a series of parallels; some of them parallels of contrast, some of similarity, and some whose subtleties cannot be caught by either term, so delicate is their blend of the like and the unlike. The groundwork of the novel, obviously, is provided by the all-pervading parallel of the lives of the two sisters. Bennett had first envisioned this as a matter of crude contrast – prim conventionality against 'guilty splendour', the goody-goody over against the baddy-baddy. This comes out clearly in the account he gives in his *Journal* (18 November 1903) of the book's genesis. This account is not as full as that given in the Preface which Bennett added to the book for the second (first American) edition of 1911, but in one respect it is more valuable. The New York Preface makes no mention of his having conceived it as the story of *two* women. He speaks of it as an account of how a slender girl, with the attractiveness of youth both in those things she is aware of and those she is unaware of, turns by small and unnoticed degrees into a heavy, clumsy, risible old woman. The *Journal* entry, written much closer to the event and with the excitement of the idea still about it, says that from that first moment 'I gave this woman a sister, fat as herself.' The point of the story was to have been, originally, that two sisters, living totally contrasting lives and acted upon by totally contrasting influences, nevertheless both finish up old and fat and fussy, dropping parcels in restaurants, and that after all there is, in their later years, nothing much to tell them apart. Not merely death, but age, is seen as the great leveller. Here is the *Journal* entry.

Wednesday, 18 November – Last night, when I went into the Duval for dinner, a middle-aged woman, inordinately stout and with pendent cheeks, had taken the seat opposite to my prescriptive seat. I hesitated, as there were plenty of empty places, but my waitress requested me to take my usual chair. I did so, and immediately thought: 'With *that* thing opposite to me my dinner will be spoilt!' But the woman was evidently also cross at my filling up her table, and she went away, picking up all her belongings, to another part of the restaurant, breathing hard. Then she abandoned her second choice for a third one. My waitress was scornful and angry at this desertion, but laughing also. Soon all the waitresses were privately laughing at the goings-on of the fat woman, who was being served by the most beautiful waitress I have ever seen in any Duval. The fat woman was clearly a crotchet, a 'maniaque', a woman who lived much alone. Her cloak (she displayed on taking it off a simply awful light

puce flannel dress) and her parcels were continually the object of her
attention and she was always arguing with her waitress. And the whole
restaurant secretly made a butt of her. She was repulsive; no one could
like her or sympathize with her. But I thought – she has been young and
slim once. And I immediately thought of a long 10 or 15 thousand words
short story, 'The History of Two Old Women'. I gave this woman a sister,
fat as herself. And the first chapter would be in the restaurant (both
sisters) something like to-night – and written rather cruelly. Then I would
go back to the infancy of these two, and sketch it all. One should have
lived ordinarily, married prosaically, and become a widow. The other
should have become a whore and all that; 'guilty splendour'. Both are
overtaken by fat. And they live together again in old age, not too rich, a
nuisance to themselves and to others. Neither has any imagination. For
'tone' I thought of 'Ivan Ilytch', and for technical arrangement I thought
of that and also of 'Histoire d'une fille de ferme'. The two lives would
have to intertwine. I saw the whole work quite clearly, and hope to do
it.

But as the book matured in his mind during the four years
between the initial conception and the writing, he came to see it as
something more interesting and more profoundly true – a contrast
of circumstances encasing a basic similarity of life-style. Constance and Sophia, products of the hard-working, respectable
trading class, imbued from birth with the values of 'the Square',
turn out in the end to have lived the same life despite their utterly
different paths. Sophia has looked after her Paris hotel with
exactly the same thrift and devotion that Constance has shown in
managing the affairs of household and drapery shop; she has
refused to be tempted down the by-paths of sensual indulgence or
mercenary vice for the same reason that these things have never
entered Constance's life – because they are not part of her
tradition, they do not belong within her scheme of realistic
alternatives. She is a Baines, and she lives out her life as a Baines.
And in this she resembles Constance so deeply that the differences
between them are differences of the surface. When they meet
again on Knype station, Constance is vaguely shocked at the
modish semi-nakedness of the poodle Fossette, and impressed by
Sophia's Paris clothes, but Sophia has not changed – she is a
Baines with a poodle, a Baines decked in *haute couture*.

On a minor scale, episode and detail balance each other in the
two stories. Chirac meets his fate in a balloon, attempting to

escape from beleaguered Paris; the irrepressible Dick Povey, archetype of the provincial 'card', sails over the Potteries in a balloon to advertise the cause of Federation. Daniel Povey is taken away after murdering his wife, and a crowd gathers in St Luke's Square to stare unwaveringly at his house; a crowd likewise gathers to watch the execution by guillotine of the murderer Rivain. Rivain has murdered a courtesan; that is, a woman who, however necessary the part she plays in sustaining the fabric of society, is conventionally seen as morally worthless; Daniel Povey's wife was in practice hardly any better, 'the dishonour of her sex, her situation, and her years', whose husband 'for thirty years had marshalled all his immense pride to suffer this woman'.

Sometimes the parallels and repetitions are striking because of the immense distance of years, the heavy flowing tide of experience, that separates them. The irresistible charm of Gerald Scales, a young man of style in a *milieu* that, as Bennett would probably say, 'recks naught' of style, leads Sophia to linger in the shop, prolonging their delicious conversation, for the fatal few minutes that lead to her father's death. The shop is empty because one of the trio of elephants at a circus has turned wild and had to be destroyed, and the staff have hastened out to see the carcass; Mrs Baines's only moment of collapse is when she sobs in her sister's arms, 'If only it had been anything else than that elephant!' Years pass, mountain ranges of experience are traversed, and the grown-up Sophia is dining in Paris; not, this time, with a man she is in love with, but one who is in love with her. The city is starving, but they get a good dinner, and as the proprietor of the restaurant places before them 'an unnamed soup' he remarks casually that he is friendly with the butcher who has purchased the bodies of the three elephants from the Jardin des Plantes. More years pass, the story is curving towards its close, the sisters are united again in the Five Towns, and as Sophia looks through the window of the Loop Line train, she suddenly sees the surprising sight of 'two camels and an elephant in a field close to the line'. That the animals once again go in threes is probably an accidental, unimportant detail; but the recurrence of the elephant motif, I will wager, is not; it is the kind of detail that Bennett sowed scrupulously in his fictions, to add texture by a subdued pattern of recurrence. Such effects work subliminally, whether or not the reader notices them. They give the novel the density, the slow and rich unfolding, of life itself.

Again, Bennett clearly admires, and indicates that we are to admire, the pertinacity and pluck with which Sophia, when left on her own, learns the hotel business and becomes a success at it, till finally 'her Pension consisted of two floors instead of one, and she had turned the two hundred pounds stolen from Gerald into over two thousand'. He does not shrink from the word; she has stolen the money, though some of us might think, as the law thinks, that a wife has as good a right to the contents of a man's pockets as he has himself. It is a good thing, in Bennett's eyes, that Sophia has committed this theft; it has helped her to survive. 'The act,' he says, 'was characteristic of her enterprise and of her fundamental prudence.' But of course we remember that in Book Two, describing Constance's life as wife and mother, no domestic episode is treated at greater length, or given more prominence, than Cyril's 'crime', the theft of some cash from the till. In a commercial society, stealing money is the one unforgivable offence; you can rob someone of dignity, leisure, reputation, and some excuses will be forthcoming, but steal his money and you are in the dock straight away.

> If Cyril had stolen cakes, jam, string, cigars, Mr Povey would never have said 'thief' as he did say it. But money! Money was different. And a till was not a cupboard or a larder. A till was a till. Cyril had struck at the very basis of society.
>
> 'And on your mother's birthday!' Mr Povey said further.

These parallels, and the general scrupulousness of design and balance, testify to Bennett's faithfulness to the writer's craft. The book is like the kind of clothes and furniture favoured by the respectable inhabitants of the Square – plain, never showy, but 'good', made of the best materials and wrought to last. The same care is evident in the historical references that come down through the story like a hand-rail on a long staircase. Some of these are the routine references to public events that any historical novel uses – the Great Exhibition, Inkerman, the Dreyfus Case, Federation in the Potteries. All we need notice about them is that they are absolutely reliable. If Bennett brings in a piece of factual information from outside the story, the reader can be assured of its accuracy. If he says that electric tramcars appeared between Bursley and Hanbridge at a certain time, they did appear at that time. If Dick Povey can drive his motor car from the Potteries to Manchester in an hour and three quarters, that will be the time taken by a car of those days on the roads of those days. Others are slighter, more glancing; they challenge the reader to keep awake. Cyril Povey as a young man, cosmopolitan, sophisticated and incomprehensible to his mother, has only one picture up in his studio, 'a Japanese print, which struck [Constance] as entirely preposterous, considered as a picture'. Dating and detail are exactly right. Japanese art, through the medium of the print, made its first Western impact in Paris, became an important ingredient in the work of the Post-Impressionists, and baffled the lay mind by its entirely unfamiliar approach to perspective.

In fact Bennett's working rule, and perhaps the rule of any novelist in this documentary tradition, is never to invent anything if it can be found ready-made in reality. The two rival marching songs, for instance, sung in the streets of the Potteries as people went to vote for or against Federation (p. 605), sound like a novelist's picturesque inventions, but they really were sung and the words were reported in the *Staffordshire Sentinel* (Bennett's *Signal*) for 25 November 1907. Character and episode, of course, have to come from the writer's imagination; but the factual husk is more effective if it is transferred straight from life.

In making use of this husk, the only freedom Bennett permits himself here is a freedom now and then to bend chronology a little. In describing the execution of Rivain, Bennett, since he himself had never seen an execution, had to rely on written descriptions, and tells us explicitly in his Preface that he took his material from 'a series of articles . . . in the Paris *Matin*'. These articles are actually concerned with an execution that took place in 1891, and the song chanted by the crowd,

> Le voilà!
> Nicolas!
> Ah! Ah! Ah!

comes in fact from a popular song of the nineties. To suit his narrative, Bennett has transferred the whole episode back into the sixties, and has kept the song, which in fact had not yet been composed at the time when he set his scene, because it is too good a detail to resist.

Another instance of the same freedom, this time so minor as to be almost microscopic, concerns a garment. When Gerald Scales drapes himself picturesquely over the snowy doorstep of the Baines house, and spins them his no doubt fanciful tale of having been set on by muggers, he is wearing 'an ulster, and a maud over the ulster'. A 'maud' is, or was, a grey striped plaid worn by shepherds in the Scottish lowlands, hence any travelling-rug or shawl resembling this. So far, so good; but the 'ulster', a long travelling-coat of rough serge, often with a belt, was first introduced by the Belfast firm of J. G. M'Gee in 1867 – and Gerald Scales is depicted as wearing one on New Year's Eve 1865. Bennett correctly sees Gerald as the kind of young man who would certainly have worn an ulster for winter travel, when they were new and fashionable; and, if told that he had dated it a few months too soon, would no doubt have replied imperturbably that young Scales, being a traveller for a clothing firm, had probably got hold of an advance model.

In accordance with this general faithfulness to realism, the novel has its own consistent time-scheme, indicated to the watchful reader though never heavily insisted on. From the pointers scattered through the book, we can date every important event: death of John Baines, 1864; elopement of Sophia, July 1866; Constance and Samuel married, 27 May 1867; Cyril Povey born, 1874; death of Mrs Baines, 1875; Constance and Sophia meet again, 1896. Since the sisters are sixteen and fifteen when the book opens, they must have been born around 1847 and 1848, so that their lives span the distance between Early Victorian and Edwardian. So keenly did Bennett bring the book's forward frontier right up to his own day that the last public event that occupies his characters, the Federation of the Five Towns, did not in fact take legal effect until after the novel was published. He knew it was coming, and that was enough.

IV

So far, I have been writing about Bennett as if everything he did
had been achieved by working to a formula. Imitate the French
novel. Keep your prose grey and truthful. Make use of home
background. Focus on middling humanity. In fact, of course, all
art, in proportion as it *is* art, achieves its enduring vitality by
virtue of the individuality, the indispensable crumb of uniqueness, that the artist puts into it. The mark of any genuine work of
art is that it could only have come from that one person, among
all the teeming millions who inhabit the earth.

The sources of Arnold Bennett's inspiration, and the tradition
in which he placed himself, are clear enough to see. Equally
obvious is the high seriousness of his objectives. In that *Journal*
entry about the germ of *The Old Wives' Tale*, one notices the
willingness to measure himself against the highest standards of
European letters. The two works that occur to him as pace-setters
are Tolstoy's 'The Death of Ivan Ilytch', possibly the greatest
short story ever written, and Maupassant's 'Histoire d'une fille de
ferme', a classic story of Normandy peasant life. He did not,
however, propose to scale the heights merely by imitating the
best models. He had something uniquely his own to contribute;
there is a Bennett flavour as there is a Fielding flavour or a Jane
Austen flavour or a Conrad flavour. It inheres partly in his
honesty, partly in his compassion, but perhaps most of all in his
irony.

An ironist Bennett certainly was. Almost every sentence he
wrote is tinged with an irony that must have been an integral part
of the constitution of his mind, as natural to him as breathing. It is
never easy to define irony, unless it is the *saeva indignatio* of Swift
or the delicate rapier-play of Wilde. I think the nearest I can get to
it is to say that Bennett's was a kindly, a tolerant irony. He saw
human beings as inclined to be silly and fussy, but he did not hate
them for it. He was free of any temptation to set himself on a
pedestal and look down on the rest of humanity; he knew that,
seen through any other pair of eyes, he was just as funny as
anyone. Beyond that, his touch is so light as to make critical
description seem ponderous and blundering. Take, for instance,

the moment when Mrs Baines and her sister are preparing for the funeral of John Baines.

> Dress and the repast exceeded all other matters in complexity and difficulty. But on the morning of the funeral Aunt Harriet had the satisfaction of beholding her younger sister the centre of a tremendous cocoon of crape, whose slightest pleat was perfect. Aunt Harriet seemed to welcome her then, like a veteran, formally into the august army of relicts.

This is undoubtedly ironic, and irony is always to some extent associated with mockery, but if we ask, 'What is being mocked here?' we see at once that the question is much too crude. Nothing is actually ridiculed. Human beings react to great issues, like death, by concentrating very hard on small issues, like the meticulous pleating of a crape garment. Widows live out their widowhood with a kind of disciplined dignity that makes them, in some ways, resemble an army. The word 'relict' itself, much used in self-approvingly formal, not to say pompous, Victorian circles, rests on certain assumptions about marriage that now seem comical, and did in fact seem so to Bennett (if the surviving female partner is a 'relict', the implication is that the active, responsible partner was the male; a widower is never described as a relict). All this clutter of social and sartorial procedure, set against the stark backdrop of eternity, makes human beings appear somewhat small-scale, like scurrying Lilliputians. Bennett sees this, but he sees it with kindliness. If human beings are Lilliputian, that is not their fault. He noted in his *Journal* his firmly held belief that the 'distinguishing mark of a great novelist' was 'a Christ-like, all-embracing compassion'.

This compassion is so closely interwoven with Bennett's ironic attitude that the two are a seamless fabric. Where we find the one, we find the other, except on the exceedingly rare occasions when he is writing about something he wishes overtly to attack and feels the need to make his irony cutting. (Example: the description of the thought-processes of the Marquess of Welwyn on p. 268.)

Setting aside such very rare sallies, Bennett's irony, which makes up the greater part of his individual flavour, is pronounced and all-pervading without being hostile or condescending. Take, as a slightly more extended example, his description of the betrothal of Miss Elizabeth Chetwynd, the remote and formidable aunt of Sophia's schoolmistress, to the celebrated preacher Archibald Jones.

For Archibald Jones was one of the idols of the Wesleyan Methodist Connexion, a special preacher famous throughout England. At 'Anniversaries' and 'Trust sermons', Archibald Jones had probably no rival. His Christian name helped him; it was a luscious, resounding mouthful for admirers. He was not an itinerant minister, migrating every three years. His function was to direct the affairs of the 'Book Room', the publishing department of the Connexion. He lived in London, and shot out into the provinces at week-ends, preaching on Sundays and giving a lecture, tinctured with bookishness, 'in the chapel' on Monday evenings. In every town he visited there was competition for the privilege of entertaining him. He had zeal, indefatigable energy, and a breezy wit. He was a widower of fifty, and his wife had been dead for twenty years. It had seemed as if women were not for this bright star. And here Elizabeth Chetwynd, who had left the Five Towns a quarter of a century before at the age of twenty, had caught him! Austere, moustached, formidable, dessicated, she must have done it with her powerful intellect! It must be a union of intellects! He had been impressed by hers, and she by his, and then their intellects had kissed. Within a week fifty thousand women in forty counties had pictured to themselves this osculation of intellects, and shrugged their shoulders, and decided once more that men were incomprehensible. These great ones in London, falling in love like the rest! But no! Love was a ribald and voluptuous word to use in such a matter as this. It was generally felt that the Reverend Archibald Jones and Miss Chetwynd the elder would lift marriage to what would now be termed an astral plane.

Who is the target here? The dignified couple? The women all over the country who picture this 'osculation of intellects'? The airs and graces of successful preachers, in that day when successful preachers were much as television personalities are now? Marriage itself, even? Yes, all of them. One is, in the end, driven back on the banal statement that Bennett's irony is directed at life itself. But it is an irony of acceptance, not of rejection.

There remains the question of Bennett's success in depicting female characters from within rather than, as most male writers necessarily must do, from without. I do not know any way in which this matter can be judged except by the counting of votes. No literary judgement is capable of proof, in any case, any more than our judgements of people are capable of proof; we get to know others as well as we can, and then we like or dislike them according to our own needs and sympathies. Flaubert is generally said to have succeeded triumphantly with the character of Madame Bovary; if I say that I accept this belief, all I am actually saying is that he, a middle-aged Frenchman, drew a portrait of a young woman which I, a middle-aged Englishman, find entirely credible. On what am I basing my judgement? Simply on my own notion of what young women are like, which might be a tissue of misapprehensions. In the end it is humanity that decides. People have gone on reading about Madame Bovary because they find she comes across as a real person in a real setting, and that therefore her touching story continues to affect them.

In the case of Bennett, the same test will be applied; it has already been applied, for two generations. He wrote very often about women, putting them in the central place in his novels. These full-length portraits are not always equally successful; *The Old Wives' Tale* is the acknowledged masterpiece, *Leonora* an under-rated achievement, *Anna of the Five Towns* more interesting for its sketch of a social scene than for its portrait of Anna, while *Hilda Lessways* by common consent is, at best, a pardonable failure. But in these novels, not to mention other and slighter stories such as *Helen with the High Hand* and *Lilian*, he places the woman at the centre and devotes to her the book's main insight and sympathy. Partly he may have been following the example of the French novel (for French nineteenth-century fiction concerned itself very much with women), but the basic reason must have been his interest in them, his willingness to see their point of view. Ernest Hemingway wrote a volume of short stories called *Men Without Women*. Bennett could have reversed this and called his masterpiece *Women Without Men*. He bundles the male characters offstage as fast as possible, in order to allow the unrestricted play of feminine character. John Baines enters the story as a hopeless invalid and shortly dies. Samuel Povey hardly reaches middle age. Gerald disappears, except for one death-mask scene, after having set in motion the machinery of Sophia's life. Chirac has scarcely time to declare his love for Sophia before being whisked up in a balloon and never heard of again. Cyril Povey is an important character, but his life mainly happens offstage – indeed, it could be said that the essence of Cyril's importance, the essence of his effect on Constance, is precisely that his life happens offstage. As soon as he is old enough to study art in London, he slides gently out of the story, never having shown much wish to be in it. Only Mr Critchlow, an allegorical figure of mocking old Father Time himself, enters the book already old and survives, 'fabulously senile', determinedly occupying a central part of the stage, till the end.

This ruthless pruning away of the male characters, making us feel sometimes that we are in a world of spiders rather than human beings, leaves Bennett free to show his women as reacting to life directly, and not through the intermediary of men. I personally am convinced of the accuracy of his view of women, but, as I say, my opinion may be worthless. The best critical method, if you are a male reader, is to get your women friends to read the book and pass judgement on the female characterization. I have done this for twenty-five years, and the suffrage has been overwhelming: it is good; it tells the truth; it sees us as we are – or, bearing in mind that Bennett is an historical novelist, as we were.

V

When Arnold Bennett lay dying in his flat in Chiltern Court, Baker Street, the road under his windows was thickly spread with straw. This, a traditional method of muffling the clop of hoofs and the grinding of iron-rimmed wheels, was increasingly irrelevant in the motor age, and its employment in Bennett's case must have been one of the last. Still, employed it was, in an effort to give the dying man some rest; and in the early hours of the morning a milk van, loaded as they were in those days with heavy metal churns, capsized outside Chiltern Court – perhaps because the straw concealed the line of the kerb – with a clanging and grinding and gonging that must have been audible a mile away. Bennett's earthly existence was already over, for he had died before midnight; but perhaps his spirit, looking down, found some quiet enjoyment in the small ironic comedy. It was so much the sort of thing he always *expected* to happen.

JOHN WAIN

THE OLD WIVES' TALE

To W. W. K.

CONTENTS

BOOK THREE

SOPHIA

BOOK FOUR

WHAT LIFE IS

PREFACE

In the autumn of 1903 I used to dine frequently in a restaurant in the Rue de Clichy, Paris. Here were, among others, two waitresses that attracted my attention. One was a beautiful, pale young girl, to whom I never spoke, for she was employed far away from the table which I affected. The other, a stout, middle-aged managing Breton woman, had sole command over my table and me, and gradually she began to assume such a maternal tone towards me that I saw I should be compelled to leave that restaurant. If I was absent for a couple of nights running she would reproach me sharply: 'What! you are unfaithful to me?' Once, when I complained about some French beans, she informed me roundly that French beans were a subject which I did not understand. I then decided to be eternally unfaithful to her, and I abandoned the restaurant. A few nights before the final parting an old woman came into the restaurant to dine. She was fat, shapeless, ugly, and grotesque. She had a ridiculous voice, and ridiculous gestures. It was easy to see that she lived alone, and that in the long lapse of years she had developed the kind of peculiarity which induces guffaws among the thoughtless. She was burdened with a lot of small parcels, which she kept dropping. She chose one seat; and then, not liking it, chose another; and then another. In a few moments she had the whole restaurant laughing at her. That my middle-aged Breton should laugh was indifferent to me, but I was pained to see a coarse grimace of giggling on the pale face of the beautiful young waitress to whom I had never spoken.

I reflected, concerning the grotesque diner: 'The woman was once young, slim, perhaps beautiful; certainly free from these ridiculous mannerisms. Very probably she is unconscious of her singularities. Her case is a tragedy. One ought to be able to make

a heart-rending novel out of the history of a woman such as she.'
Every stout, ageing woman is not grotesque – far from it! – but
there is an extreme pathos in the mere fact that every stout ageing
woman was once a young girl with the unique charm of youth in
her form and movements and in her mind. And the fact that the
change from the young girl to the stout ageing woman is made up
of an infinite number of infinitesimal changes, each unperceived
by her, only intensifies the pathos.

It was at this instant that I was visited by the idea of writing the
book which ultimately became *The Old Wives' Tale*. Of course I
felt that the woman who caused the ignoble mirth in the restaurant would not serve me as a type of heroine. For she was
much too old and obviously unsympathetic. It is an absolute rule
that the principal character of a novel must not be unsympathetic, and the whole modern tendency of realistic fiction is against
oddness in a prominent figure. I knew that I must choose the sort
of woman who would pass unnoticed in a crowd.

I put the idea aside for a long time, but it was never very distant
from me. For several reasons it made a special appeal to me. I had
always been a convinced admirer of Mrs W. K. Clifford's most
precious novel, *Aunt Anne*, but I wanted to see in the story of an
old woman many things that Mrs W. K. Clifford had omitted
from *Aunt Anne*. Moreover, I had always revolted against the
absurd youthfulness, the unfading youthfulness of the average
heroine. And as a protest against this fashion, I was already, in
1903, planning a novel (*Leonora*) of which the heroine was aged
forty, and had daughters old enough to be in love. The reviewers,
by the way, were staggered by my hardihood in offering a woman
of forty as a subject of serious interest to the public. But I meant to
go much farther than forty! Finally, as a supreme reason, I had
the example and the challenge of Guy de Maupassant's *Une Vie*.
In the nineties we used to regard *Une Vie* with mute awe, as being
the summit of achievement in fiction. And I remember being very
cross with Mr Bernard Shaw because, having read *Une Vie* at the
suggestion (I think) of Mr William Archer, he failed to see in it
anything very remarkable. Here I must confess that, in 1908, I
read *Une Vie* again, and in spite of a natural anxiety to differ from
Mr Bernard Shaw, I was gravely disappointed with it. It is a fine

novel, but decidedly inferior to *Pierre et Jean* or even *Fort Comme la Mort*. To return to the year 1903. *Une Vie* relates the entire life-history of a woman. I settled in the privacy of my own head that my book about the development of a young girl into a stout old lady must be the English *Une Vie*. I have been accused of every fault except a lack of self-confidence, and in a few weeks I settled a further point, namely, that my book must 'go one better' than *Une Vie*, and that to this end it must be the life-history of two women instead of only one. Hence, *The Old Wives' Tale* has two heroines. Constance was the original; Sophia was created out of bravado, just to indicate that I declined to consider Guy de Maupassant as the last forerunner of the deluge. I was intimidated by the audacity of my project, but I had sworn to carry it out. For several years I looked it squarely in the face at intervals, and then walked away to write novels of smaller scope, of which I produced five or six. But I could not dally for ever, and in the autumn of 1907 I actually began to write it, in a village near Fontaine-bleau, where I rented half a house from a retired railway servant. I calculated that it would be 200,000 words long (which it exactly proved to be), and I had a vague notion that no novel of such dimensions (except Richardson's) had ever been written before. So I counted the words in several famous Victorian novels, and discovered to my relief that the famous Victorian novels average 400,000 words apiece. I wrote the first part of the novel in six weeks. It was fairly easy to me, because, in the seventies, in the first decade of my life, I had lived in the actual draper's shop of the Baineses, and knew it as only a child could know it. Then I went to London on a visit. I tried to continue the book in a London hotel, but London was too distracting, and I put the thing away, and during January and February of 1908, I wrote *Buried Alive*, which was published immediately, and was received with majestic indifference by the English public, an indifference which has persisted to this day.

I then returned to the Fontainebleau region and gave *The Old Wives' Tale* no rest till I finished it at the end of July 1908. It was published in the autumn of the same year, and for six weeks afterward the English public steadily confirmed an opinion expressed by a certain person in whose judgement I had confidence, to the effect that the work was honest but dull, and that when it was not dull it had a regrettable tendency to facetiousness. My publishers, though brave fellows, were somewhat disheartened; however, the reception of the book gradually became less and less frigid.

With regard to the French portion of the story, it was not until I had written the first part that I saw from a study of my chronological basis that the Siege of Paris might be brought into the tale. The idea was seductive; but I hated, and still hate, the awful business of research; and I only knew the Paris of the Twentieth Century. Now I was aware that my railway servant and his wife had been living in Paris at the time of the war. I said to the old man, 'By the way, you went through the Siege of Paris, didn't you?' He turned to his old wife and said, uncertainly, 'The Siege of Paris? Yes, we did, didn't we?' The Siege of Paris had been only one incident among many in their lives. Of course, they remembered it well, though not vividly, and I gained much information from them. But the most useful thing which I gained from them was the perception, startling at first, that ordinary people went on living very ordinary lives in Paris during the siege, and that to the vast mass of the population the siege was not the dramatic, spectacular, thrilling, ecstatic affair that is described in history. Encouraged by this perception, I decided to include the siege in my scheme. I read Sarcey's diary of the siege aloud to my wife, and I looked at the pictures in Jules Claretie's popular work on the siege and the commune, and I glanced at the printed collection of official documents, and there my research ended.

It has been asserted that unless I had actually been present at a public execution, I could not have written the chapter in which Sophia was at the Auxerre solemnity. I have not been present at a public execution, as the whole of my information about public executions was derived from a series of articles on them which I read in the Paris *Matin*. Mr Frank Harris, discussing my book in *Vanity Fair*, said it was clear that I had not seen an execution (or words to that effect), and he proceeded to give his own description of an execution. It was a brief but terribly convincing bit of writing, quite characteristic and quite worthy of the author of *Montes the Matador* and of a man who has been almost everywhere and seen almost everything. I comprehended how far short I had fallen of the truth! I wrote to Mr Frank Harris, regretting that his description had not been printed before I wrote mine, as I should assuredly have utilized it, and, of course, I admitted that I had never witnessed an execution. He simply replied: 'Neither have I.' This detail is worth preserving, for it is a reproof to that large body of readers, who, when a novelist has really carried conviction to them, assert off hand: 'Oh, that must be auto-biography!'

ARNOLD BENNETT

BOOK ONE: MRS BAINES

CHAPTER I: *The Square*

I

Those two girls, Constance and Sophia Baines, paid no heed to the manifold interest of their situation, of which, indeed, they had never been conscious. They were, for example, established almost precisely on the fifty-third parallel of latitude. A little way to the north of them, in the creases of a hill famous for its religious orgies, rose the river Trent, the calm and characteristic stream of middle England. Somewhat farther northwards, in the near neighbourhood of the highest public-house in the realm, rose two lesser rivers, the Dane and the Dove, which, quarrelling in early infancy, turned their back on each other, and, the one by favour of the Weaver and the other by favour of the Trent, watered between them the whole width of England, and poured themselves respectively into the Irish Sea and the German Ocean. What a county of modest, unnoticed rivers! What a natural, simple county, content to fix its boundaries by these tortuous island brooks, with their comfortable names – Trent, Mease, Dove, Tern, Dane, Mees, Stour, Tame, and even hasty Severn! Not that the Severn is suitable to the county! In the county excess is deprecated. The county is happy in not exciting remark. It is content that Shropshire should possess that swollen bump, the Wrekin, and that the exaggerated wildness of the Peak should lie over its border. It does not desire to be a pancake, like Cheshire. It has everything that England has, including thirty miles of Watling Street; and England can show nothing more beautiful and nothing uglier than the works of nature and the works of man to be seen within the limits of the county. It is England in little, lost in the midst of England, unsung by searchers after the extreme; perhaps occasionally somewhat sore at this neglect, but how proud in the instinctive cognizance of its representative features and traits!

Constance and Sophia, busy with the intense preoccupations of youth, recked not of such matters. They were surrounded by the county. On every side the fields and moors of Staffordshire, intersected by roads and lanes, railways, watercourses and tele-graph-lines, patterned by hedges, ornamented and made respect-able by halls and genteel parks, enlivened by villages at the intersections, and warmly surveyed by the sun, spread out un-dulating. And trains were rushing round curves in deep cuttings, and carts and waggons trotting and jingling on the yellow roads, and long, narrow boats passing in a leisure majestic and infinite over the surface of the stolid canals; the rivers had only them-selves to support, for Staffordshire rivers have remained virgin of keels to this day. One could imagine the messages concerning prices, sudden death, and horses, in their flight through the wires under the feet of birds. In the inns Utopians were shouting the universe into order over beer, and in the halls and parks the dignity of England was being preserved in a fitting manner. The villages were full of women who did nothing but fight against dirt and hunger, and repair the effects of friction on clothes. Thousands of labourers were in the fields, but the fields were so broad and numerous that this scattered multitude was totally lost therein. The cuckoo was much more perceptible than man, dominating whole square miles with his resounding call. And on the airy moors heath-larks played in the ineffaceable muletracks that had served centuries before even the Romans thought of Watling Street. In short, the usual daily life of the county was proceeding with all its immense variety and importance; but though Constance and Sophia were in it they were not of it.

The fact is, that while in the county they were also in the district; and no person who lives in the district, even if he should be old and have nothing to do but reflect upon things in general, ever thinks about the county. So far as the county goes, the district might almost as well be in the middle of the Sahara. It ignores the county, save that it uses it nonchalantly sometimes as leg-stretcher on holiday afternoons, as a man may use his back garden. It has nothing in common with the county; it is richly sufficient to itself. Nevertheless, its self-sufficiency and the true salt savour of its life can only be appreciated by picturing it hemmed in by county. It lies on the face of the county like an insignificant stain, like a dark Pleiades in a green and empty sky. And Hanbridge has the shape of a horse and its rider, Bursley of half a donkey, Knype of a pair of trousers, Longshaw of an octopus, and little Turnhill of a beetle. The Five Towns seem to cling together for safety. Yet the idea of clinging together for safety would make them laugh. They are unique and indispensable. From the north of the county right down to the south they alone stand for civilization, applied science, organized manufacture, and the century – until you come to Wolverhampton. They are unique and indispensable because you cannot drink tea out of a teacup without the aid of the Five Towns; because you cannot eat a meal in decency without the aid of the Five Towns. For this the architecture of the Five Towns is an architecture of ovens and chimneys; for this its atmosphere is as black as its mud; for this it burns and smokes all night, so that Longshaw has been compared to hell; for this it is unlearned in the ways of agriculture, never having seen corn except as packing straw and in quartern loaves; for this, on the other hand, it comprehends the mysterious habits of fire and pure, sterile earth; for this it lives crammed together in slippery streets where the housewife must change white window-curtains at least once a fortnight if she wishes to remain respectable; for this it gets up in the mass at six a.m., winter and summer, and goes to bed when the public-houses close; for this it exists – that you may drink tea out of a teacup and toy with a chop on a plate. All the everyday crockery used in the kingdom is made in the Five Towns – all, and much besides. A district capable of such gigantic manufacture, of such a perfect monopoly – and which finds energy also to produce coal and iron and great men – may be an insignificant stain on a county, considered geographically, but it is surely well justified in treating the county as its back garden once a week, and in blindly ignoring it the rest of the time.

Even the majestic thought that whenever and wherever in all England a woman washes up, she washes up the product of the district; that whenever and wherever in all England a plate is broken the fracture means new business for the district – even this majestic thought had probably never occurred to either of the girls. The fact is, that while in the Five Towns they were also in the Square. Bursley and the Square ignored the staple manufacture as perfectly as the district ignored the county. Bursley has the honours of antiquity in the Five Towns. No industrial development can ever rob it of its superiority in age, which makes it absolutely sure in its conceit. And the time will never come when the other towns – let them swell and bluster as they may – will not pronounce the name of Bursley as one pronounces the name of one's mother. Add to this that the Square was the centre of Bursley's retail trade (which scorned the staple as something wholesale, vulgar, and assuredly filthy), and you will comprehend the importance and the self-isolation of the Square in the scheme of the created universe. There you have it, embedded in the district, and the district embedded in the county, and the county lost and dreaming in the heart of England!

The Square was named after St Luke. The Evangelist might have been startled by certain phenomena in his square, but, except in Wakes Week, when the shocking always happened, St Luke's Square lived in a manner passably saintly – though it contained five public-houses. It contained five public-houses, a bank, a barber's, a confectioner's, three grocers', two chemists', an ironmonger's, a clothier's, and five drapers'. These were all the catalogue. St Luke's Square had no room for minor establishments. The aristocracy of the Square undoubtedly consisted of the drapers (for the bank was impersonal); and among the five the shop of Baines stood supreme. No business establishment could possibly be more respected than that of Mr Baines was respected. And though John Baines had been bedridden for a dozen years, he still lived on the lips of admiring, ceremonious burgesses as 'our honoured fellow-townsman'. He deserved his reputation.

The Baineses' shop, to make which three dwellings had at intervals been thrown into one, lay at the bottom of the Square. It formed about one-third of the south side of the Square, the remainder being made up of Critchlow's (chemist), the clothier's, and the Hanover Spirit Vaults. ('Vaults'[1] was a favourite synonym of the public-house in the Square. Only two of the public-houses were crude public-houses: the rest were 'vaults'.) It was a composite building of three storeys, in blackish-crimson brick, with a projecting shop-front, and, above and behind that, two rows of little windows. On the sash of each window was a red cloth roll stuffed with sawdust, to prevent draughts; plain white blinds descended about six inches from the top of each window. There were no curtains to any of the windows save one; this was the window of the drawing-room, on the first floor at the corner of the Square and King Street. Another window, on the second storey, was peculiar, in that it had neither blind nor pad, and was very dirty; this was the window of an unused room that had a separate staircase to itself, the staircase being barred by a door always locked. Constance and Sophia had lived in continual expectation of the abnormal issuing from that mysterious room, which was next to their own. But they were disappointed. The room had no shameful secret except the incompetence of the architect who had made one house out of three; it was just an empty, unemployable room. The building had also a considerable frontage on King Street, where, behind the shop, was sheltered the parlour, with a large window and a door that led directly by two steps into the street. A strange peculiarity of the shop was that it bore no signboard. Once it had had a large signboard which a memorable gale had blown into the Square. Mr Baines had decided not to replace it. He had always objected to what he called 'puffing', and for this reason would never hear of such a thing as a clearance sale. The hatred of 'puffing' grew on him until he came to regard even a sign as 'puffing'. Uninformed persons who wished to find Baines's must ask and learn. For Mr Baines, to have replaced the sign would have been to condone, yea, to participate in, the modern craze for unscrupulous self-advertisement. This abstention of Mr Baines's from indulgence in signboards was somehow accepted by the more thoughtful members of the community as evidence that the height of Mr Baines's principles was greater even than they had imagined.

Constance and Sophia were the daughters of this credit to human nature. He had no other children.

II

They pressed their noses against the window of the showroom, and gazed down into the Square as perpendicularly as the project-

ing front of the shop would allow. The showroom was over the
millinery and silken half of the shop. Over the woollen and
shirting half were the drawing-room and the chief bedroom.
When in quest of articles of coquetry, you mounted from the shop
by a curving stair, and your head gradually rose level with a large
apartment having a mahogany counter in front of the window
and along one side, yellow linoleum on the floor, many cardboard boxes, a magnificent hinged cheval glass, and two chairs.
The window-sill being lower than the counter, there was a gulf
between the panes and the back of the counter, into which
important articles such as scissors, pencils, chalk, and artificial
flowers were continually disappearing: another proof of the
architect's incompetence.

The girls could only press their noses against the window by
kneeling on the counter, and this they were doing. Constance's
nose was snub, but agreeably so. Sophia had a fine Roman nose;
she was a beautiful creature, beautiful and handsome at the same
time. They were both of them rather like racehorses, quivering
with delicate, sensitive, and luxuriant life; exquisite, enchanting
proof of the circulation of the blood; innocent, artful, roguish,
prim, gushing, ignorant, and miraculously wise. Their ages were
sixteen and fifteen; it is an epoch when, if one is frank, one must
admit that one has nothing to learn: one has learnt simply
everything in the previous six months.

'There she goes!' exclaimed Sophia.

Up the Square, from the corner of King Street, passed a woman
in a new bonnet with pink strings, and a new blue dress that
sloped at the shoulders and grew to a vast circumference at the
hem. Through the silent sunlit solitude of the Square (for it was
Thursday afternoon, and all the shops shut except the confectioner's and one chemist's) this bonnet and this dress floated
northwards in search of romance, under the relentless eyes of
Constance and Sophia. Within them, somewhere, was the soul of
Maggie, domestic servant at Baines's. Maggie had been at the
shop since before the creation of Constance and Sophia. She lived
seventeen hours of each day in an underground kitchen and
larder, and the other seven in an attic, never going out except to
chapel on Sunday evenings, and once a month on Thursday

afternoons. 'Followers' were most strictly forbidden to her; but on rare occasions an aunt from Longshaw was permitted as a tremendous favour to see her in the subterranean den. Everybody, including herself, considered that she had a good 'place', and was well treated. It was undeniable, for instance, that she was allowed to fall in love exactly as she chose, provided she did not 'carry on' in the kitchen or the yard. And as a fact, Maggie had fallen in love. In seventeen years she had been engaged eleven times. No one could conceive how that ugly and powerful organism could softly languish to the undoing of even a butty-collier, nor why, having caught a man in her sweet toils, she could ever be imbecile enough to set him free. There are, however, mysteries in the souls of Maggies. The drudge had probably been affianced oftener than any woman in Bursley. Her employers were so accustomed to an interesting announcement that for years they had taken to saying naught in reply but 'Really, Maggie!' Engagements and tragic partings were Maggie's pastime. Fixed otherwise, she might have studied the piano instead.

'No gloves, of course!' Sophia criticized.

'Well, you can't expect her to have gloves,' said Constance.

Then a pause, as the bonnet and dress neared the top of the Square.

'Supposing she turns round and sees us?' Constance suggested.

'I don't care if she does,' said Sophia, with a haughtiness almost impassioned; and her head trembled slightly.

There were, as usual, several loafers at the top of the Square, in the corner between the bank and the 'Marquis of Granby'. And one of these loafers stepped forward and shook hands with an obviously willing Maggie. Clearly it was a rendezvous, open, unashamed. The twelfth victim had been selected by the virgin of forty, whose kiss would not have melted lard! The couple disappeared together down Oldcastle Street.

'Well!' cried Constance. 'Did you ever see such a thing?'

While Sophia, short of adequate words, flushed and bit her lip.

With the profound, instinctive cruelty of youth, Constance and Sophia had assembled in their favourite haunt, the showroom, expressly to deride Maggie in her new clothes. They obscurely thought that a woman so ugly and soiled as Maggie was had no right to possess new clothes. Even her desire to take the air of a Thursday afternoon seemed to them unnatural and somewhat reprehensible. Why should she want to stir out of her kitchen? As for her tender yearnings, they positively grudged these to Maggie. That Maggie should give rein to chaste passion was more than grotesque; it was offensive and wicked. But let it not for an instant be doubted that they were nice, kind-hearted, well-behaved, and delightful girls! Because they were. They were not angels.

'It's too ridiculous!' said Sophia, severely. She had youth, beauty, and rank in her favour. And to her it really was ridiculous.

'Poor old Maggie!' Constance murmured. Constance was foolishly good-natured, a perfect manufactory of excuses for other people; and her benevolence was eternally rising up and overpowering her reason.

'What time did mother say she should be back?' Sophia asked.

'Not until supper.'

'Oh! Hallelujah!' Sophia burst out, clasping her hands in joy. And they both slid down from the counter just as if they had been little boys, and not, as their mother called them, 'great girls'.

'Let's go and play the Osborne quadrilles,' Sophia suggested (the Osborne quadrilles being a series of dances arranged to be performed on drawing-room pianos by four jewelled hands).

'I couldn't think of it,' said Constance, with a precocious gesture of seriousness. In that gesture, and in her tone, was something which conveyed to Sophia: 'Sophia, how can you be so utterly blind to the gravity of our fleeting existence as to ask me to go and strum the piano with you?' Yet a moment before she had been a little boy.

'Why not?' Sophia demanded.

'I shall never have another chance like to-day for getting on with this,' said Constance, picking up a bag from the counter.

She sat down and took from the bag a piece of loosely woven canvas, on which she was embroidering a bunch of roses in coloured wools. The canvas had once been stretched on a frame, but now, as the delicate labour of the petals and leaves was done, and nothing remained to do but the monotonous background,

Constance was content to pin the stuff to her knee. With the long needle and several skeins of mustard-tinted wool, she bent over the canvas and resumed the filling-in of the tiny squares. The whole design was in squares – the gradations of red and greens, the curves of the smallest buds – all was contrived in squares, with a result that mimicked a fragment of uncompromising Axminster carpet. Still, the fine texture of the wool, the regular and rapid grace of those fingers moving incessantly at back and front of the canvas, the gentle sound of the wool as it passed through the holes, and the intent, youthful earnestness of that lowered gaze, excused and invested with charm an activity which, on artistic grounds, could not possibly be justified. The canvas was destined to adorn a gilt firescreen in the drawing-room, and also to form a birthday gift to Mrs Baines from her elder daughter. But whether the enterprise was as secret from Mrs Baines as Constance hoped, none save Mrs Baines knew.

'Con,' murmured Sophia, 'you're too sickening sometimes.'

'Well,' said Constance, blandly, 'it's no use pretending that this hasn't got to be finished before we go back to school, because it has.'

Sophia wandered about, a prey ripe for the Evil One. 'Oh,' she exclaimed joyously – even ecstatically – looking behind the cheval glass, 'here's mother's new skirt! Miss Dunn's been putting the gimp on it! Oh, mother, what a proud thing you will be!'

Constance heard swishings behind the glass. 'What are you doing, Sophia?'

'Nothing.'

'You surely aren't putting that skirt on?'

'Why not?'

'You'll catch it finely, I can tell you!'

Without further defence, Sophia sprang out from behind the immense glass. She had already shed a notable part of her own costume, and the flush of mischief was in her face. She ran across to the other side of the room and examined carefully a large coloured print that was affixed to the wall.

This print represented fifteen sisters, all of the same height and slimness of figure, all of the same age – about twenty-five or so – and all with exactly the same haughty and bored beauty. That they were in truth sisters was clear from the facial resemblance between them; their demeanour indicated that they were princesses, offspring of some impossibly prolific king and queen. Those hands had never toiled, nor had those features ever relaxed from the smile of courts. The princesses moved in a landscape of marble steps and verandas, with a bandstand and strange trees in the distance. One was in a riding-habit, another in evening attire, another dressed for tea, another for the theatre; another seemed to be ready to go to bed. One held a little girl by the hand; it could not have been her own little girl, for these princesses were far beyond human passions. Where had she obtained the little girl? Why was one sister going to the theatre, another to tea, another to the stable, and another to bed? Why was one in a heavy mantle, and another sheltering from the sun's rays under a parasol? The picture was drenched in mystery, and the strangest thing about it was that all these highnesses were apparently content with the most ridiculous and out-moded fashions. Absurd hats, with veils flying behind; absurd bonnets, fitting close to the head, and spotted; absurd coiffures that nearly lay on the nape; absurd, clumsy sleeves; absurd waists, almost above the elbow's level; absurd scolloped jackets! And the skirts! What a sight were those skirts! They were nothing but vast decorated pyramids; on the summit of each was stuck the upper half of a princess. It was astounding that princesses should consent to be so preposterous and so uncomfortable. But Sophia perceived nothing uncanny in the picture, which bore the legend: 'Newest summer fashions from Paris. Gratis supplement to *Myra's Journal*.' Sophia had never imagined anything more stylish, lovely, and dashing than the raiment of the fifteen princesses.

For Constance and Sophia had the disadvantage of living in the middle ages. The crinoline had not quite reached its full circumference, and the dress-improver had not even been thought of. In all the Five Towns there was not a public bath, nor a free library, nor a municipal park, nor a telephone, nor yet a board-school. People had not understood the vital necessity of going away to the seaside every year. Bishop Colenso had just staggered Christianity by his shameless notions on the Pentateuch. Half

Lancashire was starving on account of the American war. Garroting was the chief amusement of the homicidal classes. Incredible as it may appear, there was nothing but a horse-tram running between Bursley and Hanbridge – and that only twice an hour; and between the other towns no stage of any kind! One went to Longshaw as one now goes to Peking. It was an era so dark and backward that one might wonder how people could sleep in their beds at night for thinking about their sad state.

Happily the inhabitants of the Five Towns in that era were passably pleased with themselves, and they never even suspected that they were not quite modern and quite awake. They thought that the intellectual, the industrial, and the social movements had gone about as far as these movements could go, and they were amazed at their own progress. Instead of being humble and ashamed they actually showed pride in their pitiful achievements. They ought to have looked forward meekly to the prodigious feats of posterity; but, having too little faith and too much conceit, they were content to look behind and make comparisons with the past. They did not foresee the miraculous generation which is us. A poor, blind, complacent people! The ludicrous horse-car was typical of them. The driver rang a huge bell, five minutes before starting, that could be heard from the Wesleyan Chapel to the Cock Yard, and then after deliberations and hesitations the vehicle rolled off on its rails into unknown dangers while passengers shouted good-bye. At Bleakridge it had to stop for the turnpike, and it was assisted up the mountains of Leveson Place and Sutherland Street (towards Hanbridge) by a third horse, on whose back was perched a tiny, whip-cracking boy; that boy lived like a shuttle on the road between Leveson Place and Sutherland Street, and even in wet weather he was the envy of all other boys. After half an hour's perilous transit the car drew up solemnly in a narrow street by the *Signal* office in Hanbridge, and the ruddy driver, having revolved many times the polished iron handle of his sole brake, turned his attention to his passengers in calm triumph, dismissing them with a sort of unsung doxology.

And this was regarded as the last word of traction! A whip-cracking boy on a tip horse! Oh, blind, blind! You could not foresee the hundred and twenty electric cars that now rush madly bumping and thundering at twenty miles an hour through all the main streets of the district!

So that naturally Sophia, infected with the pride of her period, had no misgivings whatever concerning the final elegance of the princesses. She studied them as the fifteen apostles of the *ne plus ultra*; then, having taken some flowers and plumes out of a box, amid warnings from Constance, she retreated behind the glass, and presently emerged as a great lady in the style of the princesses. Her mother's tremendous new gown ballooned about her in all its fantastic richness and expensiveness. And with the gown she had put on her mother's importance – that mien of assured authority, of capacity tested in many a crisis, which characterized Mrs Baines, and which Mrs Baines seemed to impart to her dresses even before she had regularly worn them. For it was a fact that Mrs Baines's empty garments inspired respect, as though some essence had escaped from her and remained in them.

'Sophia!'

Constance stayed her needle, and, without lifting her head, gazed, with eyes raised from the wool-work, motionless at the posturing figure of her sister. It was sacrilege that she was witnessing, a prodigious irreverence. She was conscious of an expectation that punishment would instantly fall on this daring impious child. But she, who never felt these mad, amazing impulses, could nevertheless only smile fearfully.

'Sophia!' she breathed, with an intensity of alarm that merged into condoning admiration. 'Whatever will you do next?'

Sophia's lovely flushed face crowned the extraordinary structure like a blossom, scarcely controlling its laughter. She was as tall as her mother, and as imperious, as crested, and proud; and in spite of the pigtail, the girlish semi-circular comb, and the loose foal-like limbs, she could support as well as her mother the majesty of the gimp-embroidered dress. Her eyes sparkled with all the challenges of the untried virgin as she minced about the showroom. Abounding life inspired her movements. The confident and fierce joy of youth shone on her brow. 'What thing on earth equals me?' she seemed to demand with enchanting and yet ruthless arrogance. She was the daughter of a respected, bedridden draper in an insignificant town, lost in the central labyrinth of England, if you like; yet what manner of man, confronted with her, would or could have denied her naïve claim to dominion? She stood, in her mother's hoops, for the desire of the world. And in the innocence of her soul she knew it! The heart of a young girl mysteriously speaks and tells her of her power long ere she can use her power. If she can find nothing else to subdue, you may catch her in the early years subduing a gate-post or drawing homage from an empty chair. Sophia's experimental victim was Constance, with suspended needle and soft glance that shot out from the lowered face.

Then Sophia fell, in stepping backwards; the pyramid was overbalanced; great distended rings of silk trembled and swayed gigantically on the floor, and Sophia's small feet lay like the feet of a doll on the rim of the largest circle, which curved and arched above them like a cavern's mouth. The abrupt transition of her features from assured pride to ludicrous astonishment and alarm was comical enough to have sent into wild uncharitable laughter any creature less humane than Constance. But Constance sprang to her, a single embodied instinct of benevolence, with her snub nose, and tried to raise her.

'Oh, Sophia!' she cried compassionately – that voice seemed not to know the tones of reproof – 'I do hope you've not messed it, because mother would be so –'

The words were interrupted by the sound of groans beyond the door leading to the bedrooms. The groans, indicating direct physical torment, grew louder. The two girls stared, wonderstruck and afraid, at the door, Sophia with her dark head raised, and Constance with her arms round Sophia's waist. The door opened, letting in a much-magnified sound of groans, and there entered a youngish, undersized man, who was frantically clutching his head in his hands and contorting all the muscles of his face. On perceiving the sculptural group of two prone, interlocked girls, one enveloped in a crinoline, and the other with a wool-work bunch of flowers pinned to her knee, he jumped back, ceased groaning, arranged his face, and seriously tried to pretend that it was not he who had been vocal in anguish, that, indeed, he was just passing as a casual, ordinary wayfarer through the showroom to the shop below. He blushed darkly; and the girls also blushed.

'Oh, I beg pardon, I'm sure!' said this youngish man suddenly; and with a swift turn he disappeared whence he had come.

He was Mr Povey, a person universally esteemed, both within and without the shop, the surrogate of bedridden Mr Baines, the unfailing comfort and stand-by of Mrs Baines, the fount and radiating centre of order and discipline in the shop; a quiet, diffident, secretive, tedious, and obstinate youngish man, absolutely faithful, absolutely efficient in his sphere; without brilliance, without distinction; perhaps rather little-minded, certainly narrow-minded; but what a force in the shop! The shop was inconceivable without Mr Povey. He was under twenty and not out of his apprenticeship when Mr Baines had been struck down, and he had at once proved his worth. Of the assistants, he alone slept in the house. His bedroom was next to that of his employer; there was a door between the two chambers, and the two steps led down from the larger to the less.

The girls regained their feet, Sophia with Constance's help. It was not easy to right a capsized crinoline. They both began to laugh nervously, with a trace of hysteria.

'I thought he'd gone to the dentist's,' whispered Constance.

Mr Povey's toothache had been causing anxiety in the microcosm for two days, and it had been clearly understood at dinner that Thursday morning that Mr Povey was to set forth to Oulsnam Bros, the dentists at Hillport, without any delay. Only on Thursdays and Sundays did Mr Povey dine with the family. On other days he dined later, by himself, but at the family table, when Mrs Baines or one of the assistants could 'relieve' him in the shop. Before starting out to visit her elder sister at Axe, Mrs Baines had insisted to Mr Povey that he had eaten practically nothing but 'slops' for twenty-four hours, and that if he was not careful she would have him on her hands. He had replied in his quietest, most sagacious, matter-of-fact tone – the tone that carried weight with all who heard it – that he had only been waiting for Thursday afternoon, and should of course go instantly to Oulsnams' and have the thing attended to in a proper manner. He had even added that persons who put off going to the dentist's were simply sowing trouble for themselves.

None could possibly have guessed that Mr Povey was afraid of going to the dentist's. But such was the case. He had not dared to set forth. The paragon of common sense, pictured by most people as being somehow unliable to human frailties, could not yet screw himself up to the point of ringing a dentist's door-bell.

'He did look funny,' said Sophia. 'I wonder what he thought. I couldn't help laughing!'

Constance made no answer; but when Sophia had resumed her own clothes, and it was ascertained beyond doubt that the new dress had not suffered, and Constance herself was calmly stitching again, she said, poising her needle as she had poised it to watch Sophia:

'I was just wondering whether something oughtn't to be done for Mr Povey.'

'What?' Sophia demanded.

'Has he gone back to his bedroom?'

'Let's go and listen,' said Sophia the adventuress.

They went, through the showroom door, past the foot of the stairs leading to the second storey, down the long corridor broken in the middle by two steps and carpeted with a narrow bordered carpet whose parallel lines increased its apparent length. They went on tiptoe, sticking close to one another. Mr Povey's door was slightly ajar. They listened; not a sound.

'Mr Povey!' Constance coughed discreetly.

No reply. It was Sophia who pushed the door open. Constance made an elderly prim plucking gesture at Sophia's bare arm, but she followed Sophia gingerly into the forbidden room, which was, however, empty. The bed had been ruffled, and on it lay a book, *The Harvest of a Quiet Eye*.[2]

'Harvest of a quiet tooth!' Sophia whispered, giggling very low.

'Hsh!' Constance put her lips forward.

From the next room came a regular, muffled, oratorical sound, as though someone had begun many years ago to address a meeting and had forgotten to leave off and never would leave off. They were familiar with the sound, and they quitted Mr Povey's chamber in fear of disturbing it. At the same moment Mr Povey reappeared, this time in the drawing-room doorway at the other extremity of the long corridor. He seemed to be trying ineffectually to flee from his tooth as a murderer tries to flee from his conscience.

'Oh, Mr Povey!' said Constance quickly – for he had surprised them coming out of his bedroom; 'we were just looking for you.'

'To see if we could do anything for you,' Sophia added.

'Oh no, thanks!' said Mr Povey.

Then he began to come down the corridor, slowly.

'You haven't been to the dentist's,' said Constance sympathetically.

'No, I haven't,' said Mr Povey, as if Constance was indicating a fact which had escaped his attention. 'The truth is, I thought it looked like rain, and if I'd got wet – you see –'

Miserable Mr Povey!

'Yes,' said Constance, 'you certainly ought to keep out of draughts. Don't you think it would be a good thing if you went and sat in the parlour? There's a fire there.'

'I shall be all right, thank you,' said Mr Povey. And after a pause: 'Well, thanks, I will.'

III

The girls made way for him to pass them at the head of the twisting stairs which led down to the parlour. Constance followed, and Sophia followed Constance.

'Have father's chair,' said Constance.

There were two rocking-chairs with fluted backs covered by antimacassars, one on either side of the hearth. That to the left was still entitled 'father's chair', though its owner had not sat in it since long before the Crimean war, and would never sit in it again.

'I think I'd sooner have the other one,' said Mr Povey, 'because it's on the right side, you see.' And he touched his right cheek.

Having taken Mrs Baines's chair, he bent his face down to the fire, seeking comfort from its warmth. Sophia poked the fire, whereupon Mr Povey abruptly withdrew his face. He then felt something light on his shoulders. Constance had taken the antimacassar from the back of the chair, and protected him with it from the draughts. He did not instantly rebel, and therefore was permanently barred from rebellion. He was entrapped by the antimacassar. It formally constituted him an invalid, and Constance and Sophia his nurses. Constance drew the curtain across the street door. No draught could come from the window, for the window was not 'made to open'. The age of ventilation had not arrived. Sophia shut the other two doors. And, each near a door, the girls gazed at Mr Povey behind his back, irresolute, but filled with a delicious sense of responsibility.

The situation was on a different plane now. The seriousness of Mr Povey's toothache, which became more and more manifest, had already wiped out the ludicrous memory of the encounter in the showroom. Looking at these two big girls, with their short-sleeved black frocks and black aprons, and their smooth hair, and their composed serious faces, one would have judged them incapable of the least lapse from an archangelic primness; Sophia especially presented a marvellous imitation of saintly innocence. As for the toothache, its action on Mr Povey was apparently periodic; it gathered to a crisis like a wave, gradually, the torture increasing till the wave broke and left Mr Povey exhausted, but free for a moment from pain. These crises recurred about once a minute. And now, accustomed to the presence of the young virgins, and having tacitly acknowledged by his acceptance of the antimacassar that his state was abnormal, he gave himself up frankly to affliction. He concealed nothing of his agony, which was fully displayed by sudden contortions of his frame, and frantic oscillations of the rocking-chair. Presently, as he lay back enfeebled in the wash of a spent wave, he murmured with a sick man's voice:

'I suppose you haven't got any laudanum?'

The girls started into life. 'Laudanum, Mr Povey?'

'Yes, to hold in my mouth.'

He sat up, tense; another wave was forming. The excellent fellow was lost to all self-respect, all decency.

'There's sure to be some in mother's cupboard,' said Sophia.

Constance, who bore Mrs Baines's bunch of keys at her girdle, a solemn trust, moved a little fearfully to a corner cupboard

which was hung in the angle to the right of the projecting
fireplace, over a shelf on which stood a large copper tea-urn. That
corner cupboard, of oak inlaid with maple and ebony in a simple
border pattern, was typical of the room. It was of a piece with the
deep green 'flock' wallpaper, and the tea-urn, and the rocking-
chairs with their antimacassars, and the harmonium in rose-
wood with a Chinese papier-mâché tea-caddy on the top of it;
even with the carpet, certainly the most curious parlour carpet
that ever was, being made of lengths of the stair-carpet sewn
together side by side. That corner cupboard was already old in
service; it had held the medicines of generations. It gleamed
darkly with the grave and genuine polish which comes from
ancient use alone. The key which Constance chose from her
bunch was like the cupboard, smooth and shining with years; it
fitted and turned very easily, yet with a firm snap. The single wide
door opened sedately as a portal.

The girls examined the sacred interior, which had the air of
being inhabited by an army of diminutive prisoners, each crying
aloud with the full strength of its label to be set free on a mission.

'There it is!' said Sophia eagerly.

And there it was: a blue bottle, with a saffron label, 'Caution.
POISON, Laudanum. Charles Critchlow, M.P.S. Dispensing
Chemist. St Luke's Square, Bursley.'

Those large capitals frightened the girls. Constance took the
bottle as she might have taken a loaded revolver, and she glanced
at Sophia. Their omnipotent, all-wise mother was not present to
tell them what to do. They, who had never decided, had to decide
now. And Constance was the elder. Must this fearsome stuff,
whose very name was a name of fear, be introduced in spite of
printed warnings into Mr Povey's mouth? The responsibility was
terrifying.

'Perhaps I'd just better ask Mr Critchlow,' Constance faltered.

The expectation of beneficent laudanum had enlivened Mr
Povey, had already, indeed, by a sort of suggestion, half cured his
toothache.

'Oh no!' he said. 'No need to ask Mr Critchlow . . . Two or
three drops in a little water.' He showed impatience to be at the
laudanum.

The girls knew that an antipathy existed between the chemist and Mr Povey.

'It's sure to be all right,' said Sophia. 'I'll get the water.'

With youthful cries and alarms they succeeded in pouring four mortal dark drops (one more than Constance intended) into a cup containing a little water. And as they handed the cup to Mr Povey their faces were the faces of affrighted comical conspirators. They felt so old and they looked so young.

Mr Povey inbibed eagerly of the potion, put the cup on the mantelpiece, and then tilted his head to the right so as to submerge the affected tooth. In this posture he remained, awaiting the sweet influence of the remedy. The girls, out of a nice modesty, turned away, for Mr Povey must not swallow the medicine, and they preferred to leave him unhampered in the solution of a delicate problem. When next they examined him, he was leaning back in the rocking-chair with his mouth open and his eyes shut.

'Has it done you any good, Mr Povey?'

'I think I'll lie down on the sofa for a minute,' was Mr Povey's strange reply; and forthwith he sprang up and flung himself on to the horse-hair sofa between the fireplace and the window, where he lay stripped of all his dignity, a mere beaten animal in a grey suit with peculiar coat-tails, and a very creased waistcoat, and a lapel that was planted with pins, and a paper collar and close-fitting paper cuffs.

Constance ran after him with the antimacassar, which she spread softly on his shoulders; and Sophia put another one over his thin little legs, all drawn up.

They then gazed at their handiwork, with secret self-accusations and the most dreadful misgivings.

'He surely never swallowed it!' Constance whispered.

'He's asleep, anyhow,' said Sophia, more loudly.

Mr Povey was certainly asleep, and his mouth was very wide open – like a shop-door. The only question was whether his sleep was not an eternal sleep; the only question was whether he was not out of his pain for ever.

Then he snored – horribly; his snore seemed a portent of disaster.

Sophia approached him as though he were a bomb, and stared, growing bolder, into his mouth.

'Oh, Con,' she summoned her sister, 'do come and look! It's too droll!'

In an instant all their four eyes were exploring the singular landscape of Mr Povey's mouth. In a corner, to the right of that interior, was one sizeable fragment of a tooth, that was attached to Mr Povey by the slenderest tie, so that at each respiration of Mr Povey, when his body slightly heaved and the gale moaned in the cavern, this tooth moved separately, showing that its long connexion with Mr Povey was drawing to a close.

'That's the one,' said Sophia, pointing. 'And it's as loose as anything. Did you ever see such a funny thing?'

The extreme funniness of the thing had lulled in Sophia the fear of Mr Povey's sudden death.

'I'll see how much he's taken,' said Constance, preoccupied, going to the mantelpiece.

'Why, I do believe —' Sophia began, and then stopped, glancing at the sewing-machine, which stood next to the sofa.

It was a Howe sewing-machine. It had a little tool-drawer, and in the tool-drawer was a small pair of pliers. Constance, engaged in sniffing at the lees of the potion in order to estimate its probable deadliness, heard the well-known click of the little tool-drawer, and then she saw Sophia nearing Mr Povey's mouth with the pliers.

'Sophia!' she exclaimed, aghast. 'What in the name of goodness are you doing?'

'Nothing,' said Sophia.

The next instant Mr Povey sprang out of his laudanum dream.

'It jumps!' he muttered; and, after a reflective pause, 'but it's much better.' He had at any rate escaped death.

Sophia's right hand was behind her back.

Just then a hawker passed down King Street, crying mussels and cockles.

'Oh!' Sophia almost shrieked. 'Do let's have mussels and cockles for tea!' And she rushed to the door, and unlocked and opened it, regardless of the risk of draughts to Mr Povey.

In those days people often depended upon the caprices of

hawkers for the tastiness of their teas; but it was an adventurous age, when errant knights of commerce were numerous and enterprising. You went on to your doorstep, caught your meal as it passed, withdrew, cooked it and ate it, quite in the manner of the early Briton.

Constance was obliged to join her sister on the top step. Sophia descended to the second step.

'Fresh mussels and cockles all alive, oh!' bawled the hawker, looking across the road in the April breeze. He was the celebrated Hollins, a professional Irish drunkard, aged in iniquity, who cheerfully saluted magistrates in the street, and referred to the workhouse, which he occasionally visited, as the Bastille.

Sophia was trembling from head to foot.

'What *are* you laughing at, you silly thing?' Constance demanded.

Sophia surreptitiously showed the pliers, which she had partly thrust into her pocket. Between their points was a most perceptible, and even recognizable, fragment of Mr Povey.

This was the crown of Sophia's career as a perpetrator of the unutterable.

'What!' Constance's face showed the final contortions of that horrified incredulity which is forced to believe.

Sophia nudged her violently to remind her that they were in the street, and also quite close to Mr Povey.

'Now, my little missies,' said the vile Hollins. 'Threepence a pint, and how's your honoured mother today? Yes, fresh, so help me God!'

CHAPTER 2: *The Tooth*

I

The two girls came up the unlighted stone staircase which led from Maggie's cave to the door of the parlour. Sophia, foremost, was carrying a large tray, and Constance a small one. Constance, who had nothing on her tray but a teapot, a bowl of steaming and balmy-scented mussels and cockles, and a plate of hot buttered toast, went directly into the parlour on the left. Sophia had in her arms the entire material and apparatus of a high tea for two, including eggs, jam, and toast (covered with the slop-basin turned upside-down), but not including mussels and cockles. She turned to the right, passed along the corridor by the cutting-out room, up two steps into the sheeted and shuttered gloom of the closed shop, up the showroom stairs, through the showroom, and so into the bedroom corridor. Experience had proved it easier to make this long detour than to round the difficult corner of the parlour stairs with a large loaded tray. Sophia knocked with the edge of the tray at the door of the principal bedroom. The muffled oratorical sound from within suddenly ceased, and the door was opened by a very tall, very thin, black-bearded man, who looked down at Sophia as if to demand what she meant by such an interruption.

'I've brought the tea, Mr Critchlow,' said Sophia.

And Mr Critchlow carefully accepted the tray.

'Is that my little Sophia?' asked a faint voice from the depths of the bedroom.

'Yes, father,' said Sophia.

But she did not attempt to enter the room. Mr Critchlow put the tray on a white-clad chest of drawers near the door, and then he shut the door with no ceremony. Mr Critchlow was John Baines's oldest and closest friend, though decidedly younger than the draper. He frequently 'popped in' to have a word with the invalid; but Thursday afternoon was his special afternoon, consecrated by him to the service of the sick. From two o'clock precisely till eight o'clock precisely he took charge of John Baines, reigning autocratically over the bedroom. It was known that he would not tolerate invasions, nor even ambassadorial visits. No! He gave up his weekly holiday to this business of friendship, and he must be allowed to conduct the business in his own way. Mrs Baines herself avoided disturbing Mr Critchlow's ministrations on her husband. She was glad to do so; for Mr Baines was never to be left alone under any circumstances, and the convenience of being able to rely upon the presence of a staid member of the Pharmaceutical Society for six hours of a given day every week outweighed the slight affront to her prerogatives as wife and house-mistress. Mr Critchlow was an extremely peculiar man, but when he was in the bedroom she could leave the house with an easy mind. Moreover, John Baines enjoyed these Thursday afternoons. For him, there was 'none like Charles Critchlow'. The two old friends experienced a sort of grim, desiccated happiness, cooped up together in the bedroom, secure from women and fools generally. How they spent the time did not seem to be certainly known, but the impression was that politics occupied them. Undoubtedly Mr Critchlow was an extremely peculiar man. He was a man of habits. He must always have the same things for his tea. Black-currant jam, for instance. (He called it 'preserve'.) The idea of offering Mr Critchlow a tea which did not comprise black-currant jam was inconceivable by the intelligence of St Luke's Square. Thus for years·past, in the fruit-preserving season, when all the house and all the shop smelt richly of fruit boiling in sugar, Mrs Baines had filled an extra number of jars with black-currant jam, 'because Mr Critchlow wouldn't *touch* any other sort'.

So Sophia, faced with the shut door of the bedroom, went down to the parlour by the shorter route. She knew that on going up again, after tea, she would find the devastated tray on the doormat.

Constance was helping Mr Povey to mussels and cockles. And Mr Povey still wore one of the antimacassars. It must have stuck to his shoulders when he sprang up from the sofa, woollen antimacassars being notoriously parasitic things. Sophia sat down, somewhat self-consciously. The serious Constance was also perturbed. Mr Povey did not usually take tea in the house on Thursday afternoons; his practice was to go out into the great, mysterious world. Never before had he shared a meal with the girls alone. The situation was indubitably unexpected, unforeseen; it was, too, piquant, and what added to its piquancy was the fact that Constance and Sophia were, somehow, responsible for Mr Povey. They felt that they were responsible for him. They had offered the practical sympathy of two intelligent and well-trained young women, born nurses by reason of their sex, and Mr Povey had accepted; he was now on their hands. Sophia's monstrous, sly operation in Mr Povey's mouth did not cause either of them much alarm, Constance having apparently recovered from the first shock of it. They had discussed it in the kitchen while preparing the teas. Constance's extraordinarily severe and dictatorial tone in condemning it had led to a certain heat. But the success of the impudent wench justified it despite any irrefutable argument to the contrary. Mr Povey was better already, and he evidently remained in ignorance of his loss.

'Have some?' Constance asked of Sophia, with a large spoon hovering over the bowl of shells.

'Yes, *please*,' said Sophia, positively.

Constance well knew that she would have some, and had only asked from sheer nervousness.

'Pass your plate, then.'

Now when everybody was served with mussels, cockles, tea, and toast, and Mr Povey had been persuaded to cut the crust off his toast, and Constance had, quite unnecessarily, warned Sophia against the deadly green stuff in the mussels, and Constance had further pointed out that the evenings were getting longer, and Mr Povey had agreed that they were, there remained nothing to say. An irksome silence fell on them all, and no one could lift it off. Tiny clashes of shell and crockery sounded with the terrible clearness of noises heard in the night. Each person avoided the eyes of the others. And both Constance and Sophia kept straightening their bodies at intervals, and expanding their chests, and then looking at their plates; occasionally a prim cough was discharged. It was a sad example of the difference between young women's dreams of social brilliance and the reality of life. These girls got more and more girlish, until, from being women at the administering of laudanum, they sank back to about eight years of age – perfect children – at the tea-table.

The tension was snapped by Mr Povey. 'My God!' he muttered, moved by a startling discovery to this impious and disgraceful oath (he, the pattern and exemplar – and in the presence of innocent girlhood, too!). 'I've swallowed it!'

'Swallowed what, Mr Povey?' Constance inquired.

The tip of Mr Povey's tongue made a careful voyage of inspection all round the right side of his mouth.

'Oh yes!' he said, as if solemnly accepting the inevitable. 'I've swallowed it!'

Sophia's face was now scarlet; she seemed to be looking for some place to hide it. Constance could not think of anything to say.

'That tooth has been loose for two years,' said Mr Povey, 'and now I've swallowed it with a mussel.'

'Oh, Mr Povey!' Constance cried in confusion, and added, 'There's one good thing, it can't hurt you any more now.'

'Oh!' said Mr Povey. 'It wasn't *that* tooth that was hurting me. It's an old stump at the back that's upset me so this last day or two. I wish it had been.'

Sophia had her teacup close to her red face. At these words of Mr Povey her cheeks seemed to fill out like plump apples. She dashed the cup into its saucer, spilling tea recklessly, and then ran from the room with stifled snorts.

'Sophia!' Constance protested.

'I must just –' Sophia incoherently spluttered in the doorway. 'I shall be all right. Don't –'

Constance, who had risen, sat down again.

II

Sophia fled along the passage leading to the shop and took refuge in the cutting-out room, a room which the astonishing architect had devised upon what must have been a backyard of one of the three constituent houses. It was lighted from its roof, and only a wooden partition, eight feet high, separated it from the passage. Here Sophia gave rein to her feelings; she laughed and cried together, weeping generously into her handkerchief and wildly giggling, in a hysteria which she could not control. The spectacle of Mr Povey mourning for a tooth which he thought he had swallowed, but which in fact lay all the time in her pocket, seemed to her to be by far the most ridiculous, side-splitting thing that had ever happened or could happen on earth. It utterly overcame her. And when she fancied that she had exhausted and conquered its surpassing ridiculousness, this ridiculousness seized her again and rolled her anew in depths of mad, trembling laughter.

Gradually she grew calmer. She heard the parlour door open, and Constance descend the kitchen steps with a rattling tray of tea-things. Tea, then, was finished, without her! Constance did not remain in the kitchen, because the cups and saucers were left for Maggie to wash up as a fitting *coda* to Maggie's monthly holiday. The parlour door closed. And the vision of Mr Povey in his antimacassar swept Sophia off into another convulsion of laughter and tears. Upon this the parlour door opened again, and Sophia choked herself into silence while Constance hastened along the passage. In a minute Constance returned with her woolwork, which she had got from the showroom, and the parlour received her. Not the least curiosity on the part of Constance as to what had become of Sophia!

At length Sophia, a faint meditative smile being all that was left of the storm in her, ascended slowly to the showroom, through the shop. Nothing there of interest! Thence she wandered towards the drawing-room, and encountered Mr Critchlow's tray on the mat. She picked it up and carried it by way of the showroom and shop down to the kitchen, where she dreamily munched two pieces of toast that had cooled to the consistency of leather. She mounted the stone steps and listened at the door of the parlour. No sound! This seclusion of Mr Povey and Constance was really very strange. She roved right round the house, and descended creepingly by the twisted house-stairs, and listened intently at the other door of the parlour. She now detected a faint regular snore. Mr Povey, a prey to laudanum and mussels, was sleeping while Constance worked at her firescreen! It was now in the highest degree odd, this seclusion of Mr Povey and Constance; unlike anything in Sophia's experience! She wanted to go into the parlour, but she could not bring herself to do so. She crept away again, forlorn and puzzled, and next discovered herself in the bedroom which she shared with Constance at the top of the house; she lay down in the dusk on the bed and began to read *The Days of Bruce*; but she read only with her eyes.

Later, she heard movements on the house-stairs, and the familiar whining creak of the door at the foot thereof. She skipped lightly to the door of the bedroom.

'Good night, Mr Povey. I hope you'll be able to sleep.'

Constance's voice!

'It will probably come on again.'

Mr Povey's voice, pessimistic!

Then the shutting of doors. It was almost dark. She went back to the bed, expecting a visit from Constance. But a clock struck eight, and all the various phenomena connected with the departure of Mr Critchlow occurred one after another. At the same time Maggie came home from the land of romance. Then long silences! Constance was now immured with her father, it being her 'turn' to nurse. Maggie was washing up in her cave, and Mr Povey was lost to sight in his bedroom. Then Sophia heard her mother's lively, commanding knock on the King Street door. Dusk had definitely yielded to black night in the bedroom. Sophia dozed and dreamed. When she awoke, her ear caught the sound of knocking. She jumped up, tiptoed to the landing, and looked over the balustrade, whence she had a view of all the first-floor corridor. The gas had been lighted; through the round aperture at the top of the porcelain globe she could see the wavering flame. It was her mother, still bonneted, who was knocking at the door of Mr Povey's room. Constance stood in the doorway of her parents' room. Mrs Baines knocked twice with an interval, and then said to Constance, in a resonant whisper that vibrated up the corridor –

'He seems to be fast asleep. I'd better not disturb him.'

'But suppose he wants something in the night?'

'Well, child, I should hear him moving. Sleep's the best thing for him.'

Mrs Baines left Mr Povey to the effects of laudanum, and came along the corridor. She was a stout woman, all black stuff and gold chain, and her skirt more than filled the width of the corridor. Sophia watched her habitual heavy mounting gesture as she climbed the two steps that gave variety to the corridor. At the gas-jet she paused, and, putting her hand to the tap, gazed up into the globe.

'Where's Sophia?' she demanded, her eyes fixed on the gas as she lowered the flame.

'I think she must be in bed, mother,' said Constance, non-chalantly.

The returned mistress was point by point resuming knowledge and control of that complicated machine – her household.

Then Constance and her mother disappeared into the bedroom, and the door was shut with a gentle, decisive bang that to the silent watcher on the floor above seemed to create a special excluding intimacy round about the figures of Constance and her father and mother. The watcher wondered, with a little prick of jealousy, what they would be discussing in the large bedroom, her father's beard wagging feebly and his long arms on the counterpane. Constance perched at the foot of the bed, and her mother walking to and fro, putting her cameo brooch on the dressing-table or stretching creases out of her gloves. Certainly, in some subtle way, Constance had a standing with her parents which was more confidential than Sophia's.

III

When Constance came to bed, half an hour later, Sophia was already in bed. The room was fairly spacious. It had been the girls' retreat and fortress since their earliest years. Its features seemed to them as natural and unalterable as the features of a cave to a cave-dweller. It had been repapered twice in their lives, and each papering stood out in their memories like an epoch; a third epoch was due to the replacing of a drugget by a resplendent old carpet degraded from the drawing-room. There was only one bed, the bedstead being of painted iron; they never interfered with each other in that bed, sleeping with a detachment as perfect as if they had slept on opposite sides of St Luke's Square; yet if Constance had one night lain down on the half near the window instead of on the half near the door, the secret nature of the universe would have seemed to be altered. The small fire-grate was filled with a mass of shavings of silver paper; now the rare illnesses which they had suffered were recalled chiefly as periods when that silver paper was crammed into a large slipper-case which hung by the mantelpiece, and a fire of coals unnaturally reigned in its place – the silver paper was part of the order of the world. The sash of the window would not work quite properly, owing to a slight subsidence in the wall, and even when the window was fastened there was always a narrow slit to the left hand between the window and its frame; through this slit came draughts, and thus very keen frosts were remembered by the nights when Mrs Baines caused the sash to be forced and kept at its full height by means of wedges – the slit of exposure was part of the order of the world.

They possessed only one bed, one washstand, and one dressing-table; but in some other respects they were rather fortunate girls, for they had two mahogany wardrobes; this mutual independence as regards wardrobes was due partly to Mrs Baines's strong common sense, and partly to their father's tendency to spoil them a little. They had, moreover, a chest of drawers with a curved front, of which structure Constance occupied two short drawers and one long one, and Sophia two long drawers. On it stood two fancy work-boxes, in which each sister kept jewellery, a savings-bank book, and other treasures, and these boxes were absolutely sacred to their respective owners. They were different, but one was not more magnificent than the other. Indeed, a rigid equality was the rule in the chamber, the single exception being that behind the door were three hooks, of which Constance commanded two.

'Well,' Sophia began, when Constance appeared. 'How's darling Mr Povey?' She was lying on her back, and smiling at her two hands, which she held up in front of her.

'Asleep,' said Constance. 'At least mother thinks so. She says sleep is the best thing for him.'

'"It will probably come on again,"' said Sophia.

'What's that you say?' Constance asked, undressing.

'"It will probably come on again."'

These words were a quotation from the utterances of darling Mr Povey on the stairs, and Sophia delivered them with an exact imitation of Mr Povey's vocal mannerism.

'Sophia,' said Constance, firmly, approaching the bed. 'I wish you wouldn't be so silly!' She had benevolently ignored the satirical note in Sophia's first remark, but a strong instinct in her rose up and objected to further derision. 'Surely you've done enough for one day!' she added.

For answer Sophia exploded into violent laughter, which she

made no attempt to control. She laughed too long and too freely while Constance stared at her.

'*I* don't know what's come over you!' said Constance.

'It's only because I can't look at it without simply going off into fits!' Sophia gasped out. And she held up a tiny object in her left hand.

Constance started, flushing. 'You don't mean to say you've kept it!' she protested earnestly. 'How horrid you are, Sophia! Give it me at once and let me throw it away. I never heard of such doings. Now give it me!'

'No,' Sophia objected, still laughing. 'I wouldn't part with it for worlds. It's too lovely.'

She had laughed away all her secret resentment against Constance for having ignored her during the whole evening and for being on such intimate terms with their parents. And she was ready to be candidly jolly with Constance.

'Give it me,' said Constance, doggedly.

Sophia hid her hand under the clothes. 'You can have his old stump, when it comes out, if you like. But not this. What a pity it's the wrong one!'

'Sophia, I'm ashamed of you! Give it me.'

Then it was that Sophia first perceived Constance's extreme seriousness. She was surprised and a little intimidated by it. For the expression of Constance's face, usually so benign and calm, was harsh, almost fierce. However, Sophia had a great deal of what is called 'spirit', and not even ferocity on the face of mild Constance could intimidate her for more than a few seconds. Her gaiety expired and her teeth were hidden.

'I've said nothing to mother —' Constance proceeded.

'I should hope you haven't,' Sophia put in tersely.

'But I certainly shall if you don't throw that away,' Constance finished.

'You can say what you like,' Sophia retorted, adding contemptuously a term of opprobrium which has long since passed out of us: 'Cant!'

'Will you give it me or won't you?'

'No!'

It was a battle suddenly engaged in the bedroom. The atmosphere had altered completely with the swiftness of magic. The beauty of Sophia, the angelic tenderness of Constance, and the youthful, naïve, innocent charm of both of them, were transformed into something sinister and cruel. Sophia lay back on the pillow amid her dark-brown hair, and gazed with relentless defiance into the angry eyes of Constance, who stood threatening by the bed. They could hear the gas singing over the dressing-table, and their hearts beating the blood wildly in their veins. They ceased to be young without growing old; the eternal had leapt up in them from its sleep.

Constance walked away from the bed to the dressing-table and began to loose her hair and brush it, holding back her head, shaking it, and bending forward, in the changeless gesture of that rite. She was so disturbed that she had unconsciously reversed the customary order of the toilette. After a moment Sophia slipped out of bed and, stepping with her bare feet to the chest of drawers, opened her work-box and deposited the fragment of Mr Povey therein; she dropped the lid with an uncompromising bang, as if to say, 'We shall see if I am to be trod upon, miss!' Their eyes met again in the looking-glass. Then Sophia got back into bed.

Five minutes later, when her hair was quite finished, Constance knelt down and said her prayers. Having said her prayers, she went straight to Sophia's work-box, opened it, seized the fragment of Mr Povey, ran to the window, and frantically pushed the fragment through the slit into the square.

'There!' she exclaimed nervously.

She had accomplished this inconceivable transgression of the code of honour, beyond all undoing, before Sophia could recover from the stupefaction of seeing her sacred work-box impudently violated. In a single moment one of Sophia's chief ideals had been smashed utterly, and that by the sweetest, gentlest creature she had ever known. It was a revealing experience for Sophia – and also for Constance. And it frightened them equally. Sophia, staring at the text, 'Thou God seest me,' framed in straw over the chest of drawers, did not stir. She was defeated, and so profoundly moved in her defeat that she did not even reflect upon the obvious inefficacy of illuminated texts as a deterrent from evil-doing. Not that she cared a fig for the fragment of Mr Povey! It was the moral aspect of the affair, and the astounding, inexplicable development in Constance's character that staggered her into silent acceptance of the inevitable.

Constance, trembling, took pains to finish undressing with dignified deliberation. Sophia's behaviour under the blow seemed too good to be true; but it gave her courage. At length she turned out the gas and lay down by Sophia. And there was a little shuffling, and then stillness for a while.

'And if you want to know,' said Constance in a tone that mingled amicableness with righteousness, 'mother's decided with Aunt Harriet that we are *both* to leave school next term.'

CHAPTER 3: *A Battle*

I

The day sanctioned by custom in the Five Towns for the making of pastry is Saturday. But Mrs Baines made her pastry on Friday, because Saturday afternoon was, of course, a busy time in the shop. It is true that Mrs Baines made her pastry in the morning, and that Saturday morning in the shop was scarcely different from any other morning. Nevertheless, Mrs Baines made her pastry on Friday morning instead of Saturday morning because Saturday afternoon was a busy time in the shop. She was thus free to do her marketing without breathtaking flurry on Saturday morning.

On the morning after Sophia's first essay in dentistry, therefore, Mrs Baines was making her pastry in the underground kitchen. This kitchen, Maggie's cavern-home, had the mystery of a church, and on dark days it had the mystery of a crypt. The stone steps leading down to it from the level of earth were quite unlighted. You felt for them with the feet of faith, and when you arrived in the kitchen, the kitchen, by contrast, seemed luminous and gay; the architect may have considered and intended this effect of the staircase. The kitchen saw day through a wide, shallow window whose top touched the ceiling and whose bottom had been out of the girls' reach until long after they had begun to go to school. Its panes were small, and about half of them were of the 'knot' kind, through which no object could be distinguished; the other half were of a later date, and stood for the march of civilization. The view from the window consisted of the vast plate-glass windows of the newly built Sun vaults, and of passing legs and skirts. A strong wire grating prevented any excess of illumination, and also protected the glass from the caprices of wayfarers in King Street. Boys had a habit of stopping to kick with their full strength at the grating.

Forget-me-nots on a brown field ornamented the walls of the kitchen. Its ceiling was irregular and grimy, and a beam ran across it; in this beam were two hooks; from these hooks had once depended the ropes of a swing, much used by Constance and Sophia in the old days before they were grown up. A large range stood out from the wall between the stairs and the window. The rest of the furniture comprised a table – against the wall opposite the range – a cupboard, and two Windsor chairs. Opposite the foot of the steps was a doorway, without a door, leading to two larders, dimmer even than the kitchen, vague retreats made visible by whitewash, where bowls of milk, dishes of cold bones, and remainders of fruit-pies, reposed on stillages; in the corner nearest the kitchen was a great steen in which the bread was kept. Another doorway on the other side of the kitchen led to the first coal-cellar, where was also the slopstone and tap, and thence a tunnel took you to the second coal-cellar, where coke and ashes were stored; the tunnel proceeded to a distant, infinitesimal yard, and from the yard, by ways behind Mr Critchlow's shop, you could finally emerge, astonished, upon Brougham Street. The sense of the vast-obscure of those regions which began at the top of the kitchen steps and ended in black corners of larders or abruptly in the common dailiness of Brougham Street, a sense which Constance and Sophia had acquired in infancy, remained with them almost unimpaired as they grew old.

Mrs Baines wore black alpaca, shielded by a white apron whose string drew attention to the amplitude of her waist. Her sleeves were turned up, and her hands, as far as the knuckles, covered with damp flour. Her ageless smooth paste-board occupied a corner of the table, and near it were her paste-roller, butter, some pie-dishes, shredded apples, sugar, and other things. Those rosy hands were at work among a sticky substance in a large white bowl.

'Mother, are you there?' she heard a voice from above.

'Yes, my chuck.'

Footsteps apparently reluctant and hesitating clinked on the stairs, and Sophia entered the kitchen.

'Put this curl straight,' said Mrs Baines, lowering her head slightly and holding up her floured hands, which might not touch anything but flour. 'Thank you. It bothered me. And now stand out of my light. I'm in a hurry. I must get into the shop so that I can send Mr Povey off to the dentist's. What is Constance doing?'

'Helping Maggie to make Mr Povey's bed.'

'Oh!'

Though fat, Mrs Baines was a comely woman, with fine brown hair, and confidently calm eyes that indicated her belief in her own capacity to accomplish whatever she could be called on to accomplish. She looked neither more nor less than her age, which was forty-five. She was not a native of the district, having been culled by her husband from the moorland town of Axe, twelve miles off. Like nearly all women who settle in a strange land upon marriage, at the bottom of her heart she had considered herself just a trifle superior to the strange land and its ways. This feeling, confirmed by long experience, had never left her. It was this feeling which induced her to continue making her own pastry – with two thoroughly trained 'great girls' in the house! Constance could make good pastry, but it was not her mother's pastry. In pastry-making everything can be taught except the 'hand', light and firm, which wields the roller. One is born with this hand, or without it. And if one is born without it, the highest flights of pastry are impossible. Constance was born without it. There were days when Sophia seemed to possess it; but there were other days when Sophia's pastry was uneatable by any one except Maggie. Thus Mrs Baines, though intensely proud and fond of her daughters, had justifiably preserved a certain condescension towards them. She honestly doubted whether either of them would develop into the equal of their mother.

'Now you little vixen!' she exclaimed. Sophia was stealing and eating slices of half-cooked apple. 'This comes of having no breakfast! And why didn't you come down to supper last night?'

'I don't know. I forgot.'

Mrs Baines scrutinized the child's eyes, which met hers with a sort of diffident boldness. She knew everything that a mother can know of a daughter, and she was sure that Sophia had no cause to be indisposed. Therefore she scrutinized those eyes with a faint apprehension.

'If you can't find anything better to do,' said she, 'butter me the inside of this dish. Are your hands clean? No, better not touch it.'

Mrs Baines was now at the stage of depositing little pats of butter in rows on a large plain of paste. The best fresh butter! Cooking butter, to say naught of lard, was unknown in that kitchen on Friday mornings. She doubled the expanse of paste on itself and rolled the butter in – supreme operation!

'Constance has told you about leaving school?' said Mrs Baines, in the vein of small-talk, as she trimmed the paste to the shape of a pie-dish.

'Yes,' Sophia replied shortly. Then she moved away from the table to the range. There was a toasting-fork on the rack, and she began to play with it.

'Well, are you glad? Your aunt Harriet thinks you are quite old enough to leave. And as we'd decided in any case that Constance was to leave, it's really much simpler that you should both leave together.'

'Mother,' said Sophia, rattling the toasting-fork, 'what am I going to do after I've left school?'

'I hope,' Mrs Baines answered with that sententiousness which even the cleverest of parents are not always clever enough to deny themselves, 'I hope that both of you will do what you can to help your mother – and father,' she added.

'Yes,' said Sophia, irritated. 'But what am I going to *do*?'

'That must be considered. As Constance is to learn the millinery, I've been thinking that you might begin to make yourself useful in the underwear, gloves, silks, and so on. Then between you, you would one day be able to manage quite nicely all that side of the shop, and I should be –'

'I don't want to go into the shop, mother.'

This interruption was made in a voice apparently cold and inimical. But Sophia trembled with nervous excitement as she uttered the words. Mrs Baines gave a brief glance at her, unobserved by the child, whose face was towards the fire. She deemed herself a finished expert in the reading of Sophia's moods; nevertheless, as she looked at that straight back and proud head, she had no suspicion that the whole essence and being of Sophia was silently but intensely imploring sympathy.

'I wish you would be quiet with that fork,' said Mrs Baines, with the curious, grim politeness which often characterized her relations with her daughters.

The toasting-fork fell on the brick floor, after having rebounded from the ash-tin. Sophia hurriedly replaced it on the rack.

'Then what *shall* you do?' Mrs Baines proceeded, conquering the annoyance caused by the toasting-fork. 'I think it's me that should ask you instead of you asking me. What shall you do? Your father and I were both hoping you would take kindly to the shop and try to repay us for all the –'

Mrs Baines was unfortunate in her phrasing that morning. She happened to be, in truth, rather an exceptional parent, but that morning she seemed unable to avoid the absurd pretensions which parents of those days assumed quite sincerely and which every good child with meekness accepted.

Sophia was not a good child, and she obstinately denied in her heart the cardinal principle of family life, namely, that the parent has conferred on the offspring a supreme favour by bringing it into the world. She interrupted her mother again, rudely.

'I don't want to leave school at all,' she said passionately.

'But you will have to leave school sooner or later,' argued Mrs Baines, with an air of quiet reasoning, of putting herself on a level with Sophia. 'You can't stay at school for ever, my pet, can you? Out of my way!'

She hurried across the kitchen with a pie, which she whipped into the oven, shutting the iron door with a careful gesture.

'Yes,' said Sophia. 'I should like to be a teacher. That's what I want to be.'

The tap in the coal-cellar, out of repair, could be heard

distinctly and systematically dropping water into a jar on the slopstone.

'A school-teacher?' inquired Mrs Baines.

'Of course. What other kind is there?' said Sophia, sharply. 'With Miss Chetwynd.'

'I don't think your father would like that,' Mrs Baines replied. 'I'm sure he wouldn't like it.'

'Why not?'

'It wouldn't be quite suitable.'

'Why not, mother?' the girl demanded with a sort of ferocity. She had now quitted the range. A man's feet twinkled past the window.

Mrs Baines was startled and surprised. Sophia's attitude was really very trying; her manners deserved correction. But it was not these phenomena which seriously affected Mrs Baines; she was used to them and had come to regard them as somehow the inevitable accompaniment of Sophia's beauty, as the penalty of that surpassing charm which occasionally emanated from the girl like a radiance. What startled and surprised Mrs Baines was the perfect and unthinkable madness of Sophia's infantile scheme. It was a revelation to Mrs Baines. Why in the name of heaven had the girl taken such a notion into her head? Orphans, widows, and spinsters of a certain age suddenly thrown on the world – these were the women who, naturally, became teachers, because they had to become something. But that the daughter of comfortable parents, surrounded by love and the pleasures of an excellent home, should wish to teach in a school was beyond the horizons of Mrs Baines's common sense. Comfortable parents of today who have a difficulty in sympathizing with Mrs Baines, should picture what their feelings would be if their Sophias showed a rude desire to adopt the vocation of chauffeur.

'It would take you too much away from home,' said Mrs Baines, achieving a second pie.

She spoke softly. The experience of being Sophia's mother for nearly sixteen years had not been lost on Mrs Baines, and though she was now discovering undreamt-of dangers in Sophia's erratic temperament, she kept her presence of mind sufficiently well to behave with diplomatic smoothness. It was undoubtedly humili-

ating to a mother to be forced to use diplomacy in dealing with a
girl in short sleeves. In *her* day mothers had been autocrats. But
Sophia was Sophia.

'What if it did?' Sophia curtly demanded.

'And there's no opening in Bursley,' said Mrs Baines.

'Miss Chetwynd would have me, and then after a time I could
go to her sister.'

'Her sister? What sister?'

'Her sister that has a big school in London somewhere.'

Mrs Baines covered her unprecedented emotions by gazing
into the oven at the first pie. The pie was doing well, under all the
circumstances. In those few seconds she reflected rapidly and
decided that to a desperate disease a desperate remedy must be
applied.

London! She herself had never been farther than Manchester.
London, 'after a time'! No, diplomacy would be misplaced in this
crisis of Sophia's development!

'Sophia,' she said, in a changed and solemn voice, fronting her
daughter, and holding away from her apron those floured, ringed
hands, 'I don't know what has come over you. Truly I don't!
Your father and I are prepared to put up with a certain amount,
but the line must be drawn. The fact is, we've spoilt you, and
instead of getting better as you grow up, you're getting worse.
Now let me hear no more of this, please. I wish you would imitate
your sister a little more. Of course if you won't do your share in
the shop, no one can make you. If you choose to be an idler about
the house, we shall have to endure it. We can only advise you for
your own good. But as for this . . .' She stopped, and let silence
speak, and then finished: 'Let me hear no more of it.'

It was a powerful and impressive speech enunciated clearly in
such a tone as Mrs Baines had not employed since dismissing a
young lady assistant five years ago for light conduct.

'But, mother —'

A commotion of pails resounded at the top of the stone steps. It
was Maggie in descent from the bedrooms. Now, the Baines
family passed its life in doing its best to keep its affairs to itself,
the assumption being that Maggie and all the shop-staff (Mr
Povey possibly excepted) were obsessed by a ravening appetite

for that which did not concern them. Therefore the voices of the Baineses always died away or fell to a hushed, mysterious whisper whenever the foot of the eavesdropper was heard.

Mrs Baines put a floured finger to her double chin. 'That will do,' said she, with finality.

Maggie appeared, and Sophia, with a brusque precipitation of herself, vanished upstairs.

II

'Now, really, Mr Povey, this is not like you,' said Mrs Baines, who, on her way into the shop, had discovered the Indispensable in the cutting-out room.

It is true that the cutting-out room was almost Mr Povey's sanctum, whither he retired from time to time to cut out suits of clothes and odd garments for the tailoring department. It is true that the tailoring department flourished with orders, employing several tailors who crossed legs in their own homes, and that appointments were continually being made with customers for trying-on in that room. But these considerations did not affect Mrs Baines's attitude of disapproval.

'I'm just cutting out that suit for the minister,' said Mr Povey.

The Reverend Mr Murley, superintendent of the Wesleyan Methodist circuit, called on Mr Baines every week. On a recent visit Mr Baines had remarked that the parson's coat was ageing into green, and had commanded that a new suit should be built and presented to Mr Murley. Mr Murley, who had a genuine medieval passion for souls, and who spent his money and health freely in gratifying the passion, had accepted the offer strictly on behalf of Christ, and had carefully explained to Mr Povey Christ's use for multifarious pockets.

'I see you are,' said Mrs Baines tartly. 'But that's no reason why you should be without a coat – and in this cold room too. You with toothache!'

The fact was that Mr Povey always doffed his coat when cutting out. Instead of a coat he wore a tape-measure.

'My tooth doesn't hurt me,' said he, sheepishly, dropping the great scissors and picking up a cake of chalk.

'Fiddlesticks!' said Mrs Baines.

This exclamation shocked Mr Povey. It was not unknown on the lips of Mrs Baines, but she usually reserved it for members of her own sex. Mr Povey could not recall that she had ever applied it to any statement of his. 'What's the matter with the woman?' he thought. The redness of her face did not help him to answer the question, for her face was always red after the operations of Friday in the kitchen.

'You men are all alike,' Mrs Baines continued. 'The very thought of the dentist's cures you. Why don't you go in at once to Mr Critchlow and have it out – like a man?'

Mr Critchlow extracted teeth, and his shop sign said 'Bone-setter and chemist'. But Mr Povey had his views.

'I make no account of Mr Critchlow as a dentist,' said he.

'Then for goodness' sake go up to Oulsnam's.'

'When? I can't very well go now, and tomorrow is Saturday.'

'Why can't you go now?'

'Well, of course, I *could* go now,' he admitted.

'Let me advise you to go, then, and don't come back with that tooth in your head. I shall be having you laid up next. Show some pluck, do!'

'Oh! pluck –!' he protested, hurt.

At that moment Constance came down the passage singing.

'Constance, my pet!' Mrs Baines called.

'Yes, mother.' She put her head into the room. 'Oh!' Mr Povey was assuming his coat.

'Mr Povey is going to the dentist's.'

'Yes, I'm going at once,' Mr Povey confirmed.

'Oh! I'm so *glad*!' Constance exclaimed. Her face expressed a pure sympathy, uncomplicated by critical sentiments. Mr Povey rapidly bathed in that sympathy, and then decided that he must show himself a man of oak and iron.

'It's always best to get these things done with,' said he, with stern detachment. 'I'll just slip my overcoat on.'

'Here it is,' said Constance, quickly. Mr Povey's overcoat and hat were hung on a hook immediately outside the room, in the passage. She gave him the overcoat, anxious to be of service.

'I didn't call you in here to be Mr Povey's valet,' said Mrs Baines to herself with mild grimness; and aloud: 'I can't stay in the shop long, Constance, but you can be there, can't you, till Mr Povey comes back? And if anything happens run upstairs and tell me.'

'Yes, mother,' Constance eagerly consented. She hesitated and then turned to obey at once.

'I want to speak to you first, my pet,' Mrs Baines stopped her. And her tone was peculiar, charged with import, confidential, and therefore very flattering to Constance.

'I think I'll go out by the side-door,' said Mr Povey. 'It'll be nearer.'

This was truth. He would save about ten yards, in two miles, by going out through the side-door instead of through the shop. Who could have guessed that he was ashamed to be seen going to the dentist's, afraid lest, if he went through the shop, Mrs Baines might follow him and utter some remark prejudicial to his dignity before the assistants? (Mrs Baines could have guessed, and did.)

'You won't want that tape-measure,' said Mrs Baines, dryly, as Mr Povey dragged open the side-door. The ends of the forgotten tape-measure were dangling beneath coat and overcoat.

'Oh!' Mr Povey scowled at his forgetfulness.

'I'll put it in its place,' said Constance, offering to receive the tape-measure.

'Thank you,' said Mr Povey, gravely. 'I don't suppose they'll be long over my bit of a job,' he added, with a difficult, miserable smile.

Then he went off down King Street, with an exterior of gay briskness and dignified joy in the fine May morning. But there was no May morning in his cowardly human heart.

'Hi! Povey!' cried a voice from the Square.

But Mr Povey disregarded all appeals. He had put his hand to the plough, and he would not look back.

'Hi! Povey!'

Useless!

Mrs Baines and Constance were both at the door. A middle-aged man was crossing the road from Boulton Terrace, the lofty erection of new shops which the envious rest of the Square had decided to call 'showy'. He waved a hand to Mrs Baines, who kept the door open.

'It's Dr Harrop,' she said to Constance. 'I shouldn't be surprised if that baby's come at last, and he wanted to tell Mr Povey.'

Constance blushed, full of pride. Mrs Povey, wife of 'our Mr Povey's' renowned cousin, the high-class confectioner and baker in Boulton Terrace, was a frequent subject of discussion in the Baines family, but this was absolutely the first time that Mrs Baines had acknowledged, in presence of Constance, the marked and growing change which had characterized Mrs Povey's condition during recent months. Such frankness on the part of her mother, coming after the decision about leaving school, proved indeed that Constance had ceased to be a mere girl.

'Good morning, doctor.'

The doctor, who carried a little bag and wore riding-breeches (he was the last doctor in Bursley to abandon the saddle for the dog-cart), saluted and straightened his high, black stock.

'Morning! Morning, missy! Well, it's a boy.'

'What? Yonder?' asked Mrs Baines, indicating the confectioner's.

Dr Harrop nodded. 'I wanted to inform him,' said he, jerking his shoulder in the direction of the swaggering coward.

'What did I tell you, Constance?' said Mrs Baines, turning to her daughter.

Constance's confusion was equal to her pleasure. The alert doctor had halted at the foot of the two steps, and with one hand in the pocket of his 'full-fall' breeches, he gazed up, smiling, out of little eyes, at the ample matron and the slender virgin.

'Yes,' he said. 'Been up most of th' night. Difficult! Difficult!'

'It's all *right*, I hope?'

'Oh yes. Fine child! Fine child! But he put his mother to some trouble, for all that. Nothing fresh?' This time he lifted his eyes to indicate Mr Baines's bedroom.

'No,' said Mrs Baines, with a different expression.

'Keeps cheerful?'

'Yes.'

'Good! A very good morning to you.'

He strode off towards his house, which was lower down the street.

'I hope she'll turn over a new leaf now,' observed Mrs Baines to

Constance as she closed the door. Constance knew that her mother was referring to the confectioner's wife; she gathered that the hope was slight in the extreme.

'What did you want to speak to me about, mother?' she asked, as a way out of her delicious confusion.

'Shut that door,' Mrs Baines replied, pointing to the door which led to the passage; and while Constance obeyed, Mrs Baines herself shut the staircase-door. She then said, in a low, guarded voice:

'What's all this about Sophia wanting to be a school-teacher?'

'Wanting to be a school-teacher?' Constance repeated, in tones of amazement.

'Yes. Hasn't she said anything to you?'

'Not a word!'

'Well, I never! She wants to keep on with Miss Chetwynd and be a teacher.' Mrs Baines had half a mind to add that Sophia had mentioned London. But she restrained herself. There are some things which one cannot bring one's self to say. She added, 'Instead of going into the shop!'

'I never heard of such a thing!' Constance murmured brokenly, in the excess of her astonishment. She was rolling up Mr Povey's tape-measure.

'Neither did I!' said Mrs Baines.

'And shall you let her, mother?'

'Neither your father nor I would ever dream of it!' Mrs Baines replied, with calm and yet terrible decision. 'I only mentioned it to you because I thought Sophia would have told you something.'

'No, mother!'

As Constance put Mr Povey's tape-measure neatly away in its drawer under the cutting-out counter, she thought how serious life was – what with babies and Sophias. She was very proud of her mother's confidence in her; this simple pride filled her ardent breast with a most agreeable commotion. And she wanted to help everybody, to show in some way how much she sympathized with and loved everybody. Even the madness of Sophia did not weaken her longing to comfort Sophia.

III

That afternoon there was a search for Sophia, whom no one had seen since dinner. She was discovered by her mother, sitting alone and unoccupied in the drawing-room. The circumstance was in itself sufficiently peculiar, for on weekdays the drawing-room was never used, even by the girls during their holidays, except for the purpose of playing the piano. However, Mrs Baines offered no comment on Sophia's geographical situation, nor on her idleness.

'My dear,' she said, standing at the door, with a self-conscious effort to behave as though nothing had happened, 'will you come and sit with your father a bit?'

'Yes, mother,' answered Sophia, with a sort of cold alacrity.

'Sophia is coming, father,' said Mrs Baines at the open door of the bedroom, which was at right-angles with, and close to, the drawing-room door. Then she surged swishing along the corridor and went into the showroom, whither she had been called.

Sophia passed to the bedroom, the eternal prison of John Baines. Although, on account of his nervous restlessness, Mr Baines was never left alone, it was not a part of the usual duty of the girls to sit with him. The person who undertook the main portion of the vigils was a certain Aunt Maria – whom the girls knew to be not a real aunt, not a powerful, effective aunt like Aunt Harriet of Axe – but a poor second cousin of John Baines; one of those necessitous, pitiful relatives who so often make life difficult for a great family in a small town. The existence of Aunt Maria, after being rather a 'trial' to the Baineses, had for twelve years past developed into something absolutely 'providential' for them. (It is to be remembered that in those days Providence was still busying himself with everybody's affairs, and foreseeing the future in the most extraordinary manner. Thus, having foreseen that John Baines would have a 'stroke' and need a faithful, tireless nurse, he had begun fifty years in advance by creating Aunt Maria, and had kept her carefully in misfortune's way, so that at the proper moment she would be ready to cope with the stroke. Such at least is the only theory which will explain the use by the Baineses, and indeed by all thinking Bursley, of the word 'providential' in connexion with Aunt Maria.) She was a shrivelled little woman, capable of sitting twelve hours a day in a bedroom and thriving on the *régime*. At nights she went home to her little cottage in Brougham Street; she had her Thursday afternoons and generally her Sundays, and during the school vacations she was supposed to come only when she felt inclined, or when the cleaning of her cottage permitted her to come. Hence, in holiday seasons, Mr Baines weighed more heavily on his household than at other times, and his nurses relieved each other according to the contingencies of the moment rather than by a set programme of hours.

The tragedy in ten thousand acts of which that bedroom was the scene, almost entirely escaped Sophia's perception, as it did Constance's. Sophia went into the bedroom as though it were a mere bedroom, with its majestic mahogany furniture, its crimson rep çurtains (edged with gold), and its white, heavily tasselled counterpane. She was aged four when John Baines had suddenly been seized with giddiness on the steps of his shop, and had fallen, and, without losing consciousness, had been transformed from John Baines into a curious and pathetic survival of John Baines. She had no notion of the thrill which ran through the town on that night when it was known that John Baines had had a stroke, and that his left arm and left leg and his right eyelid were paralyzed, and that the active member of the Local Board, the orator, the religious worker, the very life of the town's life, was permanently done for. She had never heard of the crisis through which her mother, assisted by Aunt Harriet, had passed, and out of which she had triumphantly emerged. She was not yet old enough even to suspect it. She possessed only the vaguest memory of her father before he had finished with the world. She knew him simply as an organism on a bed, whose left side was wasted, whose eyes were often inflamed, whose mouth was crooked, who had no creases from the nose to the corners of the mouth like other people, who experienced difficulty in eating because the food would somehow get between his gums and his cheek, who slept a great deal but was excessively fidgety while awake, who seemed to hear what was said to him a long time after it was uttered, as if the sense had to travel miles by labyrinthine passages to his brain, and who talked very, very slowly in a weak, trembling voice.

And she had an image of that remote brain as something with a red spot on it, for once Constance had said: 'Mother, why did father have a stroke?' and Mrs Baines had replied: 'It was a haemorrhage of the brain, my dear, here' – putting a thimbled finger on a particular part of Sophia's head.

Not merely had Constance and Sophia never really felt their father's tragedy; Mrs Baines herself had largely lost the sense of it – such is the effect of use. Even the ruined organism only remembered fitfully and partially that it had once been John Baines. And if Mrs Baines had not, by the habit of years, gradually built up a gigantic fiction that the organism remained ever the supreme consultative head of the family; if Mr Critchlow had not obstinately continued to treat it as a crony, the mass of living and dead nerves on the rich Victorian bedstead would have been of no more account than some Aunt Maria in similar case. These two persons, his wife and his friend, just managed to keep him morally alive by indefatigably feeding his importance and his dignity. The feat was a miracle of stubborn, self-deceiving, splendidly blind devotion, and incorrigible pride.

When Sophia entered the room, the paralytic followed her with his nervous gaze until she had sat down on the end of the sofa at the foot of the bed. He seemed to study her for a long time, and then he murmured in his slow, enfeebled, irregular voice:

'Is that Sophia?'

'Yes, father,' she answered cheerfully.

And after another pause, the old man said: 'Ay! It's Sophia.'

And later: 'Your mother said she should send ye.'

Sophia saw that this was one of his bad, dull days. He had, occasionally, days of comparative nimbleness, when his wits seized almost easily the meanings of external phenomena.

Presently his sallow face and long white beard began to slip down the steep slant of the pillows, and a troubled look came into his left eye. Sophia rose, and, putting her hands under his armpits, lifted him higher on the bed. He was not heavy, but only a strong girl of her years could have done it.

'Ay!' he muttered. 'That's it. That's it.'

And, with his controllable right hand, he took her hand as she stood by the bed. She was so young and fresh, such an incarnation of the spirit of health, and he was so far gone in decay and corruption, that there seemed in this contact of body with body something unnatural and repulsive. But Sophia did not so feel it.

'Sophia,' he addressed her, and made preparatory noises in his throat while she waited.

He continued after an interval, now clutching her arm, 'Your mother's been telling me you don't want to go in the shop.'

She turned her eyes on him, and his anxious, dim gaze met hers. She nodded.

'Nay, Sophia,' he mumbled, with the extreme of slowness. 'I'm surprised at ye . . . Trade's bad, bad! Ye know trade's bad?' He was still clutching her arm.

She nodded. She was, in fact, aware of the badness of trade, caused by a vague war in the United States. The words 'North' and 'South' had a habit of recurring in the conversation of adult persons. That was all she knew, though people were starving in the Five Towns as they were starving in Manchester.[3]

'There's your mother,' his thought struggled on, like an aged horse over a hilly road. 'There's your mother!' he repeated, as if wishful to direct Sophia's attention to the spectacle of her mother. 'Working hard! Con – Constance and you must help her . . . Trade's bad! What can I do . . . lying here?'

The heat from his dry fingers was warming her arm. She wanted to move, but she could not have withdrawn her arm without appearing impatient. For a similar reason she would not avert her glance. A deepening flush increased the lustre of her immature loveliness as she bent over him. But though it was so close he did not feel that radiance. He had long outlived a susceptibility to the strange influences of youth and beauty.

'Teaching!' he muttered. 'Nay, nay! I canna' allow that.'

Then his white beard rose at the tip as he looked up at the ceiling above his head, reflectively.

'You understand me?' he questioned finally.

She nodded again; he loosed her arm, and she turned away. She could not have spoken. Glittering tears enriched her eyes. She was saddened into a profound and sudden grief by the ridiculousness of the scene. She had youth, physical perfection; she brimmed with energy, with the sense of vital power; all existence lay before her; when she put her lips together she felt capable of outvying no matter whom in fortitude of resolution. She had always hated the shop. She did not understand how her mother and Constance could bring themselves to be deferential and flattering to every customer that entered. No, she did not understand it; but her mother (though a proud woman) and Constance seemed to practise such behaviour so naturally, so unquestionably, that she had never imparted to either of them her feelings; she guessed that she would not be comprehended. But long ago she had decided that she would never 'go into the shop'. She knew that she would be expected to do something, and she had fixed on teaching as the one possibility. These decisions had formed part of her inner life for years past. She had not mentioned them, being secretive and scarcely anxious for unpleasantness. But she had been slowly preparing herself to mention them. The extraordinary announcement that she was to leave school at the same time as Constance had taken her unawares, before the preparations ripening in her mind were complete – before, as it were, she had girded up her loins for the fray. She had been caught unready, and the opposing forces had obtained the advantage of her. But did they suppose she was beaten?

No argument from her mother! No hearing, even! Just a curt and haughty 'Let me hear no more of it'! And so the great desire of her life, nourished year after year in her inmost bosom, was to be flouted and sacrificed with a word! Her mother did not appear ridiculous in the affair, for her mother was a genuine power, commanding by turns genuine love and genuine hate, and always, till then, obedience and the respect of reason. It was her father who appeared tragically ridiculous; and, in turn, the whole movement against her grew grotesque in its absurdity. Here was this antique wreck, helpless, useless, powerless – merely pathetic – actually thinking that he had only to mumble in order to make her 'understand'! He knew nothing; he perceived nothing; he was a ferocious egoist, like most bedridden invalids, out of touch with life – and he thought himself justified in making destinies, and capable of making them! Sophia could not, perhaps, define the feelings which overwhelmed her; but she was conscious of their tendency. They aged her, by years. They aged her so that, in a kind of momentary ecstasy of insight, she felt older than her father himself.

'You will be a good girl,' he said. 'I'm sure o' that.'

It was too painful. The grotesqueness of her father's complacency humiliated her past bearing. She was humiliated, not for herself, but for him. Singular creature! She ran out of the room.

Fortunately Constance was passing in the corridor, otherwise Sophia had been found guilty of a great breach of duty.

'Go to father,' she whispered hysterically to Constance, and fled upwards to the second floor.

IV

At supper, with her red, downcast eyes, she had returned to sheer girlishness again, overawed by her mother. The meal had an unusual aspect. Mr Povey, safe from the dentist's, but having lost two teeth in two days, was being fed on 'slops' – bread and milk, to wit; he sat near the fire. The others had cold pork, half a cold apple-pie, and cheese; but Sophia only pretended to eat; each time she tried to swallow, the tears came into her eyes, and her throat shut itself up. Mrs Baines and Constance had a too careful air of eating just as usual. Mrs Baines's handsome ringlets dominated the table under the gas.

'I'm not so set up with my pastry today,' observed Mrs Baines, critically munching a fragment of pie-crust.

She rang a little hand-bell. Maggie appeared from the cave. She wore a plain white bib-less apron, but no cap.

'Maggie, will you have some pie?'

'Yes, if you can spare it, ma'am.'

This was Maggie's customary answer to offers of food.

'We can always spare it, Maggie,' said her mistress, as usual. 'Sophia, if you aren't going to use that plate, give it to me.'

Maggie disappeared with liberal pie.

Mrs Baines then talked to Mr Povey about his condition, and in particular as to the need for precautions against taking cold in the bereaved gum. She was a brave and determined woman; from start to finish she behaved as though nothing whatever in the household except her pastry and Mr Povey had deviated that day from the normal. She kissed Constance and Sophia with the most exact equality, and called them 'my chucks' when they went up to bed.

Constance, excellent kind heart, tried to imitate her mother's tactics as the girls undressed in their room. She thought she could not do better than ignore Sophia's deplorable state.

'Mother's new dress is quite finished, and she's going to wear it on Sunday,' said she, blandly.

'If you say another word I'll scratch your eyes out!' Sophia turned on her viciously, with a catch in her voice, and then began to sob at intervals. She did not mean this threat, but its utterance gave her relief. Constance, faced with the fact that her mother's shoes were too big for her, decided to preserve her eyesight.

Long after the gas was out, rare sobs from Sophia shook the bed, and they both lay awake in silence.

'I suppose you and mother have been talking me over finely today?' Sophia burst forth, to Constance's surprise, in a wet voice.

'No,' said Constance soothingly. 'Mother only told me.'

'Told you what?'

'That you wanted to be a teacher.'

'And I will be, too!' said Sophia, bitterly.

'You don't know mother,' thought Constance; but she made no audible comment.

There was another detached, hard sob. And then, such is the astonishing talent of youth, they both fell asleep.

The next morning, early, Sophia stood gazing out of the window at the Square. It was Saturday, and all over the Square little stalls, with yellow linen roofs, were being erected for the principal market of the week. In those barbaric days Bursley had a majestic edifice, black as basalt, for the sale of dead animals by the limb and rib – it was entitled 'the Shambles' – but vegetables, fruit, cheese, eggs, and pikelets were still sold under canvas. Eggs are now offered at five farthings apiece in a palace that cost twenty-five thousand pounds. Yet you will find people in Bursley ready to assert that things generally are not what they were, and that in particular the romance of life has gone. But until it has gone it is never romance. To Sophia, though she was in a mood which usually stimulates the sense of the romantic, there was nothing of romance in this picturesque tented field. It was just the market. Holl's, the leading grocer's, was already open, at the extremity of the Square, and a boy apprentice was sweeping the pavement in front of it. The public-houses were open, several of them specializing in hot rum at 5.30 a.m. The town-crier, in his blue coat with red facings, crossed the Square, carrying his big bell by the tongue. There was the same shocking hole in one of Mrs Povey's (confectioner's) window-curtains – a hole which even her recent travail could scarcely excuse. Such matters it was that Sophia noticed with dull, smarting eyes.

'Sophia, you'll take your death of cold standing there like that!'

She jumped. The voice was her mother's. That vigorous woman, after a calm night by the side of the paralytic, was already up and neatly dressed. She carried a bottle and an egg-cup, and a small quantity of jam in a table-spoon.

'Get into bed again, do! There's a dear! You're shivering.'

White Sophia obeyed. It was true; she was shivering. Constance awoke. Mrs Baines went to the dressing-table and filled the egg-cup out of the bottle.

'Who's that for, mother?' Constance asked sleepily.

'It's for Sophia,' said Mrs Baines, with good cheer. 'Now, Sophia!' and she advanced with the egg-cup in one hand and the table-spoon in the other.

'What is it, mother?' asked Sophia, who well knew what it was.

'Castor-oil, my dear,' said Mrs Baines, winningly.

The ludicrousness of attempting to cure obstinacy and yearnings for a freer life by means of castor-oil is perhaps less real than apparent. The strange interdependence of spirit and body, though only understood intelligently in these intelligent days, was guessed at by sensible medieval mothers. And certainly, at the period when Mrs Baines represented modernity, castor-oil was still the remedy of remedies. It had supplanted cupping. And, if part of its vogue was due to its extreme unpleasantness, it had at least proved its qualities in many a contest with disease. Less than two years previously old Dr Harrop (father of him who told Mrs Baines about Mrs Povey), being then aged eighty-six, had fallen from top to bottom of his staircase. He had scrambled up, taken a dose of castor-oil at once, and on the morrow was as well as if he had never seen a staircase. This episode was town property and had sunk deep into all hearts.

'I don't want any, mother,' said Sophia, in dejection. 'I'm quite well.'

'You simply ate nothing all day yesterday,' said Mrs Baines. And she added, 'Come!' As if to say, 'There's always this silly fuss with castor-oil. Don't keep me waiting.'

'I don't *want* any,' said Sophia, irritated and captious.

The two girls lay side by side, on their backs. They seemed very thin and fragile in comparison with the solidity of their mother. Constance wisely held her peace.

Mrs Baines put her lips together, meaning: 'This is becoming tedious. I shall have to be angry in another moment!'

'Come!' said she again.

The girls could hear her foot tapping on the floor.

'I really don't want it, mamma,' Sophia fought. 'I suppose I ought to know whether I need it or not!' This was insolence.

'Sophia, will you take this medicine, or won't you?'

In conflicts with her children, the mother's ultimatum always took the formula in which this phrase was cast. The girls knew, when things had arrived at the pitch of 'or won't you', spoken in Mrs Baines's firmest tone, that the end was upon them. Never had the ultimatum failed.

There was a silence.

'And I'll thank you to mind your manners,' Mrs Baines added.

'I won't take it,' said Sophia, sullenly and flatly; and she hid her face in the pillow.

It was a historic moment in the family life. Mrs Baines thought the last day had come. But still she held herself in dignity while the apocalypse roared in her ears.

'*Of course I can't force you to take it*,' she said with superb evenness, masking anger by compassionate grief. 'You're a big girl and a naughty girl. And if you will be ill you must.'

Upon this immense admission, Mrs Baines departed.

Constance trembled.

Nor was that all. In the middle of the morning, when Mrs

Baines was pricing new potatoes at a stall at the top end of the Square, and Constance choosing threepennyworth of flowers at the same stall, whom should they both see, walking all alone across the empty corner by the Bank, but Sophia Baines! The Square was busy and populous, and Sophia was only visible behind a foreground of restless, chattering figures. But she was unmistakably seen. She had been beyond the Square and was returning. Constance could scarcely believe her eyes. Mrs Baines's heart jumped. For let it be said that the girls never under any circumstances went forth without permission, and scarcely ever alone. That Sophia should be at large in the town, without leave, without notice, exactly as if she were her own mistress, was a proposition which a day earlier had been inconceivable. Yet there she was, and moving with a leisureliness that must be described as effrontery!

Red with apprehension, Constance wondered what would happen. Mrs Baines said nought of her feelings, did not even indicate that she had seen the scandalous, the breath-taking sight. And they descended the Square laden with the lighter portions of what they had bought during an hour of buying. They went into the house by the King Street door; and the first thing they heard was the sound of the piano upstairs. Nothing happened. Mr Povey had his dinner alone; then the table was laid for them, and the bell rung, and Sophia came insolently downstairs to join her mother and sister. And nothing happened. The dinner was silently eaten, and Constance having rendered thanks to God, Sophia rose abruptly to go.

'Sophia!'

'Yes, mother.'

'Constance, stay where you are,' said Mrs Baines suddenly to Constance, who had meant to flee. Constance was therefore destined to be present at the happening, doubtless in order to emphasize its importance and seriousness.

'Sophia,' Mrs Baines resumed to her younger daughter in an ominous voice. 'No, please shut the door. There is no reason why everybody in the house should hear. Come right into the room – right in! That's it. Now, what were you doing out in the town this morning?'

Sophia was fidgeting nervously with the edge of her little black apron, and worrying a seam of the carpet with her toes. She bent her head towards her left shoulder, at first smiling vaguely. She said nothing, but every limb, every glance, every curve was speaking. Mrs Baines sat firmly in her own rocking-chair, full of the sensation that she had Sophia, as it were, writhing on the end of a skewer. Constance was braced into a moveless anguish.

'I will have an answer,' pursued Mrs Baines. 'What were you doing out in the town this morning?'

'I just went out,' answered Sophia at length, still with eyes downcast, and in a rather simpering tone.

'Why did you go out? You said nothing to me about going out. I heard Constance ask you if you were coming with us to the market, and you said, very rudely, that you weren't.'

'I didn't say it rudely,' Sophia objected.

'Yes you did. And I'll thank you not to answer back.'

'I didn't mean to say it rudely, did I, Constance?' Sophia's head turned sharply to her sister. Constance knew not where to look.

'Don't answer back,' Mrs Baines repeated sternly. 'And don't try to drag Constance into this, for I won't have it.'

'Oh, of course Constance is always right!' observed Sophia, with an irony whose unparalleled impudence shook Mrs Baines to her massive foundations.

'Do you want me to have to smack you, child?'

Her temper flashed out and you could see ringlets vibrating under the provocation of Sophia's sauciness. Then Sophia's lower lip began to fall and to bulge outwards, and all the muscles of her face seemed to slacken.

'You are a very naughty girl,' said Mrs Baines, with restraint. ('I've got her,' said Mrs Baines to herself. 'I may just as well keep my temper.')

And a sob broke out of Sophia. She was behaving like a little child. She bore no trace of the young maiden sedately crossing the Square without leave and without an escort.

('I knew she was going to cry,' said Mrs Baines, breathing relief.)

'I'm waiting,' said Mrs Baines aloud.

A second sob. Mrs Baines manufactured patience to meet the demand.

'You tell me not to answer back, and then you say you're waiting,' Sophia blubbered thickly.

'What's that you say? How can I tell what you say if you talk like that?' (But Mrs Baines failed to hear out of discretion, which is better than valour.)

'It's of no consequence,' Sophia blurted forth in a sob. She was weeping now, and tears were ricocheting off her lovely crimson cheeks on to the carpet; her whole body was trembling.

'Don't be a great baby,' Mrs Baines enjoined, with a touch of rough persuasiveness in her voice.

'It's you who make me cry,' said Sophia, bitterly. 'You make me cry and then you call me a great baby!' And sobs ran through her frame like waves one after another. She spoke so indistinctly that her mother now really had some difficulty in catching her words.

'Sophia,' said Mrs Baines, with god-like calm, 'it is not I who make you cry. It is your guilty conscience makes you cry. I have merely asked you a question, and I intend to have an answer.'

'I've told you.' Here Sophia checked the sobs with an immense effort.

'What have you told me?'

'I just went out.'

'I will have no trifling,' said Mrs Baines. 'What did you go out for, and without telling me? If you had told me afterwards, when I came in, of your own accord, it might have been different. But no, not a word! It is I who have to ask! Now, quick! I can't wait any longer.'

('I gave way over the castor-oil, my girl,' Mrs Baines said in her own breast. 'But not again! Not again!')

'I don't know,' Sophia murmured.

'What do you mean – you don't know?'

The sobbing recommenced tempestuously. 'I mean I don't know. I just went out.' Her voice rose; it was noisy, but scarcely articulate. 'What if I did go out?'

'Sophia, I am not going to be talked to like this. If you think because you're leaving school you can do exactly as you like –'

'Do I want to leave school?' yelled Sophia, stamping. In a moment a hurricane of emotion overwhelmed her, as though that stamping of the foot had released the demons of the storm. Her face was transfigured by uncontrollable passion. 'You all want to make me miserable!' she shrieked with terrible violence. 'And now I can't even go out! You are a horrid, cruel woman, and I hate you! And you can do what you like! Put me in prison if you like! I know you'd be glad if I was dead!'

She dashed from the room, banging the door with a shock that made the house rattle. And she had shouted so loud that she might have been heard in the shop, and even in the kitchen. It was a startling experience for Mrs Baines. Mrs Baines, why did you saddle yourself with a witness? Why did you so positively say that you had intended to have an answer?

'Really,' she stammered, pulling her dignity about her shoulders like a garment that the wind had snatched off, 'I never dreamed that poor girl had such a dreadful temper! What a pity it is, for her *own* sake!' It was the best she could do.

Constance, who could not bear to witness her mother's humiliation, vanished very quietly from the room. She got half-way upstairs to the second floor, and then, hearing the loud, rapid, painful, regular intake of sobbing breaths, she hesitated and crept down again.

This was Mrs Baines's first costly experience of the child thankless for having been brought into the world. It robbed her of her profound, absolute belief in herself. She had thought she knew everything in her house and could do everything there. And lo! she had suddenly stumbled against an unsuspected personality at large in her house, a sort of hard marble affair that informed her by means of bumps that if she did not want to be hurt she must keep out of the way.

v

On the Sunday afternoon Mrs Baines was trying to repose a little in the drawing-room, where she had caused a fire to be lighted. Constance was in the adjacent bedroom with her father. Sophia lay between blankets in the room overhead with a feverish cold. This cold and her new dress were Mrs Baines's sole consolation at the moment. She had prophesied a cold for Sophia, refuser of castor-oil, and it had come. Sophia had received, for standing in her nightdress at a draughty window of a May morning, what Mrs Baines called 'nature's slap in the face'. As for the dress, she had worshipped God in it, and prayed for Sophia in it, before dinner; and its four double rows of gimp on the skirt had been accounted a great success. With her lace-bordered mantle and her low, stringed bonnet she had assuredly given a unique lustre to the congregation at chapel. She was stout; but the fashions, prescribing vague outlines, broad downward slopes, and vast amplitudes, were favourable to her shape. It must not be supposed that stout women of a certain age never seek to seduce the eye and trouble the meditations of man by other than moral charms. Mrs Baines knew that she was comely, natty, imposing, and elegant; and the knowledge gave her real pleasure. She would look over her shoulder in the glass as anxious as a girl: make no mistake.

She did not repose; she could not. She sat thinking in exactly the same posture as Sophia's two afternoons previously. She would have been surprised to hear that her attitude, bearing, and expression powerfully recalled those of her reprehensible daughter. But it was so. A good angel made her restless, and she went idly to the window and glanced upon the empty, shuttered Square. She too, majestic matron, had strange, brief yearnings for an existence more romantic than this; shootings across her spirit's firmament of tailed comets; soft, inexplicable melancholies. The good angel, withdrawing her from such a mood, directed her gaze to a particular spot at the top of the Square.

She passed at once out of the room – not precisely in a hurry, yet without wasting time. In a recess under the stairs, immediately outside the door, was a box about a foot square and eighteen inches deep covered with black American cloth. She bent down and unlocked this box, which was padded within and contained the Baines silver tea-service. She drew from the box teapot, sugar-bowl, milk-jug, sugar-tongs, hot-water jug, and cake-stand (a flattish dish with an arching semicircular handle) – chased vessels, silver without and silver-gilt within; glittering heirlooms that shone in the dark corner like the secret pride of respectable families. These she put on a tray that always stood on end in the recess. Then she looked upwards through the banisters to the second floor.

'Maggie!' she piercingly whispered.

'Yes, mum,' came a voice.

'Are you dressed?'

'Yes, mum. I'm just coming.'

'Well, put on your muslin.' 'Apron,' Mrs Baines implied. Maggie understood.

'Take these for tea,' said Mrs Baines when Maggie descended. 'Better rub them over. You know where the cake is – that new one. The best cups. And the silver spoons.'

They both heard a knock at the side door, far off, below.

'There!' exclaimed Mrs Baines. 'Now take these right down into the kitchen before you open.'

'Yes, mum,' said Maggie, departing.

Mrs Baines was wearing a black alpaca apron. She removed it and put on another one of black satin embroidered with yellow flowers, which, by merely inserting her arm into the chamber, she had taken from off the chest of drawers in her bedroom. Then she fixed herself in the drawing-room.

Maggie returned, rather short of breath, convoying the visitor.

'Ah! Miss Chetwynd,' said Mrs Baines, rising to welcome. 'I'm sure I'm delighted to see you. I saw you coming down the Square, and I said to myself, "Now, I do hope Miss Chetwynd isn't going to forget us."'

Miss Chetwynd, simpering momentarily, came forward with that self-conscious, slightly histrionic air, which is one of the penalties of pedagogy. She lived under the eyes of her pupils. Her life was one ceaseless effort to avoid doing anything which might influence her charges for evil or shock the natural sensitiveness of their parents. She had to wind her earthly way through a forest of the most delicate susceptibilities – fern-fronds that stretched across the path, and that she must not even accidentally disturb with her skirt as she passed. No wonder she walked mincingly! No wonder she had a habit of keeping her elbows close to her sides, and drawing her mantle tight in the streets! Her prospectus talked about 'a sound and religious course of training', 'study embracing the usual branches of English, with music by a talented master, drawing, dancing, and calisthenics'. Also 'needlework plain and ornamental'; also 'moral influence'; and finally about terms, 'which are very moderate, and every particular, with reference to parents and others, furnished on application'. (Sometimes, too, without application.) As an illustration of the delicacy of fern-fronds, that single word 'dancing' had nearly lost her Constance and Sophia seven years before!

She was a pinched virgin, aged forty, and not 'well off'; in her family the gift of success had been monopolized by her elder sister. For these characteristics Mrs Baines, as a matron in easy circumstances, pitied Miss Chetwynd. On the other hand, Miss Chetwynd could choose ground from which to look down upon Mrs Baines, who after all was in trade. Miss Chetwynd had no trace of the local accent; she spoke with a southern refinement which the Five Towns, while making fun of it, envied. All her O's had a genteel leaning towards 'ow', as ritualism leans towards Romanism. And she was the fount of etiquette, a wonder of correctness; in the eyes of her pupils' parents not so much 'a perfect *lady*' as 'a *perfect* lady'. So that it was an extremely nice question whether, upon the whole, Mrs Baines secretly condescended to Miss Chetwynd or Miss Chetwynd to Mrs Baines. Perhaps Mrs Baines, by virtue of her wifehood, carried the day.

Miss Chetwynd, carefully and precisely seated, opened the conversation by explaining that even if Mrs Baines had not written she would have called in any case, as she made a practice of calling at the home of her pupils in vacation time: which was true. Mrs Baines, it should be stated, had on Friday afternoon sent to Miss Chetwynd one of her most luxurious notes – lavender-coloured paper with scalloped edges, the selectest mode of the day – to announce, in her Italian hand, that Constance and Sophia would both leave school at the end of next term, and giving reasons in regard to Sophia.

Before the visitor had got very far, Maggie came in with a lacquered tea-caddy and the silver teapot and a silver spoon on a lacquered tray. Mrs Baines, while continuing to talk, chose a key from her bunch, unlocked the tea-caddy, and transferred four teaspoonfuls of tea from it to the teapot and relocked the caddy.

'Strawberry,' she mysteriously whispered to Maggie; and Maggie disappeared, bearing the tray and its contents.

'And how is your sister? It is quite a long time since she was down here,' Mrs Baines went on to Miss Chetwynd, after whispering 'strawberry'.

The remark was merely in the way of small-talk – for the hostess felt a certain unwilling hesitation to approach the topic of daughters – but it happened to suit the social purpose of Miss Chetwynd to a nicety. Miss Chetwynd was a vessel brimming with great tidings.

'She is very well, thank you,' said Miss Chetwynd, and her expression grew exceedingly vivacious. Her face glowed with pride as she added, 'Of course everything is changed now.'

'Indeed?' murmured Mrs Baines, with polite curiosity.

'Yes,' said Miss Chetwynd. 'You've not heard?'

'No,' said Mrs Baines. Miss Chetwynd knew that she had not heard.

'About Elizabeth's engagement? To the Reverend Archibald Jones?'

It is the fact that Mrs Baines was taken aback. She did nothing indiscreet; she did not give vent to her excusable amazement that the elder Miss Chetwynd should be engaged to anyone at all, as some women would have done in the stress of the moment. She kept her presence of mind.

'This is really *most* interesting!' said she.

It was. For Archibald Jones was one of the idols of the Wesleyan Methodist Connexion, a special preacher famous throughout England. At 'Anniversaries' and 'Trust sermons', Archibald Jones had probably no rival. His Christian name helped him; it was a luscious, resounding mouthful for admirers. He was not an itinerant minister, migrating every three years. His function was to direct the affairs of the 'Book Room', the publishing department of the Connexion. He lived in London, and shot out into the provinces at week-ends, preaching on Sundays and giving a lecture, tinctured with bookishness, 'in the chapel' on Monday evenings. In every town he visited there was competition for the privilege of entertaining him. He had zeal, indefatigable energy, and a breezy wit. He was a widower of fifty, and his wife had been dead for twenty years. It had seemed as if women were not for this bright star. And here Elizabeth Chetwynd, who had left the Five Towns a quarter of a century before at the age of twenty, had caught him! Austere, moustached, formidable, desiccated, she must have done it with her powerful intellect! It must be a union of intellects! He had been impressed by hers, and she by his, and then their intellects had kissed. Within a week fifty thousand women in forty counties had pictured to themselves this osculation of intellects, and shrugged their shoulders, and decided once more that men were incomprehensible. These great ones in London, falling in love like the rest! But no! Love was a ribald and voluptuous word to use in such a matter as this. It was generally felt that the Reverend Archibald Jones and Miss Chetwynd the elder would lift marriage to what would now be termed an astral plane.

After tea had been served, Mrs Baines gradually recovered her position, both in her own private esteem and in the deference of Miss Aline Chetwynd.

'Yes,' said she. 'You can talk about your sister, and you can call *him* Archibald, and you can mince up your words. But have you got a tea-service like this? Can you conceive more perfect strawberry jam than this? Did not my dress cost more than you spend on your clothes in a year? Has a man ever looked at you? After all, is there not something about my situation . . . in short, something . . . ?'

She did not say this aloud. She in no way deviated from the scrupulous politeness of a hostess. There was nothing in even her tone to indicate that Mrs John Baines was a personage. Yet it suddenly occurred to Miss Chetwynd that her pride in being the prospective sister-in-law of the Rev. Archibald Jones would be better for a while in her pocket. And she inquired after Mr Baines. After this the conversation limped somewhat.

'I suppose you weren't surprised by my letter?' said Mrs Baines.

'I was and I wasn't,' answered Miss Chetwynd, in her professional manner and not her manner of a prospective sister-in-law. 'Of course I am naturally sorry to lose two such good pupils, but we can't keep our pupils for ever.' She smiled; she was not

without fortitude – it is easier to lose pupils than to replace them.
'Still' – a pause – 'what you say of Sophia is perfectly true,
perfectly. She is quite as advanced as Constance. Still' – another
pause and a more rapid enunciation – 'Sophia is by no means an
ordinary girl.'

'I hope she hasn't been a very great trouble to you?'

'Oh *no!*' exclaimed Miss Chetwynd. 'Sophia and I have got on
very well together. I have always tried to appeal to her reason. I
have never *forced* her . . . Now, with some girls . . . In some ways
I look on Sophia as the most remarkable girl – not pupil – but the
most remarkable – what shall I say? – individuality, that I have
ever met with.' And her demeanour added, 'And, mind you, this
is something – from me!'

'Indeed!' said Mrs Baines. She told herself, 'I am not your
common foolish parent. I see my children impartially. I am
incapable of being flattered concerning them.'

Nevertheless she was flattered, and the thought shaped itself
that really Sophia was no ordinary girl.

'I suppose she has talked to you about becoming a teacher?'
asked Miss Chetwynd, taking a morsel of the unparalleled jam.
She held the spoon with her thumb and three fingers. Her
fourth finger, in matters of honest labour, would never associate
with the other three; delicately curved, it always drew proudly
away from them.

'Has she mentioned that to you?' Mrs Baines demanded,
startled.

'Oh yes!' said Miss Chetwynd. 'Several times. Sophia is a very
secretive girl, very – but I think I may say I have always had her
confidence. There have been times when Sophia and I have been
very near each other. Elizabeth was much struck with her.
Indeed, I may tell you that in one of her last letters to me she spoke
of Sophia and said she had mentioned her to Mr Jones, and Mr
Jones remembered her quite well.'

Impossible for even a wise, uncommon parent not to be
affected by such an announcement!

'I dare say your sister will give up her school now,' observed
Mrs Baines, to divert attention from her self-consciousness.

'Oh *no!*' And this time Mrs Baines had genuinely shocked Miss

Chetwynd. 'Nothing would induce Elizabeth to give up the cause of education. Archibald takes the keenest interest in the school. Oh no! Not for worlds!'

'*Then you think Sophia would make a good teacher?*' asked Mrs Baines with apparent inconsequence, and with a smile. But the words marked an epoch in her mind. All was over.

'I think she is very much set on it and —'

'That wouldn't affect her father — or me,' said Mrs Baines quickly.

'Certainly not! I merely say that she is very much set on it. Yes, she would, at any rate, make a teacher far superior to the average.' ('That girl has got the better of her mother without me!' she reflected.) 'Ah! Here is dear Constance!'

Constance, tempted beyond her strength by the sounds of the visit and the colloquy, had slipped into the room.

'I've left both doors open, mother,' she excused herself for quitting her father, and kissed Miss Chetwynd.

She blushed, but she blushed happily, and really made a most creditable *début* as a young lady. Her mother rewarded her by taking her into the conversation. And history was soon made.

So Sophia was apprenticed to Miss Aline Chetwynd. Mrs Baines bore herself greatly. It was Miss Chetwynd who had urged, and her respect for Miss Chetwynd . . . Also somehow the Reverend Archibald Jones came into the cause . . . Of course the idea of Sophia ever going to London was ridiculous, ridiculous! (Mrs Baines secretly feared that the ridiculous might happen; but, with the Reverend Archibald Jones on the spot, the worst could be faced.) Sophia must understand that even the apprenticeship in Bursley was merely a trial. They would see how things went on. She had to thank Miss Chetwynd . . .

'I made Miss Chetwynd come and talk to mother,' said Sophia magnificently one night to simple Constance, as if to imply, 'Your Miss Chetwynd is my washpot.'

To Constance, Sophia's mere enterprise was just as staggering as her success. Fancy her deliberately going out that Saturday morning, after her mother's definite decision, to enlist Miss Chetwynd in her aid!

There is no need to insist on the tragic grandeur of Mrs Baines's renunciation — a renunciation which implied her acceptance of a change in the balance of power in her realm. Part of its tragedy was that none, not even Constance, could divine the intensity of Mrs Baines's suffering. She had no confidant; she was incapable of showing a wound. But when she lay awake at night by the organism which had once been her husband, she dwelt long and deeply on the martyrdom of her life. What had she done to deserve it? Always had she conscientiously endeavoured to be kind, just, patient. And she knew herself to be sagacious and prudent. In the frightful and unguessed trials of her existence as a wife, surely she might have been granted consolations as a mother! Yet no; it had not been! And she felt all the bitterness of age against youth — youth egotistic, harsh, cruel, uncompromising; youth that is so crude, so ignorant of life, so slow to understand! She had Constance. Yes, but it would be twenty years before Constance could appreciate the sacrifice of judgement and of pride which her mother had made, in a sudden decision, during that rambling, starched, simpering interview with Miss Aline Chetwynd. Probably Constance thought that she had yielded to Sophia's passionate temper! Impossible to explain to Constance that she had yielded to nothing but a perception of Sophia's complete inability to hear reason and wisdom. Ah! Sometimes as she lay in the dark, she would, in fancy, snatch her heart from her bosom and fling it down before Sophia, bleeding, and cry: 'See what I carry about with me, on your account!' Then she would take it back and hide it again, and sweeten her bitterness with wise admonitions to herself.

All this because Sophia, aware that if she stayed in the house she would be compelled to help in the shop, chose an honourable activity which freed her from the danger. Heart, how absurd of you to bleed!

CHAPTER 4: *Elephant*

I

'Sophia, will you come and see the elephant? Do come!' Constance entered the drawing-room with this request on her eager lips.

'No,' said Sophia, with a touch of condescension. 'I'm far too busy for elephants.'

Only two years had passed; but both girls were grown up now; long sleeves, long skirts, hair that had settled down in life; and a demeanour immensely serious, as though existence were terrific in its responsibilities; yet sometimes childhood surprisingly broke through the crust of gravity, as now in Constance, aroused by such things as elephants, and proclaimed with vivacious gestures that it was not dead after all. The sisters were sharply differentiated. Constance wore the black alpaca apron and the scissors at the end of long black elastic, which indicated her vocation in the shop. She was proving a considerable success in the millinery department. She had learnt how to talk to people, and was, in her modest way, very self-possessed. She was getting a little stouter. Everybody liked her. Sophia had developed into the student. Time had accentuated her reserve. Her sole friend was Miss Chetwynd, with whom she was, having regard to the disparity of their ages, very intimate. At home she spoke little. She lacked amiability; as her mother said, she was 'touchy'. She required diplomacy from others, but did not render it again. Her attitude, indeed, was one of half-hidden disdain, now gentle, now coldly bitter. She would not wear an apron, in an age when aprons were almost essential to decency. No! She would *not* wear an apron, and there was an end of it. She was not so tidy as Constance, and if Constance's hands had taken on the coarse texture which comes from commerce with needles, pins, artificial flowers, and stuffs, Sophia's fine hands were seldom innocent of ink. But Sophia was splendidly beautiful. And even her mother and Constance had an instinctive idea that that face was, at any rate, a partial excuse for her asperity.

'Well,' said Constance, 'if you won't, I do believe I shall ask mother if she will.'

Sophia, bending over her books, made no answer. But the top of her head said: 'This has no interest for me whatever.'

Constance left the room, and in a moment returned with her mother.

'Sophia,' said her mother, with gay excitement, 'you might go and sit with your father for a bit while Constance and I just run up to the playground to see the elephant. You can work just as well in there as here. Your father's asleep.'

'Oh, very well!' Sophia agreed haughtily. 'Whatever is all this fuss about an elephant? Anyhow, it'll be quieter in your room. The noise here is splitting.' She gave a supercilious glance into the Square as she languidly rose.

It was the morning of the third day of Bursley Wakes; not the modern finicking and respectable, but an orgiastic carnival, gross in all its manifestations of joy. The whole centre of the town was given over to the furious pleasures of the people. Most of the Square was occupied by Wombwell's Menagerie, in a vast oblong tent, whose raging beasts roared and growled day and night. And spreading away from this supreme attraction, right up through the market-place past the Town Hall to Duck Bank, Duck Square and the waste land called the 'playground' were hundreds of booths with banners displaying all the delights of the horrible. You could see the atrocities of the French Revolution, and of the Fiji Islands, and the ravages of unspeakable diseases, and the living flesh of a nearly nude human female guaranteed to turn the scale at twenty-two stone, and the skeletons of the mysterious phantoscope, and the bloody contests of champions naked to the waist (with the chance of picking up a red tooth as a relic). You could try your strength by hitting an image of a fellow-creature in the stomach, and test your aim by knocking off the heads of other images with a wooden ball. You could also shoot with rifles at various targets. All the streets were lined with stalls loaded with food in heaps, chiefly dried fish, the entrails of animals and gingerbread. All the public-houses were crammed and frenzied jolly drunkards, men and women, lounged along the pavements everywhere, their shouts vying with the trumpets, horns, and drums of the booths, and the shrieking, rattling toys that the children carried.

It was a glorious spectacle, but not a spectacle for the leading families. Miss Chetwynd's school was closed, so that the daughters of leading families might remain in seclusion till the worst was over. The Baineses ignored the Wakes in every possible way, choosing that week to have a show of mourning goods in the left-hand window, and refusing to let Maggie outside on any pretext. Therefore the dazzling social success of the elephant, which was quite easily drawing Mrs Baines into the vortex, cannot imaginably be over-estimated.

On the previous night one of the three Wombwell elephants had suddenly knelt on a man in the tent; he had then walked out of the tent and picked up another man at haphazard from the crowd which was staring at the great pictures in front, and tried to put this second man into his mouth. Being stopped by his Indian attendant with a pitchfork, he placed the man on the ground and stuck his tusk through an artery of the victim's arm. He then, amid unexampled excitement, suffered himself to be led away. He was conducted to the rear of the tent, just in front of Baines's shuttered windows, and by means of stakes, pulleys, and ropes forced to his knees. His head was whitewashed, and six men of the Rifle Corps were engaged to shoot at him at a distance of five yards, while constables kept the crowd off with truncheons. He died instantly, rolling over with a soft thud. The crowd cheered, and intoxicated by their importance, the Volunteers fired three more volleys into the carcase, and were then borne off as heroes to different inns. The elephant, by the help of his two companions, was got on to a railway lorry[4] and disappeared into the night. Such was the greatest sensation that has ever occurred, or perhaps will ever occur, in Bursley. The excitement about the repeal of the Corn Laws, or about Inkerman, was feeble compared to that excitement. Mr Critchlow, who had been called on to put a hasty tourniquet round the arm of the second victim, had popped in afterwards to tell John Baines all about it. Mr Baines's interest, however, had been slight. Mr Critchlow succeeded better with the ladies, who, though they had witnessed the shooting from the drawing-room, were thirsty for the most trifling details.

The next day it was known that the elephant lay near the playground, pending the decision of the Chief Bailiff and the Medical Officer as to his burial. And everybody had to visit the corpse. No social exclusiveness could withstand the seduction of that dead elephant. Pilgrims travelled from all the Five Towns to see him.

'We're going now,' said Mrs Baines, after she had assumed her bonnet and shawl.

'All right,' said Sophia, pretending to be absorbed in study, as she sat on the sofa at the foot of her father's bed.

And Constance, having put her head in at the door, drew her mother after her like a magnet.

Then Sophia heard a remarkable conversation in the passage.

'Are you going up to see the elephant, Mrs Baines?' asked the voice of Mr Povey.

'Yes. Why?'

'I think I had better come with you. The crowd is sure to be very rough.' Mr Povey's tone was firm; he had a position.

'But the shop?'

'We shall not be long,' said Mr Povey.

'Oh yes, mother,' Constance added appealingly.

Sophia felt the house thrill as the side-door banged. She sprang up and watched the three cross King Street diagonally, and so plunge into the Wakes. This triple departure was surely the crowning tribute to the dead elephant! It was simply astonishing. It caused Sophia to perceive that she had miscalculated the importance of the elephant. It made her regret her scorn of the elephant as an attraction. She was left behind; and the joy of life was calling her. She could see down into the Vaults on the opposite side of the street, where working men – potters and colliers – in their best clothes, some with high hats, were drinking, gesticulating, and laughing in a row at a long counter.

She noticed, while she was thus at the bedroom window, a young man ascending King Street, followed by a porter trundling a flat barrow of luggage. He passed slowly under the very window. She flushed. She had evidently been startled by the sight

of this young man into no ordinary state of commotion. She
glanced at the books on the sofa, and then at her father. Mr
Baines, thin and gaunt, and acutely pitiable, still slept. His brain
had almost ceased to be active now; he had to be fed and tended
like a bearded baby, and he would sleep for hours at a stretch
even in the daytime. Sophia left the room. A moment later she ran
into the shop, an apparition that amazed the three young lady
assistants. At the corner near the window on the fancy side a little
nook had been formed by screening off a portion of the counter
with large flower-boxes placed end-up. This corner had come to
be known as 'Miss Baines's corner'. Sophia hastened to it,
squeezing past a young lady assistant in the narrow space between the back of the counter and the shelf-lined wall. She sat
down in Constance's chair and pretended to look for something.
She had examined herself in the cheval-glass in the showroom, on
her way from the sick-chamber. When she heard a voice near the
door of the shop asking first for Mr Povey and then for Mrs
Baines, she rose, and seizing the object nearest to her, which
happened to be a pair of scissors, she hurried towards the
showroom stairs as though the scissors had been a grail, passionately sought and to be jealously hidden away. She wanted to
stop and turn round, but something prevented her. She was at the
end of the counter, under the curving stairs, when one of the
assistants said:

'I suppose you don't know when Mr Povey or your mother are
likely to be back, Miss Sophia? Here's –'

It was a divine release for Sophia.

'They're – I –' she stammered, turning round abruptly. Luckily
she was still sheltered behind the counter.

The young man whom she had seen in the street came boldly
forward.

'Good morning, Miss Sophia,' said he, hat in hand. 'It is a long
time since I had the pleasure of seeing you.'

Never had she blushed as she blushed then. She scarcely knew
what she was doing as she moved slowly towards her sister's
corner again, the young man following her on the customers' side
of the counter.

II

She knew that he was a traveller for the most renowned and gigantic of all Manchester wholesale firms – Birkinshaws. But she did not know his name, which was Gerald Scales. He was a rather short, but extremely well-proportioned man of thirty, with fair hair, and a distinguished appearance, as became a representative of Birkinshaw's. His broad, tight necktie, with an edge of white collar showing above it, was particularly elegant. He had been on the road for Birkinshaws for several years; but Sophia had only seen him once before in her life, when she was a little girl, three years ago. The relations between the travellers of the great firms and their solid, sure clients in small towns were in those days often cordially intimate. The traveller came with the lustre of a historic reputation around him; there was no need to fawn for orders; and the client's immense and immaculate respectability made him the equal of no matter what ambassador. It was a case of mutual esteem, and of that confidence-generating phenomenon, 'an old account'. The tone in which a commercial traveller of middle age would utter the phrase 'an old account' revealed in a flash all that was romantic, prim, and stately in mid-Victorian commerce. In the days of Baines, after one of the elaborately engraved advice-circulars had arrived ('Our Mr — will have the pleasure of waiting upon you on — day next, the — inst.') John might in certain cases be expected to say, on the morning of — day, 'Missis, what have ye gotten for supper tonight?'

Mr Gerald Scales had never been asked to supper; he had never even seen John Baines; but, as the youthful successor of an aged traveller who had had the pleasure of St Luke's Square, on behalf of Birkinshaws, since before railways, Mrs Baines had treated him with a faint agreeable touch of maternal familiarity; and, both her daughters being once in the shop during his visit, she had on that occasion commanded the gawky girls to shake hands with him.

Sophia had never forgotten that glimpse. The young man without a name had lived in her mind, brightly glowing, as the very symbol and incarnation of the masculine and the elegant. The renewed sight of him seemed to have wakened her out of a sleep. Assuredly she was not the same Sophia. As she sat in her sister's chair in the corner, entrenched behind the perpendicular boxes, playing nervously with the scissors, her beautiful face was transfigured into the ravishingly angelic. It would have been impossible for Mr Gerald Scales, or anybody else, to credit, as he gazed at those lovely, sensitive, vivacious, responsive features, that Sophia was not a character of heavenly sweetness and perfection. She did not know what she was doing; she was nothing but the exquisite expression of a deep instinct to attract and charm. Her soul itself emanated from her in an atmosphere of allurement and acquiescence. Could those laughing lips hang in a heavy pout? Could that delicate and mild voice be harsh? Could those burning eyes be coldly inimical? Never! The idea was inconceivable! And Mr Gerald Scales, with his head over the top of the boxes, yielded to the spell. Remarkable that Mr Gerald Scales, with all his experience, should have had to come to Bursley to find the pearl, the paragon, the ideal! But so it was. They met in an equal abandonment; the only difference between them was that Mr Scales, by force of habit, kept his head.

'I see it's your wakes here,' said he.

He was polite to the wakes; but now, with the least inflection in the world, he put the wakes at its proper level in the scheme of things as a local unimportance! She adored him for this; she was athirst for sympathy in the task of scorning everything local.

'I expect you didn't know,' she said, implying that there was every reason why a man of his mundane interests should not know.

'I should have remembered if I had thought,' said he. 'But I didn't think. What's this about an elephant?'

'Oh!' she exclaimed. 'Have you heard of that?'

'My porter was full of it.'

'Well,' she said, 'of course it's a very big thing in Bursley.'

As she smiled in gentle pity of poor Bursley, he naturally did the same. And he thought how much more advanced and broad the younger generation was than the old! He would never have dared to express his real feelings about Bursley to Mrs Baines, or even to Mr Povey (who was, however, of no generation); yet here was a young woman actually sharing them.

She told him all the history of the elephant.

'Must have been very exciting,' he commented, despite himself.

'Do you know,' she replied, 'it *was*.'

After all, Bursley was climbing in their opinion.

'And mother and my sister and Mr Povey have all gone to see it. That's why they're not here.'

That the elephant should have caused both Mr Povey and Mrs Baines to forget that the representative of Birkinshaws was due to call was indeed a final victory for the elephant.

'But not you!' he exclaimed.

'No,' she said. 'Not me.'

'Why didn't you go too?' He continued his flattering investigations with a generous smile.

'I simply didn't care to,' said she, proudly nonchalant.

'And I suppose you are in charge here?'

'No,' she answered. 'I just happened to have run down here for these scissors. That's all.'

'I often see your sister,' said he. ' "Often" do I say? – that is, generally, when I come; but never you.'

'I'm never in the shop,' she said. 'It's just an accident today.'

'Oh! So you leave the shop to your sister?'

'Yes.' She said nothing of her teaching.

Then there was a silence. Sophia was very thankful to be hidden from the curiosity of the shop. The shop could see nothing of her, and only the back of the young man; and the conversation had been conducted in low voices. She tapped her foot, stared at the worn, polished surface of the counter, with the brass yard-measure nailed along its edge, and then she uneasily turned her gaze to the left and seemed to be examining the backs of the black bonnets which were perched on high stands in the great window. Then her eyes caught his for an important moment.

'Yes,' she breathed. Somebody had to say something. If the shop missed the murmur of their voices the shop would wonder what had happened to them.

Mr Scales looked at his watch. 'I dare say if I come in again about two –' he began.

'Oh yes, they're *sure* to be in then,' she burst out before he could finish his sentence.

He left abruptly, queerly, without shaking hands (but then it would have been difficult – she argued – for him to have put his arm over the boxes), and without expressing the hope of seeing her again. She peeped through the black bonnets, and saw the porter put the leather strap over his shoulders, raise the rear of the barrow, and trundle off; but she did not see Mr Scales. She was drunk; thoughts were tumbling about in her brain like cargo loose in a rolling ship. Her entire conception of herself was being altered; her attitude towards life was being altered. The thought which knocked hardest against its fellows was, 'Only in these moments have I begun to live!'

And as she flitted upstairs to resume watch over her father she sought to devise an innocent-looking method by which she might see Mr Scales when he next called. And she speculated as to what his name was.

III

When Sophia arrived in the bedroom, she was startled because her father's head and beard were not in their accustomed place on the pillow. She could only make out something vaguely unusual sloping off the side of the bed. A few seconds passed – not to be measured in time – and she saw that the upper part of his body had slipped down, and his head was hanging, inverted, near the floor between the bed and the ottoman. His face, neck, and hands were dark and congested; his mouth was open, and the tongue protruded between the black, swollen, mucous lips; his eyes were prominent and coldly staring. The fact was that Mr Baines had wakened up, and, being restless, had slid out partially from his bed and died of asphyxia. After having been unceasingly watched for fourteen years, he had, with an invalid's natural perverseness, taken advantage of Sophia's brief dereliction to expire. Say what you will, amid Sophia's horror, and her terrible grief and shame, she had visitings of the idea: he did it on purpose!

She ran out of the room, knowing by intuition that he was dead, and shrieked out, 'Maggie', at the top of her voice; the house echoed.

'Yes, miss,' said Maggie, quite close, coming out of Mr Povey's chamber with a slop-pail.

'Fetch Mr Critchlow at once. Be quick. Just as you are. It's father –'

Maggie, perceiving darkly that disaster was in the air, and instantly filled with importance and a sort of black joy, dropped her pail in the exact middle of the passage, and almost fell down the crooked stairs. One of Maggie's deepest instincts, always held in check by the stern dominance of Mrs Baines, was to leave pails prominent on the main routes of the house; and now, divining what was at hand, it flamed into insurrection.

No sleepless night had ever been so long to Sophia as the three minutes which elapsed before Mr Critchlow came. As she stood on the mat outside the bedroom door she tried to draw her mother and Constance and Mr Povey by magnetic force out of the wakes into the house, and her muscles were contracted in the strange effort. She felt that it was impossible to continue living if the secret of the bedroom remained unknown one instant longer, so intense was her torture, and yet that the torture which could not be borne must be borne. Not a sound in the house! Not a sound from the shop! Only the distant murmur of the wakes!

'Why did I forget father?' she asked herself with awe. 'I only meant to tell *him* that they were all out, and run back. Why did I forget father?' She would never be able to persuade anybody that she had literally forgotten her father's existence for quite ten minutes; but it was true, though shocking.

Then there were noises downstairs.

'Bless us! Bless us!' came the unpleasant voice of Mr Critchlow as he bounded up the stairs on his long legs; he strode over the pail. 'What's amiss?' He was wearing his white apron, and he carried his spectacles in his bony hand.

'It's father – he's –' Sophia faltered.

She stood away so that he should enter the room first. He glanced at her keenly, and as it were resentfully, and went in. She followed, timidly, remaining near the door while Mr Critchlow inspected her handiwork. He put on his spectacles with strange deliberation, and then, bending his knees outwards, thus lowered his body so that he could examine John Baines point-blank. He remained staring like this, his hands on his sharp apron-covered knees, for a little space; and then he seized the inert mass and restored it to the bed, and wiped those clotted lips with his apron.

Sophia heard loud breathing behind her. It was Maggie. She heard a huge, snorting sob; Maggie was showing her emotion.

'Go fetch doctor!' Mr Critchlow rasped. 'And don't stand gaping there!'

'Run for the doctor, Maggie,' said Sophia.

'How came ye to let him fall?' Mr Critchlow demanded.

'I was out of the room. I just ran down into the shop –'

'Gallivanting with that young Scales!' said Mr Critchlow, with devilish ferocity. 'Well, you've killed yer father; that's all!'

He must have been at his shop door and seen the entry of the traveller! And it was precisely characteristic of Mr Critchlow to jump in the dark at a horrible conclusion, and to be right after all. For Sophia Mr Critchlow had always been the personification of malignity and malevolence, and now these qualities in him made him, to her, almost obscene. Her pride brought up tremendous reinforcements, and she approached the bed.

'Is he dead?' she asked in a quiet tone. (Somewhere within a voice was whispering, 'So his name is Scales.')

'Don't I tell you he's dead?'

'Pail on the stairs!'

This mild exclamation came from the passage. Mrs Baines, misliking the crowds abroad, had returned alone; she had left Constance in charge of Mr Povey. Coming into her house by the shop and showroom, she had first noted the phenomenon of the pail – proof of her theory of Maggie's incurable untidiness.

'Been to see the elephant, I reckon!' said Mr Critchlow, in fierce sarcasm, as he recognized Mrs Baines's voice.

Sophia leaped towards the door, as though to bar her mother's entrance. But Mrs Baines was already opening the door.

'Well, my pet –' she was beginning cheerfully.

Mr Critchlow confronted her. And he had no more pity for the wife than for the daughter. He was furiously angry because his precious property had been irretrievably damaged by the momentary carelessness of a silly girl. Yes, John Baines was his property, his dearest toy! He was convinced that he alone had kept John Baines alive for fourteen years, that he alone had fully understood the case and sympathized with the sufferer, that none but he had been capable of displaying ordinary common sense in the sick-room. He had learned to regard John Baines as, in some sort, his creation. And now, with their stupidity, their neglect, their elephants, between them they had done for John Baines. He had always known it would come to that, and it had come to that.

'She let him fall out o'bed, and ye're a widow now, missus!' he announced with a virulence hardly conceivable. His angular features and dark eyes expressed a murderous hate for every woman named Baines.

'Mother!' cried Sophia, 'I only ran down into the shop to – to –'

She seized her mother's arm in frenzied agony.

'My child!' said Mrs Baines, rising miraculously to the situation with a calm benevolence of tone and gesture that remained for ever sublime in the stormy heart of Sophia, 'do not hold me.' With infinite gentleness she loosed herself from these clasping hands. 'Have you sent for the doctor?' she questioned Mr Critchlow.

The fate of her husband presented no mysteries to Mrs Baines. Everybody had been warned a thousand times of the danger of leaving the paralytic, whose life depended on his position, and whose fidgetiness was thereby a constant menace of death to him. For five thousand nights she had wakened infallibly every time he stirred, and rearranged him by the flicker of a little oil lamp. But Sophia, unhappy creature, had merely left him. That was all.

Mr Critchlow and the widow gazed, helplessly waiting, at the pitiable corpse, of which the salient part was the white beard. They knew not that they were gazing at a vanished era. John Baines had belonged to the past, to the age when men really did think of their souls, when orators by phrases could move crowds to fury or to pity, when no one had learnt to hurry, when Demos was only turning in his sleep, when the sole beauty of life resided in its inflexible and slow dignity, when hell really had no bottom, and a gilt-clasped Bible really was the secret of England's greatness. Mid-Victorian England lay on that mahogany bed. Ideals had passed away with John Baines. It is thus that ideals die; not in the conventional pageantry of honoured death, but sorrily, ignobly, while one's head is turned –

And Mr Povey and Constance, very self-conscious, went and saw the dead elephant, and came back; and at the corner of King Street, Constance exclaimed brightly –

'Why! who's gone out and left the side-door open?'

For the doctor had at length arrived, and Maggie, in showing him upstairs with pious haste, had forgotten to shut the door.

And they took advantage of the side-door, rather guiltily, to avoid the eyes of the shop. They feared that in the parlour they would be the centre of a curiosity half ironical and half reproving; for had they not accomplished an escapade? So they walked slowly.

The real murderer was having his dinner in the commercial room up at the Tiger, opposite the Town Hall.

IV

Several shutters were put up in the windows of the shop, to indicate a death, and the news instantly became known in trading circles throughout the town. Many people simultaneously re-marked upon the coincidence that Mr Baines should have died while there was a show of mourning goods in his establishment. This coincidence was regarded as extremely sinister, and it was apparently felt that, for the sake of the mind's peace, one ought not to inquire into such things too closely. From the moment of putting up the prescribed shutters, John Baines and his funeral began to acquire importance in Bursley, and their importance grew rapidly almost from hour to hour. The wakes continued as usual, except that the Chief Constable, upon representations being made to him by Mr Critchlow and other citizens, de-scended upon St Luke's Square and forbade the activities of Wombwell's orchestra. Wombwell and the Chief Constable dif-fered as to the justice of the decree, but every well-minded person praised the Chief Constable, and he himself considered that he had enhanced the town's reputation for a decent propriety. It was noticed, too, not without a shiver of the uncanny, that that night the lions and tigers behaved like lambs, whereas on the previous night they had roared the whole Square out of its sleep.

The Chief Constable was not the only individual enlisted by
Mr Critchlow in the service of his friend's fame. Mr Critchlow
spent hours in recalling the principal citizens to a due sense of
John Baines's past greatness. He was determined that his treasured toy should vanish underground with due pomp, and he left
nothing undone to that end. He went over to Hanbridge on the
still wonderful horse-car, and saw the editor-proprietor of the
Staffordshire Signal (then a two-penny weekly with no thought of
Football editions), and on the very day of the funeral the *Signal*
came out with a long and eloquent biography of John Baines.
This biography, giving details of his public life, definitely restored
him to his legitimate position in the civic memory as an ex-chief
bailiff, an ex-chairman of the Burial Board, and of the Five
Towns Association for the Advancement of Useful Knowledge,
and also as a 'prime mover' in the local Turnpike Act, in the
negotiations for the new Town Hall, and in the Corinthian façade
of the Wesleyan Chapel; it narrated the anecdote of his
courageous speech from the portico of the Shambles during the
riots of 1848, and it did not omit a eulogy of his steady adherence
to the wise old English maxims of commerce and his avoidance of
dangerous modern methods. Even in the sixties the modern had
reared its shameless head. The panegyric closed with an appreciation of the dead man's fortitude in the terrible affliction with
which a divine providence had seen fit to try him; and finally the
Signal uttered its absolute conviction that his native town would
raise a cenotaph to his honour. Mr Critchlow, being unfamiliar
with the word 'cenotaph', consulted Worcester's Dictionary, and
when he found that it meant 'a sepulchral monument to one who
is buried elsewhere', he was as pleased with the *Signal's* language
as with the idea, and decided that a cenotaph should come to
pass.

The house and shop were transformed into a hive of preparation for the funeral. All was changed. Mr Povey kindly slept for
three nights on the parlour sofa, in order that Mrs Baines might
have his room. The funeral grew into an obsession, for multitudinous things had to be performed and done sumptuously and in
strict accordance with precedent. There were the family mourning, the funeral repast, the choice of the text on the memorial

card, the composition of the legend on the coffin, the legal
arrangements, the letters to relations, the selection of guests, and
the questions of bell-ringing, hearse, plumes, number of horses,
and grave-digging. Nobody had leisure for the indulgence of grief
except Aunt Maria, who, after she had helped in the laying-out,
simply sat down and bemoaned unceasingly for hours her absence on the fatal morning. 'If I hadn't been so fixed on polishing
my candle-sticks,' she weepingly repeated, 'he mit ha' been alive
and well now.' Not that Aunt Maria had been informed of the
precise circumstances of the death; she was not clearly aware that
Mr Baines had died through a piece of neglect. But, like Mr
Critchlow, she was convinced that there had been only one
person in the world truly capable of nursing Mr Baines. Beyond
the family, no one save Mr Critchlow and Dr Harrop knew just
how the martyr had finished his career. Dr Harrop, having been
asked bluntly if an inquest would be necessary, had reflected a
moment and had then replied: 'No.' And he added, 'Least said
soonest mended – mark me!' They had marked him. He was
common sense in breeches.

As for Aunt Maria, she was sent about her snivelling business
by Aunt Harriet. The arrival in the house of this genuine aunt
from Axe, of this majestic and enormous widow whom even the
imperial Mrs Baines regarded with a certain awe, set a seal of
ultimate solemnity on the whole event. In Mr Povey's bedroom
Mrs Baines fell like a child into Aunt Harriet's arms and sobbed:

'If it had been anything else but that elephant!'

Such was Mrs Baines's sole weakness from first to last.

Aunt Harriet was an exhaustless fountain of authority upon
every detail concerning interments. And, to a series of questions
ending with the word 'sister', and answers ending with the word
'sister', the prodigious travail incident to the funeral was gradually and successfully accomplished. Dress and the repast exceeded
all other matters in complexity and difficulty. But on the morning
of the funeral Aunt Harriet had the satisfaction of beholding her
younger sister the centre of a tremendous cocoon of crape, whose
slightest pleat was perfect. Aunt Harriet seemed to welcome her
then, like a veteran, formally into the august army of relicts. As
they stood side by side surveying the special table which was

being laid in the showroom for the repast, it appeared inconceivable that they had reposed together in Mr Povey's limited bed. They descended from the showroom to the kitchen, where the last delicate dishes were inspected. The shop was, of course, closed for the day, but Mr Povey was busy there, and in Aunt Harriet's all-seeing glance he came next after the dishes. She rose from the kitchen to speak with him.

'You've got your boxes of gloves all ready?' she questioned him.

'Yes, Mrs Maddack.'

'You'll not forget to have a measure handy?'

'No, Mrs Maddack.'

'You'll find you'll want more of seven-and-three-quarters and eights than anything.'

'Yes. I have allowed for that.'

'If you place yourself behind the side-door and put your boxes on the harmonium, you'll be able to catch every one as they come in.'

'That is what I had thought of, Mrs Maddack.'

She went upstairs. Mrs Baines had reached the showroom again, and was smoothing out creases in the white damask cloth and arranging glass dishes of jam at equal distances from each other.

'Come, sister,' said Mrs Maddack. 'A last look.'

And they passed into the mortuary bedroom to gaze at Mr Baines before he should be everlastingly nailed down. In death he had recovered some of his earlier dignity; but even so he was a startling sight. The two widows bent over him, one on either side, and gravely stared at that twisted, worn white face all neatly tucked up in linen.

'I shall fetch Constance and Sophia,' said Mrs Maddack, with tears in her voice. 'Do you go into the drawing-room, sister.'

But Mrs Maddack only succeeded in fetching Constance.

Then there was the sound of wheels in King Street. The long rite of the funeral was about to begin. Every guest, after having been measured and presented with a pair of the finest black kid gloves by Mr Povey, had to mount the crooked stairs and gaze upon the carcase of John Baines, going afterwards to the drawing-room to condole briefly with the widow. And every guest, while conscious of the enormity of so thinking, thought what an excellent thing it was that John Baines should be at last dead and gone. The tramping on the stairs was continual, and finally Mr Baines himself went downstairs, bumping against corners, and led a *cortège* of twenty vehicles.

The funeral tea was not over at seven o'clock, five hours after the commencement of the rite. It was a gigantic and faultless meal, worthy of John Baines's distant past. Only two persons were absent from it – John Baines and Sophia. The emptiness of Sophia's chair was much noticed; Mrs Maddack explained that Sophia was very high-strung and could not trust herself. Great efforts were put forth by the company to be lugubrious and inconsolable, but the secret relief resulting from the death would not be entirely hidden. The vast pretence of acute sorrow could not stand intact against that secret relief and the lavish richness of the food.

To the offending of sundry important relatives from a distance, Mr Critchlow informally presided over that assemblage of grave men in high stocks and crinolined women. He had closed his shop, which had never before been closed on a weekday, and he had a great deal to say about this extraordinary closure. It was due as much to the elephant as to the funeral. The elephant had become a victim to the craze of souvenirs. Already in the night his tusks had been stolen; then his feet disappeared for umbrella-stands, and most of his flesh had departed in little hunks. Everybody in Bursley had resolved to participate in the elephant. One consequence was that all the chemists' shops in the town were assaulted by strings of boys. 'Please a peenorth o' alum to tak' smell out o' a bit o' elephant.' Mr Chritchlow hated boys.

' "I'll alum ye!" says I, and I did. I alummed him out o' my shop with a pestle. If there'd been one there'd been twenty between opening and nine o'clock. "George," I says to my apprentice, "shut shop up. My old friend John Baines is going to his long home today, and I'll close. I've had enough o' alum for one day." '

The elephant fed the conversation until after the second relay of hot muffins. When Mr Critchlow had eaten to his capacity, he took the *Signal* importantly from his pocket, posed his spectacles, and read the obituary all through in slow, impressive accents. Before he reached the end Mrs Baines began to perceive that familiarity had blinded her to the heroic qualities of her late husband. The fourteen years of ceaseless care were quite genuinely forgotten, and she saw him in his strength and in his glory. When Mr Critchlow arrived at the eulogy of the husband and father, Mrs Baines rose and left the showroom. The guests looked at each other in sympathy for her. Mr Critchlow shot a glance at her over his spectacles and continued steadily reading. After he had finished he approached the question of the cenotaph.

Mrs Baines, driven from the banquet by her feelings, went into the drawing-room. Sophia was there, and Sophia, seeing tears in her mother's eyes, gave a sob, and flung herself bodily against her mother, clutching her, and hiding her face in that broad crape, which abraded her soft skin.

'Mother,' she wept passionately, 'I want to leave the school now. I want to please you. I'll do anything in the world to please you. I'll go into the shop if you'd like me to!' Her voice lost itself in tears.

'Calm yourself, my pet,' said Mrs Baines, tenderly, caressing her. It was a triumph for the mother in the very hour when she needed a triumph.

CHAPTER 5: *The Traveller*

I

'Exquisite, 1s. 11d.'

These singular signs were being painted in shiny black on an unrectangular parallelogram of white cardboard by Constance one evening in the parlour. She was seated, with her left side to the fire and to the fizzing gas, at the dining-table, which was covered with a checked cloth in red and white. Her dress was of dark crimson; she wore a cameo brooch and a gold chain round her neck; over her shoulders was thrown a white knitted shawl, for the weather was extremely cold, the English climate being much more serious and downright at that day than it is now. She bent low to the task, holding her head slightly askew, putting the tip of her tongue between her lips, and expending all the energy of her soul and body in an intense effort to do what she was doing as well as it could be done.

'Splendid!' said Mr Povey.

Mr Povey was fronting her at the table; he had his elbows on the table, and watched her carefully, with the breathless and divine anxiety of a dreamer who is witnessing the realization of his dream. And Constance, without moving any part of her frame except her head, looked up at him and smiled for a moment, and he could see her delicious little nostrils at the end of her snub nose.

Those two, without knowing or guessing it, were making history – the history of commerce. They had no suspicion that they were the forces of the future insidiously at work to destroy what the forces of the past had created, but such was the case. They were conscious merely of a desire to do their duty in the shop and to the shop; probably it had not even occurred to them that this desire, which each stimulated in the breast of the other, had assumed the dimensions of a passion. It was ageing Mr Povey, and it had made of Constance a young lady tremendously industrious and preoccupied.

Mr Povey had recently been giving attention to the question of tickets. It is not too much to say that Mr Povey, to whom heaven had granted a minimum share of imagination, had nevertheless discovered his little parcel of imagination in the recesses of being, and brought it effectively to bear on tickets. Tickets ran in conventional grooves. There were heavy oblong tickets for flannels, shirting, and other stuffs in the piece; there were smaller and lighter tickets for intermediate goods; and there were diamond-shaped tickets (containing nothing but the price) for bonnets, gloves, and flim-flams generally. The legends on the tickets gave no sort of original invention. The words 'lasting', 'durable', 'unshrinkable', 'latest', 'cheap', 'stylish', 'novelty', 'choice' (as an adjective), 'new', and 'tasteful', exhausted the entire vocabulary of tickets. Now Mr Povey attached importance to tickets, and since he was acknowledged to be the best window-dresser in Bursley, his views were entitled to respect. He dreamed of other tickets, in original shapes, with original legends. In brief, he achieved, in regard to tickets, the rare feat of ridding himself of preconceived notions, and of approaching a subject with fresh, virginal eyes. When he indicated the nature of his wishes to Mr Chawner, the wholesale stationer who supplied all the Five Towns with shop-tickets, Mr Chawner grew uneasy and worried; Mr Chawner was indeed shocked. For Mr Chawner there had always been certain well-defined genera of tickets, and he could not conceive the existence of other genera. When Mr Povey suggested circular tickets – tickets with a blue and a red line round them, tickets with legends such as 'unsurpassable', 'very dainty', or 'please note', Mr Chawner hummed and hawed, and finally stated that it would be impossible to manufacture these preposterous tickets, these tickets which would outrage the decency of trade.

If Mr Povey had not happened to be an exceedingly obstinate man, he might have been defeated by the crass Toryism of Mr Chawner. But Mr Povey was obstinate, and he had resources of ingenuity which Mr Chawner little suspected. The great tramping march of progress was not to be impeded by Mr Chawner. Mr Povey began to make his own tickets. At first he suffered as all reformers and inventors suffer. He used the internal surface of collar-boxes and ordinary ink and pens, and the result was such as to give customers the idea that Baineses were too poor or too mean to buy tickets like other shops. For bought tickets had an ivory-tinted gloss, and the ink was black and glossy, and the edges were very straight and did not show yellow between two layers of white. Whereas Mr Povey's tickets were of a bluish-white, without gloss; the ink was neither black nor shiny, and the edges were amateurishly rough: the tickets had an unmistakable air of having been 'made out of something else'; moreover, the lettering had not the free, dashing style of Mr Chawner's tickets.

And did Mrs Baines encourage him in his single-minded enterprise on behalf of *her* business? Not a bit! Mrs Baines's attitude, when not disdainful, was inimical! So curious is human nature, so blind is man to his own advantage! Life was very complex for Mr Povey. It might have been less complex had Bristol board and

Chinese ink been less expensive; with these materials he could have achieved marvels to silence all prejudice and stupidity; but they were too costly. Still, he persevered, and Constance morally supported him; he drew his inspiration and his courage from Constance. Instead of the internal surface of collar-boxes, he tried the external surface, which was at any rate shiny. But the ink would not 'take' on it. He made as many experiments as Edison was to make, and as many failures. Then Constance was visited by a notion for mixing sugar with ink. Simple, innocent creature – why should providence have chosen her to be the vessel of such a sublime notion? Puzzling enigma, which, however, did not exercise Mr Povey! He found it quite natural that she should save him. Save him she did. Sugar and ink would 'take' on anything, and it shone like a 'patent leather' boot. Further, Constance developed a 'hand' for lettering which outdid Mr Povey's. Between them they manufactured tickets by the dozen and by the score – tickets which, while possessing nearly all the smartness and finish of Mr Chawner's tickets, were much superior to these in originality and strikingness. Constance and Mr Povey were delighted and fascinated by them. As for Mrs Baines, she said little, but the modern spirit was too elated by its success to care whether she said little or much. And every few days Mr Povey thought of some new and wonderful word to put on a ticket.

His last miracle was the word 'exquisite'. 'Exquisite', pinned on a piece of broad tartan ribbon, appeared to Constance and Mr Povey as the finality of appropriateness. A climax worthy to close the year! Mr Povey had cut the card and sketched the word and figures in pencil, and Constance was doing her executive portion of the undertaking. They were very happy, very absorbed, in this strictly business matter. The clock showed five minutes past ten. Stern duty, a pure desire for the prosperity of the shop, had kept them at hard labour since before eight o'clock that morning!

The stairs-door opened, and Mrs Baines appeared, in bonnet and furs and gloves, all clad for going out. She had abandoned the cocoon of crape, but still wore weeds. She was stouter than ever.

'What!' she cried. 'Not ready! Now really!'

'Oh, mother! How you made me jump!' Constance protested. 'What time is it? It surely isn't time to go yet!'

'Look at the clock!' said Mrs Baines, dryly.

'Well, I never!' Constance murmured, confused.

'Come, put your things together, and don't keep me waiting,' said Mrs Baines, going past the table to the window, and lifting the blind to peep out. 'Still snowing,' she observed. 'Oh, the band's going away at last! I wonder how they can play at all in this weather. By the way, what was that tune they gave us just now? I couldn't make out whether it was "Redhead", or –'

'Band?' questioned Constance – the simpleton!

Neither she nor Mr Povey had heard the strains of the Bursley Town Silver Prize Band which had been enlivening the season according to its usual custom. These two practical, duteous, commonsense young and youngish persons had been so absorbed in their efforts for the welfare of the shop that they had positively not only forgotten the time, but had also failed to notice the band! But if Constance had had her wits about her she would at least have pretended that she had heard it.

'What's this?' asked Mrs Baines, bringing her vast form to the table and picking up a ticket.

Mr Povey said nothing. Constance said: 'Mr Povey thought of it today. Don't you think it's very good, mother?'

'I'm afraid I don't,' Mrs Baines coldly replied.

She had mildly objected already to certain words; but 'exquisite' seemed to her silly; it seemed out of place; she considered that it would merely bring ridicule on her shop. 'Exquisite' written upon a window-ticket! No! What would John Baines have thought of 'exquisite'?

' "Exquisite"!' She repeated the word with a sarcastic inflection, putting the accent, as every one put it, on the second syllable. 'I don't think that will quite do.'

'But why not, mother?'

'It's not suitable, my dear.'

She dropped the ticket from her gloved hand. Mr Povey had darkly flushed. Though he spoke little, he was as sensitive as he was obstinate. On this occasion he said nothing. He expressed his feelings by seizing the ticket and throwing it into the fire.

The situation was extremely delicate. Priceless employees like

Mr Povey cannot be treated as machines, and Mrs Baines of course instantly saw that tact was needed.

'Go along to my bedroom and get ready, my pet,' said she to Constance. 'Sophia is there. There's a good fire. I must just speak to Maggie.' She tactfully left the room.

Mr Povey glanced at the fire and the curling red remains of the ticket. Trade was bad; owing to weather and war, destitution was abroad; and he had been doing his utmost for the welfare of the shop; and here was the reward!

Constance's eyes were full of tears. 'Never mind!' she murmured, and went upstairs.

It was all over in a moment.

II

In the Wesleyan Methodist Chapel on Duck Bank there was a full and influential congregation. For in those days influential people were not merely content to live in the town where their fathers had lived, without dreaming of country residences and smokeless air – they were content also to believe what their fathers had believed about the beginning and end of all. There was no such thing as the unknowable in those days. The eternal mysteries were as simple as an addition sum; a child could tell you with absolute certainty where you would be and what you would be doing a million years hence, and exactly what God thought of you. Accordingly, every one being of the same mind, every one met on certain occasions in certain places in order to express the universal mind. And in the Wesleyan Methodist Chapel, for example, instead of a sparse handful of persons disturbingly conscious of being in a minority, as now, a magnificent and proud majority had collected, deeply aware of its rightness and its correctness.

And the minister, backed by minor ministers, knelt and covered his face in the superb mahogany rostrum; and behind him, in what was then still called the 'orchestra' (though no musical instruments except the grand organ had sounded in it for decades), the choir knelt and covered their faces; and all around, in the richly painted gallery and on the ground-floor, multitudinous rows of people, in easy circumstances of body and soul, knelt in high pews and covered their faces. And there floated before them, in the intense and prolonged silence, the clear vision of Jehovah on a throne, a God of sixty or so with a moustache and a beard, and a non-committal expression which declined to say whether or not he would require more bloodshed; and this God, destitute of pinions, was surrounded by white-winged creatures that wafted themselves to and fro while chanting; and afar off was an obscene monstrosity, with cloven hoofs and a tail, very danger-ous and rude and interfering, who could exist comfortably in the middle of a coal-fire, and who took a malignant and exhaustless pleasure in coaxing you by false pretences into the same fire; but of course you had too much sense to swallow his wicked absurd-ities. Once a year, for ten minutes by the clock, you knelt thus, in mass, and by meditation convinced yourself that you had too much sense to swallow his wicked absurdities. And the hour was very solemn, the most solemn of all the hours.

Strange that immortal souls should be found with the temerity to reflect upon mundane affairs in that hour! Yet there were undoubtedly such in the congregation; there were perhaps many to whom the vision, if clear, was spasmodic and fleeting. And among them the inhabitants of the Baines family pew! Who would have supposed that Mr Povey, a recent convert from Primitive Methodism in King Street to Wesleyan Methodism [5] on Duck Bank, was dwelling upon window-tickets and the injus-tice of women, instead of upon his relations with Jehovah and the tailed one? Who would have supposed that the gentle-eyed Constance, pattern of daughters, was risking her eternal welfare by smiling at the tailed one, who, concealing his tail, had assumed the image of Mr Povey? Who would have supposed that Mrs Baines, instead of resolving that Jehovah and not the tailed one should have ultimate rule over her, was resolving that she and not Mr Povey should have ultimate rule over her house and shop? It was a pew-ful that belied its highly satisfactory appearance. (And possibly there were other pew-fuls equally deceptive.)

Sophia alone, in the corner next to the wall, with her beautiful stern face pressed convulsively against her hands, was truly busy with immortal things. Turbulent heart, the violence of her spiri-tual life had made her older! Never was a passionate, proud girl in a harder case than Sophia! In the splendour of her remorse for a fatal forgetfulness, she had renounced that which she loved and thrown herself into that which she loathed. It was her nature so to do. She had done it haughtily, and not with kindness, but she had done it with the whole force of her will. Constance had been compelled to yield up to her the millinery department, for Sophia's fingers had a gift of manipulating ribbons and feathers that was beyond Constance. Sophia had accomplished miracles in the millinery. Yes, and she would be utterly polite to customers; but afterwards, when the customers were gone, let mothers, sisters, and Mr Poveys beware of her fiery darts!

But why, when nearly three months had elapsed after her father's death, had she spent more and more time in the shop, secretly aflame with expectancy? Why, when one day a strange traveller entered the shop and announced himself the new representative of Birkinshaws – why had her very soul died away within her and an awful sickness seized her? She knew then that she had been her own deceiver. She recognized and admitted, abasing herself lower than the lowest, that her motive in leaving Miss Chetwynd's and joining the shop had been, at the best, very mixed, very impure. Engaged at Miss Chetwynd's, she might easily have never set eyes on Gerald Scales again. Employed in the shop, she could not fail to meet him. In this light was to be seen the true complexion of the splendour of her remorse. A terrible thought for her! And she could not dismiss it. It contaminated her existence, this thought! And she could confide in no one. She was incapable of showing a wound. Quarter had succeeded quarter, and Gerald Scales was no more heard of. She had sacrificed her life for worse than nothing. She had made her own tragedy. She had killed her father, cheated and shamed herself with a remorse horribly spurious, exchanged content for misery and pride for humiliation – and with it all, Gerald Scales had vanished! She was ruined.

She took to religion, and her conscientious Christian virtues, practised with stern inclemency, were the canker of the family. Thus a year and a half had passed.

And then, on this last day of the year, the second year of her shame and of her heart's widowhood, Mr Scales had reappeared.

She had gone casually into the shop and found him talking to her mother and Mr Povey. He had come back to the provincial round and to her. She shook his hand and fled, because she could not have stayed. None had noticed her agitation, for she had held her body as in a vice. She knew the reason neither of his absence nor of his return. She knew nothing. And not a word had been said at meals. And the day had gone and the night come; and now she was in chapel, with Constance by her side and Gerald Scales in her soul! Happy beyond previous conception of happiness! Wretched beyond an unutterable woe! And none knew! What was she to pray for? To what purpose and end ought she to steel herself? Ought she to hope, or ought she to despair? 'O God, help me!' she kept whispering to Jehovah whenever the heavenly vision shone through the wrack of her meditation. 'O God, help me!' She had a conscience that, when it was in the mood for severity, could be unspeakably cruel to her.

And whenever she looked, with dry, hot eyes, through her gloved fingers, she saw in front of her on the wall a marble tablet inscribed in gilt letters, the cenotaph! She knew all the lines by heart, in their spacious grandiloquence; lines such as:

EVER READY WITH HIS TONGUE HIS PEN AND HIS PURSE
TO HELP THE CHURCH OF HIS FATHERS
IN HER HE LIVED AND IN HER HE DIED
CHERISHING A DEEP AND ARDENT AFFECTION
FOR HIS BELOVED FAITH AND CREED

And again:

HIS SYMPATHIES
EXTENDED BEYOND HIS OWN COMMUNITY
HE WAS ALWAYS TO THE FORE IN GOOD WORKS
AND HE SERVED THE CIRCUIT THE TOWN AND THE
DISTRICT WITH GREAT ACCEPTANCE AND USEFULNESS

Thus had Mr Critchlow's vanity been duly appeased.

As the minutes sped in the breathing silence of the chapel the emotional tension grew tighter; worshippers sighed heavily, or called upon Jehovah for a sign, or merely coughed an invocation. And then at last the clock in the middle of the balcony gave forth the single stroke to which it was limited; the ministers rose, and the congregation after them; and everybody smiled as though it was the millennium, and not simply the new year, that had set in. Then, faintly, through walls and shut windows, came the sound of bells and of steam sirens and whistles. The superintendent minister opened his hymn-book, and the hymn was sung which had been sung in Wesleyan Chapels on New Year's morn since the era of John Wesley himself. The organ finished with a clangour of all its pipes; the minister had a few last words with Jehovah, and nothing was left to do except to persevere in well-doing. The people leaned towards each other across the high backs of the pews.

'A happy New Year!'

'Eh, thank ye! The same to you!'

'Another Watch-Night service over!'

'Eh, yes!' And a sigh.

Then the aisles were suddenly crowded, and there was a good-humoured, optimistic pushing towards the door. In the Corinthian porch occurred a great putting-on of cloaks, ulsters, goloshes, and even pattens, and a great putting-up of umbrellas. And the congregation went out into the whirling snow, dividing into several black, silent-footed processions, down Trafalgar Road, up towards the playground, along the market-place, and across Duck Square in the direction of St Luke's Square.

Mr Povey was between Mrs Baines and Constance.

'You must take my arm, my pet,' said Mrs Baines to Sophia.

Then Mr Povey and Constance waded on in front through the drifts. Sophia balanced that enormous swaying mass, her mother. Owing to their hoops, she had much difficulty in keeping close to her. Mrs Baines laughed with the complacent ease of obesity, yet a fall would have been almost irremediable for her; and so Sophia had to laugh too. But, though she laughed, God had not helped her. She did not know where she was going, nor what might happen to her next.

'Why, bless us!' exclaimed Mrs Baines, as they turned the corner into King Street. 'There's someone sitting on our door-step!'

There was: a figure swathed in an ulster, a maud over the

ulster, and a high hat on the top of all. It could not have been there very long, because it was only speckled with snow. Mr Povey plunged forward.

'It's Mr Scales, of all people!' said Mr Povey.

'Mr Scales!' cried Mrs Baines.

And, 'Mr Scales!' murmured Sophia, terribly afraid.

Perhaps she was afraid of miracles. Mr Scales sitting on her mother's doorstep in the middle of the snowy night had assuredly the air of a miracle, of something dreamed in a dream, of something pathetically and impossibly appropriate – 'pat', as they say in the Five Towns. But he was a tangible fact there. And years afterwards, in the light of further knowledge of Mr Scales, Sophia came to regard his being on the doorstep as the most natural and characteristic thing in the world. Real miracles never seem to be miracles, and that which at the first blush resembles one usually proves to be an instance of the extremely prosaic.

III

'Is that you, Mrs Baines?' asked Gerald Scales, in a half-witted voice, looking up, and then getting to his feet. 'Is this your house? So it is! Well, I'd no idea I was sitting on your doorstep.'

He smiled timidly, nay, sheepishly, while the women and Mr Povey surrounded him with their astonished faces under the light of the gas-lamp. Certainly he was very pale.

'But whatever is the matter, Mr Scales?' Mrs Baines demanded in an anxious tone. 'Are you ill? Have you been suddenly –'

'Oh no,' said the young man lightly. 'It's nothing. Only I was set on just now, down there' – he pointed to the depths of King Street.

'Set on!' Mrs Baines repeated, alarmed.

'That makes the fourth case in a week, that we *know* of!' said Mr Povey. 'It really is becoming a scandal.'

The fact was that, owing to depression of trade, lack of employment, and rigorous weather, public security in the Five Towns was at that period not as perfect as it ought to have been. In the stress of hunger the lower classes were forgetting their manners – and this in spite of the altruistic and noble efforts of their social superiors to relieve the destitution due, of course, to short-sighted improvidence. When (the social superiors were asking in despair) will the lower classes learn to put by for a rainy day? (They might have said a snowy and a frosty day.) It was 'really too bad' of the lower classes, when everything that could be done was being done for them, to kill, or even attempt to kill, the goose that lays the golden eggs! And especially in a respectable town! What, indeed, were things coming to? Well, here was Mr Gerald Scales, gentleman from Manchester, a witness and victim to the deplorable moral condition of the Five Towns. What would he think of the Five Towns? The evil and the danger had been a topic of discussion in the shop for a week past, and now it was brought home to them.

'I hope you weren't –' said Mrs Baines, apologetically and sympathetically.

'Oh no!' Mr Scales interrupted her quite gaily. 'I managed to beat them off. Only my elbow –'

Meanwhile it was continuing to snow.

'Do come in!' said Mrs Baines.

'I couldn't think of troubling you,' said Mr Scales. 'I'm all right now, and I can find my way to the Tiger.'

'You must come in, if it's only for a minute,' said Mrs Baines, with decision. She had to think of the honour of the town.

'You're very kind,' said Mr Scales.

The door was suddenly opened from within, and Maggie surveyed them from the height of the two steps.

'A happy New Year, mum, to all of you.'

'Thank you, Maggie,' said Mrs Baines, and primly added: 'The same to you!' And in her own mind she said that Maggie could best prove her desire for a happy new year by contriving in future not to 'scamp her corners', and not to break so much crockery.

Sophia, scarce knowing what she did, mounted the steps.

'Mr Scales ought to let our New Year in, my pet,' Mrs Baines stopped her.

'Oh, of course, mother!' Sophia concurred with a gasp, springing back nervously.

Mr Scales raised his hat, and duly let the new year, and much snow, into the Baines parlour. And there was a vast deal of stamping of feet, agitating of umbrellas, and shaking of cloaks

and ulsters on the doormat in the corner by the harmonium. And
Maggie took away an armful of everything snowy, including
goloshes, and received instructions to boil milk and to bring
'mince'. Mr Povey said 'B-r-r-r!' and shut the door (which was
bordered with felt to stop ventilation); Mrs Baines turned up the
gas till it sang, and told Sophia to poke the fire, and actually told
Constance to light the second gas.

Excitement prevailed.

The placidity of existence had been agreeably disturbed (yes,
agreeably, in spite of horror at the attack on Mr Scales's elbow)
by an adventure. Moreover, Mr Scales proved to be in evening-
dress. And nobody had ever worn evening-dress in that house
before.

Sophia's blood was in her face, and it remained there, enhanc-
ing the vivid richness of her beauty. She was dizzy with a strange
and disconcerting intoxication. She seemed to be in a world of
unrealities and incredibilities. Her ears heard with indistinctness,
and the edges of things and people had a prismatic colouring.
She was in a state of ecstatic, unreasonable, inexplicable happiness. All her misery, doubts, despair, rancour, churlish-
ness, had disappeared. She was as softly gentle as Constance.
Her eyes were the eyes of a fawn, and her gestures delicious in
their modest and sensitive grace. Constance was sitting on the
sofa, and, after glancing about as if for shelter, she sat down on
the sofa by Constance's side. She tried not to stare at Mr Scales,
but her gaze would not leave him. She was sure that he was the
most perfect man in the world. A shortish man, perhaps, but a
perfect. That such perfection could be was almost past her belief.
He excelled all her dreams of the ideal man. His smile, his voice,
his hand, his hair – never were such! Why, when he spoke – it was
positively music! When he smiled – it was heaven! His smile, to
Sophia, was one of those natural phenomena which are so lovely
that they make you want to shed tears. There is no hyperbole in
this description of Sophia's sensation, but rather an under-
statement of them. She was utterly obsessed by the unique
qualities of Mr Scales. Nothing would have persuaded her that
the peer of Mr Scales existed among men, or could possibly exist.
And it was her intense and profound conviction of his complete

pre-eminence that gave him, as he sat there in the rocking-chair in her mother's parlour, that air of the unreal and the incredible.

'I stayed in the town on purpose to go to a New Year's party at Mr Lawton's,' Mr Scales was saying.

'Ah! So you know Lawyer Lawton!' observed Mrs Baines, impressed, for Lawyer Lawton did not consort with trades-people. He was jolly with them, and he did their legal business for them, but he was not of them. His friends came from afar.

'My people are old acquaintances of his,' said Mr Scales, sipping the milk which Maggie had brought.

'Now, Mr Scales, you must taste my mince. A happy month for every tart you eat, you know,' Mrs Baines reminded him.

He bowed. 'And it was as I was coming away from there that I got into difficulties.' He laughed.

Then he recounted the struggle, which had, however, been brief, as the assailants lacked pluck. He had slipped and fallen on his elbow on the kerb, and his elbow might have been broken, had not the snow been so thick. No, it did not hurt him now; doubtless a mere bruise. It was fortunate that the miscreants had not got the better of him, for he had in his pocket-book a considerable sum of money in notes – accounts paid! He had often thought what an excellent thing it would be if commercials could travel with dogs, particularly in winter. There was nothing like a dog.

'You are fond of dogs?' asked Mr Povey, who had always had a secret but impracticable ambition to keep a dog.

'Yes,' said Mr Scales, turning now to Mr Povey.

'Keep one?' asked Mr Povey, in a sporting tone.

'I have a fox-terrier bitch,' said Mr Scales, 'that took a first at Knutsford; but she's getting old now.'

The sexual epithet fell queerly on the room. Mr Povey, being a man of the world, behaved as if nothing had happened; but Mrs Baines's curls protested against this unnecessary coarseness. Constance pretended not to hear. Sophia did not understandingly hear. Mr Scales had no suspicion that he was transgressing a convention by virtue of which dogs have no sex. Further, he had no suspicion of the local fame of Mrs Baines's mince-tarts. He had already eaten more mince-tarts than he could enjoy, before beginning upon hers, and Mrs Baines missed the enthusiasm to which she was habituated from consumers of her pastry.

Mr Povey, fascinated, proceeded in the direction of dogs, and it grew more and more evident that Mr Scales, who went out to parties in evening dress, instead of going in respectable broadcloth to watch-night services, who knew the great ones of the land, and who kept dogs of an inconvenient sex, was neither an ordinary commercial traveller nor the kind of man to which the Square was accustomed. He came from a different world.

'Lawyer Lawton's party broke up early – at least I mean, considering –' Mrs Baines hesitated.

After a pause Mr Scales replied, 'Yes, I left immediately the clock struck twelve. I've a heavy day tomorrow – I mean today.'

It was not an hour for a prolonged visit, and in a few minutes Mr Scales was ready again to depart. He admitted a certain feebleness ('wankiness', he playfully called it, being proud of his skill in the dialect), and a burning in his elbow; but otherwise he was quite well – thanks to Mrs Baines's most kind hospitality . . . He really didn't know how he came to be sitting on her doorstep. Mrs Baines urged him, if he met a policeman on his road to the Tiger, to furnish all particulars about the attempted highway robbery, and he said he decidedly would.

He took his leave with distinguished courtliness.

'If I have a moment I shall run in tomorrow morning just to let you know I'm all right,' said he, in the white street.

'Oh, do!' said Constance. Constance's perfect innocence made her strangely forward at times.

'A happy New Year and many of them!'

'Thanks! Same to you! Don't get lost.'

'Straight up the Square and first on the right,' called the commonsense of Mr Povey.

Nothing else remained to say, and the visitor disappeared silently in the whirling snow. 'Brrr!' murmured Mr Povey, shutting the door. Everybody felt: 'What a funny ending of the old year!'

'Sophia, my pet,' Mrs Baines began.

But Sophia had vanished to bed.

'Tell her about her new night-dress,' said Mrs Baines to Constance.

'Yes, mother.'

'I don't know that I'm so set up with that young man, after all,' Mrs Baines reflected aloud.

'Oh, mother!' Constance protested. 'I think he's just lovely.'

'He never looks you straight in the face,' said Mrs Baines.

'Don't tell *me*!' laughed Constance, kissing her mother good night. 'You're only on your high horse because he didn't praise your mince. *I* noticed it.'

IV

'If anybody thinks I'm going to stand the cold in this showroom any longer, they're mistaken,' said Sophia the next morning loudly, and in her mother's hearing. And she went down into the shop carrying bonnets.

She pretended to be angry, but she was not. She felt, on the contrary, extremely joyous, and charitable to all the world. Usually she would take pains to keep out of the shop; usually she was preoccupied and stern. Hence her presence on the ground-floor, and her demeanour, excited interest among the three young lady assistants who sat sewing round the stove in the middle of the shop, sheltered by the great piles of shirtings and linseys that fronted the entrance.

Sophia shared Constance's corner. They had hot bricks under their feet, and fine-knitted wraps on their shoulders. They would have been more comfortable near the stove, but greatness has its penalties. The weather was exceptionally severe. The windows were thickly frosted over, so that Mr Povey's art in dressing them was quite wasted. And – rare phenomenon! – the doors of the shop were shut. In the ordinary way they were not merely open, but hidden by a display of 'cheap lines'. Mr Povey, after consulting Mrs Baines, had decided to close them, foregoing the customary display. Mr Povey had also, in order to get a little warmth into his limbs, personally assisted two casual labourers to scrape the thick frozen snow off the pavement; and he wore his kid mittens. All these things together proved better than the evidence of barometers how the weather nipped.

Mr Scales came about ten o'clock. Instead of going to Mr Povey's counter, he walked boldly to Constance's corner, and looked over the boxes, smiling and saluting. Both the girls candidly delighted in his visit. Both blushed; both laughed – without knowing why they laughed. Mr Scales said he was just departing and had slipped in for a moment to thank all of them for their kindness of last night – 'or rather this morning'. The girls laughed again at this witticism. Nothing could have been more simple than this speech. Yet it appeared to them magically attractive. A customer entered, a lady; one of the assistants rose from the neighbourhood of the stove, but the daughters of the house ignored the customer; it was part of the etiquette of the shop that customers, at any rate chance customers, should not exist for the daughters of the house, until an assistant had formally drawn attention to them. Otherwise every one who wanted a pennyworth of tape would be expecting to be served by Miss Baines, or Miss Sophia, if Miss Sophia were there. Which would have been ridiculous.

Sophia, glancing sidelong, saw the assistant parleying with the customer; and then the assistant came softly behind the counter and approached the corner.

'Miss Constance, can you spare a minute?' the assistant whispered discreetly.

Constance extinguished her smile for Mr Scales, and, turning away, lighted an entirely different and inferior smile for the customer.

'Good morning, Miss Baines. Very cold, isn't it?'

'Good morning, Mrs Chatterley. Yes, it is. I suppose you're getting anxious about those –' Constance stopped.

Sophia was now alone with Mr Scales, for in order to discuss the unnameable freely with Mrs Chatterley her sister was edging up the counter. Sophia had dreamed of a private conversation as something delicious and impossible. But chance had favoured her. She was alone with him. And his neat fair hair and his blue eyes and his delicate mouth were as wonderful to her as ever. He was gentlemanly to a degree that impressed her more than anything had impressed her in her life. And all the proud and aristocratic instinct that was at the base of her character sprang up and seized on his gentlemanliness like a famished animal seizing on food.

'The last time I saw you,' said Mr Scales, in a new tone, 'you said you were never in the shop.'

'What? Yesterday? Did I?'

'No, I mean the last time I saw you alone,' said he.

'Oh!' she exclaimed. 'It's just an accident.'

'That's exactly what you said last time.'

'Is it?'

Was it his manner, or what he said, that flattered her, that intensified her beautiful vivacity?

'I suppose you don't often go out?' he went on.

'What? In this weather?'

'Any time.'

'I go to chapel,' said she, 'and marketing with mother.' There was a little pause. 'And to the Free Library.'

'Oh yes. You've got a Free Library here now, haven't you?'

'Yes. We've had it over a year.'

'And you belong to it? What do you read?'

'Oh, stories, you know. I get a fresh book out once a week.'

'Saturdays, I suppose?'

'No,' she said. 'Wednesdays.' And she smiled. 'Usually.'

'It's Wednesday today,' said he. 'Not been already?'

She shook her head. 'I don't think I shall go today. It's too cold. I don't *think* I shall venture out today.'

'You must be very fond of reading,' said he.

Then Mr Povey appeared, rubbing his mittened hands. And Mrs Chatterley went.

'I'll run and fetch mother,' said Constance.

Mrs Baines was very polite to the young man. He related his interview with the police, whose opinion was that he had been attacked by stray members of a gang from Hanbridge. The young lady assistants, with ears cocked, gathered the nature of Mr Scales's adventure, and were thrilled to the point of questioning Mr Povey about it after Mr Scales had gone. His farewell was marked by much handshaking, and finally Mr Povey ran after him into the Square to mention something about dogs.

At half past one, while Mrs Baines was dozing after dinner,

Sophia wrapped herself up, and with a book under her arm went forth into the world, through the shop. She returned in less than twenty minutes. But her mother had already awakened, and was hovering about the back of the shop. Mothers have supernatural gifts.

Sophia nonchalantly passed her and hurried into the parlour, where she threw down her muff and a book and knelt before the fire to warm herself.

Mrs Baines followed her. 'Been to the Library?' questioned Mrs Baines.

'Yes, mother. And it's simply perishing.'

'I wonder at your going on a day like today. I thought you always went on Thursdays?'

'So I do. But I'd finished my book.'

'What is this?' Mrs Baines picked up the volume, which was covered with black oil-cloth.

She picked it up with a hostile air. For her attitude towards the Free Library was obscurely inimical. She never read anything herself except *The Sunday at Home*, and Constance never read anything except *The Sunday at Home*. There were scriptural commentaries, Dugdale's Gazetteer, Culpeper's Herbal, and work by Bunyan and Flavius Josephus in the drawing-room bookcase; also *Uncle Tom's Cabin*. And Mrs Baines, in considering the welfare of her daughters, looked askance at the whole remainder of printed literature. If the Free Library had not formed part of the Famous Wedgwood Institution, which had been opened with immense *éclat* by the semi-divine Gladstone; if the first book had not been ceremoniously 'taken out' of the Free Library by the Chief Bailiff in person – a grandfather of stainless renown – Mrs Baines would probably have risked her authority in forbidding the Free Library.

'You needn't be afraid,' said Sophia, laughing. 'It's Miss Sewell's *Experience of Life*.'

'A novel, I see,' observed Mrs Baines, dropping the book.

Gold and jewels would probably not tempt a Sophia of these days to read *Experience of Life*; but to Sophia Baines the bland story had the piquancy of the disapproved.

The next day Mrs Baines summoned Sophia into her bedroom.

'Sophia,' she said, trembling, 'I shall be glad if you will not walk about the streets with young men until you have my permission.'

The girl blushed violently. 'I – I –'

'You were seen in Wedgwood Street,' said Mrs Baines.

'Who's been gossiping – Mr Critchlow, I suppose?' Sophia exclaimed scornfully.

'No one has been "gossiping",' said Mrs Baines.

'Well, if I meet someone by accident in the street, I can't help it, can I?' Sophia's voice shook.

'You know what I mean, my child,' said Mrs Baines, with careful calm.

Sophia dashed angrily from the room.

'I like the idea of him having "a heavy day"!' Mrs Baines reflected ironically, recalling a phrase which had lodged in her mind. And very vaguely, with an uneasiness scarcely perceptible, she remembered that 'he', and no other, had been in the shop on the day her husband died.

CHAPTER 6: *Escapade*

I

The uneasiness of Mrs Baines flowed and ebbed, during the next three months, influenced by Sophia's moods. There were days when Sophia was the old Sophia – the forbidding, difficult, waspish, and even hedgehog Sophia. But there were other days on which Sophia seemed to be drawing joy and gaiety and good-will from some secret source, from some fount whose nature and origin none could divine. It was on these days that the uneasiness of Mrs Baines waxed. She had the wildest suspicions; she was almost capable of accusing Sophia of carrying on a clandestine correspondence; she saw Sophia and Gerald Scales deeply and wickedly in love; she saw them with their arms round each other's necks . . . And then she called herself a middle-aged fool, to base such a structure of suspicion on a brief encounter in the street and on an idea, a fancy, a curious and irrational notion!

Sophia had a certain streak of pure nobility in that exceedingly heterogeneous thing, her character. Moreover, Mrs Baines watched the posts, and she also watched Sophia – she was not the woman to trust to a streak of pure nobility – and she came to be sure that Sophia's sinfulness, if any, was not such as could be weighed in a balance, or collected together by stealth and then suddenly placed before the girl on a charger.

Still, she would have given much to see inside Sophia's lovely head. Ah! Could she have done so, what sleep-destroying wonders she would have witnessed! By what bright lamps burning in what mysterious grottoes and caverns of the brain would her mature eyes have been dazzled! Sophia was living for months on the exhaustless ardent vitality absorbed during a magical two minutes in Wedgwood Street. She was living chiefly on the flaming fire struck in her soul by the shock of seeing Gerald Scales in the porch of the Wedgwood Institution as she came out of the Free Library with *Experience of Life* tucked into her large astrakhan muff. He had stayed to meet her, then: she knew it! 'After all,' her heart said, 'I must be very beautiful, for I have attracted the pearl of men!' And she remembered her face in the glass. The value and the power of beauty were tremendously proved to her. He, the great man of the world, the handsome and elegant man with a thousand strange friends and a thousand interests far remote from her, had remained in Bursley on the mere chance of meeting her! She was proud, but her pride was drowned in bliss. 'I was just looking at this inscription about Mr Gladstone.' 'So you decided to come out as usual!' 'And may I ask what book you have chosen?' These were the phrases she heard, and to which she responded with similar phrases. And meanwhile a miracle of ecstasy had opened – opened like a flower. She was walking along Wedgwood Street, by his side slowly, on the scraped pavements, where marble bulbs of snow had defied the spade and remained. She and he were exactly of the same height, and she kept looking into his face and he into hers. This was all the miracle. Except that she was not walking on the pavement – she was walking on the intangible sward of paradise! Except that the houses had receded and faded, and the passers-by were subtilized into unnoticeable ghosts! Except that her mother and

Constance had become phantasmal beings existing at an immense distance!

What had happened? Nothing! The most commonplace occurrence! The eternal cause had picked up a commercial traveller (it might have been a clerk or curate, but it in fact was a commercial traveller), and endowed him with all the glorious, unique, incredible attributes of a god, and planted him down before Sophia in order to produce the eternal effect. A miracle performed specially for Sophia's benefit! No one else in Wedgwood Street saw the god walking along by her side. No one else saw anything but a simple commercial traveller. Yes, the most commonplace occurrence!

Of course at the corner of the street he had to go. 'Till next time!' he murmured. And fire came out of his eyes and lighted in Sophia's lovely head those lamps which Mrs Baines was mercifully spared from seeing. And he had shaken hands and raised his hat. Imagine a god raising his hat! And he went off on two legs, precisely like a dashing little commercial traveller.

And, escorted by the equivocal Angel of Eclipses, she had turned into King Street, and arranged her face, and courageously met her mother. Her mother had not at first perceived the unusual; for mothers, despite their reputation to the contrary, really are the blindest creatures. Sophia, the naïve ninny, had actually supposed that her walking along a hundred yards of pavement with a god by her side was not going to excite remark! What a delusion! It is true, certainly, that no one saw the god by direct vision. But Sophia's cheeks, Sophia's eyes, the curve of Sophia's neck as her soul yearned towards the soul of the god – these phenomena were immeasurably more notable than Sophia guessed. An account of them, in a modified form to respect Mrs Baines's notorious dignity, had healed the mother of her blindness and led to that characteristic protest from her, 'I shall be glad if you will not walk about the streets with young men,' etc.

When the period came for the reappearance of Mr Scales, Mrs Baines outlined a plan, and when the circular announcing the exact time of his arrival was dropped into the letter-box, she formulated the plan in detail. In the first place, she was determined to be indisposed and invisible herself, so that Mr Scales might be foiled in any possible design to renew social relations in the parlour. In the second place, she flattered Constance with a single hint – oh, the vaguest and briefest! – and Constance understood that she was not to quit the shop on the appointed morning. In the third place, she invented a way of explaining to Mr Povey that the approaching advent of Gerald Scales must not be mentioned. And in the fourth place, she deliberately made appointments for Sophia with two millinery customers in the showroom, so that Sophia might be imprisoned in the showroom.

Having thus left nothing to chance, she told herself that she was a foolish woman full of nonsense. But this did not prevent her from putting her lips together firmly and resolving that Mr Scales should have no finger in the pie of *her* family. She had acquired information concerning Mr Scales, at second hand, from Lawyer Pratt. More than this, she posed the question in a broader form – why should a young girl be permitted any interest in any young man whatsoever? The everlasting purpose had made use of Mrs Baines and cast her off, and, like most persons in a similar situation, she was, unconsciously and quite honestly, at odds with the everlasting purpose.

II

On the day of Mr Scales's visit to the shop to obtain orders and money on behalf of Birkinshaws, a singular success seemed to attend the machinations of Mrs Baines. With Mr Scales punctuality was not an inveterate habit, and he had rarely been known, in the past, to fulfil exactly the prophecy of the letter of advice concerning his arrival. But that morning his promptitude was unexampled. He entered the shop, and by chance Mr Povey was arranging unshrinkable flannels in the doorway. The two young-ish little men talked amiably about flannels, dogs, and quarter-day (which was just past), and then Mr Povey led Mr Scales to his desk in the dark corner behind the high pile of twills, and paid the quarterly bill, in notes and gold – as always; and then Mr Scales offered for the august inspection of Mr Povey all that Manchester had recently invented for the temptation of drapers, and Mr

Povey gave him an order which, if not reckless, was nearer 'handsome' than 'good'. During the process Mr Scales had to go out of the shop twice or three times in order to bring in from his barrow at the kerbstone certain small black boxes edged with brass. On none of these excursions did Mr Scales glance wantonly about him in satisfaction of the lust of the eye. Even if he had permitted himself this freedom he would have seen nothing more interesting than three young lady assistants seated round the stove and sewing with pricked fingers from which the chilblains were at last deciding to depart. When Mr Scales had finished writing down the details of the order with his ivory-handled stylo, and repacked his boxes, he drew the interview to a conclusion after the manner of a capable commercial traveller; that is to say, he implanted in Mr Povey his opinion that Mr Povey was a wise, a shrewd, and an upright man, and that the world would be all the better for a few more like him. He inquired for Mrs Baines, and was deeply pained to hear of her indisposition while finding consolation in the assurance that the Misses Baines were well. Mr Povey was on the point of accompanying the pattern of commercial travellers to the door, when two customers simultaneously came in – ladies. One made straight for Mr Povey, whereupon Mr Scales parted from him at once, it being a universal maxim in shops that even the most distinguished commercial shall not hinder the business of even the least distinguished customer. The other customer had the effect of causing Constance to pop up from her cloistral corner. Constance had been there all the time, but of course, though she heard the remembered voice, her maidenliness had not permitted that she should show herself to Mr Scales.

Now, as he was leaving, Mr Scales saw her, with her agreeable snub nose and her kind, simple eyes. She was requesting the second customer to mount to the showroom, where was Miss Sophia. Mr Scales hesitated a moment, and in that moment Constance, catching his eye, smiled upon him, and nodded. What else could she do? Vaguely aware though she was that her mother was not 'set up' with Mr Scales, and even feared the possible influence of the young man on Sophia, she could not exclude him from her general benevolence towards the universe. Moreover, she liked him; she liked him very much and thought him a very fine specimen of a man.

He left the door and went across to her. They shook hands and opened a conversation instantly; for Constance, while retaining all her modesty, had lost all her shyness in the shop, and could chatter with anybody. She sidled towards her corner, precisely as Sophia had done on another occasion, and Mr Scales put his chin over the screening boxes, and eagerly prosecuted the conversation.

There was absolutely nothing in the fact of the interview itself to cause alarm to a mother, nothing to render futile the precautions of Mrs Baines on behalf of the flower of Sophia's innocence. And yet it held danger for Mrs Baines, all unconscious in her parlour. Mrs Baines could rely utterly on Constance not to be led away by the dandiacal charms of Mr Scales (she knew in what quarter sat the wind for Constance); in her plan she had forgotten nothing, except Mr Povey; and it must be said that she could not possibly have foreseen the effect on the situation of Mr Povey's character.

Mr Povey, attending to his customer, had noticed the bright smile of Constance on the traveller, and his heart did not like it. And when he saw the lively gestures of a Mr Scales in apparently intimate talk with a Constance hidden behind boxes, his uneasiness grew into fury. He was a man capable of black and terrible furies. Outwardly insignificant, possessing a mind as little as his body, easily abashed, he was none the less a very susceptible young man, soon offended, proud, vain, and obscurely passionate. You might offend Mr Povey without guessing it, and only discover your sin when Mr Povey had done something too decisive as a result of it.

The reason of his fury was jealousy. Mr Povey had made great advances since the death of John Baines. He had consolidated his position, and he was in every way a personage of the first importance. His misfortune was that he could never translate his importance, or his sense of his importance, into terms of outward demeanour. Most people, had they been told that Mr Povey was seriously aspiring to enter the Baines family, would have laughed. But they would have been wrong. To laugh at Mr Povey was invariably wrong. Only Constance knew what inroads he had effected upon her.

The customer went, but Mr Scales did not go. Mr Povey, free to reconnoitre, did so. From the shadow of the till he could catch glimpses of Constance's blushing, vivacious face. She was obviously absorbed in Mr Scales. She and he had a tremendous air of intimacy. And the murmur of their chatter continued. Their chatter was nothing, and about nothing, but Mr Povey imagined that they were exchanging eternal vows. He endured Mr Scales's odious freedom until it became insufferable, until it deprived him of all his self-control; and then he retired into his cutting-out room. He meditated there in a condition of insanity for perhaps a minute, and excogitated a device. Dashing back into the shop, he spoke up, half across the shop, in a loud, curt tone:

'Miss Baines, your mother wants you at once.'

He was launched on the phrase before he noticed that during his absence, Sophia had descended from the showroom and joined her sister and Mr Scales. The danger and scandal were now less, he perceived, but he was glad he had summoned Constance away, and he was in a state to despise consequences.

The three chatterers, startled, looked at Mr Povey, who left the shop abruptly. Constance could do nothing but obey the call.

She met him at the door of the cutting-room in the passage leading to the parlour.

'Where is mother? In the parlour?' Constance inquired innocently.

There was a dark flush on Mr Povey's face. 'If you wish to know,' said he in a hard voice, 'she hasn't asked for you and she doesn't want you.'

He turned his back on her, and retreated into his lair.

'Then what –?' she began, puzzled.

He fronted her. 'Haven't you been gabbling long enough with that jackanapes?' he spit at her. There were tears in his eyes.

Constance, though without experience in these matters, comprehended. She comprehended perfectly and immediately. She ought to have put Mr Povey into his place. She ought to have protested with firm, dignified finality against such a ridiculous and monstrous outrage as that which Mr Povey had committed.

Mr Povey ought to have been ruined for ever in her esteem and in her heart. But she hesitated.

'And only last Sunday – afternoon,' Mr Povey blubbered.

(Not that anything overt had occurred, or been articulately said, between them last Sunday afternoon. But they had been alone together, and had each witnessed strange and disturbing matters in the eyes of the other.)

Tears now fell suddenly from Constance's eyes. 'You ought to be ashamed –' she stammered.

Still, the tears were in her eyes, and in his too. What he or she merely said, therefore, was of secondary importance.

Mrs Baines, coming from the kitchen, and hearing Constance's voice, burst upon the scene, which silenced her. Parents are sometimes silenced. She found Sophia and Mr Scales in the shop.

III

That afternoon Sophia, too busy with her own affairs to notice anything abnormal in the relations between her mother and Constance, and quite ignorant that there had been an unsuccessful plot against her, went forth to call upon Miss Chetwynd, with whom she had remained very friendly: she considered that she and Miss Chetwynd formed an aristocracy of intellect, and the family indeed tacitly admitted this. She practised no secrecy in her departure from the shop; she merely dressed, in her second-best hoop, and went, having been ready at any moment to tell her mother, if her mother caught her and inquired, that she was going to see Miss Chetwynd. And she did go to see Miss Chetwynd, arriving at the house-school, which lay amid trees on the road to Turnhill, just beyond the turnpike, at precisely a quarter-past four. As Miss Chetwynd's pupils left at four o'clock, and as Miss Chetwynd invariably took a walk immediately afterwards, Sophia was able to contain her surprise upon being informed that Miss Chetwynd was not in. She had not intended that Miss Chetwynd should be in.

She turned off to the right, up the side road which, starting from the turnpike, led in the direction of Moorthorne and Red Cow, two mining villages. Her heart beat with fear as she began to follow that road, for she was upon a terrific adventure. What most frightened her, perhaps, was her own astounding audacity. She was alarmed by something within herself which seemed to be no part of herself and which produced in her curious, disconcerting, fleeting impressions of unreality.

In the morning she had heard the voice of Mr Scales from the showroom – that voice whose even distant murmur caused creepings of the skin in her back. And she had actually stood on the counter in front of the window in order to see down perpendicularly into the Square; by so doing she had had a glimpse of the top of his luggage on a barrow, and of the crown of his hat occasionally when he went outside to tempt Mr Povey. She might have gone down into the shop – there was no slightest reason why she should not; three months had elapsed since the name of Mr Scales had been mentioned, and her mother had evidently forgotten the trifling incident of New Year's Day – but she was incapable of descending the stairs! She went to the head of the stairs and peeped through the balustrade – and she could not get farther. For nearly a hundred days those extraordinary lamps had been brightly burning in her head; and now the light-giver had come again, and her feet would not move to the meeting; now the moment had arrived for which alone she had lived, and she could not seize it as it passed! 'Why don't I go downstairs?' she asked herself. 'Am I afraid to meet him?'

The customer sent up by Constance had occupied the surface of her life for ten minutes, trying on hats; and during this time she was praying wildly that Mr Scales might not go, and asserting that it was impossible he should go without at least asking for her. Had she not counted the days to this day? When the customer left, Sophia followed her downstairs, and saw Mr Scales chatting with Constance. All her self-possession instantly returned to her, and she joined them with a rather mocking smile. After Mr Povey's strange summons had withdrawn Constance from the corner, Mr Scales's tone had changed; it had thrilled her. 'You are *you*,' it had said, 'there is you – and there is the rest of the universe!' Then he had not forgotten; she had lived in his heart; she had not for three months been the victim of her own fancies! . . . She saw him put a piece of folded white paper on the top edge of the screening box and flick it down to her. She blushed scarlet, staring at it as it lay on the counter. He said nothing, and she could not speak ... He had prepared that paper, then, beforehand, on the chance of being able to give it to her! This thought was exquisite but full of terror. 'I must really go,' he had said, lamely, with emotion in his voice, and he had gone – like that! And she put the piece of paper into the pocket of her apron, and hastened away. She had not even seen, as she turned up the stairs, her mother standing by the till – that spot which was the conning-tower of the whole shop. She ran, ran, breathless to the bedroom ...

'I am a wicked girl!' she said quite frankly, on the road to the rendezvous. 'It is a dream that I am going to meet him. It cannot be true. There is time to go back. If I go back I am safe. I have simply called at Miss Chetwynd's and she wasn't in, and no one can say a word. But if I go on – if I'm seen! What a fool I am to go on!'

And she went on, impelled by, amongst other things, an immense, naïve curiosity, and the vanity which the bare fact of his note had excited. The Loop railway was being constructed at that period, and hundreds of navvies were at work on it between Bursley and Turnhill. When she came to the new bridge over the cutting, he was there, as he had written that he would be.

They were very nervous, they greeted each other stiffly and as though they had met then for the first time that day. Nothing was said about his note, nor about her response to it. Her presence was treated by both of them as a basic fact of the situation which it would be well not to disturb by comment. Sophia could not hide her shame, but her shame only aggravated the stinging charm of her beauty. She was wearing a hard Amazonian hat, with a lifted veil, the final word of fashion that spring in the Five Towns; her face, beaten by the fresh breeze, shone rosily; her eyes glittered under the dark hat, and the violent colours of her Victorian frock – green and crimson – could not spoil those cheeks. If she looked earthwards, frowning, she was the more adorable so. He had come down the clayey incline from the unfinished red bridge to welcome her, and when the salutations were over they stood still, he gazing apparently at the horizon and she at the yellow marl round the edges of his boots. The encounter was as far away from Sophia's ideal conception as Manchester from Venice.

'So this is the new railway!' said she.

'Yes,' said he. 'This is your new railway. You can see it better from the bridge.'

'But it's very sludgy up there,' she objected with a pout.

'Further on it's quite dry,' he reassured her.

From the bridge they had a sudden view of a raw gash in the earth; and hundreds of men were crawling about in it, busy with minute operations, like flies in a great wound. There was a continuous rattle of picks, resembling a muffled shower of hail, and in the distance a tiny locomotive was leading a procession of tiny waggons.

'And those are the navvies!' she murmured.

The unspeakable doings of the navvies in the Five Towns had reached even her: how they drank and swore all day on Sundays, how their huts and houses were dens of the most appalling infamy, how they were the curse of a God-fearing and respectable district! She and Gerald Scales glanced down at these dangerous beasts of prey in their yellow corduroys and their open shirts revealing hairy chests. No doubt they both thought how inconvenient it was that railways could not be brought into existence without the aid of such revolting and swinish animals. They glanced down from the height of their nice decorum and felt the powerful attraction of similar superior manners. The manners of the navvies were such that Sophia could not even regard them, nor Gerald Scales permit her to regard them, without blushing.

In a united blush they turned away, up the gradual slope. Sophia knew no longer what she was doing. For some minutes she was as helpless as though she had been in a balloon with him.

'I got my work done early,' he said; and added complacently, 'As a matter of fact I've had a pretty good day.'

She was reassured to learn that he was not neglecting his duties. To be philandering with a commercial traveller who has finished a good day's work seemed less shocking than dalliance with a neglecter of business; it seemed indeed, by comparison, respectable.

'It must be very interesting,' she said primly.

'What, my trade?'

'Yes. Always seeing new places and so on.'

'In a way it is,' he admitted judicially. 'But I can tell you it was much more agreeable being in Paris.'

'Oh! Have you been in Paris?'

'Lived there for nearly two years,' he said carelessly. Then, looking at her, 'Didn't you notice I never came for a long time?'

'I didn't know you were in Paris,' she evaded him.

'I went to start a sort of agency for Birkinshaws,' he said.

'I suppose you talk French like anything.'

'Of course one has to talk French,' said he. 'I learnt French when I was a child from a governess – my uncle made me – but I forgot most of it at school, and at the Varsity you never learn anything – precious little, anyhow! Certainly not French!'

She was deeply impressed. He was a much greater personage than she had guessed. It had never occurred to her that commercial travellers had to go to a university to finish their complex education. And then, Paris! Paris meant absolutely nothing to her but pure, impossible unattainable romance. And he had been there! The clouds of glory were around him. He was a hero, dazzling. He had come to her out of another world. He was her miracle. He was almost too miraculous to be true.

She, living her humdrum life at the shop! And he, elegant, brilliant, coming from far cities! They together, side by side, strolling up the road towards the Moorthorn ridge! There was nothing quite like this in the stories of Miss Sewell.

'Your uncle . . . ?' she questioned vaguely.

'Yes, Mr Boldero. He's a partner in Birkinshaws.'

'Oh!'

'You've heard of him? He's a great Wesleyan.'

'Oh yes,' she said. 'When we had the Wesleyan Conference here, he –'

'He's always very great at Conferences,' said Gerald Scales.

'I didn't know he had anything to do with Birkinshaws.'

'He isn't a working partner of course,' Mr Scales explained. 'But he means me to be one. I have to learn the business from the bottom. So now you understand why I'm a traveller.'

'I see,' she said, still more deeply impressed.

'I'm an orphan,' said Gerald. 'And Uncle Boldero took me in hand when I was three.'

'I *see*!' she repeated.

It seemed strange to her that Mr Scales should be a Wesleyan – just like herself. She would have been sure that he was 'Church'. Her notions of Wesleyanism, with her notions of various other things, were sharply modified.

'Now tell me about you,' Mr Scales suggested.

'Oh! I'm nothing!' she burst out.

The exclamation was perfectly sincere. Mr Scales's disclosures concerning himself, while they excited her, discouraged her.

'You're the finest girl I've ever met, anyhow,' said Mr Scales with gallant emphasis, and he dug his stick into the soft ground.

She blushed and made no answer.

They walked on in silence, each wondering apprehensively what might happen next.

Suddenly Mr Scales stopped at a dilapidated low brick wall, built in a circle, close to the side of the road.

'I expect that's an old pit-shaft,' said he.

'Yes, I expect it is.'

He picked up a rather large stone and approached the wall.

'Be careful!' she enjoined him.

'Oh! It's all right,' he said lightly. 'Let's listen. Come near and listen.'

She reluctantly obeyed, and he threw the stone over the dirty ruined wall, the top of which was about level with his hat. For two or three seconds there was no sound. Then a faint reverberation echoed from the depths of the shaft. And on Sophia's brain arose dreadful images of the ghosts of miners wandering for ever in subterranean passages, far, far beneath. The noise of the falling stone had awakened for her the secret terrors of the earth. She could scarcely even look at the wall without a spasm of fear.

'How strange,' said Mr Scales, a little awe in his voice, too, 'that that should be left there like that! I suppose it's very deep.'

'Some of them are,' she trembled.

'I must just have a look,' he said, and put his hands on the top of the wall.

'Come away!' she cried.

'Oh! It's all right!' he said again, soothingly. 'The wall's as firm as a rock.' And he took a slight spring and looked over.

She shrieked loudly. She saw him at the distant bottom of the shaft, mangled, drowning. The ground seemed to quake under her feet. A horrible sickness seized her. And she shrieked again. Never had she guessed that existence could be such a pain.

He slid down from the wall and turned to her. 'No bottom to be seen!' he said. Then, observing her transformed face, he came close to her, with a superior masculine smile. 'Silly little thing!' he said coaxingly, endearingly, putting forth all his power to charm.

He perceived at once that he had miscalculated the effects of his action. Her alarm changed swiftly to angry offence. She drew back with a haughty gesture, as if he had intended actually to touch her. Did he suppose, because she chanced to be walking with him, that he had the right to address her familiarly, to tease her, to call her 'silly little thing' and to put his face against hers? She resented his freedom with quick and passionate indignation.

She showed him her proud back and nodding head and wrathful skirts; and hurried off without a word, almost running. As for him, he was so startled by unexpected phenomena that he did nothing for a moment – merely stood looking and feeling foolish.

Then she heard him in pursuit. She was too proud to stop or even to reduce her speed.

'I didn't mean to –' he muttered behind her.

No recognition from her.

'I suppose I ought to apologize,' he said.

'I should just think you ought,' she answered, furious.

'Well, I do!' said he. 'Do stop a minute.'

'I'll thank you not to follow me, Mr Scales.' She paused and scorched him with her displeasure. Then she went forward. And her heart was in torture because it could not persuade her to remain with him, and smile and forgive, and win his smile.

'I shall write to you,' he shouted down the slope.

She kept on, the ridiculous child. But the agony she had suffered as he clung to the frail wall was not ridiculous, nor her dark vision of the mine, nor her tremendous indignation when, after disobeying her, he forgot that she was a queen. To her the scene was sublimely tragic. Soon she had recrossed the bridge, but not the same she! So this was the end of the incredible adventure!

When she reached the turnpike she thought of her mother and of Constance. She had completely forgotten them; for a space they had utterly ceased to exist for her.

IV

'You've been out, Sophia?' said Mrs Baines in the parlour, questioningly. Sophia had taken off her hat and mantle hurriedly in the cutting-out room, for she was in danger of being late for tea; but her hair and face showed traces of the March breeze. Mrs Baines, whose stoutness seemed to increase, sat in the rocking-chair with a number of *The Sunday at Home* in her hand. Tea was set.

'Yes, mother. I called to see Miss Chetwynd.'

'I wish you'd tell me when you are going out.'

'I looked all over for you before I started.'

'No, you didn't, for I haven't stirred from this room since four o'clock ... You should not say things like that,' Mrs Baines added in a gentler tone.

Mrs Baines had suffered much that day. She knew that she was in an irritable, nervous state, and therefore she said to herself, in her quality of wise woman, 'I must watch myself. I mustn't let myself go.' And she thought how reasonable she was. She did not guess that all her gestures betrayed her; nor did it occur to her that few things are more galling than the spectacle of a person, actuated by lofty motives, obviously trying to be kind and patient under what he considers to be extreme provocation.

Maggie blundered up the kitchen stairs with the teapot and hot toast; and so Sophia had an excuse for silence. Sophia too had suffered much, suffered excruciatingly; she carried at that moment a whole tragedy in her young soul, unaccustomed to such burdens. Her attitude towards her mother was half fearful and half defiant; it might be summed up in the phrase which she had repeated again and again under her breath on the way home, 'Well, mother can't kill me!'

Mrs Baines put down the blue-covered magazine and twisted her rocking-chair towards the table.

'You can pour out the tea,' said Mrs Baines.

'Where's Constance?'

'She's not very well. She's lying down.'

'Anything the matter with her?'

'No.'

This was inaccurate. Nearly everything was the matter with Constance, who had never been less Constance than during that afternoon. But Mrs Baines had no intention of discussing Constance's love-affairs with Sophia. The less said to Sophia about love, the better! Sophia was excitable enough already!

They sat opposite to each other, on either side of the fire – the monumental matron whose black bodice heavily overhung the table, whose large rounded face was creased and wrinkled by what seemed countless years of joy and disillusion; and the young, slim girl, so fresh, so virginal, so ignorant, with all the pathos of an unsuspecting victim about to be sacrificed to the minotaur of Time. They both ate hot toast, with careless haste, in silence, preoccupied, worried, and outwardly non-chalant.

'And what has Miss Chetwynd got to say?' Mrs Baines inquired.

'She wasn't in.'

Here was a blow for Mrs Baines, whose suspicions about Sophia, driven off by her certainties regarding Constance, suddenly sprang forward in her mind, and prowled to and fro like a band of tigers.

Still, Mrs Baines was determined to be calm and careful. 'Oh! What time did you call?'

'I don't know. About half-past four.' Sophia finished her tea quickly, and rose. 'Shall I tell Mr Povey he can come?'

(Mr Povey had his tea after the ladies of the house.)

'Yes, if you will stay in the shop till I come. Light me the gas before you go.'

Sophia took the wax taper from a vase on the mantelpiece, stuck it in the fire and lit the gas, which exploded in its crystal cloister with a mild report.

'What's all that clay on your boots, child?' asked Mrs Baines.

'Clay?' repeated Sophia, staring foolishly at her boots.

'Yes,' said Mrs Baines. 'It looks like marl. Where on earth have you been?'

She interrogated her daughter with an upward gaze, frigid and unconsciously hostile, through her gold-rimmed glasses.

'I must have picked it up on the roads,' said Sophia, and hastened to the door.

'Sophia!'

'Yes, mother.'

'Shut the door.'

Sophia unwillingly shut the door which she had half opened.

'Come here.'

Sophia obeyed, with falling lip.

'You are deceiving me, Sophia,' said Mrs Baines, with fierce solemnity. 'Where have you been this afternoon?'

Sophia's foot was restless on the carpet behind the table. 'I haven't been anywhere,' she murmured glumly.

'Have you seen young Scales?'

'Yes,' said Sophia with grimness, glancing audaciously for an instant at her mother. ('She can't kill me: She can't kill me,' her heart muttered. And she had youth and beauty in her favour, while her mother was only a fat middle-aged woman. 'She can't kill me,' said her heart, with the trembling, cruel insolence of the mirror-flattered child.)

'How came you to meet him?'

No answer.

'Sophia, you heard what I said!'

Still no answer. Sophia looked down at the table. ('She can't kill me.')

'If you are going to be sullen, I shall have to suppose the worst,' said Mrs Baines.

Sophia kept her silence.

'Of course,' Mrs Baines resumed, 'if you choose to be wicked, neither your mother nor any one else can stop you. There are certain things I *can* do, and these I *shall* do . . . Let me warn you that young Scales is a thoroughly bad lot. I know all about him. He has been living a wild life abroad, and if it hadn't been that his uncle is a partner in Birkinshaws, they would never have taken him on again.' A pause. 'I hope that one day you will be a happy wife, but you are much too young yet to be meeting young men, and nothing would ever induce me to let you have anything to do with this Scales. I won't have it. In future you are not to go out alone. You understand me?'

Sophia kept silence.

'I hope you will be in a better frame of mind tomorrow. I can only hope so. But if you aren't, I shall take very severe measures. You think you can defy me. But you never were more mistaken in your life. I don't want to see any more of you now. Go and tell Mr Povey; and call Maggie for the fresh tea. You make me almost glad that your father died even as he did. He has, at any rate, been spared this.'

Those words 'died even as he did' achieved the intimidation of Sophia. They seemed to indicate that Mrs Baines, though she had magnanimously never mentioned the subject to Sophia, knew exactly how the old man had died. Sophia escaped from the room in fear, cowed. Nevertheless, her thought was, 'She hasn't killed me. I made up my mind I wouldn't talk, and I didn't.'

In the evening, as she sat in the shop primly and sternly sewing at hats – while her mother wept in secret on the first floor, and Constance remained hidden on the second – Sophia lived over again the scene at the old shaft; but she lived it differently, admitting that she had been wrong, guessing by instinct that she had shown a foolish mistrust of love. As she sat in the shop, she adopted just the right attitude and said just the right things. Instead of being a silly baby she was an accomplished and dazzling woman, then. When customers came in, and the young lady assistants unobtrusively turned higher the central gas, according to the *régime* of the shop, it was really extraordinary that they could not read in the heart of the beautiful Miss Baines the words which blazed there: *'You're the finest girl I ever met,'* and *'I shall write to you.'* The young lady assistants had their notions as to both Constance and Sophia, but the truth, at least as regarded Sophia, was beyond the flight of their imaginations. When eight o'clock struck and she gave the formal order for dust-sheets, the shop being empty, they never supposed that she was dreaming about posts and plotting how to get hold of the morning's letters before Mr Povey.

CHAPTER 7: *A Defeat*

I

It was during the month of June that Aunt Harriet came over from Axe to spend a few days with her little sister, Mrs Baines. The railway between Axe and the Five Towns had not yet been opened; but even if it had been opened Aunt Harriet would probably not have used it. She had always travelled from Axe to Bursley in the same vehicle, a small waggonette which she hired from Bratt's livery stables at Axe, driven by a coachman who thoroughly understood the importance, and the peculiarities, of Aunt Harriet.

Mrs Baines had increased in stoutness, so that now Aunt Harriet had very little advantage over her, physically. But the moral ascendancy of the elder still persisted. The two vast widows shared Mrs Baines's bedroom, spending much of their time there in long, hushed conversations – interviews from which Mrs Baines emerged with the air of one who had received enlightenment and Aunt Harriet with the air of one who has rendered it. The pair went about together, in the shop, the showroom, the parlour, the kitchen, and also into the town, addressing each other as 'Sister', 'Sister'. Everywhere it was 'sister', 'sister', 'my sister', 'your dear mother', 'your Aunt Harriet'. They referred to each other as oracular sources of wisdom and good taste. Respectability stalked abroad when they were afoot. The whole Square wriggled uneasily as though God's eye were peculiarly upon it. The meals in the parlour became solemn collations, at which shone the best silver and the finest diaper, but from which gaiety and naturalness seemed to be banished. (I say 'seemed' because it cannot be doubted that Aunt Harriet was natural, and there were moments when she possibly considered herself to be practising gaiety – a gaiety more desolating than her severity.) The younger generation was extinguished, pressed flat and lifeless under the ponderosity of the widows.

Mr Povey was not the man to be easily flattened by ponderosity of any kind, and his suppression was a striking proof of the prowess of the widows; who, indeed, went over Mr Povey like traction-engines, with the sublime unconsciousness of traction-engines, leaving an inanimate object in the road behind them, and scarce aware even of the jolt. Mr Povey hated Aunt Harriet, but, lying crushed there in the road, how could he rebel? He felt all the time that Aunt Harriet was adding him up, and reporting the result at frequent intervals to Mrs Baines in the bedroom. He felt that she knew everything about him – even to those tears which had been in his eyes. He felt that he could hope to do nothing right for Aunt Harriet, that absolute perfection in the performance of duty would make no more impression on her than a caress on the fly-wheel of a traction-engine. Constance, the dear Constance, was also looked at askance. There was nothing in Aunt Harriet's demeanour to her that you could take hold of, but there was emphatically something that you could not take hold of – a hint, an inkling, that insinuated to Constance, 'Have a care, lest peradventure you become the second cousin of the scarlet woman.'

Sophia was petted. Sophia was liable to be playfully tapped by Aunt Harriet's thimble when Aunt Harriet was hemming dusters (for the elderly lady could lift a duster to her own dignity). Sophia was called on two separate occasions, 'My little butterfly'. And Sophia was entrusted with the trimming of Aunt Harriet's new summer bonnet. Aunt Harriet deemed that Sophia was looking pale. As the days passed, Sophia's pallor was emphasized by Aunt Harriet until it developed into an article of faith, to which you were compelled to subscribe on pain of excommunication. Then dawned the day when Aunt Harriet said, staring at Sophia as an affectionate aunt may: 'That child would do with a change.' And then there dawned another day when Aunt Harriet, staring at Sophia compassionately, as a devoted aunt may, said: 'It's a pity that child can't have a change.' And Mrs Baines also stared and said: 'It is.'

And on another day Aunt Harriet said: 'I've been wondering

whether my little Sophia would care to come and keep her old aunt company a while.'

There were few things for which Sophia would have cared less. The girl swore to herself angrily that she would not go, that no allurement would induce her to go. But she was in a net; she was in the meshes of family correctness. Do what she would, she could not invent a reason for not going. Certainly she could not tell her aunt that she merely did not want to go. She was capable of enormities, but not of that. And then began Aunt Harriet's intricate preparations for going. Aunt Harriet never did anything simply. And she could not be hurried. Seventy-two hours before leaving she had to commence upon her trunk; but first the trunk had to be wiped by Maggie with a damp cloth under the eye and direction of Aunt Harriet. And the liveryman at Axe had to be written to, and the servants at Axe written to, and the weather prospects weighed and considered. And somehow, by the time these matters were accomplished, it was tacitly understood that Sophia should accompany her kind aunt into the bracing moorland air of Axe. No smoke at Axe! No stuffiness at Axe! The spacious existence of a wealthy widow in a residential town with a low death-rate and famous scenery! 'Have you packed your box, Sophia?' No, she had not. 'Well, I will come and help you.'

Impossible to bear up against the momentum of a massive body like Aunt Harriet's! It was irresistible.

The day of departure came, throwing the entire household into a commotion. Dinner was put a quarter of an hour earlier than usual so that Aunt Harriet might achieve Axe at her accustomed hour of tea. After dinner Maggie was the recipient of three amazing muslin aprons, given with a regal gesture. And the trunk and the box were brought down, and there was a slight odour of black kid gloves in the parlour. The waggonette was due and the waggonette appeared ('I can always rely upon Bladen!' said Aunt Harriet), and the door was opened, and Bladen, stiff on his legs, descended from the box and touched his hat to Aunt Harriet as she filled up the doorway.

'Have you baited,[6] Bladen?' asked she.

'Yes'm,' said he, assuringly.

Bladen and Mr Povey carried out the trunk and the box, and

Constance charged herself with parcels which she bestowed in the corners of the vehicle according to her aunt's prescription; it was like stowing the cargo of a vessel.

'Now, Sophia, my chuck!' Mrs Baines called up the stairs. And Sophia came slowly downstairs. Mrs Baines offered her mouth. Sophia glanced at her.

'You needn't think I don't see why you're sending me away!' exclaimed Sophia in a hard, furious voice, with glistening eyes. 'I'm not so blind as all that!' She kissed her mother – nothing but a contemptuous peck. Then, as she turned away she added: 'But you let Constance do just as she likes!'

This was her sole bitter comment on the episode, but into it she put all the profound bitterness accumulated during many mutinous nights.

Mrs Baines concealed a sigh. The explosion certainly disturbed her. She had hoped that the smooth surface of things would not be ruffled.

Sophia bounced out. And the assembly, including several urchins, watched with held breath while Aunt Harriet, after having bid majestic good-byes, got on to the step and introduced herself through the doorway of the waggonette into the interior of the vehicle; it was an operation like threading a needle with cotton too thick. Once within, her hoops distended in sudden release, filling the waggonette. Sophia followed, agilely.

As, with due formalities, the equipage drove off, Mrs Baines gave another sigh, one of relief. The sisters had won. She could now await the imminent next advent of Mr Gerald Scales with tranquillity.

II

Those singular words of Sophia's, 'But you let Constance do just as she likes,' had disturbed Mrs Baines more than was at first apparent. They worried her like a late fly in autumn. For she had said nothing to anyone about Constance's case. Mrs Maddack of course excepted. She had instinctively felt that she could not show the slightest leniency towards the romantic impulses of her elder daughter without seeming unjust to the younger, and she had acted accordingly. On the memorable morn of Mr Povey's acute jealousy, she had, temporarily at any rate, slaked the fire, banked it down, and hidden it; and since then no word had passed as to the state of Constance's heart. In the great peril to be feared from Mr Scales, Constance's heart had been put aside as a thing that could wait; so one puts aside the mending of linen when earthquake shocks are about. Mrs Baines was sure that Constance had not chattered to Sophia concerning Mr Povey. Constance, who understood her mother, had too much common-sense and too nice a sence of propriety to do that – and yet here was Sophia exclaiming, 'But you let Constance do just as she likes.' Were the relations between Constance and Mr Povey, then, common property? Did the young lady assistants discuss them?

As a fact, the young lady assistants did discuss them; not in the shop – for either one of the principal parties, or Mrs Baines herself, was always in the shop, but elsewhere. They discussed little else, when they were free; how she had looked at him today, and how he had blushed, and so forth interminably. Yet Mrs Baines really thought that she alone knew. Such is the power of the ineradicable delusion that one's own affairs, and especially one's own children, are mysteriously different from those of others.

After Sophia's departure Mrs Baines surveyed her daughter and her manager at supper-time with a curious and a diffident eye. They worked, talked, and ate just as though Mrs Baines had never caught them weeping together in the cutting-out room. They had the most matter-of-fact air. They might never have heard whispered the name of love. And there could be no deceit beneath that decorum; for Constance would not deceive. Still, Mrs Baines's conscience was unruly. Order reigned, but never-theless she knew that she ought to do something, find out something, decide something; she ought, if she did her duty, to take Constance aside and say: 'Now, Constance, my mind is freer now. Tell me frankly what has been going on between you and Mr Povey. I have never understood the meaning of that scene in the cutting-out room. Tell me.' She ought to have talked in this strain. But she could not. That energetic woman had not suf-ficient energy left. She wanted rest, rest – even though it were a coward's rest, an ostrich's tranquillity – after the turmoil of apprehensions caused by Sophia. Her soul cried out for peace. She was not, however, to have peace.

On the very first Sunday after Sophia's departure, Mr Povey did not go to chapel in the morning, and he offered no reason for his unusual conduct. He ate his breakfast with appetite, but there was something peculiar in his glance that made Mrs Baines a little uneasy; this something she could not seize upon and define. When she and Constance returned from chapel Mr Povey was playing 'Rock of Ages' on the harmonium – again unusual! The serious part of the dinner comprised roast beef and Yorkshire pudding – the pudding being served as a sweet course before the meat. Mrs Baines ate freely of these things, for she loved them, and she was always hungry after a sermon. She also did well with the Cheshire cheese. Her intention was to sleep in the drawing-room after the repast. On Sunday afternoons she invariably tried to sleep in the drawing-room, and she did not often fail. As a rule the girls accompanied her thither from the table, and either 'settled down' likewise or crept out of the room when they perceived the gradual sinking of the majestic form into the deep hollows of the easy-chair. Mrs Baines was anticipating with pleasure her somnolent Sunday afternoon.

Constance said grace after meat, and the formula on this particular occasion ran thus –

'Thank God for our good dinner, Amen. – Mother, I must just run upstairs to my room.' ('My room' – Sophia being far away.)

And off she ran, strangely girlish.

'Well, child, you needn't be in such a hurry,' said Mrs Baines, ringing the bell and rising.

She hoped that Constance would remember the conditions precedent to sleep.

'I should like to have a word with you, if it's all the same to you, Mrs Baines,' said Mr Povey suddenly, with obvious nervousness. And his tone struck a rude unexpected blow at Mrs Baines's peace of mind. It was a portentous tone.

'What about?' asked she, with an inflection subtly to remind Mr Povey what day it was.

'About Constance,' said the astonishing man.

'Constance!' exclaimed Mrs Baines with a histrionic air of bewilderment.

Maggie entered the room, solely in response to the bell, yet a thought jumped up in Mrs Baines's brain, 'How prying servants are, to be sure!' For quite five seconds she had a grievance against Maggie. She was compelled to sit down again and wait while Maggie cleared the table. Mr Povey put both his hands in his pockets, got up, went to the window, whistled, and generally behaved in a manner which foretold the worst.

At last Maggie vanished, shutting the door.

'What is it, Mr Povey?'

'Oh!' said Mr Povey, facing her with absurd nervous brusqueness, as though pretending: 'Ah, yes! We have something to say – I was forgetting!' Then he began: 'It's about Constance and me.'

Yes, they had evidently plotted this interview. Constance had evidently taken herself off on purpose to leave Mr Povey unhampered. They were in league. The inevitable had come. No sleep! No repose! Nothing but worry once more!

'I'm not at all satisfied with the present situation,' said Mr Povey, in a tone that corresponded to his words.

'I don't know what you mean, Mr Povey,' said Mrs Baines stiffly. This was a simple lie.

'Well, really, Mrs Baines!' Mr Povey protested, 'I suppose you won't deny that you know there is something between me and Constance? I suppose you won't deny that?'

'What is there between you and Constance? I can assure you I –'

'That depends on you,' Mr Povey interrupted her. When he was nervous his manners deteriorated into a behaviour that resembled rudeness. 'That depends on you!' he repeated grimly.

'But –'

'Are we to be engaged or are we not?' pursued Mr Povey, as though Mrs Baines had been guilty of some grave lapse and he was determined not to spare her. 'That's what I think ought to be settled, one way or the other. I wish to be perfectly open and above board – in the future, as I have been in the past.'

'But you have said nothing to me at all!' Mrs Baines remonstrated, lifting her eyebrows. The way in which the man had sprung this matter upon her was truly too audacious.

Mr Povey approached her as she sat at the table, shaking her ringlets and looking at her hands.

'You know there's something between us!' he insisted.

'How should I know there is something between you? Constance has never said a word to me. And have you?'

'Well,' said he. 'We've hidden nothing.'

'What is there between you and Constance? If I may ask!'

'That depends on you,' said he again.

'Have you asked her to be your wife?'

'No. I haven't exactly asked her to be my wife.' He hesitated. 'You see —'

Mrs Baines collected her forces. 'Have you kissed her?' This in a cold voice.

Mr Povey now blushed. 'I haven't exactly kissed her,' he stammered, apparently shocked by the inquisition. 'No, I should not say that I had kissed her.'

It might have been that before committing himself he felt a desire for Mrs Baines's definition of a kiss.

'You are very extraordinary,' she said loftily. It was no less than the truth.

'All I want to know is — have you got anything against me?' he demanded roughly. 'Because if so —'

'Anything against you, Mr Povey? Why should I have anything against you?'

'Then why can't we be engaged?'

She considered that he was bullying her. 'That's another question,' said she.

'Why can't we be engaged? Ain't I good enough?'

The fact was that he was not regarded as good enough. Mrs Maddack had certainly deemed that he was not good enough. He was a solid mass of excellent qualities; but he lacked brilliance, importance, dignity. He could not impose himself. Such had been the verdict.

And now, while Mrs Baines was secretly reproaching Mr Povey for his inability to impose himself, he was most patently imposing himself on her — and the phenomenon escaped her! She

felt that he was bullying her, but somehow she could not perceive
his power. Yet the man who could bully Mrs Baines was surely no
common soul!

'You know my very high opinion of you,' she said.

Mr Povey pursued in a mollified tone. 'Assuming that Constance is willing to be engaged, do I understand you consent?'

'But Constance is too young.'

'Constance is twenty. She is more than twenty.'

'In any case you won't expect me to give you an answer now.'

'Why not? You know my position.'

She did. From a practical point of view the match would be
ideal: no fault could be found with it on that side. But Mrs Baines
could not extinguish the idea that it would be a 'comedown' for
her daughter. Who, after all, was Mr Povey? Mr Povey was
nobody.

'I must think things over,' she said firmly, putting her lips
together. 'I can't reply like this. It is a serious matter.'

'When can I have your answer? Tomorrow?'

'No – really –'

'In a week, then?'

'I cannot bind myself to a date,' said Mrs Baines, haughtily. She
felt that she was gaining ground.

'Because I can't stay on here indefinitely as things are,' Mr
Povey burst out, and there was a touch of hysteria in his tone.

'Now, Mr Povey, please do be reasonable.'

'That's all very well,' he went on. 'That's all very well. But what
I say is that employers have no right to have male assistants in
their houses unless they are prepared to let their daughters marry!
That's what I say! No *right*!'

Mrs Baines did not know what to answer.

The aspirant wound up: 'I must leave if that's the case.'

'If what's the case?' she asked herself. 'What has come over
him?' And aloud: 'You know you would place me in a very
awkward position by leaving, and I hope you don't want to mix
up two quite different things. I hope you aren't trying to threaten
me.'

'Threaten you!' he cried. 'Do you suppose I should leave here
for fun? If I leave it will be because I can't *stand* it. That's all. I

can't stand it. I want Constance, and if I can't have her, then I can't *stand* it. What do you think I'm made of?'

'I'm sure –' she began.

'That's all very well!' he almost shouted.

'But please let me speak,' she said quietly.

'All I say is I can't *stand* it. That's all . . . Employers have no *right* . . . We have our feelings like other men.'

He was deeply moved. He might have appeared somewhat grotesque to the strictly impartial observer of human nature. Nevertheless he was deeply and genuinely moved, and possibly human nature could have shown nothing more human than Mr Povey at the moment when, unable any longer to restrain the paroxysm which had so surprisingly overtaken him, he fled from the parlour, passionately, to the retreat of his bed-room.

'That's the worst of those quiet calm ones,' said Mrs Baines to herself. 'You never know if they won't give way. And when they do, it's awful – awful . . . What did I do, what did I say, to bring it on? Nothing! Nothing!'

And where was her afternoon sleep? What was going to happen to her daughter? What could she say to Constance? How next could she meet Mr Povey? Ah! It needed a brave, indomit-able woman not to cry out brokenly: 'I've suffered too much. Do anything you like; only let me die in peace!' And so saying, to let everything indifferently slide!

III

Neither Mr Povey nor Constance introduced the delicate subject to her again, and she was determined not to be the first to speak of it. She considered that Mr Povey had taken advantage of his position, and that he had also been infantile and impolite. And somehow she privately blamed Constance for his behaviour. So the matter hung, as it were, suspended in the ether between the opposing forces of pride and passion.

Shortly afterwards events occurred compared to which the vicissitudes of Mr Povey's heart were of no more account than a shower of rain in April. And fate gave no warning of them; it rather indicated a complete absence of events. When the custom-

ary advice circular arrived from Birkinshaws, the name of 'our
Mr Gerald Scales' was replaced on it by another and an unfamiliar name. Mrs Baines, seeing the circular by accident, experienced
a sense of relief, mingled with the professional disappointment of a
diplomatist who has elaborately provided for contingencies which
have failed to happen. She had sent Sophia away for nothing; and
no doubt her maternal affection had exaggerated a mole-hill into
a mountain. Really, when she reflected on the past, she could not
recall a single fact that would justify her theory of an attachment
secretly budding between Sophia and the young man Scales! Not
a single little fact! All she could bring forward was that Sophia
had twice encountered Scales in the street.

She felt a curious interest in the fate of Scales, for whom in her
own mind she had long prophesied evil, and when Birkinshaws'
representative came she took care to be in the shop; her intention
was to converse with him, and ascertain as much as was ascer-
tainable, after Mr Povey had transacted business. For this purpose, at a suitable moment, she traversed the shop to Mr Povey's
side, and in so doing she had a fleeting view of King Street, and in
King Street of a familiar vehicle. She stopped, and seemed to
catch the distant sound of knocking. Abandoning the traveller,
she hurried towards the parlour, in the passage she assuredly did
hear knocking, angry and impatient knocking, the knocking of
someone who thinks he has knocked too long.

'Of course Maggie is at the top of the house!' she muttered
sarcastically.

She unchained, unbolted, and unlocked the side-door.

'At last!' It was Aunt Harriet's voice, exacerbated. 'What! You,
sister? You're soon up. What a blessing!'

The two majestic and imposing creatures met on the mat,
craning forward so that their lips might meet above their terrific
bosoms.

'What's the matter?' Mrs Baines asked, fearfully.

'Well, I do declare!' said Mrs Maddack. 'And I've driven
specially over to ask *you*!'

'Where's Sophia?' demanded Mrs Baines.

'You don't mean to say she's not come, sister?' Mrs Maddack
sank down on to the sofa.

'Come?' Mrs Baines repeated. 'Of course she's not come! What do you mean, sister?'

'The very moment she got Constance's letter yesterday, saying you were ill in bed and she'd better come over to help in the shop, she started. I got Bratt's dog-cart for her.'

Mrs Baines in her turn also sank down on to the sofa.

'I've not been ill,' she said. 'And Constance hasn't written for a week! Only yesterday I was telling her —'

'Sister — it can't be! Sophia had letters from Constance every morning. At least she said they were from Constance. I told her to be sure and write me how you were last night, and she promised faithfully she would. And it was because I got nothing by this morning's post that I decided to come over myself, to see if it was anything serious.'

'Serious it is!' murmured Mrs Baines.

'What —'

'Sophia's run off. That's the plain English of it!' said Mrs Baines with frigid calm.

'Nay! That I'll never believe. I've looked after Sophia night and day as if she was my own, and —'

'If she hasn't run off, where is she?'

Mrs Maddack opened the door with a tragic gesture.

'Bladen,' she called in a loud voice to the driver of the waggonette, who was standing on the pavement.

'Yes'm.'

'It was Pember drove Miss Sophia yesterday, wasn't it?'

'Yes'm.'

She hesitated. A clumsy question might enlighten a member of the class which ought never to be enlightened about one's private affairs.

'He didn't come all the way here?'

'No'm. He happened to say last night when he got back as Miss Sophia had told him to set her down at Knype Station.'

'I thought so!' said Mrs Maddack, courageously.

'Yes'm.'

'Sister!' she moaned, after carefully shutting the door.

They clung to each other.

The horror of what had occurred did not instantly take full

possession of them, because the power of credence, of imaginatively realizing a supreme event, whether of great grief or of great happiness, is ridiculously finite. But every minute the horror grew more clear, more intense, more tragically dominant over them. There were many things that they could not say to each other – from pride, from shame, from the inadequacy of words. Neither could utter the name of Gerald Scales. And Aunt Harriet could not stoop to defend herself from a possible charge of neglect; nor could Mrs Baines stoop to assure her sister that she was incapable of preferring such a charge. And the sheer, immense criminal folly of Sophia could not even be referred to: it was unspeakable. So the interview proceeded, lamely, clumsily, inconsequently, leading to naught.

Sophia was gone. She was gone with Gerald Scales. That beautiful child, that incalculable, untamable, impossible creature, had committed the final folly; without pretext or excuse, and with what elaborate deceit! Yes, without excuse! She had not been treated harshly; she had had a degree of liberty which would have astounded and shocked her grandmothers; she had been petted, humoured, spoilt. And her answer was to disgrace the family by an act as irrevocable as it was utterly vicious. If among her desires was the desire to humiliate those majesties, her mother and Aunt Harriet, she would have been content could she have seen them on the sofa there, humbled, shamed, mortally wounded! Ah, the monstrous Chinese cruelty of youth!

What was to be done? Tell dear Constance? No, this was not, at the moment, an affair for the younger generation. It was too new and raw for the younger generation. Moreover, capable, proud, and experienced as they were, they felt the need of a man's voice, and a man's hard, callous ideas. It was a case for Mr Critchlow. Maggie was sent to fetch him, with a particular request that he should come to the side-door. He came expectant, with the pleasurable anticipation of disaster, and he was not disappointed. He passed with the sisters the happiest hour that had fallen to him for years. Quickly he arranged the alternatives for them. Would they tell the police, or would they take the risks of waiting? They shied away, but with fierce brutality he brought them again and again to the immediate point of decision . . . Well, they could not tell the police! They simply could not . . . Then they must face another danger . . . He had no mercy for them. And while he was torturing them there arrived a telegram, despatched from Charing Cross, 'I am all right, Sophia.' That proved, at any rate, that the child was not heartless, not merely careless.

Only yesterday, it seemed to Mrs Baines, she had borne Sophia; only yesterday she was a baby, a schoolgirl to be smacked. The years rolled up in a few hours. And now she was sending telegrams from a place called Charing Cross! How unlike was the hand of the telegram to Sophia's hand! How mysteriously curt and inhuman was that official hand, as Mrs Baines stared at it through red, wet eyes!

Mr Critchlow said someone should go to Manchester, to ascertain about Scales. He went himself, that afternoon, and returned with the news that an aunt of Scales had recently died, leaving him twelve thousand pounds, and that he had, after quarrelling with his uncle Boldero, abandoned Birkinshaws at an hour's notice and vanished with his inheritance.

'It's as plain as a pikestaff,' said Mr Critchlow. 'I could ha' warned ye o' all this years ago, ever since she killed her father!'

Mr Critchlow left nothing unsaid.

During the night Mrs Baines lived through all Sophia's life, lived through it more intensely than ever Sophia had done.

The next day people began to know. A whisper almost inaudible went across the Square, and into the town: and in the stillness everyone heard it. 'Sophia Baines run off with a commercial!'

In another fortnight a note came, also dated from London.

'Dear Mother, I am married to Gerald Scales. Please don't worry about me. We are going abroad. Your affectionate Sophia. Love to Constance.' No tear-stains on that pale blue sheet! No sign of agitation!

And Mrs Baines said: 'My life is over.' It was, though she was scarcely fifty. She felt old, old and beaten. She had fought and been vanquished. The everlasting purpose had been too much for her. Virtue had gone out of her – the virtue to hold up her head and look the Square in the face. She, the wife of John Baines! She, a Syme of Axe!

Old houses, in the course of their history, see sad sights, and never forget them! And ever since, in the solemn physiognomy of the triple house of John Baines at the corner of St Luke's Square and King Street, have remained the traces of the sight it saw on the morning of the afternoon when Mr and Mrs Povey returned from their honeymoon – the sight of Mrs Baines getting into the waggonette for Axe; Mrs Baines, encumbered with trunks and parcels, leaving the scene of her struggles and her defeat, whither she had once come as slim as a wand, to return stout and heavy, and heavy-hearted, to her childhood; content to live with her grandiose sister until such time as she should be ready for burial! The grimy and impassive old house perhaps heard her heart saying: 'Only yesterday they were little girls, ever so tiny, and now –' The driving-off of a waggonette can be a dreadful thing.

BOOK TWO: CONSTANCE

CHAPTER I: *Revolution*

I

'Well,' said Mr Povey, rising from the rocking-chair that in a previous age had been John Baines's, 'I've got to make a start some time, so I may as well begin now!'

And he went from the parlour into the shop. Constance's eye followed him as far as the door, where their glances met for an instant in the transient gaze which expresses the tenderness of people who feel more than they kiss.

It was on the morning of this day that Mrs Baines, relinquishing the sovereignty of St Luke's Square, had gone to live as a younger sister in the house of Harriet Maddack at Axe. Constance guessed little of the secret anguish of that departure. She only knew that it was just like her mother, having perfectly arranged the entire house for the arrival of the honeymoon couple from Buxton, to flit early away so as to spare the natural blushing diffidence of the said couple. It was like her mother's common sense and her mother's sympathetic comprehension. Further, Constance did not pursue her mother's feelings, being far too busy with her own. She sat there full of new knowledge and new importance, brimming with experience and strange, unexpected aspirations, purposes, yes – and cunnings! And yet, though the very curves of her cheeks seemed to be mysteriously altering, the old Constance still lingered in that frame, an innocent soul hesitating to spread its wings and quit for ever the body which had been its home; you could see the timid thing peeping wistfully out of the eyes of the married woman.

Constance rang the bell for Maggie to clear the table; and as she did so she had the illusion that she was not really a married woman and a house mistress, but only a kind of counterfeit. She did most fervently hope that all would go right in the house – at any rate until she had grown more accustomed to her situation.

The hope was to be disappointed. Maggie's rather silly, obsequious smile concealed but for a moment the ineffable tragedy that had lain in wait for unarmed Constance.

'If you please, Mrs Povey,' said Maggie, as she crushed cups together on the tin tray with her great, red hands, which always looked like something out of a butcher's shop; then a pause, 'Will you please accept of this?'

Now, before the wedding Maggie had already, with tears of affection, given Constance a pair of blue glass vases (in order to purchase which she had been obliged to ask for special permission to go out), and Constance wondered what was coming now from Maggie's pocket. A small piece of folded paper came from Maggie's pocket. Constance accepted of it, and read: 'I begs to give one month's notice to leave. Signed Maggie. June 10, 1867.'

'Maggie!' exclaimed the old Constance, terrified by this incredible occurrence, ere the married woman could strangle her.

'I never give notice before, Mrs Povey,' said Maggie, 'so I don't know as I know how it ought for be done – not rightly. But I hope as you'll accept of it, Mrs Povey.'

'Oh! of course,' said Mrs Povey, primly, just as if Maggie was not the central supporting pillar of the house, just as if Maggie had not assisted at her birth, just as if the end of the world had not abruptly been announced, just as if St Luke's Square were not inconceivable without Maggie. 'But why –'

'Well, Mrs Povey, I've been a-thinking it over in my kitchen, and I said to myself: "If there's going to be one change there'd better be two," I says. Not but what I wouldn't work my fingers to the bone for ye, Miss Constance.'

Here Maggie began to cry into the tray.

Constance looked at her. Despite the special muslin of that day she had traces of the slatternliness of which Mrs Baines had never been able to cure her. She was over forty, big, gawky. She had no figure, no charms of any kind. She was what was left of a woman after twenty-two years in the cave of a philanthropic family. And in her cave she had actually been thinking things over! Constance detected for the first time, beneath the dehumanized

drudge, the stirrings of a separate and perhaps capricious individuality. Maggie's engagements had never been real to her
employers. Within the house she had never been, in practice,
anything but 'Maggie' – an organism. And now she was permitting herself ideas about changes!

'You'll soon be suited with another, Mrs Povey,' said Maggie.
'There's many a – many a –' She burst into sobs.

'But if you really want to leave, what are you crying for,
Maggie?' asked Mrs Povey, at her wisest. 'Have you told
mother?'

'No, miss,' Maggie whimpered, absently wiping her wrinkled
cheeks with ineffectual muslin. 'I couldn't seem to fancy telling
your mother. And as you're the mistress now, I thought as I'd
save if for you when you come home. I hope you'll excuse me,
Mrs Povey.'

'Of course I'm very sorry. You've been a very good servant.
And in these days –'

The child had acquired this turn of speech from her mother. It
did not appear to occur to either of them that they were living in
the sixties.

'Thank ye, miss.'

'And what are you thinking of doing, Maggie? You know you
won't get many places like this.'

'To tell ye the truth, Mrs Povey, I'm going to get married
mysen.'

'Indeed!' murmured Constance, with the perfunctoriness of
habit in replying to these tidings.

'Oh! but I am, mum,' Maggie insisted. 'It's all settled. Mr
Hollins, mum.'

'Not Hollins, the fish-hawker!'

'Yes, mum. I seem to fancy him. You don't remember as him
and me was engaged in '48. He was my first, like. I broke it off
because he was in that Chartist lot,[7] and I knew as Mr Baines
would never stand that. Now he's asked me again. He's been a
widower this long time.'

'I'm sure I hope you'll be happy, Maggie. But what about his
habits?'

'He won't have no habits with me, Mrs Povey.'

A woman was definitely emerging from the drudge.

When Maggie, having entirely ceased sobbing, had put the folded cloth in the table-drawer and departed with the tray, her mistress became frankly the girl again. No primness about her as she stood alone there in the parlour; no pretence that Maggie's notice to leave was an everyday document, to be casually glanced at as one glances at an unpaid bill! She would be compelled to find a new servant, making solemn inquiries into character, and to train the new servant, and to talk to her from heights from which she had never addressed Maggie. At that moment she had an illusion that there were no other available, suitable servants in the whole world. And the arranged marriage? She felt that this time – the thirteenth or fourteenth time – the engagement was serious and would only end at the altar. The vision of Maggie and Hollins at the altar shocked her. Marriage was a series of phenomena, and a general state, very holy and wonderful – too sacred, somehow, for such creatures as Maggie and Hollins. Her vague, instinctive revolt against such a usage of matrimony centred round the idea of a strong, eternal smell of fish. However, the projected outrage on a hallowed institution troubled her much less than the imminent problem of domestic service.

She ran into the shop – or she would have run if she had not checked her girlishness betimes – and on her lips, ready to be whispered importantly into a husband's astounded ear, were the words, 'Maggie has given notice! Yes! Truly!' But Samuel Povey was engaged. He was leaning over the counter and staring at an outspread paper upon which a certain Mr Yardley was making strokes with a thick pencil. Mr Yardley, who had a long red beard, painted houses and rooms. She knew him only by sight. In her mind she always associated him with the sign over his premises in Trafalgar Road, 'Yardley Bros, Authorized plumbers. Painters. Decorators. Paper-hangers. Facia writers.' For years, in childhood, she had passed that sign without knowing what sort of thing 'Bros' and 'Facia' were, and what was the mysterious similarity between a plumber and a version of the Bible. She could not interrupt her husband, he was wholly absorbed; nor could she stay in the shop (which appeared just a little smaller than usual), for that would have meant an unsuc-

cessful endeavour to front the young lady-assistants as though
nothing in particular had happened to her. So she went sedately
up the showroom stairs and thus to the bedroom floors of the
house – her house! Mrs Povey's house! She even climbed to
Constance's old bedroom; her mother had stripped the bed – that
was all, except a slight diminution of this room, corresponding to
that of the shop! Then to the drawing-room. In the recess outside
the drawing-room door the black box of silver plate still lay. She
had expected her mother to take it; but no! Assuredly her mother
was one to do things handsomely – when she did them. In the
drawing-room, not a tassel of an antimacassar touched! Yes, the
fire-screen, the luscious bunch of roses on an expanse of mustard,
which Constance had worked for her mother years ago, was
gone! That her mother should have clung to just that one
souvenir, out of all the heavy opulence of the drawing-room,
touched Constance intimately. She perceived that if she could not
talk to her husband she must write to her mother. And she sat
down at the oval table and wrote, 'Darling mother, I am sure you
will be very surprised to hear . . . She means it . . . I think she is
making a serious mistake. Ought I to put an advertisement in the
Signal, or will it do if . . . Please write by return. We are back, and
have enjoyed ourselves very much. Sam says he enjoys getting up
late . . .' And so on to the last inch of the fourth scolloped page.

She was obliged to revisit the shop for a stamp, stamps being
kept in Mr Povey's desk in the corner – a high desk, at which you
stood. Mr Povey was now in earnest converse with Mr Yardley at
the door, and twilight, which began a full hour earlier in the shop
than in the Square, had cast faint shadows in corners behind
counters.

'Will you just run out with this to the pillar, Miss Dadd?'

'With pleasure, Mrs Povey.'

'Where are you going to?' Mr Povey interrupted his conversation to stop the flying girl.

'She's just going to the post for me,' Constance called out from
the region of the till.

'Oh! All right!'

A trifle! A nothing! Yet somehow, in the quiet customerless
shop, the episode, with the scarce perceptible difference in

Samuel's tone at his second remark, was delicious to Constance. Somehow it was the *real* beginning of her wifehood. (There had been about nine other real beginnings in the past fortnight.)

Mr Povey came in to supper, laden with ledgers and similar works which Constance had never even pretended to understand. It was a sign from him that the honeymoon was over. He was proprietor now, and his ardour for ledgers most justifiable. Still, there was the question of her servant.

'Never!' he exclaimed, when she told him all about the end of the world. A 'never' which expressed extreme astonishment and the liveliest concern!

But Constance had anticipated that he would have been just a little more knocked down, bowled over, staggered, stunned, flabbergasted. In a swift gleam of insight she saw that she had been in danger of forgetting her *rôle* of experienced, capable married woman.

'I shall have to set about getting a fresh one,' she said hastily, with an admirable assumption of light and easy casualness.

Mr Povey seemed to think that Hollins would suit Maggie pretty well. He made no remark to the betrothed when she answered the final bell of the night.

He opened his ledgers, whistling.

'I think I shall go up, dear,' said Constance. 'I've a lot of things to put away.'

'Do,' said he. 'Call out when you've done.'

II

'Sam!' she cried from the top of the crooked stairs.

No answer. The door at the foot was closed.

'Sam!'

'Hello?' Distantly, faintly.

'I've done all I'm going to do tonight.'

And she ran back along the corridor, a white figure in the deep gloom, and hurried into bed, and drew the clothes up to her chin.

In the life of a bride there are some dramatic moments. If she has married the industrious apprentice, one of those moments occurs when she first occupies the sacred bedchamber of her ancestors, and the bed on which she was born. Her parents' room had always been to Constance, if not sacred, at least invested with a certain moral solemnity. She could not enter it as she would enter another room. The course of nature, with its succession of deaths, conceptions, and births, slowly makes such a room august with a mysterious quality which interprets the grandeur of mere existence and imposes itself on all. Constance had the strangest sensations in that bed, whose heavy dignity of ornament symbolized a past age; sensations of sacrilege and trespass, of being a naughty girl to whom punishment would accrue for this shocking freak. Not since she was quite tiny had she slept in that bed – one night with her mother, before her father's seizure, when he had been away. What a limitless, unfathomable bed it was then! Now it was just a bed – so she had to tell herself – like any other bed. The tiny child that, safely touching its mother, had slept in the vast expanse, seemed to her now a pathetic little thing; its image made her feel melancholy. And her mind dwelt on sad events: the death of her father, the flight of darling Sophia; the immense grief, and the exile, of her mother. She esteemed that she knew what life was, and that it was grim. And she sighed. But the sigh was an affectation, meant partly to convince herself that she was grown-up, and partly to keep her in countenance in the intimidating bed. This melancholy was factitious, was less than transient foam on the deep sea of her joy. Death and sorrow and sin were dim shapes to her; the ruthless egoism of happiness blew them away with a puff, and their wistful faces vanished. To see her there in the bed, framed in mahogany and tassels, lying on her side, with her young glowing cheeks, and honest but not artless gaze, and the rich curve of her hip lifting the counterpane, one would have said that she had never heard of aught but love.

Mr Povey entered, the bridegroom, quickly, firmly, carrying it off rather well, but still self-conscious. 'After all,' his shoulders were trying to say, 'what's the difference between this bedroom and the bedroom of a boarding-house? Indeed, ought we not to feel more at home here? Besides, confound it, we've been married a fortnight!'

'Doesn't it give you a funny feeling, sleeping in this room? It does me,' said Constance. Women, even experienced women, are so foolishly frank. They have no decency, no self-respect.

'Really?' replied Mr Povey, with loftiness, as who should say: 'What an extraordinary thing that a reasonable creature can have such fancies! Now to me this room is exactly like any other room.' And he added aloud, glancing away from the glass, where he was unfastening his necktie: 'It's not a bad room at all.' This, with the judicial air of an auctioneer.

Not for an instant did he deceive Constance, who read his real sensations with accuracy. But his futile poses did not in the slightest degree lessen her respect for him. On the contrary, she admired him the more for them; they were a sort of embroidery on the solid stuff of his character. At that period he could not do wrong for her. The basis of her regard for him was, she often thought, his honesty, his industry, his genuine kindliness of act, his grasp of the business, his perseverance, his passion for doing at once that which had to be done. She had the greatest admiration for his qualities, and he was in her eyes an indivisible whole; she could not admire one part of him and frown upon another. Whatever he did was good because he did it. She knew that some people were apt to smile at certain phases of his individuality; she knew that far down in her mother's heart was a suspicion that she had married ever so little beneath her. But this knowledge did not disturb her. She had no doubt as to the correctness of her own estimate.

Mr Povey was an exceedingly methodical person, and he was also one of those persons who must always be 'before-hand' with time. Thus at night he would arrange his raiment so that in the morning it might be reassumed in the minimum of minutes. He was not a man, for example, to leave the changing of studs from one shirt to another till the morrow. Had it been practicable, he would have brushed his hair the night before. Constance already loved to watch his meticulous preparations. She saw him now go into his old bedroom and return with a paper collar, which he put on the dressing-table next to a black necktie. His shop-suit was laid out on a chair.

'Oh, Sam!' she exclaimed impulsively, 'you surely aren't going to begin wearing those horrid paper collars again!' During the honeymoon he had worn linen collars.

Her tone was perfectly gentle, but the remark, nevertheless,

showed a lack of tact. It implied that all his life Mr Povey had
been enveloping his neck in something which was horrid. Like all
persons with a tendency to fall into the ridiculous, Mr Povey was
exceedingly sensitive to personal criticisms. He flushed darkly.

'I didn't know they were "horrid",' he snapped. He was hurt
and angry. Anger surprised him unawares.

Both of them suddenly saw that they were standing on the edge
of a chasm, and drew back. They had imagined themselves to be
wandering safely in a flowered meadow, and here was this
bottomless chasm! It was most disconcerting.

Mr Povey's hand hovered undecided over the collar. 'However –' he muttered.

She could feel that he was trying with all his might to be gentle
and pacific. And she was aghast at her own stupid clumsiness, she
so experienced!

'Just as you like, dear,' she said quickly. 'Please!'

'Oh no!' And he did his best to smile, and went off gawkily
with the collar and came back with a linen one.

Her passion for him burned stronger than ever. She knew then
that she did not love him for his good qualities, but for something
boyish and naïve that there was about him, an indescribable
something that occasionally, when his face was close to hers,
made her dizzy.

The chasm had disappeared. In such moments, when each
must pretend not to have seen or even suspected the chasm,
small-talk is essential.

'Wasn't that Mr Yardley in the shop tonight?' began Constance.

'Yes.'

'What did he want?'

'I'd sent for him. He's going to paint us a signboard.'

Useless for Samuel to make-believe that nothing in this world is
more ordinary than a signboard.

'Oh!' murmured Constance. She said no more, the episode of
the paper collar having weakened her self-confidence.

But a signboard!

What with servants, chasms, and signboards, Constance considered that her life as a married woman would not be de-

ficient in excitement. Long afterwards she fell asleep, thinking of Sophia.

III

A few days later Constance was arranging the more precious of her wedding presents in the parlour; some had to be wrapped in tissue and in brown paper and then tied with string and labelled; others had special cases of their own, leather without and velvet within. Among the latter was the resplendent egg-stand holding twelve silver-gilt egg-cups and twelve chased spoons to match, presented by Aunt Harriet. In the Five Towns' phrase, 'it must have cost money'. Even if Mr and Mrs Povey had ten guests or ten children, and all the twelve of them were simultaneously gripped by a desire to eat eggs at breakfast or tea – even in this remote contingency Aunt Harriet would have been pained to see the egg-stand in use; such treasures are not designed for use. The presents, few in number, were mainly of this character, because, owing to her mother's heroic cession of the entire interior, Constance already possessed every necessary. The fewness of the presents was accounted for by the fact that the wedding had been strictly private and had taken place at Axe. There is nothing like secrecy in marriage for discouraging the generous impulses of one's friends. It was Mrs Baines, abetted by both the chief parties, who had decided that the wedding should be private and secluded. Sophia's wedding had been altogether too private and secluded; but the casting of a veil over Constance's (whose union was irreproachable) somehow justified, after the event, the circumstances of Sophia's, indicating as it did that Mrs Baines believed in secret weddings on principle. In such matters Mrs Baines was capable of extraordinary subtlety.

And while Constance was thus taking her wedding presents with due seriousness, Maggie was cleaning the steps that led from the pavement of King Street to the side-door, and the door was ajar. It was a fine June morning.

Suddenly, over the sound of scouring, Constance heard a dog's low growl and then the hoarse voice of a man:

'Mester in, wench?'

'Happen he is, happen he isn't,' came Maggie's answer. She had no fancy for being called wench.

Constance went to the door, not merely from curiosity, but from a feeling that her authority and her responsibilities as housemistress extended to the pavement surrounding the house.

The famous James Boon, of Buck Row, the greatest dog-fancier in the Five Towns, stood at the bottom of the steps: a tall, fat man, clad in stiff, stained brown and smoking a black clay pipe less than three inches long. Behind him attended two bull-dogs.

'Morning, missis!' cried Boon, cheerfully. 'I've heerd tell as th' mister is looking out for a dog, as you might say.'

'I don't stay here with them animals a-sniffing at me – no, that I don't!' observed Maggie, picking herself up.

'Is he?' Constance hesitated. She knew that Samuel had vaguely referred to dogs; she had not, however, imagined that he regarded a dog as aught but a beautiful dream. No dog had ever put paw into that house, and it seemed impossible that one should ever do so. As for those beasts of prey on the pavement . . . !

'Ay!' said James Boon, calmly.

'I'll tell him you're here,' said Constance. 'But I don't know if he's at liberty. He seldom is at this time of day. Maggie, you'd better come in.'

She went slowly to the shop, full of fear for the future.

'Sam,' she whispered to her husband, who was writing at his desk, 'here's a man come to see you about a dog.'

Assuredly he was taken aback. Still, he behaved with much presence of mind.

'Oh, about a dog! Who is it?'

'It's that Jim Boon. He says he's heard you want one.'

The renowned name of Jim Boon gave him pause; but he had to go through with the affair, and he went through with it, though nervously. Constance followed his agitated footsteps to the side-door.

'Morning, Boon.'

'Morning, mester.'

They began to talk dogs, Mr Povey, for his part, with due caution.

'Now, there's a dog!' said Boon, pointing to one of the bull-dogs, a miracle of splendid ugliness.

'Yes,' responded Mr Povey, insincerely. 'He is a beauty. What's it worth now, at a venture?'

'I'll tak' a hundred and twenty sovereigns for her,' said Boon. 'Th' other's a bit cheaper – a hundred.'

'Oh, Sam!' gasped Constance.

And even Mr Povey nearly lost his nerve. 'That's more than I want to give,' said he timidly.

'But look at her!' Boon persisted, roughly snatching up the more expensive animal, and displaying her cannibal teeth.

Mr Povey shook his head. Constance glanced away.

'That's not quite the sort of dog I want,' said Mr Povey.

'Fox-terrier?'

'Yes, that's more like,' Mr Povey agreed eagerly.

'What'll ye run to?'

'Oh,' said Mr Povey, largely, 'I don't know.'

'Will ye run to a tenner?'

'I thought of something cheaper.'

'Well, hoo much? Out wi' it, mester.'

'Not more than two pounds,' said Mr Povey. He would have said one pound had he dared. The prices of dogs amazed him.

'I thowt it was a *dog* as ye wanted!' said Boon. 'Look 'ere, mester. Come up to my yard and see what I've got.'

'I will,' said Mr Povey.

'And bring missis along too. Now, what about a cat for th' missis? Or a gold-fish?'

The end of the episode was that a young lady aged some twelve months entered the Povey household on trial. Her exiguous legs twinkled all over the parlour, and she had the oddest appearance in the parlour. But she was so confiding, so affectionate, so timorous, and her black nose was so icy in that hot weather, that Constance loved her violently within an hour. Mr Povey made rules for her. He explained to her that she must never, never go into the shop. But she went, and he whipped her to the squealing point, and Constance cried an instant, while admiring her husband's firmness.

The dog was not all.

On another day Constance, prying into the least details of the parlour, discovered a box of cigars inside the lid of the harmonium, on the keyboard. She was so unaccustomed to cigars that at first she did not realize what the object was. Her father had never smoked, nor drunk intoxicants; nor had Mr Critchlow. Nobody had ever smoked in that house, where tobacco had always been regarded as equally licentious with cards, 'the devil's playthings'. Certainly Samuel had never smoked in the house, though the sight of the cigar-box reminded Constance of an occasion when her mother had announced an incredulous suspicion that Mr Povey, fresh from an excursion into the world on a Thursday evening, 'smelt of smoke'.

She closed the harmonium and kept silence.

That very night, coming suddenly into the parlour, she caught Samuel at the harmonium. The lid went down with a resonant bang that awoke sympathetic vibrations in every corner of the room.

'What is it?' Constance inquired, jumping.

'Oh, nothing!' replied Mr Povey, carelessly.

Each was deceiving the other: Mr Povey hid his crime, and Constance hid her knowledge of his crime. False, false! But this is what marriage is.

And the next day Constance had a visit in the shop from a possible new servant, recommended to her by Mr Holl, the grocer.

'Will you please step this way?' said Constance, with affable primness, steeped in the novel sense of what it is to be the sole responsible mistress of a vast household. She preceded the girl to the parlour, and as they passed the open door of Mr Povey's cutting-out room, Constance had the clear vision and titillating odour of her husband smoking a cigar. He was in his shirt-sleeves, calmly cutting out, and Fan (the lady companion), at watch on the bench, yapped at the possible new servant.

'I think I shall try that girl,' said she to Samuel at tea. She said nothing as to the cigar; nor did he.

On the following evening, after supper, Mr Povey burst out:

'I think I'll have a weed! You didn't know I smoked, did you?'

Thus Mr Povey came out in his true colours as a blood, a blade, and a gay spark.

But dogs and cigars, disconcerting enough in their degree, were to the signboard, when the signboard at last came, as skim milk is to hot brandy. It was the signboard that, more startlingly than anything else, marked the dawn of a new era in St Luke's Square. Four men spent a day and a half in fixing it; they had ladders, ropes, and pulleys, and two of them dined on the flat lead roof of the projecting shop-windows. The signboard was thirty-five feet long and two feet in depth; over its centre was a semicircle about three feet in radius; this semicircle bore the legend, judiciously disposed, 'S. Povey. Late'. All the signboard proper was devoted to the words, 'John Baines', in gold letters a foot and a half high, on a green ground.

The Square watched and wondered; and murmured: 'Well, bless us! What next?'

It was agreed that in giving paramount importance to the name of his late father-in-law, Mr Povey had displayed a very nice feeling.

Some asked with glee: 'What'll the old lady have to say?'

Constance asked herself this, but not with glee. When Constance walked down the Square homewards, she could scarcely bear to look at the sign; the thought of what her mother might say frightened her. Her mother's first visit of state was imminent, and Aunt Harriet was to accompany her. Constance felt almost sick as the day approached. When she faintly hinted her apprehensions to Samuel, he demanded, as if surprised –

'Haven't you mentioned it in one of your letters?'

'Oh *no*!'

'If that's all,' said he, with bravado, 'I'll write and tell her myself.'

IV

So that Mrs Baines was duly apprised of the signboard before her arrival. The letter written by her to Constance after receiving Samuel's letter, which was merely the amiable epistle of a son-in-

law anxious to be a little more than correct, contained no
reference to the signboard. This silence, however, did not in the
least allay Constance's apprehensions as to what might occur
when her mother and Samuel met beneath the signboard itself. It
was therefore with a fearful as well as an eager, loving heart that
Constance opened her side-door and ran down the steps when the
waggonette stopped in King Street on the Thursday morning of
the great visit of the sisters. But a surprise awaited her. Aunt
Harriet had not come. Mrs Baines explained, as she soundly
kissed her daughter, that at the last moment Aunt Harriet had not
felt well enough to undertake the journey. She sent her fondest
love, and cake. Her pains had recurred. It was these mysterious
pains which had prevented the sisters from coming to Bursley
earlier. The word 'cancer' – the continual terror of stout women –
had been on their lips, without having been actually uttered; then
there was a surcease, and each was glad that she had refrained
from the dread syllables. In view of the recurrence, it was not
unnatural that Mrs Baines's vigorous cheerfulness should be
somewhat forced.

'What is it, do you think?' Constance inquired.

Mrs Baines pushed her lips out and raised her eyebrows – a
gesture which meant that the pains might mean God knew what.

'I hope she'll be all right alone,' observed Constance.

'Of course,' said Mrs Baines quickly. 'But you don't suppose I
was going to disappoint you, do you?' she added, looking round
as if to defy the fates in general.

This speech, and its tone, gave intense pleasure to Constance;
and, laden with parcels, they mounted the stairs together, very
content with each other, very happy in the discovery that they
were still mother and daughter, very intimate in an inarticulate
way.

Constance had imagined long, detailed, absorbing, and highly
novel conversations between herself and her mother upon this
their first meeting after her marriage. But alone in the bedroom,
and with a clear half-hour to dinner, they neither of them seemed
to have a great deal to impart.

Mrs Baines slowly removed her light mantle and laid it with
precautions on the white damask counterpane. Then, fingering

her weeds, she glanced about the chamber. Nothing was changed. Though Constance had, previous to her marriage, envisaged certain alterations, she had determined to postpone them, feeling that one revolutionist in a house was enough.

'Well, my chick, you all right?' said Mrs Baines, with hearty and direct energy, gazing straight into her daughter's eyes.

Constance perceived that the question was universal in its comprehensiveness, the one unique expression that the mother would give to her maternal concern and curiosity, and that condensed into six words as much interest as would have overflowed into a whole day of the chatter of some mothers. She met the candid glance, flushing.

'Oh *yes*!' she answered with ecstatic fervour. 'Perfectly!'

And Mrs Baines nodded, as if dismissing *that*. 'You're stouter,' said she, curtly. 'If you aren't careful you'll be as big as any of us.'

'Oh, mother.'

The interview fell to a lower plane of emotion. It even fell as far as Maggie. What chiefly preoccupied Constance was a subtle change in her mother. She found her mother fussy in trifles. Her manner of laying down her mantle, of smoothing out her gloves, and her anxiety that her bonnet should not come to harm, were rather trying, were perhaps, in the very slightest degree, pitiable. It was nothing; it was barely perceptible, and yet it was enough to alter Constance's mental attitude to her mother. 'Poor dear!' thought Constance. 'I'm afraid she's not what she was.' Incredible that her mother could have aged in less than six weeks! Constance did not allow for the chemistry that had been going on in herself.

The encounter between Mrs Baines and her son-in-law was of the most satisfactory nature. He was waiting in the parlour for her to descend. He made himself exceedingly agreeable, kissing her, and flattering her by his evidently sincere desire to please. He explained that he had kept an eye open for the waggonette, but had been called away. His 'Dear me!' on learning about Aunt Harriet lacked nothing in conviction, though both women knew that his affection for Aunt Harriet would never get the better of his reason. To Constance, her husband's behaviour was marvellously perfect. She had not suspected him to be such a man of the world. And her eyes said to her mother, quite unconsciously: 'You see, after all, you didn't rate Sam as high as you ought to have done. Now you see your mistake.'

As they sat waiting for dinner, Constance and Mrs Baines on the sofa, and Samuel on the edge of the nearest rocking-chair, a small scuffling noise was heard outside the door which gave on the kitchen steps, the door yielded to pressure and Fan rushed importantly in, deranging mats. Fan's nose had been hinting to her that she was behind the times, not up-to-date in the affairs of the household, and she had hurried from the kitchen to make inquiries. It occurred to her *en route* that she had been washed that morning. The spectacle of Mrs Baines stopped her. She stood, with her legs slightly outstretched, her nose lifted, her ears raking forward, her bright eyes blinking, and her tail undecided. 'I was sure I'd never smelt anything like that before,' she was saying to herself, as she stared at Mrs Baines.

And Mrs Baines, staring at Fan, had a similar though not the same sentiment. The silence was terrible. Constance took on the mien of a culprit, and Sam had obviously lost his easy bearing of a man of the world. Mrs Baines was merely thunderstruck.

A dog!

Suddenly Fan's tail began to wag more quickly; and then, having looked in vain for encouragement to her master and mistress, she gave one mighty spring and alighted in Mrs Baines's lap. It was an aim she could not have missed. Constance emitted an 'Oh, *Fan!*' of shocked terror, and Samuel betrayed his nervous tension by an involuntary movement. But Fan had settled down into that titanic lap as into heaven. It was a greater flattery than Mr Povey's.

'So your name's Fan!' murmured Mrs Baines, stroking the animal. 'You are a dear!'

'Yes, isn't she?' said Constance, with inconceivable rapidity.

The danger was past. Thus, without any explanation, Fan became an accepted fact.

The next moment Maggie served the Yorkshire pudding.

'Well, Maggie,' said Mrs Baines. 'So you are going to get married this time? When is it?'

'Sunday, ma'am.'

'And you leave here on Saturday?'

'Yes, ma'am.'

'Well, I must have a talk with you before I go.'

During the dinner, not a word as to the signboard! Several times the conversation curved towards that signboard in the most alarming fashion, but invariably it curved away again, like a train from another train when two trains are simultaneously leaving a station. Constance had frights, so serious as to destroy her anxiety about the cookery. In the end she comprehended that her mother had adopted a silently disapproving attitude. Fan was socially very useful throughout the repast.

After dinner Constance was on pins lest Samuel should light a cigar. She had not requested him not to do so, for though she was entirely sure of his affection, she had already learned that a husband is possessed by a demon of contrariety which often forces him to violate his higher feelings. However, Samuel did not light a cigar. He went off to superintend the shutting-up of the shop, while Mrs Baines chatted with Maggie and gave her £5 for a wedding present. Then Mr Critchlow called to offer his salutations.

A little before tea Mrs Baines announced that she would go out for a short walk by herself.

'Where has she gone to?' smiled Samuel, superiorly, as with Constance at the window he watched her turn down King Street towards the church.

'I expect she has gone to look at father's grave,' said Constance.

'Oh!' muttered Samuel apologetically.

Constance was mistaken. Before reaching the church, Mrs Baines deviated to the right, got into Brougham Street and thence, by Acre Lane, into Oldcastle Street, whose steep she climbed. Now, Oldcastle Street ends at the top of St Luke's Square, and from the corner Mrs Baines had an excellent view of the signboard. It being Thursday afternoon, scarce a soul was about. She returned to her daughter's by the same extraordinary route, and said not a word on entering. But she was markedly cheerful.

The waggonette came after tea, and Mrs Baines made her final preparations to depart. The visit had proved a wonderful success;

it would have been utterly perfect if Samuel had not marred it at the very door of the waggonette. Somehow, he contrived to be talking of Christmas. Only a person of Samuel's native clumsiness would have mentioned Christmas in July.

'You know you'll spend Christmas with us!' said he into the waggonette.

'Indeed I shan't!' replied Mrs Baines. 'Aunt Harriet and I will expect you at Axe. We've already settled that.'

Mr Povey bridled. 'Oh no!' he protested, hurt by this summariness.

Having had no relatives, except his cousin the confectioner, for many years, he had dreamt of at last establishing a family Christmas under his own roof, and the dream was dear to him.

Mrs Baines said nothing. 'We couldn't possibly leave the shop,' said Mr Povey.

'Nonsense!' Mrs Baines retorted, putting her lips together. 'Christmas Day is on a Monday.'

The waggonette in starting jerked her head towards the door and set all her curls shaking. No white in those curls yet, scarcely a touch of grey!

'I shall take good care we don't go there anyway,' Mr Povey mumbled, in his heat, half to himself and half to Constance.

He had stained the brightness of the day.

CHAPTER 2: *Christmas and the Future*

I

Mr Povey was playing a hymn tune on the harmonium, it having been decided that no one should go to chapel. Constance, in mourning, with a white apron over her dress, sat on a hassock in front of the fire; and near her, in a rocking-chair, Mrs Baines swayed very gently to and fro. The weather was extremely cold. Mr Povey's mittened hands were blue and red; but, like many shopkeepers, he had apparently grown almost insensible to vagaries of temperature. Although the fire was immense and furious, its influence, owing to the fact that the medieval grate was designed to heat the flue rather than the room, seemed to die away at the borders of the fender. Constance could not have been much closer to it without being a salamander. The era of good old-fashioned Christmases, so agreeably picturesque for the poor, was not yet at an end.

Yes, Samuel Povey had won the battle concerning the *locus* of the family Christmas. But he had received the help of a formidable ally, death. Mrs Harriet Maddack had passed away, after an operation, leaving her house and her money to her sister. The solemn rite of her interment had deeply affected all the respectability of the town of Axe, where the late Mr Maddack had been a figure of consequence; it had even shut up the shop in St Luke's Square for a whole day. It was such a funeral as Aunt Harriet herself would have approved, a tremendous ceremonial which left on the crushed mind an ineffaceable, intricate impression of shiny cloth, crape, horses with arching necks and long manes, the drawl of parsons, cake, port, sighs, and Christian submission to the inscrutable decrees of Providence. Mrs Baines had borne herself with unnatural calmness until the funeral was over: and then Constance perceived that the remembered mother of her girlhood existed no longer. For the majority of human souls it would have been easier to love a virtuous principle, or a mountain, than to love Aunt Harriet, who was assuredly less a woman than an institution. But Mrs Baines had loved her, and she had been the one person to whom Mrs Baines looked for support and guidance. When she died, Mrs Baines paid the tribute of respect with the last hoarded remains of her proud fortitude, and weepingly confessed that the unconquerable had been conquered, the inexhaustible exhausted; and became old with whitening hair.

She had persisted in her refusal to spend Christmas in Bursley, but both Constance and Samuel knew that the resistance was only formal. She soon yielded. When Constance's second new servant took it into her head to leave a week before Christmas, Mrs Baines might have pointed the finger of Providence at work again, and this time in her favour. But no! With amazing pliancy she suggested that she should bring one of her own servants to 'tide Constance over' Christmas. She was met with all the forms of loving solicitude, and she found that her daughter and son-in-law had 'turned out of' the state bedroom in her favour. Intensely flattered by this attention (which was Mr Povey's magnanimous idea), she nevertheless protested strongly. Indeed she 'would not hear of it'.

'Now, mother, don't be silly,' Constance had said firmly. 'You don't expect us to be at all the trouble of moving back again, do you?' And Mrs Baines had surrendered in tears.

Thus had come Christmas. Perhaps it was fortunate that, the Axe servant being not quite the ordinary servant, but a benefactor where a benefactor was needed, both Constance and her mother thought it well to occupy themselves in household work, 'sparing' the benefactor as much as possible. Hence Constance's white apron.

'There he is!' said Mr Povey, still playing, but with his eye on the street.

Constance sprang up eagerly. Then there was a knock on the door. Constance opened, and an icy blast swept into the room. The postman stood on the steps, his instrument for knocking (like a drumstick) in one hand, a large bundle of letters in the other, and a yawning bag across the pit of his stomach.

'Merry Christmas, ma'am!' cried the postman, trying to keep warm by cheerfulness.

Constance, taking the letters, responded, while Mr Povey, playing the harmonium with his right hand, drew half a crown from his pocket with the left.

'Here you are!' he said, giving it to Constance, who gave it to the postman.

Fan, who had been keeping her muzzle warm with the extremity of her tail on the sofa, jumped down to superintend the transaction.

'Brrr!' vibrated Mr Povey as Constance shut the door.

'What lots!' Constance exclaimed, rushing to the fire. 'Here, mother! Here, Sam!'

The girl had resumed possession of the woman's body.

Though the Baines family had few friends (sustained hospitality being little practised in those days) they had, of course, many acquaintances, and, like other families, they counted their Christmas cards as an Indian counts scalps. The tale was satisfactory.

There were between thirty and forty envelopes. Constance extracted Christmas cards rapidly, reading their contents aloud, and then propping them up on the mantelpiece. Mrs Baines assisted. Fan dealt with the envelopes on the floor. Mr Povey, to prove that his soul was above toys and gewgaws, continued to play the harmonium.

'Oh, mother!' Contance murmured in a startled, hesitant voice, holding an envelope.

'What is it, my chuck?'

'It's —'

The envelope was addressed to 'Mrs and Miss Baines' in large, perpendicular, dashing characters which Constance instantly recognized as Sophia's. The stamps were strange, the postmark 'Paris'. Mrs Baines leaned forward and looked.

'Open it, child,' she said.

The envelope contained an English Christmas card of a common type, a spray of holly with greetings, and on it was written, 'I do hope this will reach you on Christmas morning. Fondest love.' No signature, nor address.

Mrs Baines took it with a trembling hand, and adjusted her spectacles. She gazed at it a long time.

'And it has done!' she said, and wept.

She tried to speak again, but not being able to command herself, held forth the card to Constance and jerked her head in the direction of Mr Povey. Constance rose and put the card on the keyboard of the harmonium.

'Sophia!' she whispered.

Mr Povey stopped playing. 'Dear, dear!' he muttered.

Fan, perceiving that nobody was interested in her feats, suddenly stood still.

Mrs Baines tried once more to speak, but could not. Then, her ringlets shaking beneath the band of her weeds, she found her feet, stepped to the harmonium, and, with a movement almost convulsive, snatched the card from Mr Povey, and returned to her chair.

Mr Povey abruptly left the room, followed by Fan. Both the women were in tears, and he was tremendously surprised to discover a dangerous lump in his own throat. The beautiful and imperious vision of Sophia, Sophia as she had left them, innocent, wayward, had swiftly risen up before him and made even him a woman too! Yet he had never liked Sophia. The awful secret wound in the family pride revealed itself to him as never before, and he felt intensely the mother's tragedy, which she carried in her breast as Aunt Harriet had carried a cancer.

At dinner he said suddenly to Mrs Baines, who still wept: 'Now, mother, you must cheer up, you know.'

'Yes, I must,' she said quickly. And she did so.

Neither Samuel nor Constance saw the card again. Little was said. There was nothing to say. As Sophia had given no address she must be still ashamed of her situation. But she had thought of her mother and sister. She . . . she did not even know that Constance was married . . . What sort of a place was Paris? To Bursley, Paris was nothing but the site of a great exhibition which had recently closed.

Through the influence of Mrs Baines a new servant was found for Constance in a village near Axe – a raw, comely girl who had never been in a 'place'. And through the post it was arranged that this innocent should come to the cave on the thirty-first of December. In obedience to the safe rule that servants should never be allowed to meet for the interchange of opinions, Mrs Baines decided to leave with her own servant on the thirtieth. She would not be persuaded to spend the New Year in the Square. On the twenty-ninth poor Aunt Maria died all of a sudden in her cottage in Brougham Street. Everybody was duly distressed, and in particular Mrs Baines's demeanour under this affliction showed the perfection of correctness. But she caused it to be understood that she should not remain for the funeral. Her nerves would be unequal to the ordeal; and, moreover, her servant must not stay to corrupt the new girl, nor could Mrs Baines think of sending her servant to Axe in advance, to spend several days in idle gossip with her colleague.

This decision took the backbone out of Aunt Maria's funeral, which touched the extreme of modesty; a hearse and a one-horse coach. Mr Povey was glad, because he happened to be very busy. An hour before his mother-in-law's departure he came into the parlour with the proof of a poster.

'What is that, Samuel?' asked Mrs Baines, not dreaming of the blow that awaited her.

'It's for my first Annual Sale,' replied Mr Povey with false tranquillity.

Mrs Baines merely tossed her head. Constance, happily for Constance, was not present at this final defeat of the old order. Had she been there, she would certainly not have known where to look.

II

'Forty next birthday!' Mr Povey exclaimed one day, with an expression and in a tone that were at once mock-serious and serious. This was on his thirty-ninth birthday.

Constance was startled. She had, of course, been aware that they were getting older, but she had never realized the phenomenon. Though customers occasionally remarked that Mr Povey was stouter, and though when she helped him to measure himself for a new suit of clothes the tape proved the fact, he had not changed for her. She knew that she too had become somewhat stouter; but for herself, she remained exactly the same Constance. Only by recalling dates and by calculations could she really grasp that she had been married a little over six years and not a little over six months. She had to admit that, if Samuel would be forty next birthday, she would be twenty-seven next birthday. But it would not be a real twenty-seven; nor would Sam's forty be a real forty, like other people's twenty-sevens and forties. Not long since she had been in the habit of regarding a man of forty as senile, as practically in his grave.

She reflected, and the more she reflected the more clearly she saw that after all the almanacs had not lied. Look at Fan! Yes, it must be five years since the memorable morning when doubt first crossed the minds of Samuel and Constance as to Fan's moral principles. Samuel's enthusiasm for dogs was equalled by his ignorance of the dangers to which a young female of tempera-ment may be exposed, and he was much disturbed as doubt developed into certainty. Fan, indeed, was the one being who did not suffer from shock and who had no fears as to the results. The animal, having a pure mind, was bereft of modesty. Sundry enormities had she committed, but none to rank with this one! The result was four quadrupeds recognizable as fox-terriers. Mr Povey breathed again. Fan had had more luck than she deserved, for the result might have been simply anything. Her owners forgave her and disposed of these fruits of iniquity, and then married her lawfully to a husband who was so high up in the world that he could demand a dowry. And now Fan was a grandmother, with fixed ideas and habits, and a son in the house, and various grandchildren scattered over the town. Fan was a sedate and disillusioned dog. She knew the world as it was, and in learning it she had taught her owners above a bit.

Then there was Maggie Hollins. Constance could still vividly recall the self-consciousness with which she had one day received Maggie and the heir of the Hollinses; but it was a long time ago. After staggering half the town by the production of this infant (of which she nearly died) Maggie allowed the angels to waft it away to heaven, and everybody said that she ought to be very thankful – at her age. Old women dug up out of their minds forgotten histories of the eccentricities of the goddess Lucina. Mrs Baines was most curiously interested; she talked freely to Constance, and Constance began to see what an incredible town Bursley had always been – and she never suspected it! Maggie was now mother of other children, and the draggled, lame mistress of a drunken home, and looked sixty. Despite her prophecy, her husband had conserved his 'habits'. The Poveys ate all the fish they could, and sometimes more than they enjoyed, because on his sober days Hollins invariably started his round at the shop, and Constance had to buy for Maggie's sake. The worst of the worthless husband was that he seldom failed to be cheery and polite. He never missed asking after the health of Mrs Baines. And when Constance replied that her mother was 'pretty well considering', but that she would not come over to Bursley again until the Axe railway was opened, as she could not stand the drive, he would shake his grey head and be sympathetically gloomy for an instant.

All these changes in six years! The almanacs were in the right of it.

But nothing had happened to her. Gradually she had obtained

a sure ascendency over her mother, yet without seeking it, merely
as the outcome of time's influences on her and on her mother
respectively. Gradually she had gained skill and use in the
management of her household and of her share of the shop, so
that these machines ran smoothly and effectively and a sudden
contretemps no longer frightened her. Gradually she had constructed a chart of Samuel's individuality, with the submerged
rocks and perilous currents all carefully marked, so that she could
now voyage unalarmed in those seas. But nothing happened.
Unless their visits to Buxton could be called happenings! Decidedly the visit to Buxton was the one little hill that rose out of
the level plain of the year. They had formed the annual habit of
going to Buxton for ten days. They had a way of saying: 'Yes, we
always go to Buxton. We went there for our honeymoon, you
know.' They had become confirmed Buxtonites, with views
concerning St Anne's Terrace, the Broad Walk and Peel's Cavern.
They could not dream of deserting their Buxton. It was the sole
possible resort. Was it not the highest town in England? Well,
then! They always stayed at the same lodgings, and grew to be
special favourites of the landlady, who whispered of them to all
her other guests as having come to her house for their honeymoon, and as never missing a year, and as being most respectable,
superior people in quite a large way of business. Each year they
walked out of Buxton station behind their luggage on a truck, full
of joy and pride because they knew all the landmarks, and the lie
of all the streets, and which were the best shops.

   At the beginning, the notion of leaving the shop to hired
custody had seemed almost fantastic, and the preparations for
absence had been very complicated. Then it was that Miss Insull
had detached herself from the other young lady assistants as a
creature who could be absolutely trusted. Miss Insull was older
than Constance; she had a bad complexion, and she was not
clever, but she was one of your reliable ones. The six years had
witnessed the slow, steady rise of Miss Insull. Her employers said
'Miss Insull' in a tone quite different from that in which they said
'Miss Hawkins' or 'Miss Dadd'. 'Miss Insull' meant the end of a
discussion. 'Better tell Miss Insull.' 'Miss Insull will see to that.' 'I
shall ask Miss Insull.' Miss Insull slept in the house ten nights

every year. Miss Insull had been called into consultation when it was decided to engage a fourth hand in the shape of an apprentice.

Trade had improved in the point of excellence. It was now admitted to be good — a rare honour for trade! The coal-mining boom was at its height, and colliers, in addition to getting drunk, were buying American organs and expensive bull-terriers. Often they would come to the shop to purchase cloth for coats for their dogs. And they would have good cloth. Mr Povey did not like this. One day a butty chose for his dog the best cloth of Mr Povey's shop — at 12s. a yard. 'Will ye make it up? I've gotten th' measurements,' asked the collier. 'No, I won't!' said Mr Povey, hotly. 'And what's more, I won't sell you the cloth either! Cloth at 12s. a yard on a dog's back indeed! I'll thank you to get out of my shop!' The incident became historic, in the Square. It finally established that Mr Povey was a worthy son-in-law and a solid and successful man. It vindicated the old pre-eminence of 'Baines's'. Some surprise was expressed that Mr Povey showed no desire nor tendency towards entering the public life of the town. But he never would, though a keen satirical critic of the Local Board in private. And at the chapel he remained a simple private worshipper, refusing stewardships and trusteeships.

III

Was Constance happy? Of course there was always something on her mind, something that had to be dealt with, either in the shop or in the house, something to employ all the skill and experience which she had acquired. Her life had much in it of laborious tedium — tedium never-ending and monotonous. And both she and Samuel worked consistently hard, rising early, 'pushing forward', as the phrase ran, and going to bed early from sheer fatigue; week after week and month after month as season changed imperceptibly into season. In June and July it would happen to them occasionally to retire before the last silver of dusk was out of the sky. They would lie in bed and talk placidly of their daily affairs. There would be a noise in the street below. 'Vaults closing!' Samuel would say, and yawn. 'Yes, it's quite late,'

Constance would say. And the Swiss clock would rapidly strike
eleven on its coil of resonant wire. And then, just before she went
to sleep, Constance might reflect upon her destiny, as even the
busiest and smoothest women do, and she would decide that it
was kind. Her mother's gradual decline and lonely life at Axe
saddened her. The cards which came now and then at extremely
long intervals from Sophia had been the cause of more sorrow
than joy. The naïve ecstasies of her girlhood had long since
departed – the price paid for experience and self-possession and a
true vision of things. The vast inherent melancholy of the universe did not exempt her. But as she went to sleep she would be
conscious of a vague contentment. The basis of this contentment
was the fact that she and Samuel comprehended and esteemed
each other, and made allowances for each other. Their characters
had been tested and had stood the test. Affection, love, was not to
them a salient phenomenon in their relations. Habit had inevitably dulled its glitter. It was like a flavouring, scarce remarked;
but had it been absent, how they would have turned from that
dish!

Samuel never, or hardly ever, set himself to meditate upon the
problem whether or not life had come up to his expectations. But
he had, at times, strange sensations which he did not analyse, and
which approached nearer to ecstasy than any feeling of Constance's. Thus, when he was in one of his dark furies, molten within and black without, the sudden thought of his wife's unalterable benignant calm, which nothing could overthrow, might
strike him into a wondering cold. For him she was astoundingly feminine. She would put flowers on the mantelpiece, and then,
hours afterwards, in the middle of a meal, ask him unexpectedly
what he thought of her 'garden'; and he gradually divined that a
perfunctory reply left her unsatisfied; she wanted a genuine
opinion; a genuine opinion mattered to her. Fancy calling flowers
on a mantelpiece a 'garden'! How charming, how childlike! Then
she had a way, on Sunday mornings, when she descended to the
parlour all ready for chapel, of shutting the door at the foot of the
stairs with a little bang, shaking herself, and turning round
swiftly as if for his inspection, as if saying: 'Well, what about this?
Will this do?' A phenomenon always associated in his mind with

the smell of kid gloves! Invariably she asked him about the colours and cut of her dresses. Would he prefer this, or that? He could not take such questions seriously until one day he happened to hint, merely hint, that he was not a thorough-going admirer of a certain new dress – it was her first new dress after the definite abandonment of crinolines. She never wore it again. He thought she was not serious at first, and remonstrated against a joke being carried too far. She said: 'It's not a bit of use you talking, I shan't wear it again.' And then he so far appreciated her seriousness as to refrain, by discretion, from any comment. The incident affected him for days. It flattered him; it thrilled him; but it baffled him. Strange that a woman subject to such caprices should be so sagacious, capable, and utterly reliable as Constance was! For the practical and commonsense side of her eternally compelled his admiration. The very first example of it – her insistence that the simultaneous absence of both of them from the shop for half an hour or an hour twice a day would not mean the immediate downfall of the business – had remained in his mind ever since. Had she not been obstinate – in her benevolent way – against the old superstition which he had acquired from his employers, they might have been eating separately to that day. Then her handling of her mother during the months of the siege of Paris, when Mrs Baines was convinced that her sinful daughter was in hourly danger of death, had been extraordinarily fine, he considered. And the sequel, a card for Constance's birthday, had completely justified her attitude.

Sometimes some blundering fool would jovially exclaim to them:

'What about that baby?'

Or a woman would remark quietly: 'I often feel sorry you've no children.'

And they would answer that really they did not know what they would do if there was a baby. What with the shop and one thing or another . . . ! And they were quite sincere.

IV

It is remarkable what a little thing will draw even the most regular and serious people from the deep groove of their habits. One

morning in March, a boneshaker, an affair on two equal wooden
wheels joined by a bar of iron, in the middle of which was a
wooden saddle, disturbed the gravity of St Luke's Square. True, it
was probably the first boneshaker that had ever attacked the
gravity of St Luke's Square. It came out of the shop of Daniel
Povey, the confectioner and baker, and Samuel Povey's celebrated cousin, in Boulton Terrace. Boulton Terrace formed nearly
a right angle with the Baines premises, and at the corner of the
angle Wedgwood Street and King Street left the Square. The
boneshaker was brought forth by Dick Povey, the only son of
Daniel, now aged eleven years, under the superintendence of his
father, and the Square soon perceived that Dick had a natural
talent for breaking-in an untrained boneshaker. After a few
attempts he could remain on the back of the machine for at least
ten yards, and his feats had the effect of endowing St Luke's
Square with the attractiveness of a circus. Samuel Povey watched
with candid interest from the ambush of his door, while the
unfortunate young lady assistants, though aware of the performance that was going on, dared not stir from the stove. Samuel was
tremendously tempted to sally out boldly, and chat with his
cousin about the toy; he had surely a better right to do so than any
other tradesman in the Square, since he was of the family; but his
diffidence prevented him from moving. Presently Daniel Povey
and Dick went to the top of the Square with the machine,
opposite Holl's, and Dick, being carefully installed in the saddle,
essayed to descend the gentle paven slopes of the Square. He
failed time after time; the machine had an astonishing way of
turning round, running uphill, and then lying calmly on its side.
At this point of Dick's life-history every shop-door in the Square
was occupied by an audience. At last the boneshaker displayed
less unwillingness to obey, and lo! in a moment Dick was riding
down the Square, and the spectators held their breath as if he had
been Blondin[8] crossing Niagara. Every second he ought to have
fallen off, but he contrived to keep upright. Already he had
accomplished twenty yards – thirty yards! It was a miracle that he
was performing! The transit continued, and seemed to occupy
hours. And then a faint hope rose in the breast of the watchers
that the prodigy might arrive at the bottom of the Square. His

speed was increasing with his 'nack'. But the Square was enormous, boundless. Samuel Povey gazed at the approaching phenomenon, as a bird at a serpent, with bulging, beady eyes. The child's speed went on increasing and his path grew straighter. Yes, he would arrive; he would do it! Samuel Povey involuntarily lifted one leg in his nervous tension. And now the hope that Dick would arrive became a fear, as his pace grew still more rapid. Everybody lifted one leg, and gaped. And the intrepid child surged on, and, finally victorious, crashed into the pavement in front of Samuel at the rate of quite six miles an hour.

Samuel picked him up, unscathed. And somehow this picking up of Dick invested Samuel with importance, gave him a share in the glory of the feat itself.

Daniel Povey came running and joyous. 'Not so bad for a start, eh?' exclaimed the great Daniel. Though by no means a simple man, his pride in his offspring sometimes made him a little naïve.

Father and son explained the machine to Samuel, Dick incessantly repeating the exceedingly strange truth that if you felt you were falling to your right you must turn to your right and *vice versa*. Samuel found himself suddenly admitted, as it were, to the inner fellowship of the boneshaker, exalted above the rest of the Square. In another adventure more thrilling events occurred. The fair-haired Dick was one of those dangerous, frenzied madcaps who are born without fear. The secret of the machine had been revealed to him in his recent transit, and he was silently determining to surpass himself. Precariously balanced, he descended the Square again, frowning hard, his teeth set, and actually managed to swerve into King Street. Constance, in the parlour, saw an incomprehensible winged thing fly past the window. The cousins Povey sounded an alarm and protest and ran in pursuit; for the gradient of King Street is, in the strict sense, steep. Half-way down King Street Dick was travelling at twenty miles an hour, and heading straight for the church, as though he meant to disestablish it and perish. The main gate of the churchyard was open, and that affrighting child, with a lunatic's luck, whizzed safely through the portals into God's acre. The cousins Povey discovered him lying on a green grave, clothed in pride. His first words were: 'Dad, did you pick my cap up?' The symbolism of the amazing ride did not escape the Square; indeed, it was much discussed.

This incident led to a friendship between the cousins. They formed a habit of meeting in the Square for a chat. The meetings were the subject of comment, for Samuel's relations with the greater Daniel had always been of the most distant. It was understood that Samuel disapproved of Mrs Daniel Povey even more than the majority of people disapproved of her. Mrs Daniel Povey, however, was away from home; probably, had she not been, Samuel would not even have gone to the length of joining Daniel on the neutral ground of the open Square. But having once broken the ice, Samuel was glad to be on terms of growing intimacy with his cousin. The friendship flattered him, for Daniel, despite his wife, was a figure in a world larger than Samuel's; moreover, it consecrated his position as the equal of no matter what tradesman (apprentice though he had been), and also he genuinely liked and admired Daniel, rather to his own astonishment.

Everyone liked Daniel Povey; he was a favourite among all ranks. The leading confectioner, a member of the Local Board, and a sidesman at St Luke's, he was, and had been for twenty-five years, very prominent in the town. He was a tall, handsome man, with a trimmed, greying beard, a jolly smile, and a flashing, dark eye. His good humour seemed to be permanent. He had dignity without the slightest stiffness; he was welcomed by his equals and frankly adored by his inferiors. He ought to have been Chief Bailiff, for he was rich enough; but there intervened a mysterious obstacle between Daniel Povey and the supreme honour, a scarcely tangible impediment which could not be definitely stated. He was capable, honest, industrious, successful, and an excellent speaker; and if he did not belong to the austerer section of society, if, for example, he thought nothing of dropping into the Tiger for a glass of beer, or of using an oath occasionally, or of telling a facetious story – well, in a busy, broad-minded town of thirty thousand inhabitants, such proclivities are no bar whatever to perfect esteem. But – how is one to phrase it without wronging Daniel Povey? He was entirely moral; his views were unexceptionable. The truth is that, for the ruling classes of Bursley, Daniel

Povey was just a little too fanatical a worshipper of the god Pan.
He was one of the remnant who had kept alive the great Pan
tradition from the days of the Regency through the vast, arid
Victorian expanse of years. The flighty character of his wife was
regarded by many as a judgement upon him for the robust
Rabelaisianism of his more private conversation, for his frank
interest in, his eternal preoccupation with, aspects of life and
human activity which, though essential to the divine purpose, are
not openly recognized as such – even by Daniel Poveys. It was not
a question of his conduct; it was a question of the cast of his mind.
If it did not explain his friendship with the rector of St Luke's, it
explained his departure from the Primitive Methodist connexion,
to which the Poveys as a family had belonged since Primitive
Methodism was created in Turnhill in 1807.

Daniel Povey had a way of assuming that every male was
boiling over with interest in the sacred cult of Pan. The assumption, though sometimes causing inconvenience at first, usually
conquered by virtue of its inherent truthfulness. Thus it fell out
with Samuel. Samuel had not suspected that Pan had silken cords
to draw him. He had always averted his eyes from the god – that
is to say, within reason. Yet now Daniel, on perhaps a couple of
fine mornings a week, in full Square, with Fan sitting behind on
the cold stones, and Mr Critchlow ironic at his door in a long
white apron, would entertain Samuel Povey for half an hour with
Pan's most intimate lore, and Samuel Povey would not blench.
He would, on the contrary, stand up to Daniel like a little man,
and pretend with all his might to be, potentially, a perfect
arch-priest of the god. Daniel taught him a lot; turned over the
page of life for him, as it were, and, showing the reverse side,
seemed to say: 'You were missing all that.' Samuel gazed upwards at the handsome long nose and rich lips of his elder cousin,
so experienced, so agreeable, so renowned, so esteemed, so
philosophic, and admitted to himself that he had lived to the age
of forty in a state of comparative boobyism. And then he would
gaze downwards at the faint patch of flour on Daniel's right leg,
and conceive that life was, and must be, life.

Not many weeks after his initiation into the cult he was startled
by Constance's preoccupied face one evening. Now, a husband of

six years' standing, to whom it has not happened to become a
father, is not easily startled by such a face as Constance wore.
Years ago he had frequently been startled, had frequently lived in
suspense for a few days. But he had long since grown impervious
to these alarms. And now he was startled again – but as a man
may be startled who is not altogether surprised at being startled.
And seven endless days passed, and Samuel and Constance
glanced at each other like guilty things, whose secret refuses to be
kept. Then three more days passed, and another three. Then
Samuel Povey remarked, in a firm, masculine, fact-fronting
tone:

'Oh, there's no doubt about it!'

And they glanced at each other like conspirators who have
lighted a fuse and cannot take refuge in flight. Their eyes said
continually, with a delicious, an enchanting mixture of ingenuous modesty and fearful joy:

'Well, we've gone and done it!'

There it was, the incredible, incomprehensible future – coming!

Samuel had never correctly imagined the matter of its herald-
ing. He had imagined in his early simplicity that one day Constance, blushing, might put her mouth to his ear and whisper –
something positive. It had not occurred in the least like that. But
things are so obstinately, so incurably unsentimental.

'I think we ought to drive over and tell mother, on Sunday,'
said Constance.

His impulse was to reply, in his grand, offhand style: 'Oh, a
letter will do!'

But he checked himself and said, with careful deference: 'You
think that will be better than writing?'

All was changed. He braced every fibre to meet destiny, and to
help Constance to meet it.

The weather threatened on Sunday. He went to Axe without
Constance. His cousin drove him there in a dog-cart, and he
announced that he should walk home, as the exercise would do
him good. During the drive Daniel, in whom he had not confided,
chattered as usual, and Samuel pretended to listen with the same
attitude as usual; but secretly he despised Daniel for a man who

has got something not of the first importance on the brain. His perspective was truer than Daniel's.

He walked home, as he had decided, over the wavy moorland of the county dreaming in the heart of England. Night fell on him in mid-career, and he was tired. But the earth, as it whirled through naked space, whirled up the moon for him, and he pressed on at a good speed. A wind from Arabia wandering cooled his face. And at last, over the brow of Toft End, he saw suddenly the Five Towns a-twinkle on their little hills down in the vast amphitheatre. And one of those lamps was Constance's lamp – one, somewhere. He lived, then. He entered into the shadow of nature. The mysteries made him solemn. What! A boneshaker, his cousin, and then this!

'Well, I'm damned! Well, I'm damned!' he kept repeating, he who never swore.

CHAPTER 3: *Cyril*

I

Constance stood at the large, many-paned window in the parlour. She was stouter. Although always plump, her figure had been comely, with a neat, well-marked waist. But now the shapeliness had gone; the waist-line no longer existed, and there were no more crinolines to create it artificially. An observer not under the charm of her face might have been excused for calling her fat and lumpy. The face, grave, kind, and expectant, with its radiant, fresh cheeks, and the rounded softness of its curves, atoned for the figure. She was nearly twenty-nine years of age.

It was late in October. In Wedgwood Street, next to Boulton Terrace, all the little brown houses had been pulled down to make room for a palatial covered market, whose foundations were then being dug. This destruction exposed a vast area of sky to the north-east. A great dark cloud with an untidy edge rose massively out of the depths and curtained off the tender blue of approaching dusk; while in the west, behind Constance, the sun was setting in calm and gorgeous melancholy on the Thursday hush of the town. It was one of those afternoons which gather up all the sadness of the moving earth and transform it into beauty.

Samuel Povey turned the corner from Wedgwood Street, and crossed King Street obliquely to the front-door, which Constance opened. He seemed tired and anxious.

'Well?' demanded Constance, as he entered.

'She's no better. There's no getting away from it, she's worse. I should have stayed, only I knew you'd be worrying. So I caught the three-fifty.'

'How is that Mrs Gilchrist shaping as a nurse?'

'She's very good,' said Samuel, with conviction. 'Very good!'

'What a blessing! I suppose you didn't happen to see the doctor?'

'Yes, I did.'

'What did he say to you?'

Samuel gave a deprecating gesture. 'Didn't say anything particular. With dropsy, at that stage, you know . . .'

Constance had returned to the window, her expectancy apparently unappeased.

'I don't like the look of that cloud,' she murmured.

'What! Are they out still?' Samuel inquired, taking off his overcoat.

'Here they are!' cried Constance. Her features suddenly transfigured, she sprang to the door, pulled it open, and descended the steps.

A perambulator was being rapidly pushed up the slope by a breathless girl.

'Amy,' Constance gently protested, 'I told you not to venture far.'

'I hurried all I could, mum, soon as I seed that cloud,' the girl puffed, with the air of one who is seriously thankful to have escaped a great disaster.

Constance dived into the recesses of the perambulator and extricated from its cocoon the centre of the universe, and scrutinized him with quiet passion, and then rushed with him into the house, though not a drop of rain had yet fallen.

'Precious!' exclaimed Amy, in ecstasy, her young virginal eyes following him till he disappeared. Then she wheeled away the perambulator, which now had no more value or interest than an egg-shell. It was necessary to take it right round to the Brougham Street yard entrance, past the front of the closed shop.

Constance sat down on the horsehair sofa and hugged and kissed her prize before removing his bonnet.

'Here's Daddy!' she said to him as if imparting strange and rapturous tidings. 'Here's Daddy come back from hanging up his coat in the passage! Daddy rubbing his hands!' And then, with a swift transition of voice and features: 'Do look at him, Sam!'

Samuel, preoccupied, stooped forward. 'Oh, you little scoundrel! Oh, you little scoundrel!' he greeted the baby, advancing his finger towards the baby's nose.

The baby, who had hitherto maintained a passive indifference to external phenomena, lifted elbows and toes, blew bubbles from his tiny mouth, and stared at the finger with the most ravishing, roguish smile, as though saying: 'I know that great sticking-out limb, and there is a joke about it which no one but me can see, and which is my secret joy that you shall never share.'

'Tea ready?' Samuel asked, resuming his gravity and his ordinary pose.

'You must give the girl time to take her things off,' said Constance. 'We'll have the table drawn away from the fire, and baby can lie on his shawl on the hearthrug while we're having tea.' Then to the baby, in rapture: 'And play with his toys; all his nice, nice toys!'

'You know Miss Insull is staying for tea?'

Constance, her head bent over the baby, who formed a white patch on her comfortable brown frock, nodded without speaking.

Samuel Povey, walking to and fro, began to enter into details of his hasty journey to Axe. Old Mrs Baines, having beheld her grandson, was preparing to quit this world. Never again would she exclaim, in her brusque tone of genial ruthlessness: 'Fiddle-sticks!' The situation was very difficult and distressing, for Constance could not leave her baby, and she would not, until the last urgency, run the risks of a journey with him to Axe. He was being weaned. In any case Constance could not have undertaken the nursing of her mother. A nurse had to be found. Mr Povey had

discovered one in the person of Mrs Gilchrist, the second wife of a
farmer at Malpas in Cheshire, whose first wife had been a sister of
the late John Baines. All the credit of Mrs Gilchrist was due to
Samuel Povey. Mrs Baines fretted seriously about Sophia, who
had given no sign of life for a very long time. Mr Povey went to
Manchester and ascertained definitely from the relatives of Scales
that nothing was known of the pair. He did not go to Manchester
especially on this errand. About once in three weeks, on Tues-
days, he had to visit the Manchester warehouses; but the tracking
of Scales's relatives cost him so much trouble and time that,
curiously, he came to believe that he had gone to Manchester one
Tuesday for no other end. Although he was very busy indeed in
the shop, he flew over to Axe and back whenever he possibly
could to the neglect of his affairs. He was glad to do all that was in
his power; even if he had not done it graciously his sensitive,
tyrannic conscience would have forced him to do it. But nevertheless he felt rather virtuous, and worry and fatigue and loss of sleep
intensified this sense of virtue.

'So that if there is any sudden change they will telegraph,' he
finished to Constance.

She raised her head. The words, clinching what had led up to
them, drew her from her dream and she saw, for a moment, her
mother in an agony.

'But you don't surely mean –?' she began, trying to disperse the
painful vision as unjustified by the facts.

'My dear girl,' said Samuel, with head singing, and hot eyes,
and a consciousness of high tension in every nerve of his body, 'I
simply mean that if there's any sudden change they will telegraph.'

While they had tea, Samuel sitting opposite to his wife, and
Miss Insull nearly against the wall (owing to the moving of the
table), the baby rolled about on the hearthrug, which had been
covered with a large soft woollen shawl, originally the property
of his great-grandmother. He had no cares, no responsibilities.
The shawl was so vast that he could not clearly distinguish
objects beyond its confines. On it lay an indiarubber ball, an
indiarubber doll, a rattle, and Fan. He vaguely recollected all four
items, with their respective properties. The fire also was an old

friend. He had occasionally tried to touch it, but a high bright fence always came in between. For ten months he had never spent a day without making experiments on this shifting universe in which he alone remained firm and stationary. The experiments were chiefly conducted out of idle amusement, but he was serious on the subject of food. Lately the behaviour of the universe in regard to his food had somewhat perplexed him, had indeed annoyed him. However, he was of a forgetful, happy disposition, and so long as the universe continued to fulfil its sole end as a machinery for the satisfaction, somehow, of his imperious desires, he was not inclined to remonstrate. He gazed at the flames and laughed, and laughed because he had laughed. He pushed the ball away and wriggled after it, and captured it with the assurance of practice. He tried to swallow the doll, and it was not until he had tried several times to swallow it that he remembered the failure of previous efforts and philosophically desisted. He rolled with a fearful shock, arms and legs in the air, against the mountainous flank of that mammoth Fan, and clutched at Fan's ear. The whole mass of Fan upheaved and vanished from his view, and was instantly forgotten by him. He seized the doll and tried to swallow it, and repeated the exhibition of his skill with the ball. Then he saw the fire again and laughed. And so he existed for centuries: no responsibilities, no appetites; and the shawl was vast. Terrific operations went on over his head. Giants moved to and fro. Great vessels were carried off and great books were brought and deep voices rumbled regularly in the spaces beyond the shawl. But he remained oblivious. At last he became aware that a face was looking down at his. He recognized it, and immediately an uncomfortable sensation in his stomach disturbed him; he tolerated it for fifty years or so, and then he gave a little cry. Life had resumed its seriousness.

'Black alpaca. B quality. Width 20, t.a. 22 yards,' Miss Insull read out of a great book. She and Mr Povey were checking stock.

And Mr Povey responded. 'Black alpaca B quality. Width 20, t.a. 22 yards. It wants ten minutes yet.' He had glanced at the clock.

'Does it?' said Constance, well knowing that it wanted ten minutes.

The baby did not guess that a high invisible god named Samuel Povey, whom nothing escaped, and who could do everything at once, was controlling his universe from an inconceivable distance. On the contrary, the baby was crying to himself. There is no God.

His weaning had reached a stage at which a baby really does not know what will happen next. The annoyance had begun exactly three months after his first tooth, such being the rule of the gods, and it had grown more and more disconcerting. No sooner did he accustom himself to a new phenomenon than it mysteriously ceased, and an old one took its place which he had utterly forgotten. This afternoon his mother nursed him, but not until she had foolishly attempted to divert him from the seriousness of life by means of gewgaws of which he was sick. Still, once at her rich breast, he forgave and forgot all. He preferred her simple natural breast to more modern inventions. And he had no shame, no modesty. Nor had his mother. It was an indecent carouse at which his father and Miss Insull had to assist. But his father had shame. His father would have preferred that, as Miss Insull had kindly offered to stop and work on Thursday afternoon, and as the shop was chilly, the due rotation should have brought the bottle round at half-past five o'clock, and not the mother's breast. He was a self-conscious parent, rather apologetic to the world, rather apt to stand off and pretend that he had nothing to do with the affair; and he genuinely disliked that anybody should witness the intimate scene of *his* wife feeding *his* baby. Especially Miss Insull, that prim, dark, moustached spinster! He would not have called it an outrage on Miss Insull, to force her to witness the scene, but his idea approached within sight of the word.

Constance blandly offered herself to the child, with the unconscious primitive savagery of a young mother, and as the baby fed, thoughts of her own mother flitted to and fro ceaselessly like vague shapes over the deep sea of content which filled her mind. This illness of her mother's was abnormal, and the baby was now, for the first time perhaps, entirely normal in her consciousness. The baby was something which could be disturbed, not something which did disturb. What a change! What a change that had seemed impossible until its full accomplishment!

For months before the birth, she had glimpsed at nights and in other silent hours the tremendous upset. She had not allowed herself to be silly in advance; by temperament she was too sagacious, too well balanced for that; but she had had fitful instants of terror, when solid ground seemed to sink away from her, and imagination shook at what faced her. Instants only! Usually she could play the comedy of sensible calmness to almost perfection. Then the appointed time drew nigh. And still she smiled, and Samuel smiled. But the preparations, meticulous, intricate, revolutionary, belied their smiles. The intense resolve to keep Mrs Baines, by methods scrupulous or unscrupulous, away from Bursley until all was over, belied their smiles. And then the first pains, sharp, shocking, cruel, heralds of torture! But when they had withdrawn, she smiled again, palely. Then she was in bed, full of the sensation that the whole house was inverted and disorganized, hopelessly. And the doctor came into the room. She smiled at the doctor apologetically, foolishly, as if saying: 'We all come to it. Here I am.' She was calm without. Oh, but what a prey of abject fear within! 'I am at the edge of the precipice,' her thought ran; 'in a moment I shall be over.' And then the pains – not the heralds but the shattering army, endless, increasing in terror as they thundered across her. Yet she could think quite clearly: 'Now I'm in the middle of it. This is *it*, the horror that I have not dared to look at. My life's in the balance. I may never get up again. All has at last come to pass. It seemed as if it would never come, as if this thing could not happen to *me*. But at last it has come to pass!'

Ah! Someone put the twisted end of a towel into her hand again – she had loosed it; and she pulled, pulled, enough to break cables. And then she shrieked. It was for pity. It was for someone to help her, at any rate to take notice of her. She was dying. Her soul was leaving her. And she was alone, panic-stricken, in the midst of a cataclysm a thousand times surpassing all that she had imagined of sickening horror. 'I cannot endure this,' she thought passionately. 'It is impossible that I should be asked to endure this!' And then she wept; beaten, terrorized, smashed and riven.

No common sense now! No wise calmness now! No self-respect now! Why, not even a woman now! Nothing but a kind of animalized victim! And then the supreme endless spasm, during which she gave up the ghost and bade good-bye to her very self . . .

She was lying quite comfortable in the soft bed; idle, silly; happiness forming like a thin crust over the lava of her anguish and her fright. And by her side was the soul that had fought its way out of her, ruthlessly; the secret disturber revealed to the light of morning. Curious to look at! Not like any baby that she had ever seen; red, creased, brutish! But – for some reason that she did not examine – she folded it in an immense tenderness.

Sam was by the bed, away from her eyes. She was so comfortable and silly that she could not move her head nor even ask him to come round to her eyes. She had to wait till he came.

In the afternoon the doctor returned, and astounded her by saying that hers had been an ideal confinement. She was too weary to rebuke him for a senseless, blind, callous old man. But she knew what she knew. 'No one will ever guess,' she thought, 'no one ever can guess, what I've been through! Talk as you like. I *know*, now.'

Gradually she had resumed cognizance of her household, perceiving that it was demoralized from top to bottom, and that when the time came to begin upon it she would not be able to settle where to begin, even supposing that the baby were not there to monopolize her attention. The task appalled her. Then she wanted to get up. Then she got up. What a blow to self-confidence! She went back to bed like a little scared rabbit to its hole, glad, glad to be on the soft pillows again. She said: 'Yet the time must come when I shall be downstairs, and walking about and meeting people, and cooking and superintending the millinery.' Well, it did come – except that she had to renounce the millinery to Miss Insull – but it was not the same. No, different! The baby pushed everything else on to another plane. He was a terrific intruder; not one minute of her old daily life was left; he made no compromise whatever. If she turned away her gaze from him he might pop off into eternity and leave her.

And now she was calmly and sensibly giving him suck in

presence of Miss Insull. She was used to his importance, to the
fragility of his organism, to waking twice every night, to being
fat. She was strong again. The convulsive twitching that for six
months had worried her repose, had quite disappeared. The state
of being a mother was normal, and the baby was so normal that
she could not conceive the house without him.

All in ten months!

When the baby was installed in his cot for the night, she came
downstairs and found Miss Insull and Samuel still working, and
harder than ever, but at addition sums now. She sat down,
leaving the door open at the foot of the stairs. She had embroidery
in hand: a cap. And while Miss Insull and Samuel combined
pounds, shillings, and pence, whispering at great speed, she bent
over the delicate, intimate, wasteful handiwork, drawing the
needle with slow exactitude. Then she would raise her head and
listen.

'Excuse me,' said Miss Insull, 'I think I hear baby crying.'

'And two are eight and three ar eleven. He must cry,' said Mr
Povey, rapidly, without looking up.

The baby's parents did not make a practice of discussing their
domestic existence even with Miss Insull; but Constance had to
justify herself as a mother.

'I've made perfectly sure he's comfortable,' said Constance.
'He's only crying because he fancies he's neglected. And we think
he can't begin too early to learn.'

'How right you are!' said Miss Insull. 'Two and carry three.'

That distant, feeble, querulous, pitiful cry continued obstinately. It continued for thirty minutes. Constance could not proceed
with her work. The cry disintegrated her will, dissolved her hard
sagacity.

Without a word she crept upstairs, having carefully deposed
the cap on her rocking-chair.

Mr Povey hesitated a moment and then bounded up after her,
startling Fan. He shut the door on Miss Insull, but Fan was too
quick for him. He saw Constance with her hand on the bedroom
door.

'My dear girl,' he protested, holding himself in. 'Now what *are*
you going to do?'

'I'm just listening,' said Constance.

'Do be reasonable and come downstairs.'

He spoke in a low voice, scarcely masking his nervous irritation, and tiptoed along the corridor towards her and up the two steps past the gas-burner. Fan followed, wagging her tail expectantly.

'Suppose he's not well?' Constance suggested.

'Pshaw!' Mr Povey exclaimed contemptuously. 'You remember what happened last night and what you said!'

They argued, subduing their tones to the false semblance of good-will, there in the closeness of the corridor. Fan, deceived, ceased to wag her tail and then trotted away. The baby's cry, behind the door, rose to a mysterious despairing howl, which had such an effect on Constance's heart that she could have walked through fire to reach the baby. But Mr Povey's will held her. And he rebelled, angry, hurt, resentful. Common sense, the ideal of mutual forbearance, had winged away from the excited pair. It would have assuredly ended in a quarrel with Samuel glaring at her in black fury from the other side of a bottomless chasm, had not Miss Insull most surprisingly burst up the stairs.

Mr Povey turned to face her, swallowing his emotion.

'A telegram!' said Miss Insull. 'The postmaster brought it down himself –'

'What? Mr Derry?' asked Samuel, opening the telegram with an affectation of majesty.

'Yes. He said it was too late for delivery by rights. But as it seemed very important . . .'

Samuel scanned it and nodded gravely; then gave it to his wife. Tears came into her eyes.

'I'll get Cousin Daniel to drive me over at once,' said Samuel, master of himself and of the situation.

'Wouldn't it be better to hire?' Constance suggested. She had a prejudice against Daniel.

Mr Povey shook his head. 'He offered,' he replied. 'I can't refuse his offer.'

'Put your thick overcoat on, dear,' said Constance, in a dream, descending with him.

'I hope it isn't –' Miss Insull stopped.

'Yes, it is, Miss Insull,' said Samuel deliberately.

In less than a minute he was gone.

Constance ran upstairs. But the cry had ceased. She turned the door-knob softly, slowly, and crept into the chamber. A night-light made large shadows among the heavy mahogany and the crimson, tasselled rep in the close-curtained room. And between the bed and the ottoman (on which lay Samuel's newly-bought family Bible) the cot loomed in the shadows. She picked up the night-light and stole round the bed. Yes, he had decided to fall asleep. The hazard of death afar off had just defeated his devilish obstinacy. Fate had bested him. How marvellously soft and delicate that tear-stained cheek; how frail that tiny, tiny clenched hand! In Constance grief and joy were mystically united.

II

The drawing-room was full of visitors, in frocks of ceremony. The old drawing-room, but newly and massively arranged with the finest Victorian furniture from dead Aunt Harriet's house at Axe; two 'Canterburys', a large bookcase, a splendid scintillant table solid beyond lifting, intricately tortured chairs and armchairs! The original furniture of the drawing-room was now down in the parlour, making it grand. All the house breathed opulence; it was gorged with quiet, restrained expensiveness; the least considerable objects, in the most modest corners, were what Mrs Baines would have termed 'good'. Constance and Samuel had half of all Aunt Harriet's money and half of Mrs Baines's; the other half was accumulating for a hypothetical Sophia, Mr Critchlow being the trustee. The business continued to flourish. People knew that Samuel Povey was buying houses. Yet Samuel and Constance had not made friends; they had not, in the Five Towns phrase, 'branched out socially', though they had very meetly branched out on subscription lists. They kept themselves to themselves (emphasizing the preposition). These guests were not their guests; they were the guests of Cyril.

He had been named Samuel because Constance would have him named after his father, and Cyril because his father secretly despised the name of Samuel; and he was called Cyril; 'Master Cyril', by Amy, definite successor to Maggie. His mother's thoughts were on Cyril as long as she was awake. His father, when not planning Cyril's welfare, was earning money whose unique object could be nothing but Cyril's welfare. Cyril was the pivot of the house; every desire ended somewhere in Cyril. The shop existed now solely for him. And those houses that Samuel bought by private treaty, or with a shamefaced air at auctions — somehow they were aimed at Cyril. Samuel and Constance had ceased to be self-justifying beings; they never thought of themselves save as the parents of Cyril.

They realized this by no means fully. Had they been accused of monomania they would have smiled the smile of people confident in their common sense and their mental balance. Nevertheless, they were monomaniacs. Instinctively they concealed the fact as much as possible. They never admitted it even to themselves. Samuel, indeed, would often say: 'That child is not everybody. That child must be kept in his place.' Constance was always teaching him consideration for his father as the most important person in the household. Samuel was always teaching him consideration for his mother as the most important person in the household. Nothing was left undone to convince him that he was a cipher, a nonentity, who ought to be very glad to be alive. But he knew all about his importance. He knew that the entire town was his. He knew that his parents were deceiving themselves. Even when he was punished he well knew that it was because he was so important. He never imparted any portion of this knowledge to his parents; a primeval wisdom prompted him to retain it strictly in his own bosom.

He was four and a half years old, dark, like his father; handsome like his aunt, and tall for his age; not one of his features resembled a feature of his mother's, but sometimes he 'had her look'. From the capricious production of inarticulate sounds, and then a few monosyllables that described concrete things and obvious desires, he had gradually acquired an astonishing idiomatic command over the most difficult of Teutonic languages; there was nothing that he could not say. He could walk and run, was full of exact knowledge about God, and entertained no doubt concerning the special partiality of a minor deity called Jesus towards himself.

Now, this party was his mother's invention and scheme. His
father, after flouting it, had said that if it was to be done at all, it
should be done well, and had brought to the doing all his
organizing skill. Cyril had accepted it at first – merely accepted it;
but, as the day approached and the preparations increased in
magnitude, he had come to look on it with favour, then with
enthusiasm. His father having taken him to Daniel Povey's
opposite, to choose cakes, he had shown, by his solemn
and fastidious waverings, how seriously he regarded the
affair.

Of course it had to occur on a Thursday afternoon. The season
was summer, suitable for pale and fragile toilettes. And the eight
children who sat round Aunt Harriet's great table glittered like
the sun. Not Constance's specially provided napkins could hide
that wealth and profusion of white lace and stitchery. Never in
after-life are the genteel children of the Five Towns so richly clad
as at the age of four or five years. Weeks of labour, thousands of
cubic feet of gas, whole nights stolen from repose, eyesight, and
general health, will disappear into the manufacture of a single
frock that accidental jam may ruin in ten seconds. Thus it was in
those old days; and thus it is today. Cyril's guests ranged in years
from four to six; they were chiefly older than their host; this was a
pity, it impaired his importance; but up to four years a child's
sense of propriety, even of common decency, is altogether too
unreliable for a respectable party.

Round about the outskirts of the table were the elders, ladies
the majority; they also in their best, for they had to meet each
other. Constance displayed a new dress, of crimson silk; after
having mourned for her mother she had definitely abandoned the
black which, by reason of her duties in the shop, she had
constantly worn from the age of sixteen to within a few months of
Cyril's birth; she never went into the shop now, except casually,
on brief visits of inspection. She was still fat; the destroyer of her
figure sat at the head of the table. Samuel kept close to her; he was
the only male, until Mr Critchlow astonishingly arrived; among
the company Mr Critchlow had a grand-niece. Samuel, if not in
his best, was certainly not in his everyday suit. With his large
frilled shirt-front, and small black tie, and his little black beard

and dark face over that, he looked very nervous and self-conscious. He had not the habit of entertaining. Nor had Constance; but her benevolence ever bubbling up to the calm surface of her personality made self-consciousness impossible for her. Miss Insull was also present, in shop-black, 'to help'. Lastly there was Amy, now as the years passed slowly assuming the character of a faithful retainer, though she was only twenty-three. An ugly, abrupt, downright girl, with convenient notions of pleasure! For she would rise early and retire late in order to contrive an hour to go out with Master Cyril; and to be allowed to put Master Cyril to bed was, really, her highest bliss.

All these elders were continually inserting arms into the fringe of fluffy children that surrounded the heaped table; removing dangerous spoons out of cups into saucers, replacing plates, passing cakes, spreading jam, whispering consolations, explanations, and sage counsel. Mr Critchlow, snow-white now but unbent, remarked that there was 'a pretty cackle', and he sniffed. Although the window was slightly open, the air was heavy with the natural human odour which young children transpire. More than one mother, pressing her nose into a lacy mass, to whisper, inhaled that pleasant perfume with a voluptuous thrill.

Cyril, while attending steadily to the demands of his body, was in a mood which approached the ideal. Proud and radiant, he combined urbanity with a certain fine condescension. His bright eyes, and his manner of scraping up jam with a spoon, said: 'I am the king of this party. This party is solely in my honour. I know that. We all know it. Still, I will pretend that we are equals, you and I.' He talked about his picture-books to a young woman on his right named Jennie, aged four, pale, pretty, the belle in fact, and Mr Critchlow's grand-niece. The boy's attractiveness was indisputable; he could put on quite an aristocratic air. It was the most delicious sight to see them, Cyril and Jennie, so soft and delicate, so infantile on their piles of cushions and books, with their white socks and black shoes dangling far distant from the carpet; and yet so old, so self-contained! And they were merely an epitome of the whole table. The whole table was bathed in the charm and mystery of young years, of helpless fragility, gentle forms, timid elegance, unshamed instincts, and waking souls.

Constance and Samuel were very satisfied; full of praise for other people's children, but with the reserve that of course Cyril was *hors concours*. They both really did believe, at that moment, that Cyril was, in some subtle way which they felt but could not define, superior to all other infants.

Someone, some officious relative of a visitor, began to pass a certain cake which had brown walls, a roof of coco-nut icing, and a yellow body studded with crimson globules. Not a conspicuously gorgeous cake, not a cake to which a catholic child would be likely to attach particular importance; a good, average cake! Who could have guessed that it stood, in Cyril's esteem, as the cake of cakes? He had insisted on his father buying it at Cousin Daniel's, and perhaps Samuel ought to have divined that for Cyril that cake was the gleam that an ardent spirit would follow through the wilderness. Samuel, however, was not a careful observer, and seriously lacked imagination. Constance knew only that Cyril had mentioned the cake once or twice. Now by the hazard of destiny that cake found much favour, helped into popularity as it was by the blundering officious relative who, not dreaming what volcano she was treading on, urged its merits with simpering enthusiasm. One boy took two slices, a slice in each hand; he happened to be the visitor of whom the cake distributor was a relative, and she protested; she expressed the shock she suffered. Whereupon both Constance and Samuel sprang forward and swore with angelic smiles that nothing could be more perfect than the propriety of that dear little fellow taking two slices of that cake. It was this hullaballoo that drew Cyril's attention to the evanescence of the cake of cakes. His face at once changed from calm pride to a dreadful anxiety. His eyes bulged out. His tiny mouth grew and grew, like a mouth in a nightmare. He was no longer human; he was a cake-eating tiger being balked of his prey. Nobody noticed him. The officious fool of a woman persuaded Jennie to take the last slice of the cake, which was quite a thin slice.

Then everyone simultaneously noticed Cyril, for he gave a yell. It was not the cry of a despairing soul who sees his beautiful irridescent dream shattered at his feet; it was the cry of the strong, masterful spirit, furious. He turned upon Jennie, sobbing, and snatched at her cake. Unaccustomed to such behaviour from hosts, and being besides a haughty put-you-in-your-place beauty of the future, Jennie defended her cake. After all, it was not she who had taken two slices at once. Cyril hit her in the eye, and then crammed most of the slice of cake into his enormous mouth. He could not swallow it, nor even masticate it, for his throat was rigid and tight. So the cake projected from his red lips, and big tears watered it. The most awful mess you can conceive! Jennie wept loudly, and one or two others joined her in sympathy, but the rest went on eating tranquilly, unmoved by the horror which transfixed their elders.

A host to snatch food from a guest! A host to strike a guest! A gentleman to strike a lady!

Constance whipped up Cyril from his chair and flew with him to his own room (once Samuel's), where she smacked him on the arm and told him he was a very, very naughty boy and that she didn't know what his father would say. She took the food out of his disgusting mouth – or as much of it as she could get at – and then she left him, on the bed. Miss Jennie was still in tears when, blushing scarlet, and trying to smile, Constance returned to the drawing-room. Jennie would not be appeased. Happily Jennie's mother (being about to present Jennie with a little brother – she hoped) was not present. Miss Insull had promised to see Jennie home, and it was decided that she should go. Mr Critchlow, in high sardonic spirits, said that he would go too; the three departed together, heavily charged with Constance's love and apologies. Then all pretended, and said loudly, that what had happened was naught, that such things were always happening at children's parties. And visitors' relatives asseverated that Cyril was a perfect darling and that really Mrs Povey must not . . .

But the attempt to keep up appearance was a failure.

The Methuselah of visitors, a gaping girl of nearly eight years, walked across the room to where Constance was standing, and said in a loud, confidential, fatuous voice:

'Cyril *has* been a rude boy, hasn't he, Mrs Povey?'

The clumsiness of children is sometimes tragic.

Later, there was a trickling stream of fluffy bundles down the crooked stairs and through the parlour and so out into King

Street. And Constance received many compliments and sundry appeals that darling Cyril should be forgiven.

'I thought you said that boy was in his bedroom,' said Samuel to Constance, coming into the parlour when the last guest had gone. Each avoided the other's eyes.

'Yes, isn't he?'

'No.'

'The little jockey!' ('Jockey', an essay in the playful, towards making light of the jockey's sin!) 'I expect he's been in search of Amy.'

She went to the top of the kitchen stairs and called out: 'Amy, is Master Cyril down there?'

'Master Cyril? No, mum. But he was in the parlour a bit ago, after the first and second lot had gone. I told him to go upstairs and be a good boy.'

Not for a few moments did the suspicion enter the minds of Samuel and Constance that Cyril might be missing, that the house might not contain Cyril. But having once entered, the suspicion became a certainty. Amy, cross-examined, burst into sudden tears, admitting that the side-door might have been open when, having sped 'the second lot', she criminally left Cyril alone in the parlour in order to descend for an instant to her kitchen. Dusk was gathering. Amy saw the defenceless innocent wandering about all night in the deserted streets of a great city. A similar vision with precise details of canals, tramcar-wheels, and cellar-flaps, disturbed Constance. Samuel said that anyhow he could not have got far, that someone was bound to remark and recognize him, and restore him. 'Yes, of course,' thought sensible Constance. 'But supposing —'

They all three searched the entire house again. Then, in the drawing-room (which was in a sad condition of anti-climax) Amy exclaimed:

'Eh, master! There's town-crier crossing the Square. Hadn't ye better have him cried?'

'Run out and stop him,' Constance commanded.

And Amy flew.

Samuel and the aged town-crier parleyed at the side-door, the women in the background.

'I canna' cry him without my bell,' drawled the crier, stroking his shabby uniform. 'My Bell's at wum [home]. I mun go and fetch my bell. Yo' write it down on a bit o' paper for me so as I can read it, and I'll foot off for my bell. Folk wouldna' listen to me if I hadna' gotten my bell.'

Thus was Cyril cried.

'Amy,' said Constance, when she and the girl were alone, 'there's no use in you standing blubbering there. Get to work and clear up that drawing-room, do! The child is sure to be found soon. Your master's gone out, too.'

Brave words! Constance aided in the drawing-room and kitchen. Theirs was the woman's lot in a great crisis. Plates have always to be washed.

Very shortly afterwards, Samuel Povey came into the kitchen by the underground passage which led past the two cellars to the yard and to Brougham Street. He was carrying in his arms an obscene black mass. This mass was Cyril, once white.

Constance screamed. She was at liberty to give way to her feelings, because Amy happened to be upstairs.

'Stand away!' cried Mr Povey. 'He isn't fit to touch.'

And Mr Povey made as if to pass directly onwards, ignoring the mother.

'Wherever did you find him?'

'I found him in the far cellar,' said Mr Povey, compelled to stop, after all. 'He was down there with me yesterday, and it just occurred to me that he might have gone there again.'

'What! All in the dark?'

'He'd lighted a candle, if you please! I'd left a candlestick and a box of matches handy because I hadn't finished that shelving.'

'Well!' Constance murmured. 'I can't think how ever he dared go there all alone!'

'Can't you?' said Mr Povey, cynically. 'I can. He simply did it to frighten us.'

'Oh, Cyril!' Constance admonished the child. 'Cyril!'

The child showed no emotion. His face was an enigma. It might have hidden sullenness or mere callous indifference, or a perfect unconsciousness of sin.

'Give him to me,' said Constance.

'I'll look after him this evening,' said Samuel, grimly.

'But you can't wash him,' said Constance, her relief yielding to apprehension.

'Why not?' demanded Mr Povey. And he moved off.

'But Sam —'

'I'll look after him, I tell you!' Mr Povey repeated, threateningly.

'But what are you going to do?' Constance asked with fear.

'Well,' said Mr Povey, 'has this sort of thing got to be dealt with, or hasn't it?' He departed upstairs.

Constance overtook him at the door of Cyril's bedroom.

Mr Povey did not wait for her to speak. His eyes were blazing.

'See here!' he admonished her cruelly. 'You get away downstairs, mother!'

And he disappeared into the bedroom with his vile and helpless victim.

A moment later he popped his head out of the door. Constance was disobeying him. He stepped into the passage and shut the door so that Cyril should not hear.

'Now please do as I tell you,' he hissed at his wife. 'Don't let's have a scene, please.'

She descended, slowly, weeping. And Mr Povey retired again to the place of execution.

Amy nearly fell on the top of Constance with a final tray of things from the drawing-room. And Constance had to tell the girl that Cyril was found. Somehow she could not resist the instinct to tell her also that the master had the affair in hand. Amy then wept.

After about an hour Mr Povey at last reappeared. Constance was trying to count silver teaspoons in the parlour.

'He's in bed now,' said Mr Povey, with a magnificent attempt to be nonchalant. 'You mustn't go near him.'

'But have you washed him?' Constance whimpered.

'I've washed him,' replied the astonishing Mr Povey.

'What have you done to him?'

'I've punished him, of course,' said Mr Povey, like a god who is above human weaknesses. 'What did you expect me to do? *Someone* had to do it.'

Constance wiped her eyes with the edge of the white apron which she was wearing over her new silk dress. She surrendered; she accepted the situation; she made the best of it. And all the evening was spent in dismally and horribly pretending that their hearts were beating as one. Mr Povey's elaborate, cheeky kindliness was extremely painful.

They went to bed, and in their bedroom Constance, as she stood close to Samuel, suddenly dropped the pretence, and with eyes and voice of anguish said:

'You must let me look at him.'

They faced each other. For a brief instant Cyril did not exist for Constance. Samuel alone obsessed her, and yet Samuel seemed a strange, unknown man. It was in Constance's life one of those crises when the human soul seems to be on the very brink of mysterious and disconcerting cognitions, and then the wave recedes as inexplicably as it surged up.

'Why, of course!' said Mr Povey, turning away lightly, as though to imply that she was making tragedies out of nothing.

She gave an involuntary gesture of almost childish relief.

Cyril slept calmly. It was a triumph for Mr Povey.

Constance could not sleep. As she lay darkly awake by her husband, her secret being seemed to be a-quiver with emotion. Not exactly sorrow; not exactly joy; an emotion more elemental than these! A sensation of the intensity of her life in that hour; troubling, anxious, yet not sad! She said that Samuel was quite right, quite right. And then she said that the poor little thing wasn't yet five years old, and that it was monstrous. The two had to be reconciled. And they never could be reconciled. Always she would be between them, to reconcile them, and to be crushed by their impact. Always she would have to bear the burden of both of them. There could be no ease for her, no surcease from a tremendous preoccupation and responsibility. She could not change Samuel; besides, he was right! And though Cyril was not yet five, she felt that she could not change Cyril either. He was just as unchangeable as a growing plant. The thought of her mother and Sophia did not present itself to her; she felt, however, somewhat as Mrs Baines had felt on historic occasions; but, being more softly kind, younger, and less chafed by destiny, she was conscious of no bitterness, conscious rather of a solemn blessedness.

CHAPTER 4: *Crime*

I

'Now, Master Cyril,' Amy protested, 'will you leave that fire alone? It's not you that can mend my fires.'

A boy of nine, great and heavy for his years, with a full face and very short hair, bent over the smoking grate. It was about five minutes to eight on a chilly morning after Easter. Amy, hastily clad in blue, with a rough brown apron, was setting the breakfast table. The boy turned his head, still bending.

'Shut up, Ame,' he replied, smiling. Life being short, he usually called her Ame when they were alone together. 'Or I'll catch you one in the eye with the poker.'

'You ought to be ashamed of yourself,' said Amy. 'And you know your mother told you to wash your feet this morning, and you haven't done. Fine clothes is all very well, but —'

'Who says I haven't washed my feet?' asked Cyril, guiltily.

Amy's mention of fine clothes referred to the fact that he was that morning wearing his Sunday suit for the first time on a week-day.

'I say you haven't,' said Amy.

She was more than three times his age still, but they had been treating each other as intellectual equals for years.

'And how do you know?' asked Cyril, tired of the fire.

'I know,' said Amy.

'Well, you just don't, then!' said Cyril. 'And what about *your* feet? I should be sorry to see your feet, Ame.'

Amy was excusably annoyed. She tossed her head. 'My feet are as clean as yours any day,' she said. 'And I shall tell your mother.'

But he would not leave her feet alone, and there ensued one of those endless monotonous altercations on a single theme which occur so often between intellectual equals when one is a young son of the house and the other an established servant who adores him. Refined minds would have found the talk disgusting, but the sentiment of disgust seemed to be unknown to either of the wranglers. At last, when Amy by superior tactics had cornered him, Cyril said suddenly:

'Oh, go to hell!'

Amy banged down the spoon for the bacon gravy. 'Now I shall tell your mother. Mark my words, this time I *shall* tell your mother.'

Cyril felt that in truth he had gone rather far. He was perfectly sure that Amy would not tell his mother. And yet, supposing that by some freak of her nature she did! The consequences would be unutterable; the consequences would more than extinguish his private glory in the use of such a dashing word. So he laughed, a rather silly, giggling laugh, to reassure himself.

'You daren't,' he said.

'Daren't I?' she said grimly. 'You'll see. *I* don't know where you learn! It fair beats me. But it isn't Amy Bates as is going to be sworn at. As soon as ever your mother comes into this room!'

The door at the foot of the stairs creaked and Constance came into the room. She was wearing a dress of magenta merino, and a gold chain descended from her neck over her rich bosom. She had scarcely aged in five years. It would have been surprising if she had altered much, for the years had passed over her head at an incredible rate. To her it appeared only a few months since Cyril's first and last party.

'Are you all ready, my pet? Let me look at you.' Constance greeted the boy with her usual bright, soft energy.

Cyril glanced at Amy, who averted her head, putting spoons into three saucers.

'Yes, mother,' he replied in a new voice.

'Did you do what I told you?'

'Yes, mother,' he said simply.

'That's right.'

Amy made a faint noise with her lips, and departed.

He was saved once more. He said to himself that never again would he permit his soul to be disturbed by any threat of 'old Ame's'.

Constance's hand descended into her pocket and drew out a hard paper packet, which she clapped on to her son's head.

'Oh, mother!' He pretended that she had hurt him, and then he opened the packet. It contained Congleton butterscotch, reputed a harmless sweetmeat.

'Good!' he cried, 'good! Oh! Thanks, mother.'

'Now don't begin eating them at once.'

'Just one, mother.'

'No! And how often have I told you to keep your feet off that fender. See how it's bent. And it's nobody but you.'

'Sorry.'

'It's no use being sorry if you persist in doing it.'

'Oh, mother, I had such a funny dream!'

They chatted until Amy came up the stairs with tea and bacon. The fire had developed from black to clear red.

'Run and tell father that breakfast is ready.'

After a little delay a spectacled man of fifty, short and stoutish, with grey hair and a small beard half grey and half black, entered from the shop. Samuel had certainly very much aged, especially in his gestures, which, however, were still quick. He sat down at once – his wife and son were already seated – and served the bacon with the rapid assurance of one who needs not to inquire about tastes and appetites. Not a word was said, except a brief grace by Samuel. But there was no restraint. Samuel had a mild, benignant air. Constance's eyes were a fountain of cheerfulness. The boy sat between them and ate steadily.

Mysterious creature, this child, mysteriously growing and growing in the house! To his mother he was a delicious joy at all times save when he disobeyed his father. But now for quite a considerable period there had been no serious collision. The boy seemed to be acquiring virtue as well as sense. And really he was charming. So big, truly enormous (everyone remarked on it), and yet graceful, lithe, with a smile that could ravish. And he was distinguished in his bearing. Without depreciating Samuel in her faithful heart, Constance saw plainly the singular differences between Samuel and the boy. Save that he was dark, and that his father's 'dangerous look' came into those childish eyes occasionally, Cyril had now scarcely any obvious resemblance to his

father. He was a Baines. This naturally deepened Constance's
family pride. Yes, he was mysterious to Constance, though
probably not more so that any other boy to any other parent. He
was equally mysterious to Samuel, but otherwise Mr Povey had
learned to regard him in the light of a parcel which he was always
attempting to wrap up in a piece of paper imperceptibly too
small. When he successfully covered the parcel at one corner it
burst out at another, and this went on for ever, and he could never
get the string on. Nevertheless, Mr Povey had unabated confidence in his skill as a parcel-wrapper. The boy was strangely
subtle at times, but then at times he was astoundingly ingenuous, and then his dodges would not deceive the dullest. Mr
Povey knew himself more than a match for his son. He was
proud of him because he regarded him as not an ordinary boy;
he took it as a matter of course that his boy should not be an
ordinary boy. He never, or very rarely, praised Cyril. Cyril
thought of his father as a man who, in response to any request,
always began by answering with a thoughtful, serious 'No, I'm
afraid not.'

'So you haven't lost your appetite!' his mother commented.

Cyril grinned. 'Did you expect me to, mother?'

'Let me see,' said Samuel, as if vaguely recalling an unimportant fact. 'It's today you begin to go to school, isn't it?'

'I wish father wouldn't be such a chump!' Cyril reflected. And,
considering that this commencement of school (real school, not a
girls' school, as once) had been the chief topic in the house for
days, weeks; considering that it now occupied and filled all
hearts, Cyril's reflection was excusable.

'Now, there's one thing you must always remember, my boy,'
said Mr Povey. 'Promptness. Never be late either in going
to school or in coming home. And in order that you may
have no excuse' – Mr Povey pressed on the word 'excuse',
as though condemning Cyril in advance – 'here's something
for you!' He said the last words quickly, with a sort of modest
shame.

It was a silver watch and chain.

Cyril was staggered. So also was Constance, for Mr Povey
could keep his own counsel. At long intervals he would prove,

thus, that he was a mighty soul, capable of sublime deeds. The watch was the unique flowering of Mr Povey's profound but harsh affection. It lay on the table like a miracle. This day was a great day, a supremely exciting day in Cyril's history, and not less so in the history of his parents.

The watch killed its owner's appetite dead.

Routine was ignored that morning. Father did not go back into the shop. At length the moment came when father put on his hat and overcoat to take Cyril, and Cyril's watch and satchel, to the Endowed School, which had quarters in the Wedgwood Institution close by. A solemn departure, and Cyril could not pretend by his demeanour that it was not! Constance desired to kiss him, but refrained. He would not have liked it. She watched them from the window. Cyril was nearly as tall as his father; that is to say, not nearly as tall, but creeping up his father's shoulder. She felt that the eyes of the town must be on the pair. She was very happy, and nervous.

At dinner-time a triumph seemed probable, and at tea-time, when Cyril came home under a mortar-board hat and with a satchel full of new books and a head full of new ideas, the triumph was actually and definitely achieved. He had been put into the third form, and he announced that he should soon be at the top of it. He was enchanted with the life of school; he liked the other boys, and it appeared that the other boys liked him. The fact was that, with a new silver watch and a packet of sweets, he had begun his new career in the most advantageous circumstances. Moreoever, he possessed qualities which ensured success at school. He was big, and easy, with a captivating smile and a marked aptitude to learn those things which boys insist on teaching to their new comrades. He had muscle, a brave demeanour, and no conceit.

During tea the parlour began to accustom itself to a new vocabulary, containing such words as 'fellows', 'kept in', 'lines', 'rot', 'recess', 'jolly'. To some of these words the parents, especially Mr Povey, had an instinct to object, but they could not object, somehow they did not seem to get an opportunity to object; they were carried away on the torrent, and after all, their excitement and pleasure in the exceeding romantic novelty of existence were just as intense and nearly as ingenuous as their son's.

He demonstrated that unless he was allowed to stay up later than aforetime he would not be able to do his home-work, and hence would not keep that place in the school to which his talents entitled him. Mr Povey suggested, but only with half a heart, that he should get up earlier in the morning. The proposal fell flat. Everybody knew and admitted that nothing save the scorpions of absolute necessity, or a tremendous occasion, such as that particular morning's, would drive Cyril from his bed until the smell of bacon rose to him from the kitchen. The parlour table was consecrated to his lessons. It became generally known that 'Cyril was doing his lessons'. His father scanned the new text-books while Cyril condescendingly explained to him that all others were superseded and worthless. His father contrived to maintain an air of preserving his mental equilibrium, but not his mother; she gave it up, she who till that day had under his father's direction taught him nearly all that he knew, and Cyril passed above her into regions of knowledge where she made no pretence of being able to follow him.

When the lessons were done, and Cyril had wiped his fingers on bits of blotting paper, and his father had expressed qualified approval and had gone into the shop, Cyril said to his mother, with that delicious hesitation which overtook him sometimes:

'Mother.'

'Well, my pet.'

'I want you to do something for me.'

'Well, what is it?'

'No, you must promise.'

'I'll do it if I can.'

'But you *can*. It isn't doing. It's *not* doing.'

'Come, Cyril, out with it.'

'I don't want you to come in and look at me after I'm asleep any more.'

'But, you silly boy, what difference can it make to you if you're asleep?'

'I don't want you to. It's like as if I was a baby. You'll *have* to stop doing it some day, and so you may as well stop now.'

It was thus he meant to turn his back on his youth.

She smiled. She was incomprehensibly happy. She continued to smile.

'Now you'll promise, won't you, mother?'

She rapped him on the head with her thimble, lovingly. He took the gesture for consent.

'You are a baby,' she murmured.

'Now I shall *trust* you,' he said, ignoring this. 'Say "honour bright".'

'Honour bright.'

With what a long caress her eyes followed him, as he went up to bed on his great sturdy legs! She was thankful that school had not contaminated her adorable innocent. If she could have been Ame for twenty-four hours, she perhaps would not have hesitated to put butter into his mouth lest it should melt.

Mr Povey and Constance talked late and low that night. They could neither of them sleep; they had little desire to sleep. Constance's face said to her husband: 'I've always stuck up for that boy, in spite of your severities, and you see how right I was!' And Mr Povey's face said: 'You see now the brilliant success of my system. You see how my educational theories have justified themselves. Never been to a school before, except that wretched little dame's school, and he goes practically straight to the top of the third form – at nine years of age!' They discussed his future. There could be no sign of lunacy in discussing his future up to a certain point, but each felt that to discuss the ultimate career of a child nine years old would not be the act of a sensible parent; only foolish parents would be so fond. Yet each was dying to discuss his ultimate career. Constance yielded first to the temptation, as became her. Mr Povey scoffed, and then, to humour Constance, yielded also. The matter was soon fairly on the carpet. Constance was relieved to find that Mr Povey had no thought whatever of putting Cyril in the shop. No; Mr Povey did not desire to chop wood with a razor. Their son must and would ascend. Doctor! Solicitor! Barrister! Not barrister – barrister was fantastic. When they had argued for about half an hour Mr Povey intimated suddenly that the conversation was unworthy of their practical common sense, and went to sleep.

II

Nobody really thought that this almost ideal condition of things would persist: an enterprise commenced in such glory must surely traverse periods of difficulty and even of temporary disaster. But no! Cyril seemed to be made specially for school. Before Mr Povey and Constance had quite accustomed themselves to being the parents of 'a great lad', before Cyril had broken the glass of his miraculous watch more than once, the summer term had come to an end and there arrived the excitations of the prize-giving, as it was called; for at that epoch the smaller schools had not found the effrontery to dub the breaking-up ceremony a 'speech-day'. This prize-giving furnished a particular joy to Mr and Mrs Povey. Although the prizes were notoriously few in number – partly to add to their significance, and partly to diminish their cost (the foundation was poor) – Cyril won a prize, a box of geometrical instruments of precision; also he reached the top of his form, and was marked for promotion to the formidable Fourth. Samuel and Constance were bidden to the large hall of the Wedgwood Institution of a summer afternoon, and they saw the whole Board of Governors raised on a rostrum, and in the middle, in front of what he referred to, in his aristocratic London accent, as 'a beggarly array of rewards' the aged and celebrated Sir Thomas Wilbraham Wilbraham, ex-M.P., last respectable member of his ancient line. And Sir Thomas gave the box of instruments to Cyril, and shook hands with him. And everybody was very well dressed. Samuel, who had never attended anything but a National School, recalled the simple rigours of his own boyhood, and swelled. For certainly, of all the parents present he was among the richest. When, in the informal promiscuities which followed the prize distribution, Cyril joined his father and mother, sheepishly they duly did their best to make light of his achievements, and failed. The walls of the hall were covered with specimens of the pupils' skill, and the headmaster was observed to direct the attention of the mighty to a map done by Cyril. Of course it was a map of Ireland, Ireland being the map chosen by every map-drawing schoolboy who is free to choose. For a third-form boy it was considered a masterpiece. In the shading of the mountains Cyril was already a prodigy. Never, it was said, had the Macgillycuddy Reeks been indicated by a member of that school with a more amazing subtle refinement than by the young Povey. From a proper pride in themselves, from a proper fear lest they should be secretly accused of ostentation by other parents, Samuel and Constance did not go near that map. For the rest, they had lived with it for weeks, and Samuel (who, after all, was determined not to be dirt under his son's feet) had scratched a blot from it with a completeness that defied inquisitive examination.

The fame of this map, added to the box of compasses and Cyril's own desire, pointed to an artistic career. Cyril had always drawn and daubed, and the drawing-master of the Endowed School, who was also headmaster of the Art School, had suggested that the youth should attend the Art School one night a week. Samuel, however, would not listen to the idea; Cyril was too young. It is true that Cyril was too young, but Samuel's real objection was to Cyril's going out alone in the evening. On that he was adamant.

The Governors had recently made the discovery that a sports department was necessary to a good school, and had rented a field for cricket, football, and rounders up at Bleakridge, an innovation which demonstrated that the town was moving with the rapid times. In June this field was open after school hours till eight p.m. as well as on Saturdays. The Squire learnt that Cyril had a talent for cricket, and Cyril wished to practise in the evenings, and was quite ready to bind himself with Bible oaths to rise at no matter what hour in the morning for the purpose of home lessons. He scarcely expected his father to say 'Yes', as his father never did say 'Yes', but he was obliged to ask. Samuel nonplussed him by replying that on fine evenings, when he could spare time from the shop, he would go up to Bleakridge with his son. Cyril did not like this in the least. Still, it might be tried. One evening they went, actually, in the new steam-car which had superseded the old horse-cars, and which travelled all the way to Longshaw, a place that Cyril had only heard of. Samuel talked of the games played in the Five Towns in his day, of the Titanic sport of prison-bars, when the team of one 'bank' went forth to the challenge of another 'bank', preceded by a drum-and-fife band, and when, in the heat of the chase, a man might jump into the canal to escape his pursuer; Samuel had never played at cricket.

Samuel, with a very young grandson of Fan (deceased), sat in dignity on the grass and watched his cricketer for an hour and a half (while Constance kept an eye on the shop and superintended its closing). Samuel then conducted Cyril home again. Two days later the father of his own accord offered to repeat the experience. Cyril refused. Disagreeable insinuations that he was a baby in arms had been made at school in the meantime.

Nevertheless, in other directions Cyril sometimes surprisingly conquered. For instance, he came home one day with the information that a dog that was not a bull-terrier was not worth calling a dog. Fan's grandson had been carried off in earliest prime by a chicken-bone that had pierced his vitals, and Cyril did indeed persuade his father to buy a bull-terrier. The animal was a superlative of forbidding ugliness, but father and son vied with each other in stern critical praise of his surpassing beauty, and Constance, from good nature, joined in the pretence. He was called Lion, and the shop, after one or two untoward episodes, was absolutely closed to him.

But the most striking of Cyril's successes had to do with the question of the annual holiday. He spoke of the sea soon after becoming a schoolboy. It appeared that his complete ignorance of the sea prejudicially affected him at school. Further, he had always loved the sea; he had drawn hundreds of three-masted ships with studding-sails set, and knew the difference between a brig and a brigantine. When he first said: 'I say, mother, why can't we go to Llandudno instead of Buxton this year?' his mother thought he was out of his senses. For the idea of going to any place other than Buxton was inconceivable! Had they not always been to Buxton? What would their landlady say? How could they ever look her in the face again? Besides . . . well . . . ! They went to Llandudno, rather scared, and hardly knowing how the change had come about. But they went. And it was the force of Cyril's will, Cyril the theoretic cipher, that took them.

III

The removal of the Endowed School to more commodious premises in the shape of Shawport Hall, an ancient mansion with fifty rooms and five acres of land round about it, was not a change that quite pleased Samuel or Constance. They admitted the hygienic advantages, but Shawport Hall was three-quarters of a mile distant from St Luke's Square – in the hollow that separates Bursley from its suburb of Hillport; whereas the Wedgwood Institution was scarcely a minute away. It was as if Cyril, when he set off to Shawport Hall of a morning, passed out of their sphere of influence. He was leagues off, doing they knew not what. Further, his dinner-hour was cut short by the extra time needed for the journey to and fro, and he arrived late for tea; it may be said that he often arrived very late for tea; the whole machinery of the meal was disturbed. These matters seemed to Samuel and Constance to be of tremendous import, seemed to threaten the very foundations of existence. Then they grew accustomed to the new order, and wondered sometimes, when they passed the Wedgwood Institution and the insalubrious Cock Yard – once sole playground of the boys – that the school could ever have 'managed' in the narrow quarters once allotted to it.

Cyril, though constantly successful at school, a rising man, an infallible bringer-home of excellent reports, and a regular taker of prizes, became gradually less satisfactory in the house. He was 'kept in' occasionally, and although his father pretended to hold that to be kept in was to slur the honour of a spotless family, Cyril continued to be kept in; a hardened sinner, lost to shame. But this was not the worst. The worst undoubtedly was that Cyril was 'getting rough'. No definite accusation could be laid against him; the offence was general, vague, everlasting; it was in all he did and said, in every gesture and movement. He shouted, whistled, sang, stamped, stumbled, lunged. He omitted such empty rites as saying 'Yes' or 'Please', and wiping his nose. He replied gruffly and nonchalantly to polite questions, or he didn't reply until the questions were repeated, and even then with a 'lost' air that was not genuine. His shoe-laces were a sad sight, and his finger-nails no sight at all for a decent woman; his hair was as rough as his

conduct; hardly at the pistol's point could he be forced to put oil
on it. In brief, he was no longer the nice boy that he used to be. He
had unmistakably deteriorated. Grievous! But what can you
expect when *your* boy is obliged, month after month and year
after year, to associate with other boys? After all, he was a *good*
boy, said Constance, often to herself and now and then to
Samuel. For Constance, his charm was eternally renewed. His
smile, his frequent ingenuousness, his funny self-conscious gesture when he wanted to 'get round' her – these characteristics
remained; and his pure heart remained; she could read that in his
eyes. Samuel was inimical to his tastes for sports and his triumphs
therein. But Constance had pride in all that. She liked to feel him
and to gaze at him, and to smell that faint, uncleanly odour of
sweat that hung in his clothes.

   In this condition he reached the advanced age of thirteen. And
his parents, who despite their notion of themselves as wideawake parents were a simple pair, never suspected that his heart,
conceived to be still pure, had become a crawling, horrible mass
of corruption.

   One day the headmaster called at the shop. Now, to see a
headmaster walking about the town during school-hours is a
startling spectacle, and is apt to give you the same uncanny
sensation as when, alone in a room, you think you see something
move which ought not to move. Mr Povey was startled. Mr Povey
had a thumping within his breast as he rubbed his hands and
drew the headmaster to the private corner where his desk was.
'What can I do for you today? he almost said to the headmaster.
But he did not say it. The boot was emphatically not on that leg.
The headmaster talked to Mr Povey in tones carefully low, for
about a quarter of an hour, and then he closed the interview. Mr
Povey escorted him across the shop and the headmaster said with
ordinary loudness: 'Of course it's nothing. But my experience is
that it's just as well to be on the safe side, and I thought I'd tell
you. Forewarned is forearmed. I have other parents to see.' They
shook hands at the door. Then Mr Povey stepped out on the
pavement and, in front of the whole Square, detained an unwilling headmaster for quite another minute.

   His face was deeply flushed as he returned into the shop. The assistants bent closer over their work. He did not instantly rush into the parlour and communicate with Constance. He had dropped into a way of conducting many operations by his own unaided brain. His confidence in his skill had increased with years. Further, at the back of his mind, there had established itself a vision of Mr Povey as the seat of government and of Constance and Cyril as a sort of permanent opposition. He would not have admitted that he saw such a vision, for he was utterly loyal to his wife; but it was there. This unconfessed vision was one of several causes which had contributed to intensify his inherent tendency towards Machiavellianism and secretiveness. He said nothing to Constance, nothing to Cyril; but, happening to encounter Amy in the showroom, he was inspired to interrogate her sharply. The result was that they descended to the cellar together, Amy weeping. Amy was commanded to hold her tongue. And as she went in mortal fear of Mr Povey she did hold her tongue.

Nothing occurred for several days. And then one morning – it was Constance's birthday: children are nearly always horribly unlucky in their choice of days for sin – Mr Povey, having executed mysterious movements in the shop after Cyril's departure to school, jammed his hat on his head and ran forth in pursuit of Cyril, whom he intercepted with two other boys, at the corner of Oldcastle Street and Acre Passage.

Cyril stood as if turned into salt. 'Come back home!' said Mr Povey, grimly; and for the sake of the other boys: 'Please.'

'But I shall be late for school, father,' Cyril weakly urged.

'Never mind.'

They passed through the shop together, causing a terrific concealed emotion, and then they did violence to Constance by appearing in the parlour. Constance was engaged in cutting straws and ribbons to make a straw-frame for a water-colour drawing of a moss-rose which her pure-hearted son had given her as a birthday present.

'Why – what –?' she exclaimed. She said no more at the moment because she was sure, from the faces of her men, that the time was big with fearful events.

'Take your satchel off,' Mr Povey ordered coldly. 'And your mortar-board,' he added with a peculiar intonation, as if glad thus to prove that Cyril was one of those rude boys who have to be told to take their hats off in a room.

'Whatever's amiss?' Constance murmured under her breath, as Cyril obeyed the command. 'Whatever's amiss?'

Mr Povey made no immediate answer. He was in charge of these proceedings, and was very anxious to conduct them with dignity and with complete effectiveness. Little fat man over fifty, with a wizened face, grey-haired and grey-bearded, he was as nervous as a youth. His heart beat furiously. And Constance, the portly matron who would never see forty again, was just as nervous as a girl. Cyril had gone very white. All three felt physically sick.

'What money have you got in your pockets?' Mr Povey demanded, as a commencement.

Cyril, who had no opportunity to prepare his case, offered no reply.

'You heard what I said,' Mr Povey thundered.

'I've got three-halfpence,' Cyril murmured glumly, looking down at the floor. His lower lip seemed to hang precariously away from his gums.

'Where did you get that from?'

'It's part of what mother gave me,' said the boy.

'I did give him a threepenny bit last week,' Constance put in guiltily. 'It was a long time since he had had any money.'

'If you gave it him, that's enough,' said Mr Povey quickly, and to the boy: 'That's all you've got?'

'Yes, father,' said the boy.

'You're sure?'

'Yes, father.'

Cyril was playing a hazardous game for the highest stakes, and under grave disadvantages; and he acted for the best. He guarded his own interests as well as he could.

Mr Povey found himself obliged to take a serious risk. 'Empty your pockets, then.'

Cyril, perceiving that he had lost that particular game, emptied his pockets.

'Cyril,' said Constance, 'how often have I told you to change your handkerchiefs oftener! Just look at this!'

Astonishing creature! She was in the seventh hell of sick apprehension, and yet she said that!

After the handkerchief emerged the common schoolboy stock of articles useful and magic, and then, last, a silver florin!

Mr Povey felt relief.

'Oh, Cyril!' whimpered Constance.

'Give it your mother,' said Mr Povey.

The boy stepped forward awkwardly, and Constance, weeping, took the coin.

'Please look at it, mother,' said Mr Povey. 'And tell me if there's a cross marked on it.'

Constance's tears blurred the coin. She had to wipe her eyes.

'Yes,' she whispered faintly. 'There's something on it.'

'I thought so,' said Mr Povey. 'Where did you steal it from?' he demanded.

'Out of the till,' answered Cyril.

'Have you ever stolen anything out of the till before?'

'Yes.'

'Yes, what.'

'Yes, father.'

'Take your hands out of your pockets and stand up straight, if you can. How often?'

'I – I don't know, father.'

'I blame myself,' said Mr Povey, frankly. 'I blame myself. The till ought always to be locked. All tills ought always to be locked. But we felt we could trust the assistants. If anybody had told me that I ought not to trust you, if anybody had told me that my own son would be the thief, I should have – well, I don't know what I should have said!'

Mr Povey was quite justified in blaming himself. The fact was that the functioning of that till was a patriarchal survival, which he ought to have revolutionized, but which it had never occurred to him to revolutionize, so accustomed to it was he. In the time of John Baines, the till, with its three bowls, two for silver and one for copper (gold had never been put into it), was invariably unlocked. The person in charge of the shop took change from it for the assistants, or temporarily authorized an assistant to do so. Gold was kept in a small linen bag in a locked drawer of the desk.

The contents of the till were never checked by any system of book-keeping, as there was no system of book-keeping; when all transactions, whether in payment or receipt, are in cash – the Baineses never owed a penny save the quarterly wholesale accounts, which were discharged instantly to the travellers – a system of book-keeping is not indispensable. The till was situate immediately at the entrance to the shop from the house; it was in the darkest part of the shop, and the unfortunate Cyril had to pass it every day on his way to school. The thing was a perfect device for the manufacture of young criminals.

'And how have you been spending this money?' Mr Povey inquired.

Cyril's hands slipped into his pockets again. Then, noticing the lapse, he dragged them out.

'Sweets,' said he.

'Anything else?'

'Sweets and things.'

'Oh!' said Mr Povey. 'Well, now you can go down into the cinder-cellar and bring up here all the things there are in that little box in the corner. Off you go!'

And off went Cyril. He had to swagger through the kitchen.

'What did I tell you, Master Cyril?' Amy unwisely asked of him. 'You've copped it finely this time.'

'Copped' was a word which she had learned from Cyril.

'Go on, you old bitch!' Cyril growled.

As he returned from the cellar, Amy said angrily:

'I told you I should tell your father the next time you called me that, and I shall. You mark my words.'

'Cant! cant!' he retorted. 'Do you think I don't know who's been canting? Cant! cant!'

Upstairs in the parlour Samuel was explaining the matter to his wife. There had been a perfect epidemic of smoking in the school. The headmaster had discovered it and, he hoped, stamped it out. What had disturbed the headmaster far more than the smoking was the fact that a few boys had been found to possess somewhat costly pipes, cigar-holders, or cigarette-holders. The headmaster, wily, had not confiscated these articles; he had merely informed the parents concerned. In his opinion the articles came from one single source, a generous thief; he left the parents to ascertain which of them had brought a thief into the world.

Further information Mr Povey had culled from Amy, and there could remain no doubt that Cyril had been providing his chums with the utensils of smoking, the till supplying the means. He had told Amy that the things which he secreted in the cellar had been presented to him by blood-brothers. But Mr Povey did not believe that. Anyhow, he had marked every silver coin in the till for three nights, and had watched the till in the mornings from behind the merino-pile; and the florin on the parlour table spoke of his success as a detective.

Constance felt guilty on behalf of Cyril. As Mr Povey outlined his case she could not free herself from an entirely irrational sensation of sin; at any rate of special responsibility. Cyril seemed to be her boy and not Samuel's boy at all. She avoided her husband's glance. This was very odd.

Then Cyril returned, and his parents composed their faces and he deposited, next to the florin, a sham meerschaum pipe in a case, a tobacco-pouch, a cigar of which one end had been charred but the other not cut, and a half-empty packet of cigarettes without a label.

Nothing could be hid from Mr Povey. The details were distressing.

'So Cyril is a liar and a thief, to say nothing of this smoking!' Mr Povey concluded.

He spoke as if Cyril had invented strange and monstrous sins. But deep down in his heart a little voice was telling him, as regards the smoking, that *he* had set the example. Mr Baines had never smoked. Mr Critchlow never smoked. Only men like Daniel smoked.

Thus far Mr Povey had conducted the proceedings to his own satisfaction. He had proved the crime. He had made Cyril confess. The whole affair lay revealed. Well – what next? Cyril ought to have dissolved in repentance; something dramatic ought to have occurred. But Cyril simply stood with hanging, sulky head, and gave no sign of proper feeling.

Mr Povey considered that, until something did happen, he must improve the occasion.

'Here we have trade getting worse every day,' said he (it was true), 'and you are robbing your parents to make a beast of yourself, and corrupting your companions! I wonder your mother never smelt you!'

'I never dreamt of such a thing!' said Constance, grievously.

Besides, a young man clever enough to rob a till is usually clever enough to find out that the secret of safety in smoking is to use cachous and not to keep the stuff in your pockets a minute longer than you can help.

'There's no knowing how much money you have stolen,' said Mr Povey. 'A thief!'

If Cyril had stolen cakes, jam, string, cigars, Mr Povey would never have said 'thief' as he did say it. But money! Money was different. And a till was not a cupboard or a larder. A till was a till. Cyril had struck at the very basis of society.

'And on your mother's birthday!' Mr Povey said further.

'There's one thing I can do!' he said. 'I can burn all this. Built on lies! How dared you?'

And he pitched into the fire — not the apparatus of crime, but the water-colour drawing of a moss-rose and the straws and the blue ribbons for bows at the corners.

'How dared you?' he repeated.

'You never gave me any money,' Cyril muttered.

He thought the marking of coins a mean trick, and the dragging-in of bad trade and his mother's birthday roused a familiar devil that usually slept quietly in his breast.

'What's that you say?' Mr Povey almost shouted.

'You never gave me any money,' the devil repeated in a louder tone than Cyril had employed.

(It was true. But Cyril 'had only to ask', and he would have received all that was good for him.)

Mr Povey sprang up. Mr Povey also had a devil. The two devils gazed at each other for an instant; and then, noticing that Cyril's head was above Mr Povey's, the elder devil controlled itself. Mr Povey had suddenly had as much drama as he wanted.

'Get away to bed!' said he with dignity.

Cyril went, defiantly.

'He's to have nothing but bread and water, mother,' Mr Povey finished. He was, on the whole, pleased with himself.

Later in the day Constance reported, tearfully, that she had been up to Cyril and that Cyril had wept. Which was to Cyril's credit. But all felt that life could never be the same again. During the remainder of existence this unspeakable horror would lift its obscene form between them. Constance had never been so unhappy. Occasionally, when by herself she would rebel for a brief moment, as one rebels in secret against a mummery which one is obliged to treat seriously. 'After all,' she would whisper, 'suppose he *has* taken a few shillings out of the till! What then? What does it matter?' But these moods of moral insurrection against society and Mr Povey were very transitory. They were come and gone in a flash.

CHAPTER 5: *Another Crime*

I

One night – it was late in the afternoon of the same year, about six months after the tragedy of the florin – Samuel Povey was wakened up by a hand on his shoulder and a voice that whispered: 'Father!'

The thief and the liar was standing in his night-shirt by the bed. Samuel's sleepy eyes could just descry him in the thick gloom.

'What – what?' questioned the father, gradually coming to consciousness. 'What are you doing there?'

'I didn't want to wake mother up,' the boy whispered. 'There's someone been throwing dirt or something at our windows, and has been for a long time.'

'Eh, what?'

Samuel stared at the dim form of the thief and liar. The boy was tall, not in the least like a little boy; and yet, then, he seemed to his father as quite a little boy, a little 'thing' in a night-shirt, with childish gestures and childish inflections, and a childish, delicious, quaint anxiety not to disturb his mother, who had lately been deprived of sleep owing to an illness of Amy's which had demanded nursing. His father had not so perceived him for years. In that instant the conviction that Cyril was permanently unfit for human society finally expired in the father's mind. Time had already weakened it very considerably. The decision that, be Cyril what he might, the summer holiday must be taken as usual, had dealt it a fearful blow. And yet, though Samuel and Constance had grown so accustomed to the companionship of a criminal that they frequently lost memory of his guilt for long periods, nevertheless the convention of his leprosy had more or less persisted with Samuel until that moment: when it vanished with strange suddenness, to Samuel's conscious relief.

There was a rain of pellets on the window.

'Hear that?' demanded Cyril, whispering dramatically. 'And it's been like that on my window too.'

Samuel arose. 'Go back to your room!' he ordered in the same dramatic whisper; but not as father to son – rather as conspirator to conspirator.

Constance slept. They could hear her regular breathing.

Barefooted, the elderly gowned figure followed the younger, and one after the other they creaked down the two steps which separated Cyril's room from his parents'.

'Shut the door quietly!' said Samuel.

Cyril observed.

And then, having lighted Cyril's gas, Samuel drew the blind, unfastened the catch of the window, and began to open it with many precautions of silence. All the sashes in that house were difficult to manage. Cyril stood close to his father, shivering without knowing that he shivered, astonished only that his father had not told him to get back into bed at once. It was, beyond doubt, the proudest hour of Cyril's career. In addition to the mysterious circumstances of the night, there was in the situation that thrill which always communicates itself to a father and son when they are afoot together upon an enterprise unsuspected by the woman from whom their lives have no secrets.

Samuel put his head out of the window.

A man was standing there.

'That you, Samuel?' The voice came low.

'Yes,' replied Samuel, cautiously. 'It's not Cousin Daniel, is it?'

'I want ye,' said Daniel Povey curtly.

Samuel paused. 'I'll be down in a minute,' he said.

Cyril at length received the command to get back into bed at once.

'Whatever's up, father?' he asked joyously.

'I don't know. I must put some things on and go and see.'

He shut down the window on all the breezes that were pouring into the room.

'Now quick, before I turn the gas out!' he admonished, his hand on the gas-tap.

'You'll tell me in the morning, won't you, father?'

'Yes,' said Mr Povey, conquering his habitual impulse to say 'No'.

He crept back to the large bedroom to grope for clothes.

When, having descended to the parlour and lighted the gas there, he opened the side-door, expecting to let Cousin Daniel in, there was no sign of Cousin Daniel. Presently he saw a figure standing at the corner of the Square. He whistled – Samuel had a singular faculty of whistling, the envy of his son – and Daniel beckoned to him. He nearly extinguished the gas and then ran out, hatless. He was wearing most of his clothes, except his linen collar and neck-tie, and the collar of his coat was turned up.

Daniel advanced before him, without waiting, into the confectioner's shop opposite. Being part of the most modern building in the Square, Daniel's shop was provided with the new roll-down iron shutter, by means of which you closed your establishment with a motion similar to the winding of a large clock, instead of putting up twenty separate shutters one by one as in the sixteenth century. The little portal in the vast sheet of armour was ajar, and Daniel had passed into the gloom beyond. At the same moment a policeman came along on his beat, cutting off Mr Povey from Daniel.

'Good night, officer! Brrr!' said Mr Povey, gathering his dignity about him and holding himself as though it was part of his normal habit to take exercise bareheaded and collarless in St Luke's Square on cold November nights. He behaved so because, if Daniel had desired the services of a policeman, Daniel would of course have spoken to this one.

'Goo' night, sir,' said the policeman, after recognizing him.

'What time is it?' asked Samuel, bold.

'A quarter-past one, sir.'

The policeman, leaving Samuel at the little open door, went forward across the lamplit Square, and Samuel entered his cousin's shop.

Daniel Povey was standing behind the door, and as Samuel came in he shut the door with a startling sudden movement. Save for the twinkle of gas, the shop was in darkness. It had the empty appearance which a well-managed confectioner's and baker's always has at night. The large brass scales near the flour-bins glinted; and the glass cake-stands, with scarce a tart among them, also caught the faint flare of the gas.

'What's the matter, Daniel? Anything wrong?' Samuel asked, feeling boyish as he usually did in the presence of Daniel.

The well-favoured white-haired man seized him with one hand by the shoulder in a grip that convicted Samuel of frailty.

'Look here, Sam'l,' said he in his low, pleasant voice, somewhat altered by excitement. 'You know as my wife drinks?'

He stared defiantly at Samuel.

'N – no,' said Samuel. 'That is – no one's ever *said* –'

This was true. He did not know that Mrs Daniel Povey, at the age of fifty, had definitely taken to drink. There had been rumours that she enjoyed a glass with too much gusto; but 'drinks' meant more than that.

'She drinks,' Daniel Povey continued. 'And has done this last two year!'

'I'm very sorry to hear it,' said Samuel, tremendously shocked by this brutal rending of the cloak of decency.

Always, everybody had feigned to Daniel, and Daniel had feigned to everybody, that his wife was as other wives. And now the man himself had torn to pieces in a moment the veil of thirty years' weaving.

'And if that was the worst!' Daniel murmured reflectively, loosening his grip.

Samuel was excessively disturbed. His cousin was hinting at matters which he himself, at any rate, had never hinted at even to Constance, so abhorrent were they; matters unutterable, which hung like clouds in the social atmosphere of the town, and of which at rare intevals one conveyed one's cognizance, not by words, but by something scarce perceptible in a glance, an accent. Not often is a town such as Bursley starred with such a woman as Mrs Daniel Povey.

'But what's wrong?' Samuel asked, trying to be firm.

And, 'What *is* wrong?' he asked himself. 'What does all this mean, at after one o'clock in the morning?'

'Look here, Sam'l,' Daniel recommenced, seizing his shoulder again. 'I went to Liverpool corn market today, and missed the last train, so I came by mail from Crewe. And what do I find? I find Dick sitting on the stairs in the dark pretty nigh naked.'

'Sitting on the stairs? Dick?'

'Ay! This is what I come home to!'

'But –'

'Hold on! He's been in bed a couple of days with a feverish cold, caught through lying in damp sheets as his mother had forgot to air. She brings him no supper tonight. He calls out. No answer. Then he gets up to go downstairs and see what's happened, and he slips on th' stairs and breaks his knee, or puts it out or summat. Sat there hours, seemingly! Couldn't walk neither up nor down.'

'And was your – wife – was Mrs –?'

'Dead drunk in the parlour, Sam'l.'

'But the servant?'

'Servant!' Daniel Povey laughed. 'We can't keep our servants. They won't stay. *You* know that.'

He did. Mrs Daniel Povey's domestic methods and idiosyncracies could at any rate be freely discussed, and they were.

'And what have you done?'

'Done? Why, I picked him up in my arms and carried him upstairs again. And a fine job I had too! Here! Come here!'

Daniel strode impulsively across the shop – the counterflap was up – and opened a door at the back. Samuel followed. Never before had he penetrated so far into his cousin's secrets. On the left, within the doorway, were the stairs, dark; on the right a shut door; and in front an open door giving on to a yard. At the extremity of the yard he discerned a building, vaguely lit, and naked figures strangely moving in it.

'What's that? Who's there?' he asked sharply.

'That's the bakehouse,' Daniel replied, as if surprised at such a question. 'It's one of their long nights.'

Never, during the brief remainder of his life, did Samuel eat a mouthful of common bread without recalling that midnight apparition. He had lived for half a century, and thoughtlessly eaten bread as though loaves grew ready-made on trees.

'Listen!' Daniel commanded him.

He cocked his ear, and caught a feeble, complaining wail from an upper floor.

'That's Dick! That is!' said Daniel Povey.

It sounded more like the distress of a child than of an adventurous young man of twenty-four or so.

'But is he in pain? Haven't you fetched the doctor?'

'Not yet,' answered Daniel, with a vacant stare.

Samuel gazed at him closely for a second. And Daniel seemed to him very old and helpless and pathetic, a man unequal to the situation in which he found himself; and yet, despite the dignified snow of his age, wistfully boyish. Samuel thought swiftly: 'This has been too much for him. He's almost out of his mind. That's the explanation. Someone's got to take charge, and I must.' And all the courageous resolution of his character braced itself to the crisis. Being without a collar, being in slippers, and his suspenders imperfectly fastened anyhow – these things seemed to be a part of the crisis.

'I'll just run upstairs and have a look at him,' said Samuel, in a matter-of-fact tone.

Daniel did not reply.

There was a glimmer at the top of the stairs. Samuel mounted, found the gas-jet, and turned it on full. A dingy, dirty, untidy passage was revealed, the very antechamber of discomfort. Guided by the moans, Samuel entered a bedroom, which was in a shameful condition of neglect, and lighted only by a nearly expired candle. Was it possible that a house-mistress could so lose her self-respect? Samuel thought of his own abode, meticu-

lously and impeccably 'kept', and a hard bitterness against Mrs
Daniel surged up in his soul.

'Is that you, doctor?' said a voice from the bed; the moans
ceased.

Samuel raised the candle.

Dick lay there, his face, on which was a beard of several days'
growth, distorted by anguish, sweating; his tousled brown hair
was limp with sweat.

'Where the hell's the doctor?' the young man demanded brusquely. Evidently he had no curiosity about Samuel's presence; the
one thing that struck him was that Samuel was not the doctor.

'He's coming, he's coming,' said Samuel, soothingly.

'Well, if he isn't here soon I shall be damn well dead,' said Dick,
in feeble resentful anger. 'I can tell you that.'

Samuel deposited the candle and ran downstairs. 'I say,
Daniel,' he said, roused and hot, 'this is really ridiculous. Why on
earth didn't you fetch the doctor while you were waiting for me?
Where's the missis?'

Daniel Povey was slowly emptying grains of Indian corn out of
his jacket-pocket into one of the big receptacles behind the
counter on the baker's side of the shop. He had provisioned
himself with Indian corn as ammunition for Samuel's bedroom
window; he was now returning the surplus.

'Are you going for Harrop?' he questioned hesitatingly.

'Why, of course!' Samuel exclaimed. 'Where's the missis?'

'Happen you'd better go and have a look at her,' said Daniel
Povey. 'She's in th' parlour.'

He preceded Samuel to the shut door on the right. When he
opened it the parlour appeared in full illumination.

'Here! Go in!' said Daniel.

Samuel went in, afraid. In a room as dishevelled and filthy as
the bedroom, Mrs Daniel Povey lay stretched awkwardly on a
worn horse-hair sofa, her head thrown back, her face discoloured,
her eyes bulging, her mouth wet and yawning: a sight horribly
offensive. Samuel was frightened; he was struck with fear and
with disgust. The singing gas beat down ruthlessly on that
dreadful figure. A wife and mother! The lady of a house! The
centre of order! The fount of healing! The balm for worry, and

the refuge of distress! She was vile. Her scanty yellow-grey hair
was dirty, her hollowed neck all grime, her hands abominable,
her black dress in decay. She was the dishonour of her sex, her
situation, and her years. She was a fouler obscenity than the
inexperienced Samuel had ever conceived. And by the door stood
her husband, neat, spotless, almost stately, the man who for
thirty years had marshalled all his immense pride to suffer this
woman, the jolly man who had laughed through thick and thin!
Samuel remembered when they were married. And he remembered when, years after their marriage, she was still as pretty,
artificial, coquettish, and adamantine in her caprices as a young
harlot with a fool at her feet. Time and the slow wrath of God had
changed her.

He remained master of himself and approached her; then
stopped.

'But –' he stammered.

'Ay, Sam'l, lad!' said the old man from the door. 'I doubt I've
killed her! I doubt I've killed her! I took and shook her. I got her
by the neck. And before I knew where I was, I'd done it. She'll
never drink brandy again. This is what it's come to!'

He moved away.

All Samuel's flesh tingled as a heavy wave of emotion rolled
through his being. It was just as if someone had dealt him a blow
unimaginably tremendous. His heart shivered, as a ship shivers at
the mountainous crash of the waters. He was numbed. He
wanted to weep, to vomit, to die, to sink away. But a voice was
whispering to him: 'You will have to go through with this. You
are in charge of this.' He thought of *his* wife and child, innocently
asleep in the cleanly pureness of *his* home. And he felt the
roughness of his coat-collar round his neck and the insecurity of
his trousers. He passed out of the room, shutting the door. And
across the yard he had a momentary glimpse of those nude
nocturnal forms, unconsciously attitudinizing in the bakehouse.
And down the stairs came the protests of Dick, driven by pain
into a monotonous silly blasphemy.

'I'll fetch Harrop,' he said, melancholily, to his cousin.

The doctor's house was less than fifty yards off, and the doctor
had a night-bell, which, though he was a much older man than his

father had been at his age, he still answered promptly. No need to bombard the doctor's premises with Indian corn! While Samuel was parleying with the doctor through a window, the question ran incessantly through his mind: 'What about telling the police?'

But when, in advance of old Harrop, he returned to Daniel's shop, lo! the policeman previously encountered had returned upon his beat, and Daniel was talking to him in the little doorway. No other soul was about. Down King Street, along Wedgwood Street, up the Square, towards Brougham Street, nothing but gas-lamps burning with their everlasting patience, and the blind façades of shops. Only in the second storey of the Bank Building at the top of the Square a light showed mysteriously through a blind. Somebody ill there!

The policeman was in a high state of nervous excitement. That had happened to him which had never happened to him before. Of the sixty policemen in Bursley, just he had been chosen by fate to fit the socket of destiny. He was startled.

'What's this, what's this, Mr Povey?' he turned hastily to Samuel. 'What's this as Mr Councillor Povey is a-telling me?'

'You come in, sergeant,' said Daniel.

'If I come in,' said the policeman to Samuel, 'you mun' go along Wedgwood Street, Mr Povey, and bring my mate. He should be on Duck Bank, by rights.'

It was astonishing, when once the stone had begun to roll, how quickly it ran. In half an hour Samuel had actually parted from Daniel at the police-office behind the Shambles, and was hurrying to rouse his wife so that she could look after Dick Povey until he might be taken off to Pirehill Infirmary, as old Harrop had instantly, on seeing him, decreed.

'Ah!' he reflected in the turmoil of his soul: 'God is not mocked!' That was his basic idea: God is not mocked! Daniel was a good fellow, honourable, brilliant; a figure in the world. But what of his licentious tongue? What of his frequenting of bars? (How had he come to miss that train from Liverpool? How?) For many years he, Samuel, had seen in Daniel a living refutation of the authenticity of the old Hebrew menaces. But he had been wrong, after all! God is not mocked! And Samuel was aware of a revulsion in himself towards that strict codified godliness from which, in thought, he had perhaps been slipping away.

And with it all he felt, too, a certain officious self-importance, as he woke his wife and essayed to break the news to her in a manner tactfully calm. He had assisted at the most overwhelming event ever known in the history of the town.

II

'Your muffler – I'll get it,' said Constance. 'Cyril, run upstairs and get father's muffler. You know the drawer.'

Cyril ran. It behoved everybody, that morning, to be prompt and efficient.

'I don't need any muffler, thank you,' said Samuel, coughing and smothering the cough.

'Oh! But, Sam –' Constance protested.

'Now please don't worry me!' said Samuel with frigid finality. 'I've got quite enough –' He did not finish.

Constance sighed as her husband stepped, nervous and self-important, out of the side-door into the street. It was early, not yet eight o'clock, and the shop still unopened.

'Your father couldn't wait,' Constance said to Cyril when he had thundered down the stairs in his heavy schoolboy boots. 'Give it to me.' She went to restore the muffler to its place.

The whole house was upset, and Amy still an invalid! Existence was disturbed; there vaguely seemed to be a thousand novel things to be done, and yet she could think of nothing whatever that she needed to do at that moment; so she occupied herself with the muffler. Before she reappeared Cyril had gone to school, he who was usually a laggard. The truth was that he could no longer contain within himself a recital of the night, and in particular of the fact that he had been the first to hear the summons of the murderer on the window-pane. This imperious news had to be imparted to somebody, as a preliminary to the thrilling of the whole school; and Cyril had issued forth in search of an appreciative and worthy confidant. He was scarcely five minutes after his father.

In St Luke's Square was a crowd of quite two hundred persons, standing moveless in the November mud. The body of Mrs

Daniel Povey had already been taken to the Tiger Hotel, and young Dick Povey was on his way in a covered waggonette to Pirehill Infirmary on the other side of Knype. The shop of the crime was closed, and the blinds drawn at the upper windows of the house. There was absolutely nothing to be seen, not even a policeman. Nevertheless the crowd stared with an extraordinary obstinate attentiveness at the fatal building in Boulton Terrace, Hypnotized by this face of bricks and mortar, it had apparently forgotten all earthly ties, and, regardless of breakfast and a livelihood, was determined to stare at it till the house fell down or otherwise rendered up its secret. Most of its component individuals wore neither overcoats nor collars, but were kept warm by a scarf round the neck and by dint of forcing their fingers into the farthest inch of their pockets. Then they would slowly lift one leg after the other. Starers of infirm purpose would occasionally detach themselves from the throng and sidle away, ashamed of their fickleness. But reinforcements were continually arriving. And to these new-comers all that had been said in gossip had to be repeated and repeated: the same questions, the same answers, the same exclamations, the same proverbial philosophy, the same prophecies recurred in all parts of the Square with an uncanny iterance. Well-dressed men spoke to mere professional loiterers; for this unparalleled and glorious sensation, whose uniqueness grew every instant more impressive, brought out the essential brotherhood of mankind. All had a peculiar feeling that the day was neither Sunday nor week-day, but some eighth day of the week. Yet in the St Luke's Covered Market close by, the stall-keepers were preparing their stalls just as though it were Saturday, just as though a Town Councillor had not murdered his wife – at last! It was stated, and restated infinitely, that the Povey baking had been taken over by Brindley, the second-best baker and confectioner, who had a stall in the market. And it was asserted, as a philosophical truth, and reasserted infinitely, that there would have been no sense in wasting good food.

Samuel's emergence stirred the multitude. But Samuel passed up the Square with a rapt expression; he might have been under an illusion, caused by the extreme gravity of his preoccupations, that he was crossing a deserted Square. He hurried past the Bank and down the Turnhill Road, to the private residence of 'Young Lawton', son of the deceased 'Lawyer Lawton'. Young Lawton followed his father's profession; he was, as his father had been, the most successful solicitor in the town (though reputed by his learned rivals to be a fool), but the custom of calling men by their occupations had died out with horse-cars. Samuel caught young Lawton at his breakfast, and presently drove with him, in the Lawton buggy, to the police-station, where their arrival electrified a crowd as large as that in St Luke's Square. Later, they drove together to Hanbridge, informally to brief a barrister; and Samuel, not permitted to be present at the first part of the interview between the solicitor and the barrister, was humbled before the pomposity of legal etiquette.

It seemed to Samuel a game. The whole rigmarole of police and police-cells and formalities seemed insincere. His cousin's case was not like any other case, and, though formalities might be necessary, it was rather absurd to pretend that it was like any other case. In what manner it differed from other cases Samuel did not analytically inquire. He thought young Lawton was self-important, and Daniel too humble, in the colloquy of these two, and he endeavoured to indicate, by the dignity of his own demeanour, that in his opinion the proper relative tones had not been set. He could not understand Daniel's attitude, for he lacked imagination to realize what Daniel had been through. After all, Daniel was not a murderer; his wife's death was due to accident, was simply a mishap.

But in the crowded and stinking court-room of the Town Hall, Samuel began to feel qualms. It occurred that the Stipendiary Magistrate was sitting that morning at Bursley. He sat alone, as not one of the Borough Justices cared to occupy the bench while a Town Councillor was in the dock. The Stipendiary, recently appointed, was a young man, from the southern part of the county; and a Town Councillor of Bursley was no more to him than a petty tradesman to a man of fashion. He was youthfully enthusiastic for the majesty and the impartiality of English justice, and behaved as though the entire responsibility for the safety of that vast fabric rested on his shoulders. He and the barrister from

Hanbridge had had a historic quarrel at Cambridge, and their behaviour to each other was a lesson to the vulgar in the art of chill and consummate politeness. Young Lawton, having been to Oxford, secretly scorned the pair of them, but, as he had engaged counsel, he of course was precluded from adding to the eloquence, which chagrined him. These three were the aristocracy of the court-room; they knew it; Samuel Povey knew it; everybody knew it, and felt it. The barrister brought an unexceptionable zeal to the performance of his duties; he referred in suitable terms to Daniel's character and high position in the town, but nothing could hide the fact that for him too his client was a petty tradesman accused of simple murder. Naturally the Stipendiary was bound to show that before the law all men are equal – the Town Councillor and the common tippler; he succeeded. The policeman gave his evidence, and the Inspector swore to what Daniel Povey had said when charged. The hearing proceeded so smoothly and quickly that it seemed naught but an empty rite, with Daniel as a lay figure in it. The Stipendiary achieved marvellously the illusion that to him a murder by a Town Councillor in St Luke's Square was quite an everyday matter. Bail was inconceivable, and the barrister, being unable to suggest any reason why the Stipendiary should grant a remand – indeed, there was no reason – Daniel Povey was committed to the Stafford Assizes for trial. The Stipendiary instantly turned to the consideration of an alleged offence against the Factory Acts by a large local firm of potters. The young magistrate had mistaken his vocation. With his steely calm, with his imperturbable detachment from weak humanity, he ought to have been a General of the Order of Jesuits.

Daniel was removed – he did not go: he was removed, by two bare-headed constables. Samuel wanted to have speech with him, and could not. And later, Samuel stood in the porch of the Town Hall, and Daniel appeared out of a corridor, still in the keeping of two policemen, helmeted now. And down below at the bottom of the broad flight of steps, up which passed dancers on the nights of subscription balls, was a dense crowd, held at bay by other policemen; and beyond the crowd a black van. And Daniel – to his cousin a sort of Christ between thieves – was hurried past the

privileged loafers in the corridor, and down the broad steps. A
murmuring wave agitated the crowd. Unkempt idlers and ne'er-
do-wells in corduroy leaped up like tigers in the air, and the
policemen fought them back furiously. And Daniel and his
guardians shot through the little living lane. Quick! Quick! For
the captive is more sacred even than a messiah. The law has him
in charge! And like a feat of prestidigitation Daniel disappeared
into the blackness of the van. A door slammed loudly, triumphantly, and a whip cracked. The crowd had been balked. It was
as though the crowd had yelled for Daniel's blood and bones, and
the faithful constables had saved him from their lust.

Yes, Samuel had qualms. He had a sickness in the stomach.

The aged Superintendent of Police walked by, with the aged
Rector. The Rector was Daniel's friend. Never before had the
Rector spoken to the Nonconformist Samuel, but now he spoke
to him; he squeezed his hand.

'Ah, Mr Povey!' he ejaculated grievously.

'I – I'm afraid it's serious!' Samuel stammered. He hated
to admit that it was serious, but the words came out of his
mouth.

He looked at the Superintendent of Police, expecting the
Superintendent to assure him that it was not serious; but the
Superintendent only raised his small white-bearded chin, saying
nothing. The Rector shook his head, and shook a senile tear out
of his eye.

After another chat with young Lawton, Samuel, on behalf of
Daniel, dropped his pose of the righteous man to whom a mere
mishap has occurred, and who is determined, with the lofty pride
of innocence, to indulge all the whims of the law, to be more
royalist than the king. He perceived that the law must be fought
with its own weapons, that no advantage must be surrendered,
and every possible advantage seized. He was truly astonished at
himself that such a pose had ever been adopted. His eyes were
opened; he saw things as they were.

He returned home through a Square that was more interested
than ever in the façade of his cousin's house. People were
beginning to come from Hanbridge, Knype, Longshaw, Turnhill,
and villages such as Moorthorne, to gaze at that façade. And the

fourth edition of the *Signal*, containing a full report of what the Stipendiary and the barrister had said to each other, was being cried.

In his shop he found customers, as absorbed in the trivialities of purchase as though nothing whatever had happened. He was shocked; he resented their callousness.

'I'm too busy now,' he said curtly to one who accosted him.

'Sam!' his wife called him in a low voice. She was standing behind the till.

'What is it?' He was ready to crush, and especially to crush indiscreet babble in the shop. He thought she was going to vent her womanly curiosity at once.

'Mr Huntbach is waiting for you in the parlour,' said Constance.

'Mr Huntbach?'

'Yes, from Longshaw.' She whispered, 'It's Mr Povey's cousin. He's come to see about the funeral and so on, the – the inquest, I suppose.'

Samuel paused. 'Oh, has he!' said he defiantly. 'Well, I'll see him. If he *wants* to see me, I'll see him.'

That evening Constance learned all that was in his mind of bitterness against the memory of the dead woman whose failings had brought Daniel Povey to Stafford gaol and Dick to the Pirehill Infirmary. Again and again, in the ensuing days, he referred to the state of foul discomfort which he had discovered in Daniel's house. He nursed a feud against all her relatives, and when, after the inquest, at which he gave evidence full of resentment, she was buried, he vented an angry sigh of relief, and said: 'Well, *she's* out of the way!' Thenceforward he had a mission, religious in its solemn intensity, to defend and save Daniel. He took the enterprise upon himself, spending the whole of himself upon it, to the neglect of his business and the scorn of his health. He lived solely for Daniel's trial, pouring out money in preparation for it. He thought and spoke of nothing else. The affair was his one preoccupation. And as the weeks passed, he became more and more sure of success, more and more sure that he would return with Daniel to Bursley in triumph after the assize. He was convinced of the impossibility that 'anything should happen' to

Daniel; the circumstances were too clear, too overwhelmingly in Daniel's favour.

When Brindley, the second-best baker and confectioner, made an offer for Daniel's business as a going concern, he was indignant at first. Then Constance, and the lawyer, and Daniel (whom he saw on every permitted occasion) between them persuaded him that if some arrangement was not made, and made quickly, the business would lose all its value, and he consented, on Daniel's behalf, to a temporary agreement under which Brindley should reopen the shop and manage it on certain terms until Daniel regained his freedom towards the end of January. He would not listen to Daniel's plaintive insistence that he would never care to be seen in Bursley again. He pooh-poohed it. He protested furiously that the whole town was seething with sympathy for Daniel; and this was true. He became Daniel's defending angel, rescuing Daniel from Daniel's own weakness and apathy. He became, indeed, Daniel.

One morning the shop-shutter was wound up, and Brindley, inflated with the importance of controlling two establishments, strutted in and out under the sign of Daniel Povey. And traffic in bread and cakes and flour was resumed. Apparently the sea of time had risen and covered Daniel and all that was his; for his wife was under earth, and Dick lingered at Pirehill, unable to stand, and Daniel was locked away. Apparently, in the regular flow of the life of the Square, Daniel was forgotten. But not in Samuel Povey's heart was he forgotten! There, before an altar erected to the martyr, the sacred flame of a new faith burned with fierce consistency. Samuel, in his greying middle-age, had inherited the eternal youth of the apostle.

III

On the dark winter morning when Samuel set off to the grand assize, Constance did not ask his views as to what protection he would adopt against the weather. She silently ranged special underclothing, and by the warmth of the fire, which for days she had kept ablaze in the bedroom, Samuel silently donned the special underclothing. Over that, with particular fastidious care, he put his best suit. Not a word was spoken. Constance and he were not estranged, but the relations between them were in a state of feverish excitation. Samuel had had a cold on his flat chest for weeks, and nothing that Constance could invent would move it. A few days in bed or even in one room at a uniform temperature would have surely worked the cure. Samuel, however, would not stay in one room; he would not stay in the house, nor yet in Bursley. He would take his lacerating cough on chilly trains to Stafford. He had no ears for reason; he simply could not listen; he was in a dream. After Christmas a crisis came. Constance grew desperate. It was a battle between her will and his that occurred one night when Constance, marshalling all her forces, suddenly insisted that he must go out no more until he was cured. In the fight Constance was scarcely recognizable. She deliberately gave way to hysteria; she was no longer soft and gentle; she flung bitterness at him like vitriol; she shrieked like a common shrew. It seems almost incredible that Constance could have gone so far; but she did. She accused him, amid sobs, of putting his cousin before his wife and son, of not caring whether or not she was left a widow as the result of his obstinacy. And she ended by crying passionately that she might as well talk to a post. She might just as well have talked to a post. Samuel answered quietly and coldly. He told her that it was useless for her to put herself about, as he should act as he thought fit. It was a most extraordinary scene, and quite unique in their annals. Constance was beaten. She accepted the defeat, gradually controlling her sobs and changing her tone to the tone of the vanquished.

She kissed him in bed, kissing the rod. And he gravely kissed her.

Henceforward she knew, in practice, what the inevitable, when you have to live with it, may contain of anguish wretched and humiliating. Her husband was risking his life, so she was absolutely convinced, and she could do nothing; she had come to the bed-rock of Samuel's character. She felt that, for the time being, she had a madman in the house, who could not be treated according to ordinary principles. The continual strain aged her. Her one source of relief was to talk with Cyril. She talked to him without reserve, and the words 'your father', 'your father', were everlastingly on her complaining tongue. Yes, she was utterly changed. Often she would weep when alone.

Nevertheless she frequently forgot that she had been beaten. She had no notion of honourable warfare. She was always beginning again, always firing under a flag of truce; and thus she constituted a very inconvenient opponent. Samuel was obliged, while hardening on the main point, to compromise on lesser questions. She too could be formidable, and when her lips took a certain pose, and her eyes glowed, he would have put on forty mufflers had she commanded. Thus it was she who arranged all the details of the supreme journey to Stafford. Samuel was to drive to Knype, so as to avoid the rigours of the Loop Line train from Bursley and the waiting on cold platforms. At Knype he was to take the express, and to travel first-class.

After he was dressed on that gas-lit morning, he learnt bit by bit the extent of her elaborate preparations. The breakfast was a special breakfast, and he had to eat it all. Then the cab came, and he saw Amy put hot bricks into it. Constance herself put goloshes over his boots, not because it was damp, but because indiarubber keeps the feet warm. Constance herself bandaged his neck, and unbottoned his waistcoat and stuck an extra flannel under his dickey. Constance herself warmed his woollen gloves, and enveloped him in his largest overcoat.

Samuel then saw Cyril getting ready to go out. 'Where are you off?' he demanded.

'He's going with you as far as Knype,' said Constance grimly. 'He'll see you into the train and then come back here in the cab.'

She had sprung this indignity upon him. She glared. Cyril glanced with timid bravado from one to the other. Samuel had to yield.

Thus in the winter darkness – for it was not yet dawn – Samuel set forth to the trial, escorted by his son. The reverberation of his appalling cough from the cab was the last thing that Constance heard.

During most of the day Constance sat in 'Miss Insull's corner' in the shop. Twenty years ago this very corner had been hers. But now, instead of large millinery-boxes enwrapped in brown paper, it was shut off from the rest of the counter by a rich screen of mahogany and ground-glass, and within the enclosed space all the apparatus necessary to the activity of Miss Insull had been provided for. However, it remained the coldest part of the whole shop, as Miss Insull's fingers testified. Constance established herself there more from a desire to do something, to interfere in something, than from a necessity of supervising the shop, though she had said to Samuel that she would keep an eye on the shop. Miss Insull, whose throne was usurped, had to sit by the stove with less important creatures; she did not like it, and her underlings suffered accordingly.

It was a long day. Towards tea-time, just before Cyril was due from school, Mr Critchlow came surprisingly in. That is to say, his arrival was less of a surprise to Miss Insull and the rest of the staff than to Constance. For he had lately formed an irregular habit of popping in at tea-time, to chat with Miss Insull. Mr Critchlow was still defying time. He kept his long, thin figure perfectly erect. His features had not altered. His hair and beard could not have been whiter than they had been for years past. He wore his long white apron, and over that a thick reefer jacket. In his long, knotty fingers he carried a copy of the *Signal*.

Evidently he had not expected to find the corner occupied by Constance. She was sewing.

'So it's you!' he said, in his unpleasant, grating voice, not even glancing at Miss Insull. He had gained the reputation of being the rudest old man in Bursley. But his general demeanour expressed indifference rather than rudeness. It was a manner that said: 'You've got to take me as I am. I may be an egotist, hard, mean, and convinced; but those who don't like it can lump it. I'm indifferent.'

He put one elbow on the top of the screen, showing the *Signal*.

'Mr Critchlow!' said Constance, primly; she had acquired Samuel's dislike of him.

'It's begun!' he observed with mysterious glee.

'Has it?' Constance said eagerly. 'Is it in the paper already?'

She had been far more disturbed about her husband's health than about the trial of Daniel Povey for murder, but her interest in the trial was of course tremendous. And this news, that it had actually begun, thrilled her.

'Ay!' said Mr Critchlow. 'Didn't ye hear the *Signal* boy holler-ing just now all over the Square?'

'No,' said Constance. For her, newspapers did not exist. She never had the idea of opening one, never felt any curiosity which she could not satisfy, if she could satisfy it at all, without the powerful aid of the Press. And even on this day it had not occurred to her that the *Signal* might be worth opening.

'Ay!' repeated Mr Critchlow. 'Seemingly it began at two o'clock – or thereabouts.' He gave a moment of his attention to a noisy gas-jet, which he carefully lowered.

'What does it say?'

'Nothing yet!' said Mr Critchlow; and they read the few brief sentences, under their big heading, which described the formal commencement of the trial of Daniel Povey for the murder of his wife. 'There was some as said,' he remarked, pushing up his spectacles, 'that grand jury would alter the charge, or summat!' He laughed, grimly tolerant of the extreme absurdity. 'Ah!' he added contemplatively, turning his head to see if the assistants were listening. They were. It would have been too much, on such a day, to expect a strict adherence to the etiquette of the shop.

Constance had been hearing a good deal lately of grand juries, but she had understood nothing, nor had she sought to under-stand.

'I'm very glad it's come on so soon,' she said. 'In a sense, that is! I was afraid Sam might be kept at Stafford for days. Do you think it will last long?'

'Not it!' said Mr Critchlow, positively. 'There's naught in it to spin out.'

Then a silence, punctuated by the sound of stitching.

Constance would really have preferred not to converse with the old man; but the desire for reassurance, for the calming of her own fears, forced her to speak, though she knew well that Mr Critchlow was precisely the last man in the town to give moral assistance if he thought it was wanted.

'I do hope everything will be all right!' she murmured.

'Everything'll be all right!' he said gaily. 'Everything'll be all right. Only it'll be all wrong for Dan.'

'Whatever do you mean, Mr Critchlow?' she protested. Nothing, she reflected, could rouse pity in that heart, not even a tragedy like Daniel's. She bit her lip for having spoken.

'Well,' he said in loud tones, frankly addressing the girls round the stove as much as Constance. 'I've met with some rare good arguments this new year, no mistake! There's been some as say that Dan never meant to do it. That's as may be. But if it's a good reason for not hanging, there's an end to capital punishment in this country. "Never meant"! There's a lot of 'em as "never meant"! Then I'm told as she was a gallivanting woman and no housekeeper, and as often drunk as sober. I'd no call to be told that. If strangling is a right punishment for a wife as spends her time in drinking brandy instead of sweeping floors and airing sheets, then Dan's safe. But I don't seem to see Judge Lindley telling the jury as it is. I've been a juryman under Judge Lindley myself – and more than once – and I don't seem to see him, like!' He paused with his mouth open. 'As for all them nobs,' he continued, 'including th' rector, as have gone to Stafford to kiss the book and swear that Dan's reputation is second to none – if they could ha' sworn as Dan wasn't in th' house at all that night, if they could ha' sworn he was in Jericho, there'd ha' been some sense in their going. But as it is, they'd ha' done better to stop at home and mind their business. Bless us! Sam wanted *me* to go!'

He laughed again, in the faces of the horrified and angry women.

'I'm surprised at you, Mr Critchlow! I really am!' Constance exclaimed.

And the assistants inarticulately supported her with vague sounds. Miss Insull got up and poked the stove. Every soul in the establishment was loyally convinced that Daniel Povey would be acquitted, and to breathe a doubt on the brightness of this certainty was a hideous crime. The conviction was not within the domain of reason; it was an act of faith; and arguments merely fretted, without in the slightest degree disturbing it.

'Ye may be!' Mr Critchlow gaily concurred. He was very content.

Just as he shuffled round to leave the shop, Cyril entered.

'Good afternoon, Mr Critchlow,' said Cyril, sheepishly polite. Mr Critchlow gazed hard at the boy, then nodded his head several times rapidly, as though to say: 'Here's another fool in the making! So the generations follow one another!' He made no answer to the salutation, and departed.

Cyril ran round to his mother's corner, pitching his bag on to the showroom stairs as he passed them. Taking off his hat, he kissed her, and she unbuttoned his overcoat with her cold hands.

'What's old Methuselah after?' he demanded.

'Hush!' Constance softly corrected him. 'He came in to tell me the trial had started.'

'Oh, I knew that! A boy bought a paper and I saw it. I say, mother, will father be in the paper?' And then in a different tone: 'I say, mother, what is there for tea?'

When his stomach had learnt exactly what there was for tea, the boy began to show an immense and talkative curiosity in the trial. He would not set himself to his home-lessons. 'It's no use, mother,' he said, 'I can't.' They returned to the shop together, and Cyril would go every moment to the door to listen for the cry of a newsboy. Presently he hit upon the idea that perhaps newsboys might be crying the special edition of the *Signal* in the market-place, in front of the Town Hall, to the neglect of St Luke's Square. And nothing would satisfy him but he must go forth and see. He went, without his overcoat, promising to run. The shop waited with a strange anxiety. Cyril had created, by his restless movements to and fro, an atmosphere of strained expectancy. It seemed now as if the whole town stood with beating heart, fearful of tidings and yet burning to get them. Constance pictured Stafford, which she had never seen, and a court of justice, which she had never seen, and her husband and Daniel in it. And she waited.

Cyril ran in. 'No!' he announced breathlessly. 'Nothing yet.'

'Don't take cold, now you're hot,' Constance advised.

But he would keep near the door. Soon he ran off again.

And perhaps fifteen seconds after he had gone, the strident cry of a *Signal* boy was heard in the distance, faint and indistinct at first, then clearer and louder.

'There's a paper!' said the apprentice.

'Sh!' said Constance, listening.

'Sh!' echoed Miss Insull.

'Yes, it is!' said Constance. 'Miss Insull, just step out and get a paper. Here's a halfpenny.'

The halfpenny passed quickly from one thimbled hand to another. Miss Insull scurried.

She came in triumphantly with the sheet, which Constance tremblingly took. Constance could not find the report at first. Miss Insull pointed to it, and read —

' "Summing up"! Lower down, lower down! "After an absence of thirty-five minutes the jury found the prisoner guilty of murder, with a recommendation to mercy. The judge assumed the black cap and pronounced sentence of death, saying that he would forward the recommendation to the proper quarter." '

Cyril returned. 'Not yet!' he was saying — when he saw the paper lying on the counter. His crest fell.

Long after the shop was shut, Constance and Cyril waited in the parlour for the arrival of the master of the house. Constance was in the blackest despair. She saw nothing but death around her. She thought: misfortunes never come singly. Why did not Samuel come? All was ready for him, everything that her imagination could suggest, in the way of food, remedies, and the means of warmth. Amy was not allowed to go to bed, lest she might be needed. Constance did not even hint that Cyril should go to bed. The dark, dreadful minutes ticked themselves off on the mantelpiece until only five minutes separated Constance from the moment when she would not know what to do next. It was twenty-five minutes past eleven. If at half-past Samuel did not appear, then he could not come that night, unless the last train from Stafford was inconceivably late.

The sound of a carriage! It ceased at the door. Mother and son sprang up.

Yes, it was Samuel! She beheld him once more. And the sight of his condition, moral and physical, terrified her. His great strapping son and Amy helped him upstairs. 'Will he ever come down those stairs again?' This thought lanced Constance's heart. The pain was come and gone in a moment, but it had surprised her tranquil common sense, which was naturally opposed to, and gently scornful of, hysterical fears. As she puffed, with her stoutness, up the stairs, that bland cheerfulness of hers cost her an immense effort of will. She was profoundly troubled; great disasters seemed to be slowly approaching her from all quarters.

Should she send for the doctor? No. To do so would only be a concession to the panic instinct. She knew exactly what was the matter with Samuel: a severe cough persistently neglected, no more. As she had expressed herself many times to inquirers, 'He's never been what you may call ill.' Nevertheless, as she laid him in bed and posseted him, how frail and fragile he looked! And he was so exhausted that he would never even talk about the trial.

'If he's not better tomorrow I *shall* send for the doctor!' she said to herself. As for his getting up, she swore she would keep him in bed by force if necessary.

IV

The next morning she was glad and proud that she had not yielded to a scare. For he was most strangely and obviously better. He had slept heavily, and she had slept a little. True that Daniel was condemned to death! Leaving Daniel to his fate, she was conscious of joy springing in her heart. How absurd to have asked herself: 'Will he ever come down those stairs again?'!

A message reached her from the forgotten shop during the morning, that Mr Lawton had called to see Mr Povey. Already Samuel had wanted to arise, but she had forbidden it in the tone of a woman who is dangerous, and Samuel had been very reasonable. He now said that Mr Lawton must be asked up. She glanced round the bedroom. It was 'done'; it was faultlessly correct as a sick chamber. She agreed to the introduction into it of the man from another sphere, and after a preliminary minute she left the two to talk together. This visit of young Lawton's was a dramatic proof of Samuel's importance, and of the importance of the matter in hand. The august occasion demanded etiquette, and etiquette said that a wife should depart from her husband when he had to transact affairs beyond the grasp of a wife.

The idea of a petition to the Home Secretary took shape at this interview, and before the day was out it had spread over the town and over the Five Towns, and it was in the *Signal*. The *Signal* spoke of Daniel Povey as 'the condemned man'. And the phrase startled the whole district into an indignant agitation for his reprieve. The district woke up to the fact that a Town Councillor, a figure in the world, an honest tradesman of unspotted character, was cooped solitary in a little cell at Stafford, waiting to be hanged by the neck till he was dead. The district determined that this must not and should not be. Why! Dan Povey had actually once been Chairman of the Bursley Society for the Prosecution of Felons, that association for annual eating and drinking, whose members humorously called each other 'felons'! Impossible, monstrous, that an ex-chairman of the 'Felons' should be a sentenced criminal!

However, there was nothing to fear. No Home Secretary would dare to run counter to the jury's recommendation and the expressed wish of the whole district. Besides, the Home Secretary's nephew was M.P. for the Knype division. Of course a verdict of guilty had been inevitable. Everybody recognized that now. Even Samuel and all the hottest partisans of Daniel Povey recognized it. They talked as if they had always foreseen it, directly contradicting all that they had said on only the previous day. Without any sense of any inconsistency or of shame, they took up an absolutely new position. The structure of blind faith had once again crumbled at the assault of realities, and unhealthy, un-English truths, the statement of which would have meant ostracism twenty-four hours earlier, became suddenly the platitudes of the Square and the market-place.

Despatch was necessary in the affair of the petition, for the condemned man had but three Sundays. But there was delay at the beginning, because neither young Lawton nor any of his colleagues was acquainted with the proper formula of a petition to the Home Secretary for the reprieve of a criminal condemned to death. No such petition had been made in the district within living memory. And at first young Lawton could not get sight or copy of any such petition anywhere, in the Five Towns or out of them. Of course there must exist a proper formula, and of course that formula and no other could be employed. Nobody was bold enough to suggest that young Lawton should commence the petition, 'To the Most Noble the Marquess of Welwyn, K.C.B., May it please your Lordship,' and end it, 'And your petitioners will ever pray!' and insert between those phrases a simple appeal for the reprieve, with a statement of reasons. No! the formula consecrated by tradition must be found. And, after Daniel had arrived a day and a half nearer death, it was found. A lawyer at Alnwick had the draft of a petition which had secured for a murderer in Northumberland twenty years' penal servitude instead of sudden death, and on request he lent it to young Lawton. The prime movers in the petition felt that Daniel Povey was now as good as saved. Hundreds of forms were printed to receive signatures, and these forms, together with copies of the petition, were laid on the counters of all the principal shops, not merely in Bursley, but in the other towns. They were also to be found at the offices of the *Signal*, in railway waiting-rooms, and in the various reading-rooms; and on the second of Daniel's three Sundays they were exposed in the porches of Churches and chapels. Chapel-keepers and vergers would come to Samuel and ask with the heavy inertia of their stupidity: 'About pens and ink, sir?' These officials had the air of audaciously disturbing the sacrosanct routine of centuries in order to confer a favour.

Samuel continued to improve. His cough shook him less, and his appetite increased. Constance allowed him to establish himself in the drawing-room, which was next to the bedroom, and of which the grate was particularly efficient. Here, in an old winter overcoat, he directed the vast affair of the petition, which grew daily to vaster proportions. Samuel dreamed of twenty thousand signatures. Each sheet held twenty signatures, and several times a day he counted the sheets; the supply of forms actually failed once, and Constance herself had to hurry to the printers to order more. Samuel was put into a passion by this carelessness of the printers. He offered Cyril sixpence for every sheet of signatures which the boy would obtain. At first Cyril was too shy to canvass, but his father made him blush, and in a few hours Cyril had developed into an eager canvasser. One whole day he stayed away from school to canvass. Altogether he earned over fifteen shillings, quite honestly except that he got a companion to forge a couple of signatures with addresses lacking at the end of a last sheet, generously rewarding him with sixpence, the value of the entire sheet.

When Samuel had received a thousand sheets with twenty

thousand signatures, he set his heart on twenty-five thousand signatures. And he also announced his firm intention of accompanying young Lawton to London with the petition. The petition had, in fact, become one of the most remarkable petitions of modern times. So the *Signal* said. The *Signal* gave a daily account of its progress, and its progress was astonishing. In certain streets every householder had signed it. The first sheets had been reserved for the signatures of members of Parliament, ministers of religion, civic dignitaries, justices of the peace, etc. These sheets were nobly filled. The aged rector of Bursley signed first of all; after him the Mayor of Bursley, as was right; then sundry M.P.s.

Samuel emerged from the drawing-room. He went into the parlour, and, later, into the shop; and no evil consequence followed. His cough was nearly, but not quite, cured. The weather was extraordinarily mild for the season. He repeated that he should go with the petition to London; and he went; Constance could not validly oppose the journey. She, too, was a little intoxicated by the petition. It weighed considerably over a hundredweight. The crowning signature, that of the M.P. for Knype, was duly obtained in London, and Samuel's one disappointment was that his hope of twenty-five thousand signatures had fallen short of realization – by only a few score. The few score could have been got had not time urgently pressed. He returned from London a man of mark, full of confidence; but his cough was worse again.

His confidence in the power of public opinion and the inherent virtue of justice might have proved to be well placed, had not the Home Secretary happened to be one of your humane officials. The Marquess of Welwyn was celebrated through every stratum of the governing classes for his humane instincts, which were continually fighting against his sense of duty. Unfortunately his sense of duty, which he had inherited from several centuries of ancestors, made havoc among his humane instincts on nearly every occasion of conflict. It was reported that he suffered horribly in consequence. Others also suffered, for he was never known to advise a remission of a sentence of flogging. Certain capital sentences he had commuted, but he did not commute Daniel Povey's. He could not permit himself to be influenced by a

wave of popular sentiment, and assuredly not by his own
nephew's signature. He gave to the case the patient, remorseless
examination which he gave to every case. He spent a sleepless
night in trying to discover a reason for yielding to his humane
instincts, but without success. As Judge Lindley remarked in his
confidential report, the sole arguments in favour of Daniel were
provocation and his previous high character; and these were no
sort of an argument. The provocation was utterly inadequate,
and the previous high character was quite too ludicrously beside
the point. So once more the Marquis's humane instincts were
routed and he suffered horribly.

V

On the Sunday morning after the day on which the *Signal* had
printed the menu of Daniel Povey's supreme breakfast, and the
exact length of the 'drop' which the executioner had administered to him, Constance and Cyril stood together at the window
of the large bedroom. The boy was in his best clothes; but
Constance's garments gave no sign of the Sabbath. She wore a
large apron over an old dress that was rather tight for her. She
was pale and looked ill.

'Oh, mother!' Cyril exclaimed suddenly. 'Listen! I'm sure I can
hear the band.'

She checked him with a soundless movement of her lips; and
they both glanced anxiously at the silent bed, Cyril with a gesture
of apology for having forgotten that he must make no noise.

The strains of the band came from down King Street, in the
direction of St Luke's Church. The music appeared to linger a
long time in the distance, and then it approached, growing
louder, and the Bursley Town Silver Prize Band passed under the
window at the solemn pace of Handel's 'Dead March'. The effect
of that requiem, heavy with its own inherent beauty and with the
vast weight of harrowing tradition, was to wring the tears from
Constance's eyes; they fell on her aproned bosom, and she sank
into a chair. And though the cheeks of the trumpeters were puffed
out, and though the drummer had to protrude his stomach and
arch his spine backwards lest he should tumble over his drum,
there was majesty in the passage of the band. The boom of the

drum, desolating the interruptions of the melody, made sick the heart, but with a lofty grief; and the dirge seemed to be weaving a purple pall that covered every meanness.

The bandsmen were not all in black, but they all wore crape on their sleeves and their instruments were knotted with crape. They carried in their hats a black-edged card. Cyril held one of these cards in his hands. It ran thus:

SACRED TO THE MEMORY OF
DANIEL POVEY
A TOWN COUNCILLOR OF THIS TOWN
JUDICIALLY MURDERED AT 8 O'CLOCK IN THE MORNING
8TH FEBRUARY 1888
'HE WAS MORE SINNED AGAINST THAN SINNING'

In the wake of the band came the aged Rector, bareheaded, and wearing a surplice over his overcoat; his thin white hair was disarranged by the breeze that played in the chilly sunshine; his hands were folded on a gilt-edged book. A curate, churchwardens, and sidesmen followed. And after these, tramping through the dark mud in a procession that had apparently no end, wound the unofficial male multitude, nearly all in mourning, and all, save the more aristocratic, carrying the memorial card in their hats. Loafers, women, and children had collected on the drying pavements, and a window just opposite Constance was ornamented with the entire family of the landlord of the Sun Vaults. In the great bar of the Vaults a barman was craning over the pitch-pine screen that secured privacy to drinkers. The procession continued without break, eternally rising over the verge of King Street 'bank', and eternally vanishing round the corner into St Luke's Square; at intervals it was punctuated by a clergyman, a Nonconformist minister, a town crier, a group of foremen, or a few Rifle Volunteers. The watching crowd grew as the procession lengthened. Then another band was heard, also playing the march from *Saul*. The first band had now reached the top of the Square, and was scarcely audible from King Street. The reiterated glitter in the sun of memorial cards in hats gave the fanciful illusion of an impossible whitish snake that was straggling across the town. Three-quarters of an hour elapsed before the tail of the snake came into view, and a rabble of unkempt boys closed in upon it, filling the street.

'I shall go to the drawing-room window, mother,' said Cyril. She nodded. He crept out of the bedroom.

St Luke's Square was a sea of hats and memorial cards. Most of the occupiers of the Square had hung out flags at half-mast, and a flag at half-mast was flying over the Town Hall in the distance. Sightseers were at every window. The two bands had united at the top of the Square; and behind them, on a North Staffordshire Railway lorry, stood the white-clad Rector and several black figures. The Rector was speaking; but only those close to the lorry could hear his feeble treble voice.

Such was the massive protest of Bursley against what Bursley regarded as a callous injustice. The execution of Daniel Povey had most genuinely excited the indignation of the town. That execution was not only an injustice; it was an insult, a humiliating snub. And the worst was that the rest of the country had really discovered no sympathetic interest in the affair. Certain London papers, indeed, in commenting casually on the execution, had slurred the morals and manners of the Five Towns, professing to regard the district as notoriously beyond the realm of the Ten Commandments. This had helped to render furious the townsmen. This, as much as anything, had encouraged the spontaneous outburst of feeling which had culminated in a St Luke's Square full of people with memorial cards in their hats. The demonstration had scarcely been organized; it had somehow organized itself, employing the places of worship and a few clubs as centres of gathering. And it proved an immense success. There were seven or eight thousand people in the Square, and the pity was that England as a whole could not have had a glimpse of the spectacle. Since the execution of the elephant, nothing had so profoundly agitated Bursley. Constance, who left the bedroom momentarily for the drawing-room, reflected that the death and burial of Cyril's honoured grandfather, though a resounding event, had not caused one-tenth of the stir which she beheld. But then John Baines had killed nobody.

The Rector spoke too long; everyone felt that. But at length he finished. The bands performed the Doxology, and the immense multitudes began to disperse by the eight streets that radiate from the Square. At the same time one o'clock struck, and the public-houses opened with their customary admirable promptitude. Respectable persons, of course, ignored the public-houses and hastened homewards to a delayed dinner. But in a town of over thirty thousand souls there are sufficient dregs to fill all the public-houses on an occasion of ceremonial excitement. Constance saw the bar of the Vaults crammed with individuals whose sense of decent fitness was imperfect. The barman and the landlord and the principal members of the landlord's family were hard put to it to quench that funereal thirst. Constance, as she ate a little meal in the bedroom, could not but witness the orgy. A bandsman with his silver instrument was prominent at the counter. At five minutes to three the Vaults spewed forth a squirt of roysterers who walked on the pavement as on a tight-rope; among them was the bandsman, his silver instrument only half enveloped in its bag of green serge. He established an equilibrium in the gutter. It would not have mattered so seriously if he had not been a bandsman. The barman and the landlord pushed the ultimate sot by force into the street and bolted the door (till six o'clock) just as a policeman strolled along, the first policeman of the day. It became known that similar scenes were enacting at the thresholds of other inns. And the judicious were sad.

VI

When the altercation between the policeman and the musician in the gutter was at its height, Samuel Povey became restless; but since he had scarcely stirred through the performances of the bands, it was probably not the cries of the drunkard that had aroused him.

He had shown very little interest in the preliminaries of the great demonstration. The flame of his passion for the case of Daniel Povey seemed to have shot up on the day before the execution, and then to have expired. On that day he went to Stafford in order, by permit of the prison governor, to see his cousin for the last time. His condition then was undoubtedly not far removed from monomania. 'Unhinged' was the conventional expression which frequently rose in Constance's mind as a description of the mind of her husband; but she fought it down; she would not have it; it was too crude – with its associations. She would only admit that the case had 'got on' his mind. A startling proof of this was that he actually suggested taking Cyril with him to see the condemned man. He wished Cyril to see Daniel; he said gravely that he thought Cyril ought to see him. The proposal was monstrous, inexplicable – or explicable only by the assumption that his mind, while not unhinged, had temporarily lost its balance. Constance opposed an absolute negative, and Samuel being in every way enfeebled, she overcame. As for Cyril, he was divided between fear and curiosity. On the whole, perhaps Cyril regretted that he would not be able to say at school that he had had speech with the most celebrated killer of the age on the day before his execution.

Samuel returned hysterical from Stafford. His account of the scene, which he gave in a very loud voice, was a most absurd and yet pathetic recital, obviously distorted by memory. When he came to the point of the entrance of Dick Povey, who was still at the hospital, and who had been specially driven to Stafford and carried into the prison, he wept without restraint. His hysteria was painful in a very high degree.

He went to bed – of his own accord, for his cough had improved again. And on the following day, the day of the execution, he remained in bed till the afternoon. In the evening the Rector sent for him to the Rectory to discuss the proposed demonstration. On the next day, Saturday, he said he should not get up. Icy showers were sweeping the town, and his cough was worse after the evening visit to the Rector. Constance had no apprehension about him. The most dangerous part of the winter was over, and there was nothing now to force him into indiscretions. She said to herself calmly that he should stay in bed as long as he liked, that he could not have too much repose after the cruel fatigues, physical and spiritual, which he had suffered. His cough was short, but not as troublesome as in the past; his face flushed, dusky, and settled in gloom; and he was slightly feverish, with quick pulse and quick breathing – the symptoms of a renewed cold. He passed a wakeful night, broken by brief dreams in which he talked. At dawn he had some hot food, asked what day it was, frowned, and seemed to doze off at once. At eleven o'clock he had refused food. And he had intermittently dozed during the progress of the demonstration and its orgiastic sequel.

Constance had food ready for his waking, and she approached the bed and leaned over him. The fever had increased somewhat, the breathing was more rapid, and his lips were covered with tiny purple pimples. He feebly shook his head with a disgusted air, at her mention of food. It was this obstinate refusal of food which first alarmed her. A little uncomfortable suspicion shot up in her: Surely there's nothing the *matter* with him?

Something – impossible to say what – caused her to bend still lower, and put her ear to his chest. She heard within that mysterious box a rapid succession of thin, dry, crackling sounds: sounds such as she would have produced by rubbing her hair between her fingers close to her ear. The crepitation ceased, then recommenced, and she perceived that it coincided with the intake of his breath. He coughed; the sounds were intensified; a spasm of pain ran over his face; and he put his damp hand to his side.

'Pain in my side!' he whispered with difficulty.

Constance stepped into the drawing-room, where Cyril was sketching by the fire.

'Cyril,' she said, 'go across and ask Dr Harrop to come round at once. And if he isn't in, then his new partner.'

'Is it for father?'

'Yes.'

'What's the matter?'

'Now do as I say, please,' said Constance, sharply, adding: 'I don't know what's the matter. Perhaps nothing. But I'm not satisfied.'

The venerable Harrop pronounced the word 'pneumonia'. It was acute double pneumonia that Samuel had got. During the three worst months of the year, he had escaped the fatal perils which await a man with a flat chest and a chronic cough, who ignores his condition and defies the weather. But a journey of five hundred yards to the Rectory had been one journey too many. The Rectory was so close to the shop that he had not troubled to wrap himself up as for an excursion to Stafford. He survived the crisis of the disease and then died of toxaemia, caused by a heart that would not do its duty by the blood. A casual death, scarce noticed in the reaction after the great febrile demonstration! Besides, Samuel Povey never could impose himself on the burgesses. He lacked individuality. He was little. I have often laughed at Samuel Povey. But I liked and respected him. He was a very honest man. I have always been glad to think that, at the end of his life, destiny took hold of him and displayed, to the observant, the vein of greatness which runs through every soul without exception. He embraced a cause, lost it, and died of it.

CHAPTER 6: *The Widow*

I

Constance, alone in the parlour, stood expectant by the set tea-table. She was not wearing weeds; her mother and she, on the death of her father, had talked of the various disadvantages of weeds; her mother had worn them unwillingly, and only because a public opinion not sufficiently advanced had intimidated her. Constance had said: 'If ever I'm a widow I won't wear them,' positively, in the tone of youth; and Mrs Baines had replied: 'I hope you won't, my dear.' That was over twenty years ago, but Constance perfectly remembered. And now, she was a widow! How strange and how impressive was life! And she had kept her word; not positively, not without hesitations; for though times were changed, Bursley was still Bursley; but she had kept it.

This was the first Monday after Samuel's funeral. Existence in the house had been resumed on the plane which would henceforth be the normal plane. Constance had put on for tea a dress of black silk with a jet brooch of her mother's. Her hands, just meticulously washed, had that feeling of being dirty which comes from roughening of the epidermis caused by a day spent in fingering stuffs. She had been 'going through' Samuel's things, and her own, and ranging all anew. It was astonishing how little the man had collected, of 'things', in the course of over half a century. All his clothes were contained in two long drawers and a short one. He had the least possible quantity of haberdashery and linen, for he invariably took from the shop such articles as he required, when he required them, and he would never preserve what was done with. He possessed no jewellery save a set of gold studs, a scarf-ring, and a wedding-ring; the wedding-ring was buried with him. Once, when Constance had offered him her father's gold watch and chain, he had politely refused it, saying that he preferred his own – a silver watch (with a black cord) which kept excellent time; he had said later that she might save the gold watch and chain for Cyril when he was twenty-one. Beyond these trifles and a half-empty box of cigars and a pair of spectacles, he left nothing personal to himself. Some men leave behind them a litter which takes months to sift and distribute. But Samuel had not the mania for owning. Constance put his clothes in a box, to be given away gradually (all except an overcoat and handkerchiefs which might do for Cyril); she locked up the watch and its black cord, the spectacles and the scarf-ring; she gave the gold studs to Cyril; she climbed on a chair and hid the cigar-box on the top of her wardrobe; and scarce a trace of Samuel remained!

By his own wish the funeral had been as simple and private as possible. One or two distant relations, whom Constance scarcely knew and who would probably not visit her again, until she too was dead, came – and went. And lo! the affair was over. The simple celerity of the funeral would have satisfied even Samuel, whose tremendous self-esteem hid itself so effectually behind such externals that nobody had ever fully perceived it. Not even Constance quite knew Samuel's secret opinion of Samuel. Constance was aware that he had a ridiculous side, that his greatest lack had been a lack of spectacular dignity. Even in the coffin, where nevertheless most people are finally effective, he had not been imposing – with his finicky little grey beard persistently sticking up.

The vision of him in his coffin – there in the churchyard, just at the end of King Street! – with the lid screwed down on that unimportant beard, recurred frequently in the mind of the widow, as something untrue and misleading. She had to say to herself: 'Yes, he is really there! And that is why I have this particular feeling in my heart.' She saw him as an object pathetic and wistful, not majestic. And yet she genuinely thought that there could not exist another husband quite so honest, quite so just, quite so reliable, quite so good, as Samuel had been. What a conscience he had! How he would try, and try, to be fair with her! Twenty years she could remember, of ceaseless, constant endeavour on his part to behave rightly to her! She could recall many an occasion when he had obviously checked himself, striving against his tendency to cold abruptness and to sullenness, in order to give her the respect due to a wife. What loyalty was his! How she could *depend on* him! How much better he was than herself (she thought with modesty)!

His death was an amputation for her. But she faced it with calmness. She was not bowed with sorrow. She did not nurse the idea that her life was at an end; on the contrary, she obstinately put it away from her, dwelling on Cyril. She did not indulge in the enervating voluptuousness of grief. She had begun in the first hours of bereavement by picturing herself as one marked out for the blows of fate. She had lost her father and her mother, and now her husband. Her career seemed to be punctuated by interments. But after a while her gentle common sense came to insist that most human beings lose their parents, and that every marriage must end in either a widower or a widow, and that all careers are punctuated by interments. Had she not had nearly twenty-one years of happy married life? (Twenty-one years – rolled up! The sudden thought of their naïve ignorance of life, hers and his, when they were first married, brought tears into her eyes. How wise and experienced she was now!) And had she not Cyril? Compared to many women, she was indeed very fortunate.

The one visitation which had been specially hers was the disappearance of Sophia. And yet even that was not worse than the death outright of Sophia, was perhaps not so bad. For Sophia might return out of the darkness. The blow of Sophia's flight had seemed unique when it was fresh, and long afterwards; had seemed to separate the Baines family from all other families in a particular shame. But at the age of forty-three Constance had learnt that such events are not uncommon in families, and strange sequels to them not unknown. Thinking often of Sophia, she hoped wildly and frequently.

She looked at the clock; she had a little spasm of nervousness lest Cyril might fail to keep his word on that first day of their new regular life together. And at the instant he burst into the room, invading it like an armed force, having previously laid waste the shop in his passage.

'I'm not late, mother! I'm not late!' he cried proudly.

She smiled warmly, happy in him, drawing out of him balm and solace. He did not know that in that stout familiar body before him was a sensitive, trembling soul that clutched at him ecstatically as the one reality in the universe. He did not know that that evening meal, partaken of without hurry after school had released him to her, was to be the ceremonial sign of their intimate unity and their interdependence, a tender and delicious proof that they were 'all in all to each other'; he saw only his tea, for which he was hungry – just as hungry as though his father were not scarcely yet cold in the grave.

But he saw obscurely that the occasion demanded something not quite ordinary, and so he exerted himself to be boyishly charming to his mother. She said to herself 'how good he was'. He felt at ease and confident in the future, because he detected beneath her customary judicial, impartial mask a dear desire to spoil him.

After tea, she regretfully left him, at his home-lessons, in order to go into the shop. The shop was the great unsolved question. What was she to do with the shop? Was she to continue the business or to sell it? With the fortunes of her father and her aunt, and the economies of twenty years, she had more than sufficient means. She was indeed rich, according to the standards of the Square; nay, wealthy! Therefore she was under no material compulsion to keep the shop. Moreover, to keep it would mean personal superintendence and the burden of responsibility, from which her calm lethargy shrank. On the other hand, to dispose of the business would mean the breaking of ties and leaving the premises; and from this also she shrank. Young Lawton, without being asked, had advised her to sell. But she did not want to sell. She wanted the impossible: that matters should proceed in the future as in the past, that Samuel's death should change nothing save in her heart.

In the meantime Miss Insull was priceless. Constance thoroughly understood one side of the shop; but Miss Insull understood both, and the finance of it also. Miss Insull could have directed the establishment with credit, if not with brilliance. She was indeed directing it at that moment. Constance, however, felt jealous of Miss Insull; she was conscious of a slight antipathy towards the faithful one. She did not care to be in the hands of Miss Insull.

There were one or two customers at the millinery counter. They greeted her with a deplorable copiousness of tact. Most tactfully they avoided any reference to Constance's loss; but by their tone, their glances, at Constance and at each other, and their heroically restrained sighs, they spread desolation as though they had been spreading ashes instead of butter on bread. The assistants, too, had a special demeanour for the poor lone widow which was excessively trying to her. She wished to be natural, and she would have succeeded, had they not all of them apparently conspired together to make her task impossible.

She moved away to the other side of the shop, to Samuel's desk, at which he used to stand, staring absently out of the little window into King Street while murmurously casting figures. She lighted the gas-jet there, arranged the light exactly to suit her, and then lifted the large flap of the desk and drew forth some account books.

'Miss Insull!' she called, in a low, clear voice, with a touch of haughtiness and a touch of command in it. The pose, a comical contradiction of Constance's benevolent character, was deliberately adopted; it illustrated the effects of jealousy on even the softest disposition.

Miss Insull responded. She had no alternative but to respond. And she gave no sign of resenting her employer's attitude. But then Miss Insull seldom did give any sign of being human.

The customers departed, one after another, obsequiously sped by the assistants, who thereupon lowered the gases somewhat, according to saecular rule; and in the dim eclipse, as they restored boxes to shelves, they could hear the tranquil, regular, half-whispered conversation of the two women at the desk, discussing accounts; and then the chink of gold.

Suddenly there was an irruption. One of the assistants sprang instinctively to the gas; but on perceiving that the disturber of peace was only a slatternly girl, hatless and imperfectly clean, she decided to leave the gas as it was, and put on a condescending, suspicious demeanour.

'If you please, can I speak to the missis?' said the girl, breathlessly.

She seemed to be about eighteen years of age, fat and plain. Her blue frock was torn, and over it she wore a rough brown apron, caught up at one corner to the waist. Her bare forearms were of brick-red colour.

'What is it?' demanded the assistant.

Miss Insull looked over her shoulder across the shop. 'It must be Maggie's – Mrs Hollins's daughter!' said Miss Insull under her breath.

'What can she want?' said Constance, leaving the desk instantly; and to the girl, who stood sturdily holding her own against the group of assistants, 'You are Mrs Hollins's daughter, aren't you?'

'Yes, mum.'

'What's your name?'

'Maggie, mum. And, if you please, mother's sent me to ask if you'll kindly give her a funeral card.'

'A funeral card?'

'Yes. Of Mr Povey. She's been expecting of one, and she thought as how perhaps you'd forgotten it, especially as she wasn't asked to the funeral.'

The girl stopped.

Constance perceived that by mere negligence she had seriously wounded the feelings of Maggie, senior. The truth was, she had never thought of Maggie. She ought to have remembered that funeral cards were almost the sole ornamentation of Maggie's abominable cottage.

'Certainly,' she replied after a pause. 'Miss Insull, there are a few cards left in the desk, aren't there? Please put me one in an envelope for Mrs Hollins.'

She gave the heavily bordered envelope to the ruddy wench, who enfolded it in her apron, and with hurried, shy thanks ran off.

'Tell your mother I send her a card with pleasure,' Constance
called after the girl.

The strangeness of the hazards of life made her thoughtful. She,
to whom Maggie had always seemed an old woman, was a
widow, but Maggie's husband survived as a lusty invalid. And
she guessed that Maggie, vilely struggling in squalor and poverty,
was somehow happy in her frowsy, careless way.

She went back to the accounts, dreaming.

II

When the shop had been closed, under her own critical and
precise superintendence, she extinguished the last gas in it and
returned to the parlour, wondering where she might discover
some entirely reliable man or boy to deal with the shutters night
and morning. Samuel had ordinarily dealt with the shutters
himself, and on extraordinary occasions and during holidays
Miss Insull and one of her subordinates had struggled with their
unwieldiness. But the extraordinary occasion had now become
ordinary, and Miss Insull could not be expected to continue
indefinitely in the functions of a male. Constance had a mind to
engage an errand-boy, a luxury against which Samuel had always
set his face. She did not dream of asking the herculean Cyril to
open and shut the shop.

He had apparently finished his home-lessons. The books were
pushed aside, and he was sketching in lead-pencil on a drawing-
block. To the right of the fireplace, over the sofa, there hung an
engraving after Landseer, showing a lonely stag paddling into a
lake. The stag at eve had drunk or was about to drink his fill, and
Cyril was copying him. He had already indicated a flight of birds
in the middle distance; vague birds on the wing being easier than
detailed stags, he had begun with the birds.

Constance put a hand on his shoulder. 'Finished your lessons?'
she murmured caressingly.

Before speaking, Cyril gazed up at the picture with a frowning,
busy expression, and then replied in an absent-minded voice:

'Yes.' And after a pause: 'Except my arithmetic. I shall do that
in the morning before breakfast.'

'Oh, Cyril!' she protested.

It had been a positive ordinance, for a long time past, that there should be no sketching until lessons were done. In his father's lifetime Cyril had never dared to break it.

He bent over his block, feigning an intense absorption. Constance's hand slipped from his shoulder. She wanted to command him formally to resume his lessons. But she could not. She feared an argument; she mistrusted herself. And, moreover, it was so soon after his father's death!

'You know you won't have time tomorrow morning!' she said weakly.

'Oh, mother!' he retorted superiorly. 'Don't worry.' And then, in a cajoling tone: 'I've wanted to do that stag for ages.'

She sighed and sat down in her rocking-chair. He went on sketching, rubbing out, and making queer expostulatory noises against his pencil, or against the difficulties needlessly invented by Sir Edwin Landseer. Once he rose and changed the position of the gas-bracket, staring fiercely at the engraving as though it had committed a sin.

Amy came to lay the supper. He did not acknowledge that she existed.

'Now, Master Cyril, after you with that table, if you please!' She announced herself brusquely, with the privilege of an old servant and a woman who would never see thirty again.

'What a nuisance you are, Amy!' he gruffly answered. 'Look here, mother, can't Amy lay the cloth on that half of the table? I'm right in the middle of my drawing. There's plenty of room there for two.'

He seemed not to be aware that, in the phrase 'plenty of room for two', he had made a callous reference to their loss. The fact was, there *was* plenty of room for two.

Constance said quickly: 'Very well, Amy. For this once.'

Amy grunted, but obeyed.

Constance had to summon him twice from art to nourishment. He ate with rapidity, frequently regarding the picture with half-shut, searching eyes. When he had finished, he refilled his glass with water, and put it next to his sketching-block.

'You surely aren't thinking of beginning to paint at this time of night!' Constance exclaimed, astonished.

'Oh *yes*, mother!' he fretfully appealed. 'It's not late.'

Another positive ordinance of his father's had been that there should be nothing after supper except bed. Nine o'clock was the latest permissible moment for going to bed. It was now less than a quarter to.

'It only wants twelve minutes to nine,' Constance pointed out.

'Well, what if it does?'

'Now, Cyril,' she said, 'I do hope you are going to be a good boy, and not cause your mother anxiety.'

But she said it too kindly.

He said sullenly: 'I do think you might let me finish it. I've begun it. It won't take me long.'

She made the mistake of leaving the main point. 'How can you possibly choose your colours properly by gas-light?' she said.

'I'm going to do it in sepia,' he replied in triumph.

'It mustn't occur again,' she said.

He thanked God for a good supper, and sprang to the harmonium, where his paint-box was. Amy cleared away. Constance did crochet-work. There was silence. The clock struck nine, and it also struck half-past nine. She warned him repeatedly. At ten minutes to ten she said persuasively:

'Now, Cyril, when the clock strikes ten I shall really put the gas out.'

The clock struck ten.

'Half a mo, half a mo!' he cried. 'I've done! I've done!'

Her hand was arrested.

Another four minutes elapsed, and then he jumped up. 'There you are!' he said proudly, showing her the block. And all his gestures were full of grace and cajolery.

'Yes, it's very good,' Constance said, rather indifferently.

'I don't believe you care for it!' he accused her, but with a bright smile.

'I care for your health,' she said. 'Just look at that clock!'

He sat down in the other rocking-chair, deliberately.

'Now, Cyril!'

'Well, mother, I suppose you'll let me take my boots off!' He said it with teasing good-humour.

When he kissed her good night, she wanted to cling to him, so affectionate was his kiss; but she could not throw off the habits of restraint which she had been originally taught and had all her life practised. She keenly regretted the inability.

In her bedroom, alone, she listened to his movements as he undressed. The door between the two rooms was unlatched. She had to control a desire to open it ever so little and peep at him. He would not have liked that. He could have enriched her heart beyond all hope, and at no cost to himself; but he did not know his power. As she could not cling to him with her hands, she clung to him with that heart of hers, while moving sedately up and down the room, alone. And her eyes saw him through the solid wood of the door. At last she got heavily into bed. She thought with placid anxiety, in the dark: 'I shall have to be firm with Cyril.' And she thought also, simultaneously: 'He really must be a good boy. He *must*.' And clung to him passionately, without shame! Lying alone there in the dark, she could be as unrestrained and girlish as her heart chose. When she loosed her hold she instantly saw the boy's father arranged in his coffin, or flitting about the room. Then she would hug that vision too, for the pleasure of the pain it gave her.

III

She was reassured as to Cyril during the next few days. He did not attempt to repeat his ingenious naughtiness of the Monday evening, and he came directly home for tea; moreover he had, as a kind of miracle performed to dazzle her, actually risen early on the Tuesday morning and done his arithmetic. To express her satisfaction she had manufactured a specially elaborate straw-frame for the sketch after Sir Edwin Landseer, and had hung it in her bedroom: an honour which Cyril appreciated. She was as happy as a woman suffering from a recent amputation can be: and compared with the long nightmare created by Samuel's monomania and illness, her existence seemed to be now a bene-ficent calm.

Cyril, she thought, had realized the importance in her eyes of tea, of that evening hour and that companionship which were for her the flowering of the day. And she had such confidence in his goodness that she would pour the boiling water on the Horniman tea-leaves even before he arrived: certainty could not be more sure. And then, on the Friday of the first week, he was late! He bounded in, after dark, and the state of his clothes indicated too clearly that he had been playing football in the mud that was a grassy field in summer.

'Have you been kept in, my boy?' she asked, for the sake of form.

'No, mother,' he said casually. 'We were just kicking the ball about a bit. Am I late?'

'Better go and tidy yourself,' she said, not replying to his question. 'You can't sit down in that state. And I'll have some fresh tea made. This is spoilt.'

'Oh, very well!'

Her sacred tea – the institution which she wanted to hallow by long habit, and which was to count before everything with both of them – had been carelessly sacrificed to the kicking of a football in mud! And his father buried not ten days! She was wounded: a deep, clean, dangerous wound that would not bleed. She tried to be glad that he had not lied; he might easily have lied, saying that he had been detained for a fault and could not help being late. No! He was not given to lying; he would lie, like any human being, when a great occasion demanded such prudence, but he was not a liar; he might fairly be called a truthful boy. She tried to be glad, and did not succeed. She would have preferred him to have lied.

Amy, grumbling, had to boil more water.

When he returned to the parlour, superficially cleaned, Constance expected him to apologize in his roundabout boyish way; at any rate to woo and wheedle her, to show by some gesture that he was conscious of having put an affront on her. But his attitude was quite otherwise. His attitude was rather brusque and over-bearing and noisy. He ate a very considerable amount of jam, far too quickly, and then asked for more, in a tone of a monarch who calls for his own. And ere tea was finished he said boldly, apropos of nothing:

'I say, mother, you'll just have to let me go to the School of Art after Easter.'

And stared at her with a fixed challenge in his eyes.

He meant, by the School of Art, the evening classes at the School of Art. His father had decided absolutely against the project. His father had said that it would interfere with his lessons, would keep him up too late at night, and involve absence from home in the evening. The last had always been the real objection. His father had not been able to believe that Cyril's desire to study art sprang purely from his love of art; he could not avoid suspecting that it was a plan to obtain freedom in the evenings – that freedom which Samuel had invariably forbidden. In all Cyril's suggestions Samuel had been ready to detect the same scheme lurking. He had finally said that when Cyril left school and took to a vocation, then he could study art at night if he chose, but not before.

'You know what your father said!' Constance replied.

'But, mother! That's all very well! I'm sure father would have agreed. If I'm going to take up drawing I ought to do it at once. That's what the drawing-master says, and I suppose he ought to know.' He finished on a tone of insolence.

'I can't allow you to do it yet,' said Constance, quietly. 'It's quite out of the question. Quite!'

He pouted and then he sulked. It was war between them.

At times he was the image of his Aunt Sophia. He would not leave the subject alone; but he would not listen to Constance's reasoning. He openly accused her of harshness. He asked her how she could expect him to get on if she thwarted him in his most earnest desires. He pointed to other boys whose parents were wiser.

'It's all very fine of you to put it on father!' he observed sarcastically.

He gave up his drawing entirely.

When she hinted that if he attended the School of Art she would be condemned to solitary evenings, he looked at her as though saying: 'Well, and if you are –?' He seemed to have no heart.

After several weeks of intense unhappiness she said: 'How many evenings do you want to go?'

The war was over.

He was charming again. When she was alone she could cling to

him again. And she said to herself: 'If we can be happy together
only when I give way to him, I must give way to him.' And there
was ecstasy in her yielding. 'After all,' she said to herself, 'perhaps
it's very important that he should go to the School of Art.' She
solaced herself with such thoughts on three solitary evenings a
week, waiting for him to come home.

CHAPTER 7: *Bricks and Mortar*

I

In the summer of that year the occurrence of a white rash of
posters on hoardings and on certain houses and shops, was
symptomatic of organic change in the town. The posters were
iterations of a mysterious announcement and summons, which
began with the august words: 'By Order of the Trustees of the late
William Clews Mericarp, Esq.' Mericarp had been a considerable
owner of property in Bursley. After a prolonged residence at
Southport, he had died, at the age of eighty-two, leaving his
property behind. For sixty years he had been a name, not a figure;
and the news of his death, which was assuredly an event, incited
the burgesses to gossip, for they had come to regard him as one of
the invisible immortals. Constance was shocked, though she had
never seen Mericarp. ('Everybody dies nowadays!' she thought.)
He owned the Baines-Povey shop, and also Mr Critchlow's shop.
Constance knew not how often her father and, later, her husband, had renewed the lease of those premises that were now
hers; but from her earliest recollections rose a vague memory of
her father talking to her mother about 'Mericarp's rent', which
was and always had been a hundred a year. Mericarp had earned
the reputation of being 'a good landlord'. Constance said sadly:
'We shall never have another as good!' When a lawyer's clerk
called and asked her to permit the exhibition of a poster in each of
her shop-windows, she had misgivings for the future; she was
worried; she decided that she would determine the lease next
year, so as to be on the safe side; but immediately afterwards she
decided that she could decide nothing.

The posters continued: 'To be sold by auction at the Tiger Hotel at six-thirty for seven o'clock precisely.' What six-thirty had to do with seven o'clock precisely no one knew. Then, after stating the name and credentials of the auctioneer, the posters at length arrived at the objects to be sold: 'All those freehold messuages and shops and copyhold tenements namely.' Houses were never sold by auction in Bursley. At moments of auction burgesses were reminded that the erections they lived in were not houses, as they had falsely supposed, but messuages. Having got as far as 'namely' the posters ruled a line and began afresh: 'Lot 1. All that extensive and commodious shop and messuage with the offices and appurtenances thereto belonging situate and being No. 4 St Luke's Square in the parish of Bursley in the County of Stafford and at present in the occupation of Mrs Constance Povey widow under a lease expiring in September 1889.' Thus clearly asserting that all Constance's shop was for sale, its whole entirety, and not a fraction or slice of it merely, the posters proceeded: 'Lot 2. All that extensive and commodious shop and messuage with the offices and appurtenances thereto belonging situate and being No. 3 St Luke's Square in the parish of Bursley in the County of Stafford and at present in the occupation of Charles Critchlow chemist under an agreement for a yearly tenancy.' The catalogue ran to fourteen lots. The posters, lest anyone should foolishly imagine that a non-legal intellect could have achieved such explicit and comprehensive clarity of statement, were signed by a powerful firm of solicitors in Hanbridge. Happily in the Five Towns there were no metaphysicians; otherwise the firm might have been expected to explain, in the 'further particulars and conditions' which the posters promised, how even a messuage could 'be' the thing at which it was 'situate'.

Within a few hours of the outbreak of the rash, Mr Critchlow abruptly presented himself before Constance at the millinery counter; he was waving a poster.

'Well!' he exclaimed grimly. 'What next, eh?'

'Yes, indeed!' Constance responded.

'Are ye thinking o' buying?' he asked. All the assistants, including Miss Insull, were in hearing, but he ignored their presence.

'Buying!' repeated Constance. 'Not me! I've got quite enough house property as it is.'

Like all owners of real property, she usually adopted towards her possessions an attitude implying that she would be willing to pay somebody to take them from her.

'Shall *you*?' she added, with Mr Critchlow's own brusqueness.

'Me! Buy property in St Luke's Square!' Mr Critchlow sneered. And then left the shop as suddenly as he had entered it.

The sneer at St Luke's Square was his characteristic expression of an opinion which had been slowly forming for some years. The Square was no longer what it had been, though individual business might be as good as ever. For nearly twelve months two shops had been to let in it. And once, bankruptcy had stained its annals. The tradesmen had naturally searched for a cause in every direction save the right one, the obvious one; and naturally they had found a cause. According to the tradesmen, the cause was 'this football'. The Bursley Football Club had recently swollen into a genuine rival of the ancient supremacy of the celebrated Knype Club. It had transformed itself into a limited company, and rented a ground up the Moorthorne Road, and built a grand stand. The Bursley F.C. had 'tied' with the Knype F.C. on the Knype ground – a prodigious achievement, an achievement which occupied a column of the *Athletic News* one Monday morning! But were the tradesmen civically proud of this glory? No! They said that 'this football' drew people out of the town on Saturday afternoons, to the complete abolition of shopping. They said also that people thought of nothing but 'this football'; and, nearly in the same breath, that only roughs and good-for-nothings could possibly be interested in such a barbarous game. And they spoke of gate-money, gambling, and professionalism, and the end of all true sport in England. In brief, something new had come to the front and was submitting to the ordeal of the curse.

The sale of the Mericarp estate had a particular interest for respectable stake-in-the-town persons. It would indicate to what extent, if at all, 'this football' was ruining Bursley.

Constance mentioned to Cyril that she fancied she might like to go to the sale, and as it was dated for one of Cyril's off-nights

Cyril said that he fancied he might like to go too. So they went together; Samuel used to attend property sales, but he had never taken his wife to one. Constance and Cyril arrived at the Tiger shortly after seven o'clock, and were directed to a room furnished and arranged as for a small public meeting of philanthropists. A few gentlemen were already present, but not the instigating trustees, solicitors, and auctioneers. It appeared that 'six-thirty for seven o'clock precisely' meant seven-fifteen. Constance took a Windsor chair in the corner nearest the door, and motioned Cyril to the next chair; they dared not speak; they moved on tiptoe; Cyril inadvertently dragged his chair along the floor, and produced a scrunching sound; be blushed, as though he had desecrated a church, and his mother made a gesture of horror. The remainder of the company glanced at the corner, apparently pained by this negligence. Some of them greeted Constance, but self-consciously, with a sort of shamed air; it might have been that they had all nefariously gathered together there for the committing of a crime. Fortunately Constance's widowhood had already lost its touching novelty, so that the greetings, if self-conscious, were at any rate given without unendurable commiseration and did not cause awkwardness.

When the official world arrived, fussy, bustling, bearing documents and a hammer, the general feeling of guilty shame was intensified. Useless for the auctioneer to try to dissipate the gloom by means of bright gestures and quick, cheerful remarks to his supporters! Cyril had an idea that the meeting would open with a hymn, until the apparition of a tapster with wine showed him his error. The auctioneer very particularly enjoined the tapster to see to it that no one lacked for his thirst, and the tapster became self-consciously energetic. He began by choosing Constance for service. In refusing wine, she blushed; then the fellow offered a glass to Cyril, who went scarlet, and mumbled 'No' with a lump in his throat; when the tapster's back was turned, he smiled sheepishly at his mother. The majority of the company accepted and sipped. The auctioneer sipped and loudly smacked, and said: 'Ah!'

Mr Critchlow came in.

And the auctioneer said again: 'Ah! I'm always glad when the tenants come. That's always a good sign.'

He glanced round for approval of this sentiment. But everybody seemed too stiff to move. Even the auctioneer was self-conscious.

'Waiter! Offer wine to Mr Critchlow!' he exclaimed bullyingly, as if saying: 'Man! what on earth are you thinking of to neglect Mr Critchlow?'

'Yes, sir; yes, sir,' said the waiter, who was dispensing wine as fast as a waiter can.

The auction commenced.

Seizing the hammer, the auctioneer gave a short biography of William Clews Mericarp, and, this pious duty accomplished, called upon a solicitor to read the conditions of sale. The solicitor complied and made a distressing exhibition of self-consciousness. The conditions of sale were very lengthy, and apparently composed in a foreign tongue; and the audience listened to this elocution with a stoical pretence of breathless interest.

Then the auctioneer put up all that extensive and commodious messuage and shop situate and being No. 4 St Luke's Square. Constance and Cyril moved their limbs surreptitiously, as though being at last found out. The auctioneer referred to John Baines and to Samuel Povey, with a sense of personal loss, and then expressed his pleasure in the presence of 'the ladies'; he meant Constance, who once more had to blush.

'Now, gentlemen,' said the auctioneer, 'what do you say for these famous premises? I think I do not exaggerate when I use the word "famous".'

Someone said a thousand pounds, in the terrorized voice of a delinquent.

'A thousand pounds,' repeated the auctioneer, paused, sipped, and smacked.

'Guineas,' said another voice self-accused of iniquity.

'A thousand and fifty,' said the auctioneer.

Then there was a long interval, an interval that tightened the nerves of the assembly.

'Now, ladies and gentlemen,' the auctioneer adjured.

The first voice said sulkily: 'Eleven hundred.'

And thus the bids rose to fifteen hundred, lifted bit by bit, as it were, by the magnetic force of the auctioneer's personality. The man was now standing up, in domination. He bent down to the solicitor's head; they whispered together.

'Gentlemen,' said the auctioneer, 'I am happy to inform you that the sale is now open.' His tone translated better than words his calm professional beatitude. Suddenly in a voice of wrath he hissed at the waiter: 'Waiter, why don't you serve these gentlemen?'

'Yes, sir; yes, sir.'

The auctioneer sat down and sipped at leisure, chatting with his clerk and the solicitor and the solicitor's clerk.

When he rose it was as a conqueror. 'Gentlemen, fifteen hundred is bid. Now, Mr Critchlow.'

Mr Critchlow shook his head. The auctioneer threw a courteous glance at Constance, who avoided it.

After many adjurations, he reluctantly raised his hammer, pretended to let it fall, and saved it several times.

And then Mr Critchlow said: 'And fifty.'

'Fifteen hundred and fifty is bid,' the auctioneer informed the company, electrifying the waiter once more. And when he had sipped he said, with feigned sadness: 'Come, gentlemen, you surely don't mean to let this magnificent Lot go for fifteen hundred and fifty pounds?'

But they did mean that.

The hammer fell, and the auctioneer's clerk and the solicitor's clerk took Mr Critchlow aside and wrote with him.

Nobody was surprised when Mr Critchlow bought Lot No. 2, his own shop.

Constance whispered then to Cyril that she wished to leave. They left, with unnatural precautions, but instantly regained their natural demeanour in the dark street.

'Well, I never! Well, I never!' she murmured outside, astonished and disturbed.

She hated the prospect of Mr Critchlow as a landlord. And yet she could not persuade herself to leave the place, in spite of decisions.

The sale demonstrated that football had not entirely under-

mined the commercial basis of society in Bursley; only two Lots
had to be withdrawn.

II

On Thursday afternoon of the same week the youth whom
Constance had ended by hiring for the manipulation of shutters
and others jobs unsuitable for fragile women, was closing the
shop. The clock had struck two. All the shutters were up except
the last one, in the midst of the doorway. Miss Insull and her
mistress were walking about the darkened interior, putting dust-
sheets well over the edges of exposed goods; the other assistants
had just left. The bull-terrier had wandered into the shop as he
almost invariably did at closing time – for he slept there, an
efficient guard – and had lain down by the dying stove; though
not venerable, he was stiffening into age.

'You can shut,' said Miss Insull to the youth.

But as the final shutter was ascending to its position, Mr
Critchlow appeared on the pavement.

'Hold on, young fellow!' Mr Critchlow commanded, and
stepped slowly, lifting up his long apron, over the horizontal
shutter on which the perpendicular shutters rested in the doorway.

'Shall you be long, Mr Critchlow?' the youth asked, posing the
shutter. 'Or am I to shut?'

'Shut, lad,' said Mr Critchlow, briefly. 'I'll go out by th' side
door.'

'Here's Mr Critchlow!' Miss Insull called out to Constance, in
a peculiar tone. And a flush, scarcely perceptible, crept very
slowly over her dark features. In the twilight of the shop, lit only
by a few starry holes in the shutters, and by the small side-
window, not the keenest eye could have detected that flush.

'Mr Critchlow!' Constance murmured the exclamation. She
resented his future ownership of her shop. She thought he was
come to play the landlord, and she determined to let him see that
her mood was independent and free, that she would as lief give up
the business as keep it. In particular she meant to accuse him of
having deliberately deceived her as to his intentions on his
previous visit.

'Well, missis!' the aged man greeted her. 'We've made it up between us. Happen some folk'll think we've taken our time, but I don't know as that's their affair.'

His little blinking eyes had a red border. The skin of his pale small face was wrinkled in millions of minute creases. His arms and legs were marvellously thin and sharply angular. The corners of his heliotrope lips were turned down, as usual, in a mysterious comment on the world; and his smile, as he fronted Constance with his excessive height, crowned the mystery.

Constance stared, at a loss. It surely could not after all be true, the substance of the rumours that had floated like vapours in the Square for eight years and more!

'What . . . ?' she began.

'Me, and her!' He jerked his head in the direction of Miss Insull.

The dog had leisurely strolled forward to inspect the edges of the *fiancé*'s trousers. Miss Insull summoned the animal with a noise of fingers, and then bent down and caressed it. A strange gesture proving the validity of Charles Critchlow's discovery that in Maria Insull a human being was buried!

Miss Insull was, as near as anyone could guess, forty years of age. For twenty-five years she had served in the shop, passing about twelve hours a day in the shop; attending regularly at least three religious services at the Wesleyan Chapel or School on Sundays, and sleeping with her mother, whom she kept. She had never earned more than thirty shillings a week, and yet her situation was considered to be exceptionally good. In the eternal fusty dusk of the shop she had gradually lost such sexual characteristics and charms as she had once possessed. She was as thin and flat as Charles Critchlow himself. It was as though her bosom had suffered from a prolonged drought at a susceptible period of development, and had never recovered. The one proof that blood ran in her veins was the pimply quality of her ruined complexion, and the pimples of that brickish expanse proved that the blood was thin and bad. Her hands and feet were large and ungainly; the skin of the fingers was roughened by coarse contacts to the texture of emery-paper. On six days a week she wore black; on the seventh a kind of discreet half-mourning. She was honest, capable, and industrious; and beyond the confines of her occupation she had no curiosity, no intelligence, no ideas. Superstitions and prejudices, deep and violent, served her for ideas; but she could incomparably sell silks and bonnets, braces and oilcloth; in widths, lengths, and prices she never erred; she never annoyed a customer, nor foolishly promised what could not be performed, nor was late or negligent, or disrespectful. No one knew anything about her, because there was nothing to know. Subtract the shop-assistant from her, and naught remained. Benighted and spiritually dead, she existed by habit.

But for Charles Critchlow she happened to be an illusion. He had cast eyes on her and had seen youth, innocence, virginity. During eight years the moth Charles had flitted round the lamp of her brilliance, and was now singed past escape. He might treat her with what casualness he chose; he might ignore her in public; he might talk brutally about women; he might leave her to wonder dully what he meant, for months at a stretch: but there emerged indisputable from the sum of his conduct the fact that he wanted her. He desired her; she charmed him; she was something ornamental and luxurious for which he was ready to pay – and to commit follies. He had been a widower since before she was born; to him she was a slip of a girl. All is relative in this world. As for her, she was too indifferent to refuse him. Why refuse him? Oysters do not refuse.

'I'm sure I congratulate you both,' Constance breathed, realizing the import of Mr Critchlow's laconic words. 'I'm sure I hope you'll be happy.'

'That'll be all right,' said Mr Critchlow.

'Thank you, Mrs Povey,' said Maria Insull.

Nobody seemed to know what to say next. 'It's rather sudden,' was on Constance's tongue, but did not achieve utterance, being patently absurd.

'Ah!' exclaimed Mr Critchlow, as though himself contemplating anew the situation.

Miss Insull gave the dog a final pat.

'So that's settled,' said Mr Critchlow. 'Now, missis, ye want to give up this shop, don't ye?'

'I'm not so sure about that,' Constance answered uneasily.

'Don't tell me!' he protested. 'Of course ye want to give up the shop.'

'I've lived here all my life,' said Constance.

'Ye've not lived in th' shop all your life. I said th' shop. Listen here!' he continued. 'I've got a proposal to make to you. You can keep the house, and I'll take the shop off your hands. Now?' He looked at her inquiringly.

Constance was taken aback by the brusqueness of the suggestion, which, moreover, she did not understand.

'But how —' she faltered.

'Come here,' said Mr Critchlow, impatiently, and he moved towards the house-door of the shop, behind the till.

'Come where? What do you want?' Constance demanded in a maze.

'Here!' said Mr Critchlow, with increasing impatience. 'Follow me, will ye?'

Constance obeyed. Miss Insull sidled after Constance, and the dog after Miss Insull. Mr Critchlow went through the doorway and down the corridor, past the cutting-out room to his right. The corridor then turned at a right-angle to the left and ended at the parlour door, the kitchen steps being to the left.

Mr Critchlow stopped short of the kitchen steps, and extended his arms, touching the walls on either side.

'Here!' he said, tapping the walls with his bony knuckles. 'Here! Suppose I brick ye this up, and th' same upstairs between th' showroom and th' bedroom passage, ye've got your house to yourself. Ye say ye've lived here all your life. Well, what's to prevent ye finishing up here? The fact is,' he added, 'it would only be making into two houses again what was two houses to start with, afore your time, missis.'

'And what about the shop?' cried Constance.

'Ye can sell us th' stock at a valuation.'

Constance suddenly comprehended the scheme. Mr Critchlow would remain the chemist, while Mrs Critchlow became the head of the chief drapery business in the town. Doubtless they would knock a hole through the separating wall on the other side, to balance the bricking-up on this side. They must have thought it all out in detail. Constance revolted.

'Yes!' she said, a little disdainfully. 'And my goodwill? Shall you take that at a valuation too?'

Mr Critchlow glanced at the creature for whom he was ready to scatter thousands of pounds. She might have been a Phryne and he the infatuated fool. He glanced at her as if to say: 'We expected this, and this is where we agreed it was to stop.'

'Ay!' he said to Constance. 'Show me your goodwill. Lap it up in a bit of paper and hand it over, and I'll take it at a valuation. But not afore, missis! Not afore! I'm making ye a very good offer. Twenty pound a year, I'll let ye th' house for. And take th' stock at a valuation. Think it over, my lass.'

Having said what he had to say, Charles Critchlow departed according to his custom. He unceremoniously let himself out by the side door, and passed with wavy apron round the corner of King Street into the Square and so to his own shop, which ignored the Thursday half-holiday. Miss Insull left soon afterwards.

III

Constance's pride urged her to refuse the offer. But in truth her sole objection to it was that she had not thought of the scheme herself. For the scheme really reconciled her wish to remain where she was with her wish to be free of the shop.

'I shall make him put me in a new window in the parlour – one that will open!' she said positively to Cyril, who accepted Mr Critchlow's idea with fatalistic indifference.

After stipulating for the new window, she closed with the offer. Then there was the stock-taking, which endured for weeks. And then the carpenter came and measured for the window. And a builder and a mason came and inspected doorways, and Constance felt that the end was upon her. She took up the carpet in the parlour and protected the furniture by dust-sheets. She and Cyril lived between bare boards and dust-sheets for twenty days, and neither carpenter nor mason reappeared. Then one surprising day the old window was removed by the carpenter's two journeymen, and late in the afternoon the carpenter brought the new window, and the three men worked till ten o'clock at night, fixing it. Cyril wore his cap and went to bed in his cap, and Constance wore a Paisley shawl. A painter had bound himself beyond all

possibility of failure to paint the window on the morrow. He was
to begin at six a.m., and Amy's alarm-clock was altered so that
she might be up and dressed to admit him. He came a week later,
administered one coat, and vanished for another ten days.

Then two masons suddenly came with heavy tools, and were
shocked to find that all was not prepared for them. (After three
carpetless weeks Constance had relaid her floors.) They tore off
wall-paper, sent cascades of plaster down the kitchen steps,
withdrew alternate courses of bricks from the walls, and, sated
with destruction, hastened away. After four days new red bricks
began to arrive, carried by a quite guiltless hodman who had not
visited the house before. The hodman met the full storm of
Constance's wrath. It was not a vicious wrath, rather a good-
humoured wrath; but it impressed the hodman. 'My house hasn't
been fit to live in for a month,' she said in fine. 'If these walls
aren't built tomorrow, upstairs *and* down – tomorrow, mind! –
don't let any of you dare to show your noses here again, for I
won't have you. Now you've brought your bricks. Off with you,
and tell your master what I say!'

It was effective. The next day subdued and plausible workmen
of all sorts awoke the house with knocking at six-thirty precisely,
and the two doorways were slowly bricked up. The curious thing
was that, when the barrier was already a foot high on the ground
floor Constance remembered small possessions of her own which
she had omitted to remove from the cutting-out room. Picking up
her skirts, she stepped over into the region that was no more hers,
and stepped back with the goods. She had a bandanna round her
head to keep the thick dust out of her hair. She was very busy,
very preoccupied with nothings. She had no time for sentimenta-
lities. Yet when the men arrived at the topmost course and were at
last hidden behind their own erection, and she could see only
rough bricks and mortar, she was disconcertingly overtaken by a
misty blindness and could not even see bricks and mortar. Cyril
found her, with her absurd bandanna, weeping in a sheet-covered
rocking-chair in the sacked parlour. He whistled uneasily, remarked: 'I say, mother, what about tea?' and then, hearing the
heavy voices of workmen above, ran with relief upstairs. Tea had
been set in the drawing-room, he was glad to learn that from

Amy, who informed him also that she should 'never get used to
them there new walls', not as long as she lived.

He went to the School of Art that night. Constance, alone,
could find nothing to do. She had willed that the walls should be
built, and they had been built; but days must elapse before they
could be plastered, and after the plaster still more days before the
papering. Not for another month, perhaps, would her house be
free of workmen and ripe for her own labours. She could only sit
in the dust-drifts and contemplate the havoc of change, and keep
her eyes as dry as she could. The legal transactions were all but
complete; little bills announcing the transfer of the business lay
on the counters in the shop at the disposal of customers. In two
days Charles Critchlow would pay the price of a desire realized.
The sign was painted out and new letters sketched thereon in
chalk. In future she would be compelled, if she wished to enter the
shop, to enter it as a customer and from the front. Yes, she saw
that, though the house remained hers, the root of her life had been
wrenched up.

And the mess! It seemed inconceivable that the material mess
could ever be straightened away!

Yet, ere the fields of the county were first covered with snow
that season, only one sign survived of the devastating revolution,
and that was a loose sheet of wall-paper that had been too soon
pasted on the new plaster and would not stick. Maria Insull was
Maria Critchlow. Constance had been out into the Square and
seen the altered sign, and seen Mrs Critchlow's taste in window-
curtains, and seen – most impressive sight of all – that the grimy
window of the abandoned room at the top of the abandoned
staircase next to the bedroom of her girlhood had been cleaned
and a table put in front of it. She knew that the chamber, which
she herself had never entered, was to be employed as a store-
room, but the visible proof of its conversion so strangely affected
her that she had not felt able to go boldly into the shop, as she had
meant to do, and make a few purchases in the way of friendliness.
'I'm a silly woman!' she muttered. Later, she did venture, timidly
abrupt, into the shop, and was received with fitting state by Mrs
Critchlow (as desiccated as ever), who insisted on allowing her
the special trade discount. And she carried her little friendly

purchases round to her own door in King Street. Trivial, trivial event! Constance, not knowing whether to laugh or cry, did both. She accused herself of developing a hysterical faculty in tears, and strove sagely against it.

CHAPTER 8: *The Proudest Mother*

I

In the year 1893 there was a new and strange man living at No. 4, St Luke's Square. Many people remarked on the phenomenon. Very few of his like had ever been seen in Bursley before. One of the striking things about him was the complex way in which he secured himself by means of glittering chains. A chain stretched across his waistcoat, passing through a special button-hole, without a button, in the middle. To this cable were firmly linked a watch at one end and a pencil-case at the other; the chain also served as a protection against a thief who might attempt to snatch the fancy waistcoat entire. Then there were longer chains, beneath the waistcoat, partly designed, no doubt, to deflect bullets, but serving mainly to enable the owner to haul up penknives, cigarette-cases, match-boxes, and key-rings from the profundities of hip-pockets. An essential portion of the man's braces, visible sometimes when he played at tennis, consisted of chain, and the upper and nether halves of his cuff-links were connected by chains. Occasionally he was to be seen chained to a dog.

A reversion, conceivably, to a medieval type! Yes, but also the exemplar of the excessively modern! Externally he was a consequence of the fact that, years previously, the leading tailor in Bursley had permitted his son to be apprenticed in London. The father died; the son had the wit to return and make a fortune while creating a new type in the town, a type of which multiple chains were but one feature, and that the least expensive if the most salient. For instance, up to the historic year in which the young tailor created the type, any cap was a cap in Bursley, and any collar was a collar. But thenceforward no cap was a cap, and no collar was a collar, which did not exactly conform in shape and material to certain sacred caps and collars guarded by the young tailor in his back shop. None knew why these sacred caps and collars were sacred, but they were; their sacredness endured for about six months, and then suddenly – again none knew why – they fell from their estate and became lower than offal for dogs, and were supplanted on the altar. The type brought into existence by the young tailor was to be recognized by its caps and collars, and in a similar manner by every other article of attire, except its boots. Unfortunately the tailor did not sell boots, and so imposed on his creatures no mystical creed as to boots. This was a pity, for the boot-makers of the town happened not to be inflamed by the type-creating passion as the tailor was, and thus the new type finished abruptly at the edges of the tailor's trousers.

The man at No. 4, St Luke's Square had comparatively small and narrow feet, which gave him an advantage; and as he was endowed with a certain vague general physical distinction he managed, despite the eternal untidiness of his hair, to be eminent among the type. Assuredly the frequent sight of him in her house flattered the pride of Constance's eye, which rested on him almost always with pleasure. He had come into the house with startling abruptness soon after Cyril left school and was indentured to the head designer at 'Peel's', that classic earthenware manufactory. The presence of a man in her abode disconcerted Constance at the beginning; but she soon grew accustomed to it, perceiving that a man would behave as a man, and must be expected to do so. This man, in truth, did what he liked in all things. Cyril having always been regarded by both his parents as enormous, one would have anticipated a giant in the new man; but, queerly, he was slim, and little above the average height. Neither in enormity nor in many other particulars did he resemble the Cyril whom he had supplanted. His gestures were lighter and quicker; he had nothing of Cyril's ungainliness; he had not Cyril's limitless taste for sweets, nor Cyril's terrific hatred of gloves, barbers, and soap. He was much more dreamy than Cyril, and much busier. In fact, Constance only saw him at meal-times. He was at Peel's in the day and at the School of Art every night. He would dream during a meal, even; and, without actually saying so, he gave the impression that he was the busiest man in Bursley, wrapped in occupations and preoccupations as in a blanket – a blanket which Constance had difficulty in penetrating.

Constance wanted to please him; she lived for nothing but to please him; he was, however, exceedingly difficult to please, not in the least because he was hypercritical and exacting, but because he was indifferent. Constance, in order to satisfy her desire of pleasing, had to make fifty efforts, in the hope that he might chance to notice one. He was a good man, amazingly industrious – when once Constance had got him out of bed in the morning; with no vices; kind, save when Constance mistakenly tried to thwart him; charming, with a curious strain of humour that Constance only half understood. Constance was unquestionably vain about him, and she could honestly find in him little to blame. But whereas he was the whole of her universe, she was merely a dim figure in the background of his. Every now and then, with his gentle, elegant raillery, he would apparently rediscover her, as though saying: 'Ah! You're still there, are you?' Constance could not meet him on the plane where his interests lay, and he never knew the passionate intensity of her absorption in that minor part of his life which moved on her plane. He never worried about her solitude, or guessed that in throwing her a smile and a word at supper he was paying her meagrely for three hours of lone rocking in a rocking-chair.

The worst of it was that she was quite incurable. No experience would suffice to cure her trick of continually expecting him to notice things which he never did notice. One day he said, in the midst of a silence: 'By the way, didn't father leave any boxes of cigars?' She had the steps up into her bedroom and reached down from the dusty top of the wardrobe the box which she had put there after Samuel's funeral. In handing him the box she was doing a great deed. His age was nineteen, and she was ratifying his precocious habit of smoking by this solemn gift. He entirely ignored the box for several days. She said timidly: 'Have you tried those cigars?' 'Not yet,' he replied. 'I'll try 'em one of these days.' Ten days later, on a Sunday when he chanced not to have gone out with his aristocratic friend Matthew Peel-Swynnerton, he did at length open the box and take out a cigar. 'Now,' he observed roguishly, cutting the cigar, 'we shall see, Mrs Plover!' He often called her Mrs Plover, for fun. Though she liked him to be sufficiently interested in her to tease her, she did not like being called Mrs Plover, and she never failed to say: 'I'm not Mrs Plover.' He smoked the cigar slowly, in the rocking-chair, throwing his head back and sending clouds to the ceiling. And afterwards he remarked: 'The old man's cigars weren't so bad.' 'Indeed!' she answered tartly, as if maternally resenting this easy patronage. But in secret she was delighted. There was something in her son's favourable verdict on her husband's cigars that thrilled her.

And she looked at him. Impossible to see in him any resemblance to his father! Oh! He was a far more brilliant, more advanced, more complicated, more seductive being than his homely father! She wondered where he had come from. And yet . . . ! If his father had lived, what would have occurred between them? Would the boy have been openly smoking cigars in the house at nineteen?

She laboriously interested herself, so far as he would allow, in his artistic studies and productions. A back attic on the second floor was now transformed into a studio – a naked apartment which smelt of oil and of damp clay. Often there were traces of clay on the stairs. For working in clay he demanded of his mother a smock, and she made a smock, on the model of a genuine smock which she obtained from a country-woman who sold eggs and butter in the Covered Market. Into the shoulders of the smock she put a week's fancy-stitching, taking the pattern from an old book of embroidery. One day when he had seen her stitching morn, noon, and afternoon, at the smock, he said, as she rocked idly after supper: 'I suppose you haven't forgotten all about the smock I asked you for, have you, mater?' She knew that he was teasing her; but, while perfectly realizing how foolish she was, she nearly always acted as though his teasing was serious; she picked up the smock again from the sofa. When the smock was finished he examined it intently; then exclaimed with an air of surprise: 'By Jove! That's beautiful! Where did you get this pattern?' He continued to stare at it, smiling in pleasure. He turned over the tattered leaves of the embroidery-book with the same naïve, charmed astonishment, and carried the book away to the studio. 'I must show that to Swynnerton,' he said. As for her, the epithet 'beautiful' seemed a strange epithet to apply to a mere piece of honest stitchery done in a pattern, and a stitch with which she had been familiar all her life. The fact was she understood his 'art' less and less. The sole wall decoration of his studio was a Japanese print, which struck her as being entirely preposterous, considered as a picture. She much preferred his own early drawings of moss-roses and picturesque castles – things that he now mercilessly condemned. Later, he discovered her cutting out another smock. 'What's that for?' he inquired. 'Well,' she said, 'you can't manage with one smock. What shall you do when that one has to go to the wash?' 'Wash!' he repeated vaguely. 'There's no need for it to go to the wash.' 'Cyril,' she replied, 'don't try my patience! I was thinking of making you half a dozen.' He whistled. 'With all that stitching?' he questioned, amazed at the undertaking. 'Why not?' she said. In her young days, no sempstress ever made fewer than half a dozen of anything, and it was usually a dozen; it was sometimes half a dozen. 'Well,' he murmured, 'you have got a nerve! I'll say that.'

Similar things happened whenever he showed that he was pleased. If he said of a dish, in the local tongue: 'I could do a bit of that!' or if he simply smacked his lips over it, she would surfeit him with that dish.

II

On a hot day in August, just before they were to leave Bursley for a month in the Isle of Man, Cyril came home, pale and perspiring, and dropped on to the sofa. He wore a grey alpaca suit, and, except his hair, which in addition to being very untidy was damp with sweat, he was a masterpiece of slim elegance, despite the heat. He blew out great sighs, and rested his head on the antimacassared arm of the sofa.

'Well, mater,' he said, in a voice of factitious calm, 'I've got it.' He was looking up at the ceiling.

'Got what?'

'The National Scholarship. Swynnerton says it's a sheer fluke. But I've got it. Great glory for the Bursley School of Art!'

'National Scholarship?' she said. 'What's that? What is it?'

'Now, mother!' he admonished her, not without testiness. 'Don't go and say I've never breathed a word about it!'

He lit a cigarette, to cover his self-consciousness, for he perceived that she was moved far beyond the ordinary.

Never, in fact, not even by the death of her husband, had she received such a frightful blow as that which the dreamy Cyril had just dealt her.

It was not a complete surprise, but it was nearly a complete surprise. A few months previously he certainly had mentioned, in his incidental way, the subject of a National Scholarship. Apropos of a drinking-cup which he had designed, he had said that the director of the School of Art had suggested that it was good enough to compete for the National, and that as he was otherwise qualified for the competition he might as well send the cup to South Kensington. He had added that Peel-Swynnerton had laughed at the notion as absurd. On that occasion she had comprehended that a National Scholarship involved residence in London. She ought to have begun to live in fear, for Cyril had a most disturbing habit of making a mere momentary reference to matters which he deemed very important and which occupied a large share of his attention. He was secretive by nature, and the rigidity of his father's rule had developed this trait in his character. But really he had spoken of the competition with such an extreme casualness that with little effort she had dismissed it from her anxieties as involving a contingency so remote as to be negligible. She had, genuinely, almost forgotten it. Only at rare intervals had it wakened in her a dull transitory pain – like the herald of a fatal malady. And, as a woman in the opening stage of disease, she had hastily reassured herself: 'How silly of me! This can't possibly be anything serious!'

And now she was condemned. She knew it. She knew there could be no appeal. She knew that she might as usefully have besought mercy from a tiger as from her good, industrious, dreamy son.

'It means a pound a week,' said Cyril, his self-consciousness intensified by her silence and by the dreadful look on her face. 'And of course free tuition.'

'For how long?' she managed to say.

'Well,' said he, 'that depends. Nominally for a year. But if you behave yourself it's always continued for three years.'

If he stayed for three years he would never come back: that was a certainty.

How she rebelled, furious and despairing, against the fortuitous cruelty of things! She was sure that he had not, till then, thought seriously of going to London. But the fact that the Government would admit him free to its classrooms and give him a pound a week besides, somehow forced him to go to London. It was not the lack of means that would have prevented him from going. Why, then, should the presence of means induce him to go? There was no logical reason. The whole affair was disastrously absurd. The art master at the Wedgwood Institution had chanced, merely chanced, to suggest that the drinking-cup should be sent to South Kensington. And the result of this caprice was that she was sentenced to solitude for life! It was too monstrously, too incredibly wicked!

With what futile and bitter execration she murmured in her heart the word 'If'. If Cyril's childish predilections had not been encouraged! If he had only been content to follow his father's trade! If she had flatly refused to sign his indenture at Peel's and pay the premium! If he had not turned from colour to clay! If the art master had not had that fatal 'idea'! If the judges for the competition had decided otherwise! If only she had brought Cyril up in habits of obedience, sacrificing temporary peace to permanent security!

For after all he could not abandon her without her consent. He was not of age. And he would want a lot more money, which he could obtain from none but her. She could refuse . . . No! She could not refuse. He was the master, the tyrant. For the sake of daily pleasantness she had weakly yielded to him at the start! She had behaved badly to herself and to him. He was spoiled. She had spoiled him. And he was about to repay her with life-long misery, and nothing would deflect him from his course. The usual conduct of the spoilt child! Had she not witnessed it, and moralized upon it, in other families?

'You don't seem very chirpy over it, mater!' he said.

She went out of the room. His joy in the prospect of departure

from the Five Towns, from her, though he masked it, was more
manifest than she could bear.

The *Signal*, the next day, made a special item of the news. It
appeared that no National Scholarship had been won in the Five
Towns for eleven years. The citizens were exhorted to remember
that Mr Povey had gained his success in open competition with
the cleverest young students of the entire kingdom – and in a
branch of art which he had but recently taken up; and further,
that the Government offered only eight scholarships each year.
The name of Cyril Povey passed from lip to lip. And nobody who
met Constance, in street or shop, could refrain from informing
her that she ought to be a proud mother, to have such a son, but
that truly they were not surprised . . . and how proud his poor
father would have been! A few sympathetically hinted that
maternal pride was one of those luxuries that may cost too dear.

III

The holiday in the Isle of Man was of course ruined for her. She
could scarcely walk because of the weight of a lump of lead that
she carried in her bosom. On the brightest days the lump of
lead was always there. Besides, she was so obese. In ordinary
circumstances they might have stayed beyond the month. An
indentured pupil is not strapped to the wheel like a common
apprentice. Moreover, the indentures were to be cancelled. But
Constance did not care to stay. She had to prepare for his departure to London. She had to lay the faggots for her own martyrdom.

In this business of preparation she showed as much silliness,
she betrayed as perfect a lack of perspective, as the most superior
son could desire for a topic of affectionate irony. Her preoccupation with petty things of no importance whatever was worthy of
the finest traditions of fond motherhood. However, Cyril's careless satire had no effect on her, save that once she got angry,
thereby startling him; he quite correctly and sagely laid this
unprecedented outburst to the account of her wrought nerves,
and forgave it. Happily for the smoothness of Cyril's translation
to London, young Peel-Swynnerton was acquainted with the
capital, had a brother in Chelsea, knew of reputable lodgings,

was, indeed, an encyclopaedia of the town, and would himself spend a portion of the autumn there. Otherwise, the preliminaries which his mother would have insisted on by means of tears and hysteria might have proved fatiguing to Cyril.

The day came when on that day week Cyril would be gone. Constance steadily fabricated cheerfulness against the prospect. She said:

'Suppose I come with you?'

He smiled in toleration of this joke as being a passable quality of joke. And then she smiled in the same sense, hastening to agree with him that as a joke it was not a bad joke.

In the last week he was very loyal to his tailor. Many a young man would have commanded new clothes after, not before, his arrival in London. But Cyril had faith in his creator.

On the day of departure the household, the very house itself, was in a state of excitement. He was to leave early. He would not listen to the project of her accompanying him as far as Knype, where the Loop Line joined the main. She might go to Bursley Station and no further. When she rebelled he disclosed the merest hint of his sullen-churlish side, and she at once yielded. During breakfast she did not cry, but the aspect of her face made him protest.

'Now, look here, mater! Just try to remember that I shall be back for Christmas. It's barely three months.' And he lit a cigarette.

She made no reply.

Amy lugged a Gladstone bag down the crooked stairs. A trunk was already close to the door; it had wrinkled the carpet and deranged the mat.

'You didn't forget to put the hair-brush in, did you, Amy?' he asked.

'N – no, Mr Cyril,' she blubbered.

'Amy!' Constance sharply corrected her, as Cyril ran upstairs, 'I wonder you can't control yourself better than that.'

Amy weakly apologized. Although treated almost as one of the family, she ought not to have forgotten that she was a servant. What right had she to weep over Cyril's luggage? This question was put to her in Constance's tone.

The cab came. Cyril tumbled downstairs with exaggerated carelessness, and with exaggerated carelessness he joked at the cabman.

'Now, mother!' he cried, when the luggage was stowed. 'Do you want me to miss the train?' But he knew that the margin of time was ample. It was his fun!

'Nay, I can't be hurried!' she said, fixing her bonnet. 'Amy, as soon as we are gone you can clear this table.'

She climbed heavily into the cab.

'That's it! Smash the springs!' Cyril teased her.

The horse got a stinging cut to recall him to the seriousness of life. It was a fine, bracing autumn morning, and the driver felt the need of communicating his abundant energy to someone or something. They drove off, Amy staring after them from the door. Matters had been so marvellously well arranged that they arrived at the station twenty minutes before the train was due.

'Never mind!' Cyril mockingly comforted his mother. 'You'd rather be twenty minutes too soon than one minute too late, wouldn't you?'

His high spirits had to come out somehow.

Gradually the minutes passed, and the empty slate-tinted platform became dotted with people to whom that train was nothing but a Loop Line train, people who took that train every week-day of their lives and knew all its eccentricities.

And they heard the train whistle as it started from Turnhill. And Cyril had a final word with the porter who was in charge of the luggage. He made a handsome figure, and he had twenty pounds in his pocket. When he returned to Constance she was sniffing, and through her veil he could see that her eyes were circled with red. But through her veil she could see nothing. The train rolled in, rattling to a standstill. Constance lifted her veil and kissed him; and kissed her life out. He smelt the odour of her crape. He was, for an instant, close to her, close; and he seemed to have an overwhelmingly intimate glimpse into her secrets; he seemed to be choked in the sudden strong emotion of that crape. He felt queer.

'Here you are, sir! Second smoker!' called the porter.

The daily frequenters of the train boarded it with their customary disgust.

'I'll write as soon as ever I get there!' said Cyril, of his own accord. It was the best he could muster.

With what grace he raised his hat!

A sliding-away; clouds of steam; and she shared the dead platform with milk-cans, two porters, and Smith's noisy boy!

She walked home very slowly and painfully. The lump of lead was heavier than ever before. And the townspeople saw the proudest mother in Bursley walking home.

'After all,' she argued with her soul angrily, petulantly, 'could you expect the boy to do anything else? He is a serious student, he has had a brilliant success, and is he to be tied to your apron-strings? The idea is preposterous. It isn't as if he was an idler, or a bad son. No mother could have a better son. A nice thing that he should stay all his life in Bursley simply because you don't like being left alone!'

Unfortunately one might as well argue with a mule as with one's soul. Her soul only kept on saying monotonously: 'I'm a lonely old woman now. I've nothing to live for any more, and I'm no use to anybody. Once I was young and proud. And this is what my life has come to! This is the end!'

When she reached home, Amy had not touched the breakfast things; the carpet was still wrinkled, and the mat still out of place. And, through the desolating atmosphere of reaction after a terrific crisis, she marched directly upstairs, entered his plundered room, and beheld the disorder of the bed in which he had slept.

BOOK THREE: SOPHIA

CHAPTER I: *The Elopement*

I

Her soberly rich dress had a countrified air, as she waited, ready for the streets, in the bedroom of the London hotel on the afternoon of the first of July, 1866; but there was nothing of the provincial in that beautiful face, nor in that bearing at once shy and haughty; and her eager heart soared beyond geographical boundaries.

It was the Hatfield Hotel, in Salisbury Street, between the Strand and the river. Both street and hotel are now gone, lost in the vast foundations of the Savoy and the Cecil; but the type of the Hatfield lingers with ever-increasing shabbiness in Jermyn Street. In 1866, with its dark passages and crooked stairs, its candles, its carpets and stuffs which had outlived their patterns, its narrow dining-room where a thousand busy flies ate together at one long table, its acrid stagnant atmosphere, and its disturbing sensation of dirt everywhere concealing itself, it stood forth in rectitude as a good average modern hotel. The patched and senile drabness of the bedroom made an environment that emphasized Sophia's flashing youth. She alone in it was unsullied.

There was a knock at the door, apparently gay and jaunty. But she thought, truly: 'He's nearly as nervous as I am!' And in her sick nervousness she coughed, and then tried to take full possession of herself. The moment had at last come which would divide her life as a battle divides the history of a nation. Her mind in an instant swept backwards through an incredible three months.

The schemings to obtain and to hide Gerald's letters at the shop, and to reply to them! The far more complex and dangerous duplicity practised upon her majestic aunt at Axe! The visits to the Axe post-office! The three divine meetings with Gerald at early morning by the canal-feeder, when he had told her of his inheritance and of the harshness of his uncle Boldero, and with a rush of words had spread before her the prospect of eternal bliss! The nights of fear! The sudden, dizzy acquiescence in his plan, and the feeling of universal unreality which obsessed her! The audacious departure from her aunt's, showering a cascade of appalling lies! Her dismay at Knype Station! Her blush as she asked for a ticket to London! The ironic, sympathetic glance of the porter, who took charge of her trunk! And then the thunder of the incoming train! Her renewed dismay when she found that it was very full, and her distracted plunge into a compartment with six people already in it! And the abrupt reopening of the carriage-door and that curt inquisition from an inspector: 'Where for, please? Where for? Where for?' Until her turn was reached: 'Where for, miss?' and her weak little reply: 'Euston!' And more violent blushes! And then the long, steady beating of the train over the rails, keeping time to the rhythm of the unanswerable voice within her breast: 'Why are you here? Why are you here?' And then Rugby; and the awful ordeal of meeting Gerald, his entry into the compartment, the rearrangement of seats, and their excruciatingly painful attempts at commonplace conversation in the publicity of the carriage! (She had felt that that part of the enterprise had not been very well devised by Gerald.) And at last London; the thousands of cabs, the fabulous streets, the general roar, all dream-surpassing, intensifying to an extraordinary degree the obsession of unreality, the illusion that she could not really have done what she had done, that she was not really doing what she was doing!

Supremely and finally, the delicious torture of the clutch of terror at her heart as she moved by Gerald's side through the impossible adventure! Who was this rash, mad Sophia? Surely not herself!

The knock at the door was impatiently repeated.

'Come in,' she said timidly.

Gerald Scales came in. Yes, beneath that mien of a commercial traveller who has been everywhere and through everything, he was very nervous. It was her privacy that, with her consent, he had invaded. He had engaged the bedroom only with the intention of using it as a retreat for Sophia until the evening, when they were to resume their travels. It ought not to have had any disturbing significance. But the mere disorder on the wash-stand, a towel lying on one of the cane chairs, made him feel that he was affronting decency, and so increased his jaunty nervousness. The moment was painful; the moment was difficult beyond his skill to handle it naturally.

Approaching her with factitious ease, he kissed her through her veil, which she then lifted with an impulsive movement, and he kissed her again, more ardently, perceiving that her ardour was exceeding his. This was the first time they had been alone together since her flight from Axe. And yet, with his worldly experience, he was naïve enough to be surprised that he could not put all the heat of passion into his embrace, and he wondered why he was not thrilled at the contact with her! However, the powerful clinging of her lips somewhat startled his senses, and also delighted him by its silent promise. He could smell the stuff of her veil, the sarsenet of her bodice, and, as it were wrapped in these odours as her body was wrapped in its clothes, the faint fleshly perfume of her body itself. Her face, viewed so close that he could see the almost imperceptible down on those fruit-like cheeks, was astonishingly beautiful; the dark eyes were exquisitely misted; and he could feel the secret loyalty of her soul ascending to him. She was very slightly taller than her lover; but somehow she hung from him, her body curved backwards, and her bosom pressed against his, so that instead of looking up at her gaze he looked down at it. He preferred that; perfectly proportioned though he was, his stature was a delicate point with him. His spirits rose by the uplift of his senses. His fears slipped away; he began to be very satisfied with himself. He was the inheritor of twelve thousand pounds, and he had won this unique creature. She was his capture; he held her close, permittedly scanning the minutiae of her skin, permittedly crushing her flimsy silks. Something in him had forced her to lay her modesty on the altar of his desire. And the sun brightly shone. So he kissed her yet more ardently, and with the slightest touch of a victor's condescension; and her burning response more than restored the self-confidence which he had been losing.

'I've got no one but you now,' she murmured in a melting voice.

She fancied in her ignorance that the expression of this sentiment would please him. She was not aware that a man is usually rather chilled by it, because it proves to him that the other is thinking about his responsibilities and not about his privileges. Certainly it calmed Gerald, though without imparting to him her sense of his responsibilities. He smiled vaguely. To Sophia his smile was a miracle continually renewed; it mingled dashing gaiety with a hint of wistful appeal in a manner that never failed to bewitch her. A less innocent girl than Sophia might have divined from that adorable half-feminine smile that she could do anything with Gerald except rely on him. But Sophia had to learn.

'Are you ready?' he asked, placing his hands on her shoulders and holding her away from him.

'Yes,' she said, nerving herself. Their faces were still very near together.

'Well, would you like to go and see the Doré pictures?'

A simple enough question! A proposal felicitous enough! Doré was becoming known even in the Five Towns, not, assuredly, by his illustrations to the *Contes Drolatiques* of Balzac, but by his shuddering Biblical conceits. In pious circles Doré was saving art from the reproach of futility and frivolity. It was indubitably a tasteful idea on Gerald's part to take his love of a summer's afternoon to gaze at the originals of those prints which had so deeply impressed the Five Towns. It was an idea that sanctified the profane adventure.

Yet Sophia showed signs of affliction. Her colour went and came; her throat made the motion of swallowing; there was a muscular contraction over her whole body. And she drew herself from him. Her glance, however, did not leave him, and his eyes fell before hers.

'But what about the wedding?' she breathed.

That sentence seemed to cost all her pride; but she was obliged to utter it, and to pay for it.

'Oh,' he said lightly and quickly, just as though she had reminded him of a detail that might have been forgotten, 'I was just going to tell you. It can't be done here. There's been some change in the rules. I only found out for certain late last night. But I've ascertained that it'll be as simple as A B C before the English

Consul in Paris; and as I've got the tickets for us to go over tonight, as we arranged . . .' He stopped.

She sat down on the towel-covered chair, staggered. She believed what he said. She did not suspect that he was using the classic device of the seducer. It was his casualness that staggered her. Had it really been his intention to set off on an excursion and remark as an afterthought: '*By the way*, we can't be married as I told you at half-past two today'? Despite her extreme ignorance and innocence, Sophia held a high opinion of her own common sense and capacity for looking after herself, and she could scarcely believe that he was expecting her to go to Paris, and at night, without being married. She looked pitiably young, virgin, raw, unsophisticated; helpless in the midst of dreadful dangers. Yet her head was full of a blank astonishment at being mistaken for a simpleton! The sole explanation could be that Gerald, in some matters, must himself be a confiding simpleton. He had not reflected. He had not sufficiently realized the immensity of her sacrifice in flying with him even to London. She felt sorry for him. She had the woman's first glimpse of the necessity for some adjustment of outlook as an essential preliminary to uninterrupted happiness.

'It'll be all right!' Gerald persuasively continued.

He looked at her, as she was not looking at him. She was nineteen. But she seemed to him utterly mature and mysterious. Her face baffled him; her mind was a foreign land. Helpless in one sense she might be; yet she, and not he, stood for destiny; the future lay in the secret and capricious workings of that mind.

'Oh no!' she exclaimed curtly. 'Oh no!'

'Oh no what?'

'We can't possibly go like that,' she said.

'But don't I tell you it'll be all right?' he protested. 'If we stay here and they come after you . . . ! Besides, I've got the tickets and all.'

'Why didn't you tell me sooner?' she demanded.

'But how could I?' he grumbled. 'Have we had a single minute alone?'

This was nearly true. They could not have discussed the formalities of marriage in the crowded train, nor during the hurried lunch with a dozen cocked ears at the same table. He saw himself on sure ground here.

'Now, could we?' he pressed.

'And you talk about going to see pictures!' was her reply.

Undoubtedly this had been a grave error of tact. He recognized that it was a stupidity. And so he resented it, as though she had committed it and not he.

'My dear girl,' he said, hurt, 'I acted for the best. It isn't my fault if rules are altered and officials silly.'

'You ought to have told me before,' she persisted sullenly.

'But how *could* I?'

He almost believed in that moment that he had really intended to marry her, and that the ineptitudes of red-tape had prevented him from achieving his honourable purpose; whereas he had done nothing whatever towards the marriage.

'Oh no! Oh no!' she repeated, with heavy lip and liquid eye. 'Oh no!'

He gathered that she was flouting his suggestion of Paris.

Slowly and nervously he approached her. She did not stir or look up. Her glance was fixed on the washstand. He bent down and murmured:

'Come, now. It'll be all right. You'll travel in the ladies' saloon on the steam-packet.'

She did not stir. He bent lower and touched the back of her neck with his lips. And she sprang up, sobbing and angry. Because she was mad for him she hated him furiously. All tenderness had vanished.

'I'll thank you not to touch me!' she said fiercely. She had given him her lips a moment ago, but now to graze her neck was an insult.

He smiled sheepishly. 'But really you must be reasonable,' he argued. 'What have I done?'

'It's what you haven't done, I think!' she cried. 'Why didn't you tell me while we were in the cab?'

'I didn't care to begin worrying you just then,' he replied: which was exactly true.

The fact was, he had of course shirked telling her that no marriage would occur that day. Not being a professional seducer of young girls, he lacked skill to do a difficult thing simply.

'Now come along, little girl,' he went on, with just a trifle of impatience. 'Let's go out and enjoy ourselves. I assure you that everything will be all right in Paris.'

'That's what you said about coming to London,' she retorted sarcastically through her sobs. 'And look at you!'

Did he imagine for a single instant that she would have come to London with him save on the understanding that she was to be married immediately upon arrival? This attitude of an indignant question was not to be reconciled with her belief that his excuses for himself were truthful. But she did not remark the discrepancy.

Her sarcasm wounded his vanity.

'Oh, very well!' he muttered. 'If you don't choose to believe what I say!' He shrugged his shoulders.

She said nothing; but the sobs swept at intervals through her frame, shaking it.

Reading hesitation in her face, he tried again. 'Come along, little girl. And wipe your eyes.' And he approached her. She stepped back.

'No, no!' she denied him, passionately. He had esteemed her too cheaply. And she did not care to be called 'little girl'.

'Then what shall you do?' he inquired, in a tone which blended mockery and bullying. She was making a fool of him.

'I can tell you what I shan't do,' she said. 'I shan't go to Paris.' Her sobs were less frequent.

'That's not my question,' he said icily. 'I want to know what you will do.'

There was now no pretence of affectionateness either on her part or on his. They might, to judge from their attitudes, have been nourished from infancy on mutual hatred.

'What's that got to do with you?' she demanded.

'It's got everything to do with me,' he said.

'Well, you can go and find out!' she said.

It was girlish; it was childish; it was scarcely according to the canons for conducting a final rupture; but it was not the less tragically serious. Indeed, the spectacle of this young girl absurdly behaving like one in a serious crisis increased the tragicalness of the situation even if it did not heighten it. The idea that ran through Gerald's brain was the ridiculous folly of having anything to do with young girls. He was quite blind to her beauty.

'"Go"?' he repeated her word. 'You mean that?'

'Of course I mean it,' she answered promptly.

The coward in him urged him to take advantage of her ignorant, helpless pride, and leave her at her word. He remembered the scene she had made at the pit shaft, and he said to himself that her charm was not worth her temper, and that he was a fool ever to have dreamed that it was, and that he would be doubly a fool now not to seize the opportunity of withdrawing from an insane enterprise.

'I am to go?' he asked, with a sneer.

She nodded.

'Of course if you order me to leave you, I must. Can I do anything for you?'

She signified that he could not.

'Nothing? You're sure?'

She frowned.

'Well, then, good-bye.' He turned towards the door.

'I suppose you'd leave me here without money or anything?' she said in a cold, cutting voice. And her sneer was far more destructive than his. It destroyed in him the last trace of compassion for her.

'Oh, I beg pardon!' he said, and swaggeringly counted out five sovereigns on to a chest of drawers.

She rushed at them. 'Do you think I'll take your odious money?' she snarled, gathering the coins in her gloved hand.

Her first impulse was to throw them in his face; but she paused and then flung them into a corner of the room.

'Pick them up!' she commanded him.

'No, thanks,' he said briefly; and left, shutting the door.

Only a very little while, and they had been lovers, exuding tenderness with every gesture, like a perfume! Only a very little while, and she had been deciding to telegraph condescendingly to her mother that she was 'all right'! And now the dream was utterly dissolved. And the voice of that hard common sense which spake to her in her wildest moods grew loud in asserting that the enterprise could never have come to any good, that it was from its inception an impossible enterprise, unredeemed by the slightest justification. An enormous folly! Yes, an elopement; but not like a real elopement; always unreal! She had always known that it was only an imitation of an elopement, and must end in some awful disappointment. She had never truly wanted to run away; but something within her had pricked her forward in spite of her protests. The strict notions of her elderly relatives were right after all. It was she who had been wrong. And it was she who would have to pay.

'I've been a wicked girl,' she said to herself grimly, in the midst of her ruin.

She faced the fact. But she would not repent; at any rate she would never sit on that stool. She would not exchange the remains of her pride for the means of escape from the worst misery that life could offer. On that point she knew herself. And she set to work to repair and renew her pride.

Whatever happened she would not return to the Five Towns. She could not, because she had stolen money from her Aunt Harriet. As much as she had thrown back at Gerald, she had filched from her aunt, but in the form of a note. A prudent, mysterious instinct had moved her to take this precaution. And she was glad. She would never have been able to dart that sneer at Gerald about money if she had really needed money. So she rejoiced in her crime; though since Aunt Harriet would assuredly discover the loss at once, the crime eternally prevented her from going back to her family. Never, never would she look at her mother with the eyes of a thief!

(In truth Aunt Harriet did discover the loss, and very creditably said naught about it to anybody. The knowledge of it would have twisted the knife in the maternal heart.)

Sophia was also glad that she had refused to proceed to Paris. The recollection of her firmness in refusing flattered her vanity as a girl convinced that she could take care of herself. To go to Paris unmarried would have been an inconceivable madness. The mere thought of the enormity did outrage to her moral susceptibilities. No, Gerald had most perfectly mistaken her for another sort of girl; as, for instance, a shop-assistant or a barmaid!

With this the catalogue of her satisfactions ended. She had no idea at all as to what she ought to do, or could do. The mere prospect of venturing out of the room intimidated her. Had Gerald left her trunk in the hall? Of course he had. What a question! But what would happen to her? London . . . London had merely dazed her. She could do nothing for herself. She was as helpless as a rabbit in London. She drew aside the window-curtain and had a glimpse of the river. It was inevitable that she should think of suicide; for she could not suppose that any girl had ever got herself into a plight more desperate than hers. 'I could slip out at night and drown myself,' she thought seriously. 'A nice thing that would be for Gerald!'

Then loneliness, like a black midnight, overwhelmed her, swiftly wasting her strength, disintegrating her pride in its horrid flood. She glanced about for support, as a woman in the open street who feels she is going to faint, and went blindly to the bed, falling on it with the upper part of her body, in an attitude of abandonment. She wept, but without sobbing.

II

Gerald Scales walked about the Strand, staring up at its high narrow houses, crushed one against another as though they had been packed, unsorted, by a packer who thought of nothing but economy of space. Except by Somerset House, King's College, and one or two theatres and banks, the monotony of mean shops, with several storeys unevenly perched over them, was unbroken. Then Gerald encountered Exeter Hall, and examined its prominent façade with a provincial's eye; for despite his travels he was not very familiar with London. Exeter Hall naturally took his mind back to his Uncle Boldero, that great and ardent Nonconformist, and his own godly youth. It was laughable to muse upon what his uncle would say and think, did the old man know that his nephew had run away with a girl, meaning to seduce her in Paris? It was enormously funny!

However, he had done with all that. He was well out of it. She had told him to go, and he had gone. She had money to get home; she had nothing to do but use the tongue in her head. The rest was her affair. He would go to Paris alone, and find another amuse-

ment. It was absurd to have supposed that Sophia would ever
have suited him. Not in such a family as the Baineses could one
reasonably expect to discover an ideal mistress. No! there had
been a mistake. The whole business was wrong. She had nearly
made a fool of him. But he was not the man to be made a fool of.
He had kept his dignity intact.

So he said to himself. Yet all the time his dignity, and his pride
also, were bleeding, dropping invisible blood along the length of
the Strand pavements.

He was at Salisbury Street again. He pictured her in the
bedroom. Damn her! He wanted her. He wanted her with an
excessive desire. He hated to think that he had been baulked. He
hated to think that she would remain immaculate. And he
continued to picture her in the exciting privacy of that cursed
bedroom.

Now he was walking down Salisbury Street. He did not wish to
be walking down Salisbury Street; but there he was!

'Oh, hell!' he murmured. 'I suppose I must go through with it.'

He felt desperate. He was ready to pay any price in order to be
able to say to himself that he had accomplished what he had set
his heart on.

'My wife hasn't gone out, has she?' he asked of the hall-porter.

'I'm not sure, sir; I think not,' said the hall-porter.

The fear that Sophia had already departed made him sick.
When he noticed her trunk still there, he took hope and ran
upstairs.

He saw her, a dark, crumpled, sinuous piece of humanity, half
on and half off the bed, silhouetted against the bluish-white
counterpane; her hat was on the floor, with the spotted veil
trailing away from it. This sight seemed to him to be the most
touching that he had ever seen, though her face was hidden. He
forgot everything except the deep and strange emotion which
affected him. He approached the bed. She did not stir.

Having heard the entry and knowing that it must be Gerald
who had entered, Sophia forced herself to remain still. A wild,
splendid hope shot up in her. Constrained by all the power of her
will not to move, she could not stifle a sob that had lain in ambush
in her throat.

The sound of the sob fetched tears to the eyes of Gerald.

'Sophia!' he appealed to her.

But she did not stir. Another sob shook her.

'Very well, then,' said Gerald. 'We'll stay in London till we can be married. I'll arrange it. I'll find a nice boarding-house for you, and I'll tell the people you're my cousin. I shall stay on at this hotel, and I'll come and see you every day.'

A silence.

'Thank you!' she blubbered. 'Thank you!'

He saw that her little gloved hand was stretching out towards him, like a feeler; and he seized it, and knelt down and took her clumsily by the waist. Somehow he dared not kiss her yet.

An immense relief surged very slowly through them both.

'I – I – really –' She began to say something, but the articulation was lost in her sobs.

'What? What do you say, dearest?' he questioned eagerly.

And she made another effort. 'I really couldn't have gone to Paris with you without being married,' she succeeded at last. 'I really couldn't.'

'No, no!' he soothed her. 'Of course you couldn't. It was I who was wrong. But you didn't know how I felt . . . Sophia, it's all right now, isn't it?'

She sat up and kissed him fairly.

It was so wonderful and startling that he burst openly into tears. She saw in the facile intensity of his emotion a guarantee of their future happiness. And as he had soothed her, so now she soothed him. They clung together, equally surprised at the sweet, exquisite, blissful melancholy which drenched them through and through. It was remorse for having quarrelled, for having lacked faith in the supreme rightness of the high adventure. Everything was right, and would be right; and they had been criminally absurd. It was remorse; but it was pure bliss, and worth the quarrel! Gerald resumed his perfection again in her eyes! He was the soul of goodness and honour! And for him she was again the ideal mistress, who would, however, be also a wife. As in his mind he rapidly ran over the steps necessary to their marriage, he kept saying to himself, far off in some remote cavern of the brain: 'I shall have her! I shall have her!' He did not reflect that this fragile slip of the Baines stock, unconsciously drawing upon the accumulated strength of generations of honest living, had put a defeat upon him.

After tea, Gerald, utterly content with the universe, redeemed his word and found an irreproachable boarding-house for Sophia in Westminster, near the Abbey. She was astonished at the glibness of his lies to the landlady about her, and about their circumstances generally. He also found a church and a parson, close by, and in half an hour the formalities preliminary to a marriage were begun. He explained to her that as she was now resident in London, it would be simpler to recommence the business entirely. She sagaciously agreed. As she by no means wished to wound him again, she made no inquiry about those other formalities which, owing to red-tape, had so unexpectedly proved abortive! She knew she was going to be married, and that sufficed. The next day she carried out her filial idea of tele-graphing to her mother.

CHAPTER 2: *Supper*

I

They had been to Versailles and had dined there. A tram had sufficed to take them out; but for the return, Gerald, who had been drinking champagne, would not be content with less than a carriage. Further, he insisted on entering Paris by way of the Bois and the Arc de Triomphe. Thoroughly to appease his conceit, it would have been necessary to swing open the gates of honour in the Arc and allow his fiacre to pass through; to be forced to drive round the monument instead of under it hurt the sense of fitness which champagne engenders. Gerald was in all his pride that day. He had been displaying the wonders to Sophia, and he could not escape the cicerone's secret feeling: that he himself was somehow responsible for the wonders. Moreover, he was exceedingly satisfied with the effect produced by Sophia.

Sophia, on arriving in Paris with the ring on her triumphant finger, had timidly mentioned the subject of frocks. None would

have guessed from her tone that she was possessed by the desire
for French clothes as by a devil. She had been surprised and
delighted by the eagerness of Gerald's response. Gerald, too, was
possessed by a devil. He thirsted to see her in French clothes. He
knew some of the shops and ateliers in the Rue de la Paix, the Rue
de la Chaussée d'Antin, and the Palais Royal. He was much more
skilled in the lore of frocks than she, for his previous business in
Paris had brought him into relations with the great firms; and
Sophia suffered a brief humiliation in the discovery that his
private opinion of her dresses was that they were not dresses at
all. She had been aware that they were not Parisian, nor even of
London; but she had thought them pretty good. It healed her
wound, however, to reflect that Gerald had so marvellously kept
his own counsel in order to spare her self-love. Gerald had taken
her to an establishment in the Chaussée d'Antin. It was not one of
what Gerald called *les grandes maisons*, but it was on the very
fringe of them, and the real *haute couture* was practised therein;
and Gerald was remembered there by name.

Sophia had gone in trembling and ashamed, yet in her heart
courageously determined to emerge uncompromisingly French.
But the models frightened her. They surpassed even the most
fantastic things that she had seen in the streets. She recoiled
before them and seemed to hide for refuge in Gerald, as it were
appealing to him for moral protection, and answering to him
instead of to the saleswoman when the saleswoman offered
remarks in stiff English. The prices also frightened her. The
simplest trifle here cost sixteen pounds; and her mother's historic
'silk', whose elaborateness had cost twelve pounds, was supposed to have approached the inexpressible! Gerald said that she
was not to think about prices. She was, however, forced by some
instinct to think about prices – she who at home had scorned the
narrowness of life in the Square. In the Square she was understood to be quite without common sense, hopelessly imprudent;
yet here, a spring of sagacity seemed to be welling up in her all the
time, a continual antidote against the general madness in which
she found herself. With extraordinary rapidity she had formed a
habit of preaching moderation to Gerald. She hated to 'see money
thrown away', and her notion of the boundary line between

throwing money away and judiciously spending it was still the notion of the Square.

Gerald would laugh. But she would say, piqued and blushing, but self-sure: 'You can laugh!' It was all deliciously agreeable.

On this evening she wore the first of the new costumes. She had worn it all day. Characteristically she had chosen something which was not too special for either afternoon or evening, for either warm or cold weather. It was of pale blue taffetas striped in a darker blue, with the corsage cut in basques, and the underskirt of a similar taffetas, but unstriped. The effect of the ornate overskirt falling on the plain underskirt with its small double *volant* was, she thought, and Gerald too, adorable. The waist was higher than any she had had before, and the crinoline expansive. Tied round her head with a large bow and flying blue ribbons under the chin, was a fragile flat *capote* like a baby's bonnet, which allowed her hair to escape in front and her great chignon behind. A large spotted veil flew out from the *capote* over the chignon. Her double skirts waved amply over Gerald's knees in the carriage, and she leaned back against the hard cushions and put an arrogant look into her face, and thought of nothing, but the intense throbbing joy of life, longing with painful ardour for more and more pleasure, then and for ever.

As the carriage slipped downwards through the wide, empty gloom of the Champs Elysées into the brilliant Paris that was waiting for them, another carriage drawn by two white horses flashed upwards and was gone in dust. Its only occupant, except the coachman and footman, was a woman. Gerald stared after it.

'By Jove!' he exclaimed. 'That's Hortense!'

It might have been Hortense, or it might not. But he instantly convinced himself that it was. Not every evening did one meet Hortense driving alone in the Champs Elysées, and in August too!

'Hortense?' Sophia asked simply.

'Yes. Hortense Schneider.'

'Who is she?'

'You've never heard of Hortense Schneider?'

'No!'

'Well! Have you ever heard of Offenbach?'

'I – I don't know. I don't think so.'

He had the mien of utter incredulity. 'You don't mean to say you've never heard of *Bluebeard*?'

'I've heard of Bluebeard, of course,' said she. 'Who hasn't?'

'I mean the opera – Offenbach's.'

She shook her head, scarce knowing even what an opera was.

'Well, well! What next?'

He implied that such ignorance stood alone in his experience. Really he was delighted at the cleanness of the slate on which he had to write. And Sophia was not a bit alarmed. She relished instruction from his lips. It was a pleasure to her to learn from that exhaustless store of worldly knowledge. To the world she would do her best to assume omniscience in its ways, but to him, in her present mood, she liked to play the ignorant, uninitiated little thing.

'Why,' he said, 'the Schneider has been the rage since last year but one. Absolutely the *rage*.'

'I do wish I'd noticed her!' said Sophia.

'As soon as the Variétés reopens we'll go and see her,' he replied, and then gave his detailed version of the career of Hortense Schneider.

More joys for her in the near future! She had yet scarcely penetrated the crust of her bliss. She exulted in the dazzling destiny which comprised freedom, fortune, eternal gaiety, and the exquisite Gerald.

As they crossed the Place de la Concorde, she inquired, 'Are we going back to the hotel?'

'No,' he said. 'I thought we'd go and have supper somewhere, if it isn't too early.'

'After all that dinner?'

'All what dinner? You ate about five times as much as me, anyhow!'

'Oh, *I'm* ready!' she said.

She was. This day, because it was the first day of her French frock, she regarded as her *début* in the dizzy life of capitals. She existed in a rapture of bliss, an ecstasy which could feel no fatigue, either of body or spirit.

II

It was after midnight when they went into the Restaurant
Sylvain; Gerald, having decided not to go to the hotel, had
changed his mind and called there, and having called there, had
remained a long time: this of course! Sophia was already ac-
customing herself to the idea that, with Gerald, it was impossible
to predict accurately more than five minutes of the future.

As the *chasseur* held open the door for them to enter, and
Sophia passed modestly into the glowing yellow interior of the
restaurant, followed by Gerald in his character of man-of-the-
world, they drew the attention of Sylvain's numerous and glittering guests. No face could have made a more provocative contrast
to the women's faces in those screened rooms than the face of
Sophia, so childlike between the baby's bonnet and the huge bow
of ribbon, so candid, so charmingly conscious of its own pure
beauty and of the fact that she was no longer a virgin, but the
equal in knowledge of any woman alive. She saw around her,
clustered about the white tables, multitudes of violently red lips,
powdered cheeks, cold, hard eyes, self-possessed arrogant faces,
and insolent bosoms. What had impressed her more than anything else in Paris, more even than the three-horsed omnibuses,
was the extraordinary self-assurance of all the women, their
unashamed posing, their calm acceptance of the public gaze.
They seemed to say: 'We are the renowned Parisiennes.' They
frightened her: they appeared to her so corrupt and so proud in
their corruption. She had already seen a dozen women in various
situations of conspicuousness apply powder to their complexions
with no more ado than if they had been giving a pat to their hair.
She could not understand such boldness. As for them, they
marvelled at the phenomena presented in Sophia's person; they
admired; they admitted the style of the gown; but they envied
neither her innocence nor her beauty; they envied nothing but her
youth and the fresh tint of her cheeks.

'Encore des Anglais!' said some of them, as if that explained all.

Gerald had a very curt way with waiters; and the more
obsequious they were, the haughtier he became; and a head-
waiter was no more to him than a scullion. He gave loud-voiced

orders in French of which both he and Sophia were proud, and a table was laid for them in a corner near one of the large windows. Sophia settled herself on the bench of green velvet, and began to ply the ivory fan which Gerald had given her. It was very hot; all the windows were wide open, and the sounds of the street mingled clearly with the tinkle of the supper-room. Outside, against a sky of deepest purple, Sophia could discern the black skeleton of a gigantic building; it was the new opera house.

'All sorts here!' said Gerald, contentedly, after he had ordered iced soup and sparkling Moselle. Sophia did not know what Moselle was, but she imagined that anything would be better than champagne.

Sylvain's was then typical of the Second Empire, and particularly famous as a supper-room. Expensive and gay, it provided, with its discreet decorations, a sumptuous scene where lorettes,[9] actresses, respectable women, and an occasional grisette in luck, could satisfy their curiosity as to each other. In its catholicity it was highly correct as a resort; not many other restaurants in the centre could have successfully fought against the rival attractions of the Bois and the dim groves of the Champs Elysées on a night in August. The complicated richness of the dresses, the yards and yards of fine stitchery, the endless ruching, the hints, more or less incautious, nether treasures of embroidered linen; and, leaping over all this to the eye, the vivid colourings of silks and muslins, veils, plumes, and flowers, piled as it were pell-mell in heaps on the universal green cushions to the farthest vista of the restaurant, and all multiplied in gilt mirrors – the spectacle intoxicated Sophia. Her eyes gleamed. She drank the soup with eagerness, and tasted the wine, though no desire on her part to like wine could make her like it; and then, seeing pineapples on a large table covered with fruits, she told Gerald that she should like some pineapple, and Gerald ordered one.

She gathered her self-esteem and her wits together, and began to give Gerald her views on the costumes. She could do so with impunity, because her own was indubitably beyond criticism. Some she wholly condemned, and there was not one which earned her unreserved approval. All the absurd fastidiousness of her schoolgirlish provinciality emerged in that eager, affected torrent of remarks. However, she was clever enough to read, after a time, in Gerald's tone and features, that she was making a tedious fool of herself. And she adroitly shifted her criticism from the taste to the *work* – she put a strong accent on the word – and pronounced that to be miraculous beyond description. She reckoned that she knew what dressmaking and millinery were, and her little fund of expert knowledge caused her to picture a whole necessary cityful of girls stitching, stitching, and stitching day and night. She had wondered, during the few odd days that they had spent in Paris, between visits to Chantilly and other places, at the massed luxury of the shops; she had wondered, starting with St Luke's Square as a standard, how they could all thrive. But now in her first real glimpse of the banal and licentious profusion of one among a hundred restaurants, she wondered that the shops were so few. She thought how splendid was all this expensiveness for trade. Indeed, the notions chasing each other within that lovely and foolish head were a surprising medley.

'Well, what do you think of Sylvain's?' Gerald asked, impatient to be assured that his Sylvain's had duly overwhelmed her.

'Oh, Gerald!' she murmured, indicating that speech was inadequate. And she just furtively touched his hand with hers.

The ennui due to her critical disquisition on the shortcomings of Parisian costume cleared away from Gerald's face.

'What do you suppose those people are talking about?' he said with a jerk of the head towards a chattering group of three gorgeous lorettes and two middle-aged men at the next table but one.

'What are they talking about?'

'They're talking about the execution of the murderer Rivain that takes place at Auxerre the day after tomorrow. They're arranging to make up a party and go and see it.'

'Oh, what a horrid idea!' said Sophia.

'Guillotine, you know!' said Gerald.

'But can people see it?'

'Yes, of course.'

'Well, I think it's horrible.'

'Yes, that's why people like to go and see it. Besides, the man isn't an ordinary sort of criminal at all. He's very young and good looking, and well-connected. And he killed the celebrated Claudine . . .'

'Claudine?'

'Claudine Jacquinot. Of course you wouldn't know. She was a tremendous – er – wrong 'un here in the forties. Made a lot of money, and retired to her native town.'

Sophia, in spite of her efforts to maintain the *rôle* of a woman who has nothing to learn, blushed.

'Then she was older than he is.'

'Thirty-five years older, if a day.'

'What did he kill her for?'

'She wouldn't give him enough money. She was his mistress – or rather one of 'em. He wanted money for a young lady friend, you see. He killed her and took all the jewels she was wearing. Whenever he went to see her she always wore all her best jewels – and you may bet a woman like that had a few. It seems she had been afraid for a long time that he meant to do for her.'

'Then why did she see him? And why did she wear her jewels?'

'Because she liked being afraid, goose! Some women only enjoy themselves when they're terrified. Queer, isn't it?'

Gerald insisted on meeting his wife's gaze as he finished these revelations. He pretended that such stories were the commonest things on earth, and that to be scandalized by them was infantile. Sophia, thrust suddenly into a strange civilization perfectly frank in its sensuality and its sensuousness, under the guidance of a young man to whom her half-formed intelligence was a most diverting toy – Sophia felt mysteriously uncomfortable, disturbed by sinister, flitting phantoms of ideas which she only dimly apprehended. Her eyes fell. Gerald laughed self-consciously. She would not eat any more pineapple.

Immediately afterwards there came into the restaurant an apparition which momentarily stopped every conversation in the room. It was a tall and mature woman who wore over a dress of purplish-black silk a vast flowing *sortie de bal* of vermilion velvet, looped and tasselled with gold. No other costume could live by the side of that garment, Arab in shape, Russian in colour, and Parisian in style. It blazed. The woman's heavy coiffure was bound with fillets of gold braid and crimson rosettes. She was

followed by a young Englishman in evening dress and whiskers of
the most exact correctness. The woman sailed, a little breathlessly, to a table next to Gerald's, and took possession of it with an air
of use, almost of tedium. She sat down, threw the cloak from her
majestic bosom, and expanded her chest. Seeming to ignore the
Englishman, who superciliously assumed the seat opposite to her,
she let her large scornful eyes travel round the restaurant, slowly
and imperiously meeting the curiosity which she had evoked. Her
beauty had undoubtedly been dazzling, it was still effulgent; but
the blossom was about to fall. She was admirably rouged and
powdered; her arms were glorious; her lashes were long. There
was little fault, save the excessive ripeness of a blonde who fights
in vain against obesity. And her clothes combined audacity with
the propriety of fashion. She carelessly deposed costly trinkets on
the table, and then, having intimidated the whole company,
she accepted the menu from the head-waiter and began to study
it.

'That's one of 'em!' Gerald whispered to Sophia.

'One of what?' Sophia whispered.

Gerald raised his eyebrows warningly, and winked. The Englishman had overheard; and a look of frigid displeasure passed
across his proud face. Evidently he belonged to a rank much
higher than Gerald's; and Gerald, though he could always comfort himself by the thought that he had been to a university with
the best, felt his own inferiority and could not hide that he felt it.
Gerald was wealthy; he came of a wealthy family; but he had not
the habit of wealth. When he spent money furiously, he did it
with bravado, too conscious of grandeur and too conscious of the
difficulties of acquiring that which he threw away. For Gerald
had earned money. This whiskered Englishman had never earned
money, never known the value of it, never imagined himself
without as much of it as he might happen to want. He had the face
of one accustomed to give orders and to look down upon
inferiors. He was absolutely sure of himself. That his companion
chiefly ignored him did not appear to incommode him in the least.
She spoke to him in French. He replied in English, very briefly;
and then, in English, he commanded the supper. As soon as the
champagne was served he began to drink; in the intervals of

drinking he gently stroked his whiskers. The woman spoke no more.

Gerald talked more loudly. With that aristocratic Englishman observing him, he could not remain at ease. And not only did he talk more loudly; he brought into his conversation references to money, travels, and worldly experiences. While seeking to impress the Englishman, he was merely becoming ridiculous to the Englishman; and obscurely he was aware of this. Sophia noticed and regretted it. Still, feeling very unimportant herself, she was reconciled to the superiority of the whiskered Englishman as to a natural fact. Gerald's behaviour slightly lowered him in her esteem. Then she looked at him – at his well-shaped neatness, his vivacious face, his excellent clothes, and decided that he was much to be preferred to any heavy-jawed, long-nosed aristocrat alive.

The woman whose vermilion cloak lay around her like a fortification spoke to her escort. He did not understand. He tried to express himself in French, and failed. Then the woman recommenced, talking at length. When she had done he shook his head. His acquaintance with French was limited to the vocabulary of food.

'Guillotine!' he murmured, the sole word of her discourse that he had understood.

'Oui, oui! Guillotine. Enfin . . . !' cried the woman excitedly. Encouraged by her success in conveying even one word of her remarks, she began a third time.

'Excuse me,' said Gerald. 'Madame is talking about the execution at Auxerre the day after tomorrow. N'est-ce-pas, madame, que vous parliez de Rivain?'

The Englishman glared angrily at Gerald's officious interruption. But the woman smiled benevolently on Gerald, and insisted on talking to her friend through him. And the Englishman had to make the best of the situation.

'There isn't a restaurant in Paris tonight where they aren't talking about that execution,' said Gerald on his own account.

'Indeed!' observed the Englishman.

Wine affected them in different ways.

Now a fragile, short young Frenchman, with an extremely pale face ending in a thin black imperial, appeared at the entrance. He looked about, and, recognizing the woman of the scarlet cloak, very discreetly saluted her. Then he saw Gerald, and his worn, fatigued features showed a sudden startled smile. He came rapidly forward, hat in hand, seized Gerald's palm and greeted him effusively.

'My wife,' said Gerald, with the solemn care of a man who is determined to prove that he is entirely sober.

The young man became grave and excessively ceremonious. He bowed low over Sophia's hand and kissed it. Her impulse was to laugh, but the gravity of the young man's deference stopped her. She glanced at Gerald, blushing, as if to say: 'This comedy is not my fault.' Gerald said something, the young man turned to him and his face resumed its welcoming smile.

'This is Monsieur Chirac,' Gerald at length completed the introduction, 'a friend of mine when I lived in Paris.'

He was proud to have met by accident an acquaintance in a restaurant. It demonstrated that he was a Parisian, and improved his standing with the whiskered Englishman and vermilion cloak.

'It is the first time you come Paris, madame?' Chirac addressed himself to Sophia, in limping, timorous English.

'Yes,' she giggled. He bowed again.

Chirac, with his best compliments, felicitated Gerald upon his marriage.

'Don't mention it!' said the humorous Gerald in English, amused at his own wit; and then: 'What about this execution?'

'Ah!' replied Chirac, breathing out a long breath, and smiling at Sophia. 'Rivain! Rivain!' He made a large, important gesture with his hand.

It was at once to be seen that Gerald had touched the topic which secretly ravaged the supper-world as a subterranean fire ravages a mine.

'I go!' said Chirac, with pride, glancing at Sophia, who smiled, self-consciously.

Chirac entered upon a conversation with Gerald in French. Sophia comprehended that Gerald was surprised and impressed by what Chirac told him and that Chirac in turn was surprised. Then Gerald laboriously found his pocket-book, and after some

fumbling with it handed it to Chirac so that the latter might write
in it.

'Madame!' murmured Chirac, resuming his ceremonious stiffness in order to take leave. 'Alors, c'est entendu, mon cher ami!'
he said to Gerald, who nodded phlegmatically. And Chirac went
away to the next table but one, where were the three lorettes and
the two middle-aged men. He was received there with enthusiasm.

Sophia began to be teased by a little fear that Gerald was not
quite his usual self. She did not think of him as tipsy. The idea of
his being tipsy would have shocked her. She did not think clearly
at all. She was lost and dazed in the labyrinth of new and vivid
impressions into which Gerald had led her. But her prudence was
awake.

'I think I'm tired,' she said in a low voice.

'You don't want to go, do you?' he asked, hurt.

'Well –'

'Oh, wait a bit!'

The owner of the vermilion cloak spoke again to Gerald, who
showed that he was flattered. While talking to her he ordered a
brandy-and-soda. And then he could not refrain from displaying
to her his familiarity with Parisian life, and he related how he had
met Hortense Schneider behind a pair of white horses. The
vermilion cloak grew even more sociable at the mention of this
resounding name, and chattered with the most agreeable vivacity. Her friend stared inimically.

'Do you hear that?' Gerald explained to Sophia, who was
sitting silent. 'About Hortense Schneider – you know, we met her
tonight. It seems she made a bet of a louis with some fellow, and
when he lost he sent her the louis set in diamonds worth a
hundred thousand francs. That's how they go on here.'

'Oh!' cried Sophia, farther than ever in the labyrinth.

' 'Scuse me,' the Englishman put in heavily. He had heard the
words 'Hortense Schneider', 'Hortense Schneider', repeating
themselves in the conversation, and at last it had occurred to him
that the conversation was about Hortense Schneider. ' 'Scuse me,'
he began again. 'Are you – do you mean Hortense Schneider?'

'Yes,' said Gerald. 'We met her tonight.'

'She's in Trouville,' said the Englishman, flatly.

Gerald shook his head positively.

'I gave a supper to her in Trouville last night,' said the Englishman. 'And she plays at the Casino Theatre tonight.'

Gerald was repulsed but not defeated. 'What is she playing in tonight? Tell me that!' he sneered.

'I don't see why I sh'd tell you.'

'Hm!' Gerald retorted. 'If what you say is true, it's a very strange thing I should have seen her in the Champs Elysées tonight, isn't it?'

The Englishman drank more wine. 'If you want to insult me, sir –' he began coldly.

'Gerald!' Sophia urged in a whisper.

'Be quiet!' Gerald snapped.

A fiddler in fancy costume plunged into the restaurant at that moment and began to play wildly. The shock of his strange advent momentarily silenced the quarrel; but soon it leaped up again, under the shelter of the noisy music – the common, tedious, tippler's quarrel. It rose higher and higher. The fiddler looked askance at it over his fiddle. Chirac cautiously observed it. Instead of attending to the music, the festal company attended to the quarrel. Three waiters in a group watched it with an impartial sporting interest. The English voices grew more menacing.

Then suddenly the whiskered Englishman, jerking his head towards the door, said more quietly:

'Hadn't we better settle thish outside?'

'At your service!' said Gerald, rising.

The owner of the vermilion cloak lifted her eyebrows to Chirac in fatigued disgust, but she said nothing. Nor did Sophia say anything. Sophia was overcome by terror.

The swain of the cloak, dragging his coat after him across the floor, left the restaurant without offering any apology or explanation to his lady.

'Wait here for me,' said Gerald defiantly to Sophia. 'I shall be back in a minute.'

'But, Gerald!' She put her hand on his sleeve.

He snatched his arm away. 'Wait here for me, I tell you,' he repeated.

The doorkeeper obsequiously opened the door to the two unsteady carousers, for whom the fiddler drew back still playing.

Thus Sophia was left side by side with the vermilion cloak. She was quite helpless. All the pride of a married woman had abandoned her. She stood transfixed by intense shame, staring painfully at a pillar, to avoid the universal assault of eyes. She felt like an indiscreet little girl, and she looked like one. No youthful radiant beauty of features, no grace and style of a Parisian dress, no certificate of a ring, no premature initiation into the mysteries, could save her from the appearance of a raw fool whose foolishness had been her undoing. Her face changed to its reddest, and remained at that, and all the fundamental innocence of her nature, which had been overlaid by the violent experiences of her brief companionship with Gerald, rose again to the surface with that blush. Her situation drew pity from a few hearts and a careless contempt from the rest. But since once more it was a question of *ces Anglais*, nobody could be astonished.

Without moving her head, she twisted her eyes to the clock: half-past two. The fiddler ceased his dance and made a collection in his tasselled cap. The vermilion cloak threw a coin into the cap. Sophia stared at it moveless, until the fiddler, tired of waiting, passed to the next table and relieved her agony. She had no money at all. She set herself to watch the clock; but its fingers would not stir.

With an exclamation the lady of the cloak got up and peered out of the window, chatted with waiters, and then removed herself and her cloak to the next table, where she was received with amiable sympathy by the three lorettes, Chirac, and the other two men. The party surreptitiously examined Sophia from time to time. Then Chirac went outside with the head-waiter, returned, consulted with his friends, and finally approached Sophia. It was twenty minutes past three.

He renewed his magnificent bow. 'Madame,' he said carefully, 'will you allow me to bring you to your hotel?'

He made no reference to Gerald, partly, doubtless, because his English was treacherous on difficult ground.

Sophia had not sufficient presence of mind to thank her saviour.

'But the bill?' she stammered. 'The bill isn't paid.'

He did not instantly understand her. But one of the waiters had caught the sound of a familiar word, and sprang forward with a slip of paper on a plate.

'I have no money,' said Sophia, with a feeble smile.

'Je vous arrangerai ça,' he said. 'What name of the hotel? Meurice, is it not?'

'Hotel Meurice,' said Sophia. 'Yes.'

He spoke to the head-waiter about the bill, which was carried away like something obscene; and on his arm, which he punctiliously offered and she could not refuse, Sophia left the scene of her ignominy. She was so distraught that she could not manage her crinoline in the doorway. No sign anywhere outside of Gerald or his foe!

He put her into an open carriage, and in five minutes they had clattered down the brilliant silence of the Rue de la Paix, through the Place Vendôme into the Rue de Rivoli; and the night-porter of the hotel was at the carriage-step.

'I tell them at the restaurant where you gone,' said Chirac, bare-headed under the long colonnade of the street. 'If your husband is there, I tell him. Till tomorrow . . . !'

His manners were more wonderful than any that Sophia had ever imagined. He might have been in the dark Tuileries on the opposite side of the street, saluting an empress, instead of taking leave of a raw little girl, who was still too disturbed even to thank him.

She fled, candle in hand, up the wide, many-cornered stairs; Gerald might be already in the bedroom . . . drunk! There was a chance. But the gilt-fringed bedroom was empty. She sat down at the velvet-covered table amid the shadows cast by the candle that wavered in the draught from the open window. And she set her teeth and a cold fury possessed her in the hot and languorous night. Gerald was an imbecile. That he should have allowed himself to get tipsy was bad enough, but that he should have exposed her to the horrible situation from which Chirac had extricated her, was unspeakably disgraceful. He was an imbecile. He had no common sense. With all his captivating charm, he could not be relied upon not to make himself ridiculous, tragically ridiculous. Compare him with Mr Chirac! She leaned despairingly on the table. She would not undress. She would not move. She had to realize her position; she had to see it.

Folly! Folly! Fancy a commercial traveller throwing a compromising piece of paper to the daughter of his customer in the shop itself: that was the incredible folly with which their relations had begun! And his mad gesture at the pit-shaft! And his scheme for bringing her to Paris unmarried! And then tonight! Monstrous folly! Alone in the bedroom she was a wise and disillusioned woman, wiser than any of those dolls in the restaurant.

And had she not gone to Gerald, as it were, over the dead body of her father, through lies and lies and again lies? That was how she phrased it to herself . . . Over the dead body of her father! How could such a venture succeed? How could she ever have hoped that it would succeed? In that moment she saw her acts with the terrible vision of a Hebrew prophet.

She thought of the Square and of her life there with her mother and Constance. Never would her pride allow her to return to that life, not even if the worst happened to her that could happen. She was one of those who are prepared to pay without grumbling for what they have had.

There was a sound outside. She noticed that the dawn had begun. The door opened and disclosed Gerald.

They exchanged a searching glance, and Gerald shut the door. Gerald infected the air, but she perceived at once that he was sobered. His lip was bleeding.

'Mr Chirac brought me home,' she said.

'So it seems,' said Gerald, curtly. 'I asked you to wait for me. Didn't I say I should come back?'

He was adopting the injured magisterial tone of the man who is ridiculously trying to conceal from himself and others that he has recently behaved like an ass.

She resented the injustice. 'I don't think you need talk like that,' she said.

'Like what?' he bullied her, determined that she should be in the wrong.

And what a hard look on his pretty face!

Her prudence bade her accept the injustice. She was his. Rapt away from her own world, she was utterly dependent on his good nature.

'I knocked my chin against the damned balustrade, coming upstairs,' said Gerald, gloomily.

She knew that was a lie. 'Did you?' she replied kindly. 'Let me bathe it.'

CHAPTER 3: *An Ambition Satisfied*

I

She went to sleep in misery. All the glory of her new life had been eclipsed. But when she woke up, a few hours later, in the large, velvety stateliness of the bedroom for which Gerald was paying so fantastic a price per day, she was in a brighter mood, and very willing to reconsider her verdicts. Her pride induced her to put Gerald in the right and herself in the wrong, for she was too proud to admit that she had married a charming and irresponsible fool. And, indeed, ought she not to put herself in the wrong? Gerald had told her to wait, and she had not waited. He had said that he should return to the restaurant, and he had returned. Why had she not waited? She had not waited because she had behaved like a simpleton. She had been terrified about nothing. Had she not been frequenting restaurants now for a month past? Ought not a married woman to be capable of waiting an hour in a restaurant for her lawful husband without looking a ninny? And as for Gerald's behaviour, how could he have acted differently? The other Englishman was obviously a brute and had sought a quarrel. His contradiction of Gerald's statements was extremely offensive. On being invited by the brute to go outside, what could Gerald do but comply? Not to have complied might have meant a fight in the restaurant, as the brute was certainly drunk. Compared to the brute, Gerald was not at all drunk, merely a little gay and talkative. Then Gerald's fib about his chin was natural; he simply wished to minimize the fuss and to spare her feelings. It was, in fact, just like Gerald to keep perfect silence as to what had passed between himself and the brute. However, she was convinced that Gerald, so lithe and quick, had given that great brute with his supercilious ways as good as he received, if not better.

And if she were a man and had asked her wife to wait in a restaurant, and the wife had gone home under the escort of another man, she would most assuredly be much more angry than Gerald had been. She was very glad that she had controlled herself and exercised a meek diplomacy. A quarrel had thus been avoided. Yes, the finish of the evening could not be called a quarrel; after her nursing of his chin, nothing but a slight coolness on his part had persisted.

She arose silently and began to dress, full of a determination to treat Gerald as a good wife ought to treat a husband. Gerald did not stir; he was an excellent sleeper: one of those organisms that never want to go to bed and never want to get up. When her toilet was complete save for her bodice, there was a knock at the door. She started.

'Gerald!' She approached the bed, and leaned her nude bosom over her husband, and put her arms round his neck. This method of being brought back to consciousness did not displease him.

The knock was repeated. He gave a grunt.

'Someone's knocking at the door,' she whispered.

'Then why don't you open it?' he asked dreamily.

'I'm not dressed, darling.'

He looked at her. 'Stick something on your shoulders, girl!' said he. 'What does it matter?'

There she was, being a simpleton again, despite her resolution!

She obeyed, and cautiously opened the door, standing behind it.

A middle-aged whiskered servant, in a long white apron, announced matters in French which passed her understanding. But Gerald had heard from the bed, and he replied.

'Bien, monsieur!' The servant departed, with a bow, down the obscure corridor.

'It's Chirac,' Gerald explained when she had shut the door. 'I was forgetting I asked him to come and have lunch with us, early.

He's waiting in the drawing-room. Just put your bodice on, and go and talk to him till I come.'

He jumped out of bed, and then, standing in his night-garb, stretched himself and terrifically yawned.

'Me?' Sophia questioned.

'Who else?' said Gerald with that curious satiric dryness which he would sometimes import into his tone.

'But I can't speak French!' she protested.

'I didn't suppose you could,' said Gerald, with an increase of dryness; 'but you know as well as I do that he can speak English.'

'Oh, very well, then!' she murmured with agreeable alacrity.

Evidently Gerald had not yet quite recovered from his legitimate displeasure of the night. He minutely examined his mouth in the glass of the Louis Philippe wardrobe. It showed scarcely a trace of battle.

'I say!' he stopped her, as, nervous at the prospect before her, she was leaving the room. 'I was thinking of going to Auxerre today.'

'Auxerre?' she repeated, wondering under what circumstances she had recently heard that name. Then she remembered: it was the place of execution of the murderer Rivain.

'Yes,' he said. 'Chirac has to go. He's on a newspaper now. He was an architect when I knew him. He's got to go and he thinks himself jolly lucky. So I thought I'd go with him.'

The truth was that he had definitely arranged to go.

'Not to see the execution?' she stammered.

'Why not? I've always wanted to see an execution, especially with the guillotine. And executions are public in France. It's quite the proper thing to go to them.'

'But why do you want to see an execution?'

'It just happens that I do want to see an execution. It's a fancy of mine, that's all. I don't know that any reason is necessary,' he said, pouring out water into the diminutive ewer.

She was aghast. 'And shall you leave me here alone?'

'Well,' said he, 'I don't see why my being married should prevent me from doing something that I've always wanted to do. Do you?'

'Oh *no*!' she eagerly concurred.

'That's all right,' he said. 'You can do exactly as you like. Either stay here, or come with me. If you go to Auxerre there's no need at all for you to see the execution. It's an interesting old town – cathedral and so on. But of course if you can't bear to be in the same town as a guillotine, I'll go alone. I shall come back tomorrow.'

It was plain where his wish lay. She stopped the phrases that came to her lips, and did her best to dismiss the thoughts which prompted them.

'Of course I'll go,' she said quietly. She hesitated, and then went up to the washstand and kissed a part of his cheek that was not soapy. That kiss, which comforted and somehow reassured her, was the expression of a surrender whose monstrousness she would not admit to herself.

In the rich and dusty drawing-room Chirac and Chirac's exquisite formalities awaited her. Nobody else was there.

'My husband . . .' she began, smiling and blushing. She liked Chirac.

It was the first time she had had the opportunity of using that word to other than a servant. It soothed her and gave her confidence. She perceived after a few moments that Chirac did genuinely admire her; more, that she inspired him with something that resembled awe. Speaking very slowly and distinctly she said that she should travel with her husband to Auxerre, as he saw no objection to that course; implying that if he saw no objection she was perfectly satisfied. Chirac was concurrence itself. In five minutes it seemed to be the most natural and proper thing in the world that, on her honeymoon, she should be going with her husband to a particular town because a notorious murderer was about to be decapitated there in public.

'My husband has always wanted to see an execution,' she said, later. 'It would be a pity to . . .'

'As psychological experience,' replied Chirac, pronouncing the *p* of the adjective, 'it will be very *intéressant* . . . To observe one's self, in such circumstances . . .' He smiled enthusiastically.

She thought how strange even nice Frenchmen were. Imagine going to an execution in order to observe yourself!

What continually impressed Sophia as strange, in the behaviour not only of Gerald but of Chirac and other people with whom she came into contact, was its quality of casualness. She had all her life been accustomed to see enterprises, even minor ones, well pondered and then carefully schemed beforehand. In St Luke's Square there was always, in every head, a sort of time-table of existence prepared at least one week in advance. But in Gerald's world nothing was prearranged. Elaborate affairs were decided in a moment and undertaken with extraordinary lightness. Thus the excursion to Auxerre! During lunch scarcely a word was said as to it; the conversation, in English for Sophia's advantage, turning, as usual under such circumstances, upon the difficulty of languages and the differences between countries. Nobody would have guessed that any member of the party had any preoccupation whatever for the rest of the day. The meal was delightful to Sophia; not merely did she find Chirac comfortingly kind and sincere, but Gerald was restored to the perfection of his charm and his good humour. Then suddenly, in the midst of coffee, the question of trains loomed up like a swift crisis. In five minutes Chirac had departed – whether to his office or his home Sophia did not understand – and within a quarter of an hour she and Gerald were driving rapidly to the Gare de Lyon, Gerald stuffing into his pocket a large envelope full of papers which he had received by registered post. They caught the train by about a minute, and Chirac by a few seconds. Yet neither he nor Gerald seemed to envisage the risk of inconvenience and annoyance which they had incurred and escaped. Chirac chattered through the window with another journalist in the next compartment. When she had leisure to examine him, Sophia saw that he must have called at his home to put on old clothes. Everybody except herself and Gerald seemed to travel in his oldest clothes.

The train was hot, noisy, and dusty. But, one after another, all three of them fell asleep and slept heavily, calmly, like healthy and exhausted young animals. Nothing could disturb them for more than a moment. To Sophia it appeared to be by simple chance that Chirac aroused himself and them at Laroche and

sleepily seized her valise and got them all on the platform, where
they yawned and smiled, full of the deep, half-realized satisfaction of repose. They drank nectar from a wheeled buffet, drank it
eagerly, in thirsty gulps, and sighed with pleasure and relief, and
Gerald threw down a coin, refusing change with a lord's gesture.
The local train to Auxerre was full, and with a varied and sinister
cargo. At length they were in the zone of the waiting guillotine.
The rumour ran that the executioner was on the train. No one
had seen him; no one was sure of recognizing him, but everyone
hugged the belief that he was on the train. Although the sun was
sinking the heat seemed not to abate. Attitudes grew more limp,
more abandoned. Soot and prickly dust flew in unceasingly at
the open windows. The train stopped at Bonnard, Chemilly, and
Moneteau, each time before a waiting crowd that invaded it. And
at last, in the great station at Auxerre, it poured out an incredible
mass of befouled humanity that spread over everything like an
inundation. Sophia was frightened. Gerald left the initiative to
Chirac, and Chirac took her arm and led her forward, looking
behind him to see that Gerald followed with the valise. Frenzy
seemed to reign in Auxerre.

The driver of a cab demanded ten francs for transporting them
to the Hotel de l'Épée.

'Bah!' scornfully exclaimed Chirac, in his quality of experienced Parisian who is not to be exploited by heavy-witted
provincials.

But the driver of the next cab demanded twelve francs.

'Jump in,' said Gerald to Sophia. Chirac lifted his eyebrows.

At the same moment a tall, stout man with the hard face of a
flourishing scoundrel, and a young, pallid girl on his arm, pushed
aside both Gerald and Chirac and got into the cab with his
companion.

Chirac protested, telling him that the cab was already engaged.

The usurper scowled and swore, and the young girl laughed
boldly.

Sophia, shrinking, expected her escort to execute justice heroic
and final; but she was disappointed.

'Brute!' murmured Chirac, and shrugged his shoulders as the
carriage drove off, leaving them foolish on the kerb.

By this time all the other cabs had been seized. They walked to the Hotel de l'Épée, jostled by the crowd, Sophia and Chirac in front, and Gerald following with the valise, whose weight caused him to lean over to the right and his left arm to rise. The avenue was long, straight, and misty with a floating dust. Sophia had a vivid sense of the romantic. They saw towers and spires, and Chirac talked to her slowly and carefully of the cathedral and the famous churches. He said that the stained glass was marvellous, and with much care he catalogued for her all the things she must visit. They crossed a river. She felt as though she was stepping into the middle age. At intervals Gerald changed the valise from hand to hand; obstinately, he would not let Chirac touch it. They struggled upwards, through narrow curving streets.

'Voilà!' said Chirac.

They were in front of the Hotel de l'Épée. Across the street was a café crammed with people. Several carriages stood in front. The Hotel de l'Épée had a reassuring air of mellow respectability, such as Chirac had claimed for it. He had suggested this hotel for Madame Scales because it was not near the place of execution. Gerald had said, 'Of course! Of course!' Chirac, who did not mean to go to bed, required no room for himself.

The Hotel de l'Épée had one room to offer, at the price of twenty-five francs.

Gerald revolted at the attempted imposition. 'A nice thing!' he grumbled, 'that ordinary travellers can't get a decent room at a decent price just because someone's going to be guillotined tomorrow! We'll try elsewhere!'

His features expressed disgust, but Sophia fancied that he was secretly pleased.

They swaggered out of the busy stir of the hotel, as those must who, having declined to be swindled, wish to preserve their importance in the face of the world. In the street a cabman solicited them, and filled them with hope by saying that he knew of an hotel that might suit them and would drive them there for five francs. He furiously lashed his horse. The mere fact of being in a swiftly moving carriage which wayfarers had to avoid nimbly, maintained their spirits. They had a near glimpse of the cathedral. The cab halted with a bump, in a small square, in front of a repellent building which bore the sign, 'Hotel de Vézelay'. The horse was bleeding. Gerald instructed Sophia to remain where she was, and he and Chirac went up four stone steps into the hotel. Sophia, stared at by loose crowds that were promenading, gazed about her, and saw that all the windows of the square were open and most of them occupied by people who laughed and chattered. Then there was a shout: Gerald's voice. He had appeared at a window on the second floor of the hotel with Chirac and a very fat woman. Chirac saluted, and Gerald laughed carelessly, and nodded.

'It's all right,' said Gerald, having descended.

'How much do they ask?' Sophia inquired indiscreetly.

Gerald hesitated, and looked self-conscious. 'Thirty-five francs,' he said. 'But I've had enough of driving about. It seems we're lucky to get it even at that.'

And Chirac shrugged his shoulders as if to indicate that the situation and the price ought to be accepted philosophically. Gerald gave the driver five francs. He examined the piece and demanded a pourboire.

'Oh! Damn!' said Gerald, and, because he had no smaller change, parted with another two francs.

'Is anyone coming out for this damned valise?' Gerald demanded, like a tyrant whose wrath would presently fall, if the populace did not instantly set about minding their p's and q's.

But nobody emerged, and he was compelled to carry the bag himself.

The hotel was dark and malodorous, and every room seemed to be crowded with giggling groups of drinkers.

'We can't both sleep in this bed, surely,' said Sophia when, Chirac having remained downstairs, she faced Gerald in a small, mean bedroom.

'You don't suppose I shall go to bed, do you?' said Gerald, rather brusquely. 'It's for you. We're going to eat now. Look sharp.'

III

It was night. She lay in the narrow, crimson-draped bed. The heavy crimson curtains had been drawn across the dirty lace curtains of the window, but the lights of the little square faintly penetrated through chinks into the room. The sounds of the square also penetrated, extraordinarily loud and clear, for the unabated heat had compelled her to leave the window open. She could not sleep. Exhausted though she was, there was no hope of her being able to sleep.

Once again she was profoundly depressed. She remembered the dinner with horror. The long, crowded table, with semicircular ends, in the oppressive and reeking dining-room lighted by oil-lamps! There must have been at least forty people at that table. Most of them ate disgustingly, as noisily as pigs, with the ends of the large coarse napkins tucked in at their necks. All the service was done by the fat woman whom she had seen at the window with Gerald, and a young girl whose demeanour was candidly brazen. Both these creatures were slatterns. Everything was dirty. But the food was good. Chirac and Gerald were agreed that the food was good, as well as the wine. 'Remarquable!' Chirac had said, of the wine. Sophia, however, could neither eat nor drink with relish. She was afraid. The company shocked her by its gestures alone. It was very heterogeneous in appearance, some of the diners being well dressed, approaching elegance, and others shabby. But all the faces, to the youngest, were brutalized, corrupt, and shameless. The juxtaposition of old men and young women was odious to her, especially when those pairs kissed, as they did frequently towards the end of the meal. Happily she was placed between Chirac and Gerald. That situation seemed to shelter her even from the conversation. She would have comprehended nothing of the conversation, had it not been for the presence of a middle-aged Englishman who sat at the opposite end of the table with a youngish, stylish Frenchwoman whom she had seen at Sylvain's on the previous night. The Englishman was evidently under a promise to teach English to the Frenchwoman. He kept translating for her into English, slowly and distinctly, and she would repeat the phrases after him, with strange contortions of the mouth.

Thus Sophia gathered that the talk was exclusively about assassinations, executions, criminals, and executioners. Some of the people there made a practice of attending every execution. They were fountains of interesting gossip, and the lions of the meal. There was a woman who could recall the dying words of all the victims of justice for twenty years past. The table roared with hysteric laughter at one of this woman's anecdotes. Sophia learned that she had related how a criminal had said to the priest who was good-naturedly trying to screen the sight of the guillotine from him with his body: 'Stand away now, parson. Haven't I paid to see it?' Such was the Englishman's rendering. The wages of the executioners and their assistants were discussed, and differences of opinion led to ferocious arguments. A young and dandiacal fellow told, as a fact which he was ready to vouch for with a pistol, how Cora Pearl, the renowned English courtesan, had through her influence over a prefect of police succeeded in visiting a criminal alone in his cell during the night preceding his execution, and had only quitted him an hour before the final summons. The tale won the honours of the dinner. It was regarded as truly impressive, and inevitably it led to the general inquiry: what could the highest personages in the empire see to admire in that red-haired Englishwoman? And of course Rivain himself, the handsome homicide, the centre and hero of the fête, was never long out of the conversation. Several of the diners had seen him; one or two knew him and could give amazing details of his prowess as a man of pleasure. Despite his crime, he seemed to be the object of sincere idolatry. It was said positively that a niece of his victim had been promised a front place at the execution.

Apropos of this, Sophia gathered, to her intense astonishment and alarm, that the prison was close by and that the execution would take place at the corner of the square itself in which the hotel was situated. Gerald must have known; he had hidden it from her. She regarded him sideways, with distrust. As the dinner finished, Gerald's pose of a calm, disinterested, scientific observer of humanity gradually broke down. He could not maintain it in front of the increasing license of the scene round the table. He was at length somewhat ashamed of having exposed his wife to the view of such an orgy; his restless glance carefully avoided both Sophia and Chirac. The latter, whose unaffected simplicity of interest in the affair had more than anything helped to keep Sophia in countenance, observed the change in Gerald and Sophia's excessive discomfort, and suggested that they should leave the table without waiting for the coffee. Gerald agreed quickly. Thus had Sophia been released from the horror of the dinner. She did not understand how a man so thoughtful and kindly as Chirac – he had bidden her good night with the most distinguished courtesy – could tolerate, much less pleasurably savour, the gluttonous, drunken, and salacious debauchery of the Hotel de Vézelay; but his theory was, so far as she could judge from his imperfect English, that whatever existed might be admitted and examined by serious persons interested in the study of human nature. His face seemed to say: 'Why not?' His face seemed to say to Gerald and to herself: 'If this incommodes you, what did you come for?'

Gerald had left her at the bedroom door with a self-conscious nod. She had partly undressed and lain down, and instantly the hotel had transformed itself into a kind of sounding-box. It was as if, beneath and within all the noises of the square, every movement in the hotel reached her ears through cardboard walls: distant shoutings and laughter below; rattlings of crockery below; stampings up and down stairs; stealthy creepings up and down stairs; brusque calls; fragments of song, whisperings; long sighs suddenly stifled; mysterious groans as of torture, broken by a giggle; quarrels and bickerings – she was spared nothing in the strangely resonant darkness.

Then there came out of the little square a great uproar and commotion, with shrieks, and under the shrieks a confused din. In vain she pressed her face into the pillow and listened to the irregular, prodigious noise of her eyelashes as they scraped the rough linen. The thought had somehow introduced itself into her head that she must arise and go to the window and see all that was to be seen. She resisted. She said to herself that the idea was absurd, that she did not *wish* to go to the window. Nevertheless, while arguing with herself, she well knew that resistance to the thought was useless and that ultimately her legs would obey its command.

When ultimately she yielded to the fascination and went to the window and pulled aside one of the curtains, she had a feeling of relief.

The cool, grey beginnings of dawn were in the sky, and every detail of the square was visible. Without exception all the windows were wide open and filled with sightseers. In the background of many windows were burning candles or lamps that the far-distant approach of the sun was already killing. In front of these, on the frontier of two mingling lights, the attentive figures of the watchers were curiously silhouetted. On the red-tiled roofs, too, was a squatted population. Below, a troop of gendarmes, mounted on caracoling horses stretched in line across the square, was gradually sweeping the entire square of a packed, gesticulating, cursing crowd. The operation of this immense besom was very slow. As the spaces of the square were cleared they began to be dotted by privileged persons, journalists or law officers or their friends, who walked to and fro in conscious pride; among them Sophia descried Gerald and Chirac, strolling arm-in-arm and talking to two elaborately clad girls, who were also arm-in-arm.

Then she saw a red reflection coming from one of the side streets of which she had a vista; it was the swinging lantern of a waggon drawn by a gaunt grey horse. The vehicle stopped at the end of the square from which the besom had started, and it was immediately surrounded by the privileged, who, however, were soon persuaded to stand away. The crowd, amassed now at the principal inlets of the square, gave a formidable cry and burst into the refrain –

'Le voilà!
Nicolas!
Ah! Ah! Ah!'

The clamour became furious as a group of workmen in blue blouses drew piece by piece all the components of the guillotine from the waggon and laid them carefully on the ground, under the superintendence of a man in a black frock-coat and a silk hat

with broad flat brim; a little fussy man of nervous gestures. And
presently the red columns had risen upright from the ground and
were joined at the top by an acrobatic climber. As each part was
bolted and screwed to the growing machine the man in the high
hat carefully tested it. In a short time that seemed very long, the
guillotine was finished save for the triangular steel blade which
lay shining on the ground, a cynosure. The executioner pointed to
it, and two men picked it up and slipped it into its groove, and
hoisted it to the summit of the machine. The executioner peered
at it interminably amid a universal silence. Then he actuated the
mechanism, and the mass of metal fell with a muffled, reverberat-
ing thud. There were a few faint shrieks, blended together, and
then an overpowering racket of cheers, shouts, hootings, and
fragments of song. The blade was again lifted, instantly repro-
ducing silence, and again it fell, liberating a new bedlam. The
executioner made a movement of satisfaction. Many women at
the windows clapped enthusiastically, and the gendarmes had to
fight brutally against the fierce pressure of the crowd. The
workmen doffed their blouses and put on coats, and Sophia was
disturbed to see them coming in single file towards the hotel,
followed by the executioner in the silk hat.

IV

There was a tremendous opening of doors in the Hotel de
Vézelay, and much whispering on thresholds, as the executioner
and his band entered solemnly. Sophia heard them tramp upstairs; they seemed to hesitate, and then apparently went into a
room on the same landing as hers. A door banged. But Sophia
could hear the regular sound of new voices talking, and then the
rattling of glasses on a tray. The conversation which came to her
from the windows of the hotel now showed a great increase of
excitement. She could not see the people at these neighbouring
windows without showing her own head, and this she would
not do. The boom of a heavy bell striking the hour vibrated
over the roofs of the square; she supposed that it might be the
cathedral clock. In a corner of the square she saw Gerald talking
vivaciously alone with one of the two girls who had been
together. She wondered vaguely how such a girl had been

brought up, and what her parents thought – or knew! And she was conscious of an intense pride in herself, of a measureless haughty feeling of superiority.

Her eye caught the guillotine again, and was held by it. Guarded by gendarmes, that tall and simple object did most menacingly dominate the square with its crude red columns. Tools and a large open box lay on the ground beside it. The enfeebled horse in the waggon had an air of dozing on his twisted legs. Then the first rays of the sun shot lengthwise across the square at the level of the chimneys; and Sophia noticed that nearly all the lamps and candles had been extinguished. Many people at the windows were yawning; they laughed foolishly after they had yawned. Some were eating and drinking. Some were shouting conversations from one house to another. The mounted gendarmes were still pressing back the feverish crowds that growled at all the inlets to the square. She saw Chirac walking to and fro alone. But she could not find Gerald. He could not have left the square. Perhaps he had returned to the hotel and would come up to see if she was comfortable or if she needed anything. Guiltily she sprang back into bed. When last she had surveyed the room it had been dark; now it was bright and every detail stood clear. Yet she had the sensation of having been at the window only a few minutes.

She waited. But Gerald did not come. She could hear chiefly the steady hum of the voices of the executioner and his aids. She reflected that the room in which they were must be at the back. The other sounds in the hotel grew less noticeable. Then, after an age, she heard a door open, and a low voice say something commandingly in French, and then a 'Oui, monsieur', and a general descent of the stairs. The executioner and his aids were leaving. 'You,' cried a drunken English voice from an upper floor – it was the middle-aged Englishman translating what the executioner had said – 'you, you will take the head.' Then a rough laugh, and the repeating voice of the Englishman's girl, still pursuing her studies in English: 'You will take ze 'ead. Yess, sair.' And another laugh. At length quiet reigned in the hotel. Sophia said to herself: 'I won't stir from this bed till it's all over and Gerald comes back!'

She dozed, under the sheet, and was awakened by a tremendous shrieking, growling, and yelling: a phenomenon of human bestiality that far surpassed Sophia's narrow experiences. Shut up though she was in a room, perfectly secure, the mad fury of that crowd, balked at the inlets to the square, thrilled and intimidated her. It sounded as if they would be capable of tearing the very horses to pieces. 'I must stay where I am,' she murmured. And even while saying it she rose and went to the window again and peeped out. The torture involved was extreme, but she had not sufficient force within her to resist the fascination. She stared greedily into the bright squre. The first thing she saw was Gerald coming out of a house opposite, followed after a few seconds by the girl with whom he had previously been talking. Gerald glanced hastily up at the façade of the hotel, and then approached as near as he could to the red columns, in front of which were now drawn up a line of gendarmes with naked swords. A second and larger wagon, with two horses, waited by the side of the other one. The racket beyond the square continued and even grew louder. But the couple of hundred persons within the cordons, and all the inhabitants of the windows, drunk and sober, gazed in a fixed and sinister enchantment at the region of the guillotine, as Sophia gazed. 'I cannot stand this!' she told herself in horror, but she could not move; she could not move even her eyes.

At intervals the crowd would burst out in a violent staccato —

'Le voilà!
Nicolas!
Ah! Ah! Ah!'

And the final 'Ah' was devilish.

Then a gigantic passionate roar, the culmination of the mob's fierce savagery, crashed against the skies. The line of maddened horses swerved and reared, and seemed to fall on the furious multitude while the statue-like gendarmes rocked over them. It was a last effort to break the cordon, and it failed.

From the little street at the rear of the guillotine appeared a priest, walking backwards and holding a crucifix high in his right hand, and behind him came the handsome hero, his body all crossed with cords, between two warders, who pressed against him and supported him on either side. He was certainly very young. He lifted his chin gallantly, but his face was incredibly white. Sophia discerned that the priest was trying to hide the sight of the guillotine from the prisoner with his body, just as in the story which she had heard at dinner.

Except the voice of the priest, indistinctly rising and falling in the prayer for the dying, there was no sound in the square or its environs. The windows were now occupied by groups turned to stone with distended eyes fixed on the little procession. Sophia had a tightening of the throat, and the hand trembled by which she held the curtain. The central figure did not seem to her to be alive; but rather a doll, a marionette wound up to imitate the action of a tragedy. She saw the priest offer the crucifix to the mouth of the marionette, which with a clumsy unhuman shoving of its corded shoulders butted the thing away. And as the procession turned and stopped she could plainly see that the marionette's nape and shoulders were bare, his shirt having been slit. It was horrible. 'Why do I stay here?' she asked herself hysterically. But she did not stir. The victim had disappeared now in the midst of a group of men. Then she perceived him prone under the red column, between the grooves. The silence was now broken only by the tinkling of the horses' bits in the corners of the square. The line of gendarmes in front of the scaffold held their swords tightly and looked over their noses, ignoring the privileged groups that peered almost between their shoulders.

And Sophia waited, horror-struck. She saw nothing but the gleaming triangle of metal that was suspended high above the prone, attendant victim. She felt like a lost soul, torn too soon from shelter, and exposed for ever to the worst hazards of destiny. Why was she in this strange, incomprehensible town, foreign and inimical to her, watching with agonized glance this cruel, obscene spectacle? Her sensibilities were all a bleeding mass of wounds. Why? Only yesterday, and she had been an innocent, timid creature in Bursley, in Axe, a foolish creature who deemed the concealment of letters a supreme excitement. Either that day or this day was not real. Why was she imprisoned alone in that odious, indescribably odious hotel, with no one to soothe and comfort her, and carry her away?

The distant bell boomed once. Then a monosyllabic voice sounded, sharp, low, nervous; she recognized the voice of the executioner, whose name she had heard but could not remember. There was a clicking noise . . .

She shrank down to the floor in terror and loathing, and hid her face, and shuddered. Shriek after shriek, from various windows, rang on her ears in a fusillade; and then the mad yell of the penned crowd, which, like herself, had not seen but had heard, extinguished all other noise. Justice was done. The great ambition of Gerald's life was at last satisfied.

V

Later, amid the stir of the hotel, there came a knock at her door, impatient and nervous. Forgetting, in her tribulation, that she was without her bodice, she got up from the floor in a kind of miserable dream, and opened. Chirac stood on the landing, and he had Gerald by the arm. Chirac looked worn out, curiously fragile and pathetic; but Gerald was the very image of death. The attainment of ambition had utterly destroyed his equilibrium; his curiosity had proved itself stronger than his stomach. Sophia would have pitied him had she in that moment been capable of pity. Gerald staggered past her into the room, and sank with a groan on to the bed. Not long since he had been proudly conversing with impudent women. Now, in swift collapse, he was as flaccid as a sick hound and as disgusting as an aged drunkard.

'He is some little *souffrant*,' said Chirac, weakly.

Sophia perceived in Chirac's tone the assumption that of course her present duty was to devote herself to the task of restoring her shamed husband to his manly pride.

'And what about me?' she thought bitterly.

The fat woman ascended the stairs like a tottering blancmange, and began to gabble to Sophia, who understood nothing whatever.

'She wants sixty francs,' Chirac said, and in answer to Sophia's startled question, he explained that Gerald had agreed to pay a hundred francs for the room, which was the landlady's own — fifty francs in advance and the fifty after the execution. The other ten was for the dinner. The landlady, distrusting the whole of her *clientèle*, was collecting her accounts instantly on the completion of the spectacle.

Sophia made no remark as to Gerald's lie to her. Indeed, Chirac had heard it. She knew Gerald for a glib liar to others, but she was naïvely surprised when he practised upon herself.

'Gerald! Do you hear?' she said coldly.

The amateur of severed heads only groaned.

With a movement of irritation she went to him and felt in his pockets for his purse; he acquiesced, still groaning. Chirac helped her to choose and count the coins.

The fat woman, appeased, pursued her way.

'Good-bye, madame!' said Chirac, with his customary courtliness, transforming the landing of the hideous hotel into some imperial antechamber.

'Are you going away?' she asked, in surprise. Her distress was so obvious that it tremendously flattered him. He would have stayed if he could. But he had to return to Paris to write and deliver his article.

'Tomorrow, I hope!' he murmured sympathetically, kissing her hand. The gesture atoned somewhat for the sordidness of her situation, and even corrected the faults of her attire. Always afterwards it seemed to her that Chirac was an old and intimate friend; he had successfully passed through the ordeal of seeing 'the wrong side' of the stuff of her life.

She shut the door on him with a lingering glance, and reconciled herself to her predicament.

Gerald slept. Just as he was, he slept heavily.

This was what he had brought her to, then! The horrors of the night, of the dawn, and of the morning! Ineffable suffering and humiliation; anguish and torture that could never be forgotten! And after a fatuous vigil of unguessed license, he had tottered back, an offensive beast, to sleep the day away in that filthy chamber! He did not possess even enough spirit to play the *rôle* of roysterer to the end. And she was bound to him; far, far from any other human aid; cut off irrevocably by her pride from those who perhaps would have protected her from his dangerous folly. The deep conviction henceforward formed a permanent part of her general consciousness that he was simply an irresponsible and thoughtless fool! He was without *sense*. Such was her brilliant and godlike husband, the man who had given her the right to call herself a married woman! He was a fool. With all her ignorance of the world she could see that nobody but an arrant imbecile could have brought her to the present pass. Her native sagacity revolted. Gusts of feeling came over her in which she could have thrashed him into the realization of his responsibilities.

Sticking out of the breast pocket of his soiled coat was the packet which he had received on the previous day. If he had not already lost it, he could only thank his luck. She took it. There were English bank-notes in it for two hundred pounds, a letter from a banker, and other papers. With precautions against noise she tore the envelope and the letter and papers into small pieces, and then looked about for a place to hide them. A cupboard suggested itself. She got on a chair, and pushed the fragments out of sight on the topmost shelf, where they may well be to this day. She finished dressing, and then sewed the notes into the lining of her skirt. She had no silly, delicate notions about stealing. She obscurely felt that, in the care of a man like Gerald, she might find herself in the most monstrous, the most impossible dilemmas. Those notes, safe and secret in her skirt, gave her confidence, reassured her against the perils of the future, and endowed her with independence. The act was characteristic of her enterprise and of her fundamental prudence. It approached the heroic. And her conscience hotly defended its righteousness.

She decided that when he discovered his loss, she would merely deny all knowledge of the envelope, for he had not spoken a word to her about it. He never mentioned the details of money; he had a fortune. However, the necessity for this untruth did not occur. He made no reference whatever to his loss. The fact was, he thought he had been careless enough to let the envelope be filched from him during the excess of the night.

All day till evening Sophia sat on a dirty chair, without food, while Gerald slept. She kept repeating to herself, in amazed resentment: 'A hundred francs for this room! A hundred francs! And he hadn't the pluck to tell me!' She could not have expressed her contempt.

Long before sheer ennui forced her to look out of the window again, every sign of justice had been removed from the square. Nothing whatever remained in the heavy August sunshine save gathered heaps of filth where the horses had reared and caracoled.

CHAPTER 4: *A Crisis for Gerald*

I

For a time there existed in the minds of both Gerald and Sophia the remarkable notion that twelve thousand pounds represented the infinity of wealth, that this sum possessed special magical properties which rendered it insensible to the process of subtraction. It seemed impossible that twelve thousand pounds, while continually getting less, could ultimately quite disappear. The notion lived longer in the mind of Gerald than in that of Sophia; for Gerald would never look at a disturbing fact, whereas Sophia's gaze was morbidly fascinated by such phenomena. In a life devoted to travel and pleasure Gerald meant not to spend more than six hundred a year, the interest on his fortune. Six hundred a year is less than two pounds a day, yet Gerald never paid less than two pounds a day in hotel bills alone. He hoped that he was living on a thousand a year, had a secret fear that he might be spending fifteen hundred, and was really spending about two thousand five hundred. Still, the remarkable notion of the inexhaustibility of twelve thousand pounds always reassured him. The faster the money went, the more vigorously this notion flourished in Gerald's mind. When twelve had unaccountably dwindled to three, Gerald suddenly decided that he must act, and in a few months he lost two thousand on the Paris Bourse. The adventure frightened him, and in his panic he scattered a couple of hundred in a frenzy of high living.

But even with only twenty thousand francs left out of three hundred thousand, he held closely to the belief that natural laws would in his case somehow be suspended. He had heard of men who were once rich begging bread and sweeping crossings, but he

felt quite secure against such risks, by simple virtue of the axiom
that he was he. However, he meant to assist the axiom by efforts
to earn money. When these continued to fail, he tried to assist the
axiom by borrowing money; but he found that his uncle had
definitely done with him. He would have assisted the axiom by
stealing money, but he had neither the nerve nor the knowledge
to be a swindler; he was not even sufficiently expert to cheat at
cards.

He had thought in thousands. Now he began to think in
hundreds, in tens, daily and hourly. He paid two hundred francs
in railway fares in order to live economically in a village, and
shortly afterwards another two hundred francs in railway fares in
order to live economically in Paris. And to celebrate the arrival in
Paris and the definite commencement of an era of strict economy
and serious search for a livelihood, he spent a hundred francs on a
dinner at the Maison Dorée and two balcony stalls at the
Gymnase. In brief, he omitted nothing – no act, no resolve, no
self-deception – of the typical fool in his situation; always
convinced that his difficulties and his wisdom were quite exceptional.

In May 1870, on an afternoon, he was ranging nervously to
and fro in a three-cornered bedroom of a little hotel at the angle
of the Rue Fontaine and the Rue Laval (now the Rue Victor Massé),
within half a minute of the Boulevard de Clichy. It had come to
that – an exchange of the 'grand boulevard' for the 'boulevard
extérieur'! Sophia sat on a chair at the grimy window, glancing
down in idle disgust of life at the Clichy-Odéon omnibus which
was casting off its tip-horse at the corner of the Rue Chaptal. The
noise of petty, hurried traffic over the bossy paving stones was
deafening. The locality was not one to correspond with an ideal.
There was too much humanity crowded into those narrow hilly
streets; humanity seemed to be bulging out at the windows of the
high houses. Gerald healed his pride by saying that this was, after
all, the real Paris, and that the cookery was as good as could be
got anywhere, pay what you would. He seldom ate a meal in the
little salons on the first floor without becoming ecstatic upon the
cookery. To hear him, he might have chosen the hotel on its
superlative merits, without regard to expense. And with his air of

use and custom, he did indeed look like a connoisseur of Paris who knew better than to herd with vulgar tourists in the pens of the Madeleine quarter. He was dressed with some distinction; good clothes, when put to the test, survive a change of fortune, as a Roman arch survives the luxury of departed empire. Only his collar, large V-shaped front, and wrist-bands, which bore the ineffaceable signs of cheap laundering, reflected the shadow of impending disaster.

He glanced sideways, stealthily, at Sophia. She, too, was still dressed with distinction; in the robe of black *faille*, the cashmere shawl, and the little black hat with its falling veil, there was no apparent symptom of beggary. She would have been judged as one of those women who content themselves with few clothes but good, and, greatly aided by nature, make a little go a long way. Good black will last for eternity; it discloses no secrets of modification and mending, and it is not transparent.

At last Gerald, resuming a suspended conversation, said as it were doggedly:

'I tell you I haven't got five francs altogether! and you can feel my pockets if you like,' added the habitual liar in him, fearing incredulity.

'Well, and what do you expect *me* to do?' Sophia inquired.

The accent, at once ironic and listless, in which she put this question, showed that strange and vital things had happened to Sophia in the four years which had elapsed since her marriage. It did really seem to her, indeed, that the Sophia whom Gerald had espoused was dead and gone, and that another Sophia had come into her body: so intensely conscious was she of a fundamental change in herself under the stress of continuous experience. And though this was but a seeming, though she was still the same Sophia more fully disclosed, it was a true seeming. Indisputably more beautiful than when Gerald had unwillingly made her his legal wife, she was now nearly twenty-four, and looked perhaps somewhat older than her age. Her frame was firmly set, her waist thicker, neither slim nor stout. The lips were rather hard, and she had a habit of tightening her mouth, on the same provocation as sends a snail into its shell. No trace was left of immature gawkiness in her gestures or of simplicity in her intonations. She was a woman of commanding and slightly arrogant charm, not in the least degree the charm of innocence and ingenuousness. Her eyes were the eyes of one who has lost her illusions too violently and too completely. Her gaze, coldly comprehending, implied familiarity with the abjectness of human nature. Gerald had begun and had finished her education. He had not ruined her, as a bad professor may ruin a fine voice, because her moral force immeasurably exceeded his; he had unwittingly produced a masterpiece, but it was a tragic masterpiece. Sophia was such a woman as, by a mere glance as she utters an opinion, will make a man say to himself, half in desire and half in alarm lest she reads him too: 'By Jove! she must have been through a thing or two. She knows what people are!'

The marriage was, of course, a calamitous folly. From the very first, from the moment when the commercial traveller had with incomparable rash fatuity thrown the paper pellet over the counter, Sophia's awakening common sense had told her that in yielding to her instinct she was sowing misery and shame for herself: but she had gone on, as if under a spell. It had needed the irretrievableness of flight from home to begin the breaking of the trance. Once fully awakened out of the trance, she had recognized her marriage for what it was. She had made neither the best nor the worst of it. She had accepted Gerald as one accepts a climate. She saw again and again that he was irreclaimably a fool and a prodigy of irresponsibleness. She tolerated him, now with sweetness, now bitterly; accepting always his caprices, and not permitting herself to have wishes of her own. She was ready to pay the price of pride and of a moment's imbecility with a lifetime of self-repression. It was high, but it was the price. She had acquired nothing but an exceptionally good knowledge of the French language (she soon learnt to scorn Gerald's glib maltreatment of the tongue), and she had conserved nothing but her dignity. She knew that Gerald was sick of her, that he would have danced for joy to be rid of her; that he was constantly unfaithful; that he had long since ceased to be excited by her beauty. She knew also that at bottom he was a little afraid of her; here was her sole moral consolation. The thing that sometimes struck her as surprising was that he had not abandoned her, simply and crudely walked off one day and forgotten to take her with him.

They hated each other, but in different ways. She loathed him, and he resented her.

'What do I expect you to do?' he repeated after her. 'Why don't you write home to your people and get some money out of them?'

Now that he had said what was in his mind, he faced her with a bullying swagger. Had he been a bigger man he might have tried the effect of physical bullying on her. One of his numerous reasons for resenting her was that she was the taller of the two.

She made no reply.

'Now you needn't turn pale and begin all that fuss over again. What I'm suggesting is a perfectly reasonable thing. If I haven't got money I haven't got it. I can't invent it.'

She perceived that he was ready for one of their periodical tempestuous quarrels. But that day she felt too tired and unwell to quarrel. His warning against a repetition of 'fuss' had reference to the gastric dizziness from which she had been suffering for two years. It would take her usually after a meal. She did not swoon, but her head swam and she could not stand. She would sink down wherever she happened to be, and, her face alarmingly white, murmur faintly: 'My salts.' Within five minutes the attack had gone and left no trace. She had been through one just after lunch. He resented this affection. He detested being compelled to hand the smelling-bottle to her, and he would have avoided doing so if her pallor did not always alarm him. Nothing but this pallor convinced him that the attacks were not a deep ruse to impress him. His attitude invariably implied that she could cure the malady if she chose, but that through obstinacy she did not choose.

'Are you going to have the decency to answer my question, or aren't you?'

'What question?' Her vibrating voice was low and restrained.

'Will you write to your people?'

'For money?'

The sarcasm of her tone was diabolic. She could not have kept the sarcasm out of her tone; she did not attempt to keep it out. She cared little if it whipped him to fury. Did he imagine, seriously, that she would be capable of going on her knees to her family? She? Was he unaware that his wife was the proudest and the most obstinate woman on earth, that all her behaviour to him was the expression of her pride and her obstinacy? Ill and weak though she felt, she marshalled together all the forces of her character to defend her resolve never, never to eat the bread of humiliation. She was absolutely determined to be dead to her family. Certainly, one December, several years previously, she had seen English Christmas cards in an English shop in the Rue de Rivoli, and in a sudden gush of tenderness towards Constance, she had despatched a coloured greeting to Constance and her mother. And having initiated the custom, she had continued it. That was not like asking a kindness; it was bestowing a kindness. But except for the annual card, she was dead to St Luke's Square. She was one of those daughters who disappear and are not discussed in the family circle. The thought of her immense foolishness, the little tender thoughts of Constance, some flitting souvenir, full of unwilling admiration, of a regal gesture of her mother – these things only steeled her against any sort of resurrection after death.

And he was urging her to write home for money! Why, she would not even have paid a visit in splendour to St Luke's Square. Never should they know what she had suffered! And especially her Aunt Harriet, from whom she had stolen!

'Will you write to your people?' he demanded yet again, emphasizing and separating each word.

'No,' she said shortly, with terrible disdain.

'Why not?'

'Because I won't.' The curling line of her lips, as they closed on each other, said all the rest; all the cruel truths about his unspeakable, inane, coarse follies, his laziness, his excesses, his lies, his deceptions, his bad faith, his truculence, his improvidence, his shameful waste and ruin of his life and hers. She doubted whether he realized his baseness and her wrongs, but if he could not read them in her silent contumely, she was too proud to recite them to him. She had never complained, save in uncontrolled moments of anger.

'If that's the way you're going to talk – all right!' he snapped, furious. Evidently he was baffled.

She kept silence. She was determined to see what he would do in the face of her inaction.

'You know, I'm not joking,' he pursued. 'We shall starve.'

'Very well,' she agreed. 'We shall starve.'

She watched him surreptitiously, and she was almost sure that he really had come to the end of his tether. His voice, which never alone convinced, carried a sort of conviction now. He was penniless. In four years he had squandered twelve thousand pounds, and had nothing to show for it except an enfeebled digestion and a tragic figure of a wife. One small point of satisfaction there was – and all the Baines in her clutched at it and tried to suck satisfaction from it – their manner of travelling about from hotel to hotel had made it impossible for Gerald to run up debts. A few debts he might have, unknown to her, but they could not be serious.

So they looked at one another, in hatred and despair. The inevitable had arrived. For months she had fronted it in bravado, not concealing from herself that it lay in waiting. For years he had been sure that though the inevitable might happen to others it could not happen to him. There it was! He was conscious of a heavy weight in his stomach, and she of a general numbness, enwrapping her fatigue. Even then he could not believe that it was true, this disaster. As for Sophia, she was reconciling herself with bitter philosophy to the eccentricities of fate. Who would have dreamed that she, a young girl brought up, etc.? Her mother could not have improved the occasion more uncompromisingly than Sophia did – behind that disdainful mask.

'Well – if that's it . . . !' Gerald exploded at length, puffing. And he puffed out of the room and was gone in a second.

II

She languidly picked up a book, the moment Gerald had departed, and tried to prove to herself that she was sufficiently in command of her nerves to read. For a long time reading had been her chief solace. But she could not read. She glanced round the inhospitable chamber, and thought of the hundreds of rooms –

some splendid and some vile, but all arid in their unwelcoming aspect – through which she had passed in her progress from mad exultation to calm and cold disgust. The ceaseless din of the street annoyed her jaded ears. And a great wave of desire for peace, peace of no matter what kind, swept through her. And then her deep distrust of Gerald reawakened; in spite of his seriously desperate air, which had a quality of sincerity quite new in her experience of him, she could not be entirely sure that, in asserting utter penury, he was not after all merely using a trick to get rid of her.

She sprang up, threw the book on the bed, and seized her gloves. She would follow him, if she could. She would do what she had never done before – she would spy on him. Fighting against her lassitude, she descended the long winding stairs, and peeped forth from the doorway into the street. The ground floor of the hotel was a wine-shop; the stout landlord was lightly flicking one of the three little yellow tables that stood on the pavement. He smiled with his customary benevolence, and silently pointed in the direction of the Rue Notre Dame de Lorette. She saw Gerald down there in the distance. He was smoking a cigar.

He seemed to be a little man without a care. The smoke of the cigar came first round his left cheek and then round his right, sailing away into nothing. He walked with a gay spring, but not quickly, flourishing his cane as freely as the traffic of the pavement would permit, glancing into all the shop windows and into the eyes of all the women under forty. This was not at all the same man as had a moment ago been spitting angry menaces at her in the bedroom of the hotel. It was a fellow of blithe charm, ripe for any adventurous joys that destiny had to offer.

Supposing he turned round and saw her?

If he turned round and saw her and asked her what she was doing there in the street, she would tell him plainly: 'I'm following you, to find out what you do.'

But he did not turn. He went straight forward, deviating at the church, where the crowd became thicker, into the Rue du Faubourg Montmartre, and so to the boulevard, which he crossed. The whole city seemed excited and vivacious. Cannons boomed in slow succession, and flags were flying. Sophia had no

conception of the significance of those guns, for, though she read
a great deal, she never read a newspaper; the idea of opening a
newspaper never occurred to her. But she was accustomed to the
feverish atmosphere of Paris. She had lately seen regiments of
cavalry flashing and prancing in the Luxembourg Gardens, and
had much admired the fine picture. She accepted the booming as
another expression of the high spirits that had to find vent
somehow in this feverish empire. She so accepted it and forgot it,
using all the panorama of the capital as a dim background for her
exacerbated egoism.

She was obliged to walk slowly, because Gerald walked slowly.
A beautiful woman, or any woman not positively hag-like or
venerable, who walks slowly in the streets of Paris becomes at
once the cause of inconvenient desires, as representing the main
objective on earth, always transcending in importance politics and
affairs. Just as a true patriotic Englishman cannot be too busy to
run after a fox, so a Frenchman is always ready to forsake all in
order to follow a woman whom he has never before set eyes on.
Many men thought twice about her, with her romantic Saxon
mystery of temperament, and her Parisian clothes; but all refrained from affronting her, not in the least out of respect for the
gloom in her face, but from an expert conviction that those rapt
eyes were fixed immovably on another male. She walked unscathed amid the frothing hounds as though protected by a spell.

On the south side of the boulevard, Gerald proceeded down
the Rue Montmartre, and then turned suddenly into the Rue
Croissant. Sophia stopped and asked the price of some combs
which were exposed outside a little shop. Then she went on,
boldly passing the end of the Rue Croissant. No shadow of
Gerald! She saw the signs of newspapers all along the street, *Le
Bien Public*, *La Presse Libre*, *La Patrie*. There was a creamery at
the corner. She entered it, asked for a cup of chocolate, and sat
down. She wanted to drink coffee, but every doctor had forbidden coffee to her, on account of her attacks of dizziness. Then,
having ordered chocolate, she felt that, on this occasion, when
she had need of strength in her great fatigue, only coffee could
suffice her, and she changed the order. She was close to the door,
and Gerald could not escape her vigilance if he emerged at that

end of the street. She drank the coffee with greedy satisfaction, and waited in the creamery till she began to feel conspicuous there. And then Gerald went by the door, within six feet of her. He turned the corner and continued his descent of the Rue Montmartre. She paid for her coffee and followed the chase. Her blood seemed to be up. Her lips were tightened, and her thought was: 'Wherever he goes, I'll go, and I don't care what happens.' She despised him. She felt herself above him. She felt that somehow, since quitting the hotel, he had been gradually growing more and more vile and meet to be exterminated. She imagined infamies as to the Rue Croissant. There was no obvious ground for this intensifying of her attitude towards him; it was merely the result of the chase. All that could be definitely charged against him was the smoking of a cigar.

He stepped into a tobacco-shop, and came out with a longer cigar than the first one, a more expensive article, stripped off its collar, and lighted it as a millionaire might have lighted it. This was the man who swore that he did not possess five francs.

She tracked him as far as the Rue de Rivoli, and then lost him. There were vast surging crowds in the Rue de Rivoli, and much bunting, and soldiers and gesticulatory policemen. The general effect of the street was that all things were brightly waving in the breeze. She was caught in the crowd as in the current of a stream, and when she tried to sidle out of it into a square, a row of smiling policemen barred her passage; she was a part of the traffic that they had to regulate. She drifted till the Louvre came into view. After all, Gerald had only strolled forth to see the sight of the day, whatever it might be! She knew not what it was. She had no curiosity about it. In the middle of all that thickening mass of humanity, staring with one accord at the vast monument of royal and imperial vanities, she thought, with her characteristic grimness, of the sacrifice of her whole career as a school-teacher for the chance of seeing Gerald once a quarter in the shop. She gloated over that, as a sick appetite will gloat over tainted food. And she saw the shop, and the curve of the stairs up to the showroom, and the pier-glass in the showroom.

Then the guns began to boom again, and splendid carriages swept one after another from under a majestic archway and glittered westward down a lane of spotless splendid uniforms. The carriages were laden with still more splendid uniforms, and with enchanting toilettes. Sophia, in her modestly stylish black, mechanically noticed how much easier it was for attired women to sit in a carriage now that crinolines had gone. That was the sole impression made upon her by this glimpse of the last fête of the Napoleonic Empire. She knew not that the supreme pillars of imperialism were exhibiting themselves before her; and that the eyes of those uniforms and those toilettes were full of the legendary beauty of Eugénie, and their ears echoing to the long phrases of Napoleon the Third about his gratitude to his people for their confidence in him as shown by the plebiscite, and about the ratification of constitutional reforms guaranteeing order, and about the empire having been strengthened at its base, and about showing force by moderation and envisaging the future without fear, and about the bosom of peace and liberty, and the eternal continuance of his dynasty.

She just wondered vaguely what was afoot.

When the last carriage had rolled away, and the guns and acclamations had ceased, the crowd at length began to scatter. She was carried by it into the Place du Palais Royal, and in a few moments she managed to withdraw into the Rue des Bons Enfants and was free.

The coins in her purse amounted to three sous, and therefore, though she felt exhausted to the point of illness, she had to return to the hotel on foot. Very slowly she crawled upwards in the direction of the Boulevard, through the expiring gaiety of the city. Near the Bourse a fiacre overtook her, and in the fiacre were Gerald and a woman. Gerald had not seen her; he was talking eagerly to his ornate companion. All his body was alive. The fiacre was out of sight in a moment, but Sophia judged instantly the grade of the woman, who was evidently of the discreet class that frequented the big shops of an afternoon with something of their own to sell.

Sophia's grimness increased. The pace of the fiacre, her fatigued body, Gerald's delightful, careless vivacity, the attractive streaming veil of the nice, modest courtesan — everything conspired to increase it.

III

Gerald returned to the bedroom which contained his wife and all else that he owned in the world at about nine o'clock that evening. Sophia was in bed. She had been driven to bed by weariness. She would have preferred to sit up to receive her husband, even if it had meant sitting up all night, but her body was too heavy for her spirit. She lay in the dark. She had eaten nothing. Gerald came straight into the room. He struck a match, which burned blue, with a stench, for several seconds, and then gave a clear, yellow flame. He lit a candle; and saw his wife.

'Oh!' he said; 'you're there, are you?'

She offered no reply.

'Won't speak, eh?' he said. 'Agreeable sort of wife! Well, have you made up your mind to do what I told you? I've come back especially to know.'

She still did not speak.

He sat down, with his hat on, and stuck out his feet, wagging them to and fro on the heels.

'I'm quite without money,' he went on. 'And I'm sure your people will be glad to lend us a bit till I get some. Especially as it's a question of you starving as well as me. If I had enough to pay your fares to Bursley I'd pack you off. But I haven't.'

She could only hear his exasperating voice. The end of the bed was between her eyes and his.

'Liar!' she said, with uncompromising distinctness. The word reached him barbed with all the poison of her contempt and disgust.

There was a pause.

'Oh! I'm a liar, am I? Thanks. I lied enough to get you, I'll admit. But you never complained of that. I remember beginning the New Year well with a thumping lie just to have a sight of you, my vixen. But you didn't complain then. I took you with only the clothes on your back. And I've spent every cent I had on you. And now I'm spun, you call me a liar.'

She said nothing.

'However,' he went on, 'this is going to come to an end, this is!'

He rose, changed the position of the candle, putting it on a chest of drawers, and then drew his trunk from the wall, and knelt in front of it.

She gathered that he was packing his clothes. At first she did not comprehend his reference to beginning the New Year. Then his meaning revealed itself. That story to her mother about having been attacked by ruffians at the bottom of King Street had been an invention, a ruse to account plausibly for his presence on her mother's doorstep! And she had never suspected that the story was not true. In spite of her experience of his lying, she had never suspected that that particular statement was a lie. What a simpleton she was!

There was a continual movement in the room for about a quarter of an hour. Then a key turned in the lock of the trunk.

His head popped up over the foot of the bed. 'This isn't a joke, you know,' he said.

She kept silence.

'I give you one more chance. Will you write to your mother – or Constance if you like – or won't you?'

She scorned to reply in any way.

'I'm your husband,' he said. 'And it's your duty to obey me, particularly in an affair like this. I order you to write to your mother.'

The corners of her lips turned downwards.

Angered by her mute obstinacy, he broke away from the bed with a sudden gesture.

'You do as you like,' he cried, putting on his overcoat, 'and I shall do as I like. You can't say I haven't warned you. It's your own deliberate choice, mind you! Whatever happens to you you've brought on yourself.' He lifted and shrugged his shoulders, to get the overcoat exactly into place on his shoulders.

She would not speak a word, not even to insist that she was indisposed.

He pushed his trunk outside the door, and returned to the bed.

'You understand,' he said menacingly: 'I'm off.'

She looked up at the foul ceiling.

'Hm!' he sniffed, bringing his reserves of pride to combat the persistent silence that was damaging his dignity. And he went off, sticking his head forward like a pugilist.

'Here!' she muttered. 'You're forgetting this.'

He turned.

She stretched her hand to the night-table and held up a red circlet.

'What is it?'

'It's the bit of paper off the cigar you bought in the Rue Montmartre this afternoon,' she answered, in a significant tone.

He hesitated, then swore violently, and bounced out of the room. He had made her suffer, but she was almost repaid for everything by that moment of cruel triumph. She exulted in it, and never forgot it.

Five minutes later, the gloomy menial in felt slippers and alpaca jacket, who seemed to pass the whole of his life flitting in and out of bedrooms like a rabbit in a warren, carried Gerald's trunk downstairs. She recognized the peculiar tread of his slippers.

Then there was a knock at the door. The landlady entered, actuated by a legitimate curiosity.

'Madame is suffering?' the landlady began.

Sophia refused offers of food and nursing.

'Madame knows without doubt that monsieur has gone away?'

'Has he paid the bill?' Sophia asked bluntly.

'But yes, madame, till tomorrow. Then madame has want of nothing?'

'If you will extinguish the candle,' said Sophia.

He had deserted her, then!

'All this,' she reflected, listening in the dark to the ceaseless rattle of the street, 'because mother and Constance wanted to see the elephant, and I had to go into father's room! I should never have caught sight of him from the drawing-room window!'

IV

She passed a night of physical misery, exasperated by the tireless rattling vitality of the street. She kept saying to herself: 'I'm all alone now, and I'm going to be ill. I am ill.' She saw herself dying in Paris, and heard the expressions of facile sympathy and idle curiosity drawn forth by the sight of the dead body of this foreign woman in a little Paris hotel. She reached the stage, in the gradual excruciation of her nerves, when she was obliged to concentrate her agonized mind on an intense and painful expectancy of the next new noise, which when it came increased her torture and decreased her strength to support it. She went through all the interminable dilatoriness of the dawn, from the moment when she could scarcely discern the window to the moment when she could read the word 'Bock' on the red circlet of paper which had tossed all night on the sea of the counterpane. She knew she would never sleep again. She could not imagine herself asleep; and then she was startled by a sound that seemed to clash with the rest of her impressions. It was a knocking at the door. With a start she perceived that she must have been asleep.

'Enter,' she murmured.

There entered the menial in alpaca. His waxen face showed a morose commiseration. He noiselessly approached the bed – he seemed to have none of the characteristics of a man, but to be a creature infinitely mysterious and aloof from humanity – and held out to Sophia a visiting card in his grey hand.

It was Chirac's card.

'Monsieur asked for monsieur,' said the waiter. 'And then, as monsieur had gone away, he demanded to see madame. He says it is very important.'

Her heart jumped, partly in vague alarm, and partly with a sense of relief at this chance of speaking to someone whom she knew. She tried to reflect rationally.

'What time is it?' she inquired.

'Eleven o'clock, madame.'

This was surprising. The fact that it was eleven o'clock destroyed the remains of her self-confidence. How could it be eleven o'clock, with the dawn scarcely finished?

'He says it is very important,' repeated the waiter, imperturbably and solemnly. 'Will madame see him an instant?'

Between resignation and anticipation she said: 'Yes.'

'It is well, madame,' said the waiter, disappearing without a sound.

She sat up and managed to drag her *matinée* from a chair and put it around her shoulders. Then she sank back from weakness, physical and spiritual. She hated to receive Chirac in a bedroom, and particularly in that bedroom. But the hotel had no public room except the dining-room, which began to be occupied after eleven o'clock. Moreover, she could not possibly get up. Yes, on the whole she was pleased to see Chirac. He was almost her only acquaintance, assuredly the only being whom she could by any stretch of meaning call a friend, in the whole of Europe. Gerald and she had wandered to and fro, skimming always over the real life of nations, and never penetrating into it. There was no place for them, because they had made none. With the exception of Chirac, whom an accident of business had thrown into Gerald's company years before, they had no social relations. Gerald was not a man to make friends; he did not seem to need friends, or at any rate to feel the want of them. But as chance had given him Chirac, he maintained the connexion whenever they came to Paris. Sophia, of course, had not been able to escape from the solitude imposed by existence in hotels. Since her marriage she had never spoken to a woman in the way of intimacy. But once or twice she had approached intimacy with Chirac, whose wistful admiration of her always aroused into activity her desire to charm.

Preceded by the menial, he came into the room hurriedly, apologetically, with an air of acute anxiety. And as he saw her lying on her back, with flushed features, her hair disarranged, and only the grace of the silk ribbons of her *matinée* to mitigate the melancholy repulsiveness of her surroundings, that anxiety seemed to deepen.

'Dear madame,' he stammered, 'all my excuses!' He hastened to the bedside and kissed her hand – a little peck, according to his custom. 'You are ill?'

'I have my migraine,' she said. 'You want Gerald?'

'Yes,' he said diffidently. 'He had promised –'

'He has left me,' Sophia interrupted him in her weak and fatigued voice. She closed her eyes as she uttered the words.

'Left you?' He glanced round to be sure that the waiter had retired.

'Quitted me! Abandoned me. Last night!'

'Not possible!' he breathed.

She nodded. She felt intimate with him. Like all secretive persons, she could be suddenly expansive at times.

'It is serious?' he questioned.

'All that is most serious,' she replied.

'And you ill! Ah, the wretch! Ah, the wretch! That, for example!' He waved his hat about.

'What is it you want, Chirac?' she demanded, in a confidential tone.

'Eh, well,' said Chirac. 'You do not know where he has gone?'

'No. What do you want?' she insisted.

He was nervous. He fidgeted. She guessed that, though warm with sympathy for her plight, he was preoccupied by interests and apprehensions of his own. He did not refuse her request temporarily to leave the astonishing matter of her situation in order to discuss the matter of his visit.

'Eh, well! He came to me yesterday afternoon in the Rue Croissant to borrow some money.'

She understood then the object of Gerald's stroll on the previous afternoon.

'I hope you didn't lend him any,' she said.

'Eh, well! It was like this. He said he ought to have received five thousand francs yesterday morning, but that he had had a telegram that it would not arrive till today. And he had need of five hundred francs at once. I had not five hundred francs' – he smiled sadly, as if to insinuate that he did not handle such sums – 'but I borrowed it from the cash-box of the journal. It is necessary, absolutely, that I should return it this morning.' He spoke with increased seriousness. 'Your husband said he would take a cab and bring me the money immediately on the arrival of the post this morning – about nine o'clock. Pardon me for deranging you with such a –'

He stopped. She could see that he really was grieved to 'derange' her, but that circumstances pressed.

'At my paper,' he murmured, 'it is not so easy as that to – in fine –!'

Gerald had genuinely been at his last francs. He had not lied when she thought he had lied. The nakedness of his character showed now. Instantly upon the final and definite cessation of the lawful supply of money, he had set his wits to obtain money unlawfully. He had, in fact, simply stolen it from Chirac, with the ornamental addition of endangering Chirac's reputation and situation – as a sort of reward to Chirac for the kindness! And, further, no sooner had he got hold of the money than it had intoxicated him, and he had yielded to the first fatuous temptation. He had no sense of responsibility, no scruple. And as for common prudence – had he not risked permanent disgrace and even prison for a paltry sum which he would certainly squander in two or three days? Yes, it was indubitable that he would stop at nothing, at nothing whatever.

'You did not know that he was coming to me?' asked Chirac, pulling his short, silky brown beard.

'No,' Sophia answered.

'But he said that you had charged him with your friendlinesses to me!' He nodded his head once or twice, sadly but candidly accepting, in his quality of a Latin, the plain facts of human nature – reconciling himself to them at once.

Sophia revolted at this crowning detail of the structure of Gerald's rascality.

'It is fortunate that I can pay you,' she said.

'But –' he tried to protest.

'I have quite enough money.'

She did not say this to screen Gerald, but merely from *amour-propre*. She would not let Chirac think that she was the wife of a man bereft of all honour. And so she clothed Gerald with the rag of having, at any rate, not left her in destitution as well as in sickness. Her assertion seemed a strange one, in view of the fact that he had abandoned her on the previous evening – that is to say, immediately after the borrowing from Chirac. But Chirac did not examine the statement.

'Perhaps he has the intention to send me the money. Perhaps, after all, he is now at the offices –'

'No,' said Sophia. 'He is gone. Will you go downstairs and wait for me. We will go together to Cook's[10] office. It is English money I have.'

'Cook's?' he repeated. The word now so potent had then little significance. 'But you are ill. You cannot –'

'I feel better.'

She did. Or rather, she felt nothing except the power of her resolve to remove the painful anxiety from that wistful brow. The shame of the trick played on Chirac awakened new forces in her. She dressed in a physical torment which, however, had no more reality than a nightmare. She searched in a place where even an inquisitive husband would not think of looking, and then, painfully, she descended the long stairs, holding to the rail, which swam round and round her, carrying the whole staircase with it. 'After all,' she thought, 'I can't be seriously ill, or I shouldn't have been able to get up and go out like this. I never guessed early this morning that I could do it! I can't possibly be as ill as I thought I was!'

And in the vestibule she encountered Chirac's face, lightening at the sight of her, which proved to him that his deliverance was really to be accomplished.

'Permit me –'

'I'm all right,' she smiled, tottering. 'Get a cab.' It suddenly occurred to her that she might quite as easily have given him the money in English notes; he could have changed them. But she had not thought. Her brain would not operate. She was dreaming and waking together.

He helped her into the cab.

V

In the *bureau de change* there was a little knot of English people, with naïve, romantic, and honest faces, quite different from the faces outside in the street. No corruption in those faces, but a sort of wondering and infantile sincerity, rather out of its element and lost in a land too unsophisticated, seeming to belong to an earlier age! Sophia liked their tourist stare, and their plain and ugly clothes. She longed to be back in England, longed for a moment with violence, drowning in that desire.

The English clerk behind his brass bars took her notes, and carefully examined them one by one. She watched him, not entirely convinced of his reality, and thought vaguely of the detestable morning when she had abstracted the notes from Gerald's pocket. She was filled with pity for the simple, ignorant

Sophia of those days, the Sophia who still had a few ridiculous illusions concerning Gerald's character. Often, since, she had been tempted to break into the money, but she had always withstood the temptation, saying to herself that an hour of more urgent need would come. It had come. She was proud of her firmness, of the force of will which had enabled her to reserve the fund intact. The clerk gave her a keen look, and then asked her how she would take the French money. And she saw the notes falling down one after another on to the counter as the clerk separated them with a snapping sound of the paper.

Chirac was beside her.

'Does that make the count?' she said, having pushed towards him five hundred-franc notes.

'I should not know how to thank you,' he said, accepting the notes. 'Truly –'

His joy was unmistakably eager. He had had a shock and a fright, and he now saw the danger past. He could return to the cashier of his newspaper, and fling down the money with a lordly and careless air, as if to say: 'When it is a question of these English, one can always be sure!' But first he would escort her to the hotel. She declined – she did not know why, for he was her sole point of moral support in all France. He insisted. She yielded. So she turned her back, with regret, on that little English oasis in the Sahara of Paris, and staggered to the fiacre.

And now that she had done what she had to do, she lost control of her body, and reclined flaccid and inert. Chirac was evidently alarmed. He did not speak, but glanced at her from time to time with eyes full of fear. The carriage appeared to her to be swimming amid waves over great depths. Then she was aware of a heavy weight against her shoulder: she had slipped down upon Chirac, unconscious.

CHAPTER 5: *Fever*

I

Then she was lying in bed in a small room, obscure because it was heavily curtained; the light came through the inner pair of curtains of *écru* lace, with a beautiful soft silvery quality. A man was standing by the side of the bed – not Chirac.

'Now, madame,' he said to her, with kind firmness, and speaking with a charming exaggerated purity of the vowels. 'You have the mucous fever. I have had it myself. You will be forced to take baths, very frequently. I must ask you to reconcile yourself to that, to be good.'

She did not reply. It did not occur to her to reply. But she certainly thought that this doctor – he was probably a doctor – was overestimating her case. She felt better than she had felt for two days. Still, she did not desire to move, nor was she in the least anxious as to her surroundings. She lay quiet.

A woman in a rather coquettish deshabille watched over her with expert skill.

Later, Sophia seemed to be revisiting the sea on whose waves the cab had swum; but now she was under the sea, in a watery gulf, terribly deep; and the sounds of the world came to her through the water, sudden and strange. Hands seized her and forced her from the subaqueous grotto where she had hidden into new alarms. And she briefly perceived that there was a large bath by the side of the bed, and that she was being pushed into it. The water was icy cold. After that her outlook upon things was for a time clearer and more precise. She knew from fragments of talk which she heard that she was put into the cold bath by her bed every three hours, night and day, and that she remained in it for ten minutes. Always, before the bath, she had to drink a glass of wine, and sometimes another glass while she was in the bath. Beyond this wine, and occasionally a cup of soup, she took nothing, had no wish to take anything. She grew perfectly accustomed to these extraordinary habits of life, to this merging of night and day into one monotonous and endless repetition of the same rite amid the same circumstances on exactly the same spot. Then followed a period during which she objected to being constantly wakened up for this annoying immersion. And she fought against it even in her dreams. Long days seemed to pass when she could not be sure whether she had been put into the bath or not, when all external phenomena were disconcertingly interwoven with matters which she knew to be merely fanciful. And then she was overwhelmed by the hopeless gravity of her state. She felt that her state was desperate. She felt that she was dying. Her unhappiness was extreme, not because she was dying, but because the veils of sense were so puzzling, so exasperating, and because her exhausted body was so vitiated, in every fibre, by disease. She was perfectly aware that she was going to die. She cried aloud for a pair of scissors. She wanted to cut off her hair, and to send part of it to Constance and part of it to her mother, in separate packages. She insisted upon separate packages. Nobody would give her a pair of scissors. She implored, meekly, haughtily, furiously, but nobody would satisfy her. It seemed to her shocking that all her hair should go with her into her coffin while Constance and her mother had nothing by which to remember her, no tangible souvenir of her beauty. Then she fought for the scissors. She clutched at someone – always through those baffling veils – who was putting her into the bath by the bedside, and fought frantically. It appeared to her that this someone was the rather stout woman who had supped at Sylvain's with the quarrelsome Englishman four years ago. She could not rid herself of this singular conceit, though she knew it to be absurd . . .

A long time afterwards – it seemed like a century – she did actually and unmistakably see the woman sitting by her bed, and the woman was crying.

'Why are you crying?' Sophia asked wonderingly.

And the other, younger, woman, who was standing at the foot of the bed, replied:

'You do well to ask! It is you who have hurt her, in your delirium, when you so madly demanded the scissors.'

The stout woman smiled with the tears on her cheeks; but Sophia wept, from remorse. The stout woman looked old, worn, and untidy. The other one was much younger. Sophia did not trouble to inquire from them who they were.

That little conversation formed a brief interlude in the delirium, which overtook her again and distorted everything. She forgot, however, that she was destined to die.

One day her brain cleared. She could be sure that she had gone to sleep in the morning and not wakened till the evening. Hence she had not been put into the bath.

'Have I had my baths?' she questioned.

It was the doctor who faced her.

'No,' he said, 'the baths are finished.'

She knew from his face that she was out of danger. Moreover, she was conscious of a new feeling in her body, as though the fount of physical energy within her, long interrupted, had recommenced to flow – but very slowly, a trickling. It was a rebirth. She was not glad, but her body itself was glad; her body had an existence of its own.

She was now often left by herself in the bedroom. To the right of the foot of the bed was a piano in walnut, and to the left a chimney-piece with a large mirror. She wanted to look at herself in the mirror. But it was a very long way off. She tried to sit up, and could not. She hoped that one day she would be able to get as far as the mirror. She said not a word about this to either of the two women.

Often they would sit in the bedroom and talk without ceasing. Sophia learnt that the stout woman was named Foucault, and the other Laurence. Sometimes Laurence would address Madame Foucault as Aimée, but usually she was more formal. Madame Foucault always called the other Laurence.

Sophia's curiosity stirred and awoke. But she could not obtain any very exact information as to where she was, except that the house was in the Rue Bréda, off the Rue Notre Dame de Lorette. She recollected vaguely that the reputation of the street was sinister. It appeared that, on the day when she had gone out with Chirac, the upper part of the Rue Notre Dame de Lorette was closed for repairs – (this she remembered) – and that the cabman had turned up the Rue Bréda in order to make a détour, and that it was just opposite to the house of Madame Foucault that she had lost consciousness. Madame Foucault happened to be getting into a cab at the moment; but she had told Chirac nevertheless to carry Sophia into the house, and a policeman had helped. Then, when the doctor came, it was discovered that she could not be moved, save to a hospital, and both Madame Foucault and Laurence were determined that no friend of Chirac's should be committed to the horrors of a Paris hospital. Madame Foucault had suffered in one as a patient, and Laurence had been a nurse in another . . .

Chirac was now away. The women talked loosely of a war.

'How kind you have been!' murmured Sophia, with humid eyes.

But they silenced her with gestures. She was not to talk. They seemed to have nothing further to tell her. They said Chirac would be returning perhaps soon, and that she could talk to him. Evidently they both held Chirac in affection. They said often that he was a charming boy.

Bit by bit Sophia comprehended the length and the seriousness of her illness, and the immense devotion of the two women, and the terrific disturbance of their lives, and her own debility. She saw that the women were strongly attached to her, and she could not understand why, as she had never done anything for them, whereas they had done everything for her. She had not learnt that benefits rendered, not benefits received, are the cause of such attachments.

All the time she was plotting, and gathering her strength to disobey orders and get as far as the mirror. Her preliminary studies and her preparations were as elaborate as those of a prisoner arranging to escape from a fortress. The first attempt was a failure. The second succeeded. Though she could not stand without support, she managed by clinging to the bed to reach a chair, and to push the chair in front of her until it approached the mirror. The enterprise was exciting and terrific. Then she saw a face in the glass: white, incredibly emaciated, with great, wild, staring eyes; and the shoulders were bent as though with age. It was a painful; almost a horrible sight. It frightened her so that in her alarm she recoiled from it. Not attending sufficiently to the chair, she sank to the ground. She could not pick herself up, and she was caught there, miserably, by her angered gaolers. The vision of her face taught her more efficiently than anything else the gravity of her adventure. As the women lifted her inert, repentant mass into the bed, she reflected, 'How queer my life is!' It seemed to her that she ought to have been trimming hats in the showroom instead of being in that curtained, mysterious, Parisian interior.

II

One day Madame Foucault knocked at the door of Sophia's little room (this ceremony of knocking was one of the indications that Sophia, convalescent, had been reinstated in her rights as an individual), and cried:

'Madame, one is going to leave you all alone for some time.'

'Come in,' said Sophia, who was sitting up in an armchair, and reading.

Madame Foucault opened the door. 'One is going to leave you all alone for some time,' she repeated in a low, confidential voice, sharply contrasting with her shriek behind the door.

Sophia nodded and smiled, and Madame Foucault also nodded and smiled. But Madame Foucault's face quickly resumed its anxious expression.

'The servant's brother marries himself today, and she implored me to accord her two days – what would you? Madame Laurence is out. And I must go out. It is four o'clock. I shall re-enter at six o'clock striking. Therefore . . .'

'Perfectly,' Sophia concurred.

She looked curiously at Madame Foucault, who was carefully made up and arranged for the street, in a dress of yellow tussore with blue ornaments, bright lemon-coloured gloves, a little blue bonnet, and a little white parasol not wider when opened than her shoulders. Cheeks, lips, and eyes were heavily charged with rouge, powder, or black. And that too abundant waist had been most cunningly confined in a belt that descended beneath, instead of rising above, the lower masses of the vast torso. The general effect was worthy of the effort that must have gone to it. Madame

Foucault was not rejuvenated by her toilette, but it almost procured her pardon for the crime of being over forty, fat, creased, and worn out. It was one of those defeats that are a triumph.

'You are very chic,' said Sophia, uttering her admiration.

'Ah!' said Madame Foucault, shrugging the shoulders of disillusion. 'Chic! What does that do?'

But she was pleased.

The front-door banged. Sophia, by herself for the first time in the flat into which she had been carried unconscious and which she had never since left, had the disturbing sensation of being surrounded by mysterious rooms and mysterious things. She tried to continue reading, but the sentences conveyed nothing to her. She rose – she could walk now a little – and looked out of the window, through the interstices of the pattern of the lace curtains. The window gave on the courtyard, which was about sixteen feet below her. A low wall divided the courtyard from that of the next house. And the windows of the two houses, only to be distinguished by the different tints of their yellow paint, rose tier above tier in level floors, continuing beyond Sophia's field of vision. She pressed her face against the glass, and remembered the St Luke's Square of her childhood; and just as there from the showroom window she could not even by pressing her face against the glass see the pavement, so here she could not see the roof; the courtyard was like the bottom of a well. There was no end to the windows; six storeys she could count, and the sills of a seventh were the limit of her view. Every window was heavily curtained, like her own. Some of the upper ones had green sunblinds. Scarcely any sound! Mysteries brooded without as well as within the flat of Madame Foucault. Sophia saw a bodiless hand twitch at a curtain and vanish. She noticed a green bird in a tiny cage on a sill in the next house. A woman whom she took to be the concierge appeared in the courtyard, deposited a small plant in the track of a ray of sunshine that lighted a corner for a couple of hours in the afternoon, and disappeared again. Then she heard a piano – somewhere. That was all. The feeling that secret and strange lives were being lived behind those baffling windows, that humanity was everywhere intimately pulsing around her, oppressed her spirit yet not quite unpleasantly. The environment softened her glance upon the spectacle of existence, insomuch that sadness became a voluptuous pleasure. And the environment threw her back on herself, into a sensuous contemplation of the fundamental fact of Sophia Scales, formerly Sophia Baines.

She turned to the room, with the marks of the bath on the floor by the bed, and the draped piano that was never opened, and her two trunks filling up the corner opposite the door. She had the idea of thoroughly examining those trunks, which Chirac or somebody else must have fetched from the hotel. At the top of one of them was her purse, tied up with old ribbon and ostentatiously sealed! How comical these French people were when they deemed it necessary to be serious! She emptied both trunks, scrutinizing minutely all her goods, and thinking of the varied occasions upon which she had obtained them. Then she carefully restored them, her mind full of souvenirs newly awakened.

She sighed as she straightened her back. A clock struck in another room. It seemed to invite her towards discoveries. She had been in no other room of the flat. She knew nothing of the rest of the flat save by sound. For neither of the other women had ever described it, nor had it occurred to them that Sophia might care to leave her room though she could not leave the house.

She opened her door, and glanced along the dim corridor, with which she was familiar. She knew that the kitchen lay next to her little room, and that next to the kitchen came the front-door. On the opposite side of the corridor were four double-doors. She crossed to the pair of doors facing her own little door, and quietly turned the handle, but the doors were locked; the same with the next pair. The third pair yielded, and she was in a large bedroom, with three windows on the street. She saw that the second pair of doors, which she had failed to unfasten, also opened into this room. Between the two pairs of doors was a wide bed. In front of the central window was a large dressing-table. To the left of the bed, half hiding the locked doors, was a large screen. On the marble mantelpiece, reflected in a huge mirror, that ascended to the ornate cornice, was a gilt-and-basalt clock, with pendants to match. On the opposite side of the room from this was a long wide couch. The floor was of polished oak, with a skin on either side of the bed. At the foot of the bed was a small writing-table, with a penny bottle of ink on it. A few coloured prints and engravings – representing, for example, Louis Philippe and his family, and people perishing on a raft – broke the tedium of the walls. The first impression on Sophia's eye was one of sombre splendour. Everything had the air of being richly ornamented, draped, looped, carved, twisted, brocaded into gorgeousness. The dark crimson bed-hangings fell from massive rosettes in majestic folds. The counterpane was covered with lace. The window-curtains had amplitude beyond the necessary, and they were suspended from behind fringed and pleated valances. The green sofa and its sateen cushions were stiff with applied embroidery. The chandelier hanging from the middle of the ceiling, modelled to represent cupids holding festoons, was a glittering confusion of gilt and lustres: the lustres tinkled when Sophia stood on a certain part of the floor. The cane-seated chairs were completely gilded. There was an effect of spaciousness. And the situation of the bed between the two double-doors, with the three windows in front and other pairs of doors communicating with other rooms on either hand, produced in addition an admirable symmetry.

But Sophia, with the sharp gaze of a woman brought up in the traditions of a modesty so proud that it scorns ostentation, quickly tested and condemned the details of this chamber that imitated every luxury. Nothing in it, she found, was 'good'. And in St Luke's Square 'goodness' meant honest workmanship, permanence, the absence of pretence. All the stuffs were cheap and showy and shabby; all the furniture was cracked, warped or broken. The clock showed five minutes past twelve at five o'clock. And further, dust was everywhere, except in those places where even the most perfunctory cleaning could not have left it. In the obscurer pleatings of draperies it lay thick. Sophia's lip curled, and instinctively she lifted her peignoir. One of her mother's phrases came into her head: 'a lick and a promise'. And then another: 'If you want to leave dirt, leave it where everybody can see it, not in the corners.'

She peeped behind the screen, and all the horrible welter of a *cabinet de toilette* met her gaze: a repulsive medley of foul waters, stained vessels and cloths, brushes, sponges, powders, and pastes. Clothes were hung up in disorder on rough nails; among them she recognized a dressing-gown of Madame Foucault's, and, behind affairs of later date, the dazzling scarlet cloak in which she had first seen Madame Foucault, dilapidated now. So this was Madame Foucault's room! This was the bower from which that elegance emerged, the filth from which had sprung the mature blossom!

She passed from that room direct to another, of which the shutters were closed, leaving it in twilight. This room too was a bedroom, rather smaller than the middle one, and having only one window, but furnished with the same dubious opulence. Dust covered it everywhere, and small footmarks were visible in the dust on the floor. At the back was a small door, papered to match the wall, and within this door was a *cabinet de toilette*, with no light and no air; neither in the room nor in the closet was there any sign of individual habitation. She traversed the main bedroom again and found another bedroom to balance the second one, but open to the full light of day, and in a state of extreme disorder; the double-pillowed bed had not even been made; clothes and towels draped all the furniture; shoes were about the floor, and on a piece of string tied across the windows hung a single white stocking, wet. At the back was a *cabinet de toilette*, as dark as the other one, a vile malodorous mess of appliances whose familiar forms loomed vague and extra-ordinarily sinister in the dense obscurity. Sophia turned away with the righteous disgust of one whose preparations for the gaze of the world are as candid and simple as those of a child. Concealed dirt shocked her as much as it would have shocked her mother; and as for the trickeries of the toilette table, she contemned them as harshly as a young saint who has never been tempted contemns moral weakness. She thought of the strange flaccid daily life of those two women, whose hours seemed to slip unprofitably away without any result of achievement. She had actually witnessed nothing; but since the beginning of her convalescence her ears had heard, and she could piece the evidences together. There was never any sound in the flat, outside the

kitchen, until noon. Then vague noises and smells would commence. And about one o'clock Madame Foucault, disarrayed,
would come to inquire if the servant had attended to the needs of
the invalid. Then the odours of cookery would accentuate themselves; bells rang; fragments of conversations escaped through
doors ajar; occasionally a man's voice or a heavy step; then the
fragrance of coffee; sometimes the sound of a kiss, the banging of
the front door, the noise of brushing, or of the shaking of a carpet,
a little scream as at some trifling domestic contretemps. Laurence, still in a dressing-gown, would lounge into Sophia's room,
dirty, haggard, but polite with a curious stiff ceremony, and
would drink her coffee there. This wandering in peignoirs would
continue till three o'clock, and then Laurence might say, as if
nerving herself to an unusual and immense effort: 'I must be
dressed by five o'clock. I have not a moment.' Often Madame
Foucault did not dress at all; on such days she would go to bed
immediately after dinner, with the remark that she didn't know
what was the matter with her, but she was exhausted. And then
the servant would retire to her seventh floor, and there would be
silence until, now and then, faint creepings were heard at midnight or after. Once or twice, through the chinks of her door,
Sophia had seen a light at two o'clock in the morning, just before
the dawn.

Yet these were the women who had saved her life, who
between them had put her into a cold bath every three hours night
and day for weeks. Surely it was impossible after that to despise
them for shiftlessness and talkative idling in peignoirs; impossible to despise them for anything whatever! But Sophia, conscious
of her inheritance of strong and resolute character, did despise
them as poor things. The one point on which she envied them was
their formal manners to her, which seemed to become more
dignified and graciously distant as her health improved. It was
always 'Madame', 'Madame', to her, with an intonation of increasing deference. They might have been apologizing to her for
themselves.

She prowled into all the corners of the flat; but she discovered
no more rooms, nothing but a large cupboard crammed with
Madame Foucault's dresses. Then she went back to the large

bedroom, and enjoyed the busy movement and rattle of the sloping street, and had long, vague yearnings for strength and for freedom in wide, sane places. She decided that on the morrow she would dress herself 'properly', and never again wear a peignoir; the peignoir, and all that it represented, disgusted her. And while looking at the street she ceased to see it and saw Cook's office and Chirac helping her into the carriage. Where was he? Why had he brought her to this impossible abode? What did he mean by such conduct? . . . But could he have acted otherwise? He had done the one thing that he could do . . . Chance! . . . Chance! And why an impossible abode? Was one place more impossible that another? . . . All this came of running away from home with Gerald. It was remarkable that she seldom thought of Gerald. He had vanished from her life as he had come into it – madly, preposterously. She wondered what the next stage in her career would be. She certainly could not forecast it. Perhaps Gerald was starving, or in prison . . . Bah! That exclamation expressed her appalling disdain of Gerald and of the Sophia who had once deemed him the paragon of men. Bah!

A carriage stopping in front of the house awakened her from her meditation. Madame Foucault and a man very much younger than Madame Foucault got out of it. Sophia fled. After all, this prying into other people's rooms was quite inexcusable. She dropped on to her own bed and picked up a book, in case Madame Foucault should come in.

III

In the evening, just after night had fallen, Sophia on the bed heard the sound of raised and acrimonious voices in Madame Foucault's room. Nothing except dinner had happened since the arrival of Madame Foucault and the young man. These two had evidently dined informally in the bedroom on a dish or so prepared by Madame Foucault, who had herself served Sophia with her invalid's repast. The odours of cookery still hung in the air.

The noise of virulent discussion increased and continued, and then Sophia could hear sobbing, broken by short and fierce phrases from the man. Then the door of the bedroom opened brusquely. 'J'en ai soupé!' exclaimed the man, in tones of angry disgust. 'Laisse-moi, je te prie!' And then a soft muffled sound, as of a struggle, a quick step, and the very violent banging of the front door. After that there was a noticeable silence, save for the regular sobbing. Sophia wondered when it would cease, that monotonous sobbing.

'What is the matter?' she called out from her bed.

The sobbing grew louder, like the sobbing of a child who has detected an awakening of sympathy and instinctively begins to practise upon it. In the end Sophia arose and put on the peignoir which she had almost determined never to wear again.

The broad corridor was lighted by a small, smelling oil-lamp with a crimson globe. That soft, transforming radiance seemed to paint the whole corridor with voluptuous luxury: so much so that it was impossible to believe that the smell came from the lamp. Under the lamp lay Madame Foucault on the floor, a shapeless mass of lace, frilled linen, and corset; her light brown hair was loose and spread about the floor. At the first glance, the creature abandoned to grief made a romantic and striking picture, and Sophia thought for an instant that she had at length encountered life on a plane that would correspond to her dreams of romance. And she was impressed, with a feeling somewhat akin to that of a middling commoner when confronted with a viscount. There was, in the distance, something imposing and sensational about that prone, trembling figure. The tragic works of love were therein apparently manifest, in a sort of dignified beauty. But when Sophia bent over Madame Foucault, and touched her flabbiness, this illusion at once vanished; and instead of being dramatically pathetic the woman was ridiculous. Her face, especially as damaged by tears, could not support the ordeal of inspection; it was horrible; not a picture, but a palette; or like the coloured design of a pavement artist after a heavy shower. Her great, relaxed eyelids alone would have rendered any face absurd; and there were monstrous details far worse than the eyelids. Then she was amazingly fat; her flesh seemed to be escaping at all ends from a corset strained to the utmost limit. And above her boots – she was still wearing dainty, high-heeled, tightly laced boots – the calves bulged suddenly out.

As a woman of between forty and fifty, the obese sepulchre of a dead vulgar beauty, she had no right to passions and tears and homage, or even the means of life; she had no right to expose herself picturesquely beneath a crimson glow in all the panoply of ribboned garters and lacy seductiveness. It was silly; it was disgraceful. She ought to have known that only youth and slimness have the right to appeal to the feelings by indecent abandonments.

Such were the thoughts that mingled with the sympathy of the beautiful and slim Sophia as she bent down to Madame Foucault. She was sorry for her landlady, but at the same time she despised her, and resented her woe.

'What is the matter?' she asked quietly.

'He has chucked me!' stammered Madame Foucault. 'And he's the last. I have no one now!'

She rolled over in the most grotesque manner, kicking up her legs, with a fresh outburst of sobs. Sophia felt quite ashamed for her.

'Come and lie down. Come now!' she said, with a touch of sharpness. 'You mustn't lie there like that.'

Madame Foucault's behaviour was really too outrageous. Sophia helped her, morally rather than physically, to rise, and then persuaded her into the large bedroom. Madame Foucault fell on the bed, of which the counterpane had been thrown over the foot. Sophia covered the lower part of her heaving body with the counterpane.

'Now, calm yourself, please!'

This room too was lit in crimson, by a small lamp that stood on the night-table, and though the shade of the lamp was cracked, the general effect of the great chamber was incontestably romantic. Only the pillows of the wide bed and a small semicircle of floor were illuminated, all the rest lay in shadow. Madame Foucault's head had dropped between the pillows. A tray containing dirty plates and glasses and a wine-bottle was speciously picturesque on the writing-table.

Despite her genuine gratitude to Madame Foucault for astounding care during her illness, Sophia did not like her landlady, and the present scene made her coldly wrathful. She saw the probability of having another's troubles piled on the top of her own. She did not, in her mind, actively object, because she felt that she could not be more hopelessly miserable than she was; but she passively resented the imposition. Her reason told her that she ought to sympathize with this ageing, ugly, disagreeable, undignified woman; but her heart was reluctant; her heart did not want to know anything at all about Madame Foucault, nor to enter in any way into her private life.

'I have not a single friend now,' stammered Madame Foucault.

'Oh, yes, you have,' said Sophia, cheerfully. 'You have Madame Laurence.'

'Laurence – that is not a friend. You know what I mean.'

'And me! I am your friend!' said Sophia, in obedience to her conscience.

'You are very kind,' replied Madame Foucault, from the pillow. 'But you know what I mean.'

The fact was that Sophia did know what she meant. The terms of their intercourse had been suddenly changed. There was no pretentious ceremony now, but the sincerity that disaster brings. The vast structure of make-believe, which between them they had gradually built, had crumbled to nothing.

'I never treated badly any man in my life,' whimpered Madame Foucault. 'I have always been a good girl. There is not a man who can say I have not been a good girl. Never was I a girl like the rest. And everyone has said so. Ah! when I tell you that once I had a hotel in the Avenue de la Reine Hortense. Four horses . . . I have sold a horse to Madame Musard . . . You know Madame Musard . . . But one cannot make economies. Impossible to make economies! Ah! In 'fifty-six I was spending a hundred thousand francs a year. That cannot last. Always I have said to myself: "That cannot last." Always I had the intention . . . But what would you? I installed myself here, and borrowed money to pay for the furniture. There did not remain to me one jewel. The men are poltroons, all! I could let three bedrooms for three hundred and fifty francs a month, and with serving meals and so on I could live.'

'Then that,' Sophia interrupted, pointing to her own bedroom across the corridor, 'is your room?'

'Yes,' said Madame Foucault. 'I put you in it because at the

moment all these were let. They are so no longer. Only one –
Laurence – and she does not pay me always. What would you?
Tenants – that does not find itself at the present hour . . . I have
nothing, and I owe. And he quits me. He chooses this moment to
quit me! And why? For nothing. For nothing. That is not for his
money that I regret him. No, no! You know, at his age – he is
twenty-five – and with a woman like me – one is not generous!
No. I loved him. And then a man is a moral support, always. I
loved him. It is at my age, mine, that one knows how to love.
Beauty goes always, but not the temperament! Ah, that – No! . . .
I loved him. I loved him.'

Sophia's face tingled with a sudden emotion caused by the
repetition of those last three words, whose spell no usage can
mar. But she said nothing.

'Do you know what I shall become? There is nothing but that
for me. And I know of such, who are there already. A charwoman! Yes, a charwoman! More soon or more late. Well, that is
life. What would you? One exists always.' Then in a different
tone: 'I demand your pardon, madame, for talking like this. I
ought to have shame.'

And Sophia felt that in listening she also ought to be ashamed.
But she was not ashamed. Everything seemed very natural, and
even ordinary. And, moreover, Sophia was full of the sense of her
superiority over the woman on the bed. Four years ago, in the
Restaurant Sylvain, the ingenuous and ignorant Sophia had shyly
sat in awe of the resplendent courtesan, with her haughty stare,
her large, easy gestures, and her imperturbable contempt for the
man who was paying. And now Sophia knew that she, Sophia,
knew all that was to be known about human nature. She had not
merely youth, beauty, and virtue, but knowledge – knowledge
enough to reconcile her to her own misery. She had a vigorous,
clear mind, and a clean conscience. She could look anyone in the
face, and judge everyone too as a woman of the world. Whereas
this obscene wreck on the bed had nothing whatever left. She had
not merely lost her effulgent beauty, she had become repulsive.
She could never have had any common sense, nor any force of
character. Her haughtiness in the day of glory was simply
fatuous, based on stupidity. She had passed the years in idleness,

trailing about all day in stuffy rooms, and emerging at night to impress nincompoops; continually meaning to do things which she never did, continually surprised at the lateness of the hour, continually occupied with the most foolish trifles. And here she was at over forty writhing about on the bare floor because a boy of twenty-five (who *must* be a worthless idiot) had abandoned her after a scene of ridiculous shoutings and stampings. She was dependent on the caprices of a young scamp, the last donkey to turn from her with loathing! Sophia thought: 'Goodness! If I had been in her place I shouldn't have been like that. I should have been rich. I should have saved like a miser. I wouldn't have been dependent on anybody at that age. If I couldn't have made a better courtesan than this pitiable woman, I would have drowned myself.'

In the harsh vanity of her conscious capableness and young strength she thought thus, half forgetting her own follies, and half excusing them on the ground of inexperience.

Sophia wanted to go round the flat and destroy every crimson lampshade in it. She wanted to shake Madame Foucault into self-respect and sagacity. Moral reprehension, though present in her mind, was only faint. Certainly she felt the immense gulf between the honest woman and the wanton, but she did not feel it as she would have expected to feel it. 'What a fool you have been!' she thought; not 'What a sinner!' With her precocious cynicism, which was somewhat unsuited to the lovely northern youthfulness of that face, she said to herself that the whole situation and their relative attitudes would have been different if only Madame Foucault had had the wit to amass a fortune, as (according to Gerald) some of her rivals had succeeded in doing.

And all the time she was thinking, in another part of her mind: 'I ought not to be here. It's no use arguing. I ought not to be here. Chirac did the only thing for me there was to do. But I must go now.'

Madame Foucault continued to recite her woes, chiefly financial, in a weak voice damp with tears; she also continued to apologize for mentioning herself. She had finished sobbing, and lay looking at the wall, away from Sophia, who stood irresolute near the bed, ashamed for her companion's weakness and incapacity.

'You must not forget,' said Sophia, irritated by the unrelieved darkness of the picture drawn by Madame Foucault, 'that at least I owe you a considerable sum, and that I am only waiting for you to tell me how much it is. I have asked you twice already, I think.'

'Oh, you are still suffering!' said Madame Foucault.

'I am quite well enough to pay my debts,' said Sophia.

'I do not like to accept money from you,' said Madame Foucault.

'But why not?'

'You will have the doctor to pay.'

'Please do not talk in that way,' said Sophia. 'I have money, and I can pay for everything, and I shall pay for everything.'

She was annoyed because she was sure that Madame Foucault was only making a pretence of delicacy, and that in any case her delicacy was preposterous. Sophia had remarked this on the two previous occasions when she had mentioned the subject of bills. Madame Foucault would not treat her as an ordinary lodger, now that the illness was past. She wanted, as it were, to complete brilliantly what she had begun, and to live in Sophia's memory as a unique figure of lavish philanthropy. This was a sentiment, a luxury that she desired to offer herself: the thought that she had played providence to a respectable married lady in distress; she frequently hinted at Sophia's misfortunes and helplessness. But she could not afford the luxury. She gazed at it as a poor woman gazes at costly stuffs through the glass of a shop-window. The truth was, she wanted the luxury for nothing. For a double reason Sophia was exasperated: by Madame Foucault's absurd desire, and by a natural objection to the *rôle* of a subject for philanthropy. She would not admit that Madame Foucault's devotion as a nurse entitled her to the satisfaction of being a philanthropist when there was no necessity for philanthropy.

'How long have I been here?' asked Sophia.

'I don't know,' murmured Madame Foucault. 'Eight weeks — or is it nine?'

'Suppose we say nine,' said Sophia.

'Very well,' agreed Madame Foucault, apparently reluctant.

'Now, how much must I pay you per week?'

'I don't want anything – I don't want anything! You are a friend of Chirac's. You –'

'Not at all!' Sophia interrupted, tapping her foot and biting her lip. 'Naturally I must pay.'

Madame Foucault wept quietly.

'Shall I pay you seventy-five francs a week?' said Sophia, anxious to end the matter.

'It is too much!' Madame Foucault protested, insincerely.

'What? For all you have done for me?'

'I speak not of that,' Madame Foucault modestly replied.

If the devotion was not to be paid for, then seventy-five francs a week was assuredly too much, as during more than half the time Sophia had had almost no food. Madame Foucault was therefore within the truth when she again protested, at sight of the bank-notes which Sophia brought from her trunk:

'I am sure that it is too much.'

'Not at all!' Sophia repeated. 'Nine weeks at seventy-five. That makes six hundred and seventy-five. Here are seven hundreds.'

'I have no change,' said Madame Foucault. 'I have nothing.'

'That will pay for the hire of the bath,' said Sophia.

She laid the notes on the pillow. Madame Foucault looked at them gluttonously, as any other person would have done in her place. She did not touch them. After an instant she burst into wild tears.

'But why do you cry?' Sophia asked, softened.

'I – I don't know!' spluttered Madame Foucault. 'You are so beautiful. I am so content that we saved you.' Her great wet eyes rested on Sophia.

It was sentimentality. Sophia ruthlessly set it down as sentimentality. But she was touched. She was suddenly moved. Those women, such as they were in their foolishness, probably had saved her life – and she a stranger! Flaccid as they were, they had been capable of resolute perseverance there. It was possible to say that chance had thrown them upon an enterprise which they could not have abandoned till they or death had won. It was possible to say that they hoped vaguely to derive advantage from their labours. But even then? Judged by an ordinary standard,

those women had been angels of mercy. And Sophia was despising them, cruelly taking their motives to pieces, accusing them of
incapacity when she herself stood a supreme proof of their
capacity in, at any rate, one direction! In a rush of emotion she
saw her hardness and her injustice.

She bent down. 'Never can I forget how kind you have been to
me. It is incredible! Incredible!' She spoke softly, in tones loaded
with genuine feeling. It was all she said. She could not embroider
on the theme. She had no talent for thanksgiving.

Madame Foucault made the beginning of a gesture, as if she
meant to kiss Sophia with those thick, marred lips; but refrained.
Her head sank back, and then she had a recurrence of the fit of
nervous sobbing. Immediately afterwards there was the sound of
a latchkey in the front-door of the flat; the bedroom door was
open. Still sobbing very violently, she cocked her ear, and pushed
the bank-notes under the pillow.

Madame Laurence – as she was called: Sophia had never heard
her surname – came straight into the bedroom, and beheld the
scene with astonishment in her dark twinkling eyes. She was
usually dressed in black, because people said that black suited
her, and because black was never out of fashion; black was an
expression of her idiosyncrasy. She showed a certain elegance,
and by comparison with the extreme disorder of Madame
Foucault and the deshabille of Sophia her appearance, all fresh
from a modish restaurant, was brilliant; it gave her an advantage
over the other two – that moral advantage which ceremonial
raiment always gives.

'What is it that passes?' she demanded.

'He has chucked me, Laurence!' exclaimed Madame Foucault,
in a sort of hysteric scream which seemed to force its way through
her sobs. From the extraordinary freshness of Madame
Foucault's woe, it might have been supposed that her young man
had only that instant strode out.

Laurence and Sophia exchanged a swift glance; and Laurence,
of course, perceived that Sophia's relations with her landlady and
nurse were now of a different, a more candid order. She indicated
her perception of the change by a single slight movement of the
eyebrows.

'But listen, Aimée,' she said authoritatively. 'You must not let yourself go like that. He will return.'

'Never!' cried Madame Foucault. 'It is finished. And he is the last!'

Laurence, ignoring Madame Foucault, approached Sophia. 'You have an air very fatigued,' she said, caressing Sophia's shoulder with her gloved hand. 'You are pale like everything. All this not for you. It is not reasonable to remain here, you still suffering! At this hour! Truly not reasonable!'

Her hands persuaded Sophia towards the corridor. And, in fact, Sophia did then notice her own exhaustion. She departed from the room with the ready obedience of physical weakness, and shut her door.

After about half an hour, during which she heard confused noises and murmurings, her door half opened.

'May I enter, since you are not asleep?' It was Laurence's voice. Twice, now, she had addressed Sophia without adding the formal 'madame'.

'Enter, I beg you,' Sophia called from the bed. 'I am reading.'

Laurence came in. Sophia was both glad and sorry to see her. She was eager to hear gossip which, however, she felt she ought to despise. Moreover, she knew that if they talked that night they would talk as friends, and that Laurence would ever afterwards treat her with the familiarity of a friend. This she dreaded. Still, she knew that she would yield, at any rate, to the temptation to listen to gossip.

'I have put her to bed,' said Laurence, in a whisper, as she cautiously closed the door. 'The poor woman! Oh, what a charming bracelet! It is a true pearl, naturally?'

Her roving eye had immediately, with an infallible instinct, caught sight of a bracelet which, in taking stock of her possessions, Sophia had accidentally left on the piano. She picked it up, and then put it down again.

'Yes,' said Sophia. She was about to add: 'It's nearly all the jewellery I possess'; but she stopped.

Laurence moved towards Sophia's bed, and stood over it as she had often done in her quality of nurse. She had taken off her gloves, and she made a piquant, pretty show, with her thirty

years, and her agreeable, slightly roguish face, in which were
mingled the knowingness of a street boy and the confidence of a
woman who has ceased to be surprised at the influence of her
snub nose on a highly intelligent man.

'Did she tell you what they had quarrelled about?' Laurence
inquired abruptly. And not only the phrasing of the question, but
the assured tone in which it was uttered, showed that Laurence
meant to be the familiar of Sophia.

'Not a word!' said Sophia.

In this brief question and reply, all was crudely implied that
had previously been supposed not to exist. The relations between
the two women were altered irretrievably in a moment.

'It must have been her fault!' said Laurence. 'With men she is
insupportable. I have never understood how that poor woman
has made her way. With women she is charming. But she seems to
be incapable of not treating men like dogs. Some men adore that,
but they are few. Is it not?'

Sophia smiled.

'I have told her! How many times have I told her! But it is
useless. It is stronger than she is, and if she finishes on straw one
will be able to say that it was because of that. But truly she ought
not to have asked him here! Truly that was too much! If he
knew . . . !'

'Why not?' asked Sophia, awkwardly. The answer startled
her.

'Because her room has not been disinfected.'

'But I thought all the flat had been disinfected?'

'All except her room.'

'But why not her room?'

Laurence shrugged her shoulders. 'She did not want to disturb
her things! Is it that I know, I? She is like that. She takes an idea —
and then, there you are!'

'She told me every room had been disinfected.'

'She told the same to the police and the doctor.'

'Then all the disinfection is useless?'

'Perfectly! But she is like that. This flat might be very remunerative; but with her, never! She has not even paid for the furniture —
after two years!'

'But what will become of her?' Sophia asked.

'Ah – that!' Another shrug of the shoulders. 'All that I know is that it will be necessary for me to leave here. The last time I brought Monsieur Cerf here, she was excessively rude to him. She has doubtless told you about Monsieur Cerf?'

'No. Who is Monsieur Cerf?'

'Ah! She has not told you? That astonishes me. Monsieur Cerf, that is my friend, you know.'

'Oh!' murmured Sophia.

'Yes,' Laurence proceeded, impelled by a desire to impress Sophia and to gossip at large. 'That is my friend. I knew him at the hospital. It was to please him that I left the hospital. After that we quarrelled for two years; but at the end he gave me right. I did not budge. Two years! It is long. And I had left the hospital. I could have gone back. But I would not. That is not a life, to be nurse in a Paris hospital! No, I drew myself out as well as I could . . . He is the most charming boy you can imagine! And rich now; that is to say, relatively. He has a cousin infinitely more rich than he. I dined with them both tonight at the Maison Dorée. For a luxurious boy, he is a luxurious boy – the cousin I mean. It appears that he has made a fortune in Canada.'

'Truly!' said Sophia, with politeness. Laurence's hand was playing on the edge of the bed, and Sophia observed for the first time that it bore a wedding-ring.

'You remark my ring?' Laurence laughed. 'That is he – the cousin. "What!" he said, "you do not wear an *alliance*? An *alliance* is more proper. We are going to arrange that after dinner." I said that all the jewellers' shops would be closed. "That is all the same to me," he said. "We will open one." And in effect . . . it passed like that. He succeeded! Is it not beautiful?' She held forth her hand.

'Yes,' said Sophia. 'It is very beautiful.'

'Yours also is beautiful,' said Laurence, with an extremely puzzling intonation.

'It is just the ordinary English wedding-ring,' said Sophia. In spite of herself she blushed.

'"Now I have married you. It is I, the curé," said he – the cousin – when he put the ring on my finger. Oh, he is excessively

amusing! He pleases me much. And he is all alone. He asked me
whether I knew among my friends a sympathetic, pretty girl, to
make four with us three for a picnic. I said I was not sure, but I
thought not. Whom do I know? Nobody. I'm not a woman like
the rest. I am always discreet. I do not like casual relations . . . But
he is very well, the cousin. Brown eyes . . . It is an idea – will you
come, one day? He speaks English. He loves the English. He is
all that is most correct, the perfect gentleman. He would arrange
a dazzling fête. I am sure he would be enchanted to make your
acquaintance. Enchanted! . . . As for my Charles, happily he
is completely mad about me – otherwise I should have fear.'

She smiled, and in her smile was a genuine respect for Sophia's
face.

'I fear I cannot come,' said Sophia. She honestly endeavoured
to keep out of her reply any accent of moral superiority, but she
did not quite succeed. She was not at all horrified by Laurence's
suggestion. She meant simply to refuse it; but she could not do so
in a natural voice.

'It is true you are not yet strong enough,' said the imperturbable Laurence, quickly, and with a perfect imitation of naturalness. 'But soon you must make a little promenade.' She stared at
her ring. 'After all, it is more proper,' she observed judicially.
'With a wedding-ring one is less likely to be annoyed. What is
curious is that the idea never before came to me. Yet . . .'

'You like jewellery?' said Sophia.

'If I like jewellery!' – with a gesture of the hands.

'Will you pass me that bracelet?'

Laurence obeyed, and Sophia clasped it round the girl's wrist.

'Keep it,' Sophia said.

'For me?' Laurence exclaimed, ravished. 'It is too much.'

'It is not enough,' said Sophia. 'And when you look at it, you
must remember how kind you were to me, and how grateful I
am.'

'How nicely you say that!' Laurence said ecstatically.

And Sophia felt that she had indeed said it rather nicely. This
giving of the bracelet, souvenir of one of the few capricious follies
that Gerald had committed for her and not for himself, pleased
Sophia very much.

'I am afraid your nursing of me forced you to neglect Monsieur Cerf,' she added.

'Yes, a little!' said Laurence, impartially, with a small pout of haughtiness. 'It is true that he used to complain. But I soon put him straight. What an idea! He knows there are things upon which I do not joke. It is not he who will quarrel a second time! Believe me!'

Laurence's absolute conviction of her power was what impressed Sophia. To Sophia she seemed to be a vulgar little piece of goods, with dubious charm and a glance that was far too brazen. Her movements were vulgar. And Sophia wondered how she had established her empire and upon what it rested.

'I shall not show this to Aimée,' whispered Laurence, indicating the bracelet.

'As you wish,' said Sophia.

'By the way, have I told you that war is declared?' Laurence casually remarked.

'No,' said Sophia. 'What war?'

'The scene with Aimée made me forget it . . . With Germany. The city is quite excited. An immense crowd in front of the New Opéra. They say we shall be at Berlin in a month – or at most two months.'

'Oh!' Sophia muttered. 'Why is there a war?'

'Ah! It is I who asked that. Nobody knows. It is those Prussians.'

'Don't you think we ought to begin again with the disinfecting?' Sophia asked anxiously. 'I must speak to Madame Foucault.'

Laurence told her not to worry, and went off to show the bracelet to Madame Foucault. She had privately decided that this was a pleasure which, after all, she could not deny herself.

IV

About a fortnight later – it was a fine Saturday in early August – Sophia, with a large pinafore over her dress, was finishing the portentous preparations for disinfecting the flat. Part of the affair was already accomplished, her own room and the corridor

having been fumigated on the previous day, in spite of the
opposition of Madame Foucault, who had taken amiss Laurence's tale-bearing to Sophia. Laurence had left the flat – under
exactly what circumstances Sophia knew not, but she guessed
that it must have been in consequence of a scene elaborating the
tiff caused by Madame Foucault's resentment against Laurence.
The brief, factitious friendliness between Laurence and Sophia
had gone like a dream, and Laurence had gone like a dream. The
servant had been dismissed; in her place Madame Foucault
employed a charwoman each morning for two hours. Finally,
Madame Foucault had been suddenly called away that morning
by a letter to her sick father at St Mammès-sur-Seine. Sophia was
delighted at the chance. The disinfecting of the flat had become an
obsession with Sophia – the obsession of a convalescent whose
perspective unconsciously twists things to the most wry shapes.
She had had trouble on the day before with Madame Foucault,
and she was expecting more serious trouble when the moment
arrived for ejecting Madame Foucault as well as all her movable
belongings from Madame Foucault's own room. Nevertheless,
Sophia had been determined, whatever should happen, to complete an honest fumigation of the entire flat. Hence the eagerness
with which, urging Madame Foucault to go to her father, Sophia
had protested that she was perfectly strong and could manage by
herself for a couple of days. Owing to the partial suppression of
the ordinary railway services in favour of military needs,
Madame Foucault could not hope to go and return on the same
day. Sophia had lent her a louis.

Pans of sulphur were mysteriously burning in each of the three
front rooms, and two pairs of doors had been pasted over with
paper, to prevent the fumes from escaping. The charwoman had
departed. Sophia, with brush, scissors, flour-paste, and news-
sheets, was sealing the third pair of doors, when there was a ring
at the front door.

She had only to cross the corridor in order to open.

It was Chirac. She was not surprised to see him. The outbreak
of the war had induced even Sophia and her landlady to look
through at least one newspaper during the day, and she had in
this way learnt, from an article signed by Chirac, that he had

returned to Paris after a mission into the Vosges country for his paper.

He started on seeing her. 'Ah!' He breathed out the exclamation slowly. And then smiled, seized her hand, and kissed it.

The sight of his obvious extreme pleasure in meeting her again was the sweetest experience that had fallen to Sophia for years.

'Then you are cured?'

'Quite.'

He sighed. 'You know, this is an enormous relief to me, to know, veritably, that you are no longer in danger. You gave me a fright . . . but a fright, my dear madame!'

She smiled in silence.

As he glanced inquiringly up and down the corridor, she said: 'I'm all alone in the flat. I'm disinfecting it.'

'Then that is sulphur that I smell?'

She nodded. 'Excuse me while I finish this door,' she said.

He closed the front-door. 'But you seem to be quite at home here!' he observed.

'I ought to be,' said she.

He glanced again inquiringly up and down the corridor. 'And you are really all alone now?' he asked, as though to be doubly sure.

She explained the circumstances.

'I owe you my most sincere excuses for bringing you here,' he said confidentially.

'But why?' she replied, looking intently at her door. 'They have been most kind to me. Nobody could have been kinder. And Madame Laurence being such a good nurse –'

'It is true,' said he. 'That was a reason. In effect they are both very good-natured little women . . . You comprehend, as journalist it arrives to me to know all kinds of people . . .' He snapped his fingers . . . 'And as we were opposite the house. In fine, I pray you to excuse me . . .'

'Hold me this paper,' she said. 'It is necessary that every crack should be covered; also between the floor and the door.'

'You English are wonderful,' he murmured, as he took the paper. 'Imagine you doing that! Then,' he added, resuming the confidential tone, 'I suppose you will leave the Foucault now, hein?'

'I suppose so,' she said carelessly.

'You go to England?'

She turned to him, as she patted the creases out of a strip of paper with a duster, and shook her head.

'Not to England?'

'No.'

'If it is not indiscreet, where are you going?'

'I don't know,' she said candidly.

And she did not know. She was without a plan. Her brain told her that she ought to return to Bursley, or, at the least, write. But her pride would not hear of such a surrender. Her situation would have to be far more desperate than it was before she could confess her defeat to her family even in a letter. A thousand times no! That was a point which she had for ever decided. She would face any disaster, and any other shame, rather than the shame of her family's forgiving reception of her.

'And you?' she asked. 'How does it go? This war?'

He told her, in a few words, a few leading facts about himself. 'It must not be said,' he added of the war, 'but that will turn out ill! I – know, you comprehend.'

'Truly?' she answered with casualness.

'You have heard nothing of him?' Chirac asked.

'Who? Gerald?'

He gave a gesture.

'Nothing! Not a word! Nothing!'

'He will have gone back to England!'

'Never!' she said positively.

'But why not?'

'Because he prefers France. He really does like France. I think it is the only real passion he ever had.'

'It is astonishing,' reflected Chirac, 'how France is loved! And yet . . . ! But to live, what will he do? Must live!'

Sophia merely shrugged her shoulders.

'Then it is finished between you two?' he muttered awkwardly.

She nodded. She was on her knees, at the lower crack of the doors.

'There!' she said, rising. 'It's well done, isn't it? That is all.'

She smiled at him, facing him squarely, in the obscurity of the untidy and shabby corridor. Both felt that they had become very intimate. He was intensely flattered by her attitude, and she knew it.

'Now,' she said, 'I will take off my pinafore. Where can I niche you? There is only my bedroom, and I want that. What are we to do?'

'Listen,' he suggested diffidently. 'Will you do me the honour to come for a drive? That will do you good. There is sunshine. And you are always very pale.'

'With pleasure,' she agreed cordially.

While dressing, she heard him walking up and down the corridor; occasionally they exchanged a few words. Before leaving, Sophia pulled off the paper from one of the key-holes of the sealed suite of rooms, and they peered through, one after the other, and saw the green glow of the sulphur, and were troubled by its uncanniness. And then Sophia refixed the paper.

In descending the stairs of the house she felt the infirmity of her knees; but in other respects, though she had been out only once before since her illness, she was conscious of a sufficient strength. A disinclination for any enterprise had prevented her from taking the air as she ought to have done, but within the flat she had exercised her limbs in many small tasks. The little Chirac, nervously active and restless, wanted to take her arm, but she would not allow it.

The concierge and part of her family stared curiously at Sophia as she passed under the archway, for the course of her illness had excited the interest of the whole house. Just as the carriage was driving off, the concierge came across the pavement and paid her compliments, and then said:

'You do not know by hazard why Madame Foucault has not returned for lunch, madame?'

'Returned for lunch!' said Sophia. 'She will not come back till tomorrow.'

The concierge made a face. 'Ah! How curious it is! She told my husband that she would return in two hours. It is very grave! Question of business.'

'I know nothing, madame,' said Sophia. She and Chirac looked at each other. The concierge murmured thanks and went off muttering indistinctly.

The fiacre turned down the Rue Laferrière, the horse slipping and sliding as usual over the cobblestones. Soon they were on the boulevard, making for the Champs Elysées and the Bois de Boulogne.

The fresh breeze and bright sunshine and the large freedom of the streets quickly intoxicated Sophia – intoxicated her, that is to say, in quite a physical sense. She was almost drunk, with the heady savour of life itself. A mild ecstasy of well-being overcame her. She saw the flat as a horrible, vile prison, and blamed herself for not leaving it sooner and oftener. The air was medicine, for body and mind too. Her perspective was instantly corrected. She was happy, living neither in the past nor in the future, but in and for that hour. And beneath her happiness moved a wistful melancholy for the Sophia who had suffered such a captivity and such woes. She yearned for more and yet more delight, for careless orgies of passionate pleasure, in the midst of which she would forget all trouble. Why had she refused the offer of Laurence? Why had she not rushed at once into the splendid fire of joyous indulgence, ignoring everything but the crude, sensuous instinct? Acutely aware as she was of her youth, her beauty, and her charm, she wondered at her refusal. She did not regret her refusal. She placidly observed it as the result of some tremendously powerful motive in herself, which could not be questioned or reasoned with – which was, in fact, the essential *her*.

'Do I look like an invalid?' she asked, leaning back luxuriously in the carriage among the crowd of other vehicles.

Chirac hesitated. 'My faith! Yes!' he said at length. 'But it becomes you. If I did not know that you have little love for compliments, I –'

'But I adore compliments!' she exclaimed. 'What made you think that?'

'Well, then,' he youthfully burst out, 'you are more ravishing than ever.'

She gave herself up deliciously to his admiration.

After a silence, he said: 'Ah! if you knew how disquieted I was

about you, away there . . . ! I should not know how to tell you.
Veritably disquieted, you comprehend! What could I do? Tell me
a little about your illness.'

She recounted details.

As the fiacre entered the Rue Royale, they noticed a crowd of
people in front of the Madeleine shouting and cheering.

The cabman turned towards them. 'It appears there has been a
victory!' he said.

'A victory! If only it was true!' murmured Chirac, cynically.

In the Rue Royale people were running frantically to and fro,
laughing and gesticulating in glee. The customers in the cafés
stood on their chairs, and even on tables, to watch, and occasionally to join in, the sudden fever. The fiacre was slowed to a
walking pace. Flags and carpets began to show from the upper
storeys of houses. The crowd grew thicker and more febrile.
'Victory! Victory!' rang hoarsely, shrilly, and hoarsely again in
the air.

'My God!' said Chirac trembling. 'It must be a true victory! We
are saved! We are saved! . . . Oh yes, it is true!'

'But naturally it is true! What are you saying?' demanded the
driver.

At the Place de la Concorde the fiacre had to stop altogether.
The immense square was a sea of white hats and flowers and
happy faces, with carriages anchored like boats on its surface.
Flag after flag waved out from neighbouring roofs in the breeze
that tempered the August sun. Then hats began to go up, and
cheers rolled across the square like echoes of firing in an enclosed
valley. Chirac's driver jumped madly on to his seat, and cracked
his whip.

'Vive la France!' he bawled with all the force of his lungs.

A thousand throats answered him.

Then there was a stir behind them. Another carriage was being
slowly forced to the front. The crowd was pushing it, and crying,
'Marseillaise! Marseillaise!' In the carriage was a woman alone;
not beautiful, but distinguished, and with the assured gaze of one
who is accustomed to homage and multitudinous applause.

'It is Gueymard!' said Chirac to Sophia. He was very pale. And
he too shouted, 'Marseillaise!' All his features were distorted.

The woman rose and spoke to her coachman, who offered his hand, and she climbed to the box seat, and stood on it and bowed several times.

'Marseillaise!' The cry continued. Then a roar of cheers, and then silence spread round the square like an inundation. And amid this silence the woman began to sing the Marseillaise. As she sang, the tears ran down her cheeks. Everybody in the vicinity was weeping or sternly frowning. In the pauses of the first verse could be heard the rattle of horses' bits, or a whistle of a tug on the river. The refrain, signalled by a proud challenging toss of Gueymard's head, leapt up like a tropical tempest, formidable, overpowering. Sophia, who had had no warning of the emotion gathering within her, sobbed violently. At the close of the hymn Gueymard's carriage was assaulted by worshippers. All around, in the tumult of shouting, men were kissing and embracing each other; and hats went up continually in fountains. Chirac leaned over the side of the carriage and wrung the hand of a man who was standing by the wheel.

'Who is that?' Sophia asked, in an unsteady voice, to break the inexplicable tension within her.

'I don't know,' said Chirac. He was weeping like a child. And he sang out: 'Victory! To Berlin! Victory!'

v

Sophia walked alone, with tired limbs, up the damaged oak stairs to the flat. Chirac had decided that, in the circumstances of the victory, he would do well to go to the offices of his paper rather earlier than usual. He had brought her back to the Rue Bréda. They had taken leave of each other in a sort of dream or general enchantment due to their participation in the vast national delirium which somehow dominated individual feelings. They did not define their relations. They had been conscious only of emotion.

The stairs, which smelt of damp even in summer, disgusted Sophia. She thought of the flat with horror and longed for green places and luxury. On the landing were two stoutish, ill-dressed men, of middle age, apparently waiting. Sophia found her key and opened the door.

'Pardon, madame!' said one of the men, raising his hat, and they both pushed into the flat after her. They stared, puzzled, at the strips of paper pasted on the doors.

'What do you want?' she asked haughtily. She was very frightened. The extraordinary irruption brought her down with a shock to the scale of the individual.

'I am the concierge,' said the man who had addressed her. He had the air of a superior artisan. 'It was my wife who spoke to you this afternoon. This,' pointing to his companion, 'this is the law. I regret it, but . . .'

The law saluted and shut the door. Like the concierge the law emitted an odour – the odour of uncleanliness on a hot August day.

'The rent?' exclaimed Sophia.

'No, madame, not the rent: the furniture!'

Then she learnt the history of the furniture. It had belonged to the concierge, who had acquired it from a previous tenant and sold it on credit to Madame Foucault. Madame Foucault had signed bills and had not met them. She had made promises and broken them. She had done everything except discharge her liabilities. She had been warned and warned again. That day had been fixed as the last limit, and she had solemnly assured her creditor that on that day she would pay. On leaving the house she had stated precisely and clearly that she would return before lunch with all the money. She had made no mention of a sick father.

Sophia slowly perceived the extent of Madame Foucault's duplicity and moral cowardice. No doubt the sick father was an invention. The woman, at the end of a tether which no ingenuity of lies could further lengthen, had probably absented herself solely to avoid the pain of witnessing the seizure. She would do anything, however silly, to avoid an immediate unpleasantness. Or perhaps she had absented herself without any particular aim, but simply in the hope that something fortunate might occur. Perhaps she had hoped that Sophia, taken unawares, would generously pay. Sophia smiled grimly.

'Well,' she said. 'I can't do anything. I suppose you must do what you have to do. You will let me pack up my own affairs?'

'Perfectly, madame!'

She warned them as to the danger of opening the sealed rooms. The man of the law seemed prepared to stay in the corridor indefinitely. No prospect of delay disturbed him.

Strange and disturbing, the triumph of the concierge! He was a locksmith by trade. He and his wife and their children lived in two little dark rooms by the archway – an insignificant fragment of the house. He was away from home about fourteen hours every day, except Sundays, when he washed the courtyard. All the other duties of the concierge were performed by the wife. The pair always looked poor, untidy, dirty, and rather forlorn. But they were steadily levying toll on everybody in the big house. They amassed money in forty ways. They lived for money, and all men have what they live for. With what arrogant gestures Madame Foucault would descend from a carriage at the great door! What respectful attitudes and tones the ageing courtesan would receive from the wife and children of the concierge! But beneath these conventional fictions the truth was that the concierge held the whip. At last he was using it. And he had given himself a half-holiday in order to celebrate his second acquirement of the ostentatious furniture and the crimson lampshades. This was one of the dramatic crises in his career as a man of substance. The national thrill of victory had not penetrated into the flat with the concierge and the law. The emotions of the concierge were entirely independent of the Napoleonic foreign policy.

As Sophia, sick with a sudden disillusion, was putting her things together, and wondering where she was to go, and whether it would be politic to consult Chirac, she heard a fluster at the front door: cries, protestations, implorings. Her own door was thrust open, and Madame Foucault burst in.

'Save me!' exclaimed Madame Foucault, sinking to the ground.

The feeble theatricality of the gesture offended Sophia's taste. She asked sternly what Madame Foucault expected her to do. Had not Madame Foucault knowingly exposed her, without the least warning, to the extreme annoyance of this visit of the law, a visit which meant practically that Sophia was put into the street?

'You must not be hard!' Madame Foucault sobbed.

Sophia learnt the complete history of the woman's efforts to pay for the furniture: a farrago of folly and deceptions. Madame Foucault confessed too much. Sophia scorned confession for the sake of confession. She scorned the impulse which forces a weak creature to insist on its weakness, to revel in remorse, and to find an excuse for its conduct in the very fact that there is no excuse. She gathered that Madame Foucault had in fact gone away in the hope that Sophia, trapped, would pay; and that in the end, she had not even had the courage of her own trickery, and had run back, driven by panic into audacity, to fall at Sophia's feet, lest Sophia might not have yielded and the furniture have been seized. From beginning to end the conduct of Madame Foucault had been fatuous and despicable and wicked. Sophia coldly condemned Madame Foucault for having allowed herself to be brought into the world with such a weak and maudlin character, and for having allowed herself to grow old and ugly. As a sight the woman was positively disgraceful.

'Save me!' she exclaimed again. 'I did what I could for you!'

Sophia hated her. But the logic of the appeal was irresistible.

'But what can I do?' she asked reluctantly.

'Lend me the money. You can. If you don't, this will be the end for me.'

'And a good thing, too!' thought Sophia's hard sense.

'How much is it?' Sophia glumly asked.

'It isn't a thousand francs!' said Madame Foucault with eagerness. 'All my beautiful furniture will go for less than a thousand francs! Save me!'

She was nauseating Sophia.

'Please rise,' said Sophia, her hands fidgeting undecidedly.

'I shall repay you, surely!' Madame Foucault asseverated. 'I swear!'

'Does she take me for a fool?' thought Sophia, 'with her oaths!'

'No!' said Sophia. 'I won't lend you the money. But I tell you what I will do. I will buy the furniture at that price; and I will promise to re-sell it to you as soon as you can pay me. Like that, you can be tranquil. But I have very little money. I must have a guarantee. The furniture must be mine till you pay me.'

'You are an angel of charity!' cried Madame Foucault, embracing Sophia's skirts. 'I will do whatever you wish. Ah! You Englishwomen are astonishing.'

Sophia was not an angel of charity. What she had promised to do involved sacrifice and anxiety without the prospect of reward. But it was not charity. It was part of the price Sophia paid for the exercise of her logical faculty; she paid it unwillingly. 'I did what I could for you!' Sophia would have died sooner than remind anyone of a benefit conferred, and Madame Foucault had committed precisely that enormity. The appeal was inexcusable to a fine mind; but it was effective.

The men were behind the door, listening. Sophia paid out of her stock of notes. Needless to say, the total was more and not less than a thousand francs. Madame Foucault grew rapidly confidential with the man. Without consulting Sophia, she asked the bailiff to draw up a receipt transferring the ownership of all the furniture to Sophia; and the bailiff, struck into obligingness by glimpses of Sophia's beauty, consented to do so. There was much conferring upon forms of words, and flourishing of pens between thick vile fingers, and scattering of ink.

Before the men left Madame Foucault uncorked a bottle of wine for them, and helped them to drink it. Throughout the evening she was insupportably deferential to Sophia, who was driven to bed. Madame Foucault contentedly went up to the sixth floor to occupy the servant's bedroom. She was glad to get so far away from the sulphur, of which a few faint fumes had penetrated into the corridor.

The next morning, after a stifling night of bad dreams, Sophia was too ill to get up. She looked round at the furniture in the little room, and she imagined the furniture in the other rooms, and dismally thought: 'All this furniture is mine. She will never pay me! I am saddled with it.'

It was cheaply bought, but she probably could not sell it for even what she had paid. Still, the sense of ownership was reassuring.

The charwoman brought her coffee, and Chirac's newspaper; from which she learnt that the news of the victory which had sent the city mad on the previous day was utterly false. Tears came

into her eyes as she gazed absently at all the curtained windows of
the courtyard. She had youth and loveliness; according to the
rules she ought to have been irresponsible, gay, and indulgently
watched over by the wisdom of admiring age. But she felt
towards the French nation as a mother might feel towards
adorable, wilful children suffering through their own charming
foolishness. She saw France personified in Chirac. How easily,
despite his special knowledge, he had yielded to the fever! Her
heart bled for France and Chirac on that morning of reaction and
of truth. She could not bear to recall the scene in the Place de la
Concorde. Madame Foucault had not descended.

CHAPTER 6: *The Siege*

I

Madame Foucault came into Sophia's room one afternoon with a
peculiar guilty expression on her large face, and she held her
peignoir close to her exuberant body in folds consciously majestic, as though endeavouring to prove to Sophia by her carriage
that despite her shifting eyes she was the most righteous and
sincere woman that ever lived.

It was Saturday, the third of September, a beautiful day.
Sophia, suffering from an unimportant relapse, had remained in a
state of inactivity, and had scarcely gone out at all. She loathed
the flat, but lacked the energy to leave it every day. There was no
sufficiently definite object in leaving it. She could not go out and
look for health as she might have looked for flowers. So she
remained in the flat, and stared at the courtyard and the continual
mystery of lives hidden behind curtains that occasionally moved.
And the painted yellow walls of the house, and the papered walls
of her room pressed upon her and crushed her. For a few days
Chirac had called daily, animated by the most adorable solicitude. Then he had ceased to call. She had tired of reading the
journals; they lay unopened. The relations between Madame
Foucault and herself, and her status in the flat of which she now
legally owned the furniture – these things were left unsettled. But

the question of her board was arranged on the terms that she halved the cost of food and service with Madame Foucault; her expenses were thus reduced to the lowest possible – about eighteen francs a week. An idea hung in the air – like a scientific discovery on the point of being made by several independent investigators simultaneously – that she and Madame Foucault should co-operate in order to let furnished rooms at a remunerative profit. Sophia felt the nearness of the idea and she wanted to be shocked at the notion of any avowed association between herself and Madame Foucault; but she could not be.

'Here are a lady and a gentleman who want a bedroom,' began Madame Foucault, 'a nice large bedroom, furnished.'

'Oh!' said Sophia; 'who are they?'

'They will pay a hundred and thirty francs a month, in advance, for the middle bedroom.'

'You've shown it to them already?' said Sophia. And her tone implied that somehow she was conscious of a right to overlook the affairs of Madame Foucault.

'No,' said the other. 'I said to myself that first I would ask you for a counsel.'

'Then will they pay all that for a room they haven't seen?'

'The fact is,' said Madame Foucault, sheepishly, 'the lady has seen the room before. I know her a little. It is a former tenant. She lived here some weeks.'

'In that room?'

'Oh no! She was poor enough then.'

'Where are they?'

'In the corridor. She is very well, the lady. Naturally one must live, she like all the world; but she is veritably well. Quite respectable! One would never say . . . Then there would be the meals. We could demand one franc for the *café au lait*, two and a half francs for the lunch, and three francs for the dinner. Without counting other things. That would mean over five hundred francs a month, at least. And what would they cost us? Almost nothing! By what appears, he is a plutocrat . . . I could thus quickly repay you.'

'Is it a married couple?'

'Ah! You know, one cannot demand the marriage certificate.'

Madame Foucault indicated by a gesture that the Rue Bréda was not the paradise of saints.

'When she came before, this lady, was it with the same man?' Sophia asked coldly.

'Ah, my faith, no!' exclaimed Madame Foucault, bridling. 'It was a bad sort, the other, a . . . ! Ah, no.'

'Why do you ask my advice?' Sophia abruptly questioned, in a hard, inimical voice. 'Is it that it concerns me?'

Tears came at once into the eyes of Madame Foucault. 'Do not be unkind,' she implored.

'I'm not unkind,' said Sophia, in the same tone.

'Shall you leave me if I accept this offer?'

There was a pause.

'Yes,' said Sophia, bluntly. She tried to be large-hearted, large-minded, and sympathetic; but there was no sign of these qualities in her speech.

'And if you take with you the furniture which is yours . . . !'

Sophia kept silence.

'How am I to live, I demand of you?' Madame Foucault asked weakly.

'By being respectable and dealing with respectable people!' said Sophia, uncompromisingly, in tones of steel.

'I am unhappy!' murmured the elder woman. 'However, you are more strong than I!'

She brusquely dabbed her eyes, gave a little sob, and ran out of the room. Sophia listened at the door, and heard her dismiss the would-be tenants of the best bedroom. She wondered that she should possess such moral ascendancy over the woman, she so young and ingenuous! For, of course, she had not meant to remove the furniture. She could hear Madame Foucault sobbing quietly in one of the other rooms; and her lips curled.

Before evening a truly astonishing event happened. Perceiving that Madame Foucault showed no signs of bestirring herself, Sophia, with good nature in her heart but not on her tongue, went to her, and said:

'Shall I occupy myself with the dinner?'

Madame Foucault sobbed more loudly.

'That would be very amiable on your part,' Madame Foucault managed at last to reply, not very articulately.

Sophia put a hat on and went to the grocer's. The grocer, who kept a busy establishment at the corner of the Rue Clausel, was a middle-aged and wealthy man. He had sent his young wife and two children to Normandy until victory over the Prussians should be more assured, and he asked Sophia whether it was true that there was a good bedroom to let in the flat where she lived. His servant was ill of smallpox; he was attacked by anxieties and fears on all sides; he would not enter his own flat on account of possible infection; he liked Sophia, and Madame Foucault had been a customer of his, with intervals, for twenty years. Within an hour he had arranged to rent the middle bedroom at eighty francs a month, and to take his meals there. The terms were modest, but the respectability was prodigious. All the glory of this tenancy fell upon Sophia.

Madame Foucault was deeply impressed. Characteristically she began at once to construct a theory that Sophia had only to walk out of the house in order to discover ideal tenants for the rooms. Also she regarded the advent of the grocer as a reward from Providence for her self-denial in refusing the profits of sinfulness. Sophia felt personally responsible to the grocer for his comfort, and so she herself undertook the preparation of the room. Madame Foucault was amazed at the thoroughness of her housewifery, and at the ingenuity of her ideas for the arrangement of furniture. She sat and watched with admiration sycophantic but real.

That night, when Sophia was in bed, Madame Foucault came into the room, and dropped down by the side of the bed, and begged Sophia to be her moral support for ever. She confessed herself generally. She explained how she had always hated the negation of respectability; how respectability was the one thing that she had all her life passionately desired. She said that if Sophia would be her partner in the letting of furnished rooms to respectable persons, she would obey her in everything. She gave Sophia a list of all the traits in Sophia's character which she admired. She asked Sophia to influence her, to stand by her. She insisted that she would sleep on the sixth floor in the servant's tiny room; and she had a vision of three bedrooms let to successful tradesmen. She was in an ecstasy of repentance and good intentions.

Sophia consented to the business proposition; for she had nothing else whatever in prospect, and she shared Madame Foucault's rosy view about the remunerativeness of the bedrooms. With three tenants who took meals the two women would be able to feed themselves for nothing and still make a profit on the food; and the rents would be clear gain.

And she felt very sorry for the ageing, feckless Madame Foucault, whose sincerity was obvious. The association between them would be strange; it would have been impossible to explain it to St Luke's Square . . . And yet, if there was anything at all in the virtue of Christian charity, what could properly be urged against the association?

'Ah!' murmured Madame Foucault, kissing Sophia's hands, 'it is today, then, that I recommence my life. You will see – you will see! You have saved me!'

It was a strange sight, the time-worn, disfigured courtesan, half prostrate before the beautiful young creature proud and unassailable in the instinctive force of her own character. It was almost a didactic tableau, fraught with lessons for the vicious. Sophia was happier than she had been for years. She had a purpose in existence; she had a fluid soul to mould to her will according to her wisdom; and there was a large compassion to her credit. Public opinion could not intimidate her, for in her case there was no public opinion; she knew nobody; nobody had the right to question her doings.

The next day, Sunday, they both worked hard at the bedrooms from early morning. The grocer was installed in his chamber, and the two other rooms were cleansed as they had never been cleansed. At four o'clock, the weather being more magnificent than ever, Madame Foucault said:

'If we took a promenade on the boulevard?'

Sophia reflected. They were partners. 'Very well,' she agreed.

The boulevard was crammed with gay, laughing crowds. All the cafés were full. None, who did not know, could have guessed that the news of Sedan was scarcely a day old in the capital.

Delirious joy reigned in the glittering sunshine. As the two women strolled along, content with their industry and their resolves, they came to a National Guard, who, perched on a ladder, was chipping away the 'N' from the official sign of a court-tradesman. He was exchanging jokes with a circle of open mouths. It was in this way that Madame Foucault and Sophia learnt of the establishment of a republic.[11]

'Vive la république!' cried Madame Foucault, incontinently, and then apologized to Sophia for the lapse.

They listened a long while to a man who was telling strange histories of the Empress.

Suddenly Sophia noticed that Madame Foucault was no longer at her elbow. She glanced about, and saw her in earnest conversation with a young man whose face seemed familiar. She remembered it was the young man with whom Madame Foucault had quarrelled on the night when Sophia found her prone in the corridor; the last remaining worshipper of the courtesan.

The woman's face was quite changed by her agitation. Sophia drew away, offended. She watched the pair from a distance for a few moments, and then, furious in disillusion, she escaped from the fever of the boulevards and walked quietly home. Madame Foucault did not return. Apparently Madame Foucault was doomed to be the toy of chance. Two days later Sophia received a scrawled letter from her, with the information that her lover had required that she should accompany him to Brussels, as Paris would soon be getting dangerous. 'He adores me always. He is the most delicious boy. As I have always said, this is the grand passion of my life. I am happy. He would not permit me to come to you. He has spent two thousand francs on clothes for me, since naturally I had nothing.' And so on. No word of apology. Sophia, in reading the letter, allowed for a certain exaggeration and twisting of the truth.

'Young fool! Fool!' she burst out angrily. She did not mean herself; she meant the fatuous adorer of that dilapidated, horrible woman. She never saw her again. Doubtless Madame Foucault fulfilled her own prediction as to her ultimate destiny, but in Brussels.

II

Sophia still possessed about a hundred pounds, and had she chosen to leave Paris and France, there was nothing to prevent her from doing so. Perhaps if she had chanced to visit the Gare St Lazare or the Gare du Nord, the sight of tens of thousands of people flying seawards might have stirred in her the desire to flee also from the vague coming danger. But she did not visit those termini; she was too busy looking after M. Niepce, her grocer. Moreover, she would not quit her furniture, which seemed to her to be a sort of rock. With a flat full of furniture she considered that she ought to be able to devise a livelihood; the enterprise of becoming independent was already indeed begun. She ardently wished to be independent, to utilize in her own behalf the gifts of organization, foresight, common sense, and tenacity which she knew she possessed and which had lain idle. And she hated the idea of flight.

Chirac returned as unexpectedly as he had gone; an expedition for his paper had occupied him. With his lips he urged her to go, but his eyes spoke differently. He had, one afternoon, a mood of candid despair, such as he would have dared to show only to one in whom he felt great confidence. 'They will come to Paris,' he said; 'nothing can stop them. And ... then ... !' He gave a cynical laugh. But when he urged her to go she said:

'And what about my furniture? And I've promised M. Niepce to look after him.'

Then Chirac informed her that he was without a lodging, and that he would like to rent one of her rooms. She agreed.

Shortly afterwards he introduced a middle-aged acquaintance named Carlier, the secretary-general of his newspaper, who wished to rent a bedroom. Thus by good fortune Sophia let all her rooms immediately, and was sure of over two hundred francs a month, apart from the profit on meals supplied. On this latter occasion Chirac (and his companion too) was quite optimistic, reiterating an absolute certitude that Paris could never be invested. Briefly, Sophia did not believe him. She believed the candidly despairing Chirac. She had no information, no wide theory, to justify her pessimism; nothing but the inward conviction that the race capable of behaving as she had seen it behave in the Place de la Concorde, was bound to be defeated. She loved the French race; but all the practical Teutonic sagacity in her wanted to take care of it in its difficulties, and was rather angry with it for being so unfitted to take care of itself.

She let the men talk, and with careless disdain of their discussions and their certainties she went about her business of preparation. At this period, overworked and harassed by novel responsibilities and risks, she was happier, for days together, than she had ever been, simply because she had a purpose in life and was depending upon herself. Her ignorance of the military and political situation was complete; the situation did not interest her. What interested her was that she had three men to feed wholly or partially, and that the price of eatables was rising. She bought eatables. She bought fifty pecks of potatoes at a franc a peck, and another fifty pecks at a franc and a quarter – double the normal price; ten hams at two and a half francs a pound; a large quantity of tinned vegetables and fruits, a sack of flour, rice, biscuits, coffee, Lyons sausage, dried prunes, dried figs, and much wood and charcoal. But the chief of her purchases was cheese, of which her mother used to say that bread and cheese and water made a complete diet. Many of these articles she obtained from her grocer. All of them, except the flour and the biscuits, she stored in the cellar belonging to the flat; after several days' delay, for the Parisian workmen were too elated by the advent of a republic to stoop to labour, she caused a new lock to be fixed on the cellar-door. Her activities were the sensation of the house. Everybody admired, but no one imitated.

One morning, on going to do her marketing, she found a notice across the shuttered windows of her creamery in the Rue Notre Dame de Lorette: 'Closed for want of milk.' The siege had begun. It was in the closing of the creamery that the siege was figured for her; in this, and in eggs at five sous a piece. She went elsewhere for her milk and paid a franc a litre for it. That evening she told her lodgers that the price of meals would be doubled, and that if any gentleman thought that he could get equally good meals elsewhere, he was at liberty to get them elsewhere. Her position was strengthened by the appearance of another candidate for a room, a friend of Niepce. She at once offered him her own room, at a hundred and fifty francs a month.

'You see,' she said, 'there is a piano in it.'

'But I don't play the piano,' the man protested, shocked at the price.

'That is not my fault,' she said.

He agreed to pay the price demanded for the room because of the opportunity of getting good meals much cheaper than in the restaurants. Like M. Niepce, he was a 'siege-widower', his wife having been put under shelter in Brittany. Sophia took to the servant's bedroom on the sixth floor. It measured nine feet by seven, and had no window save a skylight; but Sophia was in a fair way to realize a profit of at least four pounds a week after paying for everything.

On the night when she installed herself in that chamber, amid a world of domestics and poor people, she worked very late, and the rays of her candles shot up intermittently through the skylight into a black heaven; at intervals she flitted up and down the stairs with a candle. Unknown to her a crowd gradually formed opposite the house in the street, and at about one o'clock in the morning a file of soldiers woke the concierge and invaded the courtyard, and every window was suddenly populated with heads. Sophia was called upon to prove that she was not a spy signalling to the Prussians. Three-quarters of an hour passed before her innocence was established and the staircases cleared of uniforms and dishevelled curiosity. The childish, impossible unreason of the suspicion against her completed in Sophia's mind the ruin of the reputation of the French people as a sensible race. She was extremely caustic the next day to her boarders. Except for this episode, the frequency of military uniforms in the streets, the price of food, and the fact that at least one house in four was flying either the ambulance flag or the flag of a foreign embassy (in an absurd hope of immunity from the impending bombardment) the siege did not exist for Sophia. The men often talked about their guard-duty, and disappeared for a day or two to the ramparts, but she was too busy to listen to them. She thought of nothing but her enterprise, which absorbed all her powers. She

arose at six a.m., in the dark, and by seven-thirty M. Niepce and
his friend had been served with breakfast, and much general
work was already done. At eight o'clock she went out to market.
When asked why she continued to buy at a high price, articles of
which she had a store, she would reply: 'I am keeping all that till
things are much dearer.' This was regarded as astounding astute-
ness.

On the fifteenth of October she paid the quarter's rent of the
flat, four hundred francs, and was accepted as tenant. Her ears
were soon quite accustomed to the sound of cannon, and she felt
that she had always been a citizeness of Paris, and that Paris had
always been besieged. She did not speculate about the end of the
siege; she lived from day to day. Occasionally she had a qualm of
fear, when the firing grew momentarily louder, or when she heard
that battles had been fought in such and such a suburb. But then
she said it was absurd to be afraid when you were with a couple of
million people, all in the same plight as yourself. She grew
reconciled to everything. She even began to like her tiny bedroom, partly because it was so easy to keep warm (the question of
artificial heat was growing acute in Paris), and partly because it
ensured her privacy. Down in the flat, whatever was done or said
in one room could be more or less heard in all the others, owing to
the prevalence of doors.

Her existence, in the first half of November, had become
regular with a monotony almost absolute. Only the number of
meals served to her boarders varied slightly from day to day. All
these repasts, save now and then one in the evening, were carried
into the bedrooms by the charwoman. Sophia did not allow
herself to be seen much, except in the afternoons. Though Sophia
continued to increase her prices, and was now selling her stores at
an immense profit, she never approached the prices current
outside. She was very indignant against the exploitation of Paris
by its shopkeepers, who had vast supplies of provender, and were
hoarding for the rise. But the force of their example was too great
for her to ignore it entirely; she contented herself with about half
their gains. Only to M. Niepce did she charge more than to the
others, because he was a shopkeeper. The four men appreciated
their paradise. In them developed that agreeable feeling of secur-

ity which solitary males find only under the roof of a landlady who is at once prompt, honest, and a votary of cleanliness. Sophia hung a slate near the front door, and on this slate they wrote their requests for meals, for being called, for laundry-work, etc. Sophia never made a mistake, and never forgot. The perfection of the domestic machine amazed these men, who had been accustomed to something quite different, and who every day heard harrowing stories of discomfort and swindling from their acquaintances. They even admired Sophia for making them pay, if not too high, still high. They thought it wonderful that she should tell them the price of all things in advance, and even show them how to avoid expense, particularly in the matter of warmth. She arranged rugs for each of them, so that they could sit comfortably in their rooms with nothing but a small charcoal heater for the hands. Quite naturally they came to regard her as the paragon and miracle of women. They endowed her with every fine quality. According to them there had never been such a woman in the history of mankind; there could not have been! She became legendary among their friends: a young and elegant creature, surpassingly beautiful, proud, queenly, unapproach-able, scarcely visible, a marvellous manager, a fine cook and artificer of strange English dishes, utterly reliable, utterly exact and with habits of order . . . ! They adored the slight English accent which gave a touch of the exotic to her very correct and freely idiomatic French. In short, Sophia was perfect for them, an impossible woman. Whatever she did was right.

And she went up to her room every night with limbs exhausted, but with head clear enough to balance her accounts and go through her money. She did this in bed with thick gloves on. If often she did not sleep well, it was not because of the distant guns, but because of her preoccupation with the subject of finance. She was making money, and she wanted to make more. She was always inventing ways of economy. She was so anxious to achieve independence that money was always in her mind. She began to love gold, to love hoarding it, and to hate paying it away.

One morning her charwoman, who by good fortune was nearly as precise as Sophia herself, failed to appear. When the

moment came for serving M. Niepce's breakfast, Sophia hesitated, and then decided to look after the old man personally. She
knocked at his door, and went boldly in with the tray and candle.
He started at seeing her; she was wearing a blue apron, as the
charwoman did, but there could be no mistaking her for the
charwoman. Niepce looked older in bed than when dressed.
He had a rather ridiculous, undignified appearance, common
among old men before their morning toilette is achieved; and
a nightcap did not improve it. His rotund paunch lifted the
bed-clothes, upon which, for the sake of extra warmth, he
had spread unmajestic garments. Sophia smiled to herself; but
the contempt implied by that secret smile was softened by the
thought: 'Poor old man!' She told him briefly that she supposed
the charwoman to be ill. He coughed and moved nervously.
His benevolent and simple face beamed on her paternally as
she fixed the tray by the bed.

'I really must open the window for one little second,' she said,
and did so. The chill air of the street came through the closed
shutters, and the old man made a noise of shivering. She pushed
back the shutters, and closed the window, and then did the
same with the other two windows. It was almost day in the
room.

'You will no longer need the candle,' she said, and came back
to the bedside to extinguish it.

The benign and fatherly old man put his arm round her waist.
Fresh from the tonic of pure air, and with the notion of his
ridiculousness still in her mind, she was staggered for an instant
by this gesture. She had never given a thought to the temperament
of the old grocer, the husband of a young wife. She could not
always imaginatively keep in mind the effect of her own radiance, especially under such circumstances. But after an
instant her precocious cynicism, which had slept, sprang up.
'Naturally! I might have expected it!' she thought with blasting
scorn.

'Take away your hand!' she said bitterly to the amiable old
fool. She did not stir.

He obeyed, sheepishly.

'Do you wish to remain with me?' she asked, and as he did not immediately answer, she said in a most commanding tone: 'Answer, then!'

'Yes,' he said feebly.

'Well, behave properly.'

She went towards the door.

'I wished only –' he stammered.

'I do not wish to know what you wished,' she said.

Afterwards she wondered how much of the incident had been overheard. The other breakfasts she left outside the respective doors; and in future Niepce's also.

The charwoman never came again. She had caught smallpox and she died of it, thus losing a good situation. Strange to say, Sophia did not replace her; the temptation to save her wages and food was too strong. She could not, however, stand waiting for hours at the door of the official baker and the official butcher, one of a long line of frozen women, for the daily rations of bread and tri-weekly rations of meat. She employed the concierge's boy, at two sous an hour, to do this. Sometimes he would come in with his hands so blue and cold that he could scarcely hold the precious cards which gave the right to the rations and which cost Chirac an hour or two of waiting at the mayoral offices each week. Sophia might have fed her flock without resorting to the official rations, but she would not sacrifice the economy which they represented. She demanded thick clothes for the concierge's boy, and received boots from Chirac, gloves from Carlier, and a great overcoat from Niepce. The weather increased in severity, and provisions in price. One day she sold to the wife of a chemist who lived on the first floor, for a hundred and ten francs, a ham for which she had paid less than thirty francs. She was conscious of a thrill of joy in receiving a beautiful bank-note and a gold coin in exchange for a mere ham. By this time her total cash resources had grown to nearly five thousand francs. It was astounding. And the reserves in the cellar were still considerable, and the sack of flour that encumbered the kitchen was still more than half full. The death of the faithful charwoman, when she heard of it, produced but little effect on Sophia, who was so overworked and so completely absorbed in her own affairs that she had no nervous energy to spare for sentimental regrets. The charwoman, by whose side she had regularly passed many hours in the kitchen, so that she knew every crease in her face and fold of her dress, vanished out of Sophia's memory.

Sophia cleaned and arranged two of the bedrooms in the morning, and two in the afternoon. She had stayed in hotels where fifteen bedrooms were in charge of a single chambermaid, and she thought it would be hard if she could not manage four in the intervals of cooking and other work. This she said to herself by way of excuse for not engaging another charwoman. One afternoon she was rubbing the brass knobs of the numerous doors in M. Niepce's room, when the grocer unexpectedly came in.

She glanced at him sharply. There was a self-conscious look in his eye. He had entered the flat noiselessly. She remembered having told him, in response to a question, that she now did his room in the afternoon. Why should he have left his shop? He hung up his hat behind the door, with the meticulous care of an old man. Then he took off his overcoat and rubbed his hands.

'You do well to wear gloves, madame,' he said. 'It is dog's weather.'

'I do not wear them for the cold,' she replied. 'I wear them so as not to spoil my hands.'

'Ah! truly! Very well! Very well! May I demand some wood? Where shall I find it? I do not wish to derange you.'

She refused his help, and brought wood from the kitchen, counting the logs audibly before him.

'Shall I light the fire now?' she asked.

'I will light it,' he said.

'Give me a match, please.'

As she was arranging the wood and paper, he said: 'Madame, will you listen to me?'

'What is it?'

'Do not be angry,' he said. 'Have I not proved that I am capable of respecting you? I continue in that respect. It is with all that respect that I say to you that I love you, madame . . . No, remain calm, I implore you!' The fact was that Sophia showed no sign of not remaining calm. 'It is true that I have a wife. But what do you wish . . . ? She is far away. I love you madly,' he proceeded with dignified respect. 'I know I am old; but I am rich. I understand your character. You are a lady, you are decided, direct, sincere, and a woman of business. I have the greatest respect for you. One can talk to you as one could not to another woman. You prefer directness and sincerity. Madame, I will give you two thousand francs a month, and all you require from my shop, if you will be amiable to me. I am very solitary, I need the society of a charming creature who would be sympathetic. Two thousand francs a month. It is money.'

He wiped his shiny head with his hand.

Sophia was bending over the fire. She turned her head towards him.

'Is that all?' she said quietly.

'You could count on my discretion,' he said in a low voice. 'I appreciate your scruples. I would come, very late, to your room on the sixth. One could arrange . . . You see, I am direct, like you.'

She had an impulse to order him tempestuously out of the flat; but it was not a genuine impulse. He was an old fool. Why not treat him as such? To take him seriously would be absurd. Moreover, he was a very remunerative boarder.

'Do not be stupid,' she said with cruel tranquillity. 'Do not be an old fool.'

And the benign but fatuous middle-aged lecher saw the enchanting vision of Sophia, with her natty apron and her amusing gloves, sweep and fade from the room. He left the house, and the expensive fire warmed an empty room.

Sophia was angry with him. He had evidently planned the proposal. If capable of respect, he was evidently also capable of chicane. But she supposed these Frenchmen were all alike: disgusting; and decided that it was useless to worry over a universal fact. They had simply no shame, and she had been very prudent to establish herself far away on the sixth floor. She hoped that none of the other boarders had overheard Niepce's outrageous insolence. She was not sure if Chirac was not writing in his room.

That night there was no sound of cannon in the distance, and Sophia for some time was unable to sleep. She woke up with a start, after a doze, and struck a match to look at her watch. It had stopped. She had forgotten to wind it up, which omission indicated that the grocer had perturbed her more than she thought. She could not be sure how long she had slept. The hour might be two o'clock or it might be six o'clock. Impossible for her to rest! She got up and dressed (in case it should be as late as she feared) and crept down the interminable creaking stairs with the candle. As she descended, the conviction that it was the middle of the night grew upon her, and she stepped more swiftly. There was no sound save that caused by her footfalls. With her latchkey she cautiously opened the front door of the flat and entered. She could then hear the noisy ticking of the small, cheap clock in the kitchen. At the same moment another door creaked, and Chirac, with hair all tousled, but fully dressed, appeared in the corridor.

'So you have decided to sell yourself to him!' Chirac whispered.

She drew away instinctively, and she could feel herself blushing. She was at a loss. She saw that Chirac was in a furious rage, tremendously moved. He crept towards her, half crouching. She had never seen anything so theatrical as his movement, and the twitching of his face. She felt that she too ought to be theatrical, that she ought nobly to scorn his infamous suggestion, his unwarrantable attack. Even supposing that she had decided to sell herself to the old pasha, did that concern him? A dignified silence, an annihilating glance, were all that he deserved. But she was not capable of this heroic behaviour.

'What time is it?' she added weakly.

'Three o'clock,' Chirac sneered.

'I forgot to wind up my watch,' she said. 'And so I came down to see.'

'In effect!' He spoke sarcastically, as if saying: 'I've waited for you, and here you are.'

She said to herself that she owed him nothing, but all the time she felt that he and she were the only young people in that flat, and that she did owe to him the proof that she was guiltless of the supreme dishonour of youth. She collected her forces and looked at him.

'You should be ashamed,' she said. 'You will wake the others.'

'And M. Niepce – will he need to be wakened?'

'M. Niepce is not here,' she said.

Niepce's door was unlatched. She pushed it open and went into the room, which was empty and bore no sign of having been used.

'Come and satisfy yourself!' she insisted.

Chirac did so. His face fell.

She took her watch from her pocket.

'And now wind my watch, and set it, please.'

She saw that he was in anguish. He could not take the watch. Tears came into his eyes. Then he hid his face, and dashed away. She heard a sob-impeded murmur that sounded like, 'Forgive me!' and the banging of a door. And in the stillness she heard the regular snoring of M. Carlier. She too cried. Her vision was blurred by a mist, and she stumbled into the kitchen and seized the clock, and carried it with her upstairs, and shivered in the intense cold of the night. She wept gently for a very long time. 'What a shame! What a shame!' she said to herself. Yet she did not quite blame Chirac. The frost drove her into bed, but not to sleep. She continued to cry. At dawn her eyes were inflamed with weeping. She was back in the kitchen then. Chirac's door was wide open. He had left the flat. On the slate was written, 'I shall not take meals today.'

III

Their relations were permanently changed. For several days they did not meet at all; and when at the end of the week Chirac was obliged at last to face Sophia in order to pay his bill, he had a most grievous expression. It was obvious that he considered himself a criminal without any defence to offer for his crime. He seemed to make no attempt to hide his state of mind. But he said nothing. As for Sophia, she preserved a mien of amiable cheerfulness. She exerted herself to convince him by her attitude that she bore no resentment, that she had determined to forget the incident, that in short she was the forgiving angel of his dreams. She did not, however, succeed entirely in being quite natural. Confronted by his misery, it would have been impossible for her to be quite natural, and at the same time quite cheerful!

A little later the social atmosphere of the flat began to grow querulous, disputatious, and perverse. The nerves of everybody were seriously strained. This applied to the whole city. Days of heavy rains followed the sharp frosts, and the town was, as it were, sodden with woe. The gates were closed. And though nine-tenths of the inhabitants never went outside the gates, the definite and absolute closing of them demoralized all hearts. Gas was no longer supplied. Rats, cats, and thorough-bred horses were being eaten and pronounced 'not bad'. The siege had ceased to be a novelty. Friends did not invite one another to a 'siege-dinner' as to a picnic. Sophia, fatigued by regular overwork, became weary of the situation. She was angry with the Prussians for dilatoriness, and with the French for inaction, and she poured out her English spleen on her boarders. The boarders told each other in secret that the *patronne* was growing formidable. Chiefly she bore a grudge against the shopkeepers; and when, upon a rumour of peace, the shop-windows one day suddenly blossomed with prodigious quantities of all edibles, at highest prices, thus proving that the famine was artificially created, Sophia was furious. M. Niepce in particular, though he sold goods to her at a special discount, suffered indignities. A few days later that benign and fatherly man put himself lamentably in the wrong by attempting to introduce into his room a charming young creature who knew how to be sympathetic. Sophia, by an accident unfortunate for the grocer, caught them in the corridor. She was beside herself, but the only outward symptoms were a white face and a cold, steely voice that grated like a rasp on the susceptibilities of the adherents of Aphrodite. At this period Sophia had certainly developed into a termagant – without knowing it!

She would often insist now on talking about the siege and hearing everything that the men could tell her. Her comments, made without the least regard for the justifiable delicacy of their feelings as Frenchmen, sometimes led to heated exchanges. When all Montmartre and the Quartier Bréda was impassioned by the appearance from outside of the Thirty-second battalion, she took the side of the populace, and would not credit the solemn statement of the journalists, proved by documents, that these maltreated soldiers were not cowards in flight. She supported the women who had spit in the faces of the Thirty-second. She actually said that if she had met them, she would have spit too. Really she was convinced of the innocence of the Thirty-second, but something prevented her from admitting it. The dispute ended with high words between herself and Chirac.

The next day Chirac came home at an unusual hour, knocked at the kitchen door, and said:

'I must give notice to leave you.'

'Why?' she demanded curtly.

She was kneading flour and water for a potato-cake. Her potato-cakes were the joy of the household.

'My paper has stopped!' said Chirac.

'Oh!' she added thoughtfully, but not looking at him. 'That is no reason why you should leave.'

'Yes,' he said. 'This place is beyond my means. I do not need to tell you that in ceasing to appear the paper has omitted to pay its debts. The house owes me a month's salary. So I must leave.'

'No!' said Sophia. 'You can pay me when you have money.'

He shook his head. 'I have no intention of accepting your kindness.'

'Haven't you got any money?' she abruptly asked.

'None,' said he. 'It is the disaster – quite simply!'

'Then you will be forced to get into debt somewhere.'

'Yes, but not here! Not to you!'

'Truly, Chirac,' she exclaimed, with a cajoling voice, 'you are not reasonable.'

'Nevertheless it is like that!' he said with decision.

'Eh, well!' she turned on him menacingly. 'It will not be like that! You understand me? You will stay. And you will pay me when you can. Otherwise we shall quarrel. Do you imagine I shall tolerate your childishness? Just because you were angry last night –'

'It is not that,' he protested. 'You ought to know it is not that.' (She did.) 'It is solely that I cannot permit myself to –'

'Enough!' she cried peremptorily, stopping him. And then in a quieter tone, 'And what about Carlier? Is he also in the ditch?'

'Ah, he has money,' said Chirac, with sad envy.

'You also, one day,' said she. 'You stop – in any case until after Christmas, or we quarrel. Is it agreed?' Her accent had softened.

'You are too good!' he yielded. 'I cannot quarrel with you. But it pains me to accept –'

'Oh!' she snapped, dropping into the vulgar idiom, 'you make me sweat with your stupid pride. Is it that that you call friendship? Go away now. How do you wish that I should succeed with this cake while you station yourself there to distract me?'

IV

But in three days Chirac, with amazing luck, fell into another situation, and on the *Journal des Débats*. It was the Prussians who had found him a place. The celebrated Payenneville, second greatest *chroniqueur* of his time, had caught a cold while doing his duty as a national guard, and had died of pneumonia. The weather was severe again; soldiers were being frozen to death at Aubervilliers. Payenneville's position was taken by another man, whose post was offered to Chirac. He told Sophia of his good fortune with unconcealed vanity.

'You with your smile!' she said impatiently. 'One can refuse you nothing!'

She behaved just as though Chirac had disgusted her. She humbled him. But with his fellow-lodgers his airs of importance as a member of the editorial staff of the *Débâts* were comical in their ingenuousness. On the very same day Carlier gave notice to leave Sophia. He was comparatively rich; but the habits which had enabled him to arrive at independence in the uncertain vocation of a journalist would not allow him, while he was earning nothing, to spend a sou more than was absolutely necessary. He had decided to join forces with a widowed sister, who was accustomed to parsimony as parsimony is understood in France, and who was living on hoarded potatoes and wine.

'There!' said Sophia, 'you have lost me a tenant!'

And she insisted, half jocularly and half seriously, that Carlier was leaving because he could not stand Chirac's infantile conceit. The flat was full of acrimonious words.

On Christmas morning Chirac lay in bed rather late; the newspapers did not appear that day. Paris seemed to be in a sort of stupor. About eleven o'clock he came to the kitchen door.

'I must speak with you,' he said. His tone impressed Sophia.

'Enter,' said she.

He went in, and closed the door like a conspirator. 'We must have a little fête,' he said. 'You and I.'

'Fête!' she repeated. 'What an idea! How can I leave?'

If the idea had not appealed to the secrecies of her heart, stirring desires and souvenirs upon which the dust of time lay thick, she would not have begun by suggesting difficulties; she would have begun by a flat refusal.

'That is nothing,' he said vigorously. 'It is Christmas, and I must have a chat with you. We cannot chat here. I have not had a true little chat with you since you were ill. You will come with me to a restaurant for lunch.'

She laughed. 'And the lunch of my lodgers?'

'You will serve it a little earlier. We will go out immediately afterwards, and we will return in time for you to prepare dinner. It is quite simple.'

She shook her head. 'You are mad,' she said crossly.

'It is necessary that I should offer you something,' he went on scowling. 'You comprehend me? I wish you to lunch with me today. I demand it, and you are not going to refuse me.'

He was very close to her in the little kitchen, and he spoke fiercely, bullyingly, exactly as she had spoken to him when insisting that he should live on credit with her for a while.

'You are very rude,' she parried.

'If I am rude, it is all the same to me,' he held out uncompromisingly. 'You will lunch with me; I hold to it.'

'How can I be dressed?' she protested.

'That does not concern me. Arrange that as you can.'

It was the most curious invitation to a Christmas dinner imaginable.

At a quarter past twelve they issued forth side by side, heavily clad, into the mournful streets. The sky, slate-coloured, presaged snow. The air was bitterly cold, and yet damp. There were no fiacres in the little three-cornered place which forms the mouth of the Rue Clausel. In the Rue Notre Dame de Lorette, a single empty omnibus was toiling up the steep glassy slope, the horses slipping and recovering themselves in response to the whip-cracking, which sounded in the streets as in an empty vault. Higher up, in the Rue Fontaine, one of the few shops that were open displayed this announcement: '*A large selection of cheeses for New Year's gifts.*' They laughed.

'Last year at this moment,' said Chirac, 'I was thinking of only one thing – the masked ball at the opera. I could not sleep after it. This year even the churches are not open. And you?'

She put her lips together. 'Do not ask me,' she said.

They proceeded in silence.

'We are triste, we others,' he said. 'But the Prussians, in their trenches, they cannot be so gay, either! Their families and their Christmas trees must be lacking to them. Let us laugh!'

The Place Blanche and the Boulevard de Clichy were no more lively than the lesser streets and squares. There was no life anywhere, scarcely a sound; not even the sound of cannon. Nobody knew anything; Christmas had put the city into a lugubrious trance of hopelessness. Chirac took Sophia's arm across the Place Blanche, and a few yards up the Rue Lepic he stopped at a small restaurant, famous among the initiated, and known as 'The Little Louis'. They entered, descending by two steps into a confined and sombrely picturesque interior.

Sophia saw that they were expected. Chirac must have paid a previous visit to the restaurant that morning. Several disordered tables showed that people had already lunched, and left; but in the corner was a table for two, freshly laid in the best manner of such restaurants; that is to say, with a red-and-white checked cloth, and two other red-and-white cloths, almost as large as the table-cloth, folded as serviettes and arranged flat on two thick plates between solid steel cutlery; a salt-cellar, out of which one ground rock-salt by turning a handle, a pepper-castor, two knife-rests, and two common tumblers. The phenomena which differentiated this table from the ordinary table were a champagne bottle and a couple of champagne glasses. Champagne was one of the few items which had not increased in price during the siege.

The landlord and his wife were eating in another corner, a fat, slatternly pair, whom no privations of a siege could have emaciated. The landlord rose. He was dressed as a chef, all in white, with the sacred cap; but a soiled white. Everything in the place was untidy, unkempt and more or less unclean, except just the table upon which champagne was waiting. And yet the restaurant was agreeable, reassuring. The landlord greeted his customers as honest friends. His greasy face was honest, and so was the pale, weary, humorous face of his wife. Chirac saluted her.

'You see,' said she, across from the other corner, indicating a bone on her plate. 'This is Diane!'

'Ah! the poor animal!' exclaimed Chirac, sympathetically.

'What would you?' said the landlady. 'It cost too dear to feed her. And she was so *mignonne*! One could not watch her grow thin!'

'I was saying to my wife,' the landlord put in, 'how she would have enjoyed that bone – Diane!' He roared with laughter.

Sophia and the landlady exchanged a curious sad smile at this pleasantry, which had been re-discovered by the landlord for perhaps the thousandth time during the siege, but which he evidently regarded as quite new and original.

'Eh, well!' he continued confidentially to Chirac. 'I have found for you something very good – half a duck.' And in a still lower tone: 'And it will not cost you too dear.'

No attempt to realize more than a modest profit was ever made in that restaurant. It possessed a regular *clientèle* who knew the value of the little money they had, and who knew also how to appreciate sincere and accomplished cookery. The landlord was the chef, and he was always referred to as the chef, even by his wife.

'How did you get that?' Chirac asked.

'Ah!' said the landlord, mysteriously. 'I have one of my friends, who comes from Villeneuve St Georges – refugee, you know. In fine . . .' A wave of the fat hands, suggesting that Chirac should not inquire too closely.

'In effect!' Chirac commented. 'But it is very chic, that!'

'I believe you that it is *chic*!' said the landlady, sturdily.

'It is charming,' Sophia murmured politely.

'And then a quite little salad!' said the landlord.

'But that – that is still more striking!' said Chirac.

The landlord winked. The fact was that the commerce which

resulted in fresh green vegetables in the heart of a beleaguered town was notorious.

'And then also a quite little cheese!' said Sophia, slightly imitating the tone of the landlord, as she drew from the inwardness of her cloak a small round parcel. It contained a Brie cheese, in fairly good condition. It was worth at least fifty francs, and it had cost Sophia less than two francs. The landlady joined the landlord in inspecting this wondrous jewel. Sophia seized a knife and cut a slice for the landlady's table.

'Madame is too good!' said the landlady, confused by this noble generosity, and bearing the gift off to her table as a fox-terrier will hurriedly seek solitude with a sumptuous morsel. The landlord beamed. Chirac was enchanted. In the intimate and unaffected cosiness of that interior the vast, stupefied melancholy of the city seemed to be forgotten, to have lost its sway.

Then the landlord brought a hot brick for the feet of madame. It was more an acknowledgement of the slice of cheese than a necessity, for the restaurant was very warm; the tiny kitchen opened directly into it, and the door between the two was open; there was no ventilation whatever.

'It is a friend of mine,' said the landlord, proudly, in the way of gossip, as he served an undescribed soup, 'a butcher in the Faubourg St Honoré, who has bought the three elephants of the Jardin des Plantes for twenty-seven thousand francs.'

Eyebrows were lifted. He uncorked the champagne.

As she drank the first mouthful (she had long lost her youthful aversion for wine), Sophia had a glimpse of herself in a tilted mirror hung rather high on the opposite wall. It was several months since she had attired herself with ceremoniousness. The sudden unexpected vision of elegance and pallid beauty pleased her. And the instant effect of the champagne was to renew in her mind a forgotten conception of the goodness of life and of the joys which she had so long missed.

V

At half past two they were alone in the little salon of the restaurant, and vaguely in their dreamy and feverish minds that were too preoccupied to control with precision their warm, relaxed bodies, there floated the illusion that the restaurant belonged to them and that in it they were at home. It was no longer a restaurant, but a retreat and shelter from hard life. The chef and his wife were dozing in an inner room. The champagne was drunk; the adorable cheese was eaten; and they were sipping Marc de Bourgogne. They sat at right angles to one another, close to one another, with brains aswing; full of good nature and quick sympathy; their flesh content and yet expectant. In a pause of the conversation (which, entirely banal and fragmentary, had seemed to reach the acme of agreeableness), Chirac put his hand on the hand of Sophia as it rested limp on the littered table. Accidentally she caught his eye; she had not meant to do so. They both became self-conscious. His thin, bearded face had more than ever that wistfulness which always softened towards him the uncompromisingness of her character. He had the look of a child. For her, Gerald had sometimes shown the same look. But indeed she was now one of those women for whom all men, and especially all men in a tender mood, are invested with a certain incurable quality of childishness. She had not withdrawn her hand at once, and so she could not withdraw it at all.

He gazed at her with timid audacity. Her eyes were liquid.

'What are you thinking about?' she asked.

'I was asking myself what I should have done if you had refused to come.'

'And what *should* you have done?'

'Assuredly something terribly inconvenient,' he replied, with the large importance of a man who is in the domain of pure supposition. He leaned towards her. 'My very dear friend,' he said in a different voice, getting bolder.

It was infinitely sweet to her, voluptuously sweet, this basking in the heat of temptation. It certainly did seem to her, then, the one real pleasure in the world. Her body might have been saying to his: 'See how ready I am!' Her body might have been saying to his: 'Look into my mind. For you I have no modesty. Look and see all that is there.' The veil of convention seemed to have been rent. Their attitude to each other was almost that of lover and mistress, between whom a single glance may be charged with the secrets of the past and promises for the future. Morally she was his mistress in that moment.

He released her hand and put his arm round her waist.

'I love thee,' he whispered with great emotion.

Her face changed and hardened. 'You must not do that,' she said, coldly, unkindly, harshly. She scowled. She would not abate one crease in her forehead to the appeal of his surprised glance. Yet she did not want to repulse him. The instinct which repulsed him was not within her control. Just as a shy man will obstinately refuse an invitation which he is hungering to accept, so, though not from shyness, she was compelled to repulse Chirac. Perhaps if her desires had not been laid to sleep by excessive physical industry and nervous strain, the sequel might have been different.

Chirac, like most men who have once found a woman weak, imagined that he understood women profoundly. He thought of women as the Occidental thinks of the Chinese, as a race apart, mysterious but capable of being infallibly comprehended by the application of a few leading principles of psychology. Moreover he was in earnest; he was hard driven, and he was honest. He continued, respectfully obedient in withdrawing his arm:

'Very dear friend,' he urged with undaunted confidence, 'you must know that I love you.'

She shook her head impatiently, all the time wondering what it was that prevented her from slipping into his arms. She knew that she was treating him badly by this brusque change of front; but she could not help it. Then she began to feel sorry for him.

'We have been very good friends,' he said. 'I have always admired you enormously. I did not think that I should dare to love you until that day when I overheard that old villain Niepce make his advances. Then, when I perceived my acute jealousy, I knew that I was loving you. Ever since, I have thought only of you. I swear to you that if you will not belong to me, it is already finished for me! Altogether! Never have I seen a woman like you! So strong, so proud, so kind, and so beautiful! You are astonishing, yes, astonishing! No other woman could have drawn herself out of an impossible situation as you have done, since the disappearance of your husband. For me, you are a woman unique. I am very sincere. Besides, you know it . . . Dear friend!'

She shook her head passionately.

She did not love him. But she was moved. And she wanted to love him. She wanted to yield to him, only liking him, and to love afterwards. But this obstinate instinct held her back.

'I do not say, now,' Chirac went on. 'Let me hope.'

The Latin theatricality of his gestures and his tone made her sorrowful for him.

'My poor Chirac!' she plaintively murmured, and began to put on her gloves.

'I shall hope!' he persisted.

She pursed her lips. He seized her violently by the waist. She drew her face away from his, firmly. She was not hard, not angry now. Disconcerted by her compassion, he loosed her.

'My poor Chirac,' she said, 'I ought not to have come. I must go. It is perfectly useless. Believe me.'

'No, no!' he whispered fiercely.

She stood up and the abrupt movement pushed the table gratingly across the floor. The throbbing spell of the flesh was snapped like a stretched string, and the scene over. The landlord, roused from his doze, stumbled in. Chirac had nothing but the bill as a reward for his pains. He was baffled.

They left the restaurant, silently, with a foolish air.

Dusk was falling on the mournful streets, and the lamplighters were lighting the miserable oil lamps that had replaced gas. They two, and the lamplighters, and an omnibus were alone in the streets. The gloom was awful; it was desolating. The universal silence seemed to be the silence of despair. Steeped in woe, Sophia thought wearily upon the hopeless problem of existence. For it seemed to her that she and Chirac had created this woe out of nothing, and yet it was an incurable woe!

CHAPTER 7: *Success*

I

Sophia lay awake one night in the room lately quitted by Carlier. That silent negation of individuality had come and gone, and left scarcely any record of himself either in his room or in the memories of those who had surrounded his existence in the house. Sophia had decided to descend from the sixth floor, partly because the temptation of a large room, after months in a cubicle, was rather strong; but more because of late she had been obliged to barricade the door of the cubicle with a chest of drawers, owing to the propensities of a new tenant of the sixth floor. It was useless to complain to the concierge; the sole effective argument was the chest of drawers, and even that was frailer than Sophia could have wished. Hence, finally, her retreat.

She heard the front door of the flat open; then it was shut with nervous violence. The resonance of its closing would have certainly wakened less accomplished sleepers than M. Niepce and his friend, whose snores continued with undisturbed regularity. After a pause of shuffling, a match was struck, and feet crept across the corridor with the most exaggerated precautions against noise. There followed the unintentional bang of another door. It was decidedly the entry of a man without the slightest natural aptitude for furtive irruptions. The clock in M. Niepce's room, which the grocer had persuaded to exact time-keeping, chimed three with its delicate *ting*.

For several days past Chirac had been mysteriously engaged very late at the bureaux of the *Débats*. No one knew the nature of his employment; he said nothing, except to inform Sophia that he would continue to come home about three o'clock until further notice. She had insisted on leaving in his room the materials and apparatus for a light meal. Naturally he had protested, with the irrational obstinacy of a physically weak man who sticks to it that he can defy the laws of nature. But he had protested in vain.

His general conduct since Christmas Day had frightened Sophia, in spite of her tendency to stifle alarms at their birth. He had eaten scarcely anything at all, and he went about with the face of a man dying of a broken heart. The change in him was indeed tragic. And instead of improving, he grew worse. 'Have I done this?' Sophia asked herself. 'It is impossible that I should have done this! It is absurd and ridiculous that he should behave so!' Her thoughts were employed alternately in sympathizing with him and in despising him, in blaming herself and in blaming him. When they spoke, they spoke awkwardly, as though one or both of them had committed a shameful crime, which could not even be mentioned. The atmosphere of the flat was tainted by the horror. And Sophia could not offer him a bowl of soup without wondering how he would look at her or avoid looking, and without carefully arranging in advance her own gestures and speech. Existence was a nightmare of self-consciousness.

'At last they have unmasked their batteries!' he had exclaimed with painful gaiety two days after Christmas, when the besiegers had recommenced their cannonade. He tried to imitate the strange, general joy of the city, which had been roused from apathy by the recurrence of a familiar noise; but the effort was a deplorable failure. And Sophia condemned not merely the failure of Chirac's imitation, but the thing imitated. 'Childish!' she thought. Yet, despise the feebleness of Chirac's behaviour as she might, she was deeply impressed, genuinely astonished, by the gravity and persistence of the symptoms. 'He must have been getting himself into a state about me for a long time,' she thought. 'Surely he could not have gone mad like this all in a day or two! But I never noticed anything. No; honestly I never noticed anything!' And just as her behaviour in the restaurant had shaken Chirac's confidence in his knowledge of the other sex, so now the singular behaviour of Chirac shook hers. She was taken aback. She was frightened, though she pretended not to be frightened.

She had lived over and over again the scene in the restaurant. She asked herself over and over again if really she had not beforehand expected him to make love to her in the restaurant. She could not decide exactly when she had begun to expect a declaration; but probably a long time before the meal was finished. She had foreseen it, and might have stopped it. But she had not chosen to stop it. Curiosity concerning not merely him, but also herself, had tempted her tacitly to encourage him. She asked herself over and over again why she had repulsed him. It struck her as curious that she had repulsed him. Was it because she was a married woman? Was it because she had moral scruples? Was it at bottom because she did not care for him? Was it because she could not care for anybody? Was it because his fervid manner of love-making offended her English phlegm? And did she feel pleased or displeased by his forbearance in not renewing the assault? She could not answer. She did not know.

But all the time she knew that she wanted love. Only, she conceived a different kind of love: placid, regular, somewhat stern, somewhat above the plane of whims, moods, caresses, and all mere fleshly contacts. Not that she considered that she despised these things (though she did)! What she wanted was a love that was too proud, too independent, to exhibit frankly either its joy or its pain. She hated a display of sentiment. And even in the most intimate abandonments she would have made reserves, and would have expected reserves, trusting to a lover's powers of divination, and to her own! The foundation of her character was a haughty moral independence, and this quality was what she most admired in others.

Chirac's inability to draw from his own pride strength to sustain himself against the blow of her refusal gradually killed in her the sexual desire which he had aroused, and which during a few days flickered up under the stimulus of fancy and of regret. Sophia saw with increasing clearness that her unreasoning instinct had been right in saying him nay. And when, in spite of this, regrets still visited her, she would comfort herself in thinking: 'I cannot be bothered with all that sort of thing. It is not worth while. What does it lead to? Is not life complicated enough without that? No, no! I will stay as I am. At any rate I know what I am in for, as things are!' And she would reflect upon her hopeful financial situation, and the approaching prospect of a constantly sufficient income. And a little thrill of impatience against the interminable and gigantic foolishness of the siege would take her.

But her self-consciousness in presence of Chirac did not abate. As she lay in bed she awaited accustomed sounds which should have connoted Chirac's definite retirement for the night. Her ear, however, caught no sound whatever from his room. Then she imagined that there was a smell of burning in the flat. She sat up, and sniffed anxiously, of a sudden wideawake and apprehensive. And then she was sure that the smell of burning was not in her imagination. The bedroom was in perfect darkness. Feverishly she searched with her right hand for the matches on the night-table, and knocked candle-stick and matches to the floor. She seized her dressing-gown, which was spread over the bed, and put it on, aiming for the door. Her feet were bare. She discovered the door. In the passage she could discern nothing at first, and then she made out a thin line of light, which indicated the bottom of Chirac's door. The smell of burning was strong and unmistakable. She went towards the faint light, fumbled for the door-handle with her palm, and opened. It did not occur to her to call out and ask what was the matter.

The house was not on fire; but it might have been. She had left on the table at the foot of Chirac's bed a small cooking-lamp, and a saucepan of bouillon. All that Chirac had to do was to ignite the lamp and put the saucepan on it. He had ignited the lamp, having previously raised the double wicks, and had then dropped into the chair by the table just as he was, and sunk forward and gone to sleep with his head lying sideways on the table. He had not put the saucepan on the lamp; he had not lowered the wicks, and the flames, capped with thick black smoke, were waving slowly to and fro within a few inches of his loose hair. His hat had rolled along the floor; he was wearing his great overcoat and one woollen glove; the other glove had lodged on his slanting knee. A candle was also burning.

Sophia hastened forward, as it were surreptitiously, and with a forward-reaching movement turned down the wick of the lamp; black specks were falling on the table; happily the saucepan was covered, or the bouillon would have been ruined.

Chirac made a heart-rending spectacle, and Sophia was aware of deep and painful emotion in seeing him thus. He must have been utterly exhausted and broken by loss of sleep. He was a man incapable of regular hours, incapable of treating his body with decency. Though going to bed at three o'clock, he had continued to rise at his usual hour. He looked like one dead; but more sad, more wistful. Outside in the street a fog reigned, and his thin draggled beard was jewelled with the moisture of it. His attitude had the unconsidered and violent prostration of an overspent dog. The beaten animal in him was expressed in every detail of that posture. It showed even in his white, drawn eyelids, and in the falling of a finger. All his face was very sad. It appealed for mercy as the undefended face of sleep always appeals; it was so

THE OLD WIVES' TALE

helpless, so exposed, so simple. It recalled Sophia to a sense of the inner mysteries of life, reminding her somehow that humanity walks ever on a thin crust over terrific abysses. She did not physically shudder; but her soul shuddered.

She mechanically placed the saucepan on the lamp, and the noise awakened Chirac. He groaned. At first he did not perceive her. When he saw that someone was looking down at him, he did not immediately realize who this one was. He rubbed his eyes with his fists, exactly like a baby, and sat up, and the chair cracked.

'What then?' he demanded. 'Oh, madame, I ask pardon. What?'

'You have nearly destroyed the house,' she said. 'I smelt fire, and I came in. I was just in time. There is no danger now. But please be careful.' She made as if to move towards the door.

'But what did I do?' he asked, his eyelids wavering.

She explained.

He rose from his chair unsteadily. She told him to sit down again, and he obeyed as though in a dream.

'I can go now,' she said.

'Wait a moment,' he murmured. 'I ask pardon. I should not know how to thank you. You are truly too good. Will you wait one moment?'

His tone was one of supplication. He gazed at her, a little dazzled by the light and by her. The lamp and the candle illuminated the lower part of her face, theatrically, and showed the texture of her blue flannel peignoir; the pattern of a part of the lace collar was silhouetted in shadow on her cheek. Her face was flushed, and her hair hung down unconfined. Evidently he could not recover from his excusable astonishment at the apparition of such a figure in his room.

'What is it – now?' she said. The faint, quizzical emphasis which she put on the 'now' indicated the essential of her thought. The sight of him touched her and filled her with a womanly sympathy. But that sympathy was only the envelope of her disdain of him. She could not admire weakness. She could but pity it with a pity in which scorn was mingled. Her instinct was to treat him as a child. He had failed in human dignity. And it seemed to her as if she had not previously been quite certain whether she could not love him, but that now she was quite certain. She was close to him. She saw the wounds of a soul that could not hide its wounds, and she resented the sight. She was hard. She would not make allowances. And she revelled in her hardness. Contempt – a good-natured, kindly, forgiving contempt – that was the kernel of the sympathy which exteriorly warmed her! Contempt for the lack of self-control which had resulted in this swift degeneration of a man into a tortured victim! Contempt for the lack of perspective which magnified a mere mushroom passion till it filled the whole field of life! Contempt for this feminine slavery to sentiment! She felt that she might have been able to give herself to Chirac as one gives a toy to an infant. But of loving him . . . ! No! She was conscious of an immeasurable superiority to him, for she was conscious of the freedom of a strong mind.

'I wanted to tell you,' said he, 'I am going away.'

'Where?' she asked.

'Out of Paris.'

'Out of Paris? How?'

'By balloon! My journal . . . ! It is an affair of great importance. You understand. I offered myself. What would you?'

'It is dangerous,' she observed, waiting to see if he would put on the silly air of one who does not understand fear.

'Oh!' the poor fellow muttered with a fatuous intonation and snapping of the fingers. 'That is all the same to me. Yes, it is dangerous. Yes, it is dangerous!' he repeated. 'But what would you . . . ? For me . . . !'

She wished that she had not mentioned danger. It hurt her to watch him incurring her ironic disdain.

'It will be the night after tomorrow,' he said. 'In the courtyard of the Gare du Nord. I want you to come and see me go. I particularly want you to come and see me go. I have asked Carlier to escort you.'

He might have been saying, 'I am offering myself to martyrdom, and you must assist at the spectacle.'

She despised him yet more.

'Oh! Be tranquil,' he said. 'I shall not worry you. Never shall I

speak to you again of my love. I know you. I know it would
be useless. But I hope you will come and wish me bon voyage.'

'Of course, if you really wish it,' she replied with cheerful
coolness.

He seized her hand and kissed it.

Once it had pleased her when he kissed her hand. But now she
did not like it. It seemed hysterical and foolish to her. She felt her
feet to be stone-cold on the floor.

'I'll leave you now,' she said. 'Please eat your soup.'

She escaped, hoping he would not espy her feet.

II

The courtyard of the Nord Railway Station was lighted by
oil-lamps taken from locomotives; their silvered reflectors threw
dazzling rays from all sides on the under portion of the immense
yellow mass of the balloon; the upper portion was swaying to and
fro with gigantic ungainliness in the strong breeze. It was only a
small balloon, as balloons are measured, but it seemed monstrous
as it wavered over the human forms that were agitating themselves beneath it. The cordage was silhouetted against the yellow
taffetas as high up as the widest diameter of the balloon, but
above that all was vague, and even spectators standing at a
distance could not clearly separate the summit of the great sphere
from the darkly moving sky. The car, held by ropes fastened to
stakes, rose now and then a few inches uneasily from the ground.
The sombre and severe architecture of the station buildings
enclosed the balloon on every hand; it had only one way of
escape. Over the roofs of that architecture, which shut out the
sounds of the city, came the irregular booming of the bombardment. Shells were falling in the southern quarters of Paris, doing
perhaps not a great deal of damage, but still plunging occasionally into the midst of some domestic interior and making a sad mess
of it. The Parisians were convinced that the shells were aimed
maliciously at hospitals and museums; and when a child happened to be blown to pieces their unspoken comments upon the
Prussian savagery were bitter. Their faces said: 'Those barbarians
cannot even spare our children!' They amused themselves by

creating a market in shells, paying more for a live shell than a
dead one, and modifying the tariff according to the supply. And
as the cattle-market was empty, and the vegetable market was
empty, and beasts no longer pastured on the grass of the parks,
and the twenty-five million rats of the metropolis were too
numerous to furnish interest to spectators, and the Bourse was
practically deserted, the traffic in shells sustained the starving
mercantile instinct during a very dull period. But the effect on the
nerves was deleterious. The nerves of everybody were like nothing but a raw wound. Violent anger would spring up magically
out of laughter, and blows out of caresses. This indirect consequence of the bombardment was particularly noticeable in the
group of men under the balloon. Each behaved as if he were
controlling his temper in the most difficult circumstances. Constantly they all gazed upwards into the sky, though nothing could
possibly be distinguished there save the blurred edge of a flying
cloud. But the booming came from that sky; the shells that were
dropping on Montrouge came out of that sky; and the balloon
was going up into it; the balloon was ascending into its mysteries,
to brave its dangers, to sweep over the encircling ring of fire and
savages.

Sophia stood apart with Carlier. Carlier had indicated a particular spot, under the shelter of the colonnade, where he said it
was imperative that they should post themselves. Having guided
Sophia to this spot, and impressed upon her that they were not to
move, he seemed to consider that the activity of his *rôle* was
finished, and spoke no word. With the very high silk hat which he
always wore, and a thin old-fashioned overcoat whose collar was
turned up, he made a rather grotesque figure. Fortunately the
night was not very cold, or he might have passively frozen to
death on the edge of that feverish group. Sophia soon ignored
him. She watched the balloon. An aristocratic old man leaned
against the car, watch in hand; at intervals he scowled, or
stamped his foot. An old sailor, tranquilly smoking a pipe,
walked round and round the balloon, staring at it; once he
climbed up into the rigging, and once he jumped into the car and
angrily threw out of it a bag, which someone had placed in it. But
for the most part he was calm. Other persons of authority hurried

about, talking and gesticulating; and a number of workmen waited idly for orders.

'Where is Chirac?' suddenly cried the old man with the watch.

Several voices deferentially answered, and a man ran away into the gloom on an errand.

Then Chirac appeared, nervous, self-conscious, restless. He was enveloped in a fur coat that Sophia had never seen before, and he carried dangling in his hand a cage containing six pigeons whose whiteness stirred uneasily within it. The sailor took the cage from him, and all the persons of authority gathered round to inspect the wonderful birds upon which, apparently, momentous affairs depended. When the group separated, the sailor was to be seen bending over the edge of the car to deposit the cage safely. He then got into the car, still smoking his pipe, and perched himself negligently on the wicker-work. The man with the watch was conversing with Chirac; Chirac nodded his head frequently in acquiescence, and seemed to be saying all the time: 'Yes, sir! Perfectly, sir! I understand, sir! Yes, sir!'

Suddenly Chirac turned to the car and put a question to the sailor, who shook his head. Whereupon Chirac gave a gesture of submissive despair to the man with the watch. And in an instant the whole throng was in a ferment.

'The victuals!' cried the man with the watch. 'The victuals, name of God! Must one be indeed an idiot to forget the victuals! Name of God – of God!'

Sophia smiled at the agitation, and at the inefficient management which had never thought of food. For it appeared that the food had not merely been forgotten; it was a question which had not ever been considered. She could not help despising all that crowd of self-important and fussy males to whom the idea had not occurred that even balloonists must eat. And she wondered whether everything was done like that. After a delay that seemed very long, the problem of victuals was solved, chiefly, as far as Sophia could judge, by means of cakes of chocolate and bottles of wine.

'It is enough! It is enough!' Chirac shouted passionately several times to a knot of men who began to argue with him.

Then he gazed round furtively, and with an inflation of the

chest and a patting of his fur coat he came directly towards
Sophia. Evidently Sophia's position had been prearranged between him and Carlier. They could forget food, but they could
think of Sophia's position!

All eyes followed him. Those eyes could not, in the gloom,
distinguish Sophia's beauty, but they could see that she was
young and slim and elegant, and of foreign carriage. That was
enough. The very air seemed to vibrate with the intense curiosity
of those eyes. And immediately Chirac grew into the hero of some
brilliant and romantic adventure. Immediately he was envied and
admired by every man of authority present. What was she? Who
was she? Was it a serious passion or simply a caprice? Had she
flung herself at him? It was undeniable that lovely creatures did
sometimes fling themselves at lucky mediocrities. Was she a
married woman? An artiste? A girl? Such queries thumped
beneath overcoats, while the correctness of a ceremonious demeanour was strictly observed.

Chirac uncovered, and kissed her hand. The wind disarranged
his hair. She saw that his face was very pale and anxious beneath
the swagger of a sincere desire to be brave.

'Well, it is the moment!' he said.

'Did you all forget the food?' she asked.

He shrugged his shoulders. 'What will you? One cannot think
of everything.'

'I hope you will have a safe voyage,' she said.

She had already taken leave of him once, in the house, and
heard all about the balloon and the sailor-aeronaut and the
preparations; and now she had nothing to say, nothing whatever.

He shrugged his shoulders again. 'I hope so!' he murmured, but
in a tone to convey that he had no such hope.

'The wind isn't too strong?' she suggested.

He shrugged his shoulders again. 'What would you?'

'Is it in the direction you want?'

'Yes, nearly,' he admitted unwillingly. Then rousing himself:
'Eh, well, madame. You have been extremely amiable to come. I
held to it very much – that you should come. It is because of you I
quit Paris.'

She resented the speech by a frown.

'Ah!' he implored in a whisper. 'Do not do that. Smile on me. After all, it is not my fault. Remember that this may be the last time I see you, the last time I regard your eyes.'

She smiled. She was convinced of the genuineness of the emotion which expressed itself in all this flamboyant behaviour. And she had to make excuses to herself on behalf of Chirac. She smiled to give him pleasure. The hard common sense in her might sneer, but indubitably she was the centre of a romantic episode. The balloon darkly swinging there! The men waiting! The secrecy of the mission! And Chirac, bareheaded in the wind that was to whisk him away, telling her in fatalistic accents that her image had devastated his life, while envious aspirants watched their colloquy! Yes, it was romantic. And she was beautiful! Her beauty was an active reality that went about the world playing tricks in spite of herself. The thoughts that passed through her mind were the large, splendid thoughts of romance. And it was Chirac who had aroused them! A real drama existed, then, triumphing over the accidental absurdities and pettinesses of the situation. Her final words to Chirac were tender and encouraging.

He hurried back to the balloon, resuming his cap. He was received with the respect due to one who comes fresh from conquest. He was sacred.

Sophia rejoined Carlier, who had withdrawn, and began to talk to him with a self-conscious garrulity. She spoke without reason and scarcely noticed what she was saying. Already Chirac was snatched out of her life, as other beings, so many of them, had been snatched. She thought of their first meetings, and of the sympathy which had always united them. He had lost his simplicity now, in the self-created crisis of his fate, and had sunk in her esteem. And she was determined to like him all the more because he had sunk in her esteem. She wondered whether he really had undertaken this adventure from sentimental disappointment. She wondered whether, if she had not forgotten to wind her watch one night, they would still have been living quietly under the same roof in the Rue Bréda.

The sailor climbed definitely into the car; he had covered himself with a large cloak. Chirac had got one leg over the side of the car, and eight men were standing by the rope, when a horse's hoofs clattered through the guarded entrance to the courtyard, amid an uproar of sudden excitement. The shiny chest of the horse was flecked with the classic foam.

'A telegram from the Governor of Paris!'

As the orderly, checking his mount, approached the group, even the old man with the watch raised his hat. The orderly responded, bent down to make an inquiry, which Chirac answered, and then, with another exchange of salutes, the official telegram was handed over to Chirac, and the horse backed away from the crowd. It was quite thrilling. Carlier was thrilled.

'He is never too prompt, the Governor. It is a quality!' said Carlier, with irony.

Chirac entered the car. And then the old man with the watch drew a black bag from the shadow behind him and entrusted it to Chirac, who accepted it with a profound deference and hid it. The sailor began to issue commands. The men at the ropes were bending down now. Suddenly the balloon rose about a foot and trembled. The sailor continued to shout. All the persons of authority gazed motionless at the balloon. The moment of suspense was eternal.

'Let go all!' cried the sailor, standing up, and clinging to the cordage. Chirac was seated in the car, a mass of dark fur with a small patch of white in it. The men at the ropes were a knot of struggling confused figures.

One side of the car tilted up, and the sailor was nearly pitched out. Three men at the other side had failed to free the ropes.

'Let go, corpses!' the sailor yelled at them.

The balloon jumped, as if it were drawn by some terrific impulse from the skies.

'Adieu!' called Chirac, pulling his cap off and waving it. 'Adieu!'

'Bon voyage! Bon voyage!' the little crowd cheered. And then, 'Vive la France!' Throats tightened, including Sophia's.

But the top of the ballon had leaned over, destroying its pear shape, and the whole mass swerved violently towards the wall of the station, the car swinging under it like a toy, and an anchor under the car. There was a cry of alarm. Then the great ball

leaped again, and swept over the high glass roof, escaping by
inches the spouting. The cheers expired instantly . . . The balloon
was gone. It was spirited away as if by some furious and mighty
power that had grown impatient in waiting for it. There remained
for a few seconds on the collective retina of the spectators a
vision of the inclined car swinging near the roof like the tail
of a kite. And then nothing! Blackness! Blackness! Already the
balloon was lost to sight in the vast stormy ocean of the
night, a plaything of the winds. The spectators became once
more aware of the dull booming of the cannonade. The balloon
was already perhaps flying unseen amid the wrack over those
guns.

Sophia involuntarily caught her breath. A chill sense of loneliness, of purposelessness, numbed her being.

Nobody ever saw Chirac or the old sailor again. The sea must
have swallowed them. Of the sixty-five balloons that left Paris
during the siege, two were not heard of. This was the first of the
two. Chirac had, at any rate, not magnified the peril, though his
intention was undoubtedly to magnify it.

III

This was the end of Sophia's romantic adventures in France. Soon
afterwards the Germans entered Paris, by mutual agreement, and
made a point of seeing the Louvre, and departed, amid the silence
of a city. For Sophia the conclusion of the siege meant chiefly that
prices went down. Long before supplies from outside could reach
Paris, the shop-windows were suddenly full of goods which had
arrived from the shopkeepers alone knew where. Sophia, with the
stock in her cellar, could have held out for several weeks more,
and it annoyed her that she had not sold more of her good things
while good things were worth gold. The signing of a treaty at
Versailles reduced the value of Sophia's two remaining hams
from about five pounds apiece to the usual price of hams.
However, at the end of January she found herself in possession of
a capital of about eight thousand francs, all the furniture of the
flat, and a reputation. She had earned it all. Nothing could
destroy the structure of her beauty, but she looked worn and
appreciably older. She wondered often when Chirac would re-

turn. She might have written to Carlier or to the paper; but she did not. It was Niepce who discovered in a newspaper that Chirac's balloon had miscarried. At the moment the news did not affect her at all; but after several days she began to feel her loss in a dull sort of way; and she felt it more and more, though never acutely. She was perfectly convinced that Chirac could never have attracted her powerfully. She continued to dream, at rare intervals, of the kind of passion that would have satisfied her, glowing but banked down like a fire in some fine chamber of a rich but careful household.

She was speculating upon what her future would be, and whether by inertia she was doomed to stay for ever in the Rue Bréda, when the Commune[12] caught her. She was more vexed than frightened by the Commune; vexed that a city so in need of repose and industry should indulge in such antics. For many people the Commune was a worse experience than the siege; but not for Sophia. She was a woman and a foreigner. Niepce was infinitely more disturbed than Sophia; he went in fear of his life. Sophia would go out to market and take her chance. It is true that during one period the whole population of the house went to live in the cellars, and orders to the butcher and other tradesmen were given over the party-wall into the adjoining courtyard, which communicated with an alley. A strange existence, and possibly perilous! But the women who passed through it, and had also passed through the siege, were not very much intimidated by it, unless they happened to have husbands or lovers who were active politicians.

Sophia did not cease, during the greater part of the year 1871, to make a living and to save money. She watched every sou, and she developed a tendency to demand from her tenants all that they could pay. She excused this to herself by ostentatiously declaring every detail of her prices in advance. It came to the same thing in the end, with this advantage, that the bills did not lead to unpleasantness. Her difficulties commenced when Paris at last definitely resumed its normal aspect and life, when all the women and children came back to those city termini which they had left in such huddled, hysterical throngs, when flats were re-opened that had long been shut, and men who for a whole year had had the disadvantages and the advantages of being without wife and family, anchored themselves once more to the hearth. Then it was that Sophia failed to keep all her rooms let. She could have let them easily and constantly and at high rents; but not to men without encumbrances. Nearly every day she refused attractive tenants in pretty hats, or agreeable gentlemen who only wanted a room on condition that they might offer hospitality to a dashing petticoat. It was useless to proclaim aloud that her house was 'serious'. The ambition of the majority of these joyous persons was to live in a 'serious' house, because each was sure that at bottom he or she was a 'serious' person, and quite different from the rest of the joyous world. The character of Sophia's flat, instead of repelling the wrong kind of aspirant, infallibly drew just that kind. Hope was inextinguishable in these bosoms. They heard that there would be no chance for them at Sophia's; but they tried nevertheless. And occasionally Sophia would make a mistake, and grave unpleasantness would occur before the mistake could be rectified. The fact was that the street was too much for her. Few people would credit that there was a serious boarding-house in the Rue Bréda. The police themselves would not credit it. And Sophia's beauty was against her. At that time the Rue Bréda was perhaps the most notorious street in the centre of Paris; at the height of its reputation as a warren of individual improprieties; most busily creating that prejudice against itself which, over thirty years later, forced the authorities to change its name in obedience to the wish of its tradesmen. When Sophia went out at about eleven o'clock in the morning with her reticule to buy, the street was littered with women who had gone out with reticules to buy. But whereas Sophia was fully dressed, and wore headgear, the others were in dressing-gown and slippers, or opera-cloak and slippers, having slid directly out of unspeakable beds and omitted to brush their hair out of their puffy eyes. In the little shops of the Rue Bréda, the Rue Notre Dame de Lorette, and the Rue des Martyrs, you were very close indeed to the primitive instincts of human nature. It was wonderful; it was amusing; it was excitingly picturesque; and the universality of the manners rendered moral indignation absurd. But the neighbourhood was certainly not one in which a woman of Sophia's race, training, and character could comfortably earn a living, or even exist. She could not fight against the entire street. She, and not the street, was out of place and in the wrong. Little wonder that the neighbours lifted their shoulders when they spoke of her! What beautiful woman but a mad Englishwoman would have had the idea of establishing herself in the Rue Bréda with the intention of living like a nun and compelling others to do the same?

By dint of continual ingenuity, Sophia contrived to win somewhat more than her expenses, but she was slowly driven to admit to herself that the situation could not last.

Then one day she saw in *Galignani's Messenger* an advertisement of an English Pension for sale in the Rue Lord Byron, in the Champs Elysées quarter. It belonged to some people named Frensham, and had enjoyed a certain popularity before the war. The proprietor and his wife, however, had not sufficiently allowed for the vicissitudes of politics in Paris. Instead of saving money during their popularity, they had put it on the back and on the fingers of Mrs Frensham. The siege and the Commune had almost ruined them. With capital they might have restored themselves to their former pride; but their capital was exhausted. Sophia answered the advertisement. She impressed the Frenshams, who were delighted with the prospect of dealing in business with an honest English face. Like many English people abroad, they were most strangely obsessed by the notion that they had quitted an island of honest men to live among thieves and robbers. They always implied that dishonesty was unknown in Britain. They offered, if she would take over the lease, to sell all their furniture and their renown for ten thousand francs. She declined, the price seeming absurd to her. When they asked her to name a price, she said that she preferred not to do so. Upon entreaty, she said four thousand francs. They then allowed her to see that they considered her to have been quite right in hesitating to name a price so ridiculous. And their confidence in the honest English face seemed to have been shocked. Sophia left. When she got back to the Rue Bréda she was relieved that the matter had come to nothing. She did not precisely foresee what her future was to be, but at any rate she knew she shrank from the responsibility of the Pension Frensham. The next morning she received a letter offering to accept six thousand. She wrote and declined. She was indifferent, and she would not budge from four thousand. The Frenshams gave way. They were pained, but they gave way. The glitter of four thousand francs in cash, and freedom, was too tempting.

Thus Sophia became the proprietress of the Pension Frensham in the cold and correct Rue Lord Byron. She made room in it for nearly all her other furniture, so that instead of being under-furnished, as pensions usually are, it was over-furnished. She was extremely timid at first, for the rent alone was four thousand francs a year; and the prices of the quarter were alarming-ly different from those of the Rue Bréda. She lost a lot of sleep. For some nights, after she had been installed in the Rue Lord Byron about a fortnight, she scarcely slept at all, and she ate no more than she slept. She cut down expenditure to the very lowest, and frequently walked over to the Rue Bréda to do her marketing. With the aid of a charwoman at six sous an hour she accomplished everything. And though clients were few, the feat was in the nature of a miracle; for Sophia had to cook.

The articles which George Augustus Sala[13] wrote under the title 'Paris herself again' ought to have been paid for in gold by the hotel and pension-keepers of Paris. They awakened the English curiosity and the desire to witness the scene of terrible events. Their effect was immediately noticeable. In less than a year after her adventurous purchase, Sophia had acquired confidence, and she was employing two servants, working them very hard at low wages. She had also acquired the landlady's manner. She was known as Mrs Frensham. Across the balconies of two windows the Frenshams had left a gilded sign, 'Pension Frensham', and Sophia had not removed it. She often explained that her name was not Frensham; but in vain. Every visitor inevitably and persistently addressed her according to the sign. It was past the general comprehension that the proprietress of the Pension Fren-sham might bear another name than Frensham. But later there came into being a class of persons, habitués of the Pension Frensham, who knew the real name of the proprietress and were proud of knowing it, and by this knowledge were distinguished from the herd. What struck Sophia was the astounding similarity of her guests. They all asked the same questions, made the same exclamations, went out on the same excursions, returned with the same judgements, and exhibited the same unimpaired assurance that foreigners were really very peculiar people. They never seemed to advance in knowledge. There was a constant stream of explorers from England who had to be set on their way to the Louvre or the Bon Marché.

Sophia's sole interest was in her profits. The excellence of her house was firmly established. She kept it up, and she kept the modest prices up. Often she had to refuse guests. She naturally did so with a certain distant condescension. Her manner to guests increased in stiff formality; and she was excessively firm with undesirables. She grew to be seriously convinced that no Pension as good as hers existed in the world, or ever had existed, or ever could exist. Hers was the acme of niceness and respectability. Her preference for the respectable rose to a passion. And there were no faults in her establishment. Even the once despised showy furniture of Madame Foucault had mysteriously changed into the best conceivable furniture; and its cracks were hallowed.

She never heard a word of Gerald or of her family. In the thousands of people who stayed under her perfect roof, not one mentioned Bursley or disclosed a knowledge of anybody that Sophia had known. Several men had the wit to propose marriage to her with more or less skilfulness, but none of them was skilful enough to perturb her heart. She had forgotten the face of love. She was a landlady. She was *the* landlady: efficient, stylish, diplomatic, and tremendously experienced. There was no trickery, no baseness of Parisian life that she was not acquainted with and armed against. She could not be startled and she could not be swindled.

Years passed, until there was a vista of years behind her. Sometimes she would think, in an unoccupied moment, 'How strange it is that I should be here, doing what I am doing!' But the regular ordinariness of her existence would instantly seize her again. At the end of 1878, the Exhibition Year, her Pension consisted of two floors instead of one, and she had turned the two hundred pounds stolen from Gerald into over two thousand.

BOOK FOUR: WHAT LIFE IS

CHAPTER I: *Frensham's*

I

Matthew Peel-Swynnerton sat in the long dining-room of the
Pension Frensham, Rue Lord Byron, Paris; and he looked out of
place there. It was an apartment about thirty feet in length, and of
the width of two windows, which sufficiently lighted one half of a
very long table with round ends. The gloom of the other extremity was illumined by a large mirror in a tarnished gilt frame,
which filled a good portion of the wall opposite the windows.
Near the mirror was a high folding-screen of four leaves, and
behind this screen could be heard the sound of a door continually
shutting and opening. In the long wall to the left of the windows
were two doors, one dark and important, a door of state, through
which a procession of hungry and a procession of sated solemn
self-conscious persons passed twice daily, and the other, a smaller
door, glazed, its glass painted with wreaths of roses, not an
original door of the house, but a late breach in the wall, that
seemed to lead to the dangerous and to the naughty. The wall-
paper and the window drapery were rich and forbidding, dark in
hue, mysterious of pattern. Over the state-door was a pair of
antlers. And at intervals, so high up as to defy inspection,
engravings and oil-paintings made oblong patches on the walls.
They were hung from immense nails with porcelain heads, and
they appeared to depict the more majestic aspect of man and
nature. One engraving, over the mantelpiece and nearer earth
than the rest, unmistakably showed Louis Philippe and his family
in attitudes of virtue. Beneath this royal group, a vast gilt clock,
flanked by pendants of the same period, gave the right time – a
quarter past seven.

And down the room, filling it, ran the great white table,
bordered with bowed heads and the backs of chairs. There were
over thirty people at the table, and the peculiarly restrained

noisiness of their knives and forks on the plates proved that they
were a discreet and a correct people. Their clothes – blouses,
bodices, and jackets – did not flatter the lust of the eye. Only two
or three were in evening dress. They spoke little, and generally in
a timorous tone, as though silence had been enjoined. Somebody
would half-whisper a remark, and then his neighbour, absently
fingering her bread and lifting gaze from her plate into vacancy,
would conscientiously weigh the remark and half-whisper in
reply: 'I dare say.' But a few spoke loudly and volubly, and were
regarded by the rest, who envied them, as underbred.

Food was quite properly the chief preoccupation. The diners
ate as those eat who are paying a fixed price per day for as much
as they can consume while observing the rules of the game.
Without moving their heads they glanced out of the corners of
their eyes, watching the manoeuvres of the three starched maids
who served. They had no conception of food save as portions laid
out in rows on large silver dishes, and when a maid bent over
them deferentially, balancing the dish, they summed up the
offering in an instant, and in an instant decided how much they
could decently take, and to what extent they could practise the
theoretic liberty of choice. And if the food for any reason did not
tempt them, or if it egregiously failed to coincide with their
aspirations, they considered themselves aggrieved. For, according to the game, they might not command; they had the right to
seize all that was presented under their noses, like genteel tigers;
and they had the right to refuse; that was all. The dinner was thus
a series of emotional crises for the diners, who knew only that full
dishes and clean plates came endlessly from the banging door
behind the screen, and that ravaged dishes and dirty plates
vanished endlessly through the same door. They were all eating
similar food simultaneously; they began together and they
finished together. The flies that haunted the paper-bunches which
hung from the chandeliers to the level of the flower-vases, were
more free. The sole event that chequered the exact regularity of
the repast was the occasional arrival of a wine-bottle for one of
the guests. The receiver of the wine-bottle signed a small paper in
exchange for it and wrote largely a number on the label of the
bottle; then, staring at the number and fearing that after all it

might be misread by a stupid maid or an unscrupulous compeer, he would re-write the number on another part of the label, even more largely.

Matthew Peel-Swynnerton obviously did not belong to this world. He was a young man of twenty-five or so, not handsome, but elegant. Though he was not in evening dress, though he was, as a fact, in a very light grey suit, entirely improper to a dinner, he was elegant. The suit was admirably cut, and nearly new; but he wore it as though he had never worn anything else. Also his demeanour, reserved yet free from self-consciousness, his method of handling a knife and fork, the niceties of his manner in transferring food from the silver dishes to his plate, the tone in which he ordered half a bottle of wine – all these details infallibly indicated to the company that Matthew Peel-Swynnerton was their superior. Some folks hoped that he was the son of a lord, or even a lord. He happened to be fixed at the end of the table, with his back to the window, and there was a vacant chair on either side of him; this situation favoured the hope of his high rank. In truth, he was the son, the grandson, and several times the nephew, of earthenware manufacturers. He noticed that the large 'compote' (as it was called in his trade) which marked the centre of the table, was the production of his firm. This surprised him, for Peel, Swynnerton and Co., known and revered throughout the Five Towns as 'Peels', did not cater for cheap markets.

A late guest startled the room, a fat, flabby, middle-aged man whose nose would have roused the provisional hostility of those who have convinced themselves that Jews are not as other men. His nose did not definitely brand him as a usurer and a murderer of Christ, but it was suspicious. His clothes hung loose, and might have been anybody's clothes. He advanced with brisk assurance to the table, bowed, somewhat too effusively, to several people, and sat down next to Peel-Swynnerton. One of the maids at once brought him a plate of soup, and he said: 'Thank you, Marie,' smiling at her. He was evidently a habitué of the house. His spectacled eyes beamed the superiority which comes of knowing girls by their names. He was seriously handicapped in the race for sustenance, being two and a half courses behind, but he drew level with speed and then, having accomplished this, he sighed, and pointedly engaged Peel-Swynnerton with his sociable glance.

'Ah!' he breathed out. 'Nuisance when you come in late, sir!'

Peel-Swynnerton gave a reluctant affirmative.

'Doesn't only upset you! It upsets the house. Servants don't like it!'

'No,' murmured Peel-Swynnerton, 'I suppose not.'

'However, it's not often *I*'m late,' said the man. 'Can't help it sometimes. Business! Worst of these French business people is that they've no notion of time. Appointments . . . ! God bless my soul!'

'Do you come here often?' asked Peel-Swynnerton. He detested the fellow, quite inexcusably, perhaps because his serviette was tucked under his chin; but he saw that the fellow was one of your determined talkers, who always win in the end. Moreover, as being clearly not an ordinary tourist in Paris, the fellow mildly excited his curiosity.

'I live here,' said the other. 'Very convenient for a bachelor, you know. Have done for years. My office is just close by. You may know my name – Lewis Mardon.'

Peel-Swynnerton hesitated. The hesitation convicted him of not 'knowing his Paris' well.

'House-agent,' said Lewis Mardon, quickly.

'Oh yes,' said Peel-Swynnerton, vaguely recalling a vision of the name among the advertisements on newspaper kiosks.

'I expect,' Mr Mardon went on, 'my name is as well known as anybody's in Paris.'

'I suppose so,' assented Peel-Swynnerton.

The conversation fell for a few moments.

'Staying here long?' Mr Mardon demanded, having added up Peel-Swynnerton as a man of style and of means, and being puzzled by his presence at that table.

'I don't know,' said Peel-Swynnerton.

This was a lie, justified in the utterer's opinion as a repulse to Mr Mardon's vulgar inquisitiveness, such inquisitiveness as might have been expected from a fellow who tucked his serviette under his chin. Peel-Swynnerton knew exactly how long he would stay. He would stay until the day after the morrow; he had only about fifty francs in his pocket. He had been making a fool of himself in another quarter of Paris, and he had descended to the Pension

Frensham as a place where he could be absolutely sure of spending not more than twelve francs a day. Its reputation was high, and it was convenient for the Galliéra Museum, where he was making some drawings which he had come to Paris expressly to make, and without which he could not reputably return to England. He was capable of foolishness, but he was also capable of wisdom, and scarcely any pressure of need would have induced him to write home for money to replace the money spent on making himself into a fool.

Mr Mardon was conscious of a check. But, being of an accommodating disposition, he at once tried another direction.

'Good food here, eh?' he suggested.

'Very,' said Peel-Swynnerton, with sincerity. 'I was quite –'

At that moment, a tall straight woman of uncertain age pushed open the principal door and stood for an instant in the doorway. Peel-Swynnerton had just time to notice that she was handsome and pale, and that her hair was black, and then she was gone again, followed by a clipped poodle that accompanied her. She had signed with a brief gesture to one of the servants, who at once set about lighting the gas-jets over the table.

'Who is that?' asked Peel-Swynnerton, without reflecting that it was now he who was making advances to the fellow whose napkin covered all his shirt-front.

'That's the missis, that is,' said Mr Mardon, in a lower and semi-confidential voice.

'Oh! Mrs Frensham?'

'Yes. But her real name is Scales,' said Mr Mardon, proudly.

'Widow, I suppose?'

'Yes.'

'And she runs the whole show?'

'She runs the entire contraption,' said Mr Mardon, solemnly; 'and don't you make any mistake!' He was getting familiar.

Peel-Swynnerton beat him off once more, glancing with careful, uninterested nonchalance at the gas-burners which exploded one after another with a little plop under the application of the maid's taper. The white table gleamed more whitely than ever under the flaring gas. People at the end of the room away from the window instinctively smiled, as though the sun had begun to shine. The aspect of the dinner was changed, ameliorated; and with the reiterated statement that the evenings were drawing in though it was only July, conversation became almost general. In two minutes Mr Mardon was genially talking across the whole length of the table. The meal finished in a state that resembled conviviality.

Matthew Peel-Swynnerton might not go out into the crepuscular delights of Paris. Unless he remained within the shelter of the Pension, he could not hope to complete successfully his reconversion from folly to wisdom. So he bravely passed through the small rose-embroidered door into a small glass-covered courtyard, furnished with palms, wicker armchairs, and two small tables; and he lighted a pipe and pulled out of his pocket a copy of *The Referee*. That retreat was called the Lounge; it was the only part of the Pension where smoking was not either a positive crime or a transgression against good form. He felt lonely. He said to himself grimly in one breath that pleasure was all rot, and in the next he sullenly demanded of the universe how it was that pleasure could not go on for ever, and why he was not Mr Barney Barnato.[14] Two old men entered the retreat and burnt cigarettes with many precautions. Then Mr Lewis Mardon appeared and sat down boldly next to Matthew, like a privileged friend. After all, Mr Mardon was better than nobody whatever, and Matthew decided to suffer him, especially as he began without preliminary skirmishing to talk about life in Paris. An irresistible subject! Mr Mardon said in a worldly tone that the existence of a bachelor in Paris might easily be made agreeable. But that, of course, for himself – well, he preferred, as a general rule, the Pension Frensham sort of thing; and it was excellent for his business. Still he could not . . . he knew . . . He compared the advantages of what he called 'knocking about' in Paris, with the equivalent in London. His information about London was out of date, and Peel-Swynnerton was able to set him right on important details. But his information about Paris was infinitely precious and interesting to the younger man, who saw that he had hitherto lived under strange misconceptions.

'Have a whisky?' asked Mr Mardon, suddenly. 'Very good here!' he added.

'Thanks!' drawled Peel-Swynnerton.

The temptation to listen to Mr Mardon as long as Mr Mardon would talk was not to be overcome. And presently, when the old men had departed, they were frankly telling each other stories in the dimness of the retreat. Then, when the supply of stories came to an end, Mr Mardon smacked his lips over the last drop of whisky and ejaculated: 'Yes!' as if giving a general confirmation to all that had been said.

'Do have one with me,' said Matthew, politely. It was the least he could do.

The second supply of whiskies was brought into the Lounge by Mr Mardon's Marie. He smiled on her familiarly, and remarked that he supposed she would soon be going to bed after a hard day's work. She gave a *moue* and a flounce in reply, and swished out.

'Carries herself well, doesn't she?' observed Mr Mardon, as though Marie had been an exhibit at an agricultural show. 'Ten years ago she was very fresh and pretty, but of course it takes it out of 'em, a place like this!'

'But still,' said Peel-Swynnerton, 'they must like it or they wouldn't stay – that is, unless things are very different here from what they are in England.'

The conversation seemed to have stimulated him to examine the woman question in all its bearings, with philosophic curiosity.

'Oh! They *like* it,' Mr Mardon assured him, as one who knew. 'Besides, Mrs Scales treats 'em very well. I know *that*. She's told me. She's very particular' – he looked around to see if walls had ears – 'and, by Jove, you've got to be; but she treats 'em well. You'd scarcely believe the wages they get, and pickings. Now at the Hotel Moscow – know the Hotel Moscow?'

Happily Peel-Swynnerton did. He had been advised to avoid it because it catered exclusively for English visitors, but in the Pension Frensham he had accepted something even more exclusively British than the Hotel Moscow. Mr Mardon was quite relieved at his affirmative.

'The Hotel Moscow is a limited company now,' said he; 'English.'

'Really?'

'Yes. I floated it. It was my idea. A great success! That's how I know all about the Hotel Moscow.' He looked at the walls again. 'I wanted to do the same here,' he murmured, and Peel-Swynnerton had to show that he appreciated this confidence. 'But she never would agree. I've tried her all ways. No go! It's a thousand pities.'

'Paying thing, eh?'

'This place? I should say it was! And I ought to be able to judge, I reckon. Mrs Scales is one of the shrewdest women you'd meet in a day's march. She's made a lot of money here, a lot of money. And there's no reason why a place like this shouldn't be five times as big as it is. Ten times. The scope's unlimited, my dear sir. All that's wanted is capital. Naturally she has capital of her own, and she could get more. But then, as she says, she doesn't want the place any bigger. She says it's now just as big as she can handle. That isn't so. She's a woman who could handle anything – a born manager – but even if it was so, all she would have to do would be to retire – only leave us the place and the name. It's the name that counts. And she's made the name of Frensham worth something, I can tell you!'

'Did she get the place from her husband?' asked Peel-Swynnerton. Her own name of Scales intrigued him.

Mr Mardon shook his head. 'Bought it on her own, after the husband's time, for a song – a song! I know, because I knew the original Frenshams.'

'You must have been in Paris a long time,' said Peel-Swynnerton.

Mr Mardon could never resist an opportunity to talk about himself. His was a wonderful history. And Peel-Swynnerton, while scorning the man for his fatuity, was impressed. And when that was finished –

'Yes!' said Mr Mardon after a pause, reaffirming everything in general by a single monosyllable.

Shortly afterwards he rose, saying that his habits were regular.

'Good night,' he said with a mechanical smile.

'G-good night,' said Peel-Swynnerton, trying to force the tone of fellowship and not succeeding. Their intimacy which had sprung up like a mushroom, suddenly fell into dust. Peel-

Swynnerton's unspoken comment to Mr Mardon's back was:
'Ass!' Still, the sum of Peel-Swynnerton's knowledge had indubitably been increased during the evening. And the hour was
yet early. Half past ten! The Folies-Marigny, with its beautiful
architecture and its crowds of white toilettes, and its frothing of
champagne and of beer, and its musicians in tight red coats, was
just beginning to be alive – and at a distance of scarcely a
stone's-throw! Peel-Swynnerton pictured the terraced, glittering
hall, which had been the prime origin of his exceeding foolishness. And he pictured all the other resorts, great and small,
garlanded with white lanterns, in the Champs Elysées; and the
sombre aisles of the Champs Elysées where mysterious pale figures walked troublingly under the shade of trees, while snatches
of wild song or absurd brassy music floated up from the resorts
and restaurants. He wanted to go out and spend those fifty francs
that remained in his pocket. After all, why not telegraph to
England for more money? 'Oh, damn it!' he said savagely, and
stretched his arms and got up. The Lounge was very small,
gloomy and dreary.

One brilliant incandescent light burned in the hall, crudely
illuminating the wicker fauteuils, a corded trunk with a blue-and-
red label on it, a Fitzroy barometer, a map of Paris, a coloured
poster of the Compagnie Transatlantique, and the mahogany
retreat of the hall-portress. In that retreat was not only the
hall-portress – an aged woman with a white cap above her
wrinkled pink face – but the mistress of the establishment. They
were murmuring together softly; they seemed to be well disposed
to one another. The portress was respectful, but the mistress was
respectful also. The hall, with its one light tranquilly burning,
was bathed in an honest calm, the calm of a day's work accomplished, of gradual relaxation from tension, of growing expectation of repose. In its simplicity it affected Peel-Swynnerton as a
medicine tonic for nerves might have affected him. In that hall,
though exterior nocturnal life was but just stirring into activity, it
seemed that the middle of the night had come, and that these two
women alone watched in a mansion full of sleepers. And all the
recitals which Peel-Swynnerton and Mr Mardon had exchanged
sank to the level of pitiably foolish gossip. Peel-Swynnerton felt

that his duty to the house was to retire to bed. He felt, too, that he could not leave the house without saying that he was going out, and that he lacked the courage deliberately to tell these two women he was going out – at that time of night! He dropped into one of the chairs and made a second attempt to peruse *The Referee*. Useless! Either his mind was outside in the Champs Elysées, or his gaze would wander surreptitiously to the figure of Mrs Scales. He could not well distinguish her face because it was in the shadow of the mahogany.

Then the portress came forth from her box, and, slightly bent, sped actively across the hall, smiling pleasantly at the guest as she passed him, and disappeared up the stairs. The mistress was alone in the retreat. Peel-Swynnerton jumped up brusquely, dropping the paper with a rustle, and approached her.

'Excuse me,' he said deferentially. 'Have any letters come for me tonight?'

He knew that the arrival of letters for him was impossible, since nobody knew his address.

'What name?' The question was coldly polite, and the questioner looked him full in the face. Undoubtedly she was a handsome woman. Her hair was greying at the temples, and the skin was withered and crossed with lines. But she was handsome. She was one of those women of whom to their last on earth the stranger will say: 'When she was young she must have been worth looking at!' – with a little transient regret that beautiful young women cannot remain for ever young. Her voice was firm and even, sweet in tone, and yet morally harsh from incessant traffic with all varieties of human nature. Her eyes were the impartial eyes of one who is always judging. And evidently she was a proud, even a haughty creature, with her careful, controlled politeness. Evidently she considered herself superior to no matter what guest. Her eyes announced that she had lived and learnt, that she knew more about life than anyone whom she was likely to meet, and that having pre-eminently succeeded in life, she had tremendous confidence in herself. The proof of her success was the unique Frensham's. A consciousness of the uniqueness of Frensham's was also in those eyes. Theoretically Matthew Peel-Swynnerton's mental attitude towards lodging-house keepers was condescending, but here it was not condescending. It had the real respectfulness of a man who for the moment at any rate is impressed beyond his calculations. His glance fell as he said –

'Peel-Swynnerton.' Then he looked up again.

He said the words awkwardly, and rather fearfully, as if aware that he was playing with fire. If this Mrs Scales was the long-vanished aunt of his friend, Cyril Povey, she must know those two names, locally so famous. Did she start? Did she show a sign of being perturbed? At first he thought he detected a symptom of emotion, but in an instant he was sure that he had detected nothing of the sort, and that it was silly to suppose that he was treading on the edge of a romance. Then she turned towards the letter-rack at her side, and he saw her face in profile. It bore a sudden and astonishing likeness to the profile of Cyril Povey; a resemblance unmistakable and finally decisive. The nose and the curve of the upper lip were absolutely Cyril's. Matthew Peel-Swynnerton felt very queer. He felt like a criminal in peril of being caught in the act, and he could not understand why he should feel so. The landlady looked in the 'P' pigeon-hole, and in the 'S' pigeon-hole.

'No,' she said quietly, 'I see nothing for you.'

Taken with a swift rash audacity, he said: 'Have you had anyone named Povey here recently?'

'Povey?'

'Yes. Cyril Povey, of Bursley – in the Five Towns.'

He was very impressionable, very sensitive, was Matthew Peel-Swynnerton. His voice trembled as he spoke. But hers also trembled in reply.

'Not that I remember! No! Were you expecting him to be here?'

'Well, it wasn't at all sure,' he muttered. 'Thank you. Good night.'

'Good night,' she said, apparently with the simple perfunctoriness of the landlady who says good night to dozens of strangers every evening.

He hurried away upstairs, and met the portress coming down. 'Well, well!' he thought. 'Of all the queer things –!' And he kept nodding his head. At last he had encountered something *really* strange in the spectacle of existence. It had fallen to him to discover the legendary woman who had fled from Bursley before he was born, and of whom nobody knew anything. What news for Cyril! What a staggering episode! He had scarcely any sleep that night. He wondered whether he would be able to meet Mrs Scales without self-consciousness on the morrow. However, he was spared the curious ordeal of meeting her. She did not appear at all on the following day; nor did he see her before he left. He could not find a pretext for asking why she was invisible.

II

The hansom of Matthew Peel-Swynnerton drew up in front of No. 26, Victoria Grove, Chelsea; his kit-bag was on the roof of the cab. The cabman had a red flower in his buttonhole. Matthew leaped out of the vehicle, holding his straw hat on his head with one hand. On reaching the pavement he checked himself suddenly and became carelessly calm. Another straw-hatted and grey-clad figure was standing at the side-gate of No. 26 in the act of lighting a cigarette.

'Hello, Matt!' exclaimed the second figure, languidly, and in a veiled voice due to the fact that he was still holding the match to the cigarette and puffing. 'What's the meaning of all this fluster? You're just the man I want to see.'

He threw away the match with a wave of the arm, and took Matthew's hand for a moment, blowing a double shaft of smoke through his nose.

'I want to see you, too,' said Matthew. 'And I've only got a minute. I'm on my way to Euston. I must catch the twelve-five.'

He looked at his friend, and could positively see no feature of it that was not a feature of Mrs Scales's face. Also, the elderly woman held her body in exactly the same way as the young man. It was entirely disconcerting.

'Have a cigarette,' answered Cyril Povey, imperturbably. He was two years younger than Matthew, from whom he had acquired most of his vast and intricate knowledge of life and art, with certain leading notions of deportment; whose pupil indeed he was in all the things that matter to young men. But he had already surpassed his professor. He could pretend to be old much more successfully than Matthew could.

The cabman approvingly watched the ignition of the second cigarette, and then the cabman pulled out a cigar, and showed his large, white teeth, as he bit the end off it. The appearance and manner of his fare, the quality of the kit-bag, and the opening gestures of the interview between the two young dukes, had put the cabman in an optimistic mood. He had no apprehensions of miserly and ungentlemanly conduct by his fare upon the arrival at Euston. He knew the language of the tilt of a straw hat. And it was a magnificent day in London. The group of the two elegances dominated by the perfection of the cabman made a striking tableau of triumphant masculinity, content with itself, and needing nothing.

Matthew lightly took Cyril's arm and drew him farther down the street, past the gate leading to the studio (hidden behind a house) which Cyril rented.

'Look here, my boy,' he began, 'I've found your aunt.'

'Well, that's very nice of you,' said Cyril, solemnly. 'That's a friendly act. May I ask what aunt?'

'Mrs Scales,' said Matthew. 'You know –'

'Not the –' Cyril's face changed.

'Yes, precisely!' said Matthew, feeling that he was not being cheated of the legitimate joy caused by making a sensation. Assuredly he had made a sensation in Victoria Grove.

When he had related the whole story, Cyril said: 'Then she doesn't know you know?'

'I don't think so. No, I'm sure she doesn't. She may guess.'

'But how can you be certain you haven't made a mistake? It may be that –'

'Look here, my boy,' Matthew interrupted him. 'I've not made any mistake.'

'But you've no proof.'

'Proof be damned!' said Matthew, nettled. 'I tell you it's *her*!'

'Oh! All right! All right! What puzzles me most is what the devil you were doing in a place like that. According to your description of it, it must be a –'

'I went there because I was broke,' said Matthew.

'Razzle?'

Matthew nodded.

'Pretty stiff, that!' commented Cyril, when Matthew had narrated the prologue to Frensham's.

'Well, she absolutely swore she never took less than two hundred francs. And she looked it, too! And she was worth it! I had the time of my life with that woman. I can tell you one thing – no more English for me! They simply aren't in it.'

'How old was she?'

Matthew reflected judicially. 'I should say she was thirty.' The gaze of admiration and envy was upon him. He had the legitimate joy of making a second sensation. 'I'll let you know more about that when I come back,' he added. 'I can open your eyes, my child.'

Cyril smiled sheepishly. 'Why can't you stay now?' he asked. 'I'm going to take the cast of that Verrall girl's arm this afternoon, and I know I can't do it alone. And Robson's no good. You're just the man I want.'

'Can't!' said Matthew.

'Well, come into the studio a minute, anyhow.'

'Haven't time; I shall miss my train.'

'I don't care if you miss forty trains. You must come in. You've got to see that fountain,' Cyril insisted crossly.

Matthew yielded. When they emerged into the street again, after six minutes of Cyril's savage interest in his own work, Matthew remembered Mrs Scales.

'Of course you'll write to your mother?' he said.

'Yes, said Cyril, 'I'll write; but if you happen to see her, you might tell her.'

'I will,' said Matthew. 'Shall you go over to Paris?'

'What! To see Auntie?' He smiled. 'I don't know. Depends. If the mater will fork out all my exes . . . it's an idea,' he said lightly, and then without any change of tone, 'Naturally, if you're going to idle about here all morning you aren't likely to catch the twelve-five.'

Matthew got into the cab, while the driver, the stump of a cigar between his exposed teeth, leaned forward and lifted the reins away from the tilted straw hat.

'By-the-by, lend me some silver,' Matthew demanded. 'It's a good thing I've got my return ticket. I've run it as fine as ever I did in my life.'

Cyril produced eight shillings in silver. Secure in the possession of these riches, Matthew called to the driver –

'Euston – like hell!'

'Yes, sir,' said the driver calmly.

'Not coming my way, I suppose?' Matthew shouted as an afterthought, just when the cab began to move.

'No. Barber's,' Cyril shouted in answer, and waved his hand.

The horse rattled into Fulham Road.

III

Three days later Matthew Peel-Swynnerton was walking along Bursley Market Place when, just opposite the Town Hall, he met a short, fat, middle-aged lady dressed in black, with a black embroidered mantle, and a small bonnet tied with black ribbon and ornamented with jet fruit and crape leaves. As she stepped slowly and carefully forward she had the dignified, important look of a provincial woman who has always been accustomed to deference in her native town, and whose income is ample enough to extort obsequiousness from the vulgar of all ranks. But immediately she caught sight of Matthew her face changed. She became simple and naïve. She blushed slightly, smiling with a timid pleasure. For her, Matthew belonged to a superior race. He bore the almost sacred name of Peel. His family had been distinguished in the district for generations. 'Peel!' You could without impropriety utter it in the same breath with 'Wedgwood'. And 'Swynnerton' stood not much lower. Neither her self-respect, which was great, nor her common sense, which far exceeded the average, could enable her to extend as far as the Peels the theory that one man is as good as another. The Peels never shopped in St Luke's Square. Even in its golden days the Square could not have expected such a condescension. The Peels shopped in London or in Stafford; at a pinch, in Oldcastle. That was the distinction for the ageing stout lady in black. Why, she had not in six years recovered from her surprise that her son and Matthew Peel-Swynnerton treated each other rudely as equals! She and Matthew did not often meet, but they liked each other. Her involuntary meekness flattered him. And his rather elaborate homage flattered her. He admired her fundamental goodness, and her occasional raps at Cyril seemed to put him into ecstasies of joy.

'Well, Mrs Povey,' he greeted her, standing over her with his hat raised. (It was a fashion he had picked up in Paris.) 'Here I am, you see.'

'You're quite a stranger, Mr Matthew. I needn't ask you how you are. Have you been seeing anything of my boy lately?'

'Not since Wednesday,' said Matthew. 'Of course he's written to you?'

'There's no "of course" about it,' she laughed faintly. 'I had a short letter from him on Wednesday morning. He said you were in Paris.'

'But since that – hasn't he written?'

'If I hear from him on Sunday I shall be lucky, bless ye!' said Constance, grimly. 'It's not letter-writing that will kill Cyril.'

'But do you mean to say he hasn't –' Matthew stopped.

'Whatever's amiss?' asked Constance.

Matthew was at a loss to know what to do or say. 'Oh, nothing.'

'Now, Mr Matthew, do please –' Constance's tone had suddenly quite changed. It had become firm, commanding, and gravely suspicious. The conversation had ceased to be small-talk for her.

Matthew saw how nervous and how fragile she was. He had never noticed before that she was so sensitive to trifles, though it was notorious that nobody could safely discuss Cyril with her in terms of chaff. He was really astounded at that youth's carelessness, shameful carelessness. That Cyril's attitude to his mother was marked by a certain benevolent negligence – this Matthew knew; but not to have written to her with the important news concerning Mrs Scales was utterly inexcusable, and Matthew determined that he would tell Cyril so. He felt very sorry for Mrs Povey. She seemed pathetic to him, standing there in ignorance of a tremendous fact which she ought to have been aware of. He was very content that he had said nothing about Mrs Scales to anybody except his own mother, who had prudently enjoined silence upon him, saying that his one duty, having told Cyril, was to keep his mouth shut until the Poveys talked. Had it not been for his mother's advice he would assuredly have spread the amazing tale, and Mrs Povey might have first heard of it from a stranger's gossip, which would have been too cruel upon her.

'Oh!' Matthew tried to smile gaily, archly. 'You're bound to hear from Cyril to-morrow.'

He wanted to persuade her that he was concealing merely some delightful surprise from her. But he did not succeed. With all his experience of the world and of women, he was not clever enough to deceive that simple woman.

'I'm waiting, Mr Matthew,' she said, in a tone that flattened the smile out of Matthew's sympathetic face. She was ruthless. The fact was, she had in an instant convinced herself that Cyril had met some girl and was engaged to be married. She could think of nothing else. 'What has Cyril been doing?' she added, after a pause.

'It's nothing to do with Cyril,' said he.

'Then what is it?'

'It was about – Mrs Scales,' he murmured, nearly trembling. As she offered no response, merely looking around her in a peculiar fashion, he said: 'Shall we walk along a bit?' And he turned in the direction in which she had been going. She obeyed the suggestion.

'What did ye say?' she asked. The name of Scales for a moment had no significance for her. But when she comprehended it she was afraid, and so she said vacantly, as though wishing to postpone a shock: 'What did ye say?'

'I said it was about Mrs Scales. You know I m-met her in Paris.' And he was saying to himself: 'I ought not to be telling this poor old thing here in the street. But what can I do?'

'Nay, nay!' she muttered.

She stopped and looked at him with a worried expression. Then he observed that the hand that carried her reticule was making strange purposeless curves in the air, and her rosy face went the colour of cream, as though it had been painted with one stroke of an unseen brush. Matthew was very much put about.

'Hadn't you better –' he began.

'Eh,' she said; 'I must sit me –' Her bag dropped.

He supported her to the door of Allman's shop, the iron-monger's. Unfortunately, there were two steps up into the shop, and she could not climb them. She collapsed like a sack of flour on the first step. Young Edward Allman ran to the door. He was wearing a black apron and fidgeting with it in his excitement.

'Don't lift her up – don't try to lift her up, Mr Peel-Swynnerton!' he cried, as Matthew instinctively began to do the wrong thing.

Matthew stopped, looking a fool and feeling one, and he and young Allman contemplated each other helpless for a second across the body of Constance Povey. A part of the Market Place now perceived that the unusual was occurring. It was Mr Shaw-cross, the chemist next door to Allman's, who dealt adequately with the situation. He had seen all, while selling a Kodak to a young lady, and he ran out with salts. Constance recovered very rapidly. She had not quite swooned. She gave a long sigh, and whispered weakly that she was all right. The three men helped her into the lofty dark shop, which smelt of nails and of stove-polish, and she was balanced on a rickety chair.

'My word!' exclaimed young Allman, in his loud voice, when she could smile and the pink was returning reluctantly to her cheeks. 'You mustn't frighten us like that, Mrs Povey!'

Matthew said nothing. He had at last created a genuine sensation. Once again he felt like a criminal, and could not understand why.

Constance announced that she would walk slowly home, down the Cock-yard and along Wedgwood Street. But when, glancing round in her returned strength, she saw the hedge of faces at the doorway, she agreed with Mr Shawcross that she would do better to have a cab. Young Allman went to the door and whistled to the unique cab that stands for ever at the grand entrance to the Town Hall.

'Mr Matthew will come with me,' said Constance.

'Certainly, with pleasure,' said Matthew.

And she passed through the little crowd of gapers on Mr Shawcross's arm.

'Just take care of yourself, missis,' said Mr Shawcross to her, through the window of the cab, 'It's fainting weather, and we're none of us any younger, seemingly.'

She nodded.

'I'm awfully sorry I upset you, Mrs Povey,' said Matthew, when the cab moved.

She shook her head, refusing his apology as unnecessary. Tears filled her eyes. In less than a minute the cab had stopped in front of Constance's light-grained door. She demanded her reticule from Matthew, who had carried it since it fell. She would pay the cabman. Never before had Matthew permitted a woman to pay for a cab in which he had ridden; but there was no arguing with Constance. Constance was dangerous.

Amy Bates, still inhabiting the cave, had seen the cab-wheels through the grating of her window and had panted up the kitchen stairs to open the door ere Constance had climbed the steps. Amy, decidedly over forty, was a woman of authority. She wanted to know what was the matter, and Constance had to tell her that she had 'felt unwell'. Amy took the hat and mantle and departed to prepare a cup of tea. When they were alone Constance said to Matthew:

'Now, Mr Matthew, will you please tell me?'

'It's only this,' he began.

And as he told it, in quite a few words, it indeed had the air of being 'only that'. And yet his voice shook, in sympathy with the ageing woman's controlled but visible emotion. It seemed to him that gladness should have filled the absurd little parlour, but the spirit that presided had no name; it was certainly not joy. He himself felt very sad, desolated. He would have given much money to have been spared the experience. He knew simply that in the memory of the stout, comical, nice woman in the rocking-chair he had stirred old, old things, wakened slumbers that might have been eternal. He did not know that he was sitting on the very spot where the sofa had been on which Samuel Povey lay when a beautiful and shameless young creature of fifteen extracted his tooth. He did not know that Constance was sitting in the very chair in which the memorable Mrs Baines had sat in vain conflict with that same unconquerable girl. He did not know ten thousand matters that were rushing violently about in the vast heart of Constance.

She cross-questioned him in detail. But she did not put the questions which he in his innocence expected; such as, if her sister looked old, if her hair was grey, if she was stout or thin. And until Amy, mystified and resentful, had served the tea, on a little silver tray, she remained comparatively calm. It was in the middle of a gulp of tea that she broke down, and Matthew had to take the cup from her.

'I can't thank you, Mr Matthew,' she wept. 'I couldn't thank you enough.'

'But I've done nothing,' he protested.

She shook her head. 'I never hoped for this. Never hoped for it!' she went on. 'It makes me so happy – in a way . . . You mustn't take any notice of me. I'm silly. You must kindly write down that address for me. And I must write to Cyril at once. And I must see Mr Critchlow.'

'It's really very funny that Cyril hasn't written to you,' said Matthew.

'Cyril has not been a good son,' she said with sudden, solemn coldness. 'To think that he should have kept that . . . !' She wept again.

At length Matthew saw the possibility of leaving. He felt her warm, soft, crinkled hand round his fingers.

'You've behaved very nicely over this,' she said. 'And very cleverly. In *every* thing – both over there and here. Nobody could have shown a nicer feeling than you've shown. It's a great comfort to me that my son has got you for a friend.'

When he thought of his escapades, and of all the knowledge, unutterable in Bursley, fantastically impossible in Bursley, which he had imparted to her son, he marvelled that the maternal instinct should be so deceived. Still, he felt that her praise of him was deserved.

Outside, he gave vent to a 'Phew' of relief. He smiled, in his worldliest manner. But the smile was a sham. A pretence to himself! A childish attempt to disguise from himself how profoundly he had been moved by a natural scene!

IV

On the night when Matthew Peel-Swynnerton spoke to Mrs Scales, Matthew was not the only person in the Pension Frensham who failed to sleep. When the old portress came downstairs from her errand, she observed that her mistress was leaving the mahogany retreat.

'She is sleeping tranquilly, the poor one!' said the portress, discharging her commission, which had been to learn the latest news of the mistress's indisposed dog, Fossette. In saying this her ancient, vibrant voice was rich with sympathy for the suffering animal. And she smiled. She was rather like a figure out of an almshouse, with her pink, apparently brittle skin, her tight black dress, and frilled white cap. She stooped habitually, and always walked quickly, with her head a few inches in advance of her feet. Her grey hair was scanty. She was old; nobody perhaps knew exactly how old. Sophia had taken her with the Pension, over a quarter of a century before, because she was old and could not easily have found another place. Although the *clientèle* was almost exclusively English, she spoke only French, explaining herself to Britons by means of benevolent smiles.

'I think I shall go to bed, Jacqueline,' said the mistress, in reply.

A strange reply, thought Jacqueline. The unalterable custom of Jacqueline was to retire at midnight and to rise at five-thirty. Her mistress also usually retired about midnight, and during the final hour mistress and portress saw a good deal of each other. And considering that Jacqueline had just been sent up into the mistress's own bedroom to glance at Fossette, and that the bulletin was satisfactory, and that madame and Jacqueline had several customary daily matters to discuss, it seemed odd that madame should thus be going instantly to bed. However, Jacqueline said nothing but:

'Very well, madame. And the number 32?'

'Arrange yourself as you can,' said the mistress, curtly.

'It is well, madame. Good evening, madame, and a good night.'

Jacqueline, alone in the hall, re-entered her box and set upon one of those endless, mysterious tasks which occupied her when she was not rushing to and fro or whistling up the tubes.

Sophia, scarcely troubling even to glance into Fossette's round basket, undressed, put out the light, and got into bed. She felt extremely and inexplicably gloomy. She did not wish to reflect; she strongly wished not to reflect; but her mind insisted on reflection – a monotonous, futile, and distressing reflection. Povey! Povey! Could this be Constance's Povey, the unique Samuel Povey? That is to say, not he, but his son, Constance's son. Had Constance a grown-up son? Constance must be over fifty now, perhaps a grandmother! Had she really married Samuel Povey? Possibly she was dead. Certainly her mother must be dead, and Aunt Harriet and Mr Critchlow. If alive, her mother must be at least eighty years of age.

The cumulative effect of merely remaining inactive when one ought to be active, was terrible. Undoubtedly she should have communicated with her family. It was silly not to have done so. After all, even if she had, as a child, stolen a trifle of money from her wealthy aunt, what would that have mattered? She had been proud. She was criminally proud. That was her vice. She admitted it frankly. But she could not alter her pride. Everybody had some weak spot. Her reputation for sagacity, for common sense, was, she knew, enormous; she always felt, when people were talking to her, that they regarded her as a very unusually wise woman. And yet she had been guilty of the capital folly of cutting herself off from her family. She was ageing, and she was alone in the world. She was enriching herself; she had the most perfectly managed and the most respectable Pension in the world (she sincerely believed), and she was alone in the world. Acquaintances she had – French people who never offered nor accepted hospitality other than tea or wine, and one or two members of the English commercial colony – but her one friend was Fossette, aged three years! She was the most solitary person on earth. She had heard no word of Gerald, no word of anybody. Nobody whatever could truly be interested in her fate. This was what she had achieved after a quarter of a century of ceaseless labour and anxiety, during which she had not once been away from the Rue Lord Byron for more than thirty hours at a stretch. It was appalling – the passage of years; and the passage of years would grow more appalling. Ten years hence, where would she be? She pictured herself dying. Horrible!

Of course there was nothing to prevent her from going back to Bursley and repairing the grand error of her girlhood. No, nothing except the fact that her whole soul recoiled from the mere idea of any such enterprise! She was a fixture in the Rue Lord Byron. She was a part of the street. She knew all that happened or could happen there. She was attached to it by the heavy chains of habit. In the chill way of long use she loved it. There! The incandescent gas-burner of the street lamp outside had been turned down, as it was turned down every night! If it is possible to love such a phenomenon, she loved that phenomenon. That phenomenon was a portion of her life, dear to her.

An agreeable young man, that Peel-Swynnerton! Then evidently, since her days in Bursley, the Peels and the Swynnertons, partners in business, must have intermarried or there must have been some affair of a will. Did he suspect who she was? He had had a very self-conscious, guilty look. No! He could not have suspected who she was. The idea was ridiculous. Probably he did not even know that her name was Scales. And even if he knew her name, he had probably never heard of Gerald Scales or the story of her flight. Why, he could not have been born until after she had left Bursley! Besides, the Peels were always quite aloof from the ordinary social life of the town. No! He could not have suspected her identity. It was infantile to conceive such a thing.

And yet, she inconsequently proceeded in the tangle of her afflicted mind, supposing he had suspected it! Supposing by some queer chance he had heard her forgotten story, and casually put two and two together! Supposing even that he were merely to mention in the Five Towns that the Pension Frensham was kept by a Mrs Scales. 'Scales? Scales?' people might repeat. 'Now, what does that remind me of?' And the ball might roll and roll till Constance or somebody picked it up! And then . . .

Moreover — a detail of which she had at first unaccountably failed to mark the significance — this Peel-Swynnerton was a friend of the Mr Povey as to whom he had inquired . . . In that case it could not be the same Povey. Impossible that the Peels should be on terms of friendship with Samuel Povey or his connexions! But supposing after all they were! Supposing something utterly unanticipated and revolutionary had happened in the Five Towns!

She was disturbed. She was insecure. She foresaw inquiries being made concerning her. She foresaw an immense family fuss, endless tomfoolery, the upsetting of her existence, the destruction of her calm. And she sank away from that prospect. She could not face it. She did not want to face it. 'No,' she cried passionately in her soul, 'I've lived alone, and I'll stay as I am. I can't change at my time of life.' And her attitude towards a possible invasion of her solitude became one of resentment. 'I won't have it! I won't have it! I will be left alone. Constance! What can Constance be to me, or I to her, now?' The vision of any change in her existence was in the highest degree painful to her. And not only painful. It frightened her. It made her shrink. But she could not dismiss it . . . She could not argue herself out of it. The apparition of Matthew Peel-Swynnerton had somehow altered the very stuff of her fibres.

And surging on the outskirts of the central storm of her brain were ten thousand apprehensions about the management of the Pension. All was black, hopeless. The Pension might have been the most complete business failure that gross carelessness and incapacity had ever provoked. Was it not the fact that she had to supervise everything herself, that she could depend on no one? Were she to be absent even for a single day the entire structure would inevitably fall. Instead of working less she worked harder. And who could guarantee that her investments were safe?

When dawn announced itself, slowly discovering each object in the chamber, she was ill. Fever seemed to rage in her head. And in and round her mouth she had strange sensations. Fossette stirred in the basket near the large desk on which multifarious files and papers were ranged with minute particularity.

'Fossette!' she tried to call out; but no sound issued from her lips. She could not move her tongue. She tried to protrude it, and could not. For hours she had been conscious of a headache. Her heart sank. She was sick with fear. Her memory flashed to her father and his seizure. She was his daughter! Paralysis! 'Ça serait le comble!' she thought in French, horrified. Her fear became abject! 'Can I move at all?' she thought, and madly jerked her head. Yes, she could move her head slightly on the pillow, and she could stretch her right arm, both arms. Absurd cowardice! Of course it was not a seizure! She reassured herself. Still, she could not put her tongue out. Suddenly she began to hiccough, and she had no control over the hiccough. She put her hand to the bell, whose ringing would summon the man who slept in a pantry off the hall, and suddenly the hiccough ceased. Her hand dropped. She was better. Besides, what use in ringing for a man if she could not speak to him through the door? She must wait for Jacqueline. At six o'clock every morning, summer and winter, Jacqueline entered her mistress's bedroom to release the dog for a moment's airing under her own supervision. The clock on the mantelpiece showed five minutes past three. She had three hours to wait. Fossette pattered across the room, and sprang on to the bed and nestled down. Sophia ignored her, but Fossette, being herself unwell and torpid, did not seem to care.

Jacqueline was late. In the quarter of an hour between six o'clock and a quarter past, Sophia suffered the supreme pangs of despair and verged upon insanity. It appeared to her that her cranium would blow off under pressure from within. Then the door opened silently, a few inches. Usually Jacqueline came into the room, but sometimes she stood behind the door and called in her soft, trembling voice, 'Fossette! Fossette!' And on this morning she did not come into the room. The dog did not immediately respond. Sophia was in an agony. She marshalled all her volition, all her self-control and strength, to shout:

'*Jacqueline!*'

It came out of her, a horribly difficult and misshapen birth, but it came. She was exhausted.

'Yes, madame.' Jacqueline entered.

As soon as she had a glimpse of Sophia she threw up her hands. Sophia stared at her, wordless.

'I will fetch the doctor – myself,' whispered Jacqueline, and fled.

'*Jacqueline!*' The woman stopped. Then Sophia determined to force herself to make a speech, and she braced her muscles to an unprecedented effort. 'Say not a word to the others.' She could not bear that the whole household should know of her illness. Jacqueline nodded and vanished, the dog following. Jacqueline understood. She lived in the place with her mistress as with a fellow-conspirator.

Sophia began to feel better. She could get into a sitting posture, though the movement made her dizzy. By working to the foot of the bed she could see herself in the glass of the wardrobe. And she saw that the lower part of her face was twisted out of shape.

The doctor, who knew her, and who earned a lot of money in

her house, told her frankly what had happened. *Paralysie glosso-labio-laryngée* was the phrase he used. She understood. A very slight attack; due to overwork and worry. He ordered absolute rest and quiet.

'Impossible!' she said, genuinely convinced that she alone was indispensable.

'Repose the most absolute!' he repeated.

She marvelled that a few words with a man who chanced to be named Peel-Swynnerton could have resulted in such a disaster, and drew a curious satisfaction from this fearful proof that she was so highly-strung. But even then she did not realize how profoundly she had been disturbed.

V

'My darling Sophia –'

The inevitable miracle had occurred. Her suspicions concerning that Mr Peel-Swynnerton were well-founded, after all! Here was a letter from Constance! The writing on the envelope was not Constance's; but even before examining it she had had a peculiar qualm. She received letters from England nearly every day asking about rooms and prices (and on many of them she had to pay threepence excess postage, because the writers carelessly or carefully forgot that a penny stamp was not sufficient); there was nothing to distinguish this envelope, and yet her first glance at it had startled her; and when, deciphering the smudged postmark, she made out the word 'Bursley', her heart did literally seem to stop, and she opened the letter in quite violent tremulation, thinking to herself: 'The doctor would say this is very bad for me.' Six days had elapsed since her attack, and she was wonderfully better; the distortion of her face had almost disappeared. But the doctor was grave; he ordered no medicine, merely a tonic; and monotonously insisted on 'repose the most absolute', on perfect mental calm. He said little else, allowing Sophia to judge from his silences the seriousness of her condition. Yes, the receipt of such a letter must be bad for her!

She controlled herself while she read it, lying in her dressing-gown against several pillows on the bed; a mist did not form in her eyes, nor did she sob, nor betray physically that she was not reading an order for two rooms for a week. But the expenditure of nervous force necessary to self-control was terrific.

Constance's handwriting had changed; it was, however, easily recognizable as a development of the neat calligraphy of the girl who could print window-tickets. The 'S' of Sophia was formed in the same way as she had formed it in the last letter which she had received from her at Axe!

'MY DARLING SOPHIA,

'I cannot tell you how overjoyed I was to learn that after all these years you are alive and well, and doing so well too. I long to see you, my dear sister. It was Mr Peel-Swynnerton who told me. He is a friend of Cyril's. Cyril is the name of my son. I married Samuel in 1867. Cyril was born in 1874 at Christmas. He is now twenty-two, and doing very well in London as a student of sculpture, though so young. He won a National Scholarship. There were only eight, of which he won one, in all England. Samuel died in 1888. If you read the papers you must have seen about the Povey affair. I mean of course Mr Daniel Povey, Confectioner. It was that that killed poor Samuel. Poor mother died in 1875. It doesn't seem so long. Aunt Harriet and Aunt Maria are both dead. Old Dr Harrop is dead, and his son has practically retired. He has a partner, a Scotchman. Mr Critchlow has married Miss Insull. Did you ever hear of such a thing? They have taken over the shop, and I live in the house part, the other being bricked up. Business in the Square is not what it used to be. The steam trams take all the custom to Hanbridge, and they are talking of electric trams, but I dare say it is only talk. I have a fairly good servant. She has been with me a long time, but servants are not what they were. I keep pretty well, except for my sciatica and palpitation. Since Cyril went to London I have been very lonely. But I try to cheer up and count my blessings. I am sure I have a great deal to be thankful for. And now this news of you! Please write to me a long letter, and tell me all about yourself. It is a long way to Paris. But surely now you know I am still here, you will come and pay me a visit – at least. Everybody would be *most* glad to see you. And I should be so proud and glad. As I say, I am all alone. Mr Critchlow says I am to say there is a deal of money waiting for you. You know he is the trustee. There is the half-share of mother's and also of Aunt Harriet's, and it has been accumulating. By the way, they are getting up a subscription for Miss Chetwynd, poor old thing. Her sister is dead, and she is in poverty. I have put myself down for £20. Now, my dear sister, please do write to me at once. You see it is still the old address. I remain, my darling Sophia, with much love, your affectionate sister,

'CONSTANCE POVEY.

'P.S. – I should have written yesterday, but I was not fit. Every time I sat down to write, I cried.'

'Of course,' said Sophia to Fossette, 'she expects me to go to her, instead of her coming to me! And yet who's the busiest?'

But this observation was not serious. It was merely a trifle of affectionate malicious embroidery that Sophia put on the edge of her deep satisfaction. The very spirit of simple love seemed to emanate from the paper on which Constance had written. And this spirit woke suddenly and completely Sophia's love for Constance. Constance! At that moment there was assuredly for Sophia no creature in the world like Constance. Constance personified for her the qualities of the Baines family. Constance's letter was a great letter, a perfect letter, perfect in its artlessness; the natural expression of the Baines character at its best. Not an awkward reference in the whole of it! No clumsy expression of surprise at anything that she, Sophia, had done, or failed to do! No mention of Gerald! Just a sublime acceptance of the situation as it was, and the assurance of undiminished love! Tact? No; it was something finer than tact! Tact was conscious, skilful. Sophia was certain that the notion of tactfulness had not entered Constance's head. Constance had simply written out of her heart. And that was what made the letter so splendid. Sophia was convinced that no one but a Baines could have written such a letter.

She felt that she must rise to the height of that letter, that she too must show her Baines blood. And she went primly to her desk, and began to write (on private notepaper) in that imperious large hand of hers that was so different from Constance's. She began a little stiffly, but after a few lines her generous and passionate soul was responding freely to the appeal of Constance. She asked that Mr Critchlow should pay £20 for her to the Miss Chetwynd fund. She spoke of her Pension and of Paris, and of her pleasure in Constance's letter. But she said nothing as to Gerald, nor as to the possibility of a visit to the Five Towns. She finished the letter in a blaze of love, and passed from it as from a dream to the sterile banality of the daily life of the Pension Frensham, feeling that, compared to Constance's affection, nothing else had any worth.

But she would not consider the project of going to Bursley. Never, never would she go to Bursley. If Constance chose to come to Paris and see her, she would be delighted, but she herself would not budge. The mere notion of any change in her existence intimidated her. And as for returning to Bursley itself . . . no, no!

Nevertheless, at the Pension Frensham, the future could not be as the past. Sophia's health forbade that. She knew that the doctor was right. Every time that she made an effort, she knew intimately and speedily that the doctor was right. Only her will-power was unimpaired; the machinery by which will-power is converted into action was mysteriously damaged. She was aware of the fact. But she could not face it yet. Time would have to elapse before she could bring herself to face that fact. She was getting an old woman. She could no longer draw on reserves. Yet she persisted to everyone that she was quite recovered, and was abstaining from her customary work simply from an excess of prudence. Certainly her face had recovered. And the Pension, being a machine all of whose parts were in order, continued to run, apparently, with its usual smoothness. It is true that the excellent chef began to peculate, but as his cuisine did not suffer, the result was not noticeable for a long period. The whole staff and many of the guests knew that Sophia had been indisposed; and they knew no more.

When by hazard Sophia observed a fault in the daily conduct of the house, her first impulse was to go to the root of it and cure it, her second was to leave it alone, or to palliate it by some superficial remedy. Unperceived, and yet vaguely suspected by various people, the decline of the Pension Frensham had set in. The tide, having risen to its highest, was receding, but so little that no one could be sure that it had turned. Every now and then it rushed up again and washed the farthest stone.

Sophia and Constance exchanged several letters. Sophia said repeatedly that she could not leave Paris. At length she roundly asked Constance to come and pay her a visit. She made the suggestion with fear – for the prospect of actually seeing her beloved Constance alarmed her – but she could do no less than make it. And in a few days she had a reply to say that Constance would have come, under Cyril's charge, but that her sciatica was suddenly much worse, and she was obliged to lie down every day after dinner to rest her legs. Travelling was impossible for her. The fates were combining against Sophia's decision.

And now Sophia began to ask herself about her duty to Constance. The truth was that she was groping round to find an excuse for reversing her decision. She was afraid to reverse it, yet tempted. She had the desire to do something which she objected to doing. It was like the desire to throw one's self over a high balcony. It drew her, drew her, and she drew back against it. The Pension was now tedious to her. It bored her even to pretend to be the supervising head of the Pension. Throughout the house discipline had loosened.

She wondered when Mr Mardon would renew his overtures for the transformation of her enterprise into a limited company. In spite of herself she would deliberately cross his path and give him opportunities to begin on the old theme. He had never before left her in peace for so long a period. No doubt she had, upon his last assault, absolutely convinced him that his efforts had no smallest chance of success, and he had made up his mind to cease them. With a single word she could wind him up again. The merest hint, one day when he was paying his bill, and he would be beseeching her. But she could not utter the word.

Then she began to say openly that she did not feel well, that the house was too much for her, and that the doctor had imperatively commanded rest. She said this to everyone except Mardon. And everyone somehow persisted in not saying it to Mardon. The doctor having advised that she should spend more time in the open air, she would take afternoon drives in the Bois with Fossette. It was October. But Mr Mardon never seemed to hear of those drives.

One morning he met her in the street outside the house.

'I'm sorry to hear you're so unwell,' he said confidentially, after they had discussed the health of Fossette.

'So unwell!' she exclaimed as if resenting the statement. 'Who told you I was so unwell?'

'Jacqueline. She told me you often said that what you needed was a complete change. And it seems the doctor says so, too.'

'Oh! doctors!' she murmured, without however denying the truth of Jacqueline's assertion. She saw hope in Mr Mardon's eyes.

'Of course, you know,' he said, still more confidently, 'if you *should* happen to change your mind, I'm always ready to form a little syndicate to take this' – he waved discreetly at the Pension – 'off your hands.'

She shook her head violently, which was strange, considering that for weeks she had been wishing to hear such words from Mr Mardon.

'You needn't give it up altogether,' he said. 'You could retain your hold on it. We'd make you manageress, with a salary and a share in the profits. You'd be mistress just as much as you are now.'

'Oh!' said she carelessly. '*If I gave it up, I should give it up entirely*. No half measures for me.'

With the utterance of that sentence, the history of Frensham's as a private undertaking was brought to a close. Sophia knew it. Mr Mardon knew it. Mr Mardon's heart leapt. He saw in his imagination the formation of the preliminary syndicate, with himself at its head, and then the re-sale by the syndicate to a limited company at a profit. He saw a nice little profit for his own private personal self of a thousand or so – gained in a moment. The plant, his hope, which he had deemed dead, blossomed with miraculous suddenness.

'Well,' he said. 'Give it up entirely, then! Take a holiday for life. You've deserved it, Mrs Scales.'

She shook her head once again.

'Think it over,' he said.

'I gave you my answer years ago,' she said obstinately, while fearing lest he should take her at her word.

'Oblige me by thinking it over,' he said. 'I'll mention it to you again in a few days.'

'It will be no use,' she said.

He took his leave, waddling down the street in his vague clothes, conscious of his fame as Lewis Mardon, the great house-agent of the Champs Elysées, known throughout Europe and America.

In a few days he did mention it again.

'There's only one thing that makes me dream of it even for a moment,' said Sophia. 'And that is my sister's health.'

'Your sister!' he exclaimed. He did not know she had a sister. Never had she spoken of her family.

'Yes. Her letters are beginning to worry me.'

'Does she live in Paris?'

'No. In Staffordshire. She has never left home.'

And to preserve her pride intact she led Mr Mardon to think that Constance was in a most serious way, whereas in truth Constance had nothing worse than her sciatica, and even that was somewhat better.

Thus she yielded.

CHAPTER 2: *The Meeting*

I

Soon after dinner one day in the following spring, Mr Critchlow knocked at Constance's door. She was seated in the rocking-chair in front of the fire in the parlour. She wore a large 'rough' apron, and with the outlying parts of the apron she was rubbing the moisture out of the coat of a young wire-haired fox-terrier, for whom no more original name had been found than 'Spot'. It is true that he had a spot. Constance had more than once called the world to witness that she would never have a young dog again, because, as she said, she could not be always running about after them, and they ate the stuffing out of the furniture. But her last dog had lived too long; a dog can do worse things than eat furniture; and, in her natural reaction against age in dogs, and also in the hope of postponing as long as possible the inevitable sorrow and upset which death causes when it takes off a domestic pet, she had not known how to refuse the very desirable fox-terrier aged ten months that an acquaintance had offered to her. Spot's beautiful pink skin could be seen under his disturbed hair; he was exquisitely soft to the touch, and to himself he was loathsome. His eyes continually peeped forth between corners of the agitated towel, and they were full of inquietude and shame.

Amy was assisting at this performance, gravely on the watch to see that Spot did not escape into the coal-cellar. She opened the door to Mr Critchlow's knock. Mr Critchlow entered without any formalities, as usual. He did not seem to have changed. He had the same quantity of white hair, he wore the same long white apron, and his voice (which showed, however, an occasional tendency to shrillness) had the same grating quality. He stood fairly straight. He was carrying a newspaper in his vellum hand.

'Well, missis!' he said.

'That will do, thank you, Amy,' said Constance, quietly. Amy went slowly.

'So ye're washing him for her!' said Mr Critchlow.

'Yes,' Constance admitted. Spot glanced sharply at the aged man.

'An' ye seen this bit in the paper about Sophia?' he asked, holding the *Signal* for her inspection.

'About Sophia?' cried Constance. 'What's amiss?'

'Nothing's amiss. But they've got it. It's in the "Staffordshire day by day" column. Here! I'll read it ye.' He drew a long wooden spectacle-case from his waistcoat pocket, and placed a second pair of spectacles on his nose. Then he sat down on the sofa, his knees sticking out pointedly, and read: '"We understand that Mrs Sophia Scales, proprietress of the famous Pension Frensham in the Rue Lord Byron, Paris" – it's that famous that nobody in th' Five Towns has ever heard of it – "is about to pay a visit to her native town, Bursley, after an absence of over thirty years. Mrs Scales belonged to the well-known and highly respected family of Baines. She has recently disposed of the Pension Frensham to a limited company, and we are betraying no secret in stating that the price paid ran well into five figures." So ye see!' Mr Critchlow commented.

'How do those *Signal* people find out things?' Constance murmured.

'Eh, bless ye, I don't know,' said Mr Critchlow.

This was an untruth. Mr Critchlow had himself given the information to the new editor of the *Signal*, who had soon been made aware of Critchlow's passion for the Press, and who knew how to make use of it.

'I wish it hadn't appeared just today,' said Constance.

'Why?'

'Oh! I don't know, I wish it hadn't.'

'Well, I'll be touring on, missis,' said Mr Critchlow, meaning that he would go.

He left the paper, and descended the steps with senile deliber-ation. It was characteristic that he had shown no curiosity what-ever as to the details of Sophia's arrival.

Constance removed her apron, wrapped Spot up in it, and put him in a corner of the sofa. She then abruptly sent Amy out to buy a penny time-table.

'I thought you were going by tram to Knype,' Amy observed.

'I have decided to go by train,' said Constance, with cold dignity, as if she had decided the fate of nations. She hated such observations from Amy, who unfortunately lacked, in an increasing degree, the supreme gift of unquestioning obedi-ence.

When Amy came breathlessly back, she found Constance in her bedroom, withdrawing crumpled balls of paper from the sleeves of her second-best mantle. Constance scarcely ever wore this mantle. In theory it was destined for chapel on wet Sundays; in practice it had remained long in the wardrobe, Sundays having been obstinately fine for weeks and weeks together. It was a mantle that Constance had never really liked. But she was not going to Knype to meet Sophia in her everyday mantle; and she had no intention of donning her best mantle for such an excur-sion. To make her first appearance before Sophia in the best mantle she had – this would have been a sad mistake of tactics! Not only would it have led to an anti-climax on Sunday, but it would have given to Constance the air of being in awe of Sophia. Now Constance was in truth a little afraid of Sophia; in thirty years Sophia might have grown into anything, whereas Con-stance had remained just Constance. Paris was a great place; and it was immensely far off. And the mere sound of that limited company business was intimidating. Imagine Sophia having by her own efforts created something which a real limited company wanted to buy and had bought! Yes, Constance was afraid, but she did not mean to show her fear in her mantle. After all, she was the elder. And she had her dignity too – and a lot of it – tucked away in her secret heart, hidden within the mildness of that soft exterior. So she had decided on the second-best mantle, which, being seldom used, had its sleeves stuffed with paper to the end that they might keep their shape and their 'fall'. The little balls of paper were strewed over the bed.

'There's a train at a quarter to three, gets to Knype at ten minutes past,' said Amy, officiously. 'But supposing it was only three minutes late and the London train was prompt, then you might miss her. Happen you'd better take the two fifteen to be on the safe side.'

'Let me look,' said Constance, firmly. 'Please put all this paper in the wardrobe.'

She would have preferred not to follow Amy's suggestion, but it was so incontestably wise that she was obliged to accept it.

'Unless you go by tram,' said Amy. 'That won't mean starting quite so soon.'

But Constance would not go by tram. If she took the tram she would be bound to meet people who had read the *Signal*, and who would say, with their stupid vacuity: 'Going to meet your sister at Knype?' And then tiresome conversations would follow. Whereas, in the train, she would choose a compartment, and would be far less likely to encounter chatterers.

There was now not a minute to lose. And the excitement which had been growing in that house for days past, under a pretence of calm, leapt out swiftly into the light of the sun, and was unashamed. Amy had to help her mistress make herself as comely as she could be made without her best dress, mantle, and bonnet. Amy was frankly consulted as to effects. The barrier of class was lowered for a space. Many years had elapsed since Constance had been conscious of a keen desire to look smart. She was reminded of the days when, in full fig for chapel, she would dash downstairs on a Sunday morning, and, assuming a pose for inspection at the threshold of the parlour, would demand of Samuel: 'Shall I do?' Yes, she used to dash downstairs, like a child, and yet in those days she had thought herself so sedate and mature! She sighed, half with lancinating regret, and half in gentle disdain of that mercurial creature aged less than thirty. At fifty-one she regarded herself as old. And she was old. And Amy had the tricks and manners of an old spinster. Thus the excitement in the house was

an 'old' excitement, and, like Constance's desire to look smart, it
had its ridiculous side, which was also its tragic side, the side that
would have made a boor guffaw, and a hysterical fool cry, and a
wise man meditate sadly upon the earth's fashion of renewing
itself.

At half past one Constance was dressed, with the exception of
her gloves. She looked at the clock a second time to make sure
that she might safely glance round the house without fear of
missing the train. She went up into the bedroom on the second
floor, her and Sophia's old bedroom, which she had prepared
with enormous care for Sophia. The airing of that room had been
an enterprise of days, for, save by a minister during the sittings of
the Wesleyan Methodist Conference at Bursley, it had never been
occupied since the era when Maria Insull used occasionally to
sleep in the house. Cyril clung to his old room on his visits.
Constance had an ample supply of solid and stately furniture, and
the chamber destined for Sophia was lightened in every corner by
the reflections of polished mahogany. It was also fairly impreg-
nated with the odour of furniture paste – an odour of which no
housewife need be ashamed. Further, it had been re-papered in a
delicate blue, with one of the new 'art' patterns. It was a 'Baines'
room. And Constance did not care where Sophia came from, nor
what Sophia had been accustomed to, nor into what limited
company Sophia had been transformed – that room was adequate! It could not have been improved upon. You had only to look
at the crocheted mats – even those on the washstand under the
white-and-gold ewer and other utensils. It was folly to expose
such mats to the splashings of a washstand, but it was sublime
folly. Sophia might remove them if she cared. Constance was
house-proud; house-pride had slumbered within her; now it
blazed forth.

A fire brightened the drawing-room, which was a truly magnificent apartment, a museum of valuables collected by the Baines
and the Maddack families since the year 1840, tempered by the
last novelties in antimacassars and cloths. In all Bursley there
could have been few drawing-rooms to compare with Constance's. Constance knew it. She was not afraid of her drawing-
room being seen by anybody.

She passed for an instant into her own bedroom, where Amy was patiently picking balls of paper from the bed.

'Now you quite understand about tea?' Constance asked.

'Oh yes, 'm,' said Amy, as if to say: 'How much oftener are you going to ask me that question?' 'Are you off now, 'm?'

'Yes,' said Constance. 'Come and fasten the front door after me.'

They descended together to the parlour. A white cloth for tea lay folded on the table. It was of the finest damask that skill could choose and money buy. It was fifteen years old, and had never been spread. Constance would not have produced it for the first meal, had she not possessed two others of equal eminence. On the harmonium were arranged several jams and cakes, a Bursley pork-pie, and some pickled salmon; with the necessary silver. All was there. Amy could not go wrong. And crocuses were in the vases on the mantelpiece. Her 'garden', in the phrase which used to cause Samuel to think how extraordinarily feminine she was! It was a long time since she had had a 'garden' on the mantelpiece. Her interest in her chronic sciatica and in her palpitations had grown at the expense of her interest in gardens. Often, when she had finished the complicated processes by which her furniture and other goods were kept in order, she had strength only to 'rest'. She was rather a fragile, small, fat woman, soon out of breath, easily marred. This business of preparing for the advent of Sophia had appeared to her genuinely colossal. However, she had come through it very well. She was in pretty good health; only a little tired, and more than a little anxious and nervous, as she gave the last glance.

'Take away that apron, do!' she said to Amy, pointing to the rough apron in the corner of the sofa. 'By the way, where is Spot?'

'Spot, m'm?' Amy ejaculated.

Both their hearts jumped. Amy instinctively looked out of the window. He was there, sure enough, in the gutter, studying the indescribabilities of King Street. He had obviously escaped when Amy came in from buying the time-table. The woman's face was guilty.

'Amy, I wonder *at* you!' exclaimed Constance, tragically. She opened the door.

'Well, I never did see the like of that dog!' murmured Amy.

'Spot!' his mistress commanded. 'Come here at once. Do you hear me?'

Spot turned sharply and gazed motionless at Constance. Then with a toss of the head he dashed off to the corner of the Square, and gazed motionless again. Amy went forth to catch him. After an age she brought him in, squealing. He was in a state exceedingly offensive to the eye and to the nose. He had effectively got rid of the smell of the soap, which he loathed. Constance could have wept. It did really appear to her that nothing had gone right that day. And Spot had the most innocent, trustful air. Impossible to make him realize that his aunt Sophia was coming. He would have sold his entire family into servitude in order to buy ten yards of King Street gutter.

'You must wash him in the scullery, that's all there is for it,' said Constance, controlling herself. 'Put that apron on, and don't forget one of your new aprons when you open the door. Better shut him up in Mr Cyril's bedroom when you've dried him.'

And she went, charged with worries, clasping her bag and her umbrella and smoothing her gloves, and spying downwards at the folds of her mantle.

'That's a funny way to go to Bursley Station, that is,' said Amy, observing that Constance was descending King Street instead of crossing it into Wedgwood Street. And she caught Spot 'a fair clout on the head', to indicate to him that she had him alone in the house now.

Constance was taking a round-about route to the station, so that, if stopped by acquaintances, she should not be too obviously going to the station. Her feelings concerning the arrival of Sophia, and concerning the town's attitude towards it, were very complex.

She was forced to hurry. And she had risen that morning with plans perfectly contrived for the avoidance of hurry. She disliked hurry because it always 'put her about'.

II

The express from London was late, so that Constance had three-quarters of an hour of the stony calmness of Knype platform when it is waiting for a great train. At last the porters began to cry, 'Macclesfield, Stockport, and Manchester train'; the immense engine glided round the curve, dwarfing the carriages behind it, and Constance had a supreme tremor. The calmness of the platform was transformed into a *mêlée*. Little Constance found herself left on the fringe of a physically agitated crowd which was apparently trying to scale a precipice surmounted by windows and doors from whose apertures looked forth defenders of the train. Knype platform seemed as if it would never be reduced to order again. And Constance did not estimate highly the chances of picking out an unknown Sophia from that welter. She was very seriously perturbed. All the muscles of her face were drawn as her gaze wandered anxiously from end to end of the train.

Presently she saw a singular dog. Other people also saw it. It was of the colour of chocolate; it had a head and shoulders richly covered with hair that hung down in thousands of tufts like the tufts of a modern mop such as is bought in shops. This hair stopped suddenly rather less than half-way along the length of the dog's body, the remainder of which was naked and as smooth as marble. The effect was to give to the inhabitants of the Five Towns the impression that the dog had forgotten an essential part of its attire and was outraging decency. The ball of hair which had been allowed to grow on the dog's tail, and the circles of hair which ornamented its ankles, only served to intensify the impression of indecency. A pink ribbon round its neck completed the outrage. The animal had absolutely the air of a decked trollop. A chain ran taut from the creature's neck into the middle of a small crowd of persons gesticulating over trunks, and Constance traced it to a tall and distinguished woman in a coat and skirt with a rather striking hat. A beautiful and aristocratic woman, Constance thought, at a distance! Then the strange idea came to her: 'That's Sophia!' she was sure . . . She was not sure . . . She was sure. The woman emerged from the crowd. Her eye fell on Constance. They both hesitated, and, as it were, wavered uncertainly towards each other.

'I should have known you anywhere,' said Sophia, with apparently careless tranquillity, as she stooped to kiss Constance, raising her veil.

Constance saw that this marvellous tranquillity must be imitated, and she imitated it very well. It was a 'Baines' tranquillity. But she noticed a twitching of her sister's lips. The twitching comforted Constance, proving to her that she was not alone in foolishness. There was also something queer about the permanent lines of Sophia's mouth. That must be due to the 'attack' about which Sophia had written.

'Did Cyril meet you?' asked Constance. It was all that she could think of to say.

'Oh yes!' said Sophia, eagerly. 'And I went to his studio, and he saw me off at Euston. He is a *very* nice boy. I love him.'

She said 'I love him' with the intonation of Sophia aged fifteen. Her tone and imperious gestures sent Constance flying back to the 'sixties. 'She hasn't altered one bit,' Constance thought with joy. 'Nothing could change Sophia.' And at the back of that notion was a more general notion: 'Nothing could change a Baines.' It was true that Constance's Sophia had not changed. Powerful individualities remain undisfigured by no matter what vicissitudes. After this revelation of the original Sophia, arising as it did out of praise of Cyril, Constance felt easier, felt reassured.

'This is Fossette,' said Sophia, pulling at the chain.

Constance knew not what to reply. Surely Sophia could not be aware what she did in bringing such a dog to a place where people were so particular as they are in the Five Towns.

'Fossette!' She repeated the name in an endearing accent, half stooping towards the dog. After all, it was not the dog's fault. Sophia had certainly mentioned a dog in her letters, but she had not prepared Constance for the spectacle of Fossette.

All that happened in a moment. A porter appeared with two trunks belonging to Sophia. Constance observed that they were superlatively 'good' trunks; also that Sophia's clothes, though 'on the showy side', were superlatively 'good'. The getting of

Sophia's ticket to Bursley occupied them next, and soon the first shock of meeting had worn off.

In a second-class compartment of the Loop Line train, with Sophia and Fossette opposite to her, Constance had leisure to 'take in' Sophia. She came to the conclusion that, despite her slenderness and straightness and the general effect of the long oval of her face under the hat, Sophia looked her age. She saw that Sophia must have been through a great deal; her experiences were damagingly printed in the details of feature. Seen at a distance, she might have passed for a woman of thirty, even for a girl, but seen across a narrow railway carriage she was a woman whom suffering had aged. Yet obviously her spirit was unbroken. Hear her tell a doubtful porter that of course she should take Fossette with her into the carriage! See her shut the carriage door with the expressed intention of keeping other people out! She was accustomed to command. At the same time her face had an almost set smile, as though she had said to herself: 'I will die smiling.' Constance felt sorry for her. While recognizing in Sophia a superior in charm, in experience, in knowledge of the world and in force of personality, she yet with a kind of undisturbed, fundamental superiority felt sorry for Sophia.

'What do you think?' said Sophia, absently fingering Fossette. 'A man came up to me at Euston, while Cyril was getting my ticket, and said, "Eh, Miss Baines, I haven't seen ye for over thirty years, but I know you're Miss Baines, or *were* – and you're looking bonny." Then he went off. I think it must have been Holl, the grocer.'

'Had he got a long white beard?'

'Yes.'

'Then it was Mr Holl. He's been Mayor twice. He's an alderman, you know.'

'Really!' said Sophia. 'But wasn't it queer?'

'Eh! Bless us!' exclaimed Constance. 'Don't talk about queer! It's terrible how time flies.'

The conversation stopped, and it refused to start again. Two women who are full of affectionate curiosity about each other, and who have not seen each other for thirty years, and who are anxious to confide in each other, ought to discover no difficulty in talking; but somehow these two could not talk. Constance perceived that Sophia was impeded by the same awkwardness as herself.

'Well I never!' cried Sophia, suddenly. She had glanced out of the window and had seen two camels and an elephant in a field close to the line, amid manufactories and warehouses and advertisements of soap.

'Oh!' said Constance. 'That's Barnum's, you know. They have what they called a central depôt here, because it's the middle of England.' Constance spoke proudly. (After all, there can be only one middle.) It was on her tongue to say, in her 'tart' manner, that Fossette ought to be with the camels, but she refrained. Sophia hit on the excellent idea of noting all the buildings that were new to her and all the landmarks that she remembered. It was surprising how little the district had altered.

'Same smoke!' said Sophia.

'Same smoke!' Constance agreed.

'It's even worse,' said Sophia.

'Do you think so?' Constance was slightly piqued. 'But they're doing something now for smoke abatement.'

'I must have forgotten how dirty it was!' said Sophia. 'I suppose that's it. I'd no *idea* . . . !'

'Really!' said Constance. Then, in candid admission, 'The fact is, it *is* dirty. You can't imagine what work it makes, especially with window-curtains.'

As the train puffed under Trafalgar Road, Constance pointed to a new station that was being built there, to be called 'Trafalgar Road' station.

'Won't it be strange?' said she, accustomed to the eternal sequence of Loop Line stations – Turnhill, Bursley, Bleakridge, Hanbridge, Cauldon, Knype, Trent Vale, and Longshaw. A 'Trafalgar Road' inserting itself between Bleakridge and Hanbridge seemed to her exclusively curious.

'Yes, I suppose it will,' Sophia agreed.

'But of course it's not the same to you,' said Constance, dashed. She indicated the glories of Bursley Park, as the train slackened for Bursley, with modesty. Sophia gazed, and vaguely recognized the slopes where she had taken her first walk with Gerald Scales.

Nobody accosted them at Bursley Station, and they drove to the Square in a cab. Amy was at the window; she held up Spot, who was in a plenary state of cleanliness, rivalling the purity of Amy's apron.

'Good afternon, m'm,' said Amy, officiously, to Sophia, as Sophia came up the steps.

'Good afternoon, Amy,' Sophia replied. She flattered Amy in thus showing that she was acquainted with her name; but if ever a servant was put into her place by mere tone, Amy was put into her place on that occasion. Constance trembled at Sophia's frigid and arrogant politeness. Certainly Sophia was not used to being addressed first by servants. But Amy was not quite the ordinary servant. She was much older than the ordinary servant, and she had acquired a partial moral dominion over Constance, though Constance would have warmly denied it. Hence Constance's apprehension. However, nothing happened. Amy apparently did not feel the snub.

'Take Spot and put him in Mr Cyril's bedroom,' Constance murmured to her, as if implying: 'Have I not already told you to do that?' The fact was, she was afraid for Spot's life.

'Now, Fossette!' She welcomed the incoming poodle kindly; the poodle began at once to sniff.

The fat, red cabman was handling the trunks on the pavement, and Amy was upstairs. For a moment the sisters were alone together in the parlour.

'So here I am!' exclaimed the tall, majestic woman of fifty. And her lips twitched again as she looked round the room – so small to her.

'Yes, here you are!' Constance agreed. She bit her lip, and, as a measure of prudence to avoid breaking down, she bustled out to the cabman. A passing instant of emotion, like a fleck of foam on a wide and calm sea!

The cabman blundered up and downstairs with trunks, and saluted Sophia's haughty generosity, and then there was quietness. Amy was already brewing the tea in the cave. The prepared tea-table in front of the fire made a glittering array.

'Now, what about Fossette?' Constance voiced anxieties that had been growing on her.

'Fossette will be quite all right with me,' said Sophia, firmly.

They ascended to the guest's room, which drew Sophia's admiration for its prettiness. She hurried to the window and looked out into the Square.

'Would you like a fire?' Constance asked, in a rather perfunctory manner. For a bedroom fire, in seasons of normal health, was still regarded as absurd in the Square.

'Oh, no!' said Sophia; but with a slight failure to rebut the suggestion as utterly ridiculous.

'Sure?' Constance questioned.

'Quite, thank you,' said Sophia.

'Well, I'll leave you. I expect Amy will have tea ready directly.' She went down into the kitchen. 'Amy,' she said, 'as soon as we've finished tea, light a fire in Mrs Scales's bedroom.'

'In the top bedroom, m'm?'

'Yes.'

Constance climbed again to her own bedroom, and shut the door. She needed a moment to herself, in the midst of this terrific affair. She sighed with relief as she removed her mantle. She thought: 'At any rate we've met, and I've got her here. She's very nice. No, she isn't a bit altered.' She hesitated to admit that to her Sophia was the least in the world formidable. And so she said once more: 'She's very nice. She isn't a bit altered.' And then: 'Fancy her being here! She really is here.' With her perfect simplicity it did not occur to Constance to speculate as to what Sophia thought of her.

Sophia was downstairs first, and Constance found her looking at the blank wall beyond the door leading to the kitchen steps.

'So this is where you had it bricked up?' said Sophia.

'Yes,' said Constance. 'That's the place.'

'It makes me feel like people feel when they have tickling in a limb that's been cut off!' said Sophia.

'Oh, Sophia!'

The tea received a great deal of praise from Sophia, but neither of them ate much. Constance found that Sophia was like herself: she had to be particular about her food. She tasted dainties for the sake of tasting, but it was a bird's pecking. Not the twelfth part of the tea was consumed. They dared not indulge caprices. Only their eyes could feed.

After tea they went up to the drawing-room, and in the corridor had the startling pleasure of seeing two dogs who scurried about after each other in amity. Spot had found Fossette, with the aid of Amy's incurable carelessness, and had at once examined her with great particularity. She seemed to be of an amiable disposition, and not averse from the lighter distractions. For a long time the sisters sat chatting together in the lit drawing-room to the agreeable sound of happy dogs playing in the dark corridor. Those dogs saved the situation, because they needed constant attention. When the dogs dozed, the sisters began to look through the photograph albums, of which Constance had several, bound in plush or morocco. Nothing will sharpen the memory, evoke the past, raise the dead, rejuvenate the ageing, and cause both sighs and smiles, like a collection of photographs gathered together during long years of life. Constance had an astonishing menagerie of unknown cousins and their connexions, and of townspeople; she had Cyril at all ages; she had weird daguerreotypes of her parents and their parents. The strangest of all was a portrait of Samuel Povey as an infant in arms. Sophia checked an impulse to laugh at it. But when Constance said: 'Isn't it funny?' she did allow herself to laugh. A photograph of Samuel in the year before his death was really imposing. Sophia stared at it impressed. It was the portrait of an honest man.

'How long have you been a widow?' Constance asked in a low voice, glancing at upright Sophia over her spectacles, a leaf of the album raised against her finger.

Sophia unmistakably flushed. 'I don't know that I am a widow,' said she, with an air. 'My husband left me in 1870, and I've never seen nor heard of him since.'

'Oh, my dear!' cried Constance, alarmed and deafened as by a clap of awful thunder. 'I thought ye were a widow. Mr Peel-Swynnerton said he was told positively ye were a widow. That's why I never . . .' She stopped. Her face was troubled.

'Of course I always passed for a widow, over there,' said Sophia.

'Of course,' said Constance quickly. 'I see . . .'

'And I may be a widow,' said Sophia.

Constance made no remark. This was a blow. Bursley was such a particular place. Doubtless, Gerald Scales had behaved like a scoundrel. That was sure!

When, immediately afterwards, Amy opened the drawing-room door (having first knocked – the practice of encouraging a servant to plunge without warning of any kind into a drawing-room had never been favoured in that house) she saw the sisters sitting rather near to each other at the walnut oval table, Mrs Scales very upright, and staring into the fire, and Mrs Povey 'bunched up' and staring at the photograph album; but seeming to Amy aged and apprehensive; Mrs Povey's hair was quite grey, though Mrs Scales's hair was nearly as black as Amy's own. Mrs Scales started at the sound of the knock, and turned her head.

'Here's Mr and Mrs Critchlow, m'm,' announced Amy.

The sisters glanced at one another, with lifted foreheads. Then Mrs Povey spoke to Amy as though visits at half-past eight at night were a customary phenomenon of the household. Nevertheless, she trembled to think what outrageous thing Mr Critchlow might say to Sophia after thirty years' absence. The occasion was great, and it might also be terrible.

'Ask them to come up,' she said calmly.

But Amy had the best of that encounter. 'I have done,' she replied, and instantly produced them out of the darkness of the corridor. It was providential: the sisters had made no remark that the Critchlows might not hear.

Then Maria Critchlow, simpering, had to greet Sophia. Mrs Critchlow was very agitated, from sheer nervousness. She curvetted; she almost pranced; and she made noises with her mouth as though she saw someone eating a sour apple. She wanted to show Sophia how greatly she had changed from the young, timid apprentice. Certainly since her marriage she had changed. As manager of other people's business she had not felt the necessity of being effusive to customers, but as proprietress, anxiety to succeed had dragged her out of her capable and mechanical indifference. It was a pity. Her consistent dullness had had a sort of dignity; but genial, she was merely ridiculous. Animation cruelly displayed her appalling commonness and physical shabbiness. Sophia's demeanour was not chilly; but it indicated that Sophia had no wish to be eyed over as a freak of nature.

Mr Critchlow advanced very slowly into the room. 'Ye still carry your head on a stiff neck,' said he, deliberately examining Sophia. Then with great care he put out his long thin arm and took her hand. 'Well, I'm rare and glad to see ye!'

Everyone was thunderstruck at this expression of joy. Mr Critchlow had never been known to be glad to see anybody.

'Yes,' twittered Maria, 'Mr Critchlow would come in tonight. Nothing would do but he must come in tonight.'

'You didn't tell me this afternoon,' said Constance, 'that you were going to give us the pleasure of your company like this.'

He looked momentarily at Constance. 'No,' he grated, 'I don't know as I did.'

His gaze flattered Sophia. Evidently he treated this experienced and sad woman of fifty as a young girl. And in presence of his extreme age she felt like a young girl, remembering the while how as a young girl she had hated him. Repulsing the assistance of his wife, he arranged an armchair in front of the fire and meticulously put himself into it. Assuredly he was much older in a drawing-room than behind the counter of his shop. Constance had noticed that in the afternoon. A live coal fell out of the fire. He bent forward, wet his fingers, picked up the coal and threw it back into the fire.

'Well,' said Sophia, 'I wouldn't have done that.'

'I never saw Mr Critchlow's equal for picking up hot cinders,' Maria giggled.

Mr Critchlow deigned no remark. 'When did ye leave this Paris?' he demanded of Sophia, leaning back, and putting his hands on the arms of the chair.

'Yesterday morning,' said Sophia.

'And what'n ye been doing with yeself since yesterday morning?'

'I spent last night in London,' Sophia replied.

'Oh, in London, did ye?'

'Yes. Cyril and I had an evening together.'

'Eh? Cyril! What's yer opinion o' Cyril, Sophia?'

'I'm very proud to have Cyril for a nephew,' said Sophia.

'Oh! Are ye?' The old man was obviously ironic.

'Yes I am,' Sophia insisted sharply. 'I'm not going to hear a word said against Cyril.'

She proceeded to an enthusiastic laudation of Cyril which rather overwhelmed his mother. Constance was pleased; she was delighted. And yet somewhere in her mind was an uncomfortable feeling that Cyril, having taken a fancy to his brilliant aunt, had tried to charm her as he seldom or never tried to charm his mother. Cyril and Sophia had dazzled and conquered each other; they were of the same type; whereas she, Constance, being but a plain person, could not glitter.

She rang the bell and gave instructions to Amy about food – fruit cakes, coffee and hot milk, on a tray; and Sophia also spoke to Amy, murmuring a request as to Fossette.

'Yes, Mrs Scales,' said Amy, with eager deference.

Mrs Critchlow smiled vaguely from a low chair near the curtained window. Then Constance lit another burner of the chandelier. In doing so, she gave a little sigh; it was a sigh of relief. Mr Critchlow had behaved himself. Now that he and Sophia had met, the worst was over. Had Constance known beforehand that he would pay a call, she would have been agonized by apprehensions, but now that he had actually come she was glad he had come.

When he had silently sipped some hot milk, he drew a thick bunch of papers, white and blue, from his bulging breast-pocket.

'Now, Maria Critchlow,' he called, edging round his chair slightly. 'Ye'd best go back home.'

Maria Critchlow was biting a bit of walnut cake, while in her right hand, all seamed with black lines, she held a cup of coffee.

'But, Mr Critchlow –' Constance protested.

'I've got business with Sophia, and I must get it done. I've got for to render an account of my stewardship to Sophia, under her father's will, and her mother's will, and her aunt's will, and it's nobody's business but mine and Sophia's, I reckon. Now then,' he glanced at his wife, 'off with ye!'

Maria rose, half-kittenish and half-ashamed.

'Surely you don't want to go into all that tonight,' said Sophia. She spoke softly, for she had already fully perceived that Mr Critchlow must be managed with the tact which the capricious obstinacies of advanced age demanded. 'Surely you can wait a day or two. I'm in no hurry.'

'*Haven't I waited long enough?*' he retorted fiercely.

There was a pause. Maria Critchlow moved.

'As for you being in no hurry, Sophia,' the old man went on, 'nobody can say as *you've* been in a hurry.'

Sophia had suffered a check. She glanced hesitatingly at Constance.

'Mrs Critchlow and I will go down into the parlour,' said Constance, quickly. 'There's a bit of fire there.'

'Oh no. I won't hear of such a thing!'

'Yes, we will, won't we, Mrs Critchlow?' Constance insisted, cheerfully but firmly. She was determined that in her house Sophia should have all the freedom and conveniences that she could have had in her own. If a private room was needed for discussions between Sophia and her trustee, Constance's pride was piqued to supply that room. Further, Constance was glad to get Maria out of Sophia's sight. She was accustomed to Maria; with her it did not matter; but she did not care that the teeth of Sophia should be set on edge by the ridiculous demeanour of Maria. So those two left the drawing-room, and the old man began to open the papers which he had been preparing for weeks.

There was very little fire in the parlour, and Constance, in addition to being bored by Mrs Critchlow's inane and inquisitive remarks, felt chilly, which was bad for her sciatica. She wondered whether Sophia would have to confess to Mr Critchlow that she was not certainly a widow. She thought that steps ought to be taken to ascertain, through Birkinshaws, if anything was known of Gerald Scales. But even that course was set with perils. Supposing that he still lived, an unspeakable villain (Constance could only think of him as an unspeakable villain), and supposing that he molested Sophia, – what scenes! What shame in the town! Such frightful thoughts ran endlessly through Constance's mind as she bent over the fire endeavouring to keep alive a silly conversation with Maria Critchlow.

Amy passed through the parlour to go to bed. There was no other way of reaching the upper part of the house.

'Are you going to bed, Amy?'

'Yes'm.'

'Where is Fossette?'

'In the kitchen, m'm,' said Amy, defending herself. 'Mrs Scales told me the dog might sleep in the kitchen with Spot, as they were such good friends. I've opened the bottom drawer, and Fossit is lying in that.'

'Mrs Scales has brought a dog with her!' exclaimed Maria.

'Yes'm!' said Amy, dryly, before Constance could answer. She implied everything in that affirmative.

'You *are* a family for dogs,' said Maria. 'What sort of dog is it?'

'Well,' said Constance, 'I don't know exactly what they call it. It's a French dog, one of those French dogs.' Amy was lingering at the stairfoot. 'Good night, Amy, thank you.'

Amy ascended, shutting the door.

'Oh! I see!' Maria muttered. 'Well, I never!'

It was ten o'clock before sounds above indicated that the first interview between trustee and beneficiary was finished.

'I'll be going on to open our side-door,' said Maria. 'Say good night to Mrs Scales for me.' She was not sure whether Charles Critchlow had really meant her to go home, or whether her mere absence from the drawing-room had contented him. So she departed. He came down the stairs with the most tiresome slowness, went through the parlour in silence, ignoring Constance, and also Sophia, who was at his heels, and vanished.

As Constance shut and bolted the front-door, the sisters looked at each other, Sophia faintly smiling. It seemed to them that they understood each other better when they did not speak. With a glance, they exchanged their ideas on the subject of Charles Critchlow and Maria, and learnt that their ideas were similar. Constance said nothing as to the private interview. Nor did Sophia. At present, on this the first day, they could only achieve intimacy by intermittent flashes.

'What about bed?' asked Sophia.

'You must be tired,' said Constance.

Sophia got to the stairs, which received a little light from the corridor gas, before Constance, having tested the window-fastening, turned out the gas in the parlour. They climbed the lower flight of stairs together.

'I must see that your room is all right,' Constance said.

'Must you?' Sophia smiled.

They climbed the second flight, slowly. Constance was out of breath.

'Oh, a fire! How nice!' cried Sophia. 'But why did you go to all that trouble? I told you not to.'

'It's no trouble at all,' said Constance, raising the gas in the bedroom. Her tone implied that bedroom fires were a quite ordinary incident of daily life in a place like Bursley.

'Well, my dear, I hope you'll find everything comfortable,' said Constance.

'I'm sure I shall. Good night, dear.'

'Good night, then.'

They looked at each other again, with timid affectionateness. They did not kiss. The thought in both their minds was: 'We couldn't keep on kissing every day.' But there was a vast amount of quiet restrained affection, of mutual confidence and respect, even of tenderness, in their tones.

About half an hour later a dreadful hullabaloo smote the ear of Constance. She was just getting into bed. She listened intently, in great alarm. It was undoubtedly those dogs fighting, and fighting to the death. She pictured the kitchen as a battlefield, and Spot slain. Opening the door, she stepped out into the corridor.

'Constance,' said a low voice above her. She jumped. 'Is that you?'

'Yes.'

'Well, don't bother to go down to the dogs; they'll stop in a moment. Fossette won't bite. I'm so sorry she's upsetting the house.'

Constance stared upwards, and discerned a pale shadow. The dogs did soon cease their altercation. This short colloquy in the dark affected Constance strangely.

III

The next morning, after a night varied by periods of wakefulness not unpleasant, Sophia rose and, taking due precautions against cold, went to the window. It was Saturday; she had left Paris on the Thursday. She looked forth upon the Square, holding aside the blind. She had expected, of course, to find that the Square had shrunk in size; but nevertheless she was startled to see how small it was. It seemed to her scarcely bigger than a courtyard. She could remember a winter morning when from the window she had watched the Square under virgin snow in the lamplight, and the Square had been vast, and the first wayfarer, crossing it diagonally and leaving behind him the irregular impress of his feet, had appeared to travel for hours over an interminable white waste before vanishing past Holl's shop in the direction of the Town Hall. She chiefly recalled the Square under snow; cold mornings, and the coldness of the oil-cloth at the window, and the draught of cold air through the ill-fitting sash (it was put right now)! These visions of herself seemed beautiful to her, her childish existence seemed beautiful; the storms and tempests of her girlhood seemed beautiful; even the great sterile expanse of tedium when, after giving up a scholastic career, she had served for two years in the shop – even this had a strange charm in her memory.

And she thought that not for millions of pounds would she live her life over again.

In its contents the Square had not surprisingly changed during the immense, the terrifying interval that separated her from her virginity. On the east side, several shops had been thrown into one, and forced into a semblance of eternal unity by means of a coat of stucco. And there was a fountain at the north end which was new to her. No other constructional change! But the moral change, the sad declension from the ancient proud spirit of the Square – this was painfully depressing. Several establishments lacked tenants, had obviously lacked tenants for a long time; 'To let' notices hung in their stained and dirty upper windows, and clung insecurely to their closed shutters. And on the sign-boards of these establishments were names that Sophia did not know.

The character of most of the shops seemed to have worsened; they had become pettifogging little holes, unkempt, shabby, poor; they had no brightness, no feeling of vitality. And the floor of the Square was littered with nondescript refuse. The whole scene, paltry, confined, and dull, reached for her the extreme of provinciality. It was what the French called, with a pregnant intonation, *la province*. This being said, there was nothing else to say. Bursley, of course, was in the provinces; Bursley must, in the nature of things, be typically provincial. But in her mind it had always been differentiated from the common *province*; it had always had an air, a distinction, and especially St Luke's Square! That illusion was now gone. Still, the alteration was not wholly in herself; it was not wholly subjective. The Square really had changed for the worse; it might not be smaller, but it had deteriorated. As a centre of commerce it had assuredly approached very near to death. On a Saturday morning thirty years ago it would have been covered with linen-roofed stalls, and chattering countryfolk, and the stir of bargains. Now, Saturday morning was like any other morning in the Square, and the glass-roof of St Luke's market in Wedgwood Street, which she could see from her window, echoed to the sounds of noisy commerce. In that instance business had simply moved a few yards to the east; but Sophia knew, from hints in Constance's letters and in her talk, that business in general had moved more than a few yards, it had moved a couple of miles – to arrogant and pushing Hanbridge, with its electric light and its theatres and its big, advertising shops. The heaven of thick smoke over the Square, the black deposit on painted woodwork, the intermittent hooting of steam sirens, showed that the wholesale trade of Bursley still flourished. But Sophia had no memories of the wholesale trade of Bursley; it meant nothing to the youth of her heart; she was attached by intimate links to the retail traffic of Bursley, and as a mart old Bursley was done for.

She thought: 'It would kill me if I had to live here. It's deadening. It weighs on you. And the dirt, and the horrible ugliness! And the way they talk, and the way they think! I felt it first at Knype station. The Square is rather picturesque, but it's such a poor, poor little thing! Fancy having to look at it every morning of one's life! No!' She almost shuddered.

For the time being she had no home. To Constance she was 'paying a visit'.

Constance did not appear to realize the awful conditions of dirt, decay, and provinciality in which she was living. Even Constance's house was extremely inconvenient, dark, and no doubt unhealthy. Cellar-kitchen, no hall, abominable stairs, and as to hygiene, simply medieval. She could not understand why Constance had remained in the house. Constance had plenty of money, and might live where she liked, and in a good modern house. Yet she stayed in the Square. 'I dare say she's got used to it,' Sophia thought leniently. 'I dare say I should be just the same in her place.' But she did not really think so, and she could not understand Constance's state of mind.

Certainly she could not claim to have 'added up' Constance yet. She considered that her sister was in some respects utterly provincial – what they used to call in the Five Towns a 'body'. Somewhat too diffident, not assertive enough, not erect enough; with curious provincial pronunciations, accents, gestures, mannerisms, and inarticulate ejaculations; with a curious narrowness of outlook! But at the same time Constance was very shrewd, and she was often proving by some bit of a remark that she knew what was what, despite her provinciality. In judgements upon human nature they undoubtedly thought alike, and there was a strong natural general sympathy between them. And at the bottom of Constance was something fine. At intervals Sophia discovered herself secretly patronizing Constance, but reflection would always cause her to cease from patronage and to examine her own defences. Constance, besides being the essence of kindness, was no fool. Constance could see through a pretence, an absurdity, as quickly as anyone. Constance did honestly appear to Sophia to be superior to any Frenchwoman that she had ever encountered. She saw supreme in Constance that quality which she had recognized in the porters at Newhaven on landing – the quality of an honest and naïve goodwill, of powerful simplicity. That quality presented itself to her as the greatest in the world, and it seemed to be in the very air of England. She could even detect it in Mr

Critchlow, whom, for the rest, she liked, admiring the brutal force of his character. She pardoned his brutality to his wife. She found it proper. 'After all,' she said, 'supposing he hadn't married her, what would she have been? Nothing but a slave! She's infinitely better off as his wife. In fact she's lucky. And it would be absurd for him to treat her otherwise than he does treat her.' (Sophia did not divine that her masterful Critchlow had once wanted Maria as one might want a star.)

But to be always with such people! To be always with Constance! To be always in the Bursley atmosphere, physical and mental!

She pictured Paris as it would be on that very morning – bright, clean, glittering; the neatness of the Rue Lord Byron, and the magnificent slanting splendour of the Champs Elysées. Paris had always seemed beautiful to her; but the life of Paris had not seemed beautiful to her. Yet now it did seem beautiful. She could delve down into the earlier years of her ownership of the Pension, and see a regular, placid beauty in her daily life there. Her life there, even so late as a fortnight ago, seemed beautiful; sad, but beautiful. It had passed into history. She sighed when she thought of the innumerable interviews with Mardon, the endless formalities required by the English and the French law and by the particularity of the Syndicate. She had been through all that. She had actually been through it and it was over. She had bought the Pension for a song and sold it for great riches. She had developed from a nobody into the desired of Syndicates. And after long, long, monotonous, strenuous years of possession the day had come, the emotional moment had come, when she had yielded up the keys of ownership to Mr Mardon and a man from the Hotel Moscow, and had paid her servants for the last time and signed the last receipted bill. The men had been very gallant, and had requested her to stay in the Pension as their guest until she was ready to leave Paris. But she had declined that. She could not have borne to remain in the Pension under the reign of another. She had left at once and gone to a hotel with her few goods while finally disposing of certain financial questions. And one evening Jacqueline had come to see her, and had wept.

Her exit from the Pension Frensham struck her now as poign-

antly pathetic, in its quickness and its absence of ceremonial. Ten
steps, and her career was finished, closed. Astonishing, with what
liquid tenderness she turned and looked back on that hard,
fighting, exhausting life in Paris! For, even if she had unconsciously liked it, she had never enjoyed it. She had always
compared France disadvantageously with England, always resented the French temperament in business, always been convinced that 'you never knew where you were' with French
tradespeople. And now they flitted before her endowed with a
wondrous charm; so polite in their lying, so eager to spare your
feelings and to reassure you, so neat and prim. And the French
shops, so exquisitely arranged! Even a butcher's shop in Paris was
a pleasure to the eye, whereas the butcher's shop in Wedgwood
Street, which she remembered of old, and which she had glimpsed
from the cab – what a bloody shambles! She longed for Paris
again. She longed to stretch her lungs in Paris. These people in
Bursley did not suspect what Paris was. They did not appreciate
and they never would appreciate the marvels that she had accomplished in a theatre of marvels. They probably never realized that
the whole of the rest of the world was not more or less like
Bursley. They had no curiosity. Even Constance was a thousand
times more interested in relating trifles of Bursley gossip than in
listening to details of life in Paris. Occasionally she had expressed
a mild, vapid surprise at things told to her by Sophia; but she was
not really impressed, because her curiosity did not extend beyond
Bursley. She, like the rest, had the formidable, thrice-callous
egotism of the provinces. And if Sophia had informed her that the
heads of Parisians grew out of their navels she would have
murmured: 'Well, well! Bless us! I never heard of such things!
Mrs Brindley's second boy has got his head quite crooked, poor
little fellow!'

Why should Sophia feel sorrowful? She did not know. She was
free; free to go where she liked and do what she liked. She had no
responsibilities, no cares. The thought of her husband had long
ago ceased to rouse in her any feeling of any kind. She was rich.
Mr Critchlow had accumulated for her about as much money as
she had herself acquired. Never could she spend her income! She
did not know how to spend it. She lacked nothing that was

procurable. She had no desires except the direct desire for happiness. If thirty thousand pounds or so could have bought a son like Cyril, she would have bought one for herself. She bitterly regretted that she had no child. In this she envied Constance. A child seemed to be the one commodity worth having. She was too free, too exempt from responsibilities. In spite of Constance she was alone in the world. The strangeness of the hazards of life overwhelmed her. Here she was at fifty, alone.

But the idea of leaving Constance, having once rejoined her, did not please Sophia. It disquieted her. She could not see herself living away from Constance. She was alone – but Constance was there.

She was downstairs first, and she had a little conversation with Amy. And she stood on the step of the front door while Fossette made a preliminary inspection of Spot's gutter. She found the air nipping.

Constance, when she descended, saw stretching across one side of the breakfast table an umbrella, Sophia's present to her from Paris. It was an umbrella such that a better could not be bought. It would have impressed even Aunt Harriet. The handle was of gold, set with a circlet of opalines. The tips of the ribs were also of gold. It was this detail which staggered Constance. Frankly, this development of luxury had been unknown and unsuspected in the Square. That the tips of the ribs should match the handle . . . that did truly beat everything! Sophia said calmly that the device was quite common. But she did not conceal that the umbrella was strictly of the highest class and that it might be shown to queens without shame. She intimated that the frame (a 'Fox's Paragon'), handle, and tips, would outlast many silks. Constance was childish with pleasure.

They decided to go out marketing together. The unspoken thought in their minds was that as Sophia would have to be introduced to the town sooner or later, it might as well be sooner.

Constance looked at the sky. 'It can't possibly rain,' she said. 'I shall take my umbrella.'

I

Sophia wore list slippers in the morning. It was a habit which she had formed in the Rue Lord Byron – by accident rather than with an intention to utilize list slippers for the effective supervision of servants. These list slippers were the immediate cause of important happenings in St Luke's Square. Sophia had been with Constance one calendar month – it was, of course, astonishing how quickly the time had passed! – and she had become familiar with the house. Restraint had gradually ceased to mark the relations of the sisters. Constance, in particular, hid nothing from Sophia, who was made aware of the minor and major defects of Amy and all the other creakings of the household machine. Meals were eaten off the ordinary table-cloths, and on the days for 'turning out' the parlour, Constance assumed, with a little laugh, that Sophia would excuse Amy's apron, which she had not had time to change. In brief, Sophia was no longer a stranger, and nobody felt bound to pretend that things were not exactly what they were. In spite of the foulness and the provinciality of Bursley, Sophia enjoyed the intimacy with Constance. As for Constance, she was enchanted. The inflections of their voices, when they were talking to each other very privately, were often tender, and these sudden surprising tenderness secretly thrilled both of them.

On the fourth Sunday morning Sophia put on her dressing-gown and those list slippers very early, and paid a visit to Constance's bedroom. She was somewhat concerned about Constance, and her concern was pleasurable to her. She made the most of it. Amy, with her lifelong carelessness about doors, had criminally failed to latch the street door of the parlour on the previous morning, and Constance had only perceived the omission by the phenomenon of frigidity in her legs at breakfast. She always sat with her back to the door, in her mother's fluted rocking-chair; and Sophia on the spot, but not in the chair, occupied by John Baines in the forties, and in the seventies and later by Samuel Povey. Constance had been alarmed by that frigidity. 'I shall have a return of my sciatica!' she had exclaimed, and Sophia was startled by the apprehension in her tone. Before evening the sciatica had indeed revisited Constance's sciatic nerve, and Sophia for the first time gained an idea of what a pulsating sciatica can do in the way of torturing its victim. Constance, in addition to the sciatica, had caught a sneezing cold, and the act of sneezing caused her the most acute pain. Sophia had soon stopped the sneezing. Constance was got to bed. Sophia wished to summon a doctor, but Constance assured her that the doctor would have nothing new to advise. Constance suffered angelically. The weak and exquisite sweetness of her smile, as she lay in bed under the stress of twinging pain amid hot-water bottles, was amazing to Sophia. It made her think upon the reserves of Constance's character, and upon the variety of the manifestations of the Baines blood.

So on the Sunday morning she had risen early, just after Amy.

She discovered Constance to be a little better, as regards the neuralgia, but exhausted by the torments of a sleepless night. Sophia, though she had herself not slept well, felt somehow conscience-stricken for having slept at all.

'You poor dear!' she murmured, brimming with sympathy. 'I shall make you some tea at once, myself.'

'Oh, Amy will do it,' said Constance.

Sophia repeated with a resolute intonation: 'I shall make it myself.' And after being satisfied that there was no instant need for a renewal of hot-water bottles, she went further downstairs in those list slippers.

As she was descending the dark kitchen steps she heard Amy's voice in pettish exclamation: 'Oh, get out, you!' followed by a yelp from Fossette. She had a swift movement of anger, which she controlled. The relations between her and Fossette were not marked by transports, and her rules over dogs in general were severe; even when alone she very seldom kissed the animal passionately, according to the general habit of people owning dogs. But she loved Fossette. And, moreover, her love for Fossette had been lately sharpened by the ridicule which Bursley had showered upon that strange beast. Happily for Sophia's *amour propre*, there was no means of getting Fossette shaved in Bursley, and thus Fossette was daily growing less comic to the Bursley eye. Sophia could therefore without loss of dignity yield to force of circumstances what she would not have yielded to popular opinion. She guessed that Amy had no liking for the dog, but the accent which Amy had put upon the '*you*' seemed to indicate that Amy was making distinctions between Fossette and Spot, and this disturbed Sophia much more than Fossette's yelps.

Sophia coughed, and entered the kitchen.

Spot was lapping his morning milk out of a saucer, while Fossette stood wistfully, an amorphous mass of thick hair, under the table.

'Good morning, Amy,' said Sophia, with dreadful politeness.

'Good morning, m'm,' said Amy, glumly.

Amy knew that Sophia had heard that yelp, and Sophia knew that she knew. The pretence of politeness was horrible. Both the women felt as though the kitchen was sanded with gunpowder and there were lighted matches about. Sophia had a very proper grievance against Amy on account of the open door of the previous day. Sophia thought that, after such a sin, the least Amy could do was to show contrition and amiability and an anxiety to please: which things Amy had not shown. Amy had a grievance against Sophia because Sophia had recently thrust upon her a fresh method of cooking green vegetables. Amy was a strong opponent of new or foreign methods. Sophia was not aware of this grievance, for Amy had hidden it under her customary cringing politeness to Sophia.

They surveyed each other like opposing armies.

'What a pity you have no gas stove here! I want to make some tea at once for Mrs Povey,' said Sophia, inspecting the just-born fire.

'Gas stove, m'm?' said Amy, hostilely. It was Sophia's list slippers which had finally decided Amy to drop the mask of deference.

She made no effort to aid Sophia; she gave no indication as to where the various necessaries for tea were to be found. Sophia got the kettle, and washed it out. Sophia got the smallest tea-pot, and, as the tea-leaves had been left in it, she washed out the tea-pot also, with exaggerated noise and meticulousness. Sophia got the sugar and the other trifles, and Sophia blew up the fire with the bellows. And Amy did nothing in particular except encourage Spot to drink.

'Is that all the milk you give to Fossette?' Sophia demanded coldly, when it had come to Fossette's turn. She was waiting for the water to boil. The saucer for the bigger dog, who would have made two of Spot, was not half full.

'It's all there is to spare, m'm,' Amy rasped.

Sophia made no reply. Soon afterwards she departed, with the tea successfully made. If Amy had not been a mature woman of over forty she would have snorted as Sophia went away. But Amy was scarcely the ordinary silly girl.

Save for a certain primness as she offered the tray to her sister, Sophia's demeanour gave no sign whatever that the Amazon in her was aroused. Constance's eager trembling pleasure in the tea touched her deeply, and she was exceedingly thankful that Constance had her, Sophia, as a succour in time of distress.

A few minutes later, Constance, having first asked Sophia what time it was by the watch in the watch-case on the chest of drawers (the Swiss clock had long since ceased to work), pulled the red tassel of bell-cord over her bed. A bell tinkled far away in the kitchen.

'Anything I can do?' Sophia inquired.

'Oh no, thanks,' said Constance. 'I only want my letters, if the postman has come. He ought to have been here long ago.'

Sophia had learned during her stay that Sunday morning was the morning on which Constance expected a letter from Cyril. It was a definite arrangement between mother and son that Cyril should write on Saturdays, and Constance on Sundays. Sophia knew that Constance set store by this letter, becoming more and more preoccupied about Cyril as the end of the week approached. Since Sophia's arrival Cyril's letter had not failed to come, but once it had been naught save a scribbled line or two, and Sophia gathered that it was never a certainty, and that Constance was accustomed, though not reconciled, to disappointments. Sophia had been allowed to read the letters. They left a faint impression on her mind that her favourite was perhaps somewhat negligent in his relations with his mother.

There was no reply to the bell. Constance rang again without effect.

With a brusque movement Sophia left the bedroom by way of Cyril's room.

'Amy,' she called over the banisters, 'do you not hear your mistress's bell?'

'I'm coming as quick as I can, m'm.' The voice was still very glum.

Sophia murmured something inarticulate, staying till assured that Amy really was coming, and then she passed back into Cyril's bedroom. She waited there, hesitant, not exactly on the watch, not exactly unwilling to assist at an interview between Amy and Amy's mistress; indeed, she could not have surely analysed her motive for remaining in Cyril's bedroom, with the door ajar between that room and Constance's.

Amy reluctantly mounted the stairs and went into her mistress's bedroom with her chin in the air. She thought that Sophia had gone up to the second storey, where she 'belonged'. She stood in silence by the bed, showing no sympathy with Constance, no curiosity as to the indisposition. She objected to Constance's attack of sciatica, as being a too permanent reproof of her carelessness as to doors.

Constance also waited, for the fraction of a second, as if expectant.

'Well, Amy,' she said at length in her voice weakened by fatigue and pain. 'The letters?'

'There ain't no letters,' said Amy, grimly. 'You might have known, if there'd been any, I should have brought 'em up. Postman went past twenty minutes agone. I'm always being interrupted, and it isn't as if I hadn't got enough to do – now!'

She turned to leave, and was pulling the door open.

'Amy!' said a voice sharply. It was Sophia's.

The servant jumped, and in spite of herself obeyed the implicit, imperious command to stop.

'You will please not speak to your mistress in that tone, at any rate while I'm here,' said Sophia, icily. 'You know she is ill and weak. You ought to be ashamed of yourself.'

'I never –' Amy began.

'I don't want to argue,' Sophia said angrily. 'Please leave the room.'

Amy obeyed. She was cowed, in addition to being staggered.

To the persons involved in it, this episode was intensely dramatic. Sophia had surmised that Constance permitted liberties of speech to Amy; she had even guessed that Amy sometimes took licence to be rude. But that the relations between them were such as to allow the bullying of Constance by an Amy downright insolent – this had shocked and wounded Sophia, who suddenly had a vision of Constance as the victim of a reign of terror. 'If the creature will do this while I'm here,' said Sophia to herself, 'what does she do when they are alone together in the house?'

'Well,' she exclaimed, 'I never heard of such goings-on! And you let her talk to you in that style! My dear Constance!'

Constance was sitting up in bed, the small tea-tray on her knees. Her eyes were moist. The tears had filled them when she knew that there was no letter. Ordinarily the failure of Cyril's letter would not have made her cry, but weakness had impaired her self-control. And the tears having once got into her eyes, she could not dismiss them. There they were!

'She's been with me such a long time,' Constance murmured. 'She takes liberties. I've corrected her once or twice.'

'Liberties!' Sophia repeated the word. 'Liberties!'

'Of course I really ought not to allow it,' said Constance. 'I ought to have put a stop to it long since.'

'Well,' said Sophia, rather relieved by this symptom of Constance's secret mind, 'I do hope you won't think I'm meddlesome, but truly it was too much for me. The words were out of my mouth before I –' She stopped.

'You were quite right, quite right,' said Constance, seeing before her in the woman of fifty the passionate girl of fifteen.

'I've had a good deal of experience of servants,' said Sophia.

'I know you have,' Constance put in.

'And I'm convinced that it never pays to stand any sauce.

Servants don't understand kindness and forbearance. And this sort of things grows and grows till you can't call your soul your own.'

'You are quite right,' Constance said again, with even more positiveness.

Not merely the conviction that Sophia was quite right, but the desire to assure Sophia that Sophia was not meddlesome, gave force to her utterance. Amy's allusion to extra work shamed Amy's mistress as a hostess, and she was bound to make amends.

'Now as to that woman,' said Sophia in a lower voice, as she sat down confidentially on the edge of the bed. And she told Constance about Amy and the dogs, and about Amy's rudeness in the kitchen. 'I should never have *dreamt* of mentioning such things,' she finished. 'But under the circumstances I felt it right that you should know. I feel you ought to know.'

And Constance nodded her head in thorough agreement. She did not trouble to go into articulate apologies to her guest for the actual misdeeds of her servant. The sisters were now on a plane of intimacy where such apologies would have been supererogatory. Their voices fell lower and lower, and the case of Amy was laid bare and discussed to the minutest detail.

Gradually they realized that what had occurred was a crisis. They were both very excited, apprehensive, and rather too consciously defiant. At the same time they were drawn very close to each other, by Sophia's generous indignation and by Constance's absolute loyalty.

A long time passed before Constance said, thinking about something else:

'I expect it's been delayed in the post.'

'Cyril's letter? Oh, no doubt! If you knew the posts in France, my word!'

Then they determined, with little sighs, to face the crisis cheerfully.

In truth it was a crisis, and a great one. The sensation of the crisis affected the atmosphere of the entire house. Constance got up for tea and managed to walk to the drawing-room. And when Sophia, after an absence in her own room, came down to tea and found the tea all served, Constance whispered:

'She's given notice! And Sunday too!'

'What did she say?'

'She didn't say much,' Constance replied vaguely, hiding from Sophia that Amy had harped on the too great profusion of mistresses in that house. 'After all, it's just as well. She'll be all right. She's saved a good bit of money, and she has friends.'

'But how foolish of her to give up such a good place!'

'She simply doesn't care,' said Constance, who was a little hurt by Amy's defection. 'When she takes a thing into her head she simply doesn't care. She's got no common sense. I've always known that.'

'So you're going to leave, Amy?' said Sophia that evening, as Amy was passing through the parlour on her way to bed. Constance was already arranged for the night.

'I am, m'm,' answered Amy, precisely.

Her tone was not rude, but it was firm. She had apparently reconnoitred her position in calmness.

'I'm sorry I was obliged to correct you this morning,' said Sophia, with cheerful amicableness, pleased in spite of herself with the woman's tone. 'But I think you will see that I had reason to.'

'I've been thinking it over, m'm,' said Amy, with dignity, 'and I see as I must leave.'

There was a pause.

'Well, you know best . . . Good night, Amy.'

'Good night, m'm.'

'She's a decent woman,' thought Sophia, 'but hopeless for this place now.'

The sisters were fronted with the fact that Constance had a month in which to find a new servant, and that a new servant would have to be trained in well-doing and might easily prove disastrous. Both Constance and Amy were profoundly disturbed by the prospective dissolution of a bond which dated from the seventies. And both were decided that there was no alternative to the dissolution. Outsiders knew merely that Mrs Povey's old servant was leaving. Outsiders merely saw Mrs Povey's advertisement in the *Signal* for a new servant. They could not read hearts. Some of the younger generation even said superiorly that old-fashioned women like Mrs Povey seemed to have servants on the brain, etc., etc.

II

'Well, have you got your letter?' Sophia demanded cheerfully of Constance when she entered the bedroom the next morning.

Constance merely shook her head. She was very depressed. Sophia's cheerfulness died out. As she hated to be insincerely optimistic, she said nothing. Otherwise she might have remarked: 'Perhaps the afternoon post will bring it.' Gloom reigned. To Constance particularly, as Amy had given notice and as Cyril was 'remiss', it seemed really that the time was out of joint and life unworth living. Even the presence of Sophia did not bring her much comfort. Immediately Sophia left the room Constance's sciatica began to return, and in a severe form. She had regretted this, less for the pain than because she had just assured Sophia, quite honestly, that she was not suffering; Sophia had been sceptical. After that it was of course imperative that Constance should get up as usual. She had said that she would get up as usual. Besides, there was the immense enterprise of obtaining a new servant! Worries loomed mountainous. Suppose Cyril was dangerously ill, and unable to write! Suppose something had happened to him! Supposing she never did obtain a new servant!

Sophia, up in her room, was endeavouring to be philosophical, and to see the world brightly. She was saying to herself that she must take Constance in hand, that what Constance lacked was energy, that Constance must be stirred out of her groove. And in the cavernous kitchen Amy, preparing the nine o'clock breakfast, was meditating upon the ingratitude of employers and wondering what the future held for her. She had a widowed mother in the picturesque village of Sneyd, where the mortal and immortal welfare of every inhabitant was watched over by God's vicegerent, the busy Countess of Chell; she possessed about two hundred pounds of her own; her mother for years had been begging Amy to share her home free of expense. But nevertheless Amy's mind was black with foreboding and vague dejection. The house was a house of sorrow, and these three women, each solitary, the devotees of sorrow. And the two dogs wandered disconsolate up and down, aware of the necessity for circumspection, never guessing that the highly peculiar state of the atmosphere had been brought about by nothing but a half-shut door and an incorrect tone.

As Sophia, fully dressed this time, was descending to breakfast, she heard Constance's voice, feebly calling her, and found the convalescent still in bed. The truth could not be concealed. Constance was once more in great pain, and her moral condition was not favourable to fortitude.

'I wish you had told me, to begin with,' Sophia could not help saying, 'then I should have known what to do.'

Constance did not defend herself by saying that the pain had only recurred since their first interview that morning. She just wept.

'I'm very low!' she blubbered.

Sophia was surprised. She felt that this was not 'being a Baines'.

During the progress of that interminable April morning, her acquaintance with the possibilities of sciatica as an agent destructive of moral fibre was further increased. Constance had no force at all to resist its activity. The sweetness of her resignation seemed to melt into nullity. She held to it that the doctor could do nothing for her.

About noon, when Sophia was moving anxiously around her, she suddenly screamed.

'I feel as if my leg was going to burst!' she cried.

That decided Sophia. As soon as Constance was a little easier she went downstairs to Amy.

'Amy,' she said, 'it's a Doctor Stirling that your mistress has when she's ill, isn't it?'

'Yes, m'm.'

'Where is his surgery?'

'Well, m'm, he did live just opposite, with Dr Harrop, but latterly he's gone to live at Bleakridge.'

'I wish you would put your things on, and run up there and ask him to call as soon as he can.'

'I will, m'm,' said Amy, with the greatest willingness. 'I thought

I heard missis cry out.' She was not effusive. She was better than effusive: kindly and helpful with a certain reserve.

'There's something about that woman I like,' said Sophia to herself. For a proved fool, Amy was indeed holding her own rather well.

Dr Stirling drove down about two o'clock. He had now been established in the Five Towns for more than a decade, and the stamp of success was on his brow and on the proud forehead of his trotting horse. He had, in the phrase of the *Signal*, 'identified himself with the local life of the district'. He was liked, being a man of broad sympathies. In his rich Scotch accent he could discuss with equal ability the flavour of whisky or of a sermon, and he had more than sufficient tact never to discuss either whiskies or sermons in the wrong place. He had made a speech (responding for the learned professions) at the annual dinner of the Society for the Prosecution of Felons, and this speech (in which praise of red wine was rendered innocuous by praise of books – his fine library was notorious) had classed him as a wit with the American consul, whose post-prandial manner was modelled on Mark Twain's. He was thirty-five years of age, tall and stoutish, with a chubby boyish face that the razor left chiefly blue every morning.

The immediate effect of his arrival on Constance was miraculous. His presence almost cured her for a moment, just as though her malady had been toothache and he a dentist. Then, when he had finished his examination, the pain resumed its sway over her.

In talking to her and to Sophia, he listened very seriously to all that they said; he seemed to regard the case as the one case that had ever aroused his genuine professional interest; but as it unfolded itself, in all its difficulty and urgency, so he seemed, in his mind, to be discovering wondrous ways of dealing with it; these mysterious discoveries seemed to give him confidence, and his confidence was communicated to the patient by means of faint sallies of humour. He was a highly skilled doctor. This fact, however, had no share in his popularity; which was due solely to his rare gift of taking a case very seriously while remaining cheerful.

He said he would return in a quarter of an hour, and he

returned in thirteen minutes with a hypodermic syringe, with which he attacked the pain in its central strongholds.

'What is it?' asked Constance, breathing gratitude for the relief.

He paused, looking at her roguishly from under lowered eyelids.

'I'd better not tell ye,' he said. 'It might lead ye into mischief.'

'Oh, but you must tell me doctor,' Constance insisted, anxious that he should live up to his reputation for Sophia's benefit.

'It's hydrochloride of cocaine,' he said, and lifted a finger. 'Beware of the cocaine habit. It's ruined many a respectable family. But if I hadn't a certain amount of confidence in yer strength of character, Mrs Povey, I wouldn't have risked it.'

'He will have his joke, will the doctor!' Constance smiled, in a brighter world.

He said he should come again about half-past five, and he arrived about half-past six, and injected more cocaine. The special importance of the case was thereby established. On this second visit, he and Sophia soon grew rather friendly. When she conducted him downstairs again he stopped chatting with her in the parlour for a long time, as though he had nothing else on earth to do, while his coachman walked the horse to and fro in front of the door.

His attitude to her flattered Sophia, for it showed that he took her for no ordinary woman. It implied a continual assumption that she must be a mine of interest for anyone who was privileged to delve into her memory. So far, among Constance's acquaintance, Sophia had met no one who showed more than a perfunctory curiosity as to her life. Her return was accepted with indifference. Her escapade of thirty years ago had entirely lost its dramatic quality. Many people indeed had never heard that she had run away from home to marry a commercial traveller; and to those who remembered, or had been told, it seemed a sufficiently banal exploit – after thirty years! Her fear, and Constance's, that the town would be murmurous with gossip was ludicrously unfounded. The effect of time was such that even Mr Critchlow appeared to have forgotten even that she had been indirectly responsible for her father's death. She had nearly forgotten it herself; when she happened to think of it she felt no shame, no remorse, seeing the death as purely accidental, and not altogether unfortunate. On two points only was the town inquisitive: as to her husband, and as to the precise figure at which she had sold the Pension. The town knew that she was probably not a widow, for she had been obliged to tell Mr Critchlow, and Mr Critchlow in some hour of tenderness had told Maria. But nobody had dared to mention the name of Gerald Scales to her. With her fashionable clothes, her striking mien of command, and the legend of her wealth, she inspired respect, if not awe, in the townsfolk. In the doctor's attitude there was something of amaze; she felt it. Though the dull apathy of the people she had hitherto met was assuredly not without its advantageous side for her tranquillity of mind, it had touched her vanity, and the gaze of the doctor soothed the smart. He had so obviously divined her interestingness; he so obviously wanted to enjoy it.

'I've just been reading Zola's *Downfall*,' he said.

Her mind searched backwards, and recalled a poster.

'Oh!' she replied. '*La Débâcle*?'

'Yes. What do ye think of it?' His eyes lighted at the prospect of a talk. He was even pleased to hear her give him the title in French.

'I haven't read it,' she said, and she was momentarily sorry that she had not read it, for she could see that he was dashed. The doctor had supposed that residence in a foreign country involved a knowledge of the literature of that country. Yet he had never supposed that residence in England involved a knowledge of English literature. Sophia had read practically nothing since 1870; for her the latest author was Cherbuliez.[15] Moreover, her impression of Zola was that he was not at all nice, and that he was the enemy of his race, though at that date the world had scarcely heard of Dreyfus.[16] Dr Stirling had too hastily assumed that the opinions of the bourgeois upon art differ in different countries.

'And ye actually were in the siege of Paris?' he questioned, trying again.

'Yes.'

'*And* the commune?'

'Yes, the commune too.'

'Well!' he exclaimed. 'It's incredible! When I was reading the *Downfall* the night before last, I said to myself that you must have been through a lot of all that. I didn't know I was going to have the pleasure of a chat with ye so soon.'

She smiled. 'But how did you know I was in the siege of Paris?' she asked, curious.

'How do I know? I know because I've seen that birthday card ye sent to Mrs Povey in 1871, after it was over. It's one of her possessions, that card is. She showed it me one day when she told me ye were coming.'

Sophia started. She had quite forgotten that card. It had not occurred to her that Constance would have treasured all those cards that she had despatched during the early years of her exile. She responded as well as she could to his eagerness for personal details concerning the siege and the commune. He might have been disappointed at the prose of her answers, had he not been determined not to be disappointed.

'Ye seem to have taken it all very quietly,' he observed.

'Eh yes!' she agreed, not without pride. 'But it's a long time since.'

Those events, as they existed in her memory, scarcely warranted the tremendous fuss subsequently made about them. What were they, after all? Such was her secret thought. Chirac himself was now nothing but a faint shadow. Still, were the estimate of those events true or false, she was a woman who had been through them, and Dr Stirling's high appreciation of that fact was very pleasant to her. Their friendliness approached intimacy. Night had fallen. Outside could be heard the champing of a bit.

'I must be getting on,' he said at last; but he did not move.

'Then there is nothing else I am to do for my sister?' Sophia inquired.

'I don't think so,' said he. 'It isn't a question of medicine.'

'Then what is it a question of?' Sophia demanded bluntly.

'Nerves,' he said. 'It's nearly all nerves. I know something about Mrs Povey's constitution now, and I was hoping that your visit would do her good.'

'She's been quite well – I mean what you may call quite well –

until the day before yesterday, when she sat in that draught. She was better last night, and then this morning I find her ever so much worse.'

'No worries?' The doctor looked at her confidentially.

'What *can* she have in the way of worries?' exclaimed Sophia. 'That's to say – real worries.'

'Exactly!' the doctor agreed.

'I tell her she doesn't know what worry is,' said Sophia.

'So do I!' said the doctor, his eyes twinkling.

'She was a little upset because she didn't receive her usual Sunday letter from Cyril yesterday. But then she was weak and low.'

'Clever youth, Cyril!' mused the doctor.

'I think he's a particularly nice boy,' said Sophia, eagerly.

'So you've seen him?'

'Of course,' said Sophia, rather stiffly. Did the doctor suppose that she did not know her own nephew? She went back to the subject of her sister. 'She is also a little bothered, I think, because the servant is going to leave.'

'Oh! So Amy is going to leave, is she?' He spoke still lower. 'Between you and me, it's no bad thing.'

'I'm so glad you think so.'

'In another few years the servant would have been the mistress here. One can see these things coming on, but it's so difficult to do anything. In fact ye can't do anything.'

'I did something,' said Sophia, sharply. 'I told the woman straight that it shouldn't go on while I was in the house. I didn't suspect it at first – but when I found it out . . . I can tell you!' She let the doctor imagine what she could tell him.

He smiled. 'No,' he said. 'I can easily understand that ye didn't suspect anything at first. When she's well and bright Mrs Povey could hold her own – so I'm told. But it was certainly slowly getting worse.'

'Then people talk about it?' said Sophia, shocked.

'As a native of Bursley, Mrs Scales,' said the doctor, 'ye ought to know what people in Bursley do!' Sophia put her lips together. The doctor rose, smoothing his waistcoat. 'What does she bother with servants at all for?' he burst out. 'She's perfectly free. She hasn't got a care in the world, if she only knew it. Why doesn't she go out and about, and enjoy herself? She wants stirring up, that's what your sister wants.'

'You're quite right,' Sophia burst out in her turn. 'That's precisely what I say to myself; precisely! I was thinking it over only this morning. She wants stirring up. She's got into a rut.'

'She needs to be jolly. Why doesn't she go to some seaside place, and live in a hotel, and enjoy herself? Is there anything to prevent her?'

'Nothing whatever.'

'Instead of being dependent on a servant! I believe in enjoying one's self – when ye've got the money to do it with! Can ye imagine anybody living in Bursley for pleasure? And especially in St Luke's Square, right in the thick of it all! Smoke! Dirt! No air! No light! No scenery! No amusements! What does she do it for? She's in a rut.'

'Yes, she's in a rut,' Sophia repeated her own phrase, which he had copied.

'My word!' said the doctor. 'Wouldn't I clear out and enjoy myself if I could! Your sister's a young woman.'

'Of course she is!' Sophia concurred, feeling that she herself was even younger. 'Of course she is!'

'And except that she's nervously organized, and has certain predispositions, there's nothing the matter with her. This sciatica – I don't say it would be cured, but it might be, by a complete change and throwing off all these ridiculous worries. Not only does she live in the most depressing conditions, but she suffers tortures for it, and there's absolutely no need for her to be here at all.'

'Doctor,' said Sophia, solemnly, impressed, 'you are quite right. I agree with every word you say.'

'Naturally she's attached to the place,' he continued, glancing round the room. 'I know all about that. After living here all her life! But she's got to break herself of her attachment. It's her duty to do so. She ought to show a little energy. I'm deeply attached to my bed in the morning, but I have to leave it.'

'Of course,' said Sophia, in an impatient tone, as though disgusted with every person who could not perceive, or would

not subscribe to, these obvious truths that the doctor was uttering. 'Of course!'

'What she needs is the bustle of life in a good hotel, a good
hydro, for instance. Among jolly people. Parties! Games! Excursions! She wouldn't be the same woman. You'd see. Wouldn't I
do it, if I could? Strathpeffer. She'd soon forget her sciatica. I
don't know what Mrs Povey's annual income is, but I expect that
if she took it into her head to live in the dearest hotel in England,
there would be no reason why she shouldn't.'

Sophia lifted her head and smiled in calm amusement. 'I expect
so,' she said superiorly.

'A hotel – that's the life. No worries. If ye want anything ye ring
a bell. If a waiter gives notice, it's someone else who has the
worry, not you. But you know all about that, Mrs Scales.'

'No one better,' murmured Sophia.

'Good evening,' he said abruptly, sticking out his hand. 'I'll be
down in the morning.'

'Did you ever mention this to my sister?' Sophia asked him,
rising.

'Yes,' said he. 'But it's no use. Oh yes, I've told her. But she does
really think it's quite impossible. She wouldn't even hear of going
to live in London with her beloved son. She won't listen.'

'I never thought of that,' said Sophia. 'Good night.'

Their hand-grasp was very intimate and mutually comprehending. He was pleased by the quick responsiveness of her
temperament, and the masterful vigour which occasionally
flashed out in her replies. He noticed the hardly perceptible
distortion of her handsome, worn face, and he said to himself:
'She's been through a thing or two,' and: 'She'll have to mind her
p's and q's.' Sophia was pleased because he admired her, and
because with her he dropped his bedside jocularities, and talked
plainly as a sensible man will talk when he meets an uncommonly
wise woman, and because he echoed and amplified her own
thoughts. She honoured him by standing at the door till he had
driven off.

For a few moments she mused solitary in the parlour, and then,
lowering the gas, she went upstairs to her sister, who lay in the
dark. Sophia struck a match.

'You've been having quite a long chat with the doctor,' said Constance. 'He's very good company, isn't he? What did he talk about this time?'

'He wanted to know about Paris and so on,' Sophia answered.

'Oh! I believe he's a rare student.'

Lying there in the dark, the simple Constance never suspected that those two active and strenuous ones had been arranging her life for her, so that she should be jolly and live for twenty years yet. She did not suspect that she had been tried and found guilty of sinful attachments, and of being in a rut, and of lacking the elements of ordinary sagacity. It had not occurred to her that if she was worried and ill, the reason was to be found in her own blind and stupid obstinacy. She had thought herself a fairly sensible kind of creature.

III

The sisters had an early supper together in Constance's bedroom. Constance was much easier. Having a fancy that a little movement would be beneficial, she had even got up for a few moments and moved about the room. Now she sat ensconced in pillows. A fire burned in the old-fashioned ineffectual grate. From the Sun Vaults opposite came the sound of a phonograph singing an invitation to God to save its gracious queen. This phonograph was a wonderful novelty, and filled the Sun nightly. For a few evenings it had interested the sisters, in spite of themselves, but they had soon sickened of it and loathed it. Sophia became more and more obsessed by the monstrous absurdity of the simple fact that she and Constance were there, in that dark inconvenient house, wearied by the gaiety of public-houses, blackened by smoke, surrounded by mud, instead of being luxuriously installed in a beautiful climate, amid scenes of beauty and white cleanliness. Secretly she became more and more indignant.

Amy entered, bearing a letter in her coarse hand. As Amy unceremoniously handed the letter to Constance, Sophia thought: 'If she was my servant she would hand letters on a tray.' (An advertisement had already been sent to the *Signal*.)

Constance took the letter trembling. 'Here it is at last,' she cried.

When she had put on her spectacles and read it, she exclaimed: 'Bless us! Here's news! He's coming down! That's why he didn't write on Saturday as usual.'

She gave the letter to Sophia to read. It ran —

'Sunday midnight.

'DEAR MOTHER,

'Just a line to say I am coming down to Bursley on Wednesday, on business with Peels. I shall get to Knype at 5.28, and take the Loop. I've been very busy, and as I was coming down I didn't write on Saturday. I hope you didn't worry. Love to yourself and Aunt Sophia.

'Yours, C.'

'I must send him a line,' said Constance, excitedly.

'What? Tonight?'

'Yes. Amy can easily catch the last post with it. Otherwise he won't know that I've got his letter.'

She rang the bell.

Sophia thought: 'His coming down is really no excuse for his not writing on Saturday. How could she guess that he was coming down? I shall have to put in a little word to that young man. I wonder Constance is so blind. She is quite satisfied now that his letter has come.' On behalf of the elder generation she rather resented Constance's eagerness to write in answer.

But Constance was not so blind. Constance thought exactly as Sophia thought. In her heart she did not at all justify or excuse Cyril. She remembered separately almost every instance of his carelessness in her regard. 'Hope I didn't worry, indeed!' she said to herself with a faint touch of bitterness, apropos of the phrase in his letter.

Nevertheless she insisted on writing at once. And Amy had to bring the writing materials.

'Mr Cyril is coming down on Wednesday,' she said to Amy with great dignity.

Amy's stony calmness was shaken, for Mr Cyril was a great deal to Amy. Amy wondered how she would be able to look Mr Cyril in the face when he knew that she had given notice.

In the middle of writing, on her knee, Constance looked up at Sophia, and said, as though defending herself against an accusation: 'I didn't write to him yesterday, you know, or today.'

'No,' Sophia murmured assentingly.

Constance rang the bell yet again, and Amy was sent out to the post.

Soon afterwards the bell was rung for the fourth time, and not answered.

'I suppose she hasn't come back yet. But I thought I heard the door. What a long time she is!'

'What do you want?' Sophia asked.

'I just want to speak to her,' said Constance.

When the bell had been rung seven or eight times, Amy at length reappeared, somewhat breathless.

'Amy,' said Constance, 'let me examine those sheets, will you?'

'Yes'm,' said Amy, apparently knowing what sheets, of all the various and multitudinous sheets in that house.

'And the pillow-cases,' Constance added as Amy left the room.

So it continued. The next day the fever heightened. Constance was up early, before Sophia, and trotting about the house like a girl. Immediately after breakfast Cyril's bedroom was invested and revolutionized; not till evening was order restored in that chamber. And on the Wednesday morning it had to be dusted afresh. Sophia watched the preparations, and the increasing agitation of Constance's demeanour, with an astonishment which she had real difficulty in concealing. 'Is the woman absolutely mad?' she asked herself. The spectacle was ludicrous: or it seemed so to Sophia, whose career had not embraced much experience of mothers. It was not as if the manifestations of Constance's anxiety were dignified or original or splendid. They were just silly, ordinary fussinesses; they had no sense in them. Sophia was very careful to make no observation. She felt that before she and Constance were very much older she had a very great deal to do, and that a subtle diplomacy and wary tactics would be necessary. Moreover, Constance's angelic temper was slightly affected by the strain of expectation. She had a tendency to rasp. After the high-tea was set she suddenly sprang on to the sofa and lifted down the 'Stag at Eve' engraving. The dust on the top of the frame incensed her.

'What are you going to do?' Sophia asked, in a final marvel.

'I'm going to change it with that one,' said Constance, pointing to another engraving opposite the fireplace. 'He said the effect would be very much better if they were changed. And his lordship is very particular.'

Constance did not go to Bursley station to meet her son. She explained that it upset her to do so, and that also Cyril preferred her not to come.

'Suppose I go to meet him,' said Sophia, at half-past five. The idea had visited her suddenly. She thought: 'Then I could talk to him before anyone else.'

'Oh, *do!*' Constance agreed.

Sophia put her things on with remarkable expedition. She arrived at the station a minute before the train came in. Only a few persons emerged from the train, and Cyril was not among them. A porter said that there was not supposed to be any connexion between the Loop Line trains and the main line expresses, and that probably the express had missed the Loop. She waited thirty-five minutes for the next Loop, and Cyril did not emerge from that train either.

Constance opened the front door to her, and showed a telegram –

'Sorry prevented last moment. Writing. CYRIL.'

Sophia had known it. Somehow she had known that it was useless to wait for the second train. Constance was silent and calm; Sophia also.

'What a shame! What a shame!' thumped Sophia's heart.

It was the most ordinary episode. But beneath her calm she was furious against her favourite. She hesitated.

'I'm just going out a minute,' she said.

'Where?' asked Constance. 'Hadn't we better have tea? I suppose we must have tea.'

'I shan't be long. I want to buy something.'

Sophia went to the post-office and despatched a telegram. Then, partially eased, she returned to the arid and painful desolation of the house.

IV

The next evening Cyril sat at the tea-table in the parlour with his mother and his aunt. To Constance his presence there had something of the miraculous in it. He had come, after all! Sophia was in a rich robe, and for ornament wore an old silver-gilt neck-chain, which was clasped at the throat, and fell in double to her waist, where it was caught in her belt. This chain interested Cyril. He referred to it once or twice, and then he said: 'Just let me have a *look* at that chain,' and put out his hands; and Sophia leaned forward so that he could handle it. His fingers played with it thus for some seconds; the picture strikingly affected Constance. At length he dropped it, and said: 'H'm!' After a pause he said: 'Louis Sixteenth, eh?' and Sophia said:

'They told me so. But it's nothing; it only cost thirty francs, you know.' And Cyril took her up sharply:

'What does that matter?' Then after another pause he asked: 'How often do you break a link of it?'

'Oh, often,' she said. 'It's always getting shorter.'

And he murmured mysteriously: 'H'm!'

He was still mysterious, withdrawn within himself, extraordinarily uninterested in his physical surroundings. But that evening he talked more than he usually did. He was benevolent, and showed a particular benevolence towards his mother, apparently exerting himself to answer her questions with fullness and heartiness, as though admitting frankly her right to be curious. He praised the tea; he seemed to notice what he was eating. He took Spot on his knee, and gazed in admiration at Fossette.

'By Jove!' he said, 'that's a dog, that is! . . . All the same . . .' And he burst out laughing.

'I won't have Fossette laughed at,' Sophia warned him.

'No, seriously,' he said, in his quality of an amateur of dogs; 'she is very fine.' Even then he could not help adding: 'What you can see of her!'

Whereupon Sophia shook her head, deprecating such wit. Sophia was very lenient towards him. Her leniency could be perceived in her eyes, which followed his movements all the time. 'Do you think he is like me, Constance?' she asked.

'I wish I was half as good looking,' said Cyril, quickly; and Constance said:

'As a baby he was very like you. He was a handsome baby. He wasn't at all like you when he was at school. These last few years he's begun to be like you again. He's very much changed since he left school; he was rather heavy and clumsy then.'

'Heavy and clumsy!' exclaimed Sophia. 'Well, I should never have believed it!'

'Oh, but he was!' Constance insisted.

'Now, mater,' said Cyril, 'it's a pity you don't want that cake cutting into. I think I could have eaten a bit of that cake. But of course if it's only for show . . . !'

Constance sprang up, seizing a knife.

'You shouldn't tease your mother,' Sophia told him. 'He doesn't really want any, Constance; he's regularly stuffed himself.'

And Cyril agreed, 'No, no, mater, don't cut it; I really couldn't. I was only gassing.'

But Constance could never clearly see through humour of that sort. She cut three slices of cake, and she held the plate towards Cyril.

'I tell you I really couldn't!' he protested.

'Come!' she said obstinately. 'I'm waiting! How much longer must I hold this plate?'

And he had to take a slice. So had Sophia. When she was roused, they both of them had to yield to Constance.

With the dogs, and the splendour of the tea-table under the gas, and the distinction of Sophia and Cyril, and the conversation, which on the whole was gay and free, rising at times to jolly garrulity, the scene in her parlour ought surely to have satisfied Constance utterly. She ought to have been quite happy, as her sciatica had raised the siege for a space. But she was not quite happy. The circumstances of Cyril's arrival had disturbed her; they had in fact wounded her, though she would scarcely admit the wound. In the morning she had received a brief letter from Cyril to say that he had not been able to come, and vaguely promising, or half-promising, to run down at a later date. That letter had the cardinal defects of all Cyril's relations with his mother: it was casual, and it was not candid. It gave no hint of the nature of the obstacle which had prevented him from coming. Cyril had always been too secretive. She was gravely depressed by the letter, which she did not show to Sophia, because it impaired her dignity as a mother, and displayed her son in a bad light. Then about eleven o'clock a telegram had come for Sophia.

'That's all right,' Sophia had said, on reading it. 'He'll be here this evening!' And she had handed over the telegram, which read –

'Very well. Will come same train today.'

And Constance learned that when Sophia had rushed out just before tea on the previous evening, it was to telegraph to Cyril.

'What did you say to him?' Constance asked.

'Oh!' said Sophia, with a careless air, 'I told him I thought he ought to come. After all, you're more important than any *business*, Constance! And I don't like him behaving like that. I was determined he should come!'

Sophia had tossed her proud head.

Constance had pretended to be pleased and grateful. But the existence of a wound was incontestable. Sophia, then, could do more with Cyril than she could! Sophia had only met him once, and could simply twist him round her little finger. He would never have done so much for his mother. A fine sort of an obstacle it must have been, if a single telegram from Sophia could overcome it . . . ! And Sophia, too, was secretive. She had gone out and had telegraphed, and had not breathed a word until she got the reply, sixteen hours later. She was secretive, and Cyril was secretive. They resembled one another. They had taken to one another. But Sophia was a curious mixture. When Constance had asked her if she should go to the station again to meet Cyril, she had replied scornfully: 'No, indeed! I've done going to meet Cyril. People who don't arrive must not expect to be met.'

When Cyril drove up to the door, Sophia had been in attendance. She hurried down the steps. 'Don't say anything about my telegram,' she had rapidly whispered to Cyril; there was no time for further explanation. Constance was at the top of the steps. Constance had not heard the whisper, but she had seen it; and she

saw a guilty, puzzled look on Cyril's face, afterwards an ineffectively concealed conspiratorial look on both their faces. They had
'something between them', from which she, the mother, was shut
out! Was it not natural that she should be wounded? She was far
too proud to mention the telegrams. And as neither Cyril nor
Sophia mentioned them, the circumstances leading to Cyril's
change of plan were not referred to at all, which was very curious.
Then Cyril was more sociable than he had ever been; he was
different, under his aunt's gaze. Certainly he treated his mother
faultlessly. But Constance said to herself: 'It is because she is here
that he is so specially nice to me.'

When tea was finished and they were going upstairs to the
drawing-room, she asked him, with her eye on the 'Stag at Eve'
engraving:

'Well, is it a success?'

'What?' His eye followed hers. 'Oh, you've changed it! What
did you do that for, mater?'

'You said it would be better like that,' she reminded him.

'Did I?' He seemed genuinely surprised. 'I don't remember. I
believe it is better, though,' he added. 'It might be better still if
you turned it the other way up.'

He pulled a face to Sophia, and screwed up his shoulders, as if
to indicate: 'I've done it, this time!'

'How? The other way up?' Constance queried. Then as she
comprehended that he was teasing her, she said: 'Get away with
you!' and pretended to box his ears. 'You were fond enough of
that picture at one time!' she said ironically.

'Yes, I was, mater,' he submissively agreed. 'There's no getting
over that.' And he pressed her cheeks between his hands and
kissed her.

In the drawing-room he smoked cigarettes and played the
piano – waltzes of his own composition. Constance and Sophia
did not entirely comprehend those waltzes. But they agreed that
all were wonderful and that one was very pretty indeed. (It
soothed Constance that Sophia's opinion coincided with hers.)
He said that that waltz was the worst of the lot. When he had
finished with the piano, Constance informed him about Amy.
'Oh! She told me,' he said, 'when she brought me my water. I

didn't mention it because I thought it would be rather a sore subject.' Beneath the casualness of his tone there lurked a certain curiosity, a willingness to hear details. He heard them.

At five minutes to ten, when Constance had yawned, he threw a bomb among them on the hearthrug.

'Well,' he said, 'I've got an appointment with Matthew at the Conservative Club at ten o'clock. I must go. Don't wait up for me.'

Both women protested, Sophia the more vivaciously. It was Sophia now who was wounded.

'It's business,' he said, defending himself. 'He's going away early tomorrow, and it's my only chance.' And as Constance did not brighten he went on: 'Business has to be attended to. You mustn't think I've got nothing to do but enjoy myself.'

No hint of the nature of the business! He never explained. As to business, Constance knew only that she allowed him three hundred a year, and paid his local tailor. The sum had at first seemed to her enormous, but she had grown accustomed to it.

'I should have preferred you to see Mr Peel-Swynnerton here,' said Constance. 'You could have had a room to yourselves. I do not like you going out at ten o'clock at night to a club.'

'Well, good night, mater,' he said, getting up. 'See you tomorrow. I shall take the key out of the door. It's true my pocket will never be the same again.'

Sophia saw Constance into bed, and provided her with two hot-water bottles against sciatica. They did not talk much.

V

Sophia sat waiting on the sofa in the parlour. It appeared to her that, though little more than a month had elapsed since her arrival in Bursley, she had already acquired a new set of interests and anxieties. Paris and her life there had receded in the strangest way. Sometimes for hours she would absolutely forget Paris. Thoughts of Paris were disconcerting; for either Paris or Bursley must surely be unreal! As she sat waiting on the sofa Paris kept coming into her mind. Certainly it was astonishing that she should be just as preoccupied with her schemes for the welfare of Constance as she had ever been preoccupied with schemes for the improvement of the Pension Frensham. She said to herself: 'My life has been so queer – and yet every part of it separately seemed ordinary enough – how will it end?'

Then there were footfalls on the steps outside, and a key was put in the door, which she at once opened.

'Oh!' exclaimed Cyril, startled, and also somewhat out of countenance. 'You're still up! Thanks.' He came in, smoking the end of a cigar. 'Fancy having to cart that about!' he murmured, holding up the great old-fashioned key before inserting it into the lock on the inside.

'I stayed up,' said Sophia, 'because I wanted to talk to you about your mother, and it's so difficult to get a chance.'

Cyril smiled, not without self-consciousness, and dropped into his mother's rocking-chair, which he had twisted round with his feet to face the sofa.

'Yes,' he said. 'I was wondering what was the real meaning of your telegram. What was it?' He blew out a lot of smoke and waited for her reply.

'I thought you ought to come down,' said Sophia, cheerfully but firmly. 'It was a fearful disappointment to your mother that you didn't come yesterday. And when she's expecting a letter from you and it doesn't come, it makes her ill.'

'Oh, well!' he said. 'I'm glad it's no worse. I thought from your telegram there was something seriously wrong. And then when you told me not to mention it – when I came in . . . !'

She saw that he failed to realize the situation, and she lifted her head challengingly.

'You neglect your mother, young man,' she said.

'Oh, come now, auntie!' he answered quite gently. 'You mustn't talk like that. I write to her every week. I've never missed a week. I come down as often as –'

'You miss the Sunday sometimes,' Sophia interrupted him.

'Perhaps,' he said doubtfully. 'But what –'

'Don't you understand that she simply lives for your letters? And if one doesn't come, she's very upset indeed – can't eat! And it brings on her sciatica, and I don't know what!'

He was taken aback by her boldness, her directness.

'But how silly of her! A fellow can't always –'

'It may be silly. But there it is. You can't alter her. And, after all, what would it cost you to be more attentive, even to write to her twice a week? You aren't going to tell me you're so busy as all that! I know a great deal more about young men than your mother does.' She smiled like an aunt.

He answered her smile sheepishly.

'If you'll only put yourself in your mother's place . . . !'

'I expect you're quite right,' he said at length. 'And I'm much obliged to you for telling me. How was I to know?' He threw the end of the cigar, with a large sweeping gesture, into the fire.

'Well, anyhow, you know now!' she said curtly; and she thought: 'You *ought* to have known. It was your business to know.' But she was pleased with the way in which he had accepted her criticism, and the gesture with which he threw away the cigar-end struck her as very distinguished.

'That's all right!' he said dreamily, as if to say: 'That's done with.' And he rose.

Sophia, however, did not stir.

'Your mother's health is not what it ought to be,' she went on, and gave him a full account of her conversation with the doctor.

'Really!' Cyril murmured, leaning on the mantelpiece with his elbow and looking down at her. 'Stirling said that, did he? I should have thought she would have been better where she is, in the Square.'

'Why better in the Square?'

'Oh, I don't know!'

'Neither do I!'

'She's always been here.'

'Yes,' said Sophia, 'she's been here a great deal too long.'

'What do *you* suggest?' Cyril asked, with impatience in his voice against this new anxiety that was being thrust upon him.

'Well,' said Sophia, 'what should you say to her coming to London and living with you?'

Cyril started back. Sophia could see that he was genuinely shocked. 'I don't think that would do at all,' he said.

'Why?'

'Oh! I don't think it would. London wouldn't suit her. She's not that sort of woman. I really thought she was quite all right down here. She wouldn't like London.' He shook his head, looking up at the gas; his eyes had a dangerous glare.

'But supposing she said she did?'

'Look here,' Cyril began in a new and brighter tone. 'Why don't you and she keep house together somewhere? That would be the very –'

He turned his head sharply. There was a noise on the staircase, and the staircase door opened with its eternal creak.

'Yes,' said Sophia. 'The Champs Elysées begins at the Place de la Concorde, and ends – Is that you, Constance?'

The figure of Constance filled the doorway. Her face was troubled. She had heard Cyril in the street, and had come down to see why he remained so long in the parlour. She was astounded to find Sophia with him. There they were, as intimate as cronies, chattering about Paris! Undoubtedly she was jealous! Never did Cyril talk like that to her!

'I thought you were in bed and asleep, Sophia,' she said weakly. 'It's nearly one o'clock.'

'No,' said Sophia. 'I didn't seem to feel like going to bed; and then Cyril happened to come in.'

But neither she nor Cyril could look innocent. And Constance glanced from one to the other apprehensively.

The next morning Cyril received a letter which, he said – with no further explanations – forced him to leave at once. He intimated that there had been danger in his coming just then, and that matters had turned out as he had feared.

'You think over what I said,' he whispered to Sophia when they were alone for an instant, 'and let me know.'

VI

A week before Easter the guests of the Rutland Hotel in the Broad Walk, Buxton, being assembled for afternoon tea in the 'lounge' of that establishment, witnessed the arrival of two middle-aged ladies and two dogs. Critically to examine newcomers was one of the amusements of the occupants of the lounge. This apartment, furnished 'in the oriental style', made a pretty show among the photographs in the illustrated brochure of the hotel, and, though draughty, it was of all the public rooms the favourite. It was draughty because only separated from the street (if the Broad Walk can be called a street) by two pairs of swinging-doors – in charge of two page-boys. Every visitor entering the hotel was obliged to pass through the lounge, and for newcomers the passage was an ordeal; they were made to feel that they had so much to learn, so much to get accustomed to; like passengers who join a ship at a port of call, they felt that the business lay before them of creating a niche for themselves in a hostile and haughty society. The two ladies produced a fairly favourable impression at the outset by reason of their two dogs. It is not everyone who has the courage to bring dogs into an expensive private hotel: to bring one dog indicates that you are not accustomed to deny yourself small pleasures for the sake of a few extra shillings; to bring two indicates that you have no fear of hotel-managers and that you are in the habit of regarding your own whim as nature's law. The shorter and stouter of the two ladies did not impose herself with much force on the collective vision of the Rutland; she was dressed in black, not fashionably, though with a certain unpretending richness; her gestures were timid and nervous; evidently she relied upon her tall companion to shield her in the first trying contacts of hotel life. The tall lady was of a different stamp. Handsome, stately, deliberate, and handsomely dressed in colours, she had the assured hard gaze of a person who is thoroughly habituated to the inspection of strangers. She curtly asked one of the page-boys for the manager, and the manager's wife tripped rapidly down the stairs in response, and was noticeably deferential. Her voice was quiet and commanding, the voice of one who gives orders that are obeyed. The opinion of the lounge was divided as to whether or not they were sisters.

They vanished quietly upstairs in convoy of the manager's wife, and they did not reappear for the lounge tea, which in any case would have been undrinkably stewed. It then became known, by the agency of one of those guests, to be found in every hotel, who acquire all the secrets of the hotel by the exercise of unabashed curiosity on the personnel, that the two ladies had engaged two bedrooms, Nos. 17 and 18, and the sumptuous private parlour with a balcony on the first floor, styled 'C' in the nomenclature of rooms. This fact definitely established the position of the new arrivals in the moral fabric of the hotel. They were wealthy. They had money to throw away. For even in a select hotel like the Rutland it is not everybody who indulges in a private sitting-room; there were only four such apartments in the hotel, as against fifty bedrooms.

At dinner they had a small table to themselves in a corner. The short lady wore a white shawl over her shoulders. Her almost apologetic manner during the meal confirmed the view that she must be a very simple person, unused to the world and its ways. The other continued to be imperial. She ordered half a bottle of wine and drank two glasses. She stared about her quite self-unconsciously, whereas the little woman divided her glances between her companion and her plate. They did not talk much. Immediately after dinner they retired. 'Widows in easy circumstances' was the verdict; but the contrast between the pair held puzzles that piqued the inquisitive.

Sophia had conquered again. Once more Sophia had resolved to accomplish a thing, and she had accomplished it. Events had fallen out thus. The advertisement for a general servant in the *Signal* had been a disheartening failure. A few answers were received, but of an entirely unsatisfactory character. Constance, a great deal more than Sophia, had been astounded by the bearing and the demands of modern servants. Constance was in despair. If Constance had not had an immense pride she would have been ready to suggest to Sophia that Amy should be asked to 'stay on'. But Constance would have accepted a modern impudent wench first. It was Maria Critchlow who got Constance out of her difficulty by giving her particulars of a reliable servant who was about to leave a situation in which she had stayed for eight years. Constance did not imagine that a servant recommended by Maria Critchlow would suit her, but, being in a quandary, she arranged to see the servant, and both she and Sophia were very pleased with the girl – Rose Bennion by name. The mischief was that Rose would not be free until about a month after Amy had left. Rose would have left her old situation, but she had a fancy to go and spend a fortnight with a married sister at Manchester before settling into new quarters. Constance and Sophia felt that this caprice of Rose's was really very tiresome and unnecessary. Of course Amy might have been asked to 'stay on' just for a month. Amy would probably have volunteered to do so had she been aware of the circumstances. She was not, however, aware of the circumstances. And Constance was determined not to be beholden to Amy for anything. What could the sisters do? Sophia, who had conducted all the interviews with Rose and other candidates, said that it would be a grave error to let Rose slip. Besides, they had no one to take her place, no one who could come at once.

The dilemma was appalling. At least, it seemed appalling to Constance, who really believed that no mistress had ever been so 'awkwardly fixed'. And yet, when Sophia first proposed her solution, Constance considered it to be a quite impossible solution. Sophia's idea was that they should lock up the house and leave it on the same day as Amy left it, to spend a few weeks in some holiday resort. To begin with, the idea of leaving the house empty seemed to Constance a mad idea. The house had never been left empty. And then – going for a holiday in April! Constance had never been for a holiday except in the month of August. No! The project was beset with difficulties and dangers which could not be overcome or provided against. For example, 'We can't come back to a dirty house,' said Constance. 'And we can't have a strange servant coming here before us.' To which Sophia had replied: 'Then what *shall* you do?' And Constance, after prodigious reflection on the frightful pass to which destiny had brought her, had said that she supposed she would have to manage with a charwoman until Rose's advent. She asked Sophia if she remembered old Maggie. Sophia, of course, perfectly remembered. Old Maggie was dead, as well as the drunken, amiable Hollins, but there was young Maggie (wife of a bricklayer) who went out charring in the spare time left from looking after seven children. The more Constance meditated upon young Maggie, the more was she convinced that young Maggie would meet the case. Constance felt that she could trust young Maggie.

This expression of trust in Maggie was Constance's undoing. Why should they not go away, and arrange with Maggie to come to the house a few days before their return, to clean and ventilate? The weight of reason overbore Constance. She yielded unwilling-

ly, but she yielded. It was the mention of Buxton that finally
moved her. She knew Buxton. Her old landlady at Buxton was
dead, and Constance had not visited the place since before
Samuel's death; nevertheless its name had a reassuring sound to
her ears, and for sciatica its waters and climate were admitted to
be the best in England. Gradually Constance permitted herself to
be embarked on this perilous enterprise of shutting up the house
for twenty-five days. She imparted the information to Amy, who
was astounded. Then she commenced her domestic preparations.
She wrapped Samuel's Family Bible in brown paper; she put
Cyril's straw-framed copy of Sir Edwin Landseer away in a
drawer, and she took ten thousand other precautions. It was
grotesque; it was farcical; it was what you please. And when,
with the cab at the door and the luggage on the cab, and the dogs
chained together, and Maria Critchlow waiting on the pavement
to receive the key, Constance put the key into the door on the
outside, and locked up the empty house, Constance's face was
tragic with innumerable apprehensions. And Sophia felt that she
had performed a miracle. She had.

On the whole the sisters were well received in the hotel, though
they were not at an age which commands popularity. In the
criticism which was passed upon them – the free, realistic and
relentless criticism of private hotels – Sophia was at first set down
as overbearing. But in a few days this view was modified, and
Sophia rose in esteem. The fact was that Sophia's behaviour
changed after forty-eight hours. The Rutland Hotel was very
good. It was so good as to disturb Sophia's profound beliefs that
there was in the world only one truly high-class pension, and that
nobody could teach the creator of that unique pension anything
about the art of management. The food was excellent; the
attendance on the bedrooms was excellent (and Sophia knew
how difficult of attainment was excellent bedroom attendance);
and to the eye the interior of the Rutland presented a spectacle far
richer than the Pension Frensham could show. The standard of
comfort was higher. The guests had a more distinguished appearance. It is true that the prices were much higher. Sophia was
humbled. She had enough sense to adjust her perspective. Further, she found herself ignorant of many matters which by the

other guests were taken for granted and used as a basis for conversation. Prolonged residence in Paris could not justify this ignorance; it seemed rather to intensify its strangeness. Thus, when someone of cosmopolitan experience, having learnt that she had lived in Paris for many years, asked what had been going on lately at the Comédie Française, she had to admit that she had not been in a French theatre for nearly thirty years. And when, on a Sunday, the same person questioned her about the English chaplain in Paris, lo! she knew nothing but his name, had never even seen him. Sophia's life, in its way, had been as narrow as Constance's. Though her experience of human nature was wide, she had been in a groove as deep as Constance's. She had been utterly absorbed in doing one single thing.

By tacit agreement she had charge of the expedition. She paid all the bills. Constance protested against the expensiveness of the affair several times, but Sophia quietened her by sheer force of individuality. Constance had one advantage over Sophia. She knew Buxton and its neighbourhood intimately, and she was therefore in a position to show off the sights and to deal with local peculiarities. In all other respects Sophia led.

They very soon became acclimatized to the hotel. They moved easily between Turkey carpets and sculptured ceilings; their eyes grew used to the eternal vision of themselves and other slow-moving dignities in gilt mirrors, to the heaviness of great oil-paintings of picturesque scenery, to the indications of surreptitious dirt behind massive furniture, to the grey-brown of the shirt-fronts of the waiters, to the litter of trays, boots, and pails in long corridors; their ears were always awake to the sounds of gongs and bells. They consulted the barometer and ordered the daily carriage with the perfunctoriness of habit. They discovered what can be learnt of other people's needle-work in a hotel on a wet day. They performed co-operative outings with fellow-guests. They invited fellow-guests into their sitting-room. When there was an entertainment they did not avoid it. Sophia was determined to do everything that could with propriety be done, partly as an outlet for her own energy (which since she left Paris had been accumulating), but more on Constance's account. She remembered all that Dr Stirling had said, and the heartiness of her own agreement with his opinions. It was a great day when, under tuition of an aged lady and in the privacy of their parlour, they both began to study the elements of Patience. Neither had ever played at cards. Constance was almost afraid to touch cards, as though in the very cardboard there had been something unrighteous and perilous. But the respectability of a luxurious private hotel makes proper every act that passes within its walls. And Constance plausibly argued that no harm could come from a game which you played by yourself. She acquired with some aptitude several varieties of Patience. She said: 'I think I could enjoy that, if I kept at it. But it does make my head whirl.'

Nevertheless Constance was not happy in the hotel. She worried the whole time about her empty house. She anticipated difficulties and even disasters. She wondered again and again whether she could trust the second Maggie in her house alone, whether it would not be better to return home earlier and participate personally in the cleaning. She would have decided to do so had it not been that she hesitated to subject Sophia to the inconvenience of a house upside down. The matter was on her mind, always. Always she was restlessly anticipating the day when they would leave. She had carelessly left her heart behind in St Luke's Square. She had never stayed in a hotel before, and she did not like it. Sciatica occasionally harassed her. Yet when it came to the point she would not drink the waters. She said she never had drunk them, and seemed to regard that as a reason why she never should. Sophia had achieved a miracle in getting her to Buxton for nearly a month, but the ultimate grand effect lacked brilliance.

Then came the fatal letter, the desolating letter, which vindicated Constance's dark apprehensions. Rose Bennion calmly wrote to say that she had decided not to come to St Luke's Square. She expressed regret for any inconvenience which might possibly be caused; she was polite. But the monstrousness of it! Constance felt that this actually and truly was the deepest depth of her calamities. There she was, far from a dirty home, with no servant and no prospect of a servant! She bore herself bravely, nobly; but she was stricken. She wanted to return to the dirty home at once.

Sophia felt that the situation created by this letter would demand her highest powers of dealing with situations, and she determined to deal with it adequately. Great measures were needed, for Constance's health and happiness were at stake, she alone could act. She knew that she could not rely upon Cyril. She still had an immense partiality for Cyril; she thought him the most charming young man she had ever known; she knew him to be industrious and clever; but in his relations with his mother there was a hardness, a touch of callousness. She explained it vaguely by saying that 'they did not get on well together'; which was strange, considering Constance's sweet affectionateness. Still, Constance could be a little trying – at times. Anyhow, it was soon clear to Sophia that the idea of mother and son living together in London was entirely impracticable. No! If Constance was to be saved from herself, there was no one but Sophia to save her.

After half a morning spent chiefly in listening to Constance's hopeless comments on the monstrous letter, Sophia said suddenly that she must take the dogs for an airing. Constance did not feel equal to walking out, and she would not drive. She did not want Sophia to 'venture', because the sky threatened. However, Sophia did venture, and she returned a few minutes late for lunch, full of vigour, with two happy dogs. Constance was moodily awaiting her in the dining-room. Constance could not eat. But Sophia ate, and she poured out cheerfulness and energy as from a source inexhaustible. After lunch it began to rain. Constance said she thought she should retire directly to the sitting-room. 'I'm coming too,' said Sophia, who was still wearing her hat and coat and carried her gloves in her hand. In the pretentious and banal sitting-room they sat down on either side the fire. Constance put a little shawl round her shoulders, pushed her spectacles into her grey hair, folded her hands, and sighed an enormous sigh: 'Oh, dear!' She was the tragic muse, aged, and in black silk.

'I tell you what I've been thinking,' said Sophia folding up her gloves.

'What?' asked Constance, expecting some wonderful solution to come out of Sophia's active brain.

'There's no earthly reason why you should go back to Bursley.

The house won't run away, and it's costing nothing but the rent. Why not take things easy for a bit?'

'And stay here?' said Constance, with an inflection that enlightened Sophia as to the intensity of her dislike of the existence at the Rutland.

'No, not here,' Sophia answered with quick deprecation. 'There are plenty of other places we could go to.'

'I don't think I should be easy in my mind,' said Constance. 'What with nothing being settled, the house –'

'What does it matter about the house?'

'It matters a great deal,' said Constance, seriously, and slightly hurt. 'I didn't leave things as if we were going to be away for a long time. It wouldn't do.'

'I don't see that anything could come to any harm, I really don't!' said Sophia, persuasively. 'Dirt can always be cleaned, after all. I think you ought to go about more. It would do you good – all the good in the world. And there is no reason why you shouldn't go about. You are perfectly free. Why shouldn't we go abroad together, for instance, you and I? I'm sure you would enjoy it very much.'

'Abroad?' murmured Constance, aghast, recoiling from the proposition as from a grave danger.

'Yes,' said Sophia, brightly and eagerly. She was determined to take Constance abroad. 'There are lots of places we could go to, and live very comfortably among nice English people.' She thought of the resorts she had visited with Gerald in the sixties. They seemed to her like cities of a dream. They came back to her as a dream recurs.

'I don't think going abroad would suit me,' said Constance.

'But why not? You don't know. You've never tried, my dear.' She smiled encouragingly. But Constance did not smile. Constance was inclined to be grim.

'I don't think it would,' said she, obstinately. 'I'm one of your stay-at-homes. I'm not like you. We can't all be alike,' she added, with her 'tart' accent.

Sophia suppressed a feeling of irritation. She knew that she had a stronger individuality than Constance's.

'Well, then,' she said, with undiminished persuasiveness, 'in

England or Scotland. There are several places I should like to visit – Torquay, Tunbridge Wells. I've always understood that Tunbridge Wells is a very nice town indeed, with very superior people, and a beautiful climate.'

'I think I shall have to be getting back to St Luke's Square,' said Constance, ignoring all that Sophia had said. 'There's so much to be done.'

Then Sophia looked at Constance with a more serious and resolute air; but still kindly, as though looking thus at Constance for Constance's own good.

'You are making a mistake, Constance,' she said, 'if you will allow me to say so.'

'A mistake!' exclaimed Constance, startled.

'A very great mistake,' Sophia insisted, observing that she was creating an effect.

'I don't see how I can be making a mistake,' Constance said, gaining confidence in herself, as she thought the matter over.

'No,' said Sophia, 'I'm sure you don't see it. But you are. You know, you are just a little apt to let yourself be a slave to that house of yours. Instead of the house existing for you, you exist for the house.'

'Oh! Sophia!' Constance muttered awkwardly. 'What ideas you do have, to be sure!' In her nervousness she rose and picked up some embroidery, adjusting her spectacles and coughing. When she sat down she said: 'No one could take things easier than I do as regards housekeeping. I can assure you I let dozens of little matters go, rather than bother myself.'

'Then why do you bother now?' Sophia posed her.

'I can't leave the place like that.' Constance was hurt.

'There's one thing I can't understand,' said Sophia, raising her head and gazing at Constance again, 'and that is, why you live in St Luke's Square at all.'

'I must live somewhere. And I'm sure it's very pleasant.'

'In all that smoke! And with that dirt! And the house is very old.'

'It's a great deal better built than a lot of those new houses by the Park,' Constance sharply retorted. In spite of herself she resented any criticism of her house. She even resented the obvious truth that it was old.

'You'll never get a servant to stay in that cellar-kitchen, for one thing,' said Sophia, keeping calm.

'Oh! I don't know about that! I don't know about that! That Bennion woman didn't object to it, anyway. It's all very well for you, Sophia, to talk like that. But I know Bursley perhaps better than you do.' She was tart again. 'And I can assure you that my house is looked upon as a very good house indeed.'

'Oh! I don't say it isn't; I don't say it isn't. But you would be better away from it. Everyone says that.'

'Everyone?' Constance looked up, dropping her work. 'Who? Who's been talking about me?'

'Well,' said Sophia, 'the doctor, for instance.'

'Dr Stirling? I like that! He's always saying that Bursley is one of the healthiest climates in England. He's always sticking up for Bursley.'

'Dr Stirling thinks you ought to go away more – not stay always in that dark house.' If Sophia had sufficiently reflected she would not have used the adjective 'dark'. It did not help her cause.

'Oh, does he!' Constance fairly snorted. 'Well, if it's of any interest to Dr Stirling, I like my dark house.'

'Hasn't he ever told you you ought to go away more?' Sophia persisted.

'He may have mentioned it,' Constance reluctantly admitted.

'When he was talking to me he did a good deal more than mention it. And I've a good mind to tell you what he said.'

'Do!' said Constance, politely.

'You don't realize how serious it is, I'm afraid,' said Sophia. 'You can't see yourself.' She hesitated a moment. Her blood being stirred by Constance's peculiar inflection of the phrase 'my dark house', her judgement was slightly obscured. She decided to give Constance a fairly full version of the conversation between herself and the doctor.

'It's a question of your health,' she finished. 'I think it's my duty to talk to you seriously, and I have done. I hope you'll take it as it's meant.'

'Oh, of course!' Constance hastened to say. And she thought:

'It isn't yet three months that we've been together, and she's trying already to get me under her thumb.'

A pause ensued. Sophia at length said: 'There's no doubt that both your sciatica and your palpitations are due to nerves. And you let your nerves get into a state because you worry over trifles. A change would do you a tremendous amount of good. It's just what you need. Really, you must admit, Constance, that the idea of living always in a place like St Luke's Square, when you are perfectly free to do what you like and go where you like – you must admit it's rather too much.'

Constance put her lips together and bent over her embroidery.

'Now, what do you say?' Sophia gently entreated.

'There's some of us like Bursley, black as it is!' said Constance. And Sophia was surprised to detect tears in her sister's voice.

'Now, my dear Constance,' she remonstrated.

'It's no use!' cried Constance, flinging away her work, and letting her tears flow suddenly. Her face was distorted. She was behaving just like a child. 'It's no use! I've got to go back home and look after things. It's no use. Here we are pitching money about in this place. It's perfectly sinful. Drives, carriages, extras! A shilling a day extra for each dog. I never heard of such goings-on. And I'd sooner be at home. That's it. I'd sooner be at home.' This was the first reference that Constance had made for a long time to the question of expense, and incomparably the most violent. It angered Sophia.

'We will count it that you are here as my guest,' said Sophia, loftily, 'if that is how you look at it.'

'Oh no!' said Constance. 'It isn't the money I grudge. Oh no, we won't.' And her tears were falling thick.

'Yes, we will,' said Sophia, coldly. 'I've only been talking to you for your own good. I –'

'Well,' Constance interrupted her despairingly, 'I wish you wouldn't try to domineer over me!'

'Domineer!' exclaimed Sophia, aghast. 'Well, Constance, I do think –'

She got up and went to her bedroom, where the dogs were imprisoned. They escaped to the stairs. She was shaking with emotion. This was what came of trying to help other people!

Imagine Constance . . . ! Truly Constance was most unjust, and quite unlike her usual self! And Sophia encouraged in her breast the feeling of injustice suffered. But a voice kept saying to her: 'You've made a mess of this. You've not conquered this time. You're beaten. And the situation is unworthy of you, of both of you. Two women of fifty quarrelling like this! It's undignified. You've made a mess of things.' And to strangle the voice, she did her best to encourage the feeling of injustice suffered.

'Domineer!'

And Constance was absolutely in the wrong. She had not argued at all. She had merely stuck to her idea like a mule! How difficult and painful would be the next meeting with Constance, after this grievous miscarriage!

As she was reflecting thus the door burst open, and Constance stumbled, as it were blindly, into the bedroom. She was still weeping.

'Sophia!' she sobbed, supplicatingly, and all her fat body was trembling. 'You mustn't kill me . . . I'm like that – you can't alter me. I'm like that. I know I'm silly. But it's no use!' She made a piteous figure.

Sophia was aware of a lump in her throat.

'It's all right, Constance; it's all right. I quite understand. Don't bother any more.'

Constance, catching her breath at intervals, raised her wet, worn face and kissed her.

Sophia remembered the very words, 'You can't alter her,' which she had used in remonstrating with Cyril. And now she had been guilty of precisely the same unreason as that with which she had reproached Cyril! She was ashamed, both for herself and for Constance. Assuredly it had not been such a scene as women of their age would want to go through often. It was humiliating. She wished that it could have been blotted out as though it had never happened. Neither of them ever forgot it. They had had a lesson. And particularly Sophia had had a lesson. Having learnt, they left the Rutland, amid due ceremonies, and returned to St Luke's Square.

CHAPTER 4: *End of Sophia*

I

The kitchen steps were as steep, dark, and difficult as ever. Up those steps Sophia Scales, nine years older than when she had failed to persuade Constance to leave the Square, was carrying a large basket, weighted with all the heaviness of Fossette. Sophia, despite her age, climbed the steps violently, and burst with equal violence into the parlour, where she deposited the basket on the floor near the empty fireplace. She was triumphant and breathless. She looked at Constance, who had been standing near the door in the attitude of a shocked listener.

'There!' said Sophia. 'Did you hear how she talked?'

'Yes,' said Constance. 'What shall you do?'

'Well,' said Sophia. 'I had a very good mind to order her out of the house at once. But then I thought I would take no notice. Her time will be up in three weeks. It's best to be indifferent. If once they see they can upset you . . . However, I wasn't going to leave Fossette down there to her tender mercies a moment longer. She's simply not looked after her at all.'

Sophia went on her knees to the basket, and, pulling aside the dog's hair, round about the head, examined the skin. Fossette was a sick dog and behaved like one. Fossette, too, was nine years older, and her senility was offensive. She was to no sense a pleasant object.

'See here,' said Sophia.

Constance also knelt to the basket.

'And here,' said Sophia. 'And here.'

The dog sighed, the insincere and pity-seeking sigh of a spoilt animal. Fossette foolishly hoped by such appeals to be spared the annoying treatment prescribed for her by the veterinary surgeon.

While the sisters were coddling her, and protecting her from her own paws, and trying to persuade her that all was for the best, another aged dog wandered vaguely into the room: Spot. Spot had very few teeth, and his legs were stiff. He had only one vice, jealousy. Fearing that Fossette might be receiving the entire attention of his mistresses, he had come to inquire into the situation. When he found the justification of his gloomiest apprehensions, he nosed obstinately up to Constance, and would not be put off. In vain Constance told him at length that he was interfering with the treatment. In vain Sophia ordered him sharply to go away. He would not listen to reason, being furious with jealousy. He got his foot into the basket.

'Will you!' exclaimed Sophia angrily, and gave him a clout on his old head. He barked snappishly, and retired to the kitchen again, disillusioned, tired of the world, and nursing his terrific grievance. 'I do declare,' said Sophia, 'that dog gets worse and worse.'

Constance said nothing.

When everything was done that could be done for the aged virgin in the basket, the sisters rose from their knees, stiffly; and they began to whisper to each other about the prospects of obtaining a fresh servant. They also debated whether they could tolerate the criminal eccentricities of the present occupant of the cave for yet another three weeks. Evidently they were in the midst of a crisis. To judge from Constance's face every imaginable woe had been piled on them by destiny without the slightest regard for their powers of resistance. Her eyes had the permanent look of worry, and there was in them also something of the self-defensive. Sophia had a bellicose air, as though the creature in the cave had squarely challenged her, and she was decided to take up the challenge. Sophia's tone seemed to imply an accusation of Constance. The general tension was acute.

Then suddenly their whispers expired, and the door opened and the servant came in to lay the supper. Her nose was high, her gaze cruel, radiant, and conquering. She was a pretty and an impudent girl of about twenty-three. She knew she was torturing her old and infirm mistresses. She did not care. She did it purposely. Her motto was: War on employers, get all you can out of them, for they will get all they can out of you. On principle — the sole principle she possessed — she would not stay in a place more than six months. She liked change. And employers did not like change. She was shameless with men. She ignored all orders as to what she was to eat and what she was not to eat. She lived up to the full resources of her employers. She could be to the last degree slatternly. Or she could be as neat as a pin, with an apron that symbolized purity and propriety, as tonight. She could be idle during a whole day, accumulating dirty dishes from morn till eve. On the other hand she could, when she chose, work with astonishing celerity and even thoroughness. In short, she was born to infuriate a mistress like Sophia and to wear out a mistress like Constance. Her strongest advantage in the struggle was that she enjoyed altercation; she revelled in a brawl; she found peace tedious. She was perfectly calculated to convince the sisters that times had worsened, and that the world would never again be the beautiful, agreeable place it once had been.

Her gestures as she laid the table were very graceful, in the pert style. She dropped forks into their appointed positions with disdain; she made slightly too much noise; when she turned she manoeuvred her swelling hips as though for the benefit of a soldier in a handsome uniform.

Nothing but the servant had been changed in that house. The harmonium on which Mr Povey used occasionally to play was still behind the door; and on the harmonium was the tea-caddy of which Mrs Baines used to carry the key on her bunch. In the corner to the right of the fireplace still hung the cupboard where Mrs Baines stored her pharmacopoeia. The rest of the furniture was arranged as it had been arranged when the death of Mrs Baines endowed Mr and Mrs Povey with all the treasures of the house at Axe. And it was as good as ever; better than ever. Dr Stirling often expressed the desire for a corner cupboard like Mrs Baines's corner cupboard. One item had been added: the 'Peel' compote which Matthew Peel-Swynnerton had noticed in the dining-room of the Pension Frensham. This majestic piece, which had been reserved by Sophia in the sale of the pension, stood alone on a canterbury in the drawing-room. She had stored it, with a few other trifles, in Paris, and when she sent for it and the packing-case arrived, both she and Constance became aware that they were united for the rest of their lives. Of worldly goods, except money, securities, and clothes, that compote was practically all that Sophia owned. Happily it was a first-class item, doing no shame to the antique magnificence of the drawing-room.

In yielding to Constance's terrible inertia, Sophia had meant nevertheless to work her own will on the interior of the house. She had meant to bully Constance into modernizing the dwelling. She did bully Constance, but the house defied her. Nothing could be done to that house. If only it had had a hall or lobby a complete transformation would have been possible. But there was no access to the upper floor except through the parlour. The parlour could not therefore be turned into a kitchen and the basement suppressed, and the ladies of the house could not live entirely on the upper floor. The disposition of the rooms had to remain exactly as it had always been. There was the same draught under the door, the same darkness on the kitchen stairs, the same difficulties with tradesmen in the distant backyard, the same twist in the bedroom stairs, the same eternal ascending and descending of pails. An efficient cooking-stove, instead of the large and capacious range, alone represented the twentieth century in the fixtures of the house.

Buried at the root of the relations between the sisters was Sophia's grudge against Constance for refusing to leave the Square. Sophia was loyal. She would not consciously give with one hand while taking away with the other, and in accepting Constance's decision she honestly meant to close her eyes to its stupidity. But she could not entirely succeed. She could not avoid thinking that the angelic Constance had been strangely and monstrously selfish in refusing to quit the Square. She marvelled that a woman of Constance's sweet and calm disposition should be capable of so vast and ruthless an egotism. Constance must have known that Sophia would not leave her, and that the habitation of the Square was a continual irk to Sophia. Constance had never been able to advance a single argument for remaining in the Square. And yet she would not budge. It was so inconsistent with the rest of Constance's behaviour. See Sophia sitting primly there by the table, a woman approaching sixty, with immense experience written on the fine hardness of her worn and distinguished face! Though her hair is not yet all grey, nor her figure bowed, you would imagine that she would in her passage through the world, have learnt better than to expect a character to be consistent. But no! She was ever disappointed and hurt by Constance's inconsistency! And see Constance, stout and bowed, looking more than her age, with hair nearly white and slightly trembling hands! See that face whose mark is meekness and the spirit of conciliation, the desire for peace – you would not think that that placid soul could, while submitting to it, inly rage against the imposed weight of Sophia's individuality. 'Because I wouldn't turn out of my house to please her,' Constance would say to herself, 'she fancies she is entitled to do just as she likes.' Not often did she secretly rebel thus, but it occurred sometimes. They never quarrelled. They would have regarded separation as a disaster. Considering the difference of their lives, they agreed marvellously in their judgement of things. But that buried question of domicile prevented a complete unity between them. And its subtle effect was to influence both of them to make the worst, instead of the best, of the trifling mishaps that disturbed their tranquillity. When annoyed, Sophia would meditate upon the mere fact that they lived in the Square for no reason whatever, until it grew incredibly shocking to her. After all it was scarcely conceivable that they should be living in the very middle of a dirty, ugly, industrial town simply because Constance mulishly declined to move. Another thing that curiously exasperated both of them upon occasion was that, owing to a recurrence of her old complaint of dizziness after meals, Sophia had been strictly forbidden to drink tea, which she loved. Sophia chafed under the deprivation, and Constance's pleasure was impaired because she had to drink it alone.

While the brazen and pretty servant, mysteriously smiling to herself, dropped food and utensils on to the table, Constance and Sophia attempted to converse with negligent ease upon indifferent topics, as though nothing had occurred that day to mar the beauty of ideal relations between employers and employed. The pretence was ludicrous. The young wench saw through it instantly, and her mysterious smile developed almost into a laugh.

'Please shut the door after you, Maud,' said Sophia as the girl picked up her empty tray.

'Yes, ma'am,' replied Maud, politely.

She went out and left the door open.

It was a defiance, offered from sheer, youthful, wanton mischief.

The sisters looked at each other, their faces gravely troubled, aghast, as though they had glimpsed the end of civilized society, as though they felt that they had lived too long into an age of decadence and open shame. Constance's face showed despair – she might have been about to be pitched into the gutter without a friend and without a shilling – but Sophia's had the reckless courage that disaster breeds.

Sophia jumped up, and stepped to the door. 'Maud,' she called out.

No answer.

'Maud, do you hear me?'

The suspense was fearful.

Still no answer.

Sophia glanced at Constance. 'Either she shuts this door, or she leaves this house at once, even if I have to fetch a policeman!'

And Sophia disappeared down the kitchen steps. Constance trembled with painful excitement. The horror of existence closed in upon her. She could imagine nothing more appalling than the pass to which they had been brought by the modern change in the lower classes.

In the kitchen, Sophia, conscious that the moment held the future of at least the next three weeks, collected her forces.

'Maud,' she said, 'did you not hear me call you?'

Maud looked up from a book – doubtless a wicked book.

'No, ma'am.'

'You liar!' thought Sophia. And she said: 'I asked you to shut the parlour door, and I shall be obliged if you will do so.'

Now Maud would have given a week's wages for the moral force to disobey Sophia. There was nothing to compel her to obey. She could have trampled on the fragile and weak Sophia. But something in Sophia's gaze compelled her to obey. She flounced; she bridled; she mumbled; she unnecessarily disturbed the venerable Spot; but she obeyed. Sophia had risked all, and she had won something.

'And you should light the gas in the kitchen,' said Sophia magnificently, as Maud followed her up the steps. 'Your young eyes may be very good now, but you are not going the way to preserve them. My sister and I have often told you that we do not grudge you gas.'

With stateliness she rejoined Constance, and sat down to the cold supper. And as Maud clicked the door to, the sisters breathed relief. They envisaged new tribulations, but for a brief instant there was surcease.

Yet they could not eat. Niether of them, when it came to the point, could swallow. The day had been too exciting, too distressing. They were at the end of their resources. And they did not hide from each other that they were at the end of their resources. The illness of Fossette, without anything else, had been more than enough to ruin their tranquillity. But the illness of Fossette was as nothing to the ingenious naughtiness of the servant. Maud had a sense of temporary defeat, and was planning fresh operations; but really it was Maud who had conquered. Poor old things, they were in such a 'state' that they could not eat!

'I'm not going to let her think she can spoil my appetite!' said Sophia, dauntless. Truly that woman's spirit was unquenchable.

She cut a couple of slices off the cold fowl; she cut a tomato into slices; she disturbed the butter; she crumbled bread on the cloth, and rubbed bits of fowl over the plates, and dirtied knives and forks. Then she put the slices of fowl and bread and tomato into a piece of tissue paper, and silently went upstairs with the parcel and came down again a moment afterwards emptyhanded.

After an interval she rang the bell, and lighted the gas.

'We've finished, Maud. You can clear away.'

Constance thirsted for a cup of tea. She felt that a cup of tea was the one thing that would certainly keep her alive. She longed for it passionately. But she would not demand it from Maud. Nor would she mention it to Sophia, lest Sophia, flushed by the victory of the door, should incur new risks. She simply did without. On empty stomachs they tried pathetically to help each other in games of Patience. And when the blithe Maud passed through the parlour on the way to bed, she saw two dignified and apparently calm ladies, apparently absorbed in a delightful game of cards, apparently without a worry in the world. They said 'Good night, Maud,' cheerfully, politely, and coldly. It was a heroic scene. Immediately afterwards Sophia carried Fossette up to her own bedroom.

II

The next afternoon the sisters, in the drawing-room, saw Dr Stirling's motor-car speeding down the Square. The doctor's partner, young Harrop, had died a few years before at the age of over seventy, and the practice was much larger than it had ever been, even in the time of old Harrop. Instead of two or three horses, Stirling kept a car, which was a constant spectacle in the streets of the district.

'I do hope he'll call in,' said Mrs Povey, and sighed.

Sophia smiled to herself with a little scorn. She knew that Constance's desire for Dr Stirling was due simply to the need which she felt of telling someone about the great calamity that had happened to them that morning. Constance was utterly absorbed by it, in the most provincial way. Sophia had said to herself at the beginning of her sojourn in Bursley, and long afterwards, that she should never get accustomed to the exasperating provinciality of the town, exemplified by the childish preoccupation of the inhabitants with their own two-penny affairs. No characteristic of life in Bursley annoyed her more than this. None had oftener caused her to yearn in a brief madness for the desert-like freedom of great cities. But she had got accustomed to it. Indeed, she had almost ceased to notice it. Only occasionally, when her nerves were more upset than usual, did it strike her.

She went into Constance's bedroom to see whether the doctor's car halted in King Street. It did.

'He's here,' she called out to Constance.

'I wish you'd go down, Sophia,' said Constance. 'I can't trust that minx —'

So Sophia went downstairs to superintend the opening of the door by the minx.

The doctor was radiant, according to custom.

'I thought I'd just see how that dizziness was going on,' said he as he came up the steps.

'I'm glad you've come,' said Sophia, confidentially. Since the first days of their acquaintance they had always been confidential. 'You'll do my sister good today.'

Just as Maud was closing the door a telegraph-boy arrived, with a telegram addressed to Mrs Scales. Sophia read it and then crumpled it in her hand.

'What's wrong with Mrs Povey today?' the doctor asked, when the servant had withdrawn.

'She only wants a bit of your society,' said Sophia. 'Will you go up? You know the way to the drawing-room. I'll follow.'

As soon as he had gone she sat down on the sofa, staring out of the window. Then with a grunt: 'Well, that's no use, anyway!' she went upstairs after the doctor. Already Constance had begun upon her recital.

'Yes,' Constance was saying. 'And when I went down this morning to keep an eye on the breakfast, I thought Spot was very quiet —' She paused. 'He was dead in the drawer. She pretended she didn't know, but I'm sure she did. Nothing will convince me that she didn't poison that dog with the mice-poison we had last year. She was vexed because Sophia took her up sharply about Fossette last night, and she revenged herself on the other dog. It would just be like her. Don't tell me! I know. I should have packed her off at once, but Sophia thought better not. We couldn't *prove* anything, as Sophia says. Now, what do you think of it, doctor?'

Constance's eyes suddenly filled with tears.

'Ye'd had Spot a long time, hadn't ye?' he said sympathetically.

She nodded. 'When I was married,' said she, 'the first thing my husband did was to buy a fox-terrier, and ever since we've always had a fox-terrier in the house.' This was not true, but Constance was firmly convinced of its truth.

'It's very trying,' said the doctor. 'I know when my Airedale died, I said to my wife I'd never have another dog — unless she could find me one that would live for ever. Ye remember my Airedale?'

'Oh, quite well!'

'Well, my wife said I should be bound to have another one sooner or later, and the sooner the better. She went straight off to Oldcastle and bought me a spaniel pup, and there was such a to-do training it that we hadn't too much time to think about Piper.'

Constance regarded this procedure as somewhat callous, and she said so, tartly. Then she recommenced the tale of Spot's death from the beginning, and took it as far as his burial, that afternoon, by Mr Critchlow's manager, in the yard. It had been necessary to remove and replace paving-stones.

'Of course,' said Dr Stirling, 'ten years is a long time. He was an old dog. Well, you've still got the celebrated Fossette.' He turned to Sophia.

'Oh yes,' said Constance, perfunctorily. 'Fossette's ill. The fact is that if Fossette hadn't been ill, Spot would probably have been alive and well now.'

Her tone exhibited a grievance. She could not forget that Sophia had harshly dismissed Spot to the kitchen, thus practically sending him to his death. It seemed very hard to her that Fossette, whose life had once been despaired of, should continue to exist, while Spot, always healthy and unspoilt, should die untended, and by treachery. For the rest, she had never liked Fossette. On Spot's behalf she had always been jealous of Fossette.

'Probably alive and well now!' she repeated, with a peculiar accent.

Observing that Sophia maintained a strange silence, Dr Stirling suspected a slight tension in the relations of the sisters, and he changed the subject. One of his great qualities was that he refrained from changing a subject introduced by a patient unless there was a professional reason for changing it.

'I've just met Richard Povey in the town,' said he. 'He told me to tell ye that he'll be round in about an hour or so to take you for a spin. He was in a new car, which he did his best to sell to me, but he didn't succeed.'

'It's very kind of Dick,' said Constance. 'But this afternoon really we're not –'

'I'll thank ye to take it as a prescription, then,' replied the doctor. 'I told Dick I'd see that ye went. Splendid June weather. No dust after all that rain. It'll do ye all the good in the world. I must exercise my authority. The truth is, I've gradually been losing all control over ye. Ye do just as ye like.'

'Oh, doctor, how you do run on!' murmured Constance, not quite well pleased today by his tone.

After the scene between Sophia and herself at Buxton, Constance had always, to a certain extent, in the doctor's own phrase, 'got her knife into him'. Sophia had, then, in a manner betrayed him. Constance and the doctor discussed that matter with frankness, the doctor humorously accusing her of being 'hard' on him. Nevertheless the little cloud between them was real, and the result was often a faint captiousness on Constance's part in judging the doctor's behaviour.

'He's got a surprise for ye, has Dick!' the doctor added.

Dick Povey, after his father's death and his own partial recovery, had set up in Hanbridge as a bicycle agent. He was permanently lamed, and he hopped about with a thick stick. He had succeeded with bicycles and had taken to automobiles, and he was succeeding with automobiles. People were at first startled that he should advertise himself in the Five Towns. There was an obscure general feeling that because his mother had been a drunkard and his father a murderer, Dick Povey had no right to exist. However, when it had recovered from the shock of seeing Dick Povey's announcement of bargains in the *Signal*, the district most sensibly decided that there was no reason why Dick Povey should not sell bicycles as well as a man with normal parents. He was now supposed to be acquiring wealth rapidly. It was said that he was a marvellous chauffeur, at once daring and prudent. He had one day, several years previously, overtaken the sisters in the rural neighbourhood of Sneyd, where they had been making an afternoon excursion. Constance had presented him to Sophia, and he had insisted on driving the ladies home. They had been much impressed by his cautious care of them, and their natural prejudice against anything so new as a motor-car had been conquered instantly. Afterwards he had taken them out for occasional runs. He had a great admiration for Constance, founded on gratitude to Samuel Povey; and as for Sophia, he always said to her that she would be an ornament to any car.

'You haven't heard his latest, I suppose?' said the doctor, smiling.

'What is it?' Sophia asked, perfunctorily.

'He wants to take to ballooning. It seems he's been up once.'

Constance made a deprecating noise with her lips.

'However, that's not his surprise,' the doctor added, smiling again at the floor. He was sitting on the music-stool, and saying to himself, behind his mask of effulgent good-nature: 'It gets more and more uphill work, cheering up these two women. I'll try them on Federation.'

Federation was the name given to the scheme for blending the Five Towns into one town, which would be the twelfth largest town in the kingdom. It aroused fury in Bursley, which saw in the suggestion nothing but the extinction of its ancient glory to the aggrandizement of Hanbridge. Hanbridge had already, with the assistance of electric cars that whizzed to and fro every five minutes, robbed Bursley of two-thirds of its retail trade – as witness the steady decadence of the Square! – and Bursley had no mind to swallow the insult and become a mere ward of Hanbridge. Bursley would die fighting. Both Constance and Sophia were bitter opponents of Federation. They would have been capable of putting Federationists to the torture. Sophia in particular, though so long absent from her native town, had adopted its cause with characteristic vigour. And when Dr Stirling wished to practise his curative treatment of taking the sisters 'out of themselves', he had only to start the hare of Federation and the hunt would be up in a moment. But this afternoon he did not succeed with Sophia, and only partially with Constance. When he stated that there was to be a public meeting that very night, and that Constance as a ratepayer ought to go to it and vote, if her convictions were genuine, she received his chaff with a mere murmur to the effect that she did not think she should go. Had the man forgotten that Spot was dead? At length he became grave, and examined them both as to their ailments, and nodded his head, and looked into vacancy while meditating upon each case. And then, when he had inquired where they meant to go for their summer holidays, he departed.

'Aren't you going to see him out?' Constance whispered to Sophia, who had shaken hands with him at the drawing-room door. It was Sophia who did the running about, owing to the state of Constance's sciatic nerve. Constance had, indeed, become extraordinarily inert, leaving everything to Sophia.

Sophia shook her head. She hesitated; then approached Constance, holding out her hand and disclosing the crumpled telegram.

'Look at that!' said she.

Her face frightened Constance, who was always expectant of new anxieties and troubles. Constance straightened out the paper with difficulty, and read –

Mr Gerald Scales is dangerously ill here. Boldero, 49, Deansgate, Manchester.

All through the inexpressibly tedious and quite unnecessary call of Dr Stirling – (Why had he chosen to call just then? Neither of them was ill) – Sophia had held that telegram concealed in her hand and its information concealed in her heart. She had kept her head up, offering a calm front to the world. She had given no hint of the terrible explosion – for an explosion it was. Constance was astounded at her sister's self-control, which entirely passed her comprehension. Constance felt that worries would never cease, but would rather go on multiplying until death ended all. First, there had been the frightful worry of the servant; then the extremely distressing death and burial of Spot – and now it was Gerald Scales turning up again! With what violence was the direction of their thoughts now shifted! The wickedness of maids was a trifle; the death of pets was a trifle. But the reappearance of Gerald Scales! ... That involved the possibility of consequences which could not even be named, so afflictive was the mere prospect to them. Constance was speechless, and she saw that Sophia was also speechless.

Of course the event had been bound to happen. People do not vanish never to be heard of again. The time surely arrives when the secret is revealed. So Sophia said to herself – now!

She had always refused to consider the effect of Gerald's reappearance. She had put the idea of it away from her, deter-

mined to convince herself that she had done with him finally and
for ever. She had forgotten him. It was years since he had ceased
to disturb her thoughts – many years. 'He *must* be dead,' she had
persuaded herself. 'It is inconceivable that he should have lived
on and never come across me. If he had been alive and learnt that I
had made money, he would assuredly have come to me. No, he
must be dead!'

And he was not dead! The brief telegram overwhelmingly
shocked her. Her life had been calm, regular, monotonous. And
now it was thrown into an indescribable turmoil by five words of
a telegram, suddenly, with no warning whatever. Sophia had the
right to say to herself: 'I have had my share of trouble, and more
than my share!' The end of her life promised to be as awful as the
beginning. The mere existence of Gerald Scales was a menace to
her. But it was the simple impact of the blow that affected her
supremely, beyond ulterior things. One might have pictured fate
as a cowardly brute who had struck this ageing woman full in the
face, a felling blow, which however had not felled her. She
staggered, but she stuck on her legs. It seemed a shame – one of
those crude, spectacular shames which make the blood boil – that
the gallant, defenceless creature should be so maltreated by the
bully, destiny.

'Oh, Sophia!' Constance moaned. 'What trouble is this?'

Sophia's lip curled with a disgusted air. Under that she hid her
suffering.

She had not seen him for thirty-six years. He must be over
seventy years of age, and he had turned up again like a bad penny,
doubtless a disgrace! What had he been doing in those thirty-six
years? He was an old, enfeebled man now! He must be a pretty
sight! And he lay at Manchester, not two hours away!

Whatever feelings were in Sophia's heart, tenderness was not
among them. As she collected her wits from the stroke, she was
principally aware of the sentiment of fear. She recoiled from the
future.

'What shall you do?' Constance asked. Constance was weeping.

Sophia tapped her foot, glancing out of the window.

'Shall you go to see him?' Constance continued.

'Of course,' said Sophia. 'I must!'

She hated the thought of going to see him. She flinched from it. She felt herself under no moral obligation to go. Why should she go? Gerald was nothing to her, and had no claim on her of any kind. This she honestly believed. And yet she knew that she must go to him. She knew it to be impossible that she should not go.

'Now?' demanded Constance.

Sophia nodded.

'What about the trains? . . . Oh, you poor dear!' The mere idea of the journey to Manchester put Constance out of her wits, seeming a business of unparalleled complexity and difficulty.

'Would you like me to come with you?'

'Oh no! I must go by myself.'

Constance was relieved by this. They could not have left the servant in the house alone, and the idea of shutting up the house without notice or preparation presented itself to Constance as too fantastic.

By a common instinct they both descended to the parlour.

'Now, what about a time-table? What about a time-table?' Constance mumbled on the stairs. She wiped her eyes resolutely. 'I wonder whatever in this world has brought him at last to that Mr Boldero's in Deansgate?' she asked the walls.

As they came into the parlour, a great motor-car drove up before the door, and when the pulsations of its engines had died away, Dick Povey hobbled from the driver's seat to the pavement. In an instant he was hammering at the door in his lively style. There was no avoiding him. The door had to be opened. Sophia opened it. Dick Povey was over forty, but he looked considerably younger. Despite his lameness, and the fact that his lameness tended to induce corpulence, he had a dashing air, and his face, with its short, light moustache, was boyish. He seemed to be always upon some joyous adventure.

'Well, aunties,' he greeted the sisters, having perceived Constance behind Sophia; he often so addressed them. 'Has Dr Stirling warned you that I was coming? Why haven't you got your things on?'

Sophia observed a young woman in the car.

'Yes,' said he, following her gaze, 'you may as well look. Come

down, miss. Come down, Lily. You've got to go through with it.'
The young woman, delicately confused and blushing, obeyed.
'This is Miss Lily Holl,' he went on. 'I don't know whether you
would remember her. I don't think you do. It's not often she
comes to the Square. But, of course, she knows you by sight.
Granddaughter of your old neighbour, Alderman Holl! We are
engaged to be married, if you please.'

Constance and Sophia could not decently pour out their griefs
on the top of such news. The betrothed pair had to come in and be
congratulated upon their entry into the large realms of mutual
love. But the sisters, even in their painful quandary, could not
help noticing what a nice, quiet, ladylike girl Lily Holl was. Her
one fault appeared to be that she was too quiet. Dick Povey was
not the man to pass time in formalities, and he was soon urging
departure.

'I'm sorry we can't come,' said Sophia. 'I've got to go to
Manchester now. We are in great trouble.'

'Yes, in great trouble,' Constance weakly echoed.

Dick's face clouded sympathetically. And both the affianced
began to see that to which the egotism of their happiness had
blinded them. They felt that long, long years had elapsed since
these ageing ladies had experienced the delights which they were
feeling.

'Trouble? I'm sorry to hear that!' said Dick.

'Can you tell me the trains to Manchester?' asked Sophia.

'No,' said Dick, quickly. 'But I can drive you there quicker than
any train, if it's urgent. Where do you want to go to?'

'Deansgate,' Sophia faltered.

'Look here,' said Dick, 'it's half-past three. Put yourself in my
hands; I'll guarantee at Deansgate you shall be before half-past
five. I'll look after you.'

'But –'

'There isn't any "but". I'm quite free for the afternoon and
evening.'

At first the suggestion seemed absurd, especially to Constance.
But really it was too tempting to be declined. While Sophia made
ready for the journey, Dick and Lily Holl and Constance con-
versed in low, solemn tones. The pair were waiting to be enlight-

ened as to the nature of the trouble; Constance, however, did not enlighten them. How could Constance say to them: 'Sophia has a husband that she hasn't seen for thirty-six years, and he's dangerously ill, and they've telegraphed for her to go?' Constance could not. It did not even occur to Constance to order a cup of tea.

III

Dick Povey kept his word. At a quarter past five he drew up in front of No. 49 Deansgate, Manchester. 'There you are!' he said, not without pride. 'Now, we'll come back in about a couple of hours or so, just to take your orders, whatever they are.' He was very comforting, with his suggestion that in him Sophia had a sure support in the background.

Without many words Sophia went straight into the shop. It looked like a jeweller's shop, and a shop for bargains generally. Only the conventional sign over a side-entrance showed that at heart it was a pawnbroker's. Mr Till Boldero did a nice business in the Five Towns, and in other centres near Manchester, by selling silver-ware second-hand, or nominally second-hand, to persons who wished to make presents to other persons or to themselves. He would send anything by post on approval. Occasionally he came to the Five Towns, and he had once, several years before, met Constance. They had talked. He was the son of a cousin of the late great and wealthy Boldero, sleeping partner in Birkinshaws, and Gerald's uncle. It was from Constance that he had learnt of Sophia's return to Bursley. Constance had often remarked to Sophia what a superior man Mr Till Boldero was.

The shop was narrow and lofty. It seemed like a menagerie for trapped silver-ware. In glass cases right up to the dark ceiling silver vessels and instruments of all kinds lay confined. The top of the counter was a glass prison containing dozens of gold watches, together with snuff-boxes, enamels, and other antiquities. The front of the counter was also glazed, showing vases and large pieces of porcelain. A few pictures in heavy gold frames were perched about. There was a case of umbrellas with elaborate handles and rich tassels. There were a couple of statuettes. The counter, on the customer's side, ended in a glass screen on which were the words 'Private Office'. On the seller's side the prospect was closed by a vast safe. A tall young man was fumbling in this safe. Two women sat on customers' chairs, leaning against the crystal counter. The young man came towards them from the safe, bearing a tray.

'How much is that goblet?' asked one of the women, raising her parasol dangerously among such fragility and pointing to one object among many in a case high up from the ground.

'That, madam?'

'Yes.'

'Thirty-five pounds.'

The young man disposed his tray on the counter. It was packed with more gold watches, adding to the extraordinary glitter and shimmer of the shop. He chose a small watch from the regiment.

'Now, this is something I can recommend,' he said. 'It's made by Cuthbert Butler of Blackburn. I can guarantee you that for five years.' He spoke as though he were the accredited representative of the Bank of England, with calm and absolute assurance.

The effect upon Sophia was mysteriously soothing. She felt that she was among honest men. The young man raised his head towards her with a questioning, deferential gesture.

'Can I see Mr Boldero?' she asked. 'Mrs Scales.'

The young man's face changed instantly to a sympathetic comprehension.

'Yes, madam. I'll fetch him at once,' said he, and he disappeared behind the safe. The two customers discussed the watch. Then the door opened in the glass screen, and a portly, middle-aged man showed himself. He was dressed in blue broadcloth, with a turned-down collar and a small black tie. His waistcoat displayed a plain but heavy gold watch-chain, and his cuff-links were of plain gold. His eye-glasses were gold-rimmed. He had grey hair, beard, and moustache, but on the backs of his hands grew a light brown hair. His appearance was strangely mild, dignified, and confidence-inspiring. He was, in fact, one of the most respected tradesmen in Manchester.

He peered forward, looking over his eye-glasses, which he then took off, holding them up in the air by their short handle. Sophia had approached him.

'Mrs Scales?' he said, in a very quiet, very benevolent voice.

Sophia nodded. 'Please come this way.' He took her hand, squeezing it commiseratingly, and drew her into the sanctum. 'I didn't expect you so soon,' he said. 'I looked up the trains, and I didn't see how you could get here before six.'

Sophia explained.

He led her farther, through the private office, into a sort of parlour, and asked her to sit down. And he too sat down. Sophia waited, as it were, like a suitor.

'I'm afraid I've got bad news for you, Mrs Scales,' he said, still in that mild, benevolent voice.

'He's dead?' Sophia asked.

Mr Till Boldero nodded. 'He's dead. I may as well tell you that he had passed away before I telegraphed. It all happened very, very suddenly.' He paused. 'Very, very suddenly!'

'Yes,' said Sophia, weakly. She was conscious of a profound sadness which was not grief, though it resembled grief. And she had also a feeling that she was responsible to Mr Till Boldero for anything untoward that might have occurred to him by reason of Gerald.

'Yes,' said Mr Till Boldero, deliberately and softly. 'He came in last night just as we were closing. We had very heavy rain here. I don't know how it was with you. He was wet, in a dreadful state, simply dreadful. Of course, I didn't recognize him. I'd never seen him before, so far as my recollection goes. He asked me if I was the son of Mr Till Boldero that had this shop in 1866. I said I was. "Well," he says, "you're the only connexion I've got. My name's Gerald Scales. My mother was your father's cousin. Can you do anything for me?" he says. I could see he was ill. I had him in here. When I found he couldn't eat nor drink I thought I'd happen better send for th' doctor. The doctor got him to bed. He passed away at one o'clock this afternoon. I was very sorry my wife wasn't here to look after things a bit better. But she's at Southport, not well at all.'

'What was it?' Sophia asked briefly.

Mr Boldero indicated the enigmatic. 'Exhaustion, I suppose,' he replied.

'He's here?' demanded Sophia, lifting her eyes to possible bedrooms.

'Yes,' said Mr Boldero. 'I suppose you would wish to see him?'

'Yes,' said Sophia.

'You haven't seen him for a long time, your sister told me?' Mr Boldero murmured, sympathetically.

'Not since 'seventy,' said Sophia.

'Eh, dear! Eh, dear!' ejaculated Mr Boldero. 'I fear it's been a sad business for ye, Mrs Scales. Not since 'seventy!' He sighed. 'You must take it as well as you can. I'm not one as talks much, but I sympathize with you. I do that! I wish my wife had been here to receive you.'

Tears came into Sophia's eyes.

'Nay, nay!' he said. 'You must bear up now!'

'It's you that make me cry,' said Sophia, gratefully. 'You were very good to take him in. It must have been exceedingly trying for you.'

'Oh,' he protested, 'you mustn't talk like that. I couldn't leave a Boldero on the pavement, and an old man at that! . . . Oh, to think that if he'd only managed to please his uncle he might ha' been one of the richest men in Lancashire. But then there'd ha' been no Boldero Institute at Strangeways!' he added.

They both sat silent a moment.

'Will you come now? Or will you wait a bit?' asked Mr Boldero, gently. 'Just as you wish. I'm sorry as my wife's away, that I am!'

'I'll come now,' said Sophia, firmly. But she was stricken.

He conducted her up a short, dark flight of stairs which gave on a passage, and at the end of the passage was a door ajar. He pushed the door open.

'I'll leave you for a moment,' he said, always in the same very restrained tone. 'You'll find me downstairs, there, if you want me.' And he moved away with hushed, deliberate tread.

Sophia went into the room, of which the white blind was drawn. She appreciated Mr Boldero's consideration in leaving her. She was trembling. But when she saw, in the pale gloom, the face of an aged man peeping out from under a white sheet on a naked mattress, she started back, trembling no more – rather transfixed into an absolute rigidity. That was no conventional, expected shock that she had received. It was a genuine unforeseen shock, the most violent that she had ever had. In her mind she had not pictured Gerald as a very old man. She knew that he was old; she had said to herself that he must be very old, well over seventy. But she had not pictured him. This face on the bed was painfully, pitiably old. A withered face, with the shiny skin all drawn into wrinkles! The stretched skin under the jaw was like the skin of a plucked fowl. The cheek-bones stood up, and below them were deep hollows, almost like egg-cups. A short, scraggy white beard covered the lower part of the face. The hair was scanty, irregular, and quite white; a little white hair grew in the ears. The shut mouth obviously hid toothless gums, for the lips were sucked in. The eyelids were as if pasted down over the eyes, fitting them like kid. All the skin was extremely pallid; it seemed brittle. The body, whose outlines were clear under the sheet, was very small, thin, shrunk, pitiable as the face. And on the face was a general expression of final fatigue, of tragic and acute exhaustion; such as made Sophia pleased that the fatigue and exhaustion had been assuaged in rest, while all the time she kept thinking to herself horribly: 'Oh! how tired he must have been!'

Sophia then experienced a pure and primitive emotion, uncoloured by any moral or religious quality. She was not sorry that Gerald had wasted his life, nor that he was a shame to his years and to her. The manner of his life was of no importance. What affected her was that he had once been young, and that he had grown old, and was now dead. That was all. Youth and vigour had come to that. Youth and vigour always came to that. Everything came to that. He had ill-treated her; he had abandoned her; he had been a devious rascal; but how trivial were such accusations against him! The whole of her huge and bitter grievance against him fell to pieces and crumbled. She saw him young, and proud, and strong, as for instance when he had kissed her lying on the bed in that London hotel – she forgot the name – in 1866; and now he was old, and worn, and horrible, and dead. It was the riddle of life that was puzzling and killing her. By the corner of her eye, reflected in the mirror of a wardrobe near the bed, she glimpsed a tall, forlorn woman, who had once been young and now was old; who had once exulted in abundant strength, and trodden proudly on the neck of circumstance, and now was old. He and she had once loved and burned and quarrelled in the glittering and scornful pride of youth. But time had worn them out. 'Yet a little while,' she thought, 'and I shall be lying on a bed like that! And what shall I have lived for? What is the meaning of it?' The riddle of life itself was killing her, and she seemed to drown in a sea of inexpressible sorrow.

Her memory wandered hopelessly among those past years. She saw Chirac with his wistful smile. She saw him whipped over the roof of the Gare du Nord at the tail of a balloon. She saw old Niepce. She felt his lecherous arm round her. She was as old now as Niepce had been then. Could she excite lust now? Ah! the irony of such a question! To be young and seductive, to be able to kindle a man's eye – that seemed to her the sole thing desirable. Once she had been so! . . . Niepce must certainly have been dead for years. Niepce, the obstinate and hopeful voluptuary, was nothing but a few bones in a coffin now!

She was acquainted with affliction in that hour. All that she had previously suffered sank into insignificance by the side of that suffering.

She turned to the veiled window and idly pulled the blind and looked out. Huge red and yellow cars were swimming in thunder along Deansgate; lorries jolted and rattled; the people of Manchester hurried along the pavements, apparently unconscious that all their doings were vain. Yesterday he too had been in Deansgate, hungry for life, hating the idea of death! What a figure he must have made! Her heart dissolved in pity for him. She dropped the blind.

'My life has been too terrible!' she thought. 'I wish I was dead. I have been through too much. It is monstrous, and I cannot stand it. I do not want to die, but I wish I was dead.'

There was a discreet knock on the door.

'Come in,' she said, in a calm, resigned, cheerful voice. The sound had recalled her with the swiftness of a miracle to the unconquerable dignity of human pride.

Mr Till Boldero entered.

'I should like you to come downstairs and drink a cup of tea,' he said. He was a marvel of tact and good nature. 'My wife is unfortunately not here, and the house is rather at sixes and sevens; but I have sent out for some tea.'

She followed him downstairs into the parlour. He poured out a cup of tea.

'I was forgetting,' she said. 'I am forbidden tea. I mustn't drink it.'

She looked at the cup, tremendously tempted. She longed for tea. An occasional transgression could not harm her. But no! She would not drink it.

'Then what can I get you?'

'If I could have just milk and water,' she said meekly.

Mr Boldero emptied the cup into the slop basin, and began to fill it again.

'Did he tell you anything?' she asked, after a considerable silence.

'Nothing,' said Mr Boldero in his low, soothing tones. 'Nothing except that he had come from Liverpool. Judging from his shoes I should say he must have walked a good bit of the way.'

'At his age!' murmured Sophia, touched.

'Yes,' sighed Mr Boldero. 'He must have been in great straits. You know, he could scarcely talk at all. By the way, here are his clothes. I have had them put aside.'

Sophia saw a small pile of clothes on a chair. She examined the suit, which was still damp, and its woeful shabbiness pained her. The linen collar was nearly black, its stud of bone. As for the boots, she had noticed such boots on the feet of tramps. She wept now. These were the clothes of him who had once been a dandy living at the rate of fifty pounds a week.

'No luggage or anything, of course?' she muttered.

'No,' said Mr Boldero. 'In the pockets there was nothing whatever but this.'

He went to the mantelpiece and picked up a cheap, cracked letter case, which Sophia opened. In it were a visiting card – 'Senorita Clemenzia Borja' – and a bill-head of the Hotel of the Holy Spirit, Concepcion del Uruguay, on the back of which a lot of figures had been scrawled.

'One would suppose,' said Mr Boldero, 'that he had come from South America.'

'Nothing else?'

'Nothing.'

Gerald's soul had not been compelled to abandon much in the haste of its flight.

A servant announced that Mrs Scales's friends were waiting for her outside in the motor-car. Sophia glanced at Mr Till Boldero with an exacerbated anxiety on her face.

'Surely they don't expect me to go back with them tonight!' she said. 'And look at all there is to be done!'

Mr Till Boldero's kindness was then redoubled. 'You can do nothing for *him* now,' he said. 'Tell me your wishes about the funeral. I will arrange everything. Go back to your sister tonight. She will be nervous about you. And return tomorrow or the day after . . . No! it's no trouble, I assure you!'

She yielded.

Thus towards eight o'clock, when Sophia had eaten a little under Mr Boldero's superintendence, and the pawnshop was shut up, the motor-car started again for Bursley, Lily Holl being beside her lover and Sophia alone in the body of the car. Sophia had told them nothing of the nature of her mission. She was incapable of talking to them. They saw that she was in a condition of serious mental disturbance. Under cover of the noise of the car, Lily said to Dick that she was sure Mrs Scales was ill, and Dick, putting his lips together, replied that he meant to be in King Street at nine-thirty at the latest. From time to time Lily surreptitiously glanced at Sophia – a glance of apprehensive inspection – or smiled at her silently; and Sophia vaguely responded to the smile.

In half an hour they had escaped from the ring of Manchester and were on the county roads of Cheshire, polished, flat, sinuous. It was the season of the year when there is no night – only daylight and twilight; when the last silver of dusk remains obstinately visible for hours. And in the open country, under the melancholy arch of evening, the sadness of the earth seemed to possess Sophia anew. Only then did she realize the intensity of the ordeal through which she was passing.

To the south of Congleton one of the tyres softened, immediately after Dick had lighted his lamps. He stopped the car and got down again. They were two miles from Astbury, the nearest village. He had just, with the resignation of experience, reached for the tool-bag, when Lily exclaimed: 'Is she asleep, or what?' Sophia was not asleep, but she was apparently not conscious.

It was a difficult and a trying situation for two lovers. Their voices changed momentarily to the tone of alarm and consternation, and then grew firm again. Sophia showed life but not reason. Lily could feel the poor old lady's heart.

'Well, there's nothing for it!' said Dick, briefly, when all their efforts failed to rouse her.

'What — shall you do?'

'Go straight home as quick as I can on three tyres. We must get her over to this side, and you must hold her. Like that we shall keep the weight off the other side.'

He pitched back the tool-bag into its box. Lily admired his decision.

It was in this order, no longer under the spell of the changing beauty of nocturnal landscapes, that they finished the journey. Constance had opened the door before the car came to a stop in the gloom of King Street. The young people considered that she bore the shock well, though the carrying into the house of Sophia's inert, twitching body, with its hat forlornly awry, was a sight to harrow a soul sturdier than Constance.

When that was done, Dick said curtly: 'I'm off. You stay here, of course.'

'Where are you going?' asked Lily.

'Doctor!' snapped Dick, hobbling rapidly down the steps.

IV

The extraordinary violence of the turn in affairs was what chiefly struck Constance, though it did not overwhelm her. Less than twelve hours before — nay, scarcely six hours before — she and Sophia had been living their placid and monotonous existence, undisturbed by anything worse then the indisposition or death of dogs, or the perversity of a servant. And now, the menacing

Gerald Scales having reappeared, Sophia's form lay mysterious and affrightening on the sofa; and she and Lily Holl, a girl whom she had not met till that day, were staring at Sophia side by side, intimately sharing the same alarm. Constance rose to the crisis. She no longer had Sophia's energy and decisive peremptoriness to depend on, and the Baines in her was awakened. All her daily troubles sank away to their proper scale of unimportance. Neither the young woman nor the old one knew what to do. They could loosen clothes, vainly offer restoratives to the smitten mouth: that was all. Sophia was not unconscious, as could be judged from her eyes; but she could not speak, nor make signs; her body was frequently convulsed. So the two women waited, and the servant waited in the background. The sight of Sophia had effected an astonishing transformation in Maud. Maud was a changed girl. Constance could not recognize, in her eager deferential anxiety to be of use, the pert naughtiness of the minx. She was altered as a wanton of the middle ages would have been altered by some miraculous visitation. It might have been the turning point in Maud's career!

Dr Stirling arrived in less than ten minutes. Dick Povey had had the wit to look for him at the Federation meeting in the Town Hall. And the advent of the doctor and Dick, noisily, at break-neck speed in the car, provided a second sensation. The doctor inquired quickly what had occurred. Nobody could tell him anything. Constance had already confided to Lily Holl the reason of the visit to Manchester; but that was the extent of her knowledge. Not a single person in Bursley, except Sophia, knew what had happened in Manchester. But Constance conjectured that Gerald Scales was dead – or Sophia would never have returned so soon. Then the doctor suggested that on the contrary Gerald Scales might be out of danger. And all then pictured to themselves this troubling Gerald Scales, this dark and sinister husband that had caused such a violent upheaval.

Meanwhile the doctor was at work. He sent Dick Povey to knock up Critchlow's, if the shop should be closed, and obtain a drug. Then, after a time, he lifted Sophia, just as she was, like a bundle on his shoulder, and carried her single-handed upstairs to the second floor. He had recently been giving a course of instruction to enthusiasts of the St John Ambulance Association in Bursley. The feat had an air of the superhuman. Above all else it remained printed on Constance's mind: the burly doctor treading delicately and carefully on the crooked, creaking stairs, his precautions against damaging Sophia by brusque contacts, his stumble at the two steps in the middle of the corridor; Sophia's horribly limp head and loosened hair; and then the tender placing of her on the bed, and the doctor's long breath and flourish of his large handkerchief – all that under the crude lights and shadows of gas-jets! The doctor was nonplussed. Constance gave a second-hand account of Sophia's original attack in Paris, roughly as she had heard it from Sophia. He at once said that it could not have been what the French doctor had said it was. Constance shrugged her shoulders. She was not surprised. For her there was necessarily something of the charlatan about a French doctor. She said she only knew what Sophia had told her. After a time Dr Stirling determined to try electricity, and Dick Povey drove him up to the surgery to fetch his apparatus. The women were left alone again. Constance was very deeply impressed by Lily Holl's sensible, sympathetic attitude. 'Whatever I should have done without Miss Lily I don't know!' she used to exclaim afterwards. Even Maud was beyond praise. It seemed to be the middle of the night when Dr Stirling came back, but it was barely eleven o'clock, and people were only just returning from Hanbridge Theatre and Hanbridge Music Hall. The use of the electrical apparatus was a dead spectacle. Sophia's inertness under it was agonizing. They waited, as it were, breathless for the result. And there was no result. Both injections and electricity had entirely failed to influence the paralysis of Sophia's mouth and throat. Everything had failed. 'Nothing to do but wait a bit!' said the doctor quietly. They waited in the chamber. Sophia seemed to be in a kind of coma. The distortion of her handsome face was more marked as time passed. The doctor spoke now and then in a low voice. He said that the attack had ultimately been determined by cold produced by rapid motion in the automobile. Dick Povey whispered that he must run over to Hanbridge and let Lily's parents know that there was no cause for alarm on her account, and that he would return at once. He was very devoted. On the

landing outside the bedroom, the doctor murmured to him: 'U.P.'
And Dick nodded. They were great friends.

At intervals the doctor, who never knew when he, was beaten,
essayed new methods of dealing with Sophia's case. New symptoms followed. It was half-past twelve when, after gazing with
prolonged intensity at the patient, and after having tested her
mouth and heart, he rose slowly and looked at Constance.

'It's over?' said Constance.

And he very slightly moved his head. 'Come downstairs,
please,' he enjoined her, in a pause that ensued. Constance was
amazingly courageous. The doctor was very solemn and very
kind; Constance had never before seen him to such heroic
advantage. He led her with infinite gentleness out of the room.
There was nothing to stay for; Sophia had gone. Constance
wanted to stay by Sophia's body; but it was the rule that the
stricken should be led away, the doctor observed this classic rule,
and Constance felt that he was right and that she must obey. Lily
Holl followed. The servant, learning the truth by the intuition
accorded to primitive natures, burst into loud sobs, yelling that
Sophia had been the most excellent mistress that servant ever
had. The doctor angrily told her not to stand blubbering there,
but to go into her kitchen and shut the door if she couldn't control
herself. All his accumulated nervous agitation was discharged on
Maud like a thunderclap. Constance continued to behave wonderfully. She was the admiration of the doctor and Lily Holl.
Then Dick Povey came back. It was settled that Lily should pass
the night with Constance. At last the doctor and Dick departed
together, the doctor undertaking the mortuary arrangements.
Maud was hunted to bed.

Early in the morning Constance rose up from her own bed. It
was five o'clock, and there had been daylight for two hours
already. She moved noiselessly and peeped over the foot of the
bed at the sofa. Lily was quietly asleep there, breathing with the
softness of a child. Lily would have deemed that she was a very
mature woman, who had seen life and much of it. Yet to
Constance her face and attitude had the exquisite quality of a
child's. She was not precisely a pretty girl, but her features, the
candid expression of her disposition, produced an impression

that was akin to that of beauty. Her abandonment was complete. She had gone through the night unscathed, and was now renewing herself in calm, oblivious sleep. Her ingenuous girlishness was apparent then. It seemed as if all her wise and sweet behaviour of the evening could have been nothing but so many imitative gestures. It seemed impossible that a being so young and fresh could have really experienced the mood of which her gestures had been the expression. Her strong virginal simplicity made Constance vaguely sad for her.

Creeping out of the room, Constance climbed to the second floor in her dressing-grown, and entered the other chamber. She was obliged to look again upon Sophia's body. Incredible swiftness of calamity! Who could have foreseen it? Constance was less desolated than numbed. She was as yet only touching the fringe of her bereavement. She had not begun to think of herself. She was drenched, as she gazed at Sophia's body, not by pity for herself, but by compassion for the immense disaster of her sister's life. She perceived fully now for the first time the greatness of that disaster. Sophia's charm and Sophia's beauty – what profit had they been to their owner? She saw pictures of Sophia's career, distorted and grotesque images formed in her untravelled mind from Sophia's own rare and compressed recitals. What a career! A brief passion, and then nearly thirty years in a boarding-house! And Sophia had never had a child; had never known either the joy or the pain of maternity. She had never even had a true home till, in all her sterile splendour, she came to Bursley. And she had ended – thus! This was the piteous, ignominious end of Sophia's wondrous gifts of body and soul. Hers had not been a life at all. And the reason? It is strange how fate persists in justifying the harsh generalizations of Puritan morals, of the morals in which Constance had been brought up by her stern parents! Sophia had sinned. It was therefore inevitable that she should suffer. An adventure such as she had in wicked and capricious pride undertaken with Gerald Scales, could not conclude otherwise than it had concluded. It could have brought nothing but evil. There was no getting away from these verities, thought Constance. And she was to be excused for thinking that all modern progress and cleverness was as naught, and that the world would be forced to return upon its steps and start again in the path which it had left.

Up to within a few days of her death people had been wont to remark that Mrs Scales looked as young as ever, and that she was as bright and as energetic as ever. And truly, regarding Sophia from a little distance – that handsome oval, that erect carriage of a slim body, that challenging eye! – no one would have said that she was in her sixtieth year. But look at her now, with her twisted face, her sightless orbs, her worn skin – she did not seem sixty, but seventy! She was like something used, exhausted, and thrown aside! Yes, Constance's heart melted in an anguished pity for that stormy creature. And mingled with the pity was a stern recognition of the handiwork of divine justice. To Constance's lips came the same phrase as had come to the lips of Samuel Povey on a different occasion: God is not mocked! The ideas of her parents and her grandparents had survived intact in Constance. It is true that Constance's father would have shuddered in Heaven could he have seen Constance solitarily playing cards of a night. But in spite of cards, and of a son who never went to chapel, Constance, under the various influences of destiny, had remained essentially what her father had been. Not in her was the force of evolution manifest. There are thousands such.

Lily, awake, and reclothed with that unreal mien of a grown and comprehending woman, stepped quietly into the room, searching for the poor old thing, Constance. The layer-out had come.

By the first post was delivered a letter addressed to Sophia by Mr Till Boldero. From its contents the death of Gerald Scales was clear. There seemed then to be nothing else for Constance to do. What had to be done was done for her. And stronger wills than hers put her to bed. Cyril was telegraphed for. Mr Critchlow called, Mrs Critchlow following – a fussy infliction, but useful in certain matters. Mr Critchlow was not allowed to see Constance. She could hear his high grating voice in the corridor. She had to lie calm, and the sudden tranquillity seemed strange after the feverish violence of the night. Only twenty-four hours since, and she had been worrying about the death of a dog! With a body crying for sleep, she dozed off, thoughts of the mystery of life merging into the incoherence of dreams.

The news was abroad in the Square before nine o'clock. There were persons who had witnessed the arrival of the motor-car, and the transfer of Sophia to the house. Untruthful rumours had spread as to the manner of Gerald Scales's death. Some said that he had dramatically committed suicide. But the town, though titillated, was not moved as it would have been moved by a similar event twenty years, or even ten years earlier. Times had changed in Bursley. Bursley was more sophisticated than in the old days.

Constance was afraid lest Cyril, despite the seriousness of the occasion, might exhibit his customary tardiness in coming. She had long since learnt not to rely upon him. But he came the same evening. His behaviour was in every way perfect. He showed quiet but genuine grief for the death of his aunt, and he was a model of consideration for his mother. Further, he at once assumed charge of all the arrangements, in regard both to Sophia and to her husband. Constance was surprised at the ease which he displayed in the conduct of practical affairs, and the assurance with which he gave orders. She had never seen him direct anything before. He said, indeed, that he had never directed anything before, but that there appeared to him to be no difficulties. Whereas Constance had figured a tiresome series of varied complications. As to the burial of Sophia, Cyril was vigorously in favour of an absolutely private funeral; that is to say, a funeral at which none but himself should be present. He seemed to have a passionate objection to any sort of parade. Constance agreed with him. But she said that it would be impossible not to invite Mr Critchlow, Sophia's trustee, and that if Mr Critchlow were invited certain others must be invited. Cyril asked: 'Why impossible?' Constance said: 'Because it *would* be impossible. Because Mr Critchlow would be hurt.' Cyril asked: 'What does it matter if he is hurt?' and suggested that Mr Critchlow would get over his damage. Constance grew more serious. The discussion threatened to be warm. Suddenly Cyril yielded. 'All right, Mrs Plover, all right! It shall be exactly as you choose,' he said, in a gentle, humouring tone. He had not called her 'Mrs Plover' for years. She thought the hour badly chosen for verbal pleasantry, but he was so kind that she made no complaint. Thus there were six people at

Sophia's funeral, including Mr Critchlow. No refreshments were offered. The mourners separated at the church. When both funerals were accomplished Cyril sat down and played the harmonium softly, and said that it had kept well in tune. He was extraordinarily soothing.

He had now reached the age of thirty-three. His habits were as industrious as ever, his preoccupation with his art as keen. But he had achieved no fame, no success. He earned nothing, living in comfort on an allowance from his mother. He seldom spoke of his plans and never of his hopes. He had in fact settled down into a dilettante, having learnt gently to scorn the triumphs which he lacked the force to win. He imagined that industry and a regular existence were sufficient justification in themselves for any man's life. Constance had dropped the habit of expecting him to astound the world. He was rather grave and precise in manner, courteous and tepid, with a touch of condescension towards his environment; as though he were continually permitting the perspicacious to discern that he had nothing to learn – if the truth were known! His humour had assumed a modified form. He often smiled to himself. He was unexceptionable.

On the day after Sophia's funeral he set to work to design a simple stone for his aunt's tomb. He said he could not tolerate the ordinary gravestone, which always looked, to him, as if the wind might blow it over, thus negativing the idea of solidity. His mother did not in the least understand him. She thought the lettering of his tombstone affected and finicking. But she let it pass without comment, being secretly very flattered that he should have deigned to design a stone at all.

Sophia had left all her money to Cyril, and had made him the sole executor of her will. This arrangement had been agreed with Constance. The sisters thought it was the best plan. Cyril ignored Mr Critchlow entirely, and went to a young lawyer at Hanbridge, a friend of his and of Matthew Peel-Swynnerton's. Mr Critchlow, aged and unaccustomed to interference, had to render accounts of his trusteeship to this young man, and was incensed. The estate was proved at over thirty-five thousand pounds. In the main, Sophia had been careful, and had even been parsimonious. She had often told Constance that they ought to spend money much more freely, and she had had a few brief fits of extravagance. But the habit of stern thrift, begun in 1870 and practised without any intermission till she came to England in 1897, had been too strong for her theories. The squandering of money pained her. And she could not, in her age, devise expensive tastes.

Cyril showed no emotion whatever on learning himself the inheritor of thirty-five thousand pounds. He did not seem to care. He spoke of the sum as a millionaire might have spoken of it. In justice to him it is to be said that he cared nothing for wealth, except in so far as wealth could gratify his eye and ear trained to artistic voluptuousness. But for his mother's sake, and for the sake of Bursley, he might have affected a little satisfaction. His mother was somewhat hurt. His behaviour caused her to revert in meditation again and again to the futility of Sophia's career, and the waste of her attributes. She had grown old and hard in joyless years in order to amass this money which Cyril would spend coldly and ungratefully, never thinking of the immense effort and endless sacrifice which had gone to its collection. He would spend it as carelessly as though he had picked it up in the street. As the days went by and Constance realized her own grief, she also realized more and more the completeness of the tragedy of Sophia's life. Headstrong Sophia had deceived her mother, and for the deception had paid with thirty years of melancholy and the entire frustration of her proper destiny.

After haunting Bursley for a fortnight in elegant black, Cyril said, without any warning, one night: 'I must go the day after tomorrow, mater.' And he told her of a journey to Hungary which he had long since definitely planned with Matthew Peel-Swynnerton, and which could not be postponed, as it comprised 'business'. He had hitherto breathed no word of this. He was as secretive as ever. As to her holiday, he suggested that she should arrange to go away with the Holls and Dick Povey. He approved of Lily Holl and of Dick Povey. Of Dick Povey he said: 'He's one of the most remarkable chaps in the Five Towns.' And he had the air of having made Dick's reputation. Constance, knowing there was no appeal, accepted the sentence of loneliness. Her health was singularly good.

When he was gone she said to herself: 'Scarcely a fortnight and

Sophia was here at this table!' She would remember every now and then, with a faint shock, that poor, proud, masterful Sophia was dead.

CHAPTER 5: *End of Constance*

I

When, on a June afternoon about twelve months later, Lily Holl walked into Mrs Povey's drawing-room overlooking the Square, she found a calm, somewhat optimistic old lady – older than her years, which were little more than sixty – whose chief enemies were sciatica and rheumatism. The sciatica was a dear enemy of long standing, always affectionately referred to by the forgiving Constance as '*my* sciatica'; the rheumatism was a newcomer, unprivileged, spoken of by its victim apprehensively and yet disdainfully as 'this *rheumatism*'. Constance was now very stout. She sat in a low easy-chair between the oval table and the window, arrayed in black silk. As the girl Lily came in, Constance lifted her head with a bland smile, and Lily kissed her, contentedly. Lily knew that she was a welcome visitor. These two had become as intimate as the difference between their ages would permit; of the two, Constance was the more frank. Lily as well as Constance was in mourning. A few months previously her aged grandfather, 'Holl, the grocer', had died. The second of his two sons, Lily's father, had then left the business established by the brothers at Hanbridge in order to manage, for a time, the parent business in St Luke's Square. Alderman Holl's death had delayed Lily's marriage. Lily took tea with Constance, or at any rate paid a call, four or five times a week. She listened to Constance.

Everybody considered that Constance had 'come splendidly through' the dreadful affair of Sophia's death. Indeed, it was observed that she was more philosophic, more cheerful, more sweet, than she had been for many years. The truth was that, though her bereavement had been the cause of a most genuine and durable sorrow, it had been a relief to her. When Constance was over fifty, the energetic and masterful Sophia had burst in upon her lethargic tranquillity and very seriously disturbed the flow of old habits. Certainly Constance had fought Sophia on the main point, and won; but on a hundred minor points she had either lost or had not fought. Sophia had been 'too much' for Constance, and it had been only by a wearying expenditure of nervous force that Constance had succeeded in holding a small part of her own against the unconscious domination of Sophia. The death of Mrs Scales had put an end to all strain, and Constance had been once again mistress in Constance's house. Constance would never have admitted these facts, even to herself; and no one would ever have dared to suggest them to her. For with all her temperamental mildness she had her formidable side.

She was slipping a photograph into a plush-covered photograph album.

'More photographs?' Lily questioned. She had almost exactly the same benignant smile that Constance had. She seemed to be the personification of gentleness – one of those feather-beds that some capricious men occasionally have the luck to marry. She was capable, with a touch of honest, simple stupidity. All her character was displayed in the tone in which she said: 'More photographs?' It showed an eager, responsive sympathy with Constance's cult for photographs, also a slight personal fondness for photographs, also a dim perception that a cult for photographs might be carried to the ridiculous, and a kind desire to hide all trace of this perception. The voice was thin, and matched the pale complexion of her delicate face.

Constance's eyes had a quizzical gleam behind her spectacles as she silently held up the photograph for Lily's inspection.

Lily, sitting down, lowered the corners of her soft lips when she beheld the photograph, and nodded her head several times, scarce perceptibly.

'Her ladyship has just given it to me,' whispered Constance.

'Indeed!' said Lily, with an extraordinary accent.

'Her ladyship' was the last and best of Constance's servants, a really excellent creature of thirty, who had known misfortune, and who must assuredly have been sent to Constance by the old watchful Providence. They 'got on together' nearly perfectly. Her name was Mary. After ten years of turmoil, Constance in the matter of servants was now at rest.

'Yes,' said Constance. 'She's named it to me several times – about having her photograph taken, and last week I let her go. I told you, didn't I? I always consider her in every way, all her little fancies and everything. And the copies came today. I wouldn't hurt her feelings for anything. You may be sure she'll take a look into the album next time she cleans the room.'

Constance and Lily exchanged a glance agreeing that Constance had affably stretched a point in deciding to put the photograph of a servant between the same covers with photographs of her family and friends. It was doubtful whether such a thing had ever been done before.

One photograph usually leads to another, and one photograph album to another photograph album.

'Pass me that album on the second shelf of the Canterbury, my dear,' said Constance.

Lily rose vivaciously, as though to see the album on the second shelf of the Canterbury had been the ambition of her life.

They sat side by side at the table, Lily turning over the pages. Constance, for all her vast bulk, continually made little nervous movements. Occasionally she would sniff and occasionally a mysterious noise would occur in her chest; she always pretended that this noise was a cough, and would support the pretence by emitting a real cough immediately after it.

'Why!' exclaimed Lily. 'Have I seen that before?'

'I don't know, my dear,' said Constance, '*Have* you?'

It was a photograph of Sophia taken a few years previously by 'a very nice gentleman', whose acquaintance the sisters had made during a holiday at Harrogate. It portrayed Sophia on a knoll, fronting the weather.

'It's Mrs Scales to the life – I can see that,' said Lily.

'Yes,' said Constance. 'Whenever there was a wind she always stood like that, and took long deep breaths of it.'

This recollection of one of Sophia's habits recalled the whole woman to Constance's memory, and drew a picture of her character for the girl who had scarcely known her.

'It's not like ordinary photographs. There's something special about it,' said Lily, enthusiastically. 'I don't think I ever saw a photograph like that.'

'I've got another copy of it in my bedroom,' said Constance. 'I'll give you this one.'

'Oh, Mrs Povey! I couldn't think –'

'Yes, yes!' said Constance, removing the photograph from the page.

'Oh, *thank* you!' said Lily.

'And that reminds me,' said Constance, getting up with great difficulty from her chair.

'Can I find anything for you?' Lily asked.

'No, no!' said Constance, leaving the room.

She returned in a moment with her jewel-box, a receptacle of ebony with ivory ornamentations.

'I've always meant to give you this,' said Constance, taking from the box a fine cameo brooch. 'I don't seem to fancy wearing it myself. And I should like to see you wearing it. It was mother's. I believe they're coming into fashion again. I don't see why you shouldn't wear it while you're in mourning. They aren't half so strict now about mourning as they used to be.'

'Truly!' murmured Lily, ecstatically. They kissed. Constance seemed to breathe out benevolence, as with trembling hands she pinned the brooch at Lily's neck. She lavished the warm treasure of her heart on Lily, whom she regarded as an almost perfect girl, and who had become the idol of her latter years.

'What a magnificent old watch!' said Lily, as they delved together in the lower recesses of the box. '*And* the chain to it!'

'That was father's,' said Constance. 'He always used to swear by it. When it didn't agree with the Town Hall, he used to say: "Then th' Town Hall's wrong." And it's curious, the Town Hall *was* wrong. You know the Town Hall clock has never been a good timekeeper. I've been thinking of giving that watch and chain to Dick.'

'*Have* you?' said Lily.

'Yes. It's just as good as it was when father wore it. My husband never would wear it. He preferred his own. He had little fancies like that. And Cyril takes after his father.' She spoke in her 'dry' tone. 'I've almost decided to give it to Dick – that is, if he behaves himself. Is he still on with his ballooning?'

Lily smiled guiltily: 'Oh yes!'

'Well,' said Constance, 'I never heard the like! If he's been up and come down safely, that ought to be enough for him. I wonder you let him do it, my dear.'

'But how can I stop him? I've no control over him.'

'But do you mean to say that he'd still do it if you told him seriously you didn't want him to?'

'Yes,' said Lily; and added: 'So I shan't tell him.'

Constance nodded her head, musing over the secret nature of men. She remembered too well the cruel obstinacy of Samuel, who had nevertheless loved her. And Dick Povey was a thousand times more bizarre than Samuel. She saw him vividly, a little boy, whizzing down King Street on a boneshaker, and his cap flying off. Afterwards it had been motor-cars! Now it was balloons! She sighed. She was struck by the profound instinctive wisdom just enunciated by the girl.

'Well,' she said, 'I shall see. I've not made up my mind yet. What's the young man doing this afternoon, by the way?'

'He's gone to Birmingham to try to sell two motor-lorries. He won't be back home till late. He's coming over here tomorrow.'

It was an excellent illustration of Dick Povey's methods that at this very moment Lily heard in the Square the sound of a motor-car, which happened to be Dick's car. She sprang up to look.

'Why!' she cried, flushing. 'Here he is now!'

'Bless us, bless us!' muttered Constance, closing the box.

When Dick, having left the car in King Street, limped tempestuously into the drawing-room, galvanizing it by his abundant vitality into a new life, he cried joyously: 'Sold my lorries! Sold my lorries!' And he explained that by a charming accident he had disposed of them to a chance buyer in Hanbridge, just before starting for Birmingham. So he had telephoned to Birmingham that the matter was 'off', and then, being 'at a loose end', he had come over to Bursley in search of his betrothed. At Holl's shop they had told him that she was with Mrs Povey. Constance glanced at him, impressed by his jolly air of success. He seemed

exactly like his breezy and self-confident advertisements in the
Signal. He was absolutely pleased with himself. He triumphed
over his limp – that ever-present reminder of a tragedy. Who
would dream, to look at this blond, laughing, scintillating face,
astonishingly young for his years, that he had once passed
through such a night as that on which his father had killed his
mother while he lay immovable and cursing, with a broken knee,
in bed? Constance had heard all about that scene from her
husband, and she paused in wonder at the contrasting hazards of
existence.

Dick Povey brought his hands together with a resounding
smack, and then rubbed them rapidly.

'*And* a good price, too!' he exclaimed blithely. 'Mrs Povey, I
don't mind telling you that I've netted seventy pounds odd this
afternoon.'

Lily's eyes expressed her proud joy.

'I hope pride won't have a fall,' said Constance, with a calm
smile out of which peeped a hint of a rebuke. 'That's what I hope.
I must just go and see about tea.'

'I can't stay for tea – really,' said Dick.

'Of course you can,' said Constance, positively. 'Suppose
you'd been at Birmingham? It's weeks since you stayed to tea.'

'Oh, well, thanks!' Dick yielded, rather snubbed.

'Can't I save you a journey, Mrs Povey?' Lily asked, eagerly
thoughtful.

'No, thank you, my dear. There are one or two little things that
need my attention.' And Constance departed with her jewel-box.

Dick, having assured himself that the door was closed,
assaulted Lily with a kiss.

'Been here long?' he inquired.

'About an hour and a half.'

'Glad to see me?'

'Oh, Dick!' she protested.

'Old lady's in one of her humours, eh?'

'No, no! Only she was just talking about balloons – you know.
She's very much up in arms.'

'You ought to keep her off balloons. Balloons may be the ruin
of her wedding-present to us, my child.'

'Dick! How can you talk like that? . . . It's all very well saying I ought to keep her off balloons. You try to keep her off balloons when once she begins, and see!'

'What started her?'

'She said she was thinking of giving you old Mr Baines's gold watch and chain — if you behaved yourself.'

'Thank you for nothing!' said Dick. 'I don't want it.'

'Have you seen it?'

'Have I seen it? I should say I had seen it. She's mentioned it once or twice before.'

'Oh! I didn't know.'

'I don't see myself carting that thing about. I much prefer my own. What do you think of it?'

'Of course it is rather clumsy,' said Lily. 'But if she offered it to you, you couldn't refuse it, and you'd simply have to wear it.'

'Well, then,' said Dick, 'I must try to behave myself just badly enough to keep off the watch, but not badly enough to upset her notions about wedding-presents.'

'Poor old thing!' Lily murmured, compassionately.

Then Lily put her hand silently to her neck.

'What's that?'

'She's just given it to me.'

Dick approached very near to examine the cameo brooch. 'Hm!' he murmured. It was an adverse verdict. And Lily co-incided with it by a lift of the eyebrows.

'And I suppose you'll have to wear that!' said Dick.

'She values it as much as anything she's got, poor old thing!' said Lily. 'It belonged to her mother. And she says cameos are coming into fashion again. It really is rather good, you know.'

'I wonder where she learnt that!' said Dick, dryly. 'I see you've been suffering from the photographs again.'

'Well,' said Lily, 'I much prefer the photographs to helping her to play Patience. The way she cheats herself — it's too silly! I —'

She stopped. The door, which had after all not been latched, was pushed open, and the antique Fossette introduced herself painfully into the room. Fossette had an affection for Dick Povey.

'Well, Methuselah!' he greeted the animal loudly. She could scarcely wag her tail, or shake the hair out of her dim eyes in order to look up at him. He stooped to pat her.

'That dog does smell,' said Lily, bluntly.

'What do you expect? What she wants is the least dose of prussic acid. She's a burden to herself.'

'It's funny that if you venture to hint to Mrs Povey that the dog is offensive she gets quite peppery,' said Lily.

'Well, that's very simple,' said Dick. 'Don't hint, that's all! Hold your nose and your tongue too.'

'Dick, I do wish you wouldn't be so absurd.'

Constance returned into the room, cutting short the conversation.

'Mrs Povey,' said Dick, in a voice full of gratitude, 'Lily has just been showing me her brooch.'

He noticed that she paid no heed to him, but passed hurriedly to the window.

'What's amiss in the Square?' Constance exclaimed. 'When I was in the parlour just now I saw a man running along Wedgwood Street, and I said to myself, what's amiss?'

Dick and Lily joined her at the window.

Several people were hurrying down the Square, and then a man came running with a doctor from the market-place. All these persons disappeared from view under the window of Mrs Povey's drawing-room, which was over part of Mrs Critchlow's shop. As the windows of the shop projected beyond the walls of the house it was impossible, from the drawing-room window, to see the pavement in front of the shop.

'It must be something on the pavement – or in the shop!' murmured Constance.

'Oh, ma'am!' said a startled voice behind the three. It was Mary, original of the photograph, who had run unperceived into the drawing-room. 'They say as Mrs Critchlow has tried to commit suicide!'

Constance started back. Lily went towards her, with an instinctive gesture of supporting consolation.

'Maria Critchlow tried to commit suicide!' Constance muttered.

'Yes, ma'am! But they say she's not done it.'

'By Jove! I'd better go and see if I can help, hadn't I?' cried Dick Povey, hobbling off, excited and speedy. 'Strange, isn't it?' he exclaimed afterwards, 'how I manage to come in for things? Sheer chance that I was here today! But it's always like that! Somehow something extraordinary is always happening where I am.' And this too ministered to his satisfaction, and to his zest for life.

II

When, in the evening, after all sorts of comings and goings, he finally returned to the old lady and the young one, in order to report the upshot, his demeanour was suitably toned to Constance's mood. The old lady had been very deeply disturbed by the tragedy, which, as she said, had passed under her very feet while she was calmly talking to Lily.

The whole truth came out in a short space of time. Mrs Critchlow was suffering from melancholia. It appeared that for long she had been depressed by the failing trade of the shop, which was none of her fault. The state of the Square had steadily deteriorated. Even the 'Vaults' were not what they once were. Four or five shops had been shut up, as it were definitely, the landlords having given up hope of discovering serious tenants. And, of those kept open, the majority were struggling desperately to make ends meet. Only Holl's and a new upstart draper, who had widely advertised his dressmaking department, were really flourishing. The confectionery half of Mr Brindley's business was disappearing. People would not go to Hanbridge for their bread or for their groceries, but they would go for their cakes. These electric trams had simply carried to Hanbridge the cream, and much of the milk, of Bursley's retail trade. There were unprincipled tradesmen in Hanbridge ready to pay the car-fares of any customer who spent a crown in their establishments. Hanbridge was the geographical centre of the Five Towns, and it was alive to its situation. Useless for Bursley to compete! If Mrs Critchlow had been a philosopher, if she had known that geography had always made history, she would have given up her enterprise a dozen years ago. But Mrs Critchlow was merely Maria Insull. She had seen Baines's in its magnificent prime, when Baines's almost conferred a favour on customers in serving them. At the time when she took over the business under the wing of her husband, it was still a good business. But from that instant the tide had seemed to turn. She had fought, and she kept on fighting, stupidly. She was not aware that she was fighting against evolution, not aware that evolution had chosen her for one of its victims! She could understand that all the other shops in the Square should fail, but not that Baines's should fail! She was as industrious as ever, as good a buyer, as good a seller, as keen for novelties, as economical, as methodical! And yet the returns dropped and dropped.

She naturally had no sympathy from Charles, who now took small interest even in his own business, or what was left of it, and who was coldly disgusted at the ultimate cost of his marriage. Charles gave her no money that he could avoid giving her. The crisis had been slowly approaching for years. The assistants in the shop had said nothing, or had only whispered among themselves, but now that the crisis had flowered suddenly in an attempted self-murder, they all spoke at once, and the evidences were pieced together into a formidable proof of the strain which Mrs Critchlow had suffered. It appeared that for many months she had been depressed and irritable, that sometimes she would sit down in the midst of work and declare, with every sign of exhaustion, that she could do no more. Then with equal briskness she would arise and force herself to labour. She did not sleep for whole nights. One assistant related how she had complained of having had no sleep whatever for four nights consecutively. She had noises in the ears and a chronic headache. Never very plump, she had grown thinner and thinner. And she was for ever taking pills: this information came from Charles's manager. She had had several outrageous quarrels with the redoubtable Charles, to the stupefaction of all who heard or saw them . . . Mrs Critchlow standing up to her husband! Another strange thing was that she thought the bills of several of the big Manchester firms were unpaid when as a fact they had been paid. Even when shown the receipts she would not be convinced, though she pretended to be convinced. She would recommence the next day. All this was sufficiently disconcerting for female assistants in the drapery. But what could they do?

Then Maria Critchlow had gone a step further. She had summoned the eldest assistant to her corner and had informed her, with all the solemnity of a confession made to assuage a conscience which has been tortured too long, that she had on many occasions been guilty of sexual irregularity with her late employer, Samuel Povey. There was no truth whatever in this accusation (which everybody, however, took care not to mention to Constance); it merely indicated, perhaps, the secret aspirations of Maria Insull, the virgin. The assistant was properly scandalized, more by the crudity of Mrs Critchlow's language than by the alleged sin buried in the past. Goodness knows what the assistant would have done! But two hours later Maria Critchlow tried to commit suicide by stabbing herself with a pair of scissors. There was blood in the shop.

With as little delay as possible she had been driven away to the asylum. Charles Critchlow, enveloped safely in the armour of his senile egotism, had shown no emotion, and very little activity. The shop was closed. And as a general draper's it never opened again. That was the end of Baines's. Two assistants found themselves without a livelihood. The small tumble with the great.

Constance's emotion was more than pardonable; it was justified. She could not eat and Lily could not persuade her to eat. In an unhappy moment Dick Povey mentioned – he never could remember how, afterwards – the word Federation! And then Constance, from a passive figure of grief, became a menace. She overwhelmed Dick Povey with her anathema of Federation, for Dick was a citizen of Hanbridge, where this detestable movement for Federation had had its birth. All the misfortunes of St Luke's Square were due to that great, busy, grasping, unscrupulous neighbour. Had not Hanbridge done enough, without wanting to merge all the Five Towns into one town, of which of course itself would be the centre? For Constance, Hanbridge was a borough of unprincipled adventurers, bent on ruining the ancient 'Mother of the Five Towns' for its own glory and aggrandizement. Let Constance hear no more of Federation! Her poor sister Sophia had been dead against Federation, and she had been quite right!

All really respectable people were against it! The attempted suicide of Mrs Critchlow sealed the fate of Federation and damped it for ever, in Constance's mind. Her hatred of the idea of it was intensified into violent animosity; insomuch that in the result she died a martyr to the cause of Bursley's municipal independence.

III

It was on a muddy day in October that the first great battle for and against Federation was fought in Bursley. Constance was suffering severely from sciatica. She was also suffering from disgust with the modern world.

Unimaginable things had happened in the Square. For Constance, the reputation of the Square was eternally ruined. Charles Critchlow, by that strange good fortune which always put him in the right when fairly he ought to have been in the wrong, had let the Baines shop and his own shop and house to the Midland Clothiers Company, which was establishing branches throughout Staffordshire, Warwickshire, Leicestershire, and adjacent counties. He had sold his own chemist's stock and gone to live in a little house at the bottom of King Street. It is doubtful whether he would have consented to retire had not Alderman Holl died earlier in the year, thus ending a long rivalry between the old men for the patriarchate of the Square. Charles Critchlow was as free from sentiment as any man, but no man is quite free from it, and the ancient was in a position to indulge sentiment had he chosen. His business was not a source of loss, and he could still trust his skinny hands and peering eyes to make up a prescription. However, the offer of the Midland Clothiers Company tempted him, and as the undisputed 'father' of the Square he left the Square in triumph.

The Midland Clothiers Company had no sense of the proprieties of trade. Their sole idea was to sell goods. Having possessed themselves of one of the finest sites in a town which, after all was said and done, comprised nearly forty thousand inhabitants, they set about to make the best of that site. They threw the two shops into one, and they caused to be constructed a sign compared to which the spacious old 'Baines' sign was a

postcard. They covered the entire frontage with posters of a
theatrical description – coloured posters! They occupied the
front page of the *Signal*, and from that pulpit they announced
that winter was approaching, and that they meant to sell ten
thousand overcoats at their new shop in Bursley at the price of
twelve and sixpence each. The tailoring of the world was loudly
and coarsely defied to equal the value of those overcoats. On the
day of opening they arranged an orchestra or artillery of phonographs upon the leads over the window of that part of the shop
which had been Mr Critchlow's. They also carpeted the Square
with handbills, and flew flags from their upper storeys. The
immense shop proved to be full of overcoats; overcoats were
shown in all the three great windows; in one window an overcoat
was disposed as a receptacle for water, to prove that the Midland
twelve-and-sixpenny overcoats were impermeable by rain. Overcoats flapped in the two doorways. These devices woke and drew
the town, and the town found itself received by bustling male
assistants very energetic and rapid, instead of by demure anaemic
virgins. At moments towards evening the shop was populous
with custom; the number of overcoats sold was prodigious. On
another day the Midland sold trousers in a like manner, but
without the phonographs. Unmistakably the Midland had
shaken the Square and demonstrated that commerce was still
possible to fearless enterprise.

Nevertheless the Square was not pleased. The Square was
conscious of shame, of dignity departed. Constance was divided
between pain and scornful wrath. For her, what the Midland had
done was to desecrate a shrine. She hated those flags, and those
flaring, staring posters on the honest old brick walls, and the
enormous gilded sign, and the windows all filled with a monotonous repetition of the same article, and the bustling assistants. As
for the phonographs, she regarded them as a grave insult; they
had been within twenty feet of her drawing-room window!
Twelve-and-sixpenny overcoats! It was monstrous, and equally
monstrous was the gullibility of the people. How could an
overcoat at twelve and sixpence be 'good'? She remembered the
overcoats made and sold in the shop in the time of her father and
her husband, overcoats of which the inconvenience was that they

would not wear out! The Midland, for Constance, was not a trading concern, but something between a cheap-jack and a circus. She could scarcely bear to walk down the Square, to such a degree did the ignoble frontage of the Midland offend her eye and outrage her ancestral pride. She even said that she would give up her house.

But when, on the twenty-ninth of September, she received six months' notice, signed in Critchlow's shaky hand, to quit the house – it was wanted for the Midland's manager, the Midland having taken the premises on condition that they might eject Constance if they chose – the blow was an exceedingly severe one. She had sworn to go – but to be turned out, to be turned out of the house of her birth and out of her father's home, that was different! Her pride, injured as it was, had a great deal of support. It became necessary for her to recollect that she was a Baines. She affected magnificently not to care. But she could not refrain from telling all her acquaintances that she was being turned out of her house, and asking them what they thought of *that*; and when she met Charles Critchlow in the street she seared him with the heat of her resentment. The enterprise of finding a new house and moving into it loomed before her gigantic, terrible; the idea of it was alone sufficient to make her ill.

Meanwhile, in the matter of Federation, preparations for the pitched battle had been going forward, especially in the columns of the *Signal*, where the scribes of each one of the Five Towns had proved that all the other towns were in the clutch of unscrupulous gangs of self-seekers. After months of argument and recrimination, all the towns except Bursley were either favourable or indifferent to the prospect of becoming a part of the twelfth largest town in the United Kingdom. But in Bursley the opposition was strong, and the twelfth largest town in the United Kingdom could not spring into existence without the consent of Bursley. The United Kingdom itself was languidly interested in the possibility of suddenly being endowed with a new town of a quarter of a million inhabitants. The Five Towns were frequently mentioned in the London dailies, and London journalists would write such sentences as: 'The Five Towns, which are of course, *as everybody knows*, Hanbridge, Bursley, Knype, Longshaw, and

Turnhill . . .' This was renown at last, for the most maligned
district in the country! And then a Cabinet Minister had visited
the Five Towns, and assisted at an official inquiry, and stated in
his hammering style that he meant personally to do everything
possible to accomplish the Federation of the Five Towns: an
incautious remark, which infuriated, while it flattered, the opponents of Federation in Bursley. Constance, with many other
sensitive persons, asked angrily what right a Cabinet Minister
had to take sides in a purely local affair. But the partiality of the
official world grew flagrant. The Mayor of Bursley openly proclaimed himself a Federationist, though there was a majority on
the Council against him. Even ministers of religion permitted
themselves to think and to express opinions. Well might the
indignant Old Guard imagine that the end of public decency had
come! The Federationists were very ingenious individuals. They
contrived to enrol in their ranks a vast number of leading men.
Then they hired the Covered Market, and put a platform in it,
and put all these leading men on the platform, and made them all
speak eloquently on the advantages of moving with the times.
The meeting was crowded and enthusiastic, and readers of the
Signal next day could not but see that the battle was won in
advance, and that Anti-Federation was dead. In the following
week, however, the Anti-Federationists held in the Covered
Market an exactly similar meeting (except that the display of
leading men was less brilliant), and demanded of a floor of serried
heads whether the old Mother of the Five Towns was prepared to
put herself into the hands of a crew of highly paid bureaucrats at
Hanbridge, and was answered by a wild defiant 'No', that could
be heard on Duck Bank. Readers of the *Signal* next day were fain
to see that the battle had not been won in advance. Bursley was
lukewarm on the topics of education, slums, water, gas, electricity. But it meant to fight for that mysterious thing, its identity.
Was the name of Bursley to be lost to the world? To ask the
question was to give the answer.

Then dawned the day of battle, the day of the Poll, when the
burgesses were to indicate plainly by means of a cross on a voting
paper whether or not they wanted Federation. And on this day
Constance was almost incapacitated by sciatica. It was a heroic

day. The walls of the town were covered with literature, and the streets dotted with motor-cars and other vehicles at the service of the voters. The greater number of these vehicles bore large cards with the words, 'Federation this time'. And hundreds of men walked briskly about with circular cards tied to their lapels, as though Bursley had been a race-course, and these cards too had the words, 'Federation this time'. (The reference was to a light poll which had been taken several years before, when no interest had been aroused and the immature project yet defeated by a six to one majority.) All partisans of Federation sported a red ribbon; all Anti-Federationists sported a blue ribbon. The schools were closed and the Federationists displayed their characteristic lack of scruple in appropriating the children. The Federationists, with devilish skill, had hired the Bursley Town Silver Prize Band, an organization of terrific respectability, and had set it to march playing through the town followed by wagonettes crammed with children, who sang:

> Vote, vote, vote for Federation,
> Don't be stupid, old and slow,
> We are sure that it will be
> Good for the communitie,
> So vote, vote, vote, and make it go.

How this performance could affect the decision of grave burgesses at the polls was not apparent; but the Anti-Federationists feared that it might, and before noon was come they had engaged two bands, and had composed in committee the following lyric in reply to the first one:

> Down, down, down with Federation,
> As we are we'd rather stay;
> When the vote on Saturday's read
> Federation will be dead,
> Good old Bursley's sure to win the day.

They had also composed another song, entitled 'Dear old Bursley', which, however, they made the fatal error of setting to the music of 'Auld Lang Syne'. The effect was that of a dirge, and it perhaps influenced many voters in favour of the more cheerful party. The Anti-Federationists, indeed, never regained the mean advantage filched by unscrupulous Federationists with the help of the Silver Prize Band and a few hundred infants. The odds were against the Anti-Federationists. The mayor had actually issued a letter to the inhabitants accusing the Anti-Federationists of unfair methods! This was really too much! The impudence of it knocked the breath out of its victims, and breath is very necessary in a polling contest. The Federationists, as one of their prominent opponents admitted, 'had it all their own way', dominating both the streets and the walls. And when, early in the afternoon, Mr Dick Povey sailed over the town in a balloon that was plainly decorated with the crimson of Federation, it was felt that the cause of Bursley's separate identity was for ever lost. Still, Bursley, with the willing aid of the public-houses, maintained its gaiety.

IV

Towards dusk a stout old lady, with grey hair, and a dowdy bonnet, and an expensive mantle, passed limping, very slowly, along Wedgwood Street and up the Cock Yard towards the Town Hall. Her wrinkled face had an anxious look, but it was also very determined. The busy, joyous Federationists and Anti-Federationists who knew her not saw merely a stout old lady fussing forth, and those who knew her saw merely Mrs Povey and greeted her perfunctorily, a woman of her age and gait being rather out of place in that feverish altercation of opposed principles. But it was more than a stout old lady, it was more than Mrs Povey, that waddled with such painful deliberation through the streets – it was a miracle.

In the morning Constance had been partially incapacitated by her sciatica; so much so, at any rate, that she had perceived the advisability of remaining on the bedroom floor instead of descending to the parlour. Therefore Mary had lighted the drawing-room fire, and Constance had ensconced herself by it, with Fossette in a basket. Lily Holl had called early, and had been very sympathetic, but rather vague. The truth was that she was concealing the imminent balloon ascent which Dick Povey, with his instinct for the picturesque, had somehow arranged, in conjunction with a well-known Manchester aeronaut, for the very day of the poll. That was one of various matters that had to be 'kept from' the old lady. Lily herself was much perturbed about the balloon ascent. She had to run off and see Dick before he started, at the Football Ground at Bleakridge, and then she had to live through the hours till she should receive a telegram to the effect that Dick had come down safely or that Dick had broken his leg in coming down, or that Dick was dead. It was a trying time for Lily. She had left Constance after a brief visit, with a preoccupied unusual air, saying that as the day was a special day, she should come in again 'if she could'. And she did not forget to assure Constance that Federation would beyond any question whatever be handsomely beaten at the poll; for this was another matter as to which it was deemed advisable to keep the old lady 'in the dark', lest the foolish old lady should worry and commit indiscretions.

After that Constance had been forgotten by the world of Bursley, which could pay small heed to sciatical old ladies confined to sofas and firesides. She was in acute pain, as Mary could see when at intervals she hovered round her. Assuredly it was one of Constance's bad days, one of those days on which she felt that the tide of life had left her stranded in utter neglect. The sound of the Bursley Town Silver Prize Band aroused her from her mournful trance of suffering. Then the high treble of children's voices startled her. She defied her sciatica, and, grimacing, went to the window. And at the first glimpse she could see that the Federation Poll was going to be a much more exciting affair than she had imagined. The great cards swinging from the waggonettes showed her that Federation was at all events still sufficiently alive to make a formidable impression on the eye and the ear. The Square was transformed by this clamour in favour of Federation; people cheered, and sang also, as the procession wound down the Square. And she could distinctly catch the tramping, martial syllables, '*Vote, vote, vote*'. She was indignant. The pother, once begun, continued. Vehicles flashed frequently across the Square, most of them in the crimson livery. Little knots and processions of excited wayfarers were a recurring feature of the unaccustomed traffic, and the large majority of them flaunted the colours of Federation. Mary, after some errands of shopping, came upstairs and reported that 'it was simply "Federation" every-where', and that Mr Brindley, a strong Federationist, was 'above a bit above himself'; further, that the interest in the poll was tremendous and universal. She said there were 'crowds and crowds' round the Town Hall. Even Mary, generally a little placid and dull, had caught something of the contagious vivacity.

Constance remained at the window till dinner, and after dinner she went to it again. It was fortunate that she did not think of looking up into the sky when Dick's balloon sailed westwards; she would have guessed instantly that Dick was in that balloon, and her grievances would have been multiplied. The vast griev-ance of the Federation scheme weighed on her to the extremity of her power to bear. She was not a politician; she had no general ideas; she did not see the cosmic movement in large curves. She was incapable of perceiving the absurdity involved in perpetuat-ing municipal divisions which the growth of the district had rendered artificial, vexatious, and harmful. She saw nothing but Bursley, and in Bursley nothing but the Square. She knew nothing except that the people of Bursley, who once shopped in Bursley, now shopped in Hanbridge, and that the Square was a desert infested by cheap-jacks. And there were actually people who wished to bow the neck to Hanbridge, who were ready to sacrifice the very name of Bursley to the greedy humour of that pushing Chicago! She could not understand such people. Did they know that poor Maria Critchlow was in a lunatic asylum because Hanbridge was so grasping? Ah, poor Maria was already forgotten! Did they know that, as a further indirect consequence, she, the daughter of Bursley's chief tradesman, was to be thrown out of the house in which she was born? She wished, bitterly, as she stood there at the window, watching the triumph of Federa-tion, that she had bought the house and shop at the Mericarp sale years ago. She would have shown them, as owner, what was what! She forgot that the property which she already owned in Bursley was a continual annoyance to her, and that she was always resolving to sell it at no matter what loss.

She said to herself that she had a vote, and that if she had been 'at all fit to stir out' she would certainly have voted. She said to herself that it had been her duty to vote. And then by an illusion of her wrought nerves, tightened minute by minute throughout the day, she began to fancy that her sciatica was easier. She said: 'If only I could go out!' She might have a cab, or any of the parading vehicles would be glad to take her to the Town Hall, and, perhaps, as a favour, to bring her back again. But no. She dared not go out. She was afraid, really afraid that even the mild Mary might stop her. Otherwise, she could have sent Mary for a cab. And supposing that Lily returned, and caught her going out or coming in! She ought not to go out. Yet her sciatica was strangely better. It was folly to think of going out. Yet . . . ! And Lily did not come. She was rather hurt that Lily had not paid her a second visit. Lily was neglecting her . . . She *would* go out. It was not four minutes' walk for her to the Town Hall, and she was better. And there had been no shower for a long time, and the wind was drying the mud in the roadways. Yes, she would go.

Like a thief she passed into her bedroom and put on her things; and like a thief she crept downstairs, and so, without a word to Mary, into the street. It was a desperate adventure. As soon as she was in the street she felt all her weakness, all the fatigue which the effort had already cost her. The pain returned. The streets were still wet and foul, the wind cold, and the sky menacing. She ought to go back. She ought to admit that she had been a fool to dream of the enterprise. The Town Hall seemed to be miles off, at the top of a mountain. She went forward, however, steeled to do her share in the killing of Federation. Every step caused her a gnashing of her old teeth. She chose the Cock Yard route, because if she had gone up the Square she would have had to pass Holl's shop, and Lily might have spied her.

This was the miracle that breezy politicians witnessed without being aware that it was a miracle. To have impressed them, Constance ought to have fainted before recording her vote, and made herself the centre of a crowd of gapers. But she managed, somehow, to reach home again on her own tortured feet, and an astounded and protesting Mary opened the door to her. Rain was descending. She was frightened, then, by the hardihood of her adventure, and by its atrocious results on her body. An appalling exhaustion rendered her helpless. But the deed was done.

V

The next morning, after a night which she could not have
described, Constance found herself lying flat in bed, with all her
limbs stretched out straight. She was conscious that her face was
covered with perspiration. The bell-rope hung within a foot of
her head, but she had decided that, rather than move in order to
pull it, she would prefer to wait for assistance until Mary came of
her own accord. Her experiences of the night had given her a
dread of the slightest movement; anything was better than movement. She felt vaguely ill, with a kind of subdued pain, and she
was very thirsty and somewhat cold. She knew that her left arm
and leg were extraordinarily tender to the touch. When Mary at
length entered, clean and fresh and pale in all her mildness, she
found the mistress the colour of a duck's egg, with puffed
features, and a strangely anxious expression.

'Mary,' said Constance, 'I feel so queer. Perhaps you'd better
run up and tell Miss Holl, and ask her to telephone for Dr
Stirling.'

This was the beginning of Constance's last illness. Mary most
impressively informed Miss Holl that her mistress had been out
on the previous afternoon in spite of her sciatica, and Lily
telephoned the fact to the doctor. Lily then came down to take
charge of Constance. But she dared not upbraid the invalid.

'Is the result out?' Constance murmured.

'Oh yes,' said Lily, lightly. 'There's a majority of over twelve
hundred against Federation. Great excitement last night! I told
you yesterday morning that Federation was bound to be
beaten.'

Lily spoke as though the result throughout had been a certainty; her tone to Constance indicated: 'Surely you don't imagine
that I should have told you untruths yesterday morning merely to
cheer you up!' The truth was, however, that towards the end of
the day nearly everyone had believed Federation to be carried.
The result caused great surprise. Only the profoundest philo-
sophers had not been surprised to see that the mere blind, deaf,
inert forces of reaction, with faulty organization, and quite
deprived of the aid of logic, had proved far stronger than all the

alert enthusiasm arrayed aginst them. It was a notable lesson to reformers.

'Oh,' murmured Constance, startled. She was relieved; but she would have liked the majority to be smaller. Moreover, her interest in the question had lessened. It was her limbs that preoccupied her now.

'You look tired,' she said feebly to Lily.

'Do I?' said Lily, shortly, hiding the fact that she had spent half the night in tending Dick Povey, who, in a sensational descent near Macclesfield, had been dragged through the tops of a row of elm trees to the detriment of an elbow-joint; the professional aeronaut had broken a leg.

Then Dr Stirling came.

'I'm afraid my sciatica's worse, Doctor,' said Constance, apologetically.

'Did you expect it to be better?' said he, gazing at her sternly. She knew then that someone had saved her the trouble of confessing her escapade.

However, her sciatica was not worse. Her sciatica had not behaved basely. What she was suffering from was the preliminary advances of an attack of acute rheumatism. She had indeed selected the right month and weather for her escapade! Fatigued by pain, by nervous agitation, and by the immense moral and physical effort needed to carry her to the Town Hall and back, she had caught a chill, and had got her feet damp. In such a subject as herself it was enough. The doctor used only the phrase 'acute rheumatism'. Constance did not know that acute rheumatism was precisely the same thing as that dread disease, rheumatic fever, and she was not informed. She did not surmise for a considerable period that her case was desperately serious. The doctor explained the summoning of two nurses, and the frequency of his own visits, by saying that his chief anxiety was to minimize the fearful pain as much as possible, and that this end could only be secured by incessant watchfulness. The pain was certainly formidable. But then Constance was well habituated to formidable pain. Sciatica, at its most active, cannot be surpassed even by rheumatic fever. Constance had been in nearly continuous pain for years. Her friends, however sympathetic, could not appreciate the intensity of her torture. They were just as used to it as she was. And the monotony and particularity of her complaints (slight thought the complaints were in comparison with their cause) necessarily blunted the edge of compassion. 'Mrs Povey and her sciatica again! Poor thing, she really is a little tedious!' They were apt not to realize that sciatica is even more tedious than complaints about sciatica.

She asked one day that Dick should come to see her. He came with his arm in a sling, and told her charily that he had hurt his elbow through dropping his stick and slipping downstairs.

'Lily never told me,' said Constance, suspiciously.

'Oh, it's simply nothing!' said Dick. Not even the sick-room could chasten him of his joy in the magnificent balloon adventure.

'I do hope you won't go running any risks!' said Constance.

'Never you fear!' said he. 'I shall die in my bed.'

And he was absolutely convinced that he would, and not as the result of any accident, either! The nurse would not allow him to remain in the room.

Lily suggested that Constance might like her to write to Cyril. It was only in order to make sure of Cyril's correct address. He had gone on a tour through Italy with some friends of whom Constance knew nothing. The address appeared to be very uncertain; there were several addresses, *poste restante* in various towns. Cyril had sent postcards to his mother. Dick and Lily went to the post-office and telegraphed to foreign parts.

Though Constance was too ill to know how ill she was, though she had no conception of the domestic confusion caused by her illness, her brain was often remarkably clear, and she could reflect in long sane meditations above the uneasy sea of her pain. In the earlier hours of the night, after the nurses had been changed, and Mary had gone to bed exhausted with stair-climbing, and Lily Holl was recounting the day to Dick up at the grocer's, and the day-nurse was already asleep, and the night-nurse had arranged the night, then, in the faintly lit silence of the chamber, Constance would argue with herself for an hour at a time. She frequently thought of Sophia. In spite of the fact that Sophia was dead she still pitied Sophia as a woman whose life had been wasted. This idea of Sophia's wasted and sterile life, and of the far-reaching importance of adhering to principles, recurred to her again and again. 'Why did she run away with him? If only she had not run away!' she would repeat. And yet there had been something so fine about Sophia! Which made Sophia's case all the more pitiable! Constance never pitied herself. She did not consider that Fate had treated her very badly. She was not very discontented with herself. The invincible common sense of a sound nature prevented her, in her best moments, from feebly dissolving in self-pity. She had lived in honesty and kindliness for a fair number of years, and she had tasted triumphant hours. She was justly respected, she had a position, she had dignity, she was well-off. She possessed, after all, a certain amount of quiet self-conceit. There existed nobody to whom she would 'knuckle down' or could be asked to 'knuckle down'. True, she was old! So were thousands of other people in Bursley. She was in pain. So there were thousands of other people. With whom would she be willing to exchange lots? She had many dissatisfactions. But she rose superior to them. When she surveyed her life, and life in general, she would think, with a sort of tart but not sour cheerfulness: *'Well, that is what life is!'* Despite her habit of complaining about domestic trifles, she was, in the essence of her character, 'a great body for making the best of things'. Thus she did not unduly bewail her excursion to the Town Hall to vote, which the sequel had proved to be ludicrously supererogatory. 'How was I to know?' she said.

The one matter in which she had gravely to reproach herself was her indulgent spoiling of Cyril after the death of Samuel Povey. But the end of her reproaches always was: 'I expect I should do the same again! And probably it wouldn't have made any difference if I hadn't spoiled him!' And she had paid tenfold for the weakness. She loved Cyril, but she had no illusions about him; she saw both sides of him. She remembered all the sadness and all the humiliations which he had caused her. Still, her affection was unimpaired. A son might be worse than Cyril was; he had admirable qualities. She did not resent his being away from England while she lay ill. 'If it was serious,' she said, 'he would not lose a moment.' And Lily and Dick were a treasure to her. In those two she really had been lucky. She took great pleasure in contemplating the splendour of the gift with which she would mark her appreciation of them at their approaching wedding. The secret attitude of both of them towards her was one of good-natured condescension, expressed in the tone in which they would say to each other, 'the old lady'. Perhaps they would have been startled to know that Constance lovingly looked down on both of them. She had unbounded admiration for their hearts; but she thought that Dick was a little too brusque, a little too clownish, to be quite a gentleman. And though Lily was perfectly ladylike, in Constance's opinion she lacked backbone, or grit, or independence of spirit. Further, Constance considered that the disparity of age between them was excessive. It is to be doubted whether, when all was said, Constance had such a very great deal to learn from the self-confident wisdom of these young things.

After a period of self-communion, she would sometimes fall into a shallow delirium. In all her delirium she was invariably wandering to and fro, lost, in the long underground passage leading from the scullery past the coal-cellar and the cinder-cellar to the backyard. And she was afraid of the vast-obscure of those regions, as she had been in her infancy.

It was not acute rheumatism but a supervening pericarditis that in a few days killed her. She died in the night, alone with the night-nurse. By a curious chance the Wesleyan minister, hearing that she was seriously ill, had called on the previous day. She had not asked for him; and this pastoral visit, from a man who had always said that the heavy duties of the circuit rendered pastoral visits almost impossible, made her think. In the evening she had requested that Fossette should be brought upstairs.

Thus she was turned out of her house, but not by the Midland Clothiers Company. Old people said to one another: 'Have you heard that Mrs Povey is dead? Eh, dear me! There'll be no one left soon.' These old people were bad prophets. Her friends genuinely regretted her, and forgot the tediousness of her sciatica. They tried, in their sympathetic grief, to picture to themselves all that she had been through in her life. Possibly they imagined that they succeeded in this imaginative attempt. But they did not succeed.

No one but Constance could realize all that Constance had been through, and all that life had meant to her.

Cyril was not at the funeral. He arrived three days later. (As he had no interest in the love affairs of Dick and Lily, the couple were robbed of their wedding-present. The will, fifteen years old, was in Cyril's favour.) But the immortal Charles Critchlow came to the funeral, full of calm, sardonic glee, and without being asked. Though fabulously senile, he had preserved and even improved his faculty for enjoying a catastrophe. He now went to funerals with gusto, contentedly absorbed in the task of burying his friends one by one. It was he who said, in his high, trembling, rasping, deliberate voice: 'It's a pity her didn't live long enough to hear as Federation is going on after all! That would ha' worritted her.' (For the unscrupulous advocates of Federation had discovered a method of setting at naught the decisive result of the referendum, and that day's *Signal* was fuller than ever of Federation.)

When the short funeral procession started, Mary and the infirm Fossette (sole relic of the connexion between the Baines family and Paris) were left alone in the house. The tearful servant prepared the dog's dinner and laid it before her in the customary soup-plate in the customary corner. Fossette sniffed at it, and then walked away and lay down with a dog's sigh in front of the kitchen fire. She had been deranged in her habits that day; she was conscious of neglect, due to events which passed her comprehension. And she did not like it. She was hurt, and her appetite was hurt. However, after a few minutes, she began to reconsider the matter. She glanced at the soup-plate, and, on the chance that it might after all contain something worth inspection, she awkwardly balanced herself on her old legs and went to it again.

NOTES

1 (p. 40). '*Vaults*'; Well into my lifetime, respectable working people in the Potteries never referred to licensed premises as a public house or even an inn. If it were the sort of place they could bring themselves to mention at all, they called it 'a vaults', or even more grandly 'a Wine and Vaults'. I last heard the expression in 1967, over a century after the time Bennett is describing.

2 (p. 51). *The Harvest of a Quiet Eye*: The phrase is from Words-worth, 'A Poet's Epitaph', but what book read in the Baines household had taken it as a title I cannot trace.

3 (p. 83). *people were starving . . . in Manchester*: During the Amer-ican Civil War, the Northern blockade of the Southern ports halted the flow of raw materials, principally cotton, to British industry. To their credit, the British working class never wavered in their support for the North, because slavery was the only issue between the two sides that they had grasped and they saw it as a war between slavers and emancipators.

4 (p. 103). *railway lorry*: a flat-car, term used on the railways since the 1830s.

5 (p. 124). *a recent convert from Primitive . . . to Wesleyan Method-ism*: John Wesley, who founded the Methodist church in 1784, was a highly respectable Anglican clergyman. Hugh Bourne, who founded Primitive Methodism in 1811, was a man of the people. In 1807 an American evangelist, Lorenzo Dow, introduced the Camp Meeting into English religion at Mow Cop. Hugh Bourne continued this tradition, was expelled from the Methodist ministry for it, and founded 'Camp Meeting Methodism'; cf. Bennett's cool reference on the first page to Mow Cop as 'a hill famous for its religious orgies'. Mr Povey left Primitive for Wesleyan because he was climbing up the social ladder.

6 (p. 157). *baited*: fed the horse.

7 (p. 172). *in that Chartist lot*: The six-point 'People's Charter' of 1838 demanded six reforms: universal male suffrage, equal electoral districts, annual Parliaments, secret ballot, and MPs to be paid and to have no property qualification. Support for these reforms gathered until millions of working men were 'Chartists', and in 1842 a wave of strikes 'for the Charter' swept Manchester, Cheshire, the Potteries, Lancashire,

Yorkshire, Warwickshire and South Wales. The fish-hawker Hollins, evidently, was still disapproved of as a Chartist six years later.

8 (p. 199). *Blondin*: world-famous acrobat, escape artist, stunt man.

9 (p. 328). *lorettes*: women of the town. Cf. Flaubert, *Education sentimentale*, I, 5, 'Une lorette est plus amusante que la Vénus de Milo.'

10 (p. 375). *Cook's*: Thomas Cook (1808–99) ran his first excursion out of Leicester station in 1841 (to Loughborough, one shilling return) and built up a world empire in the travel business; in 1898 he arranged a tour of the Holy Land for the Emperor and Empress of Germany.

11 (p. 418). *The establishment of a republic*: In September 1870, after the disastrous Battle of Sedan, France abandoned the Second Empire (set up in 1851 with Napoleon III as Emperor) and proclaimed the Third Republic, which lasted till 1945.

12 (p. 453). *the Commune*: The Revolutionary Commune held power in Paris, though not in France generally, for a few months in 1871, executing more Frenchmen than had died in the Franco-Prussian War.

13 (p. 456). *George Augustus Sala*: Famous journalist (1828–96), worked on *Household Words* under Dickens's editorship, went on to such exploits as reporting the American Civil War for a London paper and being arrested by the Prussians as a suspected French spy in 1870; his articles on *Paris Herself Again* appeared in book form in 1880.

14 (p. 464). *Mr Barney Barnato*: Barnett Isaacs Barnato (1852–97) sailed as a young man to South Africa with £50 capital, amassed huge wealth, spent lavishly and never lost his taste for simple pleasures such as the music-hall and boxing matches.

15 (p. 528). *Cherbuliez*: Victor Cherbuliez (1829–99) went in for stories of adventure set against colourful historical backgrounds.

16 (p. 528). *Dreyfus*: The novelist Zola was foremost among those who championed Captain Alfred Dreyfus, a Jewish officer wrongly accused of espionage and sent to Devil's Island in 1894. The French War Office suppressed subsequent evidence which would have cleared Dreyfus in 1896; he was not pardoned and reinstated until 1906, and then only after a prolonged agitation which split France into two camps. Zola would be considered 'the enemy of his race' by anti-Semites.

FOR THE BEST IN PAPERBACKS, LOOK FOR THE 🐧

In every corner of the world, on every subject under the sun, Penguin represents quality and variety – the very best in publishing today.

For complete information about books available from Penguin – including Pelicans, Puffins, Peregrines and Penguin Classics – and how to order them, write to us at the appropriate address below. Please note that for copyright reasons the selection of books varies from country to country.

In the United Kingdom: For a complete list of books available from Penguin in the U.K., please write to *Dept E.P., Penguin Books Ltd, Harmondsworth, Middlesex, UB7 0DA*

In the United States: For a complete list of books available from Penguin in the U.S., please write to *Dept BA, Penguin, 299 Murray Hill Parkway, East Rutherford, New Jersey 07073*

In Canada: For a complete list of books available from Penguin in Canada, please write to *Penguin Books Canada Ltd, 2801 John Street, Markham, Ontario L3R 1B4*

In Australia: For a complete list of books available from Penguin in Australia, please write to the *Marketing Department, Penguin Books Australia Ltd, P.O. Box 257, Ringwood, Victoria 3134*

In New Zealand: For a complete list of books available from Penguin in New Zealand, please write to the *Marketing Department, Penguin Books (NZ) Ltd, Private Bag, Takapuna, Auckland 9*

In India: For a complete list of books available from Penguin, please write to *Penguin Overseas Ltd, 706 Eros Apartments, 56 Nehru Place, New Delhi, 110019*

In Holland: For a complete list of books available from Penguin in Holland, please write to *Penguin Books Nederland B.V., Postbus 195, NL–1380AD Weesp, Netherlands*

In Germany: For a complete list of books available from Penguin, please write to *Penguin Books Ltd, Friedrichstrasse 10 – 12, D–6000 Frankfurt Main 1, Federal Republic of Germany*

In Spain: For a complete list of books available from Penguin in Spain, please write to *Longman Penguin España, Calle San Nicolas 15, E–28013 Madrid, Spain*

ANNA OF THE FIVE TOWNS

This is one of the finest of Arnold Bennett's novels, a brilliantly detailed picture of life in the Potteries; a tightly knit story of the destructive forces of evangelism and industrial expansion at work in a small community.

Arnold Bennett understood well the self-sufficiency of the people of Staffordshire. He sympathized with it and detested it. 'We are of the North, outwardly brusque, stoical, undemonstrative, scornful of the impulsive; inwardly all sentiment and crushed tenderness.' His work is filled with that secret and impulsive tenderness, and in *Anna of the Five Towns*, his central character attempts to respond to the emotions she feels but, preoccupied with sin and duty, salvation and savings, she ultimately submits to the world in which she lives.

THE GRIM SMILE OF THE FIVE TOWNS

'They joke with such extraordinary seriousness in the Five Towns that one is somehow bound to pretend that they are not joking.'

In the short stories which make up *The Grim Smile of the Five Towns* Arnold Bennett caught some of the manner of Maupassant, one of the French writers on whom he modelled his writing. The redolent tale of the coffin and the cheese, 'In a New Bottle', and 'The Silent Brothers' (who have not addressed one another for ten years) possess the true ring.

The pride, pretensions and provincial snobbery of the Potteries are handled by Arnold Bennett with amused tolerance. Most of his stories, like the four linked adventures of Vera Cheswardine, set the home life of middle-class manufacturers of earthenware and porcelain against a 'singular scenery of coal dust, potsherds, flame and steam'. But Bennett never ignores the less successful members of families in a region where 'clogs to clogs is only three generations'.

THE CARD

From the day he first saw the smoke of the Five Towns, Edward Henry Machin (his mother saved time by calling him Denry) was destined for fame. He forged his way into a scholarship and into the Municipal Ball where he danced with the Countess of Chell. He wheeled and he dealed through the length and breadth of the Five Towns and Llandudno – where he caused a sensation with lifeboat trips to the wreck of the *Hjalmar* and narrowly avoided matrimony. And he ended up as Bursley's youngest-ever Mayor.

Denry was, in short 'A Card', that strange species so beloved of the Five Towns.

Arnold Bennett used the life of a fellow-townsman, H. K. Hales, as the basis for one of his most entertaining 'larks' – the hilarious tall story of a rogue whose every bad deed turns to gold.

CLAYHANGER

Arnold Bennett's careful evocation of a boy growing to manhood during the last quarter of the nineteenth-century, with its superb portrait of an autocratic father, stands on a literary level with *The Old Wives' Tale*. Set, like its successful predecessor, in the Five Towns, *Clayhanger* was destined to be the first novel in a trilogy.

Of the book and its hero Walter Allen has written in *The English Novel*: 'He is one of the most attractive heroes in twentieth-century fiction.' Bennett, who believed inordinately in the 'interestingness' of ordinary people, was never more successful in revealing the 'interestingness' of an apparently ordinary man than in Edwin Clayhanger.

Arnold Bennett in Penguins

THE JOURNALS

Edited by Frank Swinnerton

'All London will miss him, and some Londoners will miss him very bitterly. For he abounded in kindliness.'

So wrote Rebecca West after Arnold Bennett's death in 1931, and Virginia Woolf echoed her sentiments, 'Arnold Bennett died last night, which leaves me sadder than I should have supposed. A loveable genuine man: impeded, somehow a little awkward in life; well meaning; ponderous; kindly; coarse; knowing he was coarse; dimly floundering and feeling for something else; glutted with success; wounded in his feelings . . . Some real understanding power, as well as gigantic absorbing power'.

Written almost daily from 1896, when he was twenty-nine, until his death, the *Journals* reflect the sensitive and modest side of Bennett, aspects of his character overlooked by some of his critics. In them he records his life in France and his trip to America. And later, in a style perfectly calculated to conceal emotion, he writes calmly of the tremendous waste of ammunition as shots pour round him on the road to Souchez.

Of interest not only for his impressions of well-known writers, the *Journals* are also an illuminating self-portrait of a fascinating and much loved man.

ARNOLD BENNETT

A Biography by
Margaret Drabble

A literary lion and a hugely popular novelist, a household cartoon character, a passionate cyclist, an enemy of Ezra Pound, a friend of Gide and H. G. Wells – in his time Arnold Bennett was a phenomenon.

Partly because he could not resist his own popularity, Bennett, at the height of his fame in the twenties, was continually teased by literary society over his provincialism, the pleasure he took in money, his flamboyant clothes, vulgar Empire furniture and his yacht. Yet even his wittiest sparring partner, Virginia Woolf, while mocking his stammer and his accent (in true Bloomsbury style), had to admit that 'I like the old creature. I do my best as a writer, to detect signs of genius in his smoky brown eyes . . .'

'A warm and exhilarating book, extremely enjoyable, intelligent, partisan . . . big in enthusiasm and generosity . . . she makes you want to read Bennett again' – Dennis Potter in the *Guardian*